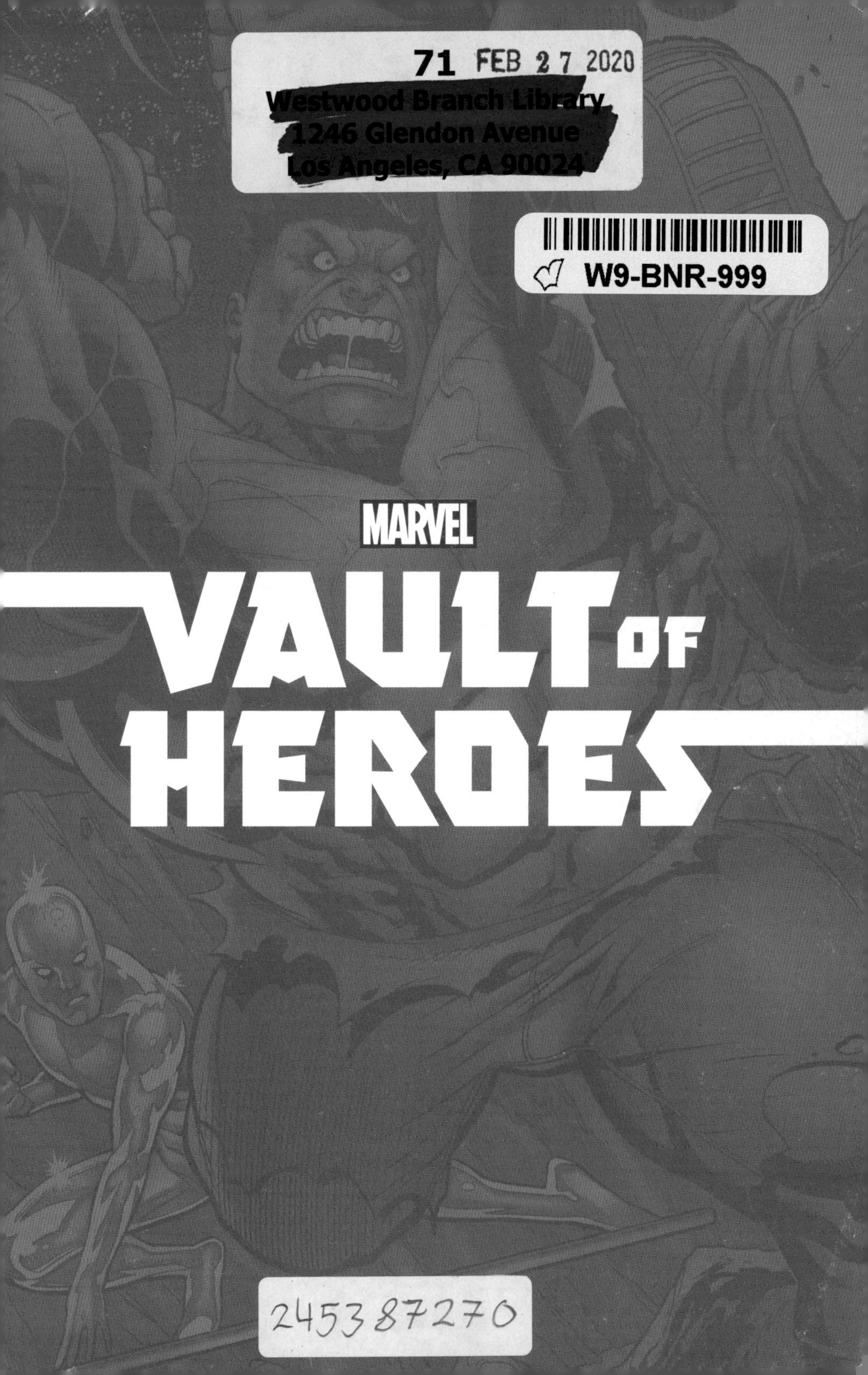

MARVEL

VAULT OF HEROES

ISBN: 978-1-68405-661-3   22 21 20 19   1 2 3 4

MARVEL VAULT OF HEROES: HULK: BIGGEST & BEST. DECEMBER 2019. FIRST PRINTING. © 2019 MARVEL.
The IDW logo is registered in the U.S. Patent and Trademark Office. IDW Publishing, a division of Idea and Design Works, LLC.
Editorial offices: 2765 Truxtun Road, San Diego, CA 92106. Any similarities to persons living or dead are purely coincidental.
With the exception of artwork used for review purposes, none of the contents of this publication may be reprinted without the
permission of Idea and Design Works, LLC.
Printed in Korea.

IDW Publishing does not read or accept unsolicited submissions of ideas, stories, or artwork.

Originally published by MARVEL as MARVEL ADVENTURES: HULK issues #1–12.

IDW

COVER ART PENCILS BY
CARLO PAGULAYAN

COVER ART INKS BY
JEFFREY HUET

COVER ART COLORS BY
CHRIS SOTOMAYOR

COLLECTION EDITS BY
JUSTIN EISINGER
AND ALONZO SIMON

COLLECTION DESIGN BY
JEFF POWELL

HULK CREATED BY
STAN LEE & JACK KIRBY

Chris Ryall, President, Publisher, & CCO

John Barber, Editor-In-Chief

Cara Morrison, Chief Financial Officer

Matt Ruzicka, Chief Accounting Officer

David Hedgecock, Associate Publisher

Jerry Bennington, VP of New Product Development

Lorelei Bunjes, VP of Digital Services

Justin Eisinger, Editorial Director, Graphic Novels & Collections

Eric Moss, Senior Director, Licensing and Business Development

Ted Adams and Robbie Robbins, IDW Founders

Marvel Publishing:

VP Production & Special Projects: Jeff Youngquist

Assistant Editor, Special Projects: Caitlin O'Connell

Director, Licensed Publishing: Sven Larsen

SVP Print, Sales & Marketing: David Gabriel

Editor In Chief: C.B. Cebulski

Chief Creative Officer: Joe Quesada

President, Marvel Entertainment: Dan Buckley

Executive Producer: Alan Fine

#71 WESTWOOD

HULK
BIGGEST & BEST

x GN H9125Va

01

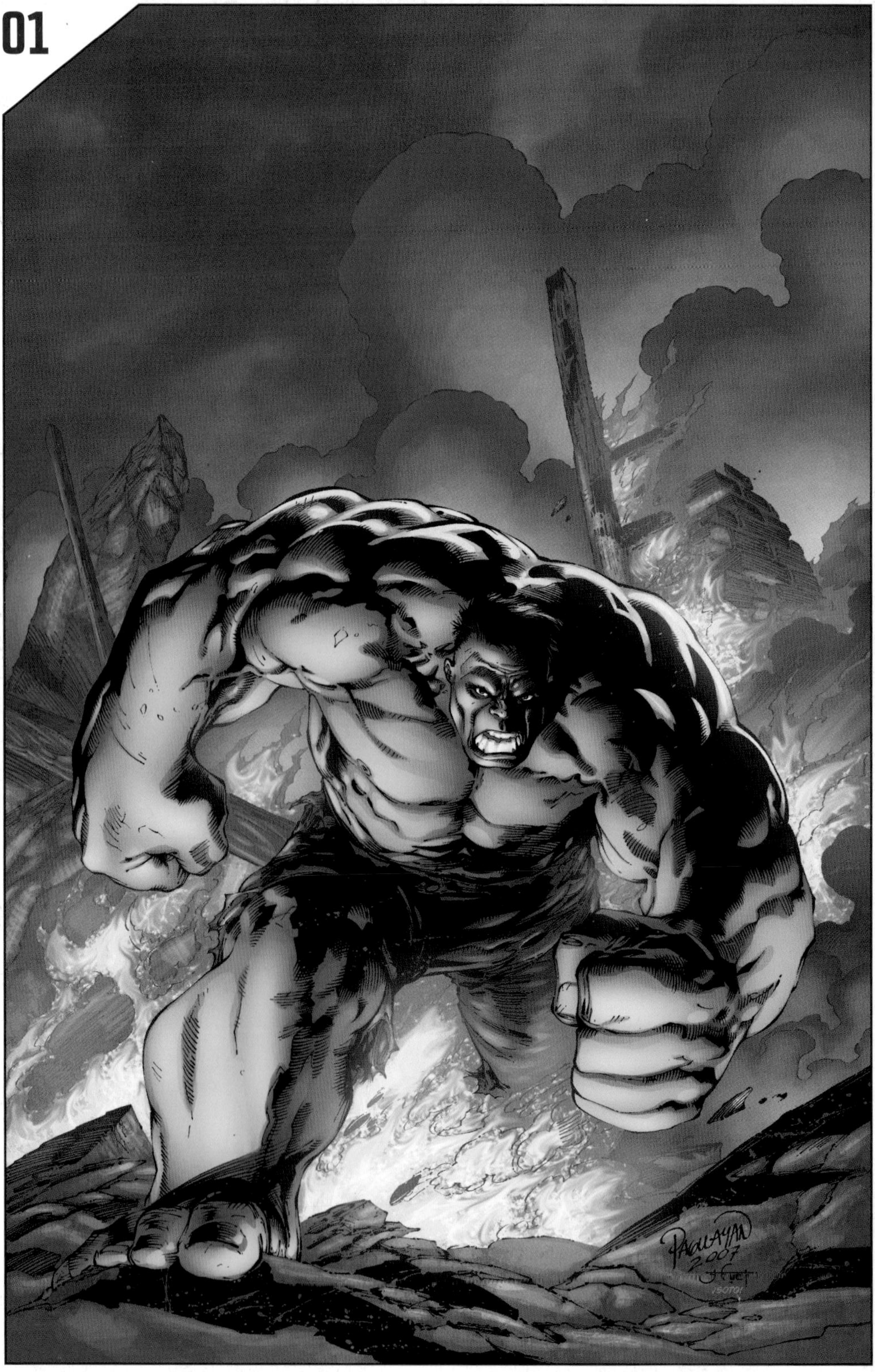
PAGULAYAN
2007

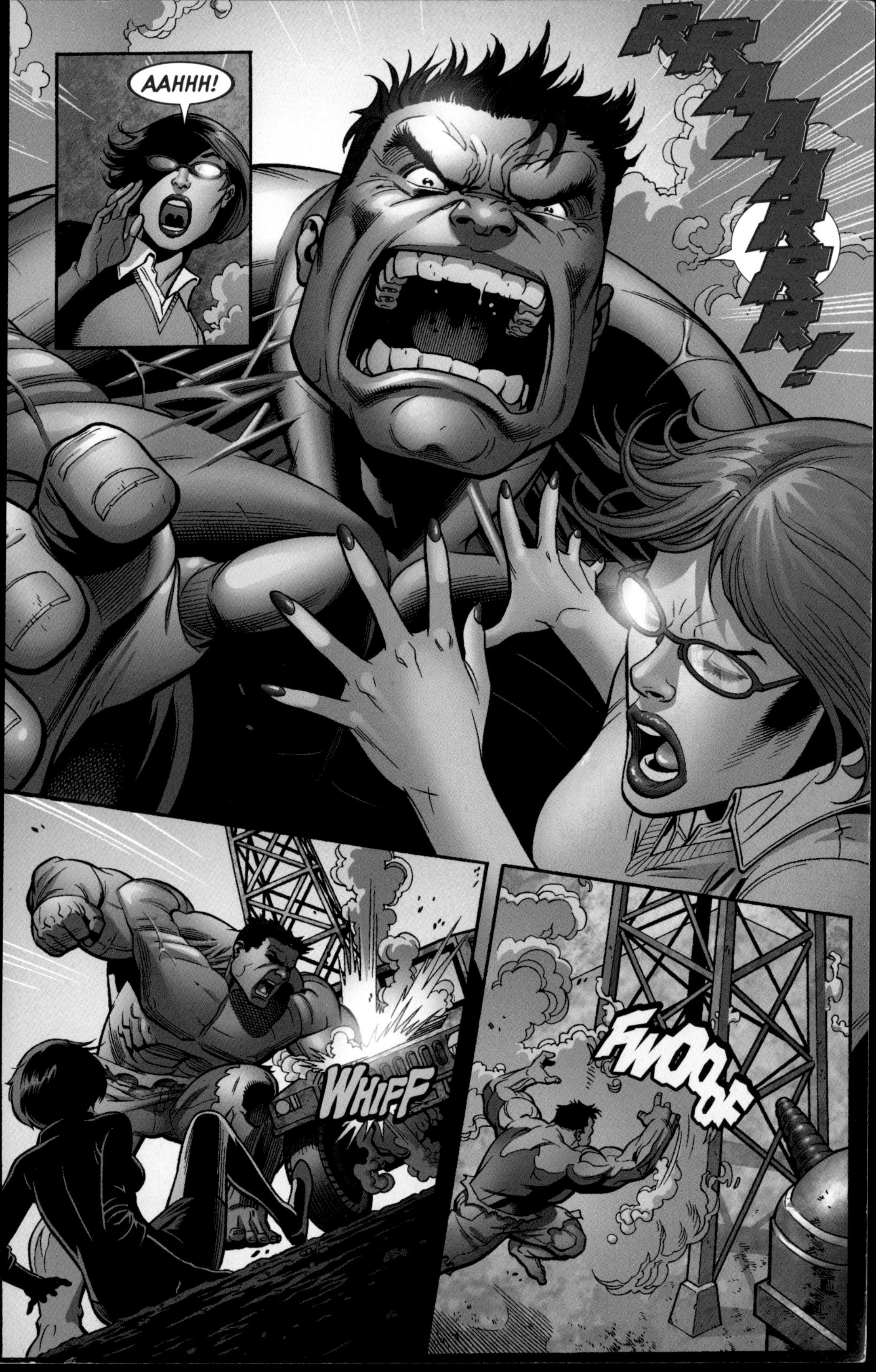

AAHHH!
RRAAARR!
WHIFF
FWOOOF

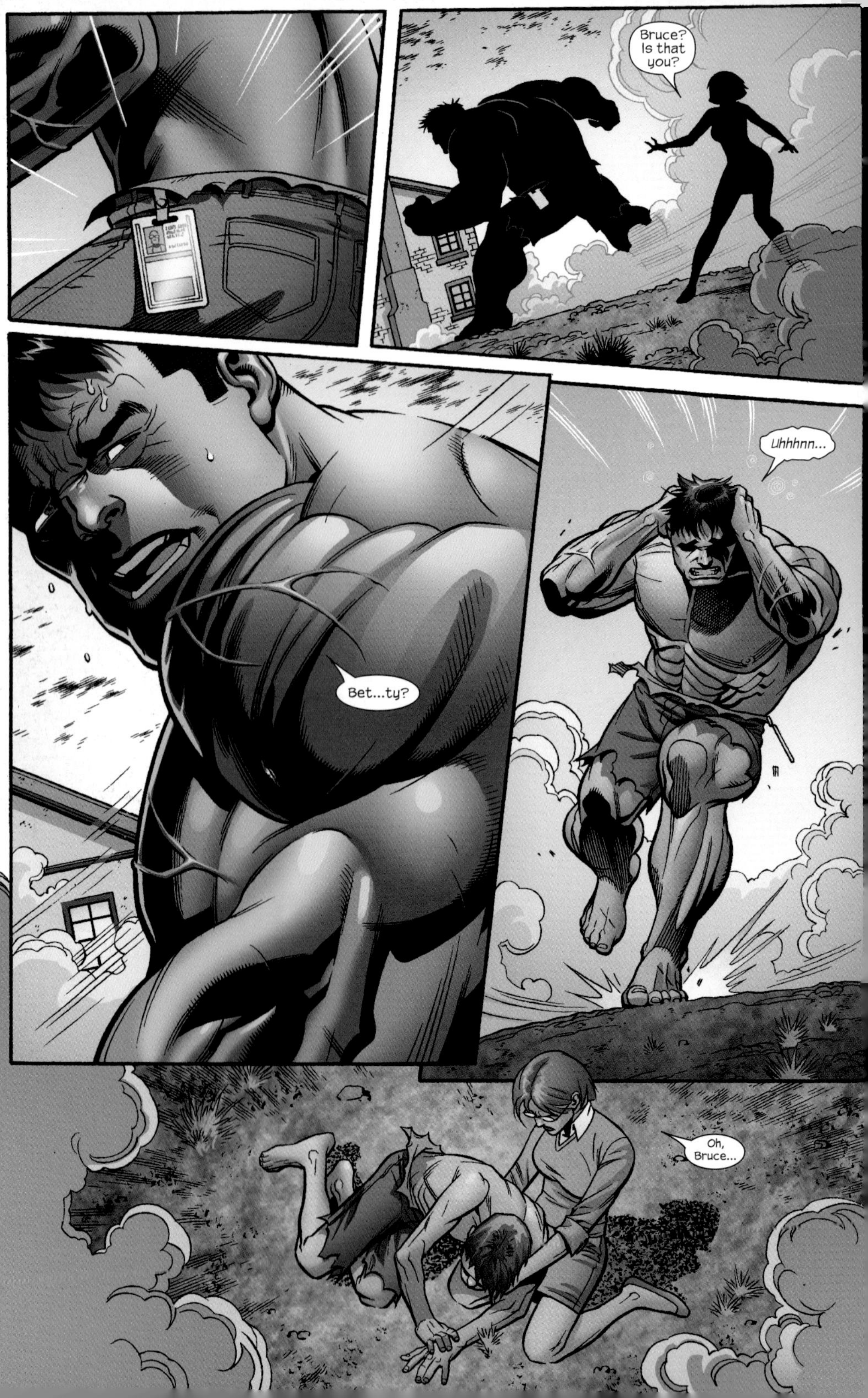
Bruce? Is that you?
Bet...ty?
Uhhhnn...
Oh, Bruce...

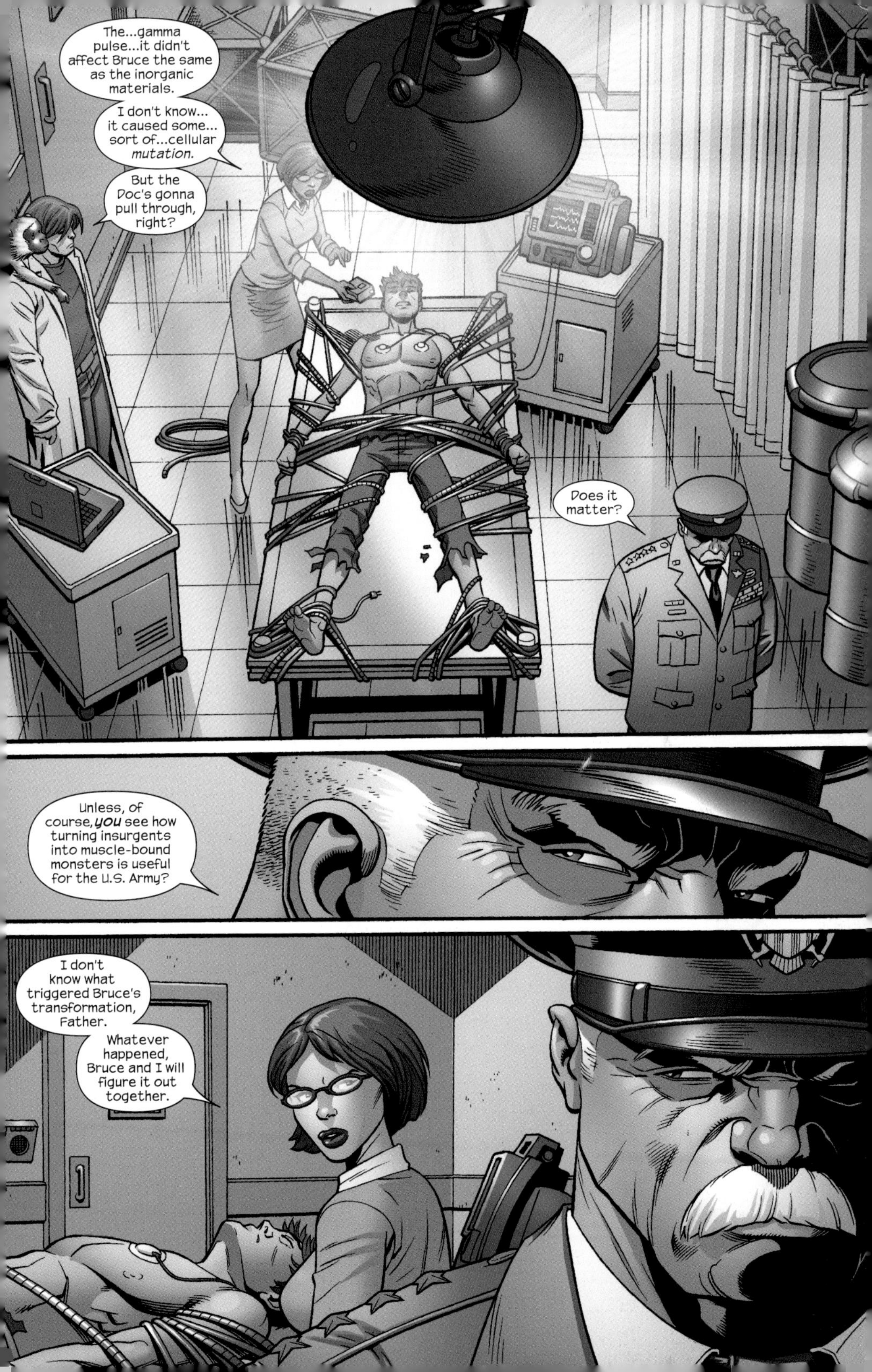
The...gamma pulse...it didn't affect Bruce the same as the inorganic materials.
I don't know... it caused some... sort of...cellular *mutation.*
But the Doc's gonna pull through, right?
Does it matter?
Unless, of course, ***YOU*** see how turning insurgents into muscle-bound monsters is useful for the U.S. Army?
I don't know what triggered Bruce's transformation, Father.
Whatever happened, Bruce and I will figure it out together.

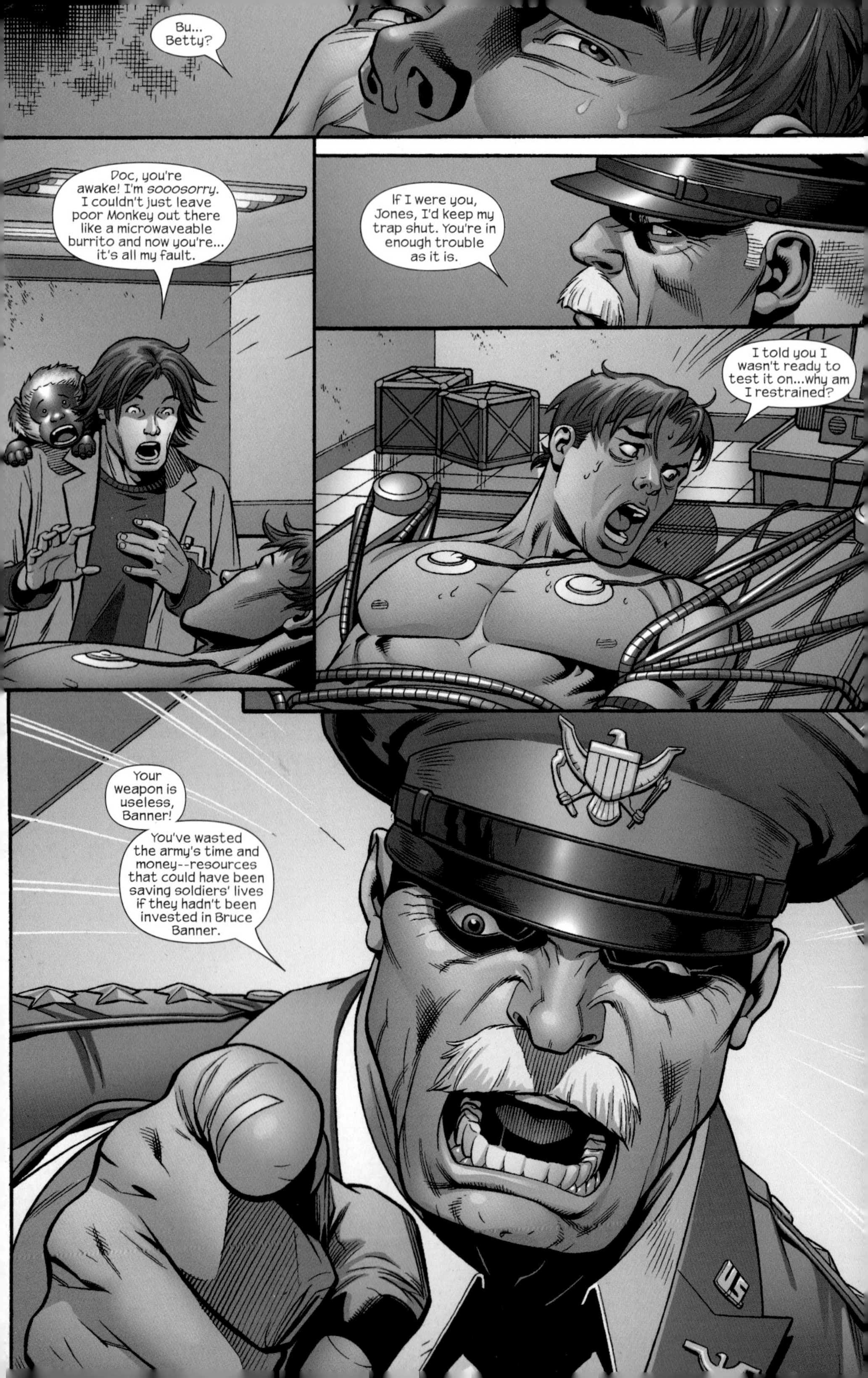
Bu... Betty?
Doc, you're awake! I'm sooosorry. I couldn't just leave poor Monkey out there like a microwaveable burrito and now you're... it's all my fault.
If I were you, Jones, I'd keep my trap shut. You're in enough trouble as it is.
I told you I wasn't ready to test it on...why am I restrained?
Your weapon is useless, Banner!
You've wasted the army's time and money--resources that could have been saving soldiers' lives if they hadn't been invested in Bruce Banner.

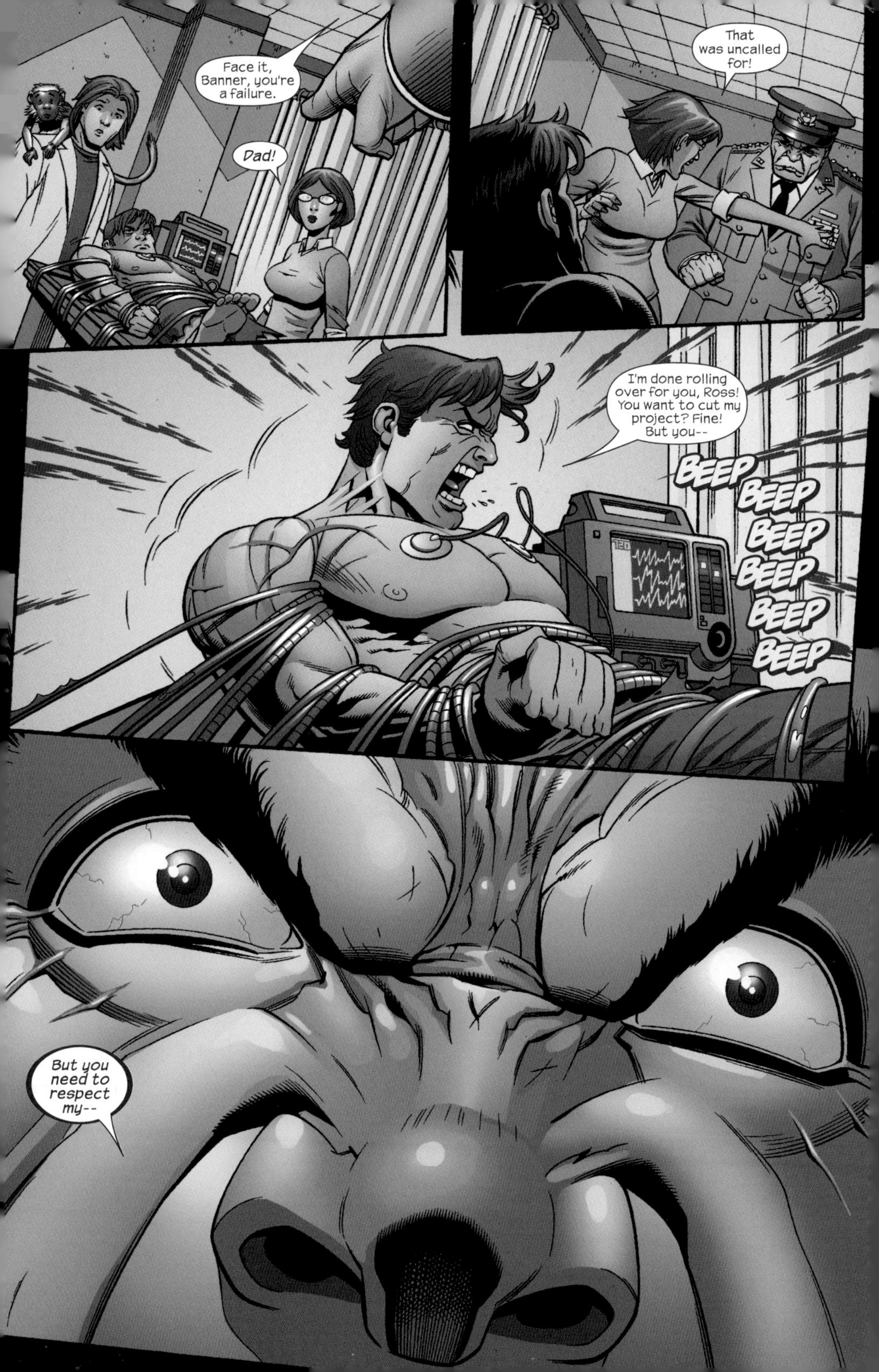
Face it, Banner, you're a failure.
Dad!
That was uncalled for!
I'm done rolling over for you, Ross! You want to cut my project? Fine! But you--
BEEP BEEP BEEP BEEP BEEP BEEP
But you need to respect my--

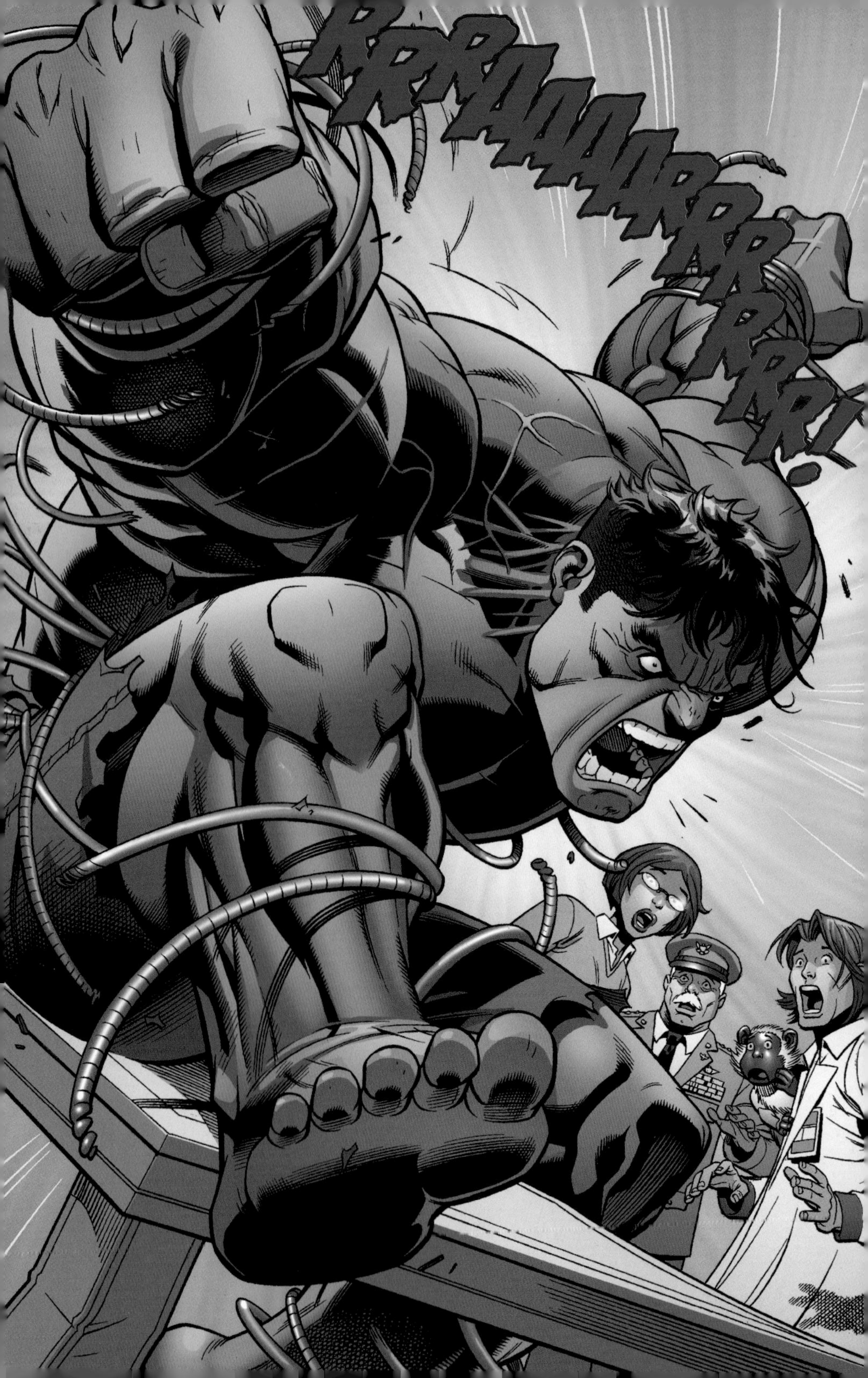
RRRAAAARRRRR!

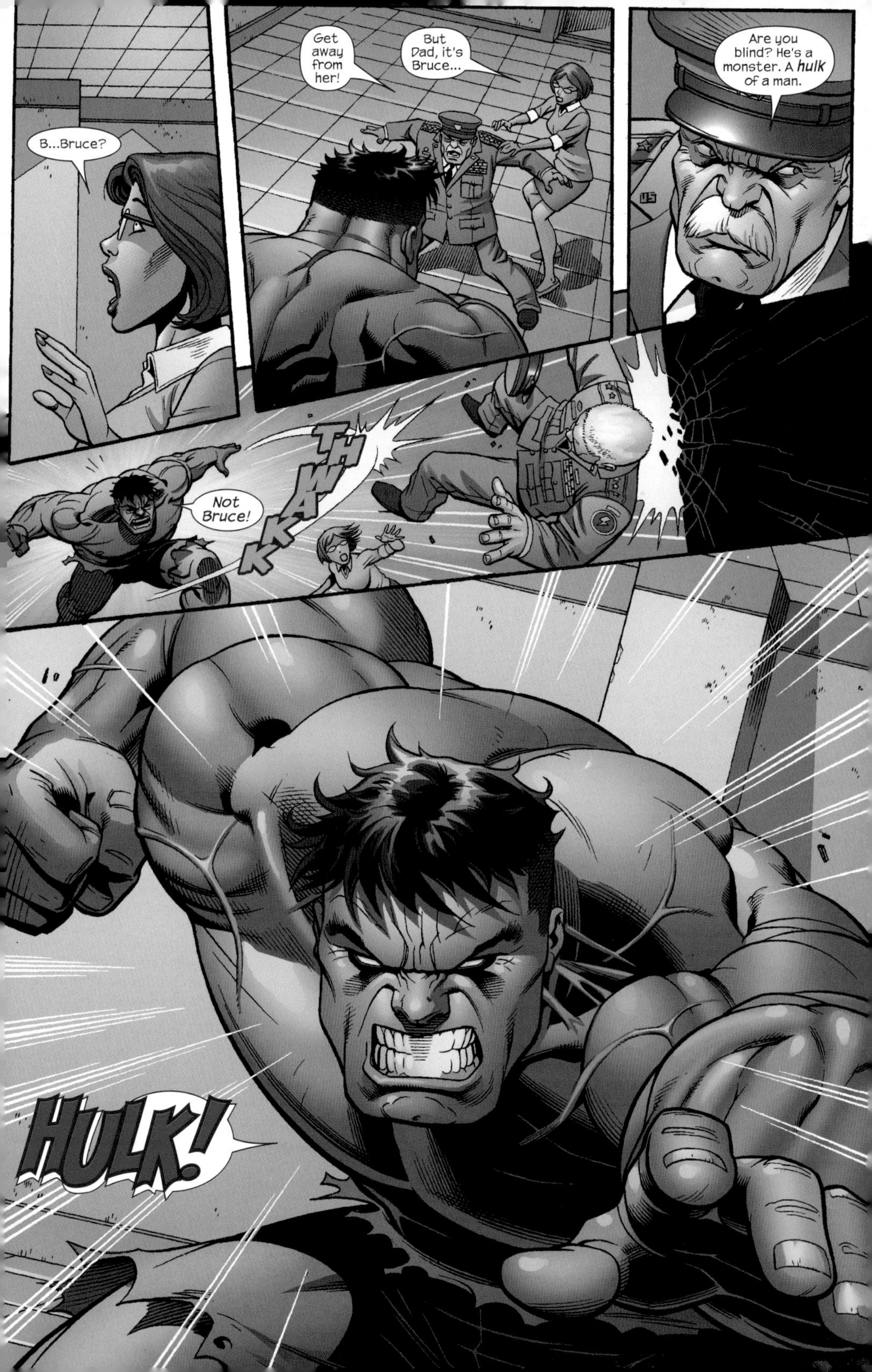
B...Bruce?
Get away from her!
But Dad, it's Bruce...
Are you blind? He's a monster. A *hulk* of a man.
THWAKKK
Not Bruce!
HULK!

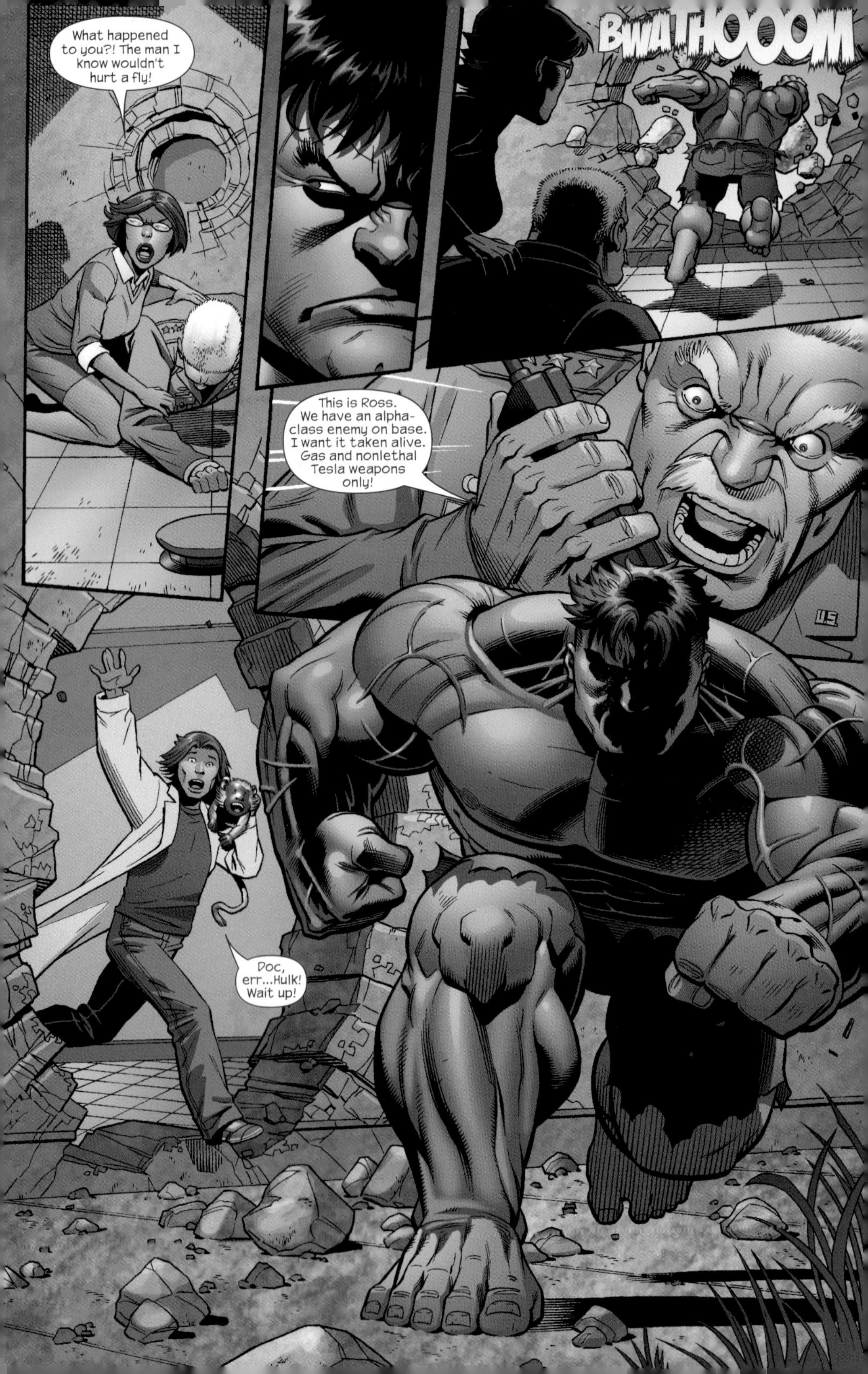
What happened to you?! The man I know wouldn't hurt a fly!
BWATHOOOM
This is Ross. We have an alpha-class enemy on base. I want it taken alive. Gas and nonlethal Tesla weapons only!
Doc, err...Hulk! Wait up!

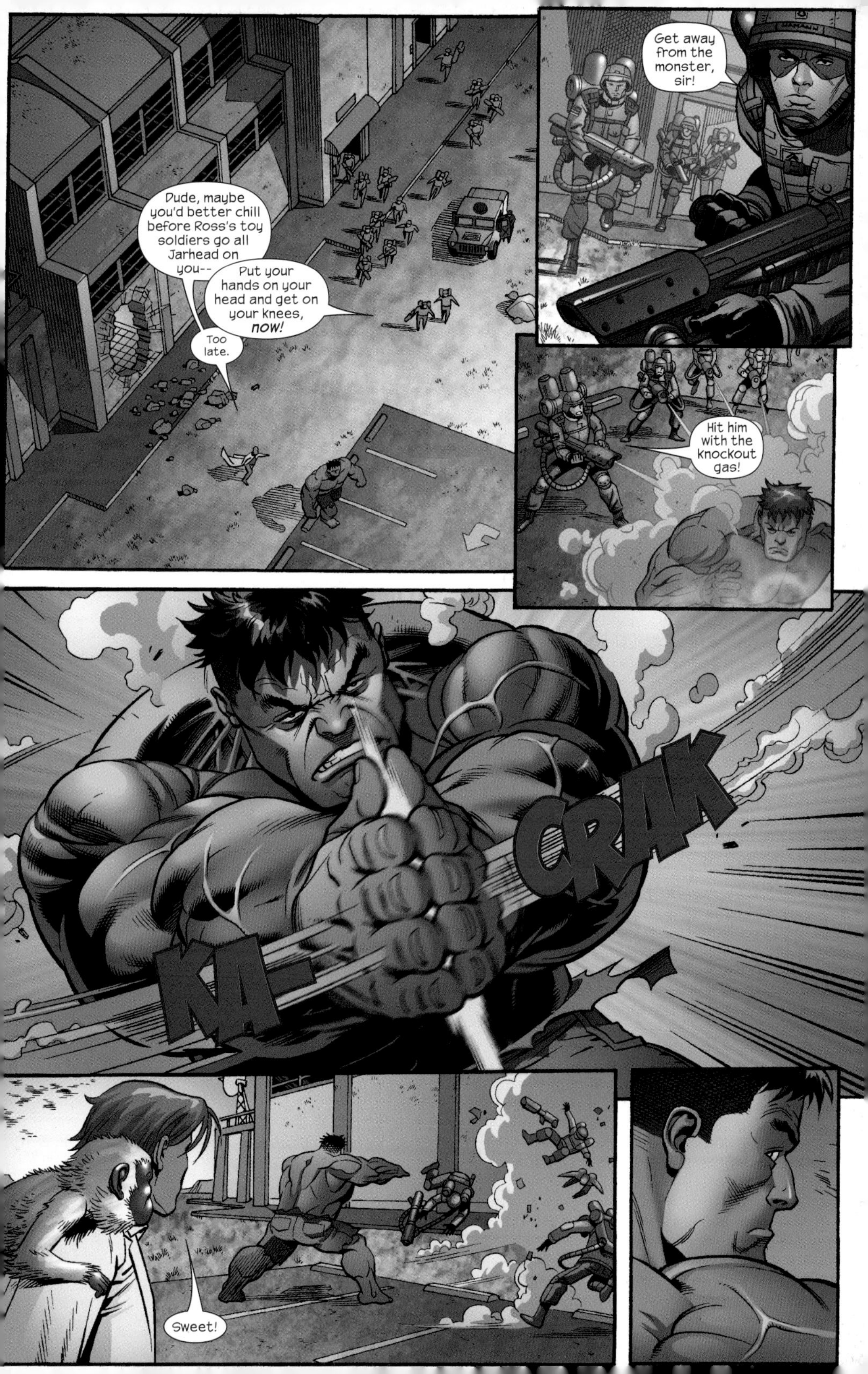
Dude, maybe you'd better chill before Ross's toy soldiers go all Jarhead on you--
Put your hands on your head and get on your knees, now!
Too late.
Get away from the monster, sir!
Hit him with the knockout gas!
KA-
CRAK
Sweet!

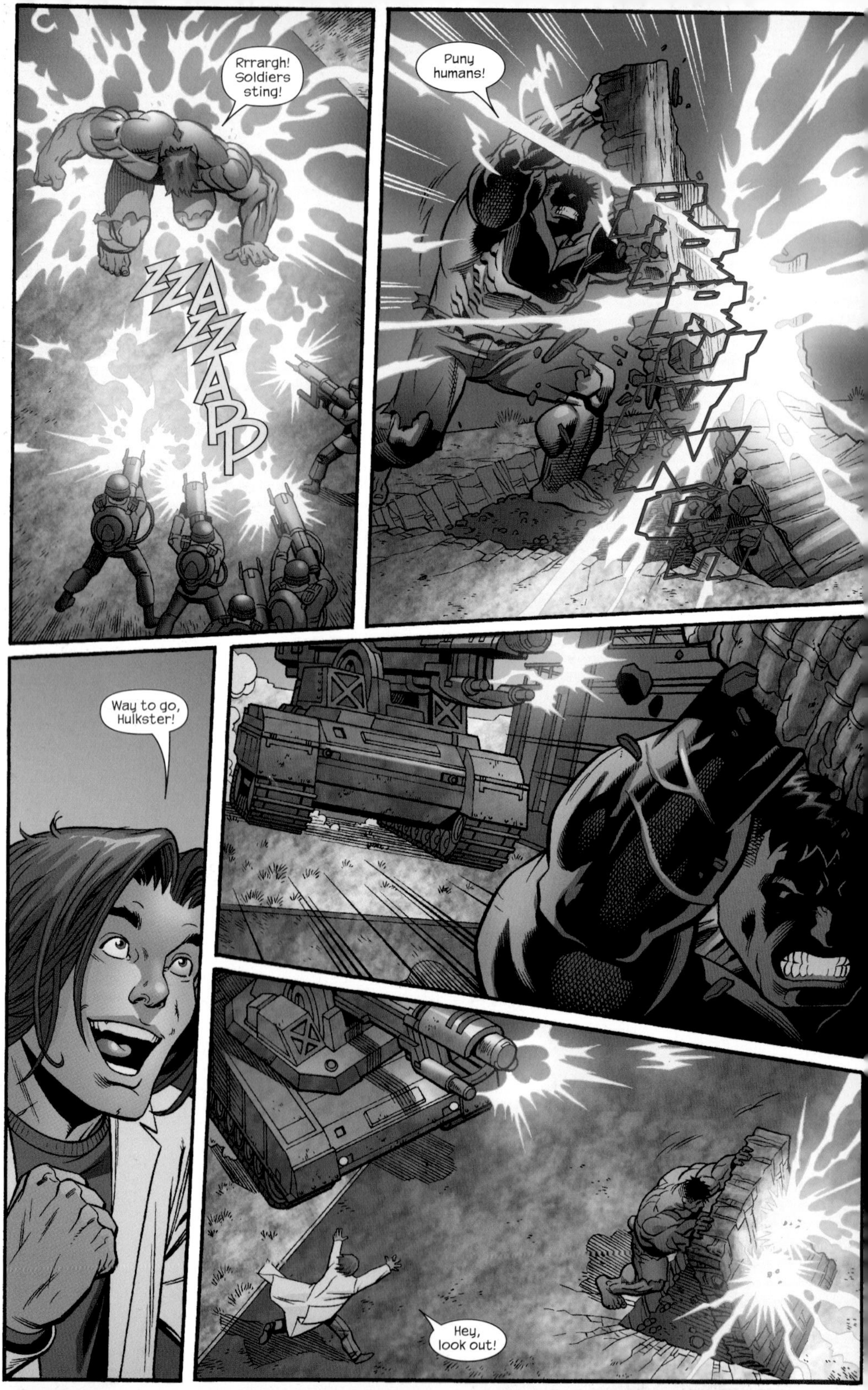
Rrrargh! Soldiers sting!
ZZZZAAP
Puny humans!
Way to go, Hulkster!
Hey, look out!

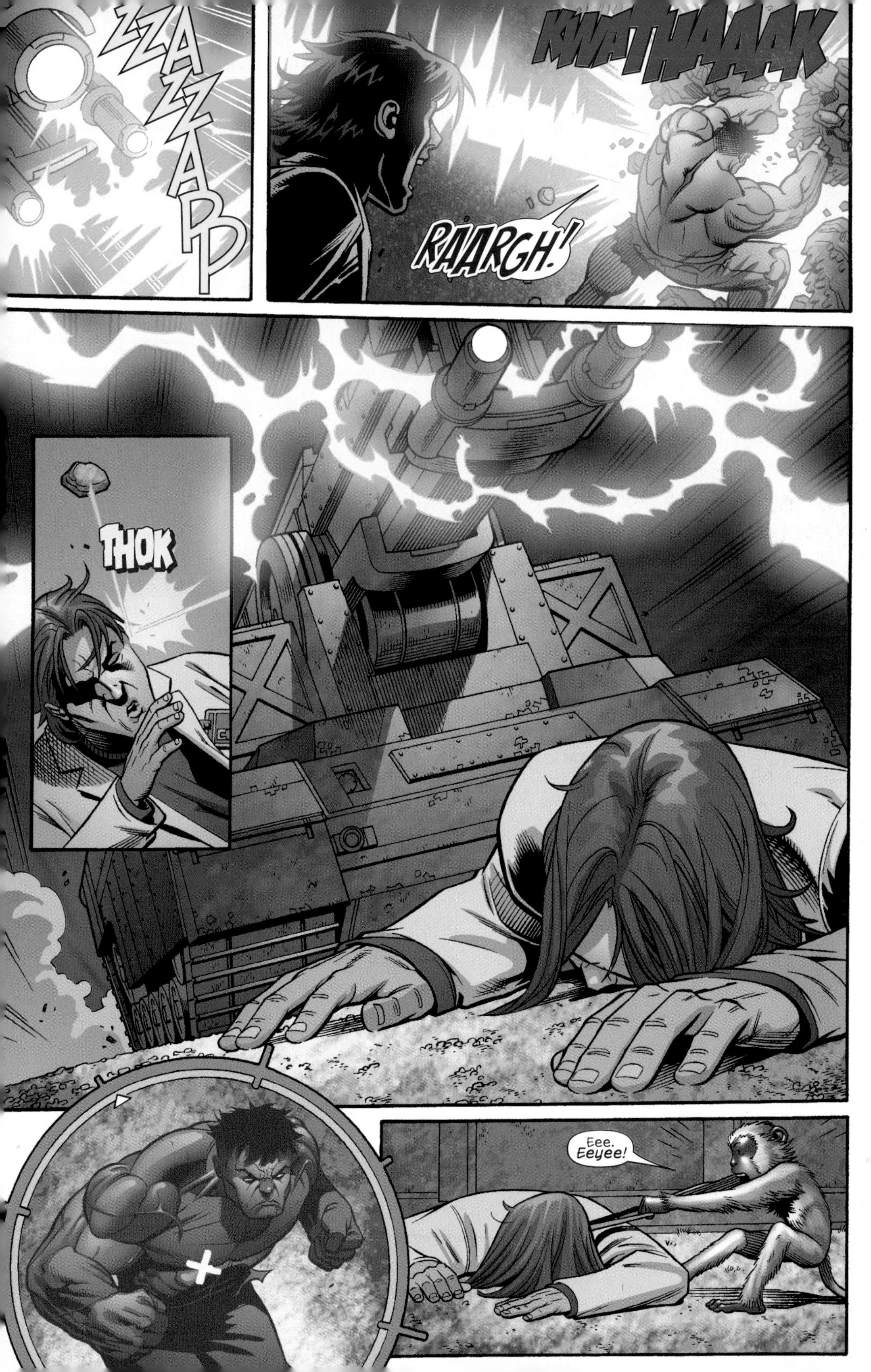
ZZAZZAP
KWATHAAAK
RAAARGH!
THOK
Eee.
Eeyee!

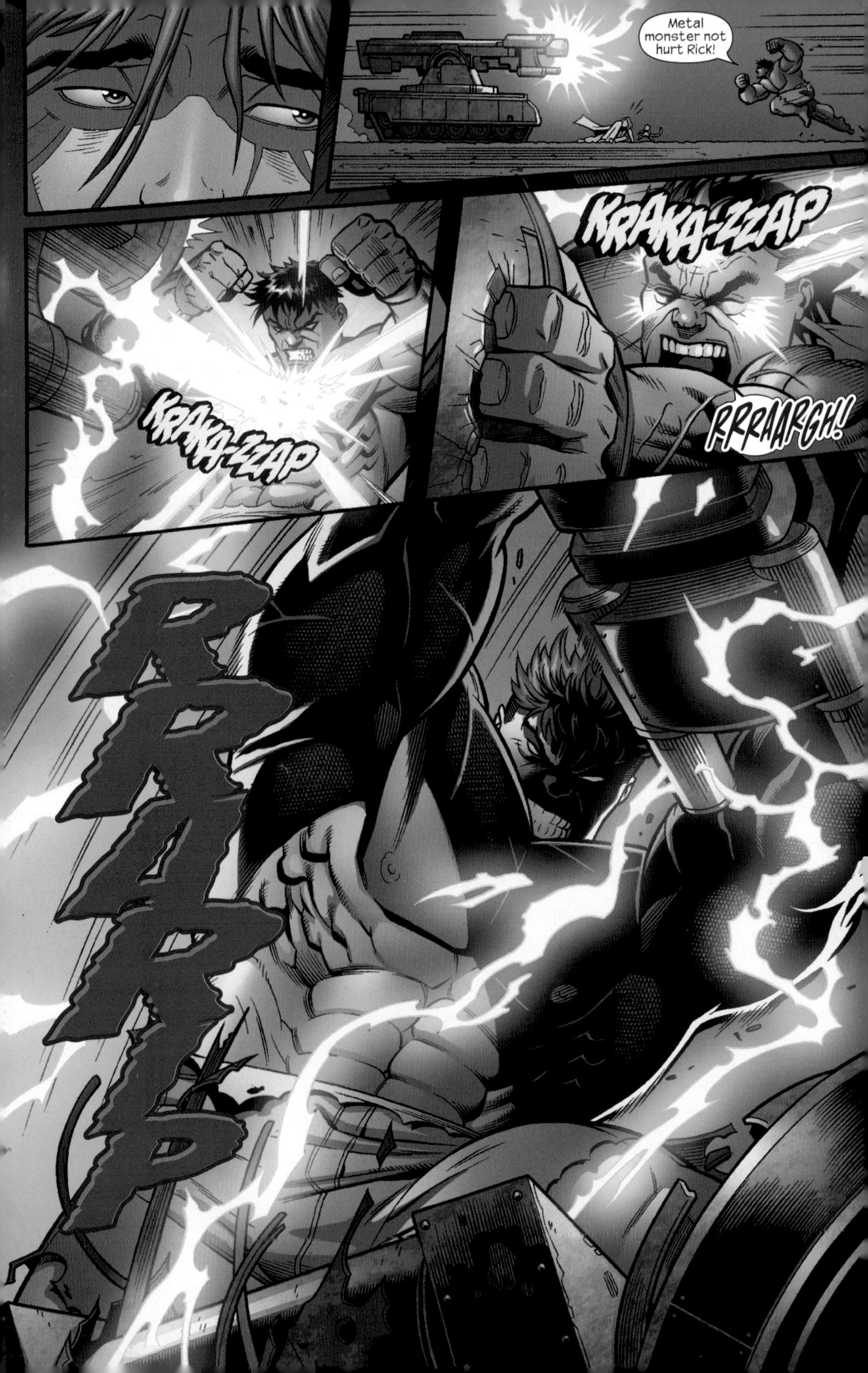
Metal monster not hurt Rick!
KRAKA-ZZAP
KRAKA-ZZAP
RRRAARGH!
RRRAAR

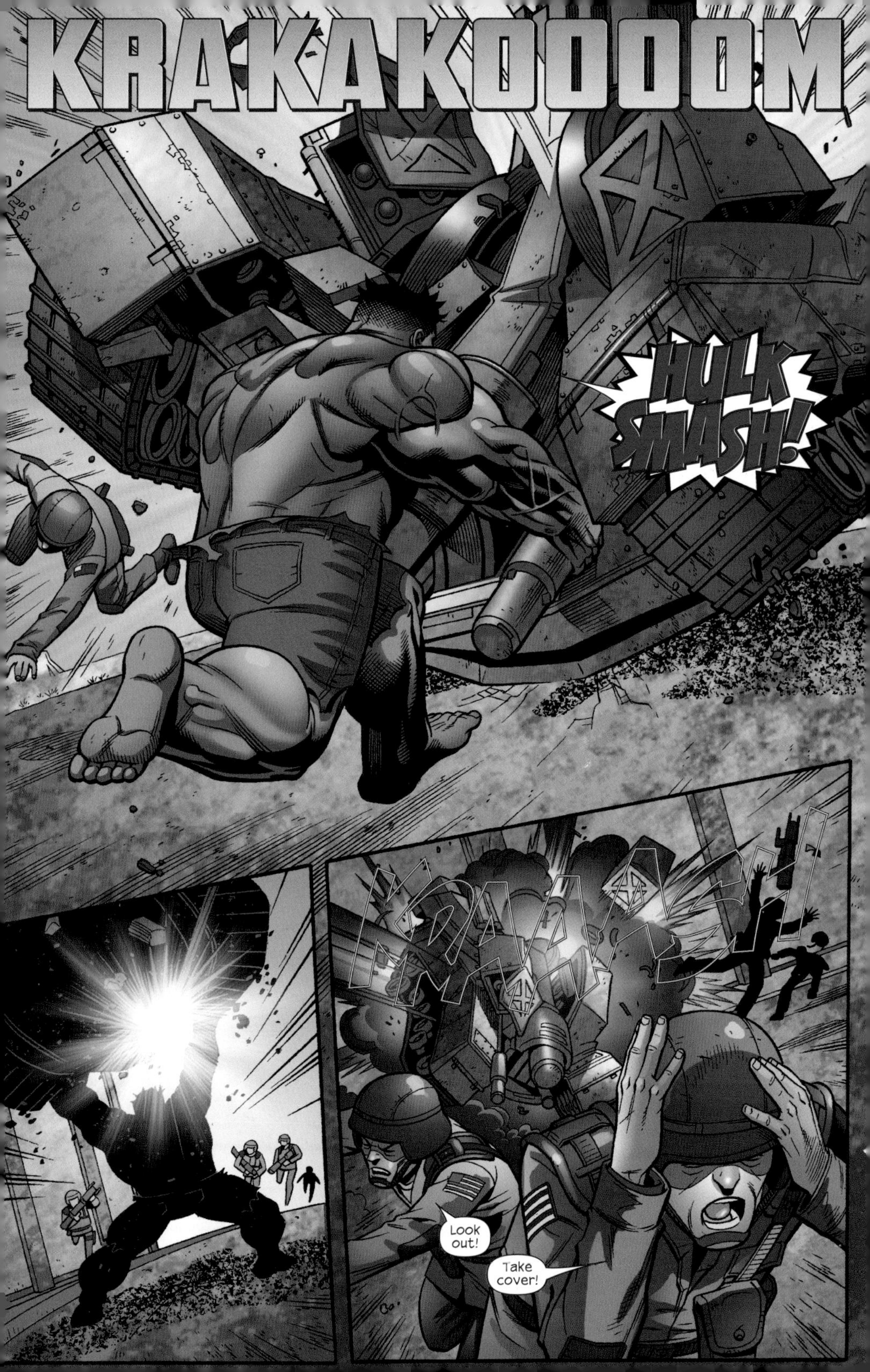
KRAKAKOOOOM
HULK SMASH!
Look out!
Take cover!

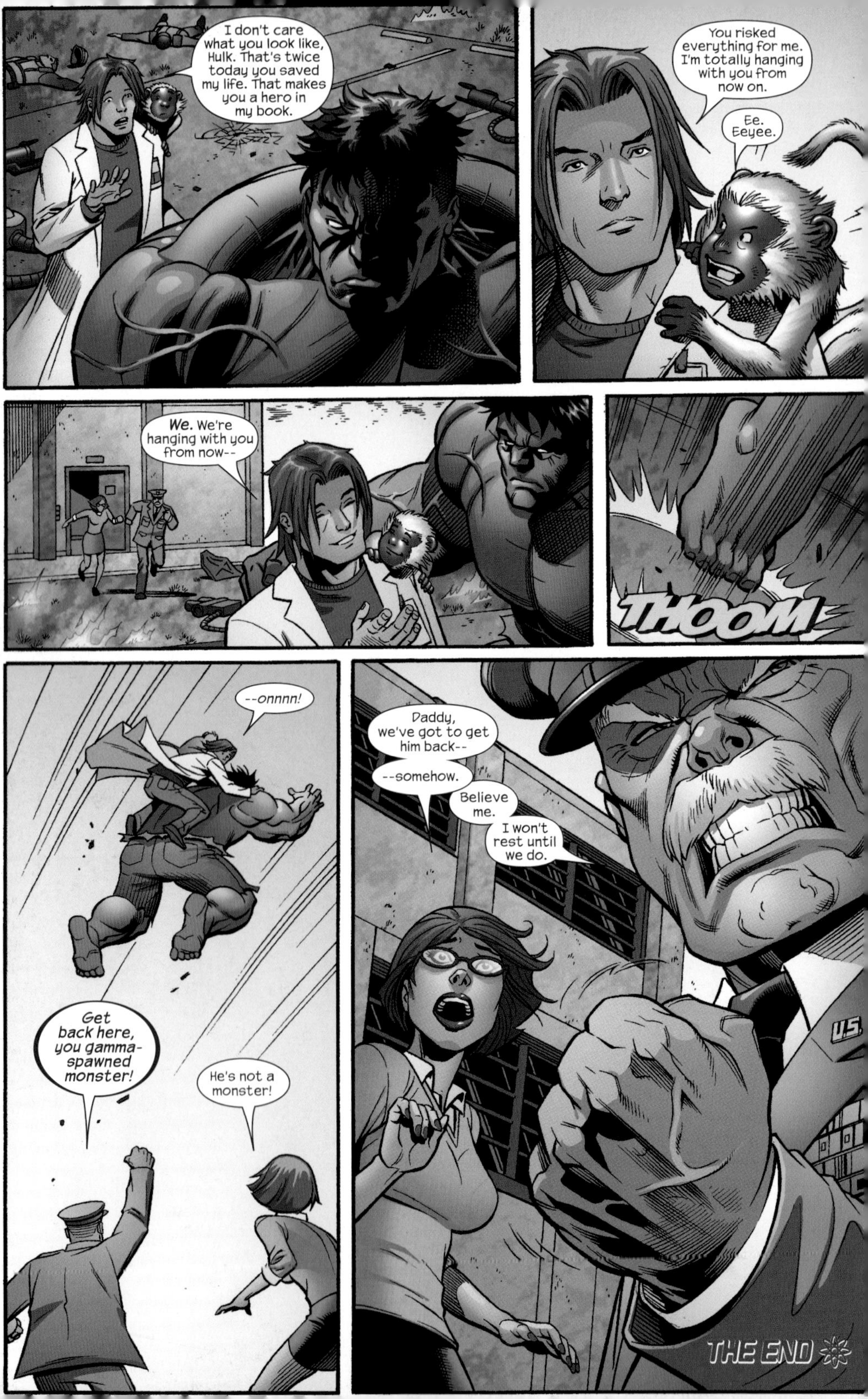
I don't care what you look like, Hulk. That's twice today you saved my life. That makes you a hero in my book.
You risked everything for me. I'm totally hanging with you from now on.
Ee. Eeyee.
We. We're hanging with you from now--
THOOM
--onnnn!
Get back here, you gamma-spawned monster!
He's not a monster!
Daddy, we've got to get him back--
--somehow.
Believe me.
I won't rest until we do.
U.S.
THE END

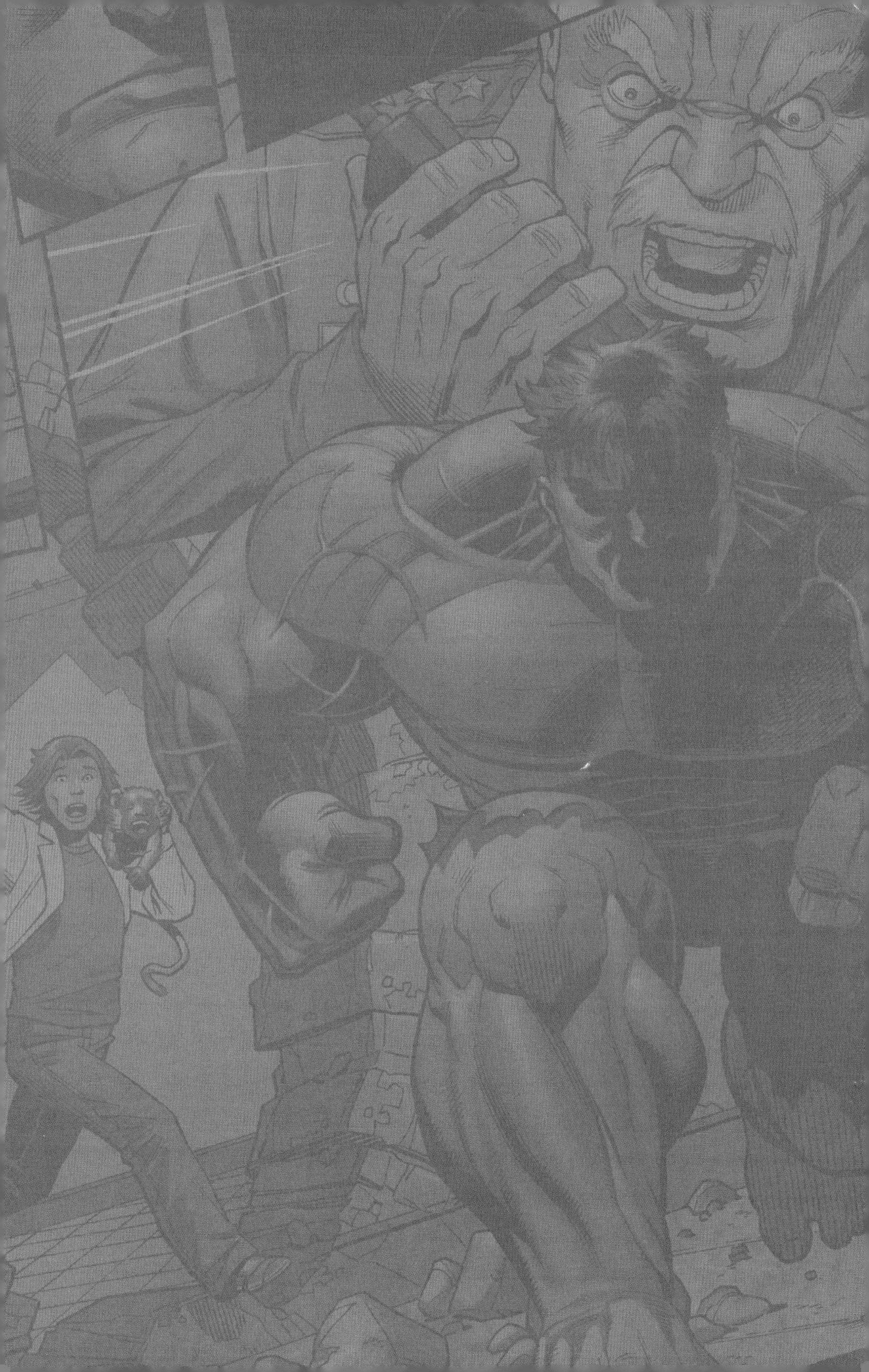

02

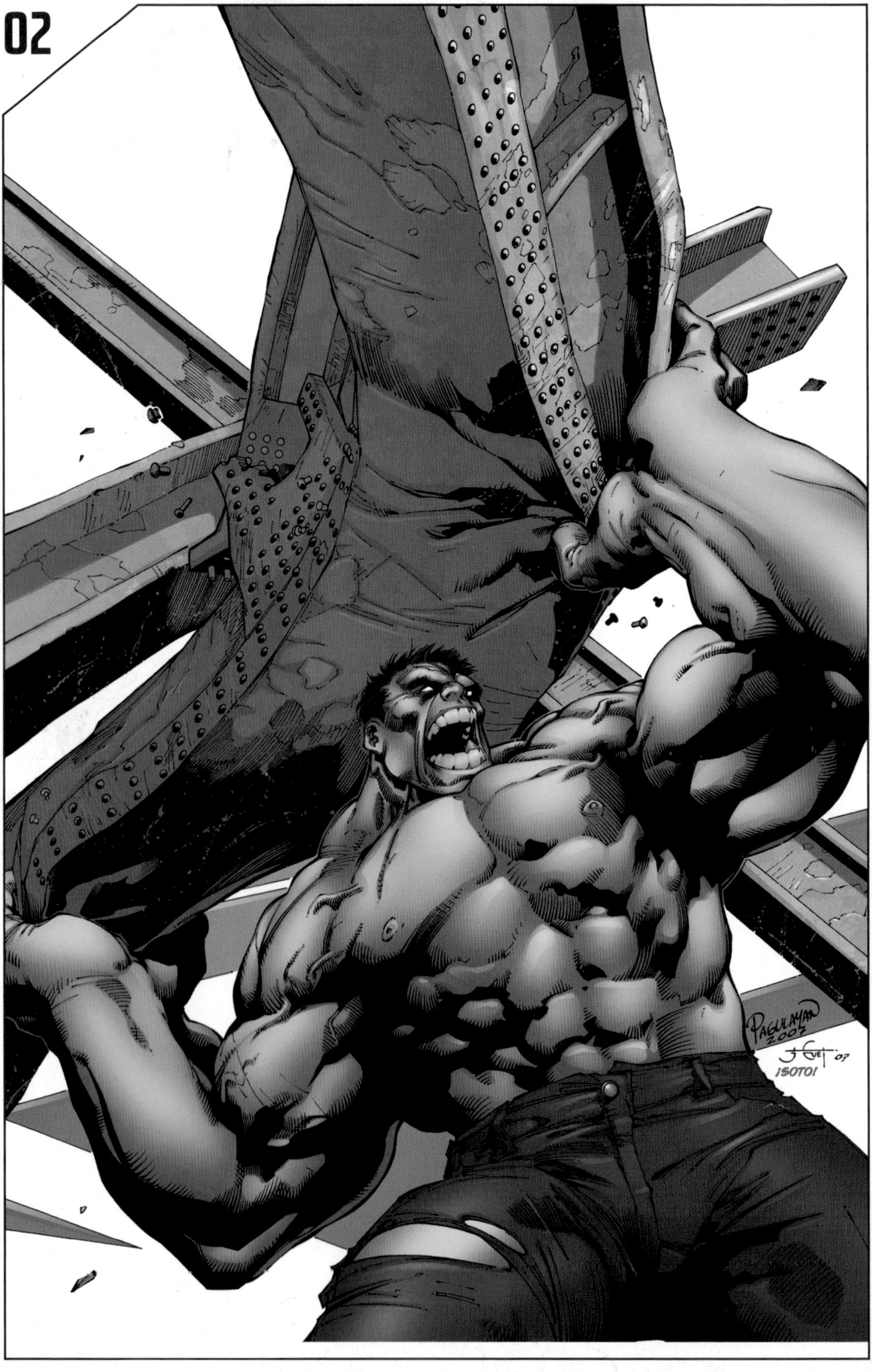
PAGULAYAN 2007
¡SOTO!

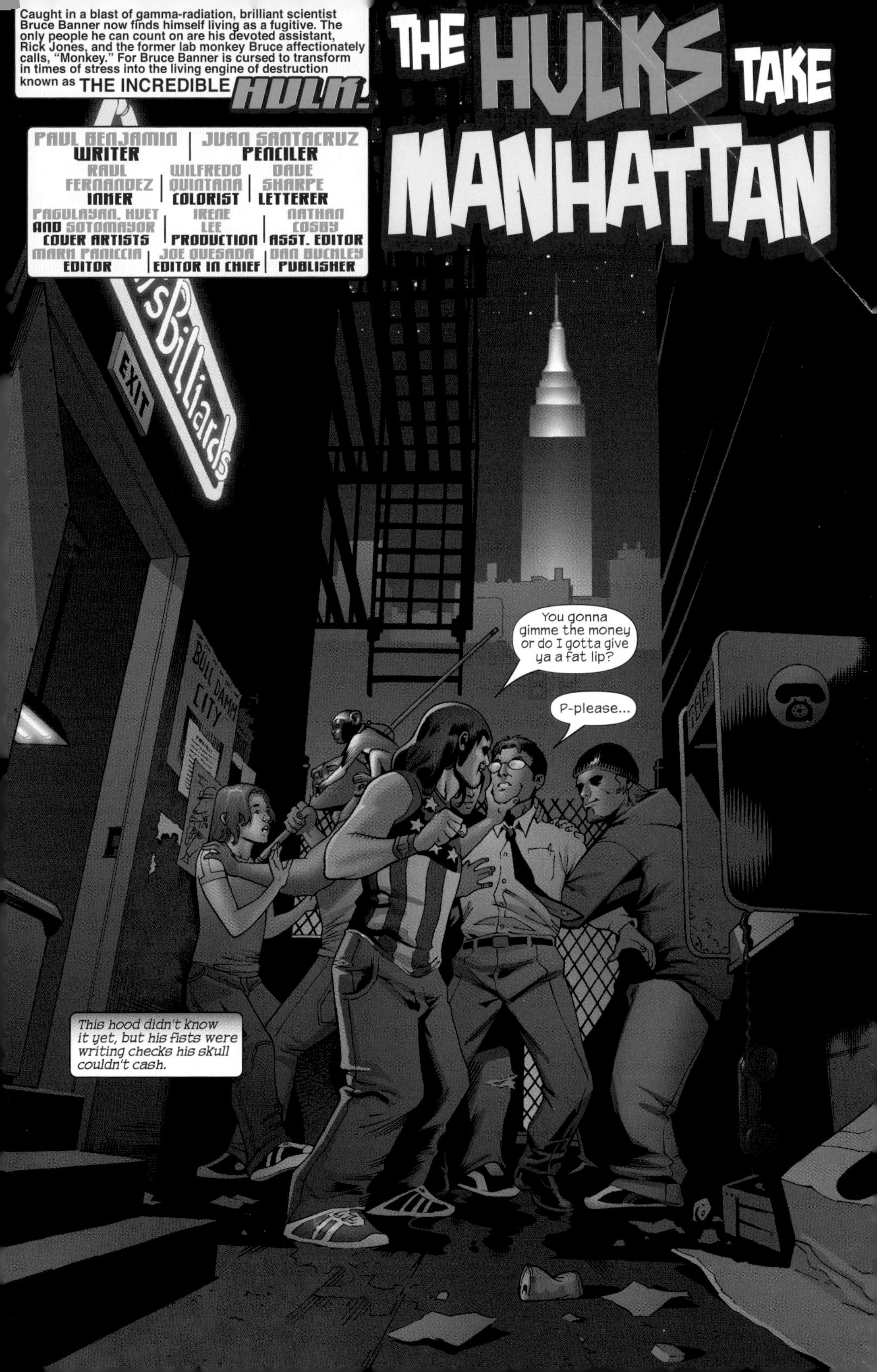

Caught in a blast of gamma-radiation, brilliant scientist Bruce Banner now finds himself living as a fugitive. The only people he can count on are his devoted assistant, Rick Jones, and the former lab monkey Bruce affectionately calls, "Monkey." For Bruce Banner is cursed to transform in times of stress into the living engine of destruction known as THE INCREDIBLE HULK!
THE HULKS TAKE MANHATTAN
PAUL BENJAMIN WRITER
JUAN SANTACRUZ PENCILER
RAUL FERNANDEZ INKER
WILFREDO QUINTANA COLORIST
DAVE SHARPE LETTERER
PAGULAYAN, HUET AND SOTOMAYOR COVER ARTISTS
IRENE LEE PRODUCTION
NATHAN COSBY ASST. EDITOR
MARK PANICCIA EDITOR
JOE QUESADA EDITOR IN CHIEF
DAN BUCKLEY PUBLISHER
EXIT
Billiards
You gonna gimme the money or do I gotta give ya a fat lip?
P-please...
This hood didn't know it yet, but his fists were writing checks his skull couldn't cash.

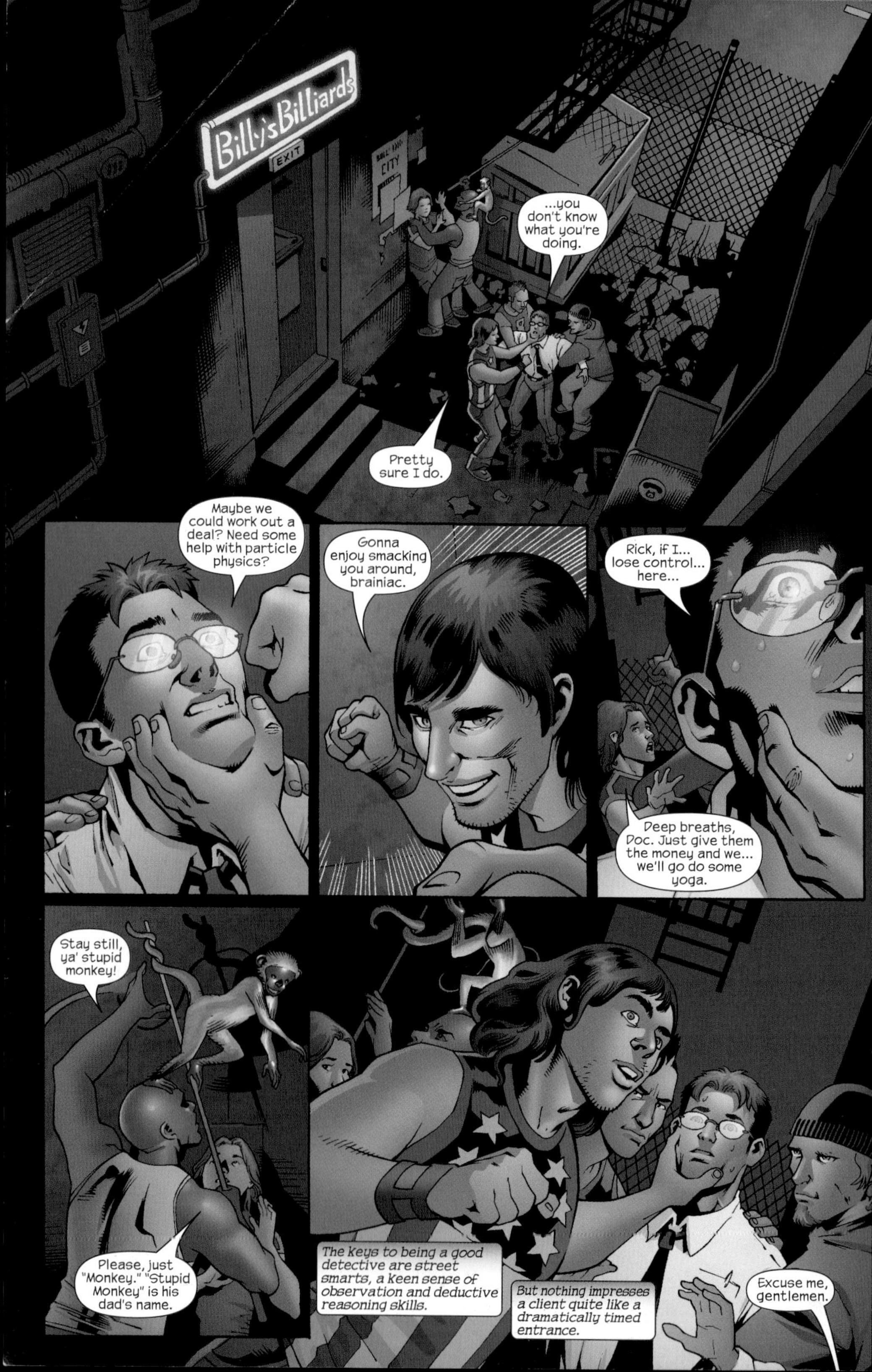
Billy's Billiards
EXIT
...you don't know what you're doing.
Pretty sure I do.
Maybe we could work out a deal? Need some help with particle physics?
Gonna enjoy smacking you around, brainiac.
Rick, if I... lose control... here...
Deep breaths, Doc. Just give them the money and we... we'll go do some yoga.
Stay still, ya' stupid monkey!
Please, just "Monkey." "Stupid Monkey" is his dad's name.
The keys to being a good detective are street smarts, a keen sense of observation and deductive reasoning skills.
But nothing impresses a client quite like a dramatically timed entrance.
Excuse me, gentlemen.

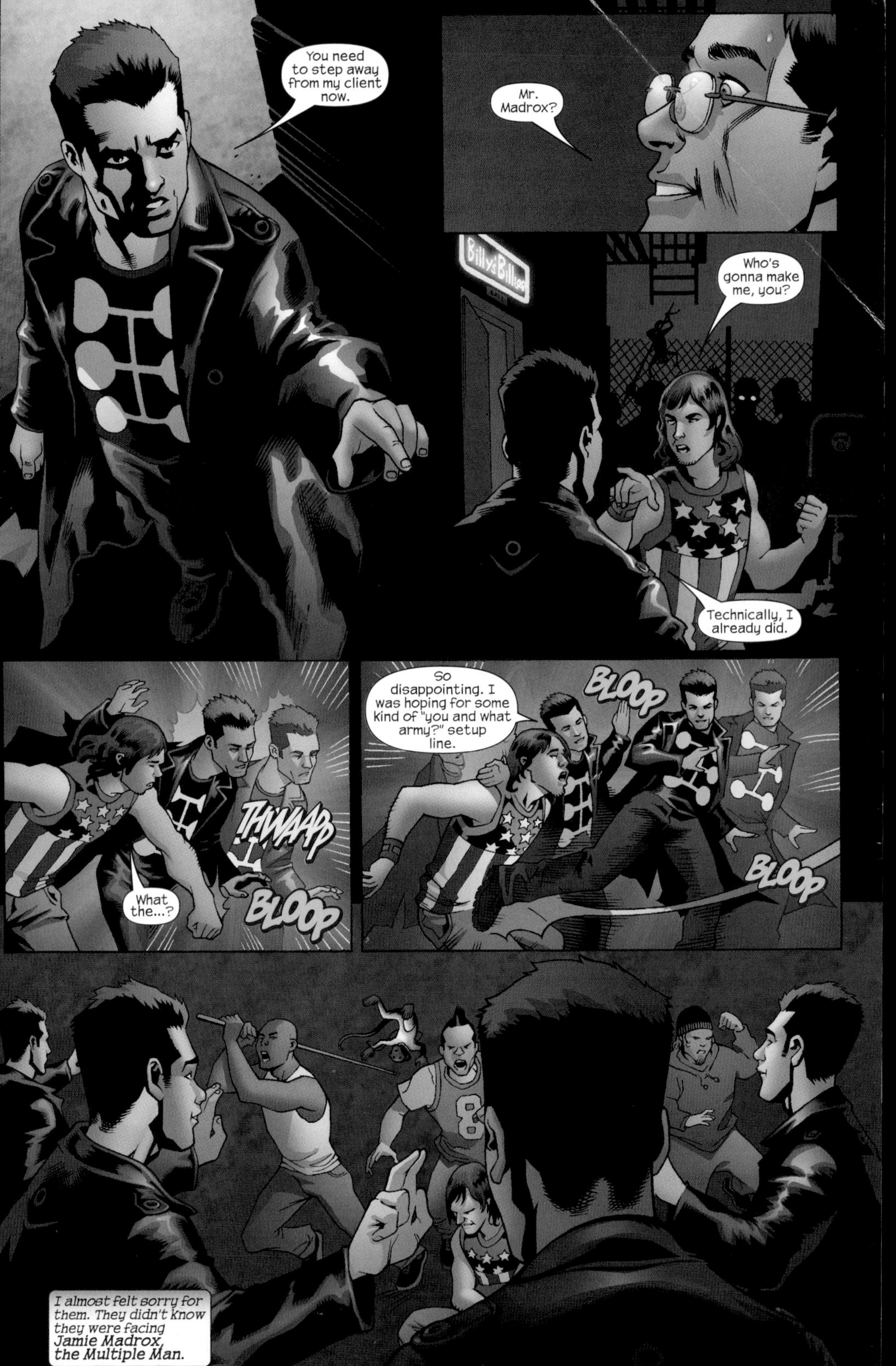
You need to step away from my client now.
Mr. Madrox?
Billy's Billiards
Who's gonna make me, you?
Technically, I already did.
THWAAPP
What the...?
BLOOP
So disappointing. I was hoping for some kind of "you and what army?" setup line.
BLOOP
BLOOP
I almost felt sorry for them. They didn't know they were facing Jamie Madrox, the Multiple Man.

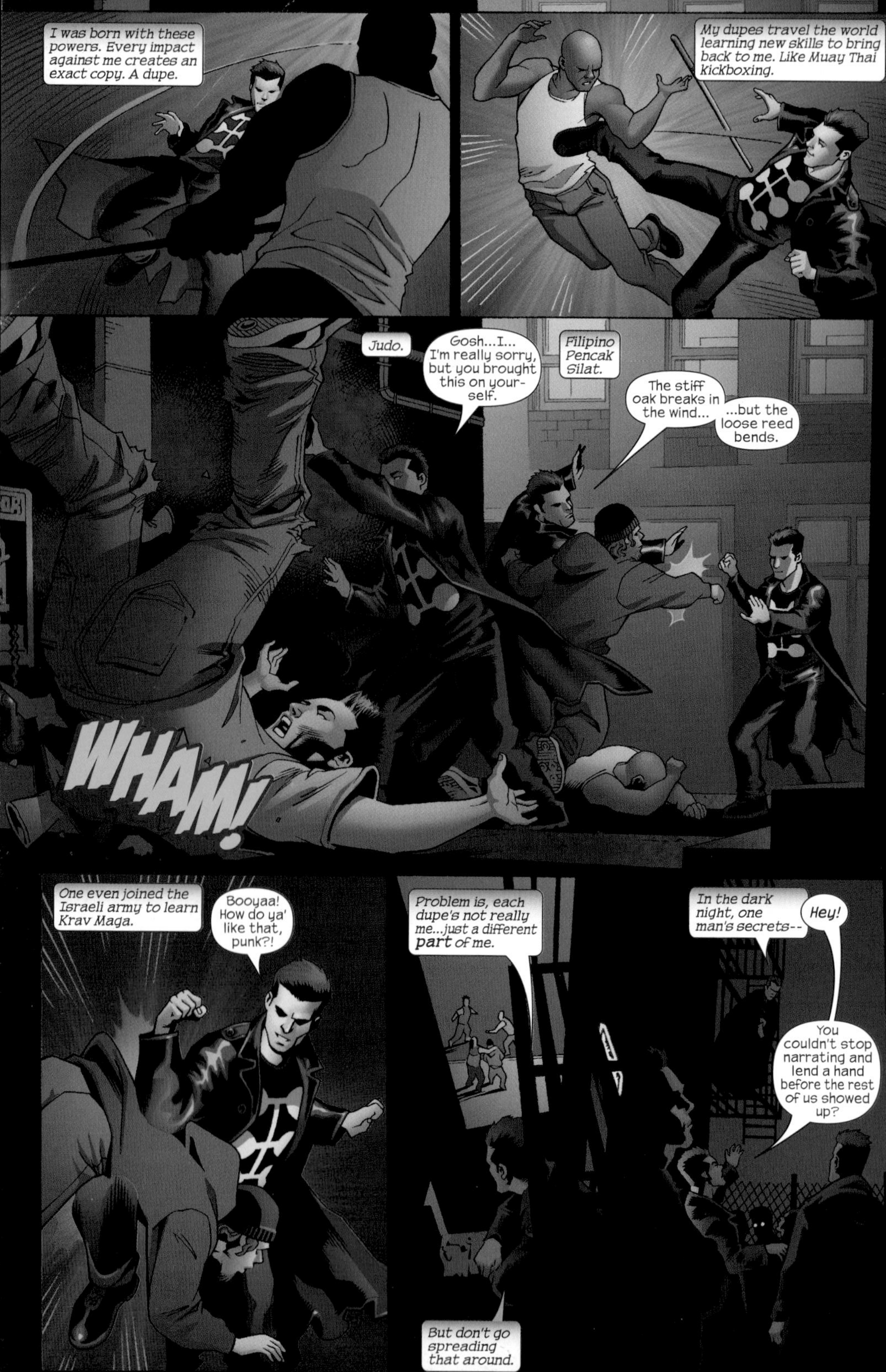

I was born with these powers. Every impact against me creates an exact copy. A dupe.
My dupes travel the world learning new skills to bring back to me. Like Muay Thai kickboxing.
Judo.
Gosh...I... I'm really sorry, but you brought this on your-self.
Filipino Pencak Silat.
The stiff oak breaks in the wind...
...but the loose reed bends.
WHAM!
One even joined the Israeli army to learn Krav Maga.
Booyaa! How do ya' like that, punk?!
Problem is, each dupe's not really me...just a different part of me.
But don't go spreading that around.
In the dark night, one man's secrets--
Hey!
You couldn't stop narrating and lend a hand before the rest of us showed up?

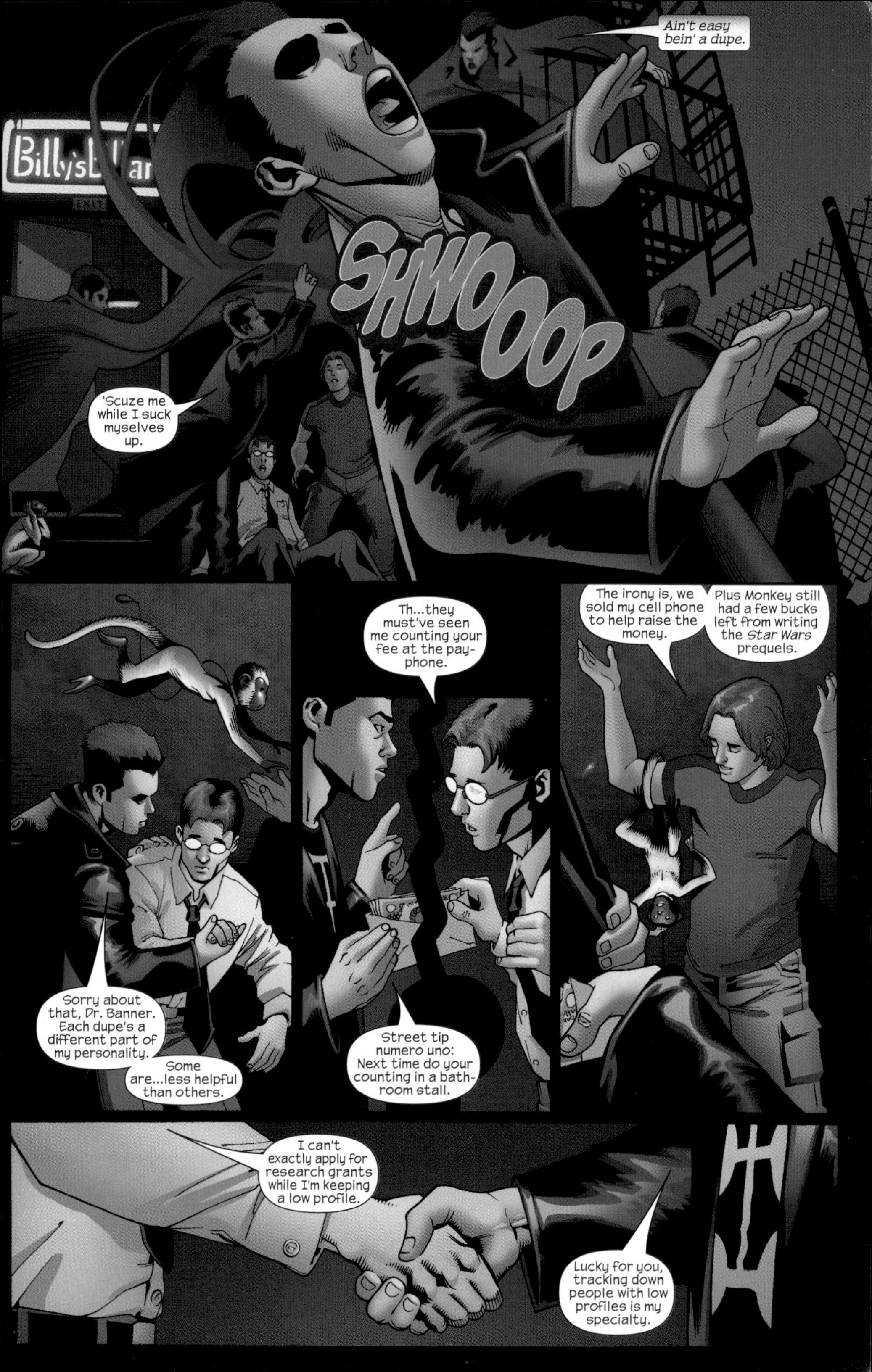
Billy's Billiards
EXIT
Ain't easy bein' a dupe.
SHWOOOP
'Scuze me while I suck myselves up.
Sorry about that, Dr. Banner. Each dupe's a different part of my personality.
Some are...less helpful than others.
Th...they must've seen me counting your fee at the pay-phone.
Street tip numero uno: Next time do your counting in a bath-room stall.
The irony is, we sold my cell phone to help raise the money.
Plus Monkey still had a few bucks left from writing the Star Wars prequels.
I can't exactly apply for research grants while I'm keeping a low profile.
Lucky for you, tracking down people with low profiles is my specialty.

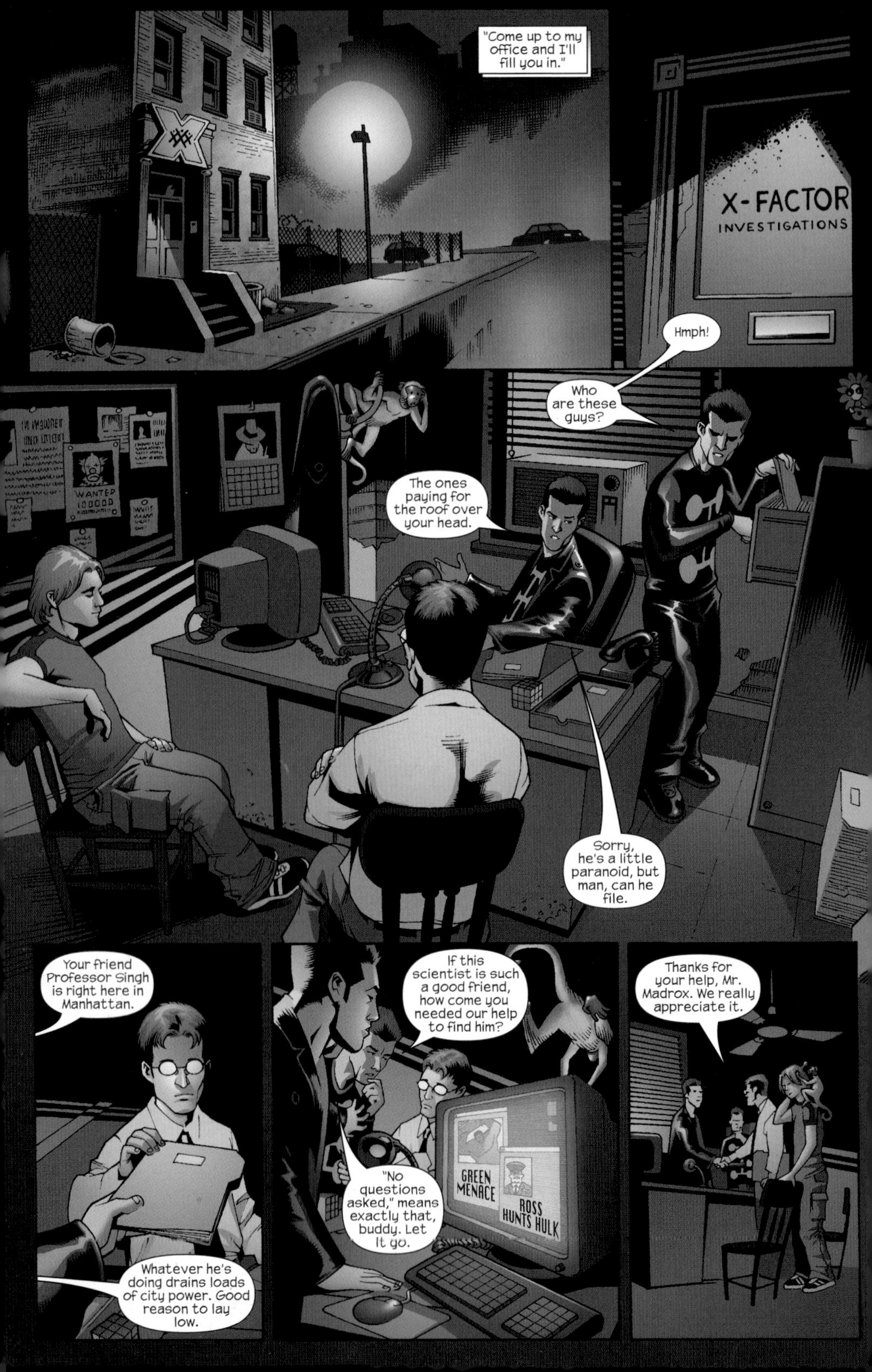
"Come up to my office and I'll fill you in."
X-FACTOR INVESTIGATIONS
Hmph!
Who are these guys?
The ones paying for the roof over your head.
Sorry, he's a little paranoid, but man, can he file.
WANTED 100000
Your friend Professor Singh is right here in Manhattan.
Whatever he's doing drains loads of city power. Good reason to lay low.
If this scientist is such a good friend, how come you needed our help to find him?
"No questions asked," means exactly that, buddy. Let it go.
GREEN MENACE
ROSS HUNTS HULK
Thanks for your help, Mr. Madrox. We really appreciate it.

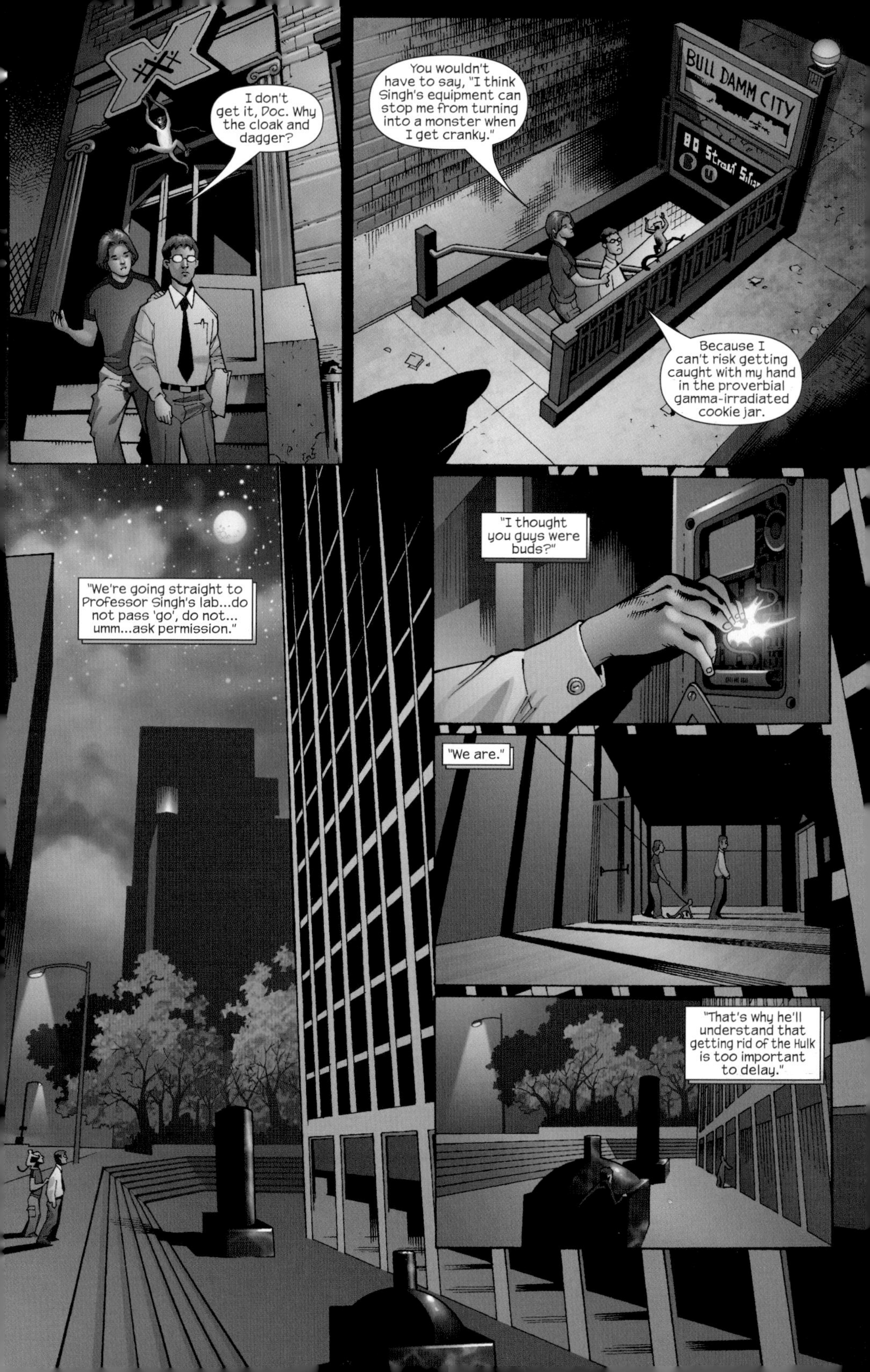

I don't get it, Doc. Why the cloak and dagger?
You wouldn't have to say, "I think Singh's equipment can stop me from turning into a monster when I get cranky."
BULL DAMM CITY
Because I can't risk getting caught with my hand in the proverbial gamma-irradiated cookie jar.
"We're going straight to Professor Singh's lab...do not pass 'go', do not... umm...ask permission."
"I thought you guys were buds?"
"We are."
"That's why he'll understand that getting rid of the Hulk is too important to delay."

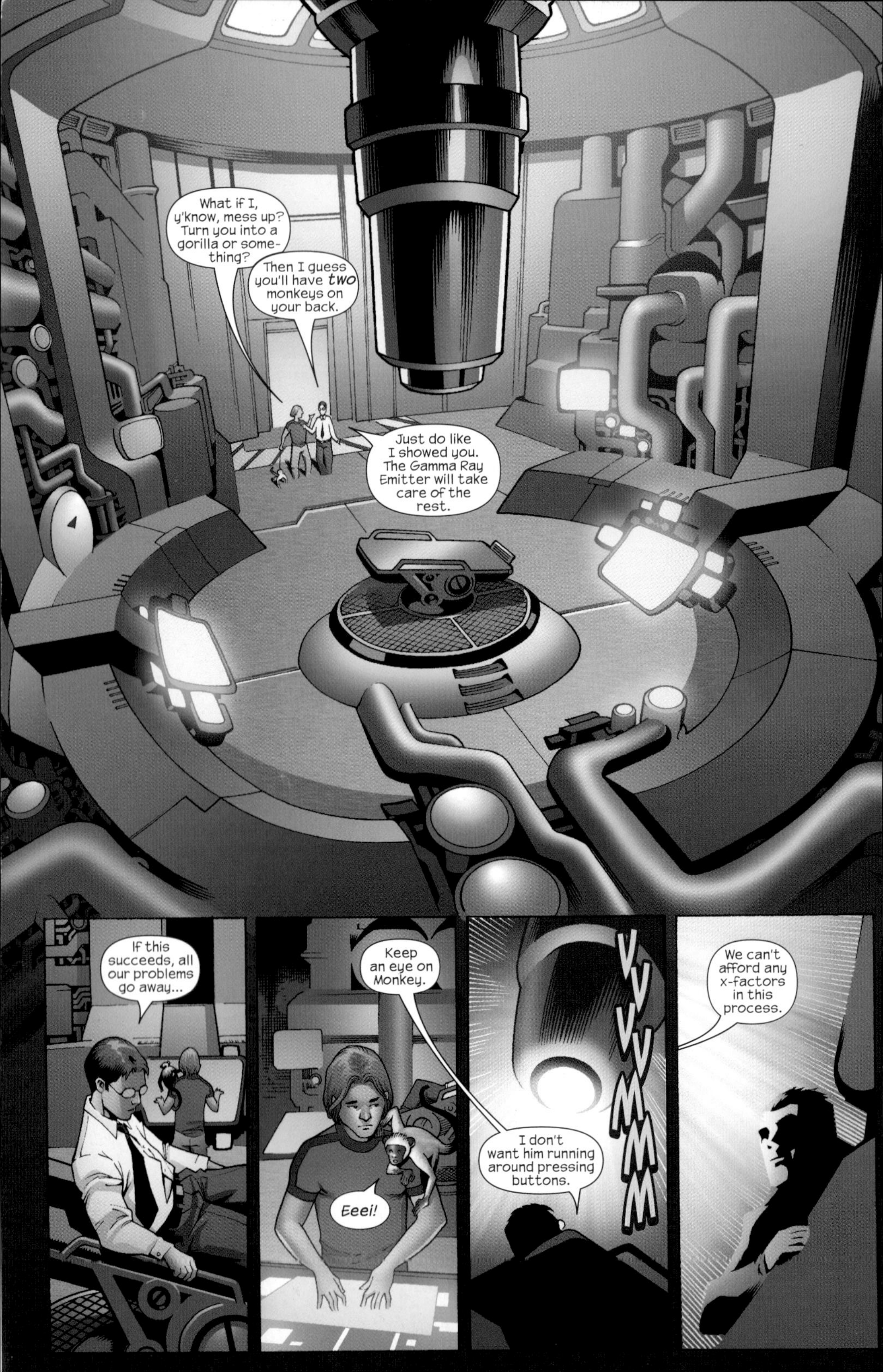
What if I, y'know, mess up? Turn you into a gorilla or some-thing?
Then I guess you'll have two monkeys on your back.
Just do like I showed you. The Gamma Ray Emitter will take care of the rest.
If this succeeds, all our problems go away...
Keep an eye on Monkey.
Eeei!
I don't want him running around pressing buttons.
VVVVVMMMM
We can't afford any x-factors in this process.

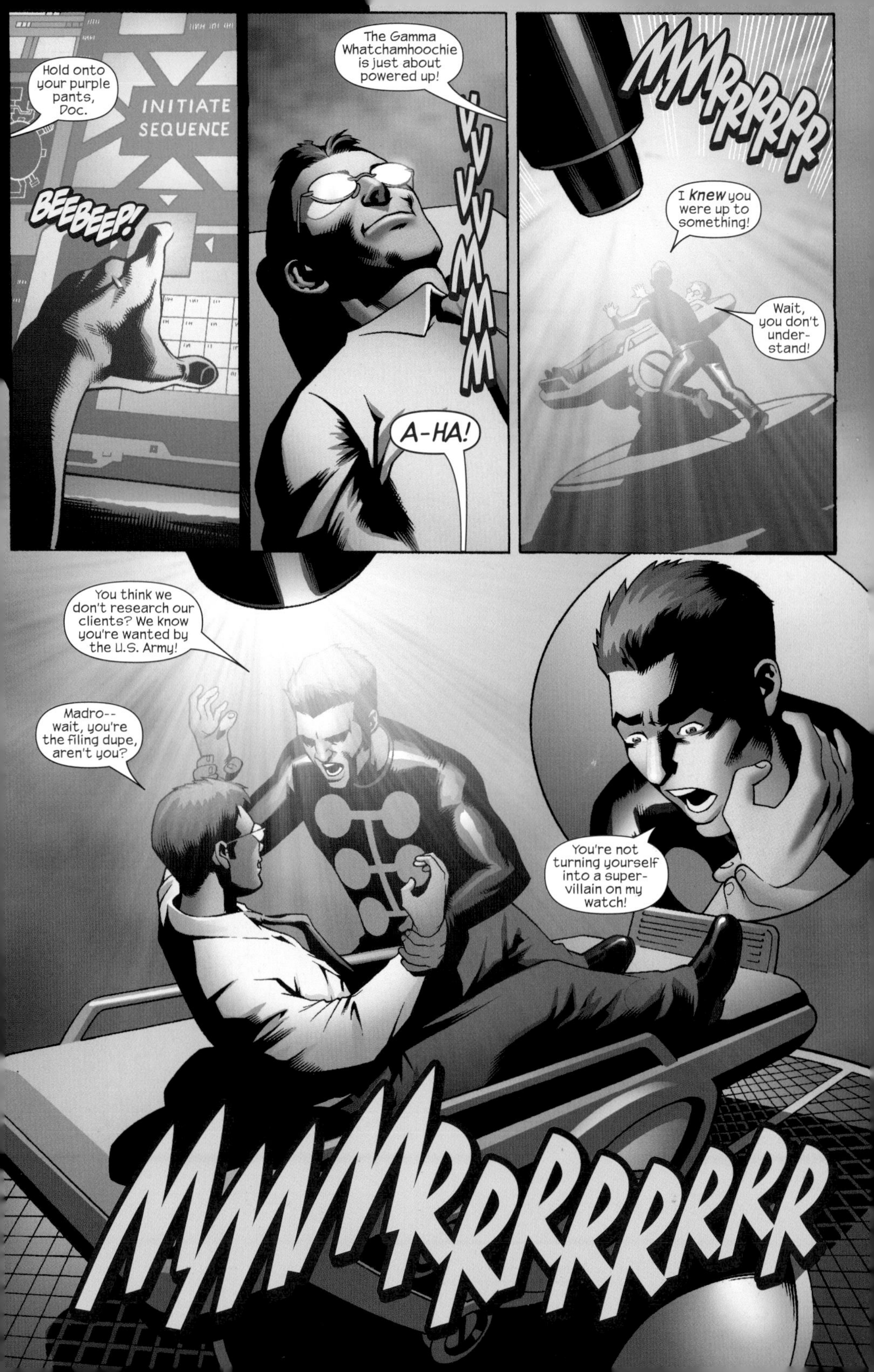
Hold onto your purple pants, Doc.
INITIATE SEQUENCE
BEEBEEP!
The Gamma Whatchamhoochie is just about powered up!
VVVVMMMM
A-HA!
MMRRRRRR
I knew you were up to something!
Wait, you don't under-stand!
You think we don't research our clients? We know you're wanted by the U.S. Army!
Madro-- wait, you're the filing dupe, aren't you?
You're not turning yourself into a super-villain on my watch!
MMMRRRRRRRR

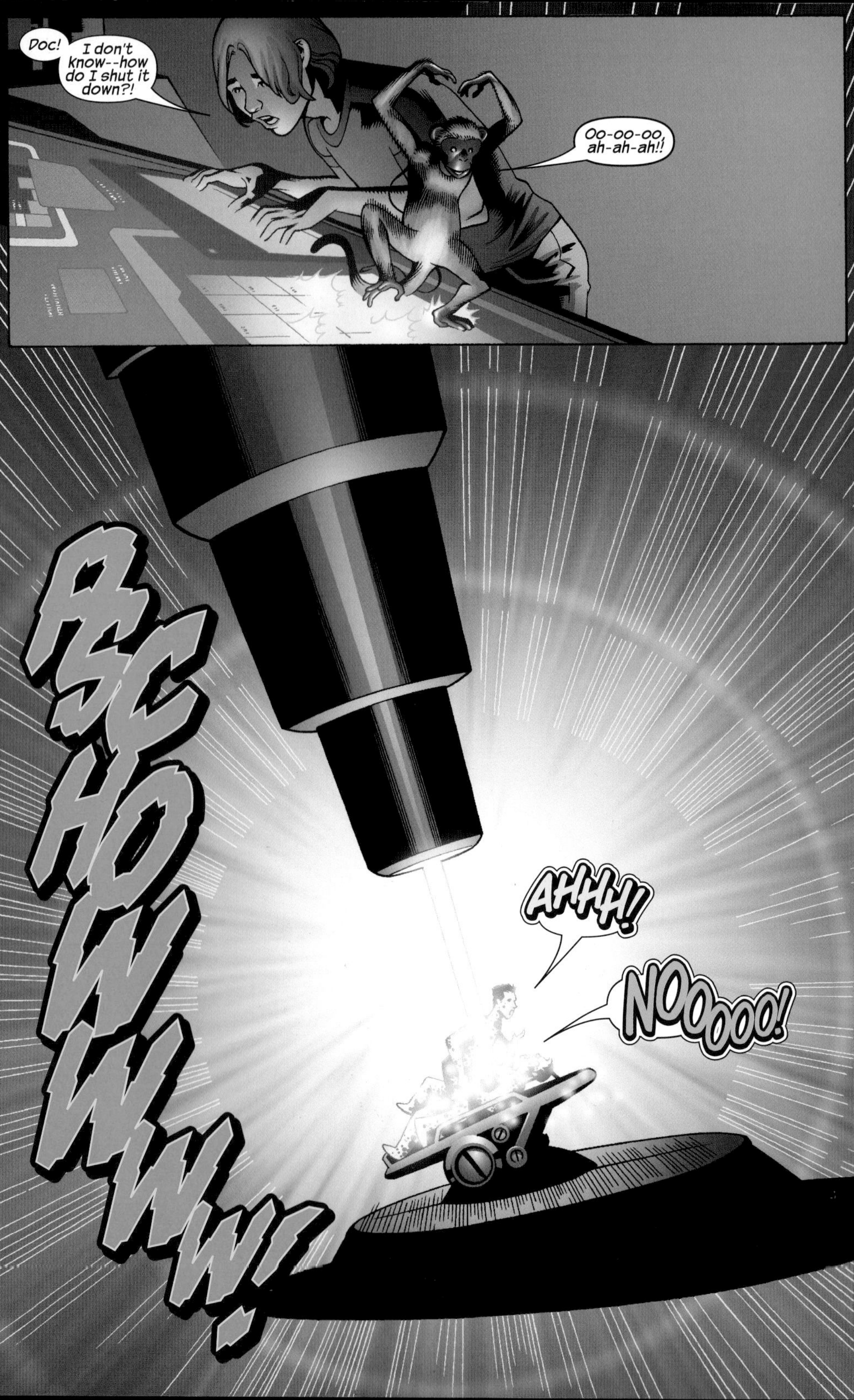
Doc!
I don't know--how do I shut it down?!
Oo-oo-oo, ah-ah-ah!!
PSCHOWWWWW!
AHHH!
NOOOOO!

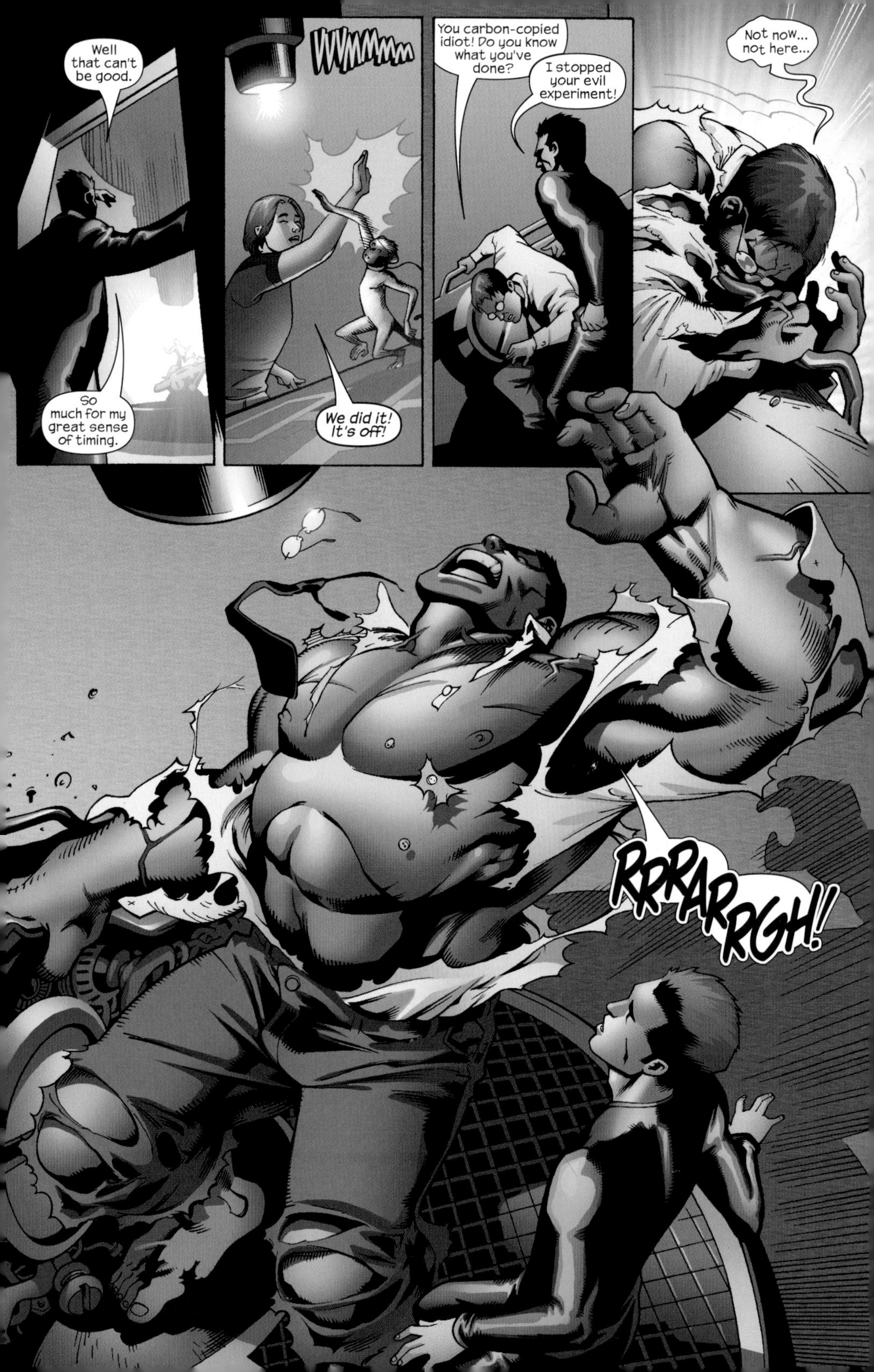

Well that can't be good.
So much for my great sense of timing.
VVVMMMmm
We did it! It's off!
You carbon-copied idiot! Do you know what you've done?
I stopped your evil experiment!
Not now... not here...
RRRARRRGH!

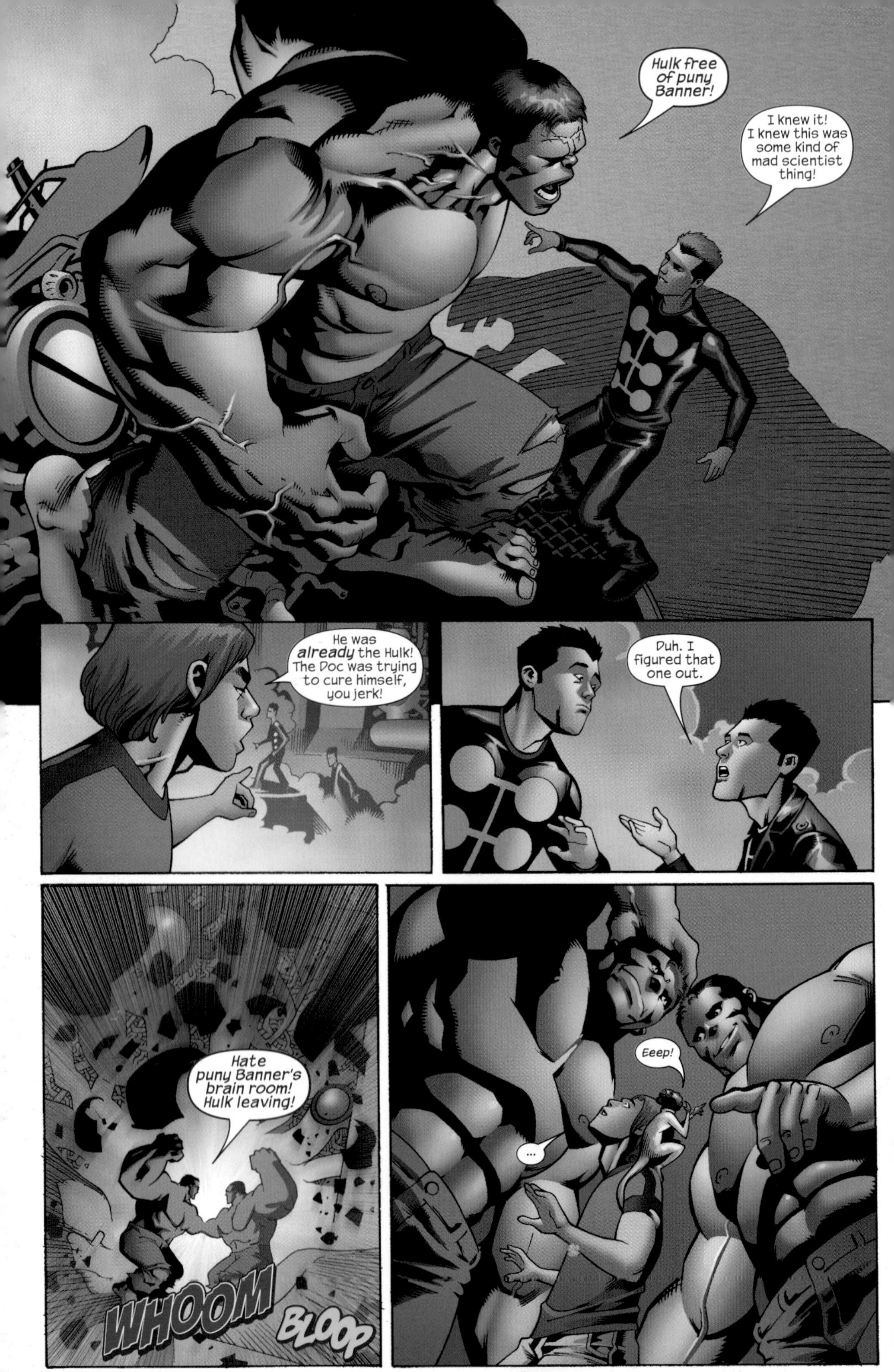
Hulk free of puny Banner!
I knew it! I knew this was some kind of mad scientist thing!
He was already the Hulk! The Doc was trying to cure himself, you jerk!
Duh. I figured that one out.
Hate puny Banner's brain room! Hulk leaving!
WHOOM
BLOOP
Eeep!
...

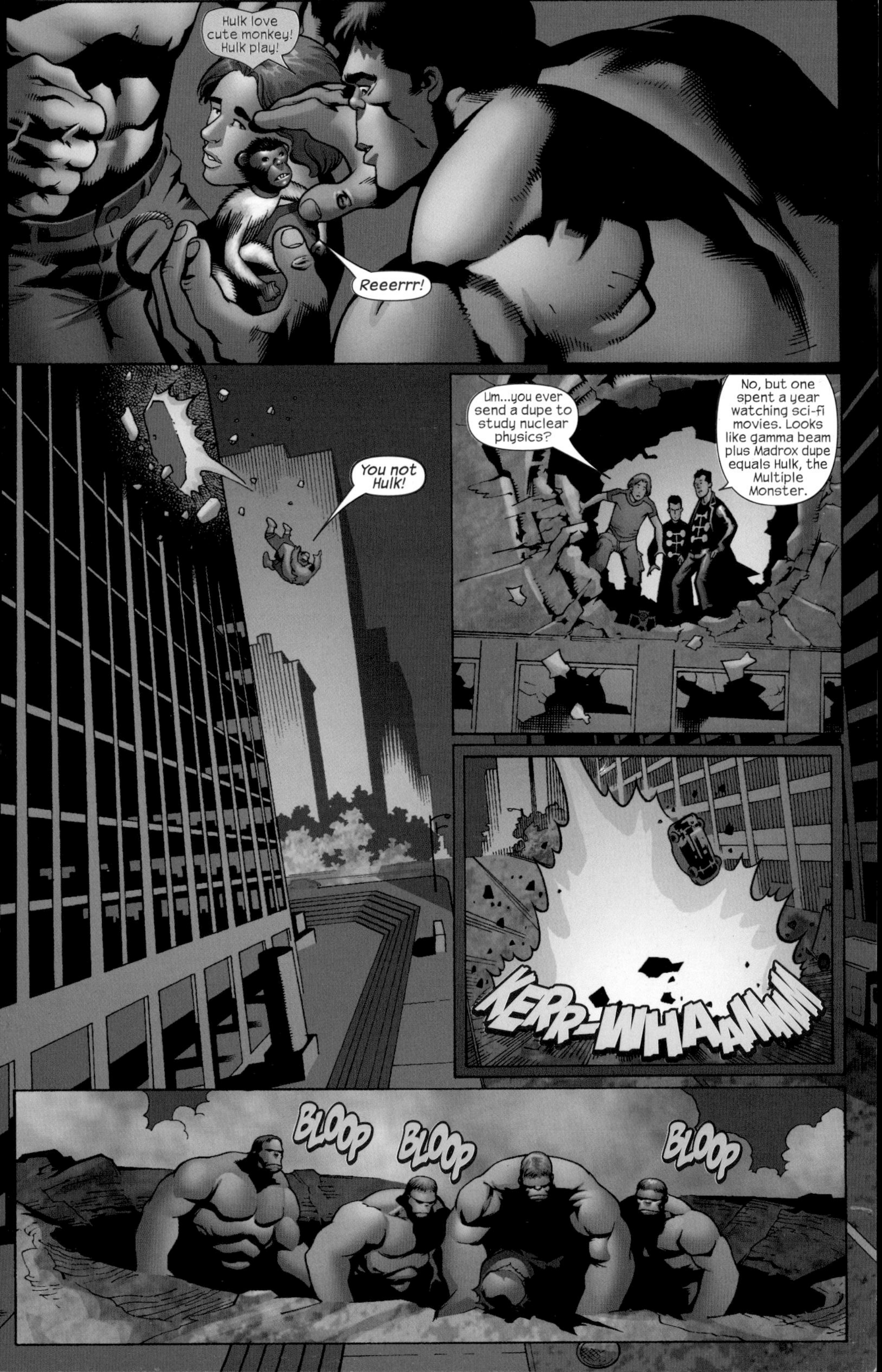

Hulk love cute monkey! Hulk play!
Reeerrr!
You not Hulk!
Um...you ever send a dupe to study nuclear physics?
No, but one spent a year watching sci-fi movies. Looks like gamma beam plus Madrox dupe equals Hulk, the Multiple Monster.
KERR-WHAAMM
BLOOP
BLOOP
BLOOP

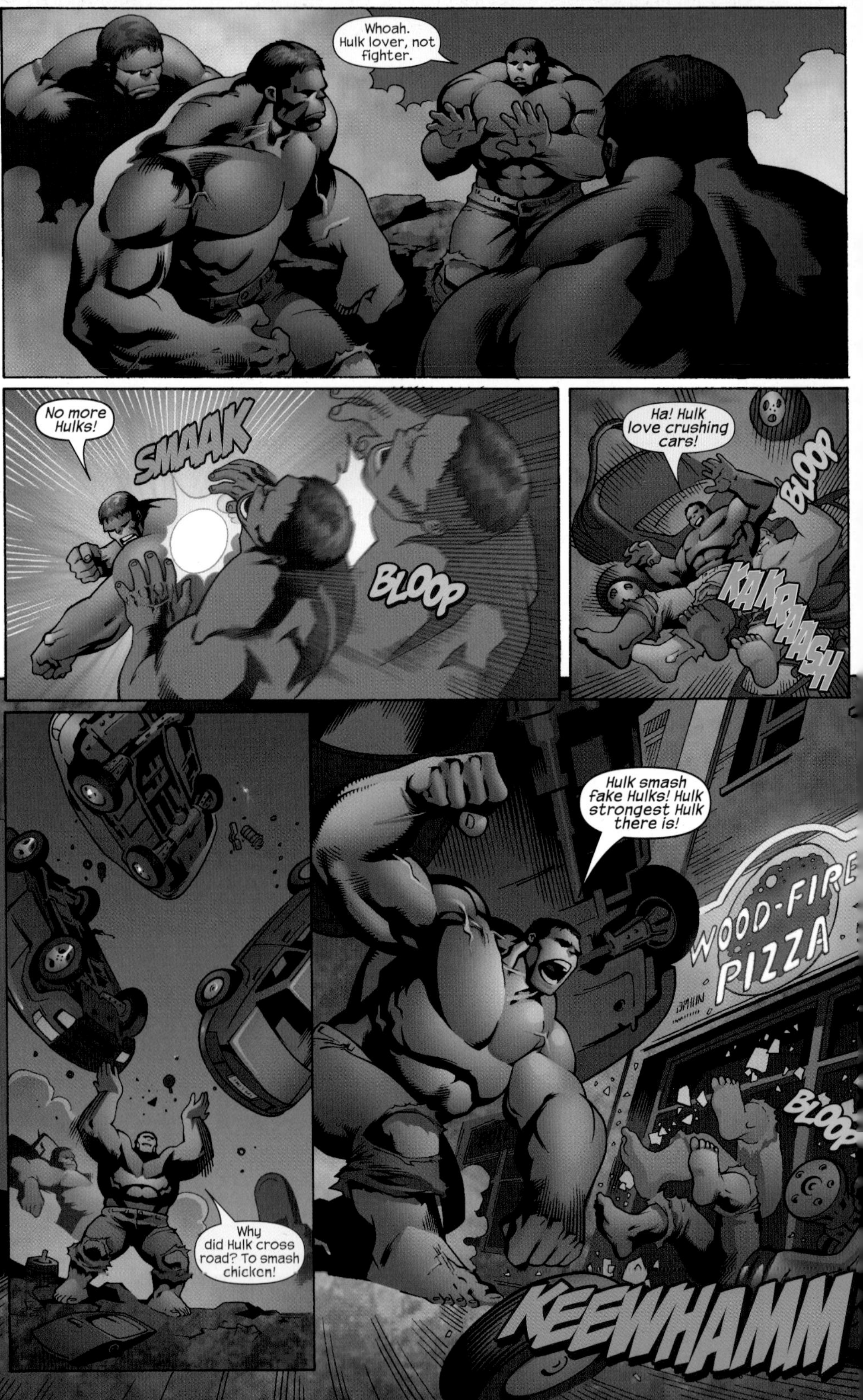
Whoah. Hulk lover, not fighter.
No more Hulks!
SMAAK
BLOOP
Ha! Hulk love crushing cars!
BLOOP
KAKRAASH
Hulk smash fake Hulks! Hulk strongest Hulk there is!
WOOD-FIRE PIZZA
BLOOP
Why did Hulk cross road? To smash chicken!
KEEWHAMM

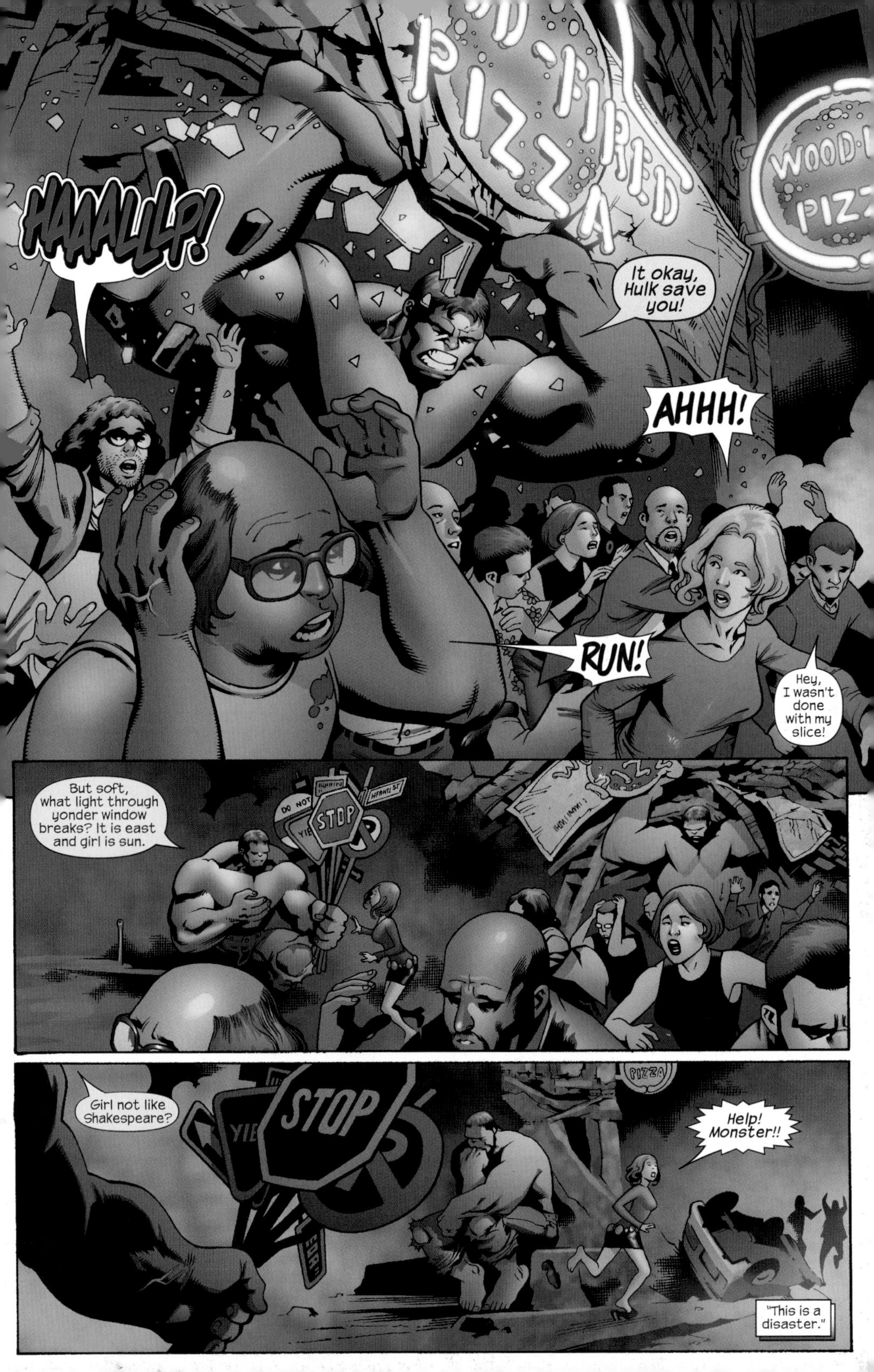
HAAAALLLP!
It okay, Hulk save you!
AHHH!
RUN!
Hey, I wasn't done with my slice!
But soft, what light through yonder window breaks? It is east and girl is sun.
STOP
Girl not like Shakespeare?
STOP
Help! Monster!!
"This is a disaster."

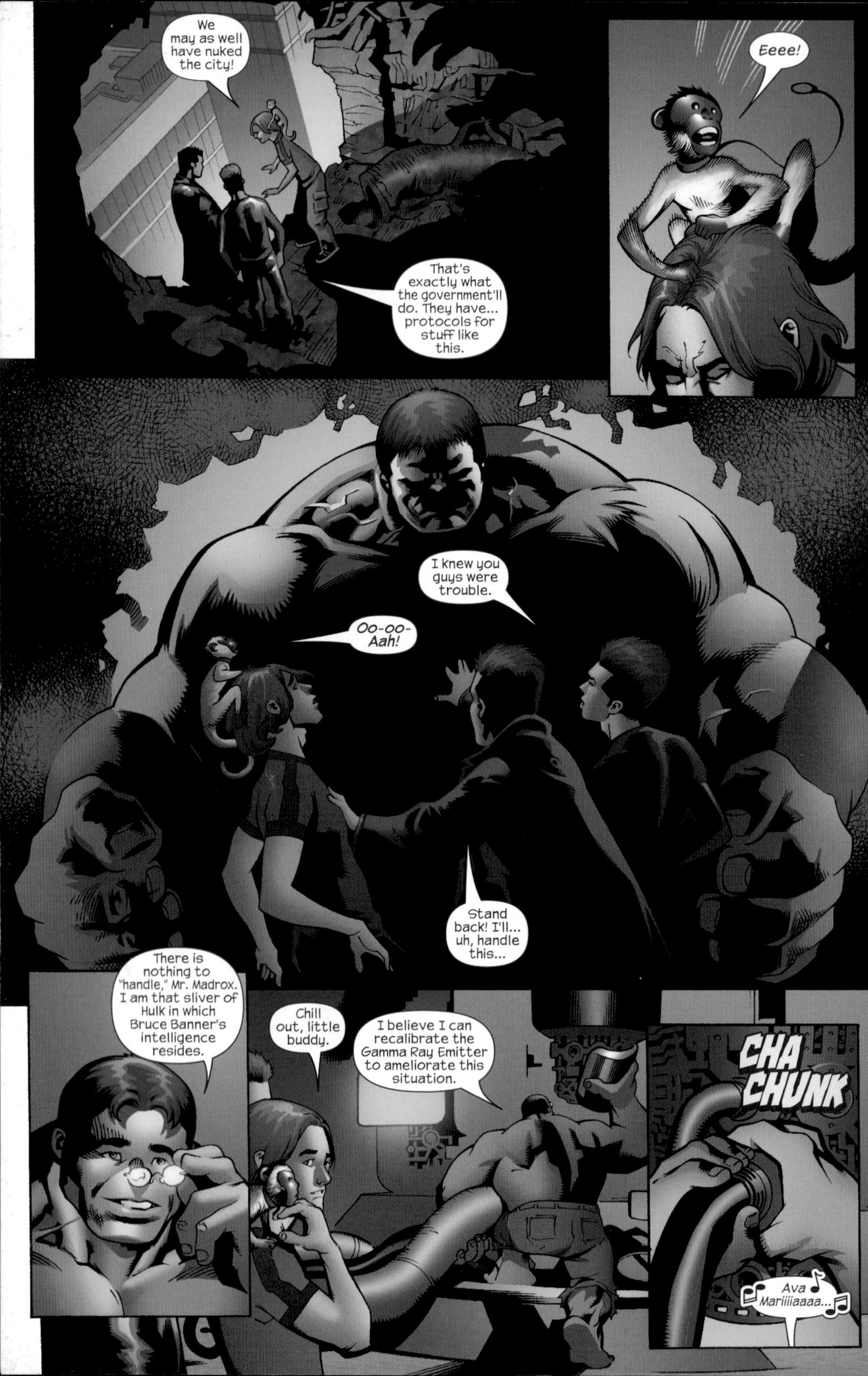
We may as well have nuked the city!
That's exactly what the government'll do. They have... protocols for stuff like this.
Eeee!
I knew you guys were trouble.
Oo-oo-Aah!
Stand back! I'll... uh, handle this...
There is nothing to "handle," Mr. Madrox. I am that sliver of Hulk in which Bruce Banner's intelligence resides.
Chill out, little buddy.
I believe I can recalibrate the Gamma Ray Emitter to ameliorate this situation.
CHA CHUNK
Ava Mariiiiaaaa...

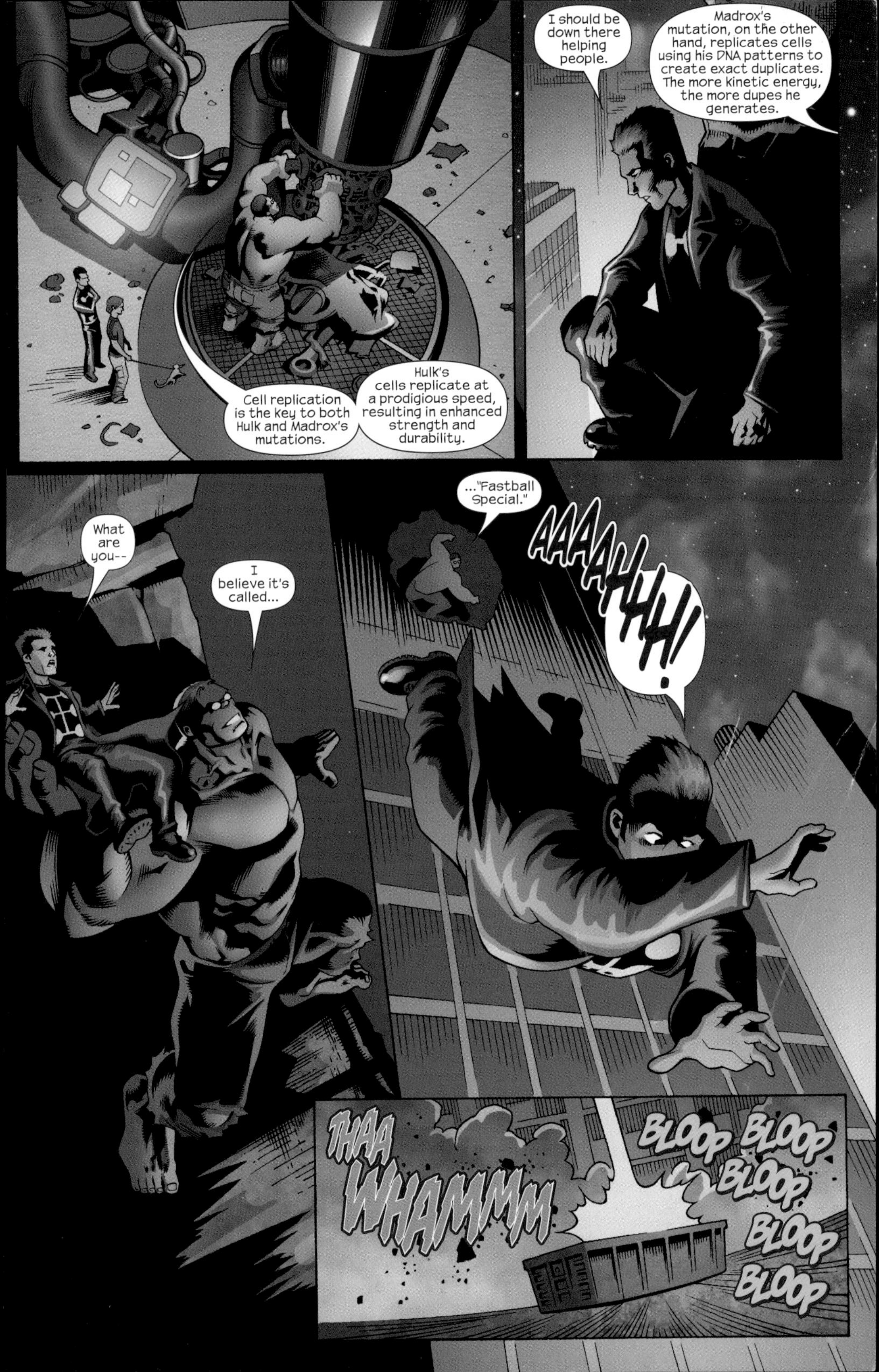
Cell replication is the key to both Hulk and Madrox's mutations.
Hulk's cells replicate at a prodigious speed, resulting in enhanced strength and durability.
I should be down there helping people.
Madrox's mutation, on the other hand, replicates cells using his DNA patterns to create exact duplicates. The more kinetic energy, the more dupes he generates.
What are you--
I believe it's called...
..."Fastball Special."
AAAAHHH!
THAA WHAMMM
BLOOP BLOOP BLOOP BLOOP BLOOP

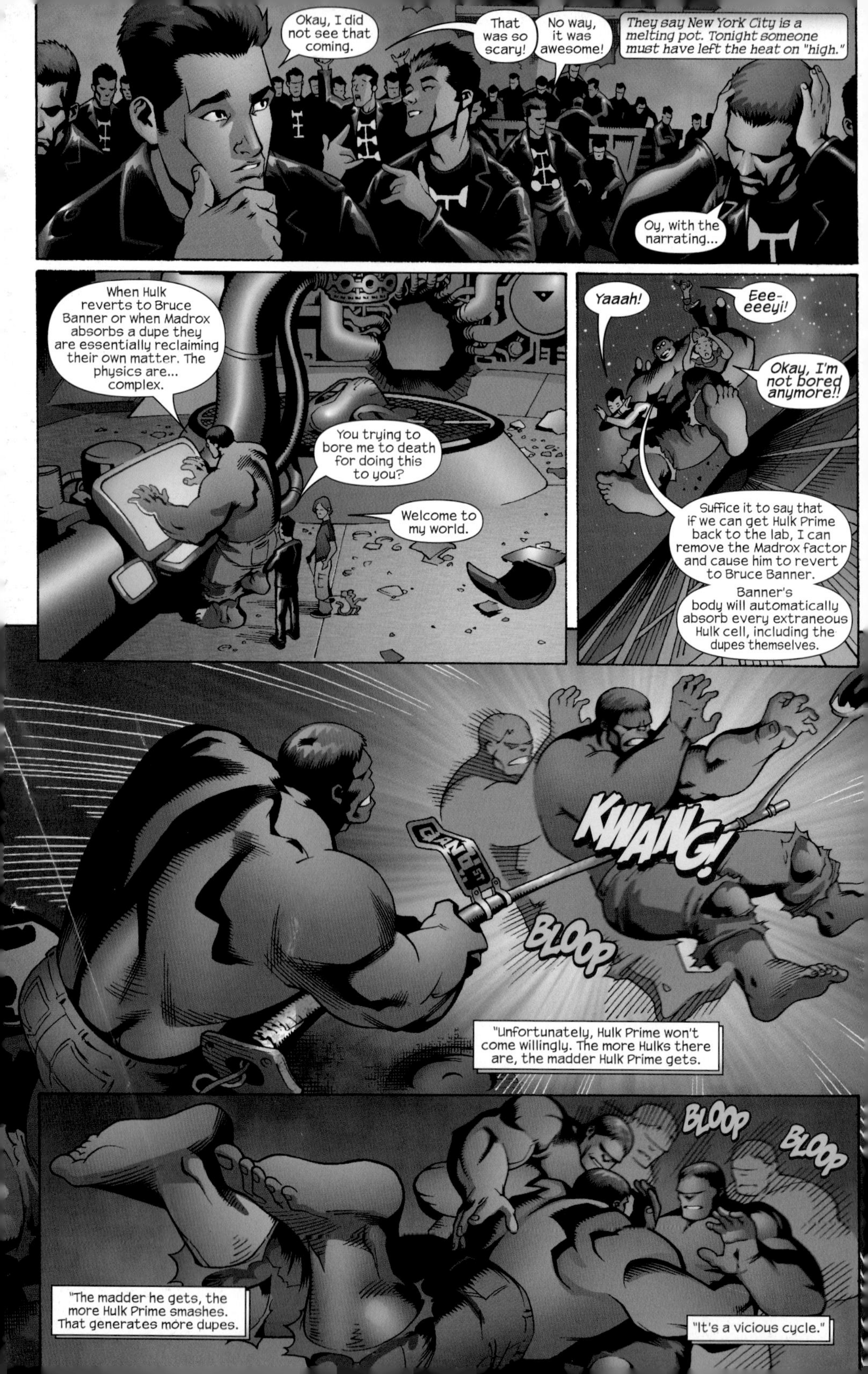
Okay, I did not see that coming.
That was so scary!
No way, it was awesome!
They say New York City is a melting pot. Tonight someone must have left the heat on "high."
Oy, with the narrating...
When Hulk reverts to Bruce Banner or when Madrox absorbs a dupe they are essentially reclaiming their own matter. The physics are... complex.
You trying to bore me to death for doing this to you?
Welcome to my world.
Yaaah!
Eee-eeeyi!
Okay, I'm not bored anymore!!
Suffice it to say that if we can get Hulk Prime back to the lab, I can remove the Madrox factor and cause him to revert to Bruce Banner.
Banner's body will automatically absorb every extraneous Hulk cell, including the dupes themselves.
KWANG!
BLOOP
"Unfortunately, Hulk Prime won't come willingly. The more Hulks there are, the madder Hulk Prime gets.
BLOOP
BLOOP
"The madder he gets, the more Hulk Prime smashes. That generates more dupes.
"It's a vicious cycle."

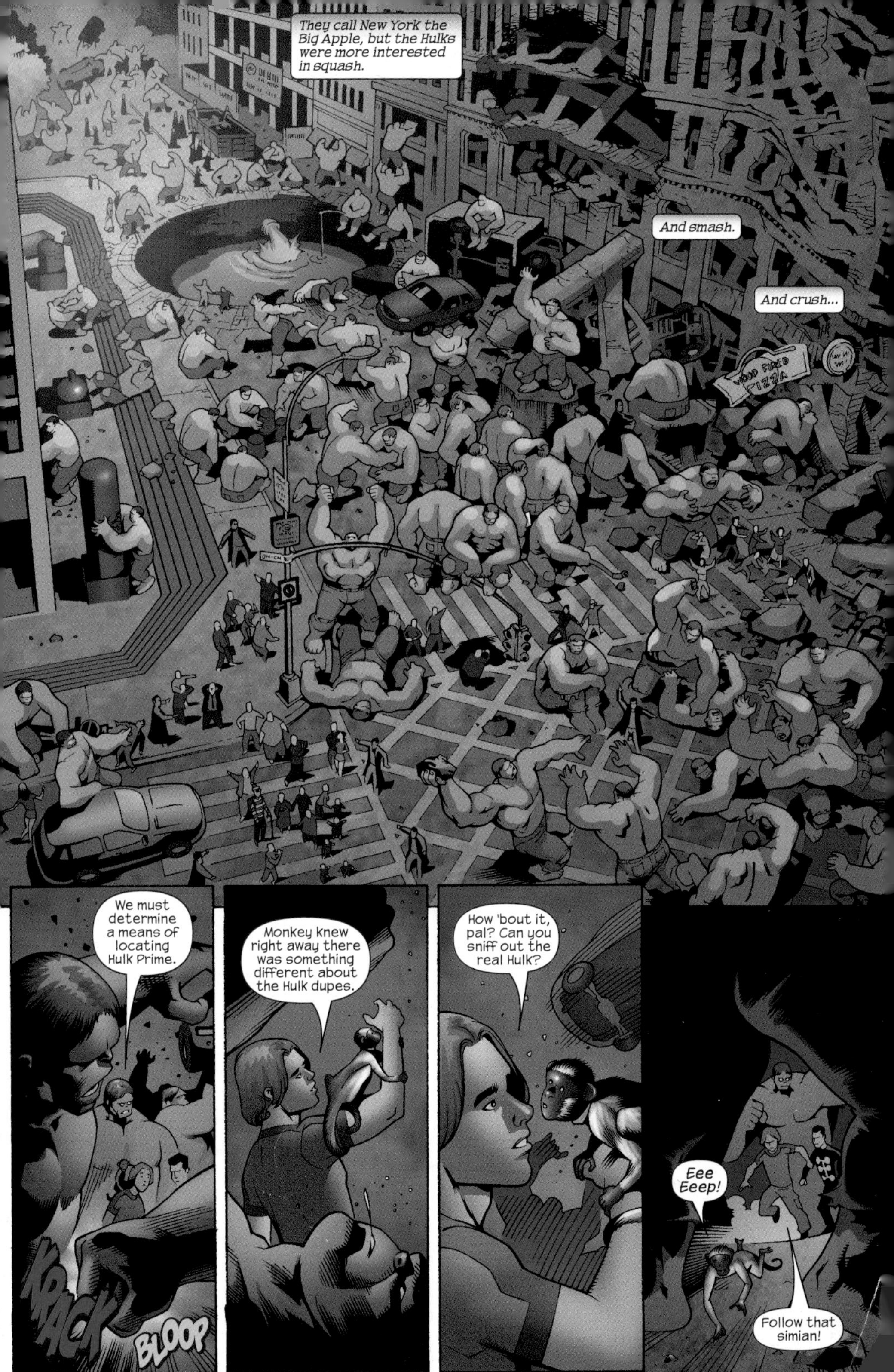
They call New York the Big Apple, but the Hulks were more interested in squash.
And smash.
And crush...
WOOD FIRED PIZZA
We must determine a means of locating Hulk Prime.
KRACK
BLOOP
Monkey knew right away there was something different about the Hulk dupes.
How 'bout it, pal? Can you sniff out the real Hulk?
Eee Eeep!
Follow that simian!

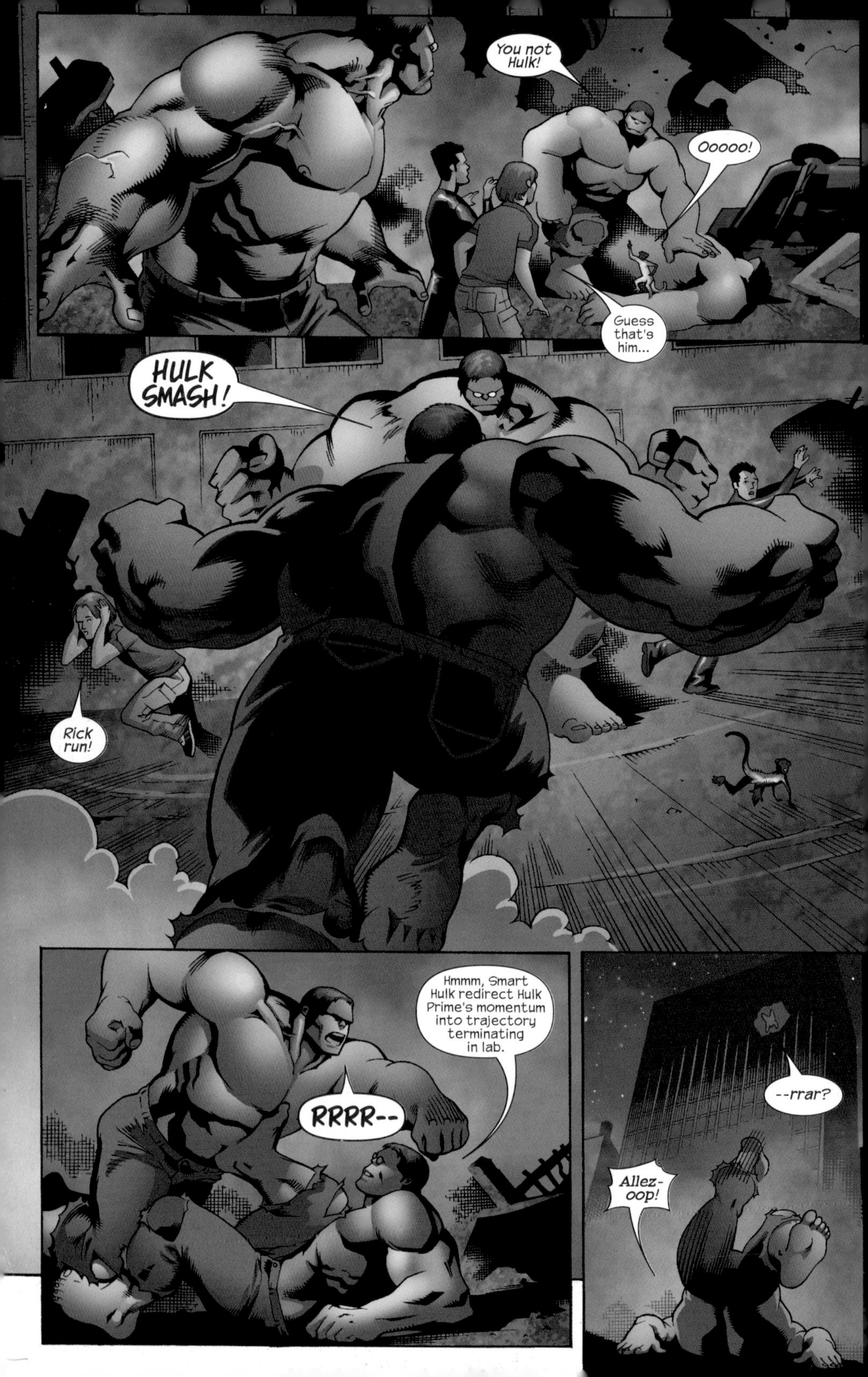
You not Hulk!
Ooooo!
Guess that's him...
HULK SMASH!
Rick run!
Hmmm, Smart Hulk redirect Hulk Prime's momentum into trajectory terminating in lab.
RRRR--
--rrar?
Allez-oop!

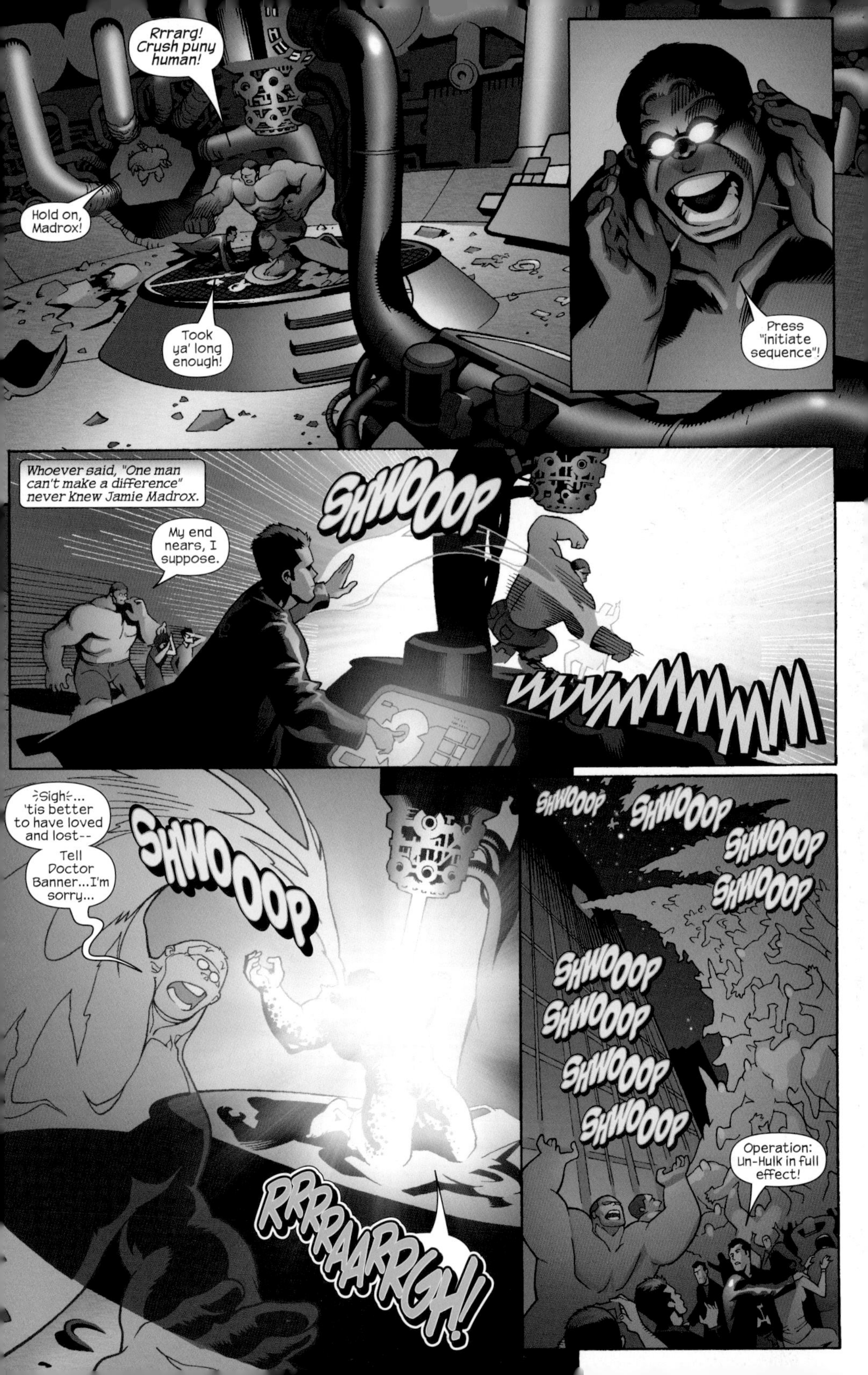
Rrrarg! Crush puny human!
Hold on, Madrox!
Took ya' long enough!
Press "initiate sequence"!
Whoever said, "One man can't make a difference" never knew Jamie Madrox.
SHWOOOP
My end nears, I suppose.
WWVMMMMMM
Sigh... 'tis better to have loved and lost--
Tell Doctor Banner...I'm sorry...
SHWOOOP
RRRRAARRGH!
SHWOOOP
SHWOOOP
SHWOOOP
SHWOOOP
SHWOOOP
SHWOOOP
SHWOOOP
SHWOOOP
Operation: Un-Hulk in full effect!

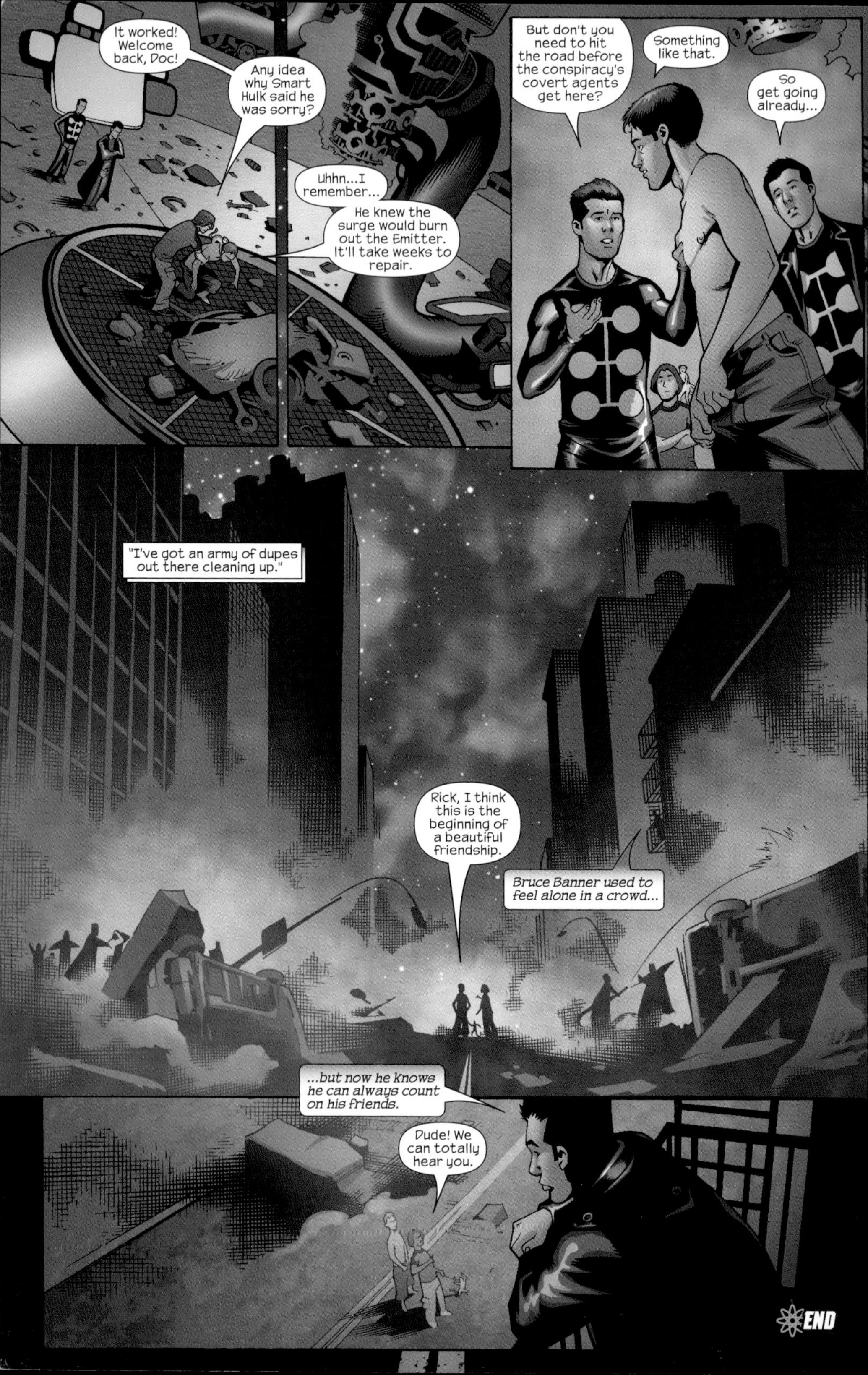
It worked! Welcome back, Doc!
Any idea why Smart Hulk said he was sorry?
Uhhn...I remember...
He knew the surge would burn out the Emitter. It'll take weeks to repair.
But don't you need to hit the road before the conspiracy's covert agents get here?
Something like that.
So get going already...
"I've got an army of dupes out there cleaning up."
Rick, I think this is the beginning of a beautiful friendship.
Bruce Banner used to feel alone in a crowd...
...but now he knows he can always count on his friends.
Dude! We can totally hear you.
END

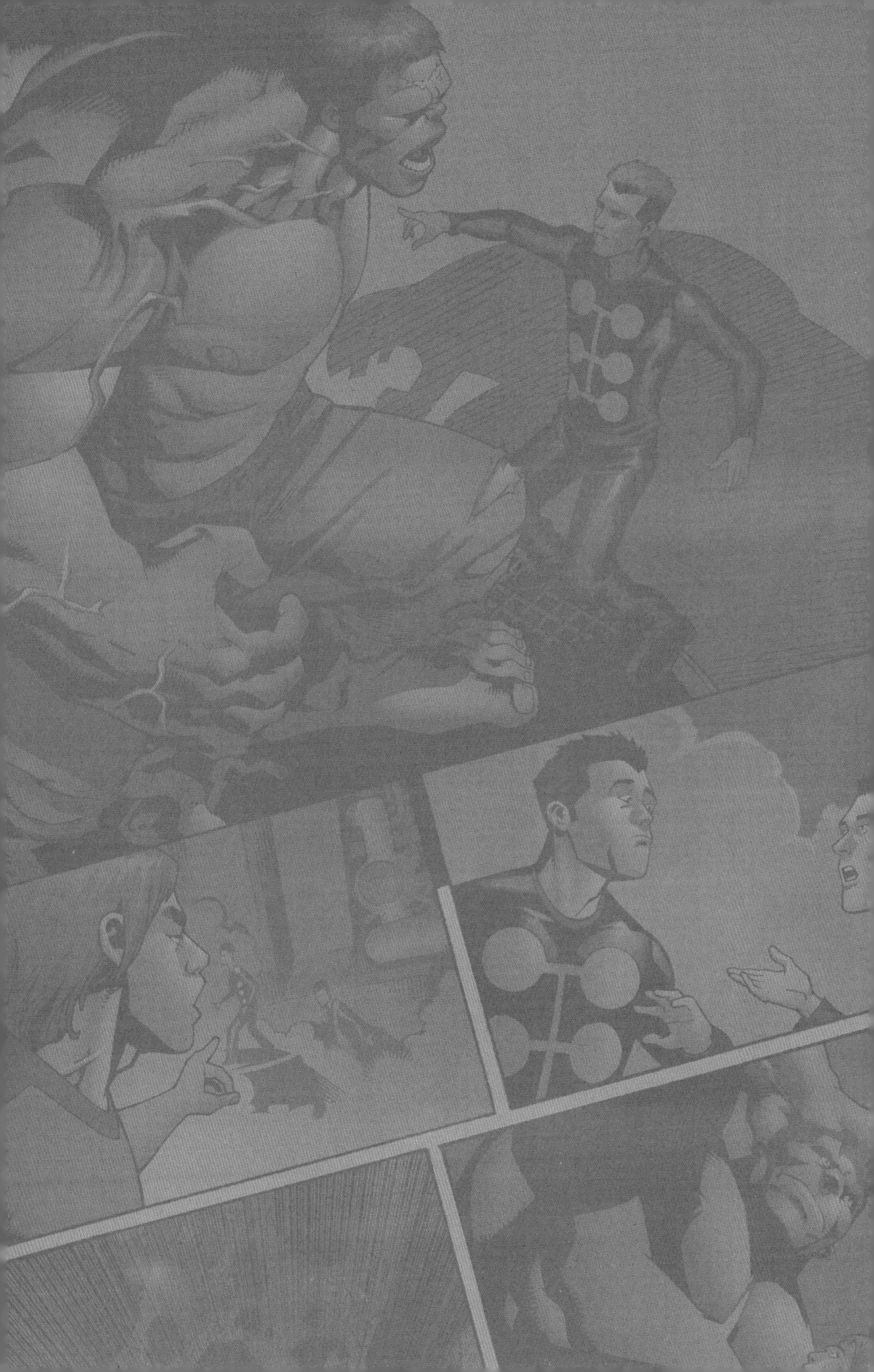

03

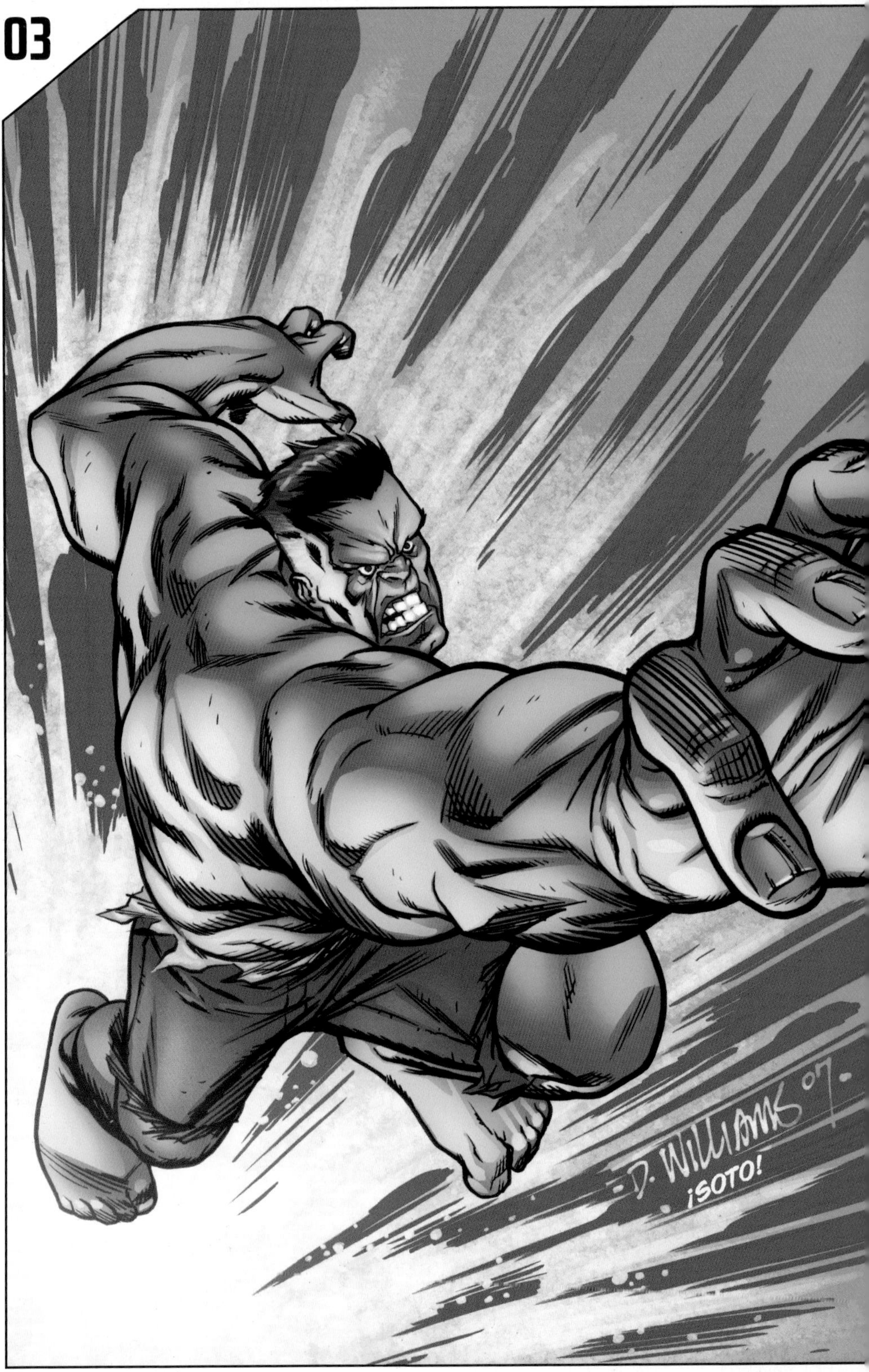
D. WILLIAMS '07
¡SOTO!

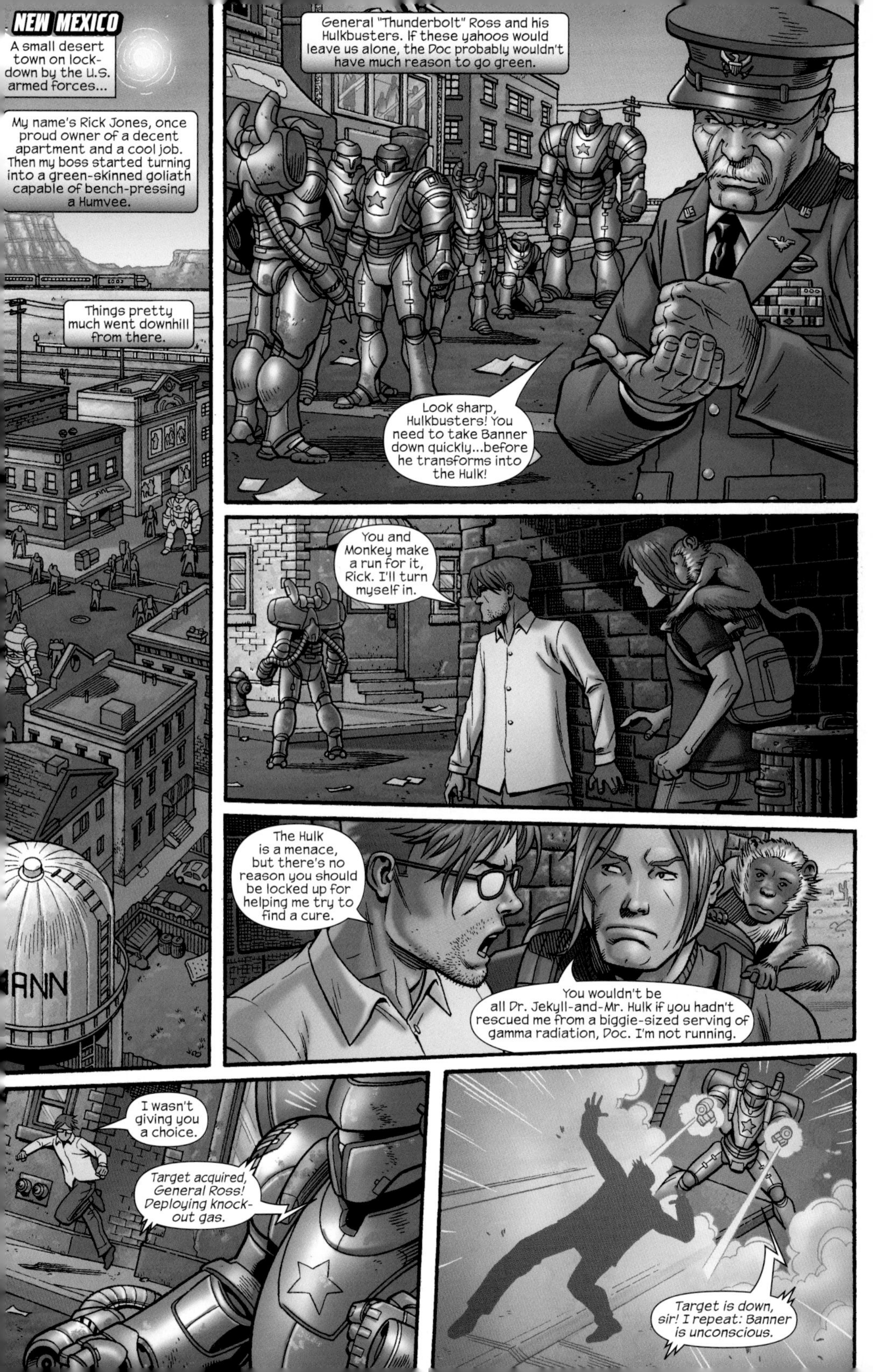
NEW MEXICO
A small desert town on lock-down by the U.S. armed forces...
My name's Rick Jones, once proud owner of a decent apartment and a cool job. Then my boss started turning into a green-skinned goliath capable of bench-pressing a Humvee.
Things pretty much went downhill from there.
General "Thunderbolt" Ross and his Hulkbusters. If these yahoos would leave us alone, the Doc probably wouldn't have much reason to go green.
Look sharp, Hulkbusters! You need to take Banner down quickly...before he transforms into the Hulk!
You and Monkey make a run for it, Rick. I'll turn myself in.
The Hulk is a menace, but there's no reason you should be locked up for helping me try to find a cure.
You wouldn't be all Dr. Jekyll-and-Mr. Hulk if you hadn't rescued me from a biggie-sized serving of gamma radiation, Doc. I'm not running.
I wasn't giving you a choice.
Target acquired, General Ross! Deploying knock-out gas.
Target is down, sir! I repeat: Banner is unconscious.

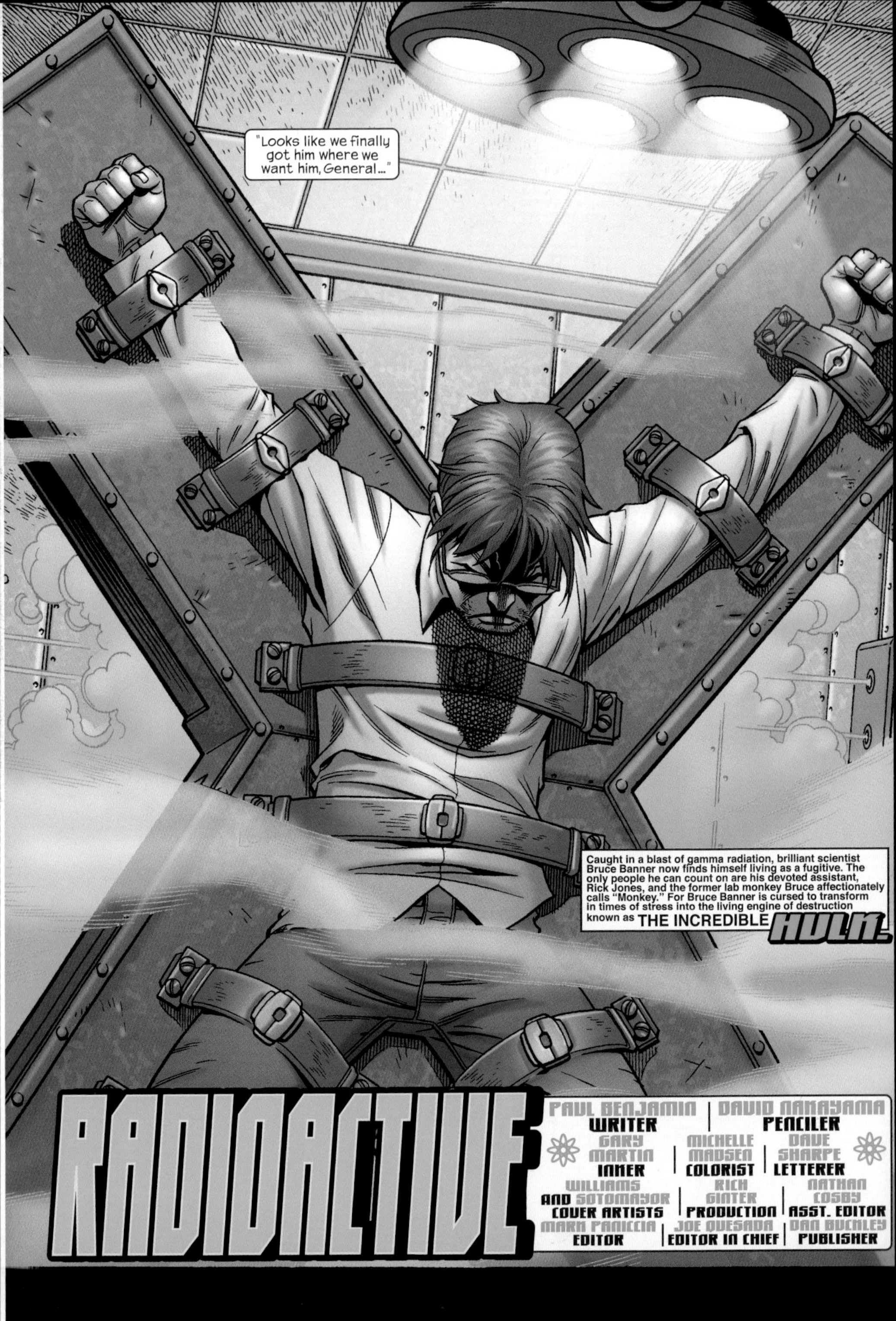

"Looks like we finally got him where we want him, General..."
Caught in a blast of gamma radiation, brilliant scientist Bruce Banner now finds himself living as a fugitive. The only people he can count on are his devoted assistant, Rick Jones, and the former lab monkey Bruce affectionately calls "Monkey." For Bruce Banner is cursed to transform in times of stress into the living engine of destruction known as THE INCREDIBLE HULK.
RADIOACTIVE
PAUL BENJAMIN WRITER
DAVID NAKAYAMA PENCILER
GARY MARTIN INKER
MICHELLE MADSEN COLORIST
DAVE SHARPE LETTERER
WILLIAMS AND SOTOMAYOR COVER ARTISTS
RICH GINTER PRODUCTION
NATHAN COSBY ASST. EDITOR
MARK PANICCIA EDITOR
JOE QUESADA EDITOR IN CHIEF
DAN BUCKLEY PUBLISHER

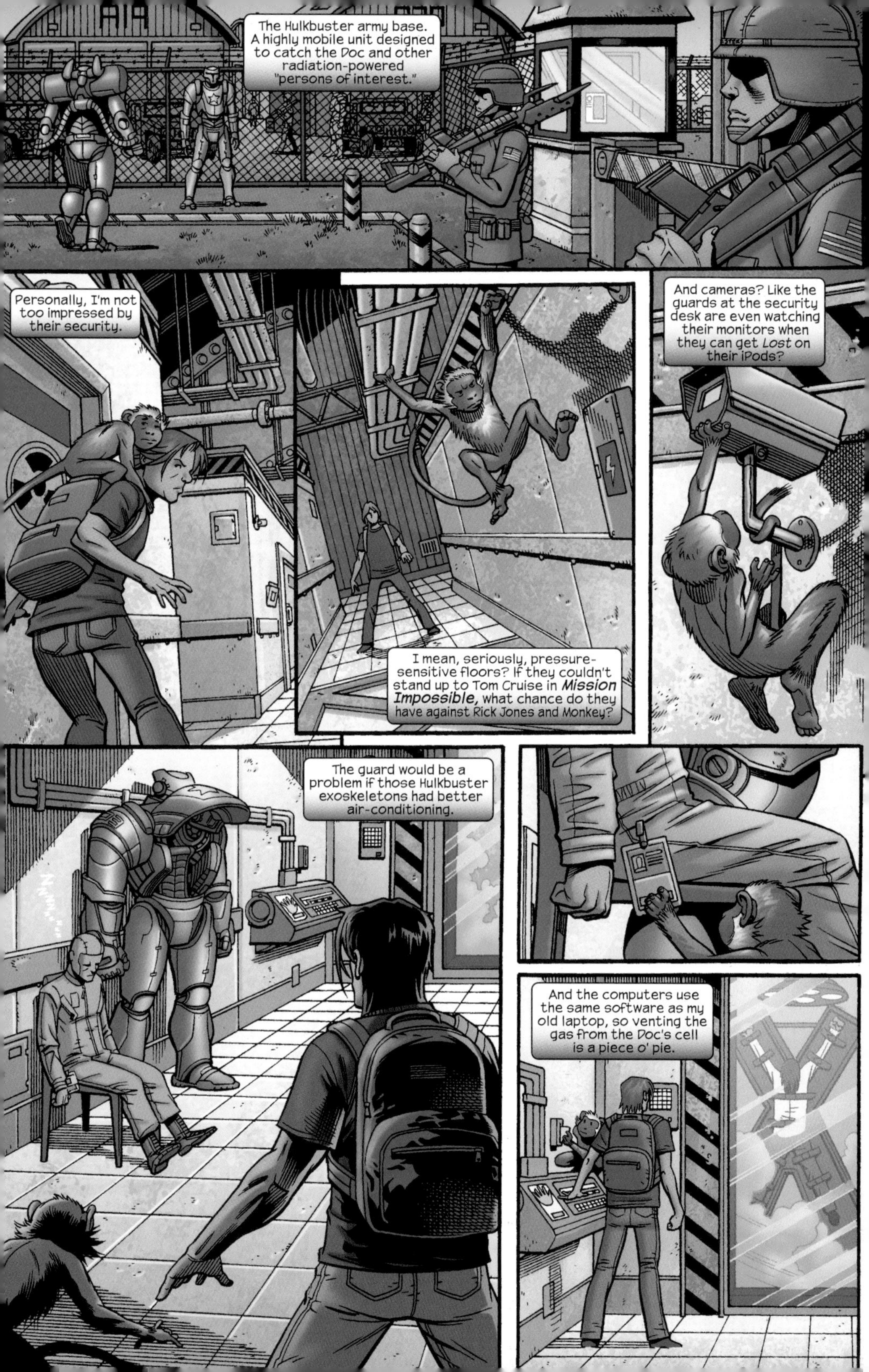
The Hulkbuster army base. A highly mobile unit designed to catch the Doc and other radiation-powered "persons of interest."
Personally, I'm not too impressed by their security.
I mean, seriously, pressure-sensitive floors? If they couldn't stand up to Tom Cruise in *Mission Impossible,* what chance do they have against Rick Jones and Monkey?
And cameras? Like the guards at the security desk are even watching their monitors when they can get *Lost* on their iPods?
The guard would be a problem if those Hulkbuster exoskeletons had better air-conditioning.
And the computers use the same software as my old laptop, so venting the gas from the Doc's cell is a piece o' pie.

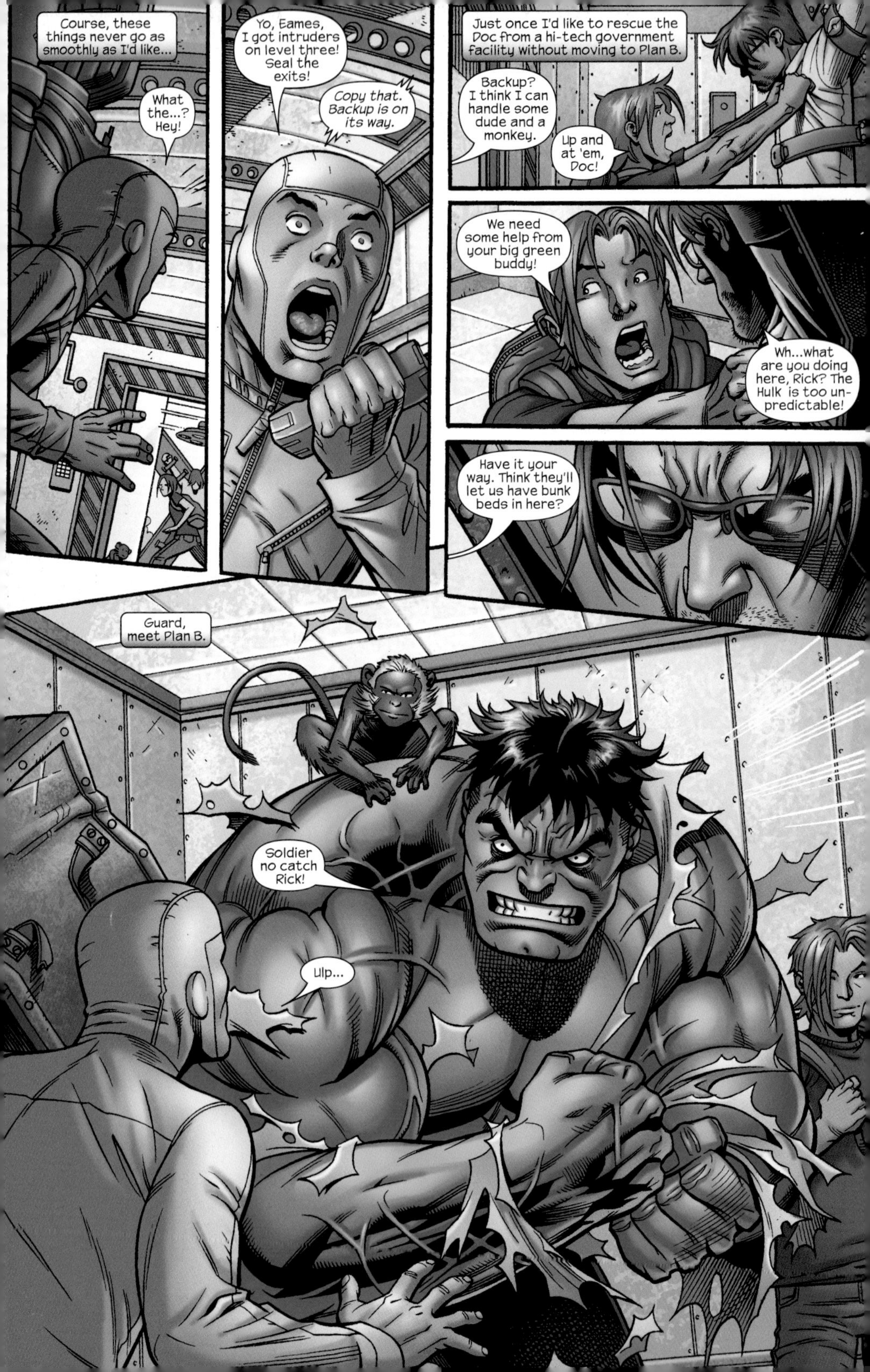
Course, these things never go as smoothly as I'd like...
What the...? Hey!
Yo, Eames, I got intruders on level three! Seal the exits!
Copy that. Backup is on its way.
Just once I'd like to rescue the Doc from a hi-tech government facility without moving to Plan B.
Backup? I think I can handle some dude and a monkey.
Up and at 'em, Doc!
We need some help from your big green buddy!
Wh...what are you doing here, Rick? The Hulk is too un-predictable!
Have it your way. Think they'll let us have bunk beds in here?
Guard, meet Plan B.
Soldier no catch Rick!
Ulp...

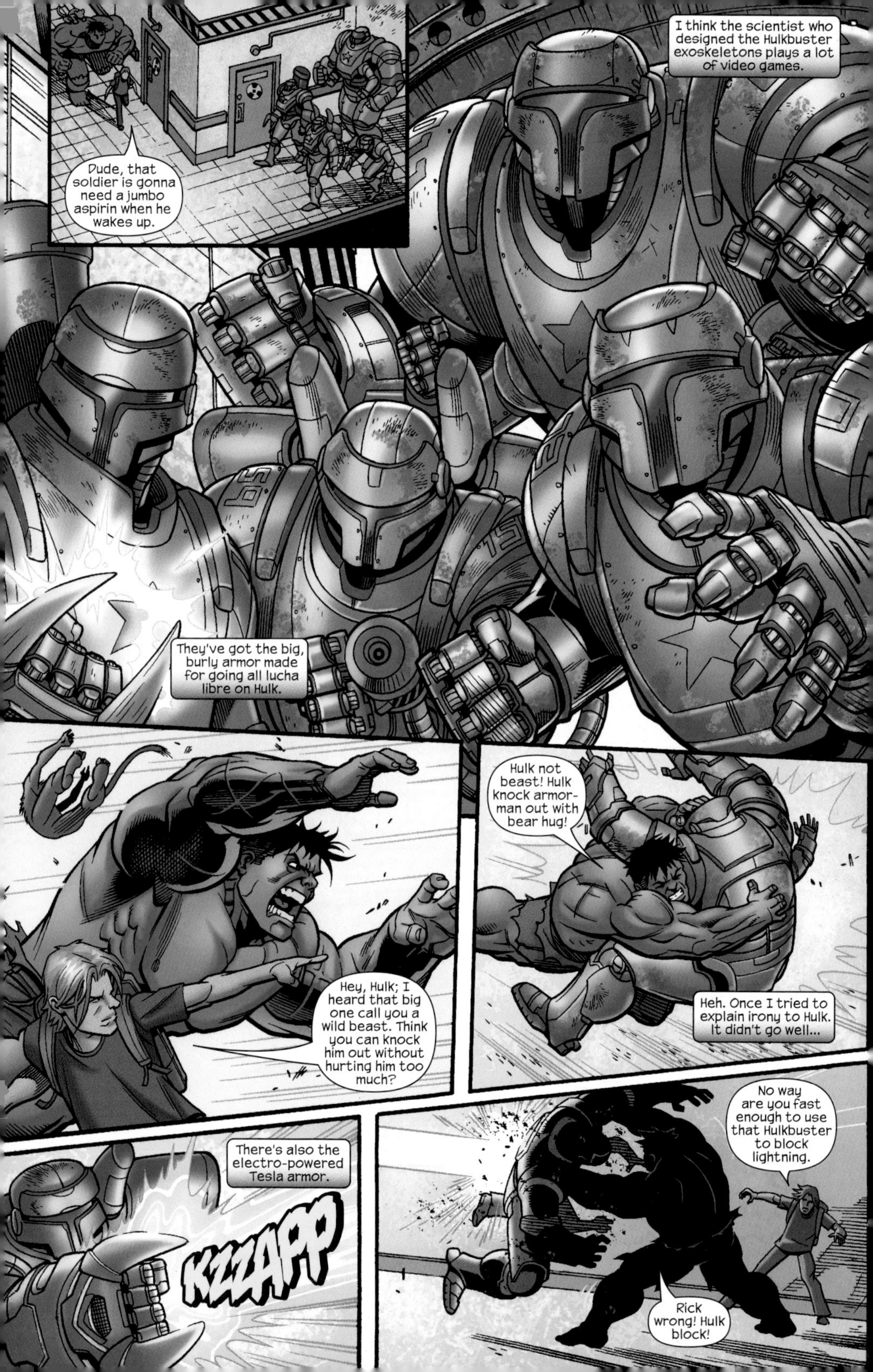
Dude, that soldier is gonna need a jumbo aspirin when he wakes up.
I think the scientist who designed the Hulkbuster exoskeletons plays a lot of video games.
They've got the big, burly armor made for going all lucha libre on Hulk.
Hey, Hulk; I heard that big one call you a wild beast. Think you can knock him out without hurting him too much?
Hulk not beast! Hulk knock armor-man out with bear hug!
Heh. Once I tried to explain irony to Hulk. It didn't go well...
There's also the electro-powered Tesla armor.
KZZAPP
No way are you fast enough to use that Hulkbuster to block lightning.
Rick wrong! Hulk block!

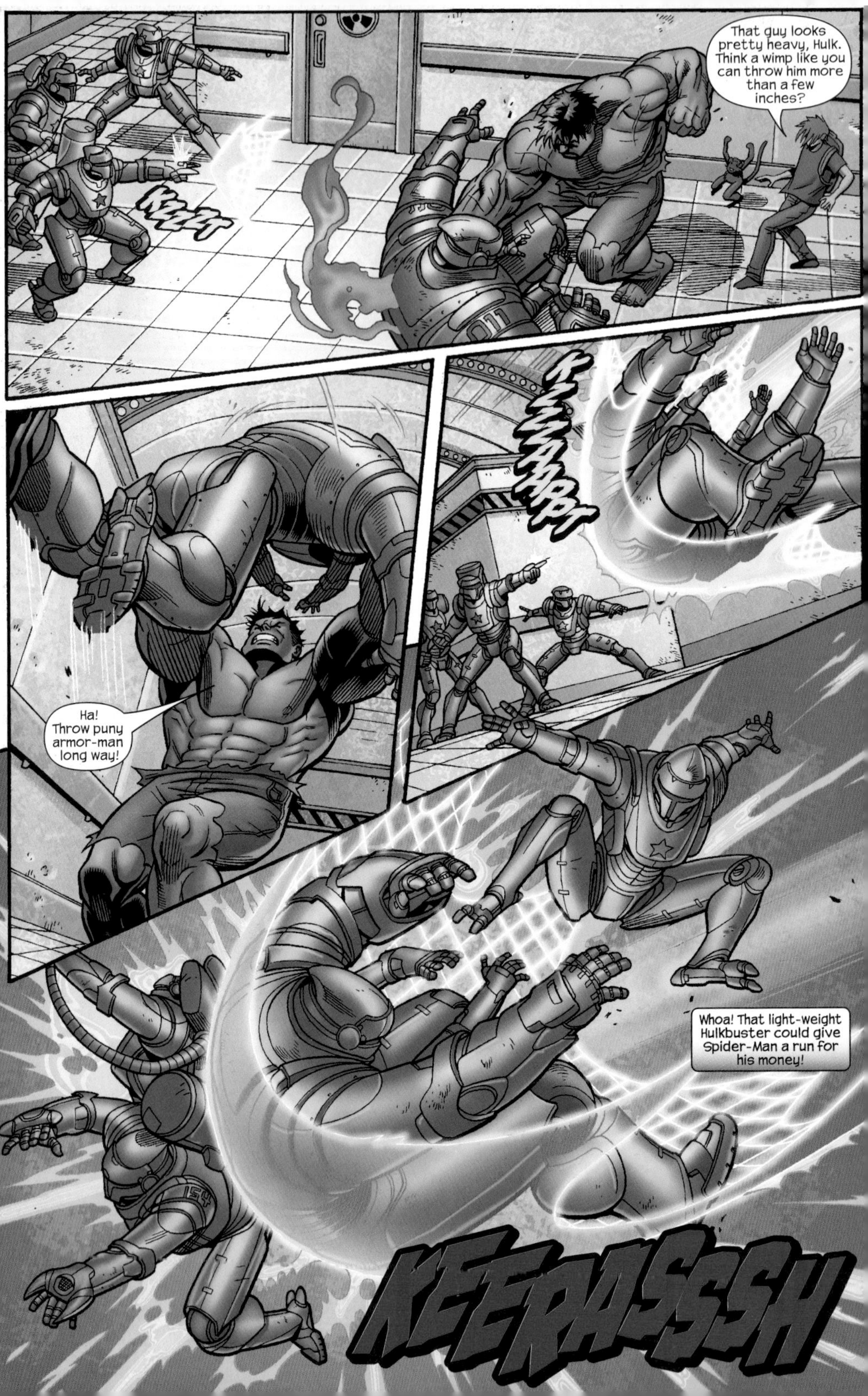
KZZZT
That guy looks pretty heavy, Hulk. Think a wimp like you can throw him more than a few inches?
Ha! Throw puny armor-man long way!
KZZZAPPT
Whoa! That light-weight Hulkbuster could give Spider-Man a run for his money!
KEERASSSH

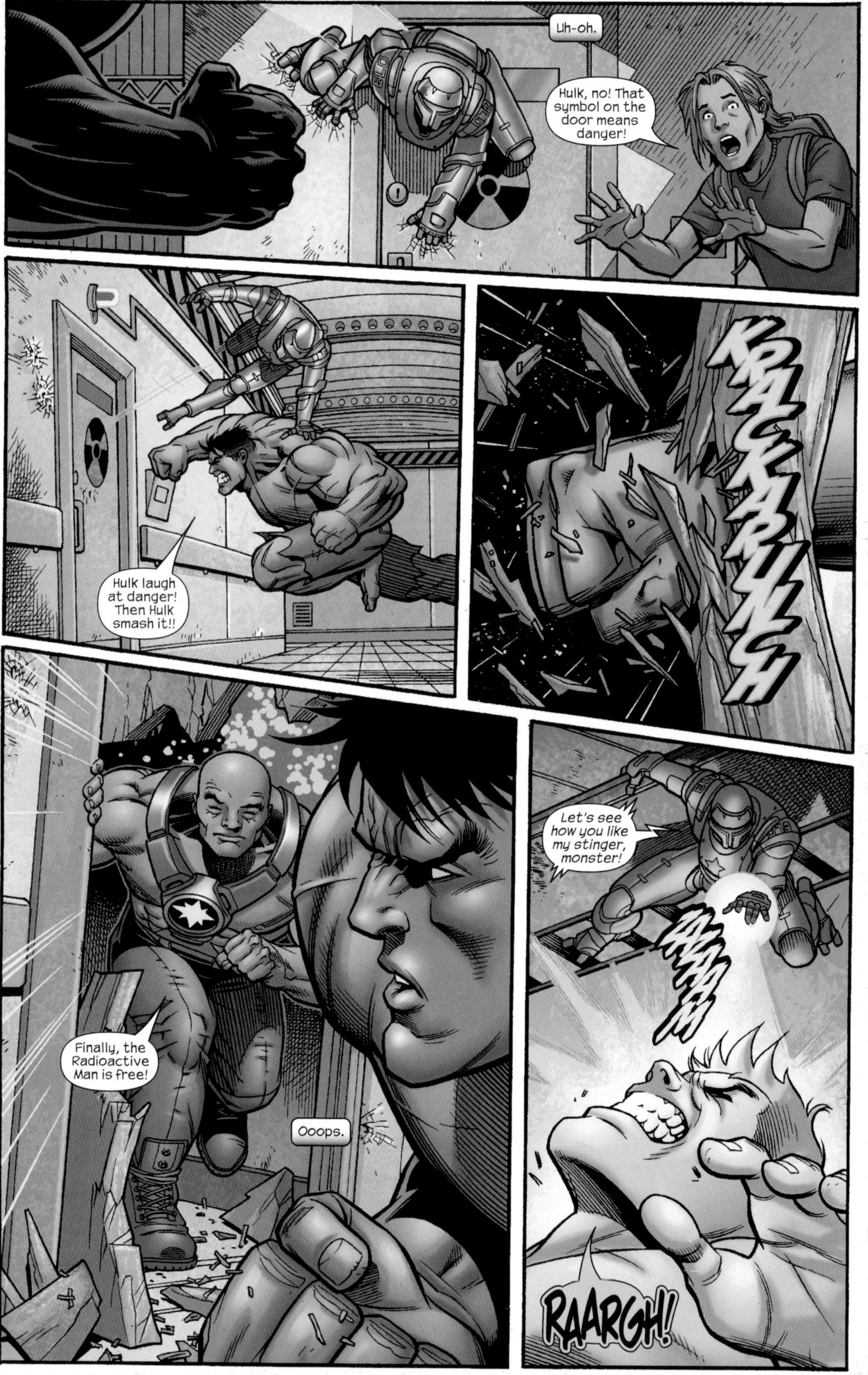
Uh-oh.
Hulk, no! That symbol on the door means danger!
Hulk laugh at danger! Then Hulk smash it!!
KRACKARUNCH
Finally, the Radioactive Man is free!
Ooops.
Let's see how you like my stinger, monster!
RAARGH!

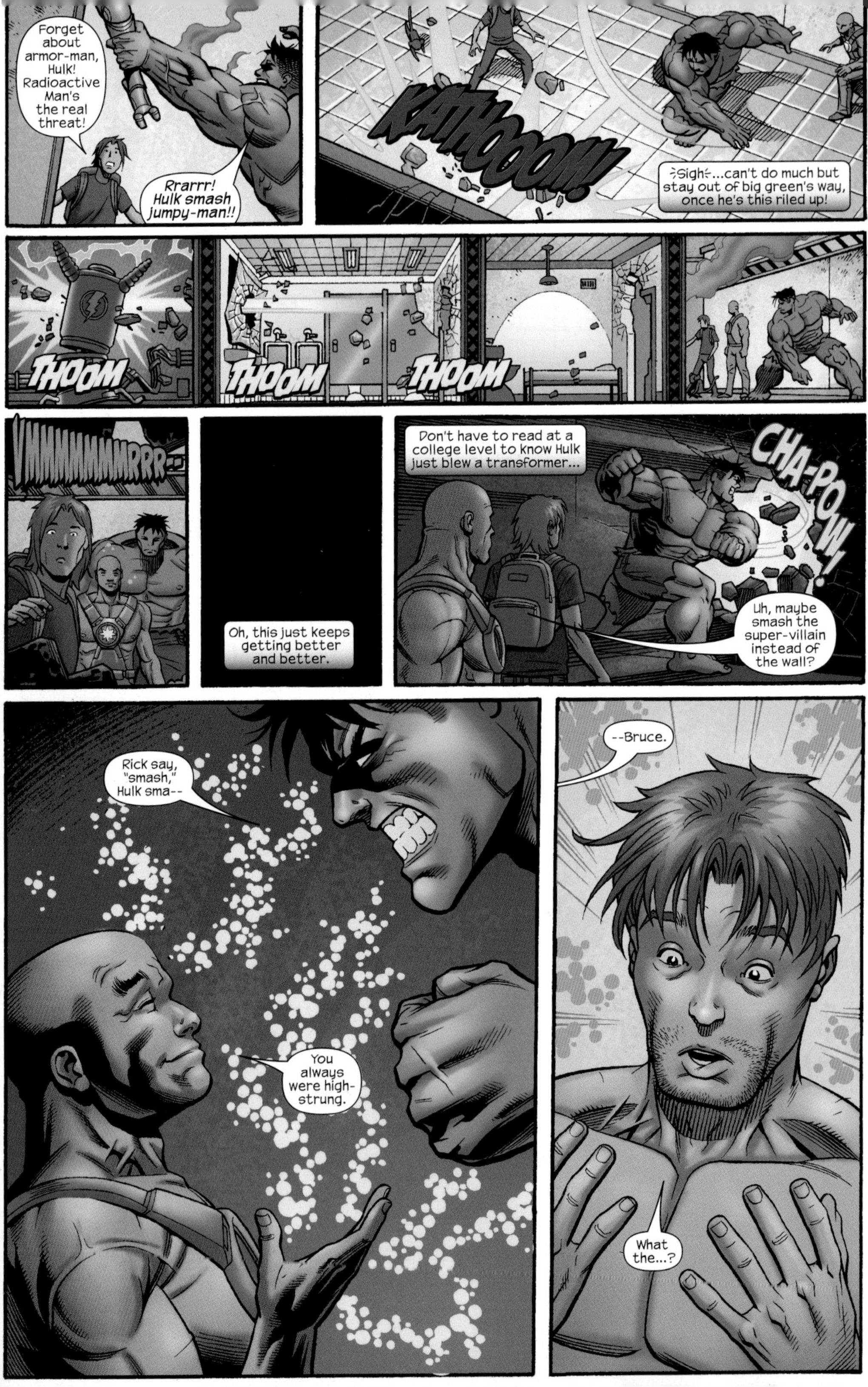
Forget about armor-man, Hulk! Radioactive Man's the real threat!
Rrarrr! Hulk smash jumpy-man!!
KATHOOOOM!!
≈Sigh≈...can't do much but stay out of big green's way, once he's this riled up!
THOOM
THOOM
THOOM
VMMMMMMMRRR
Oh, this just keeps getting better and better.
Don't have to read at a college level to know Hulk just blew a transformer...
CHA-POW!
Uh, maybe smash the super-villain instead of the wall?
Rick say, "smash," Hulk sma--
You always were high-strung.
--Bruce.
What the...?

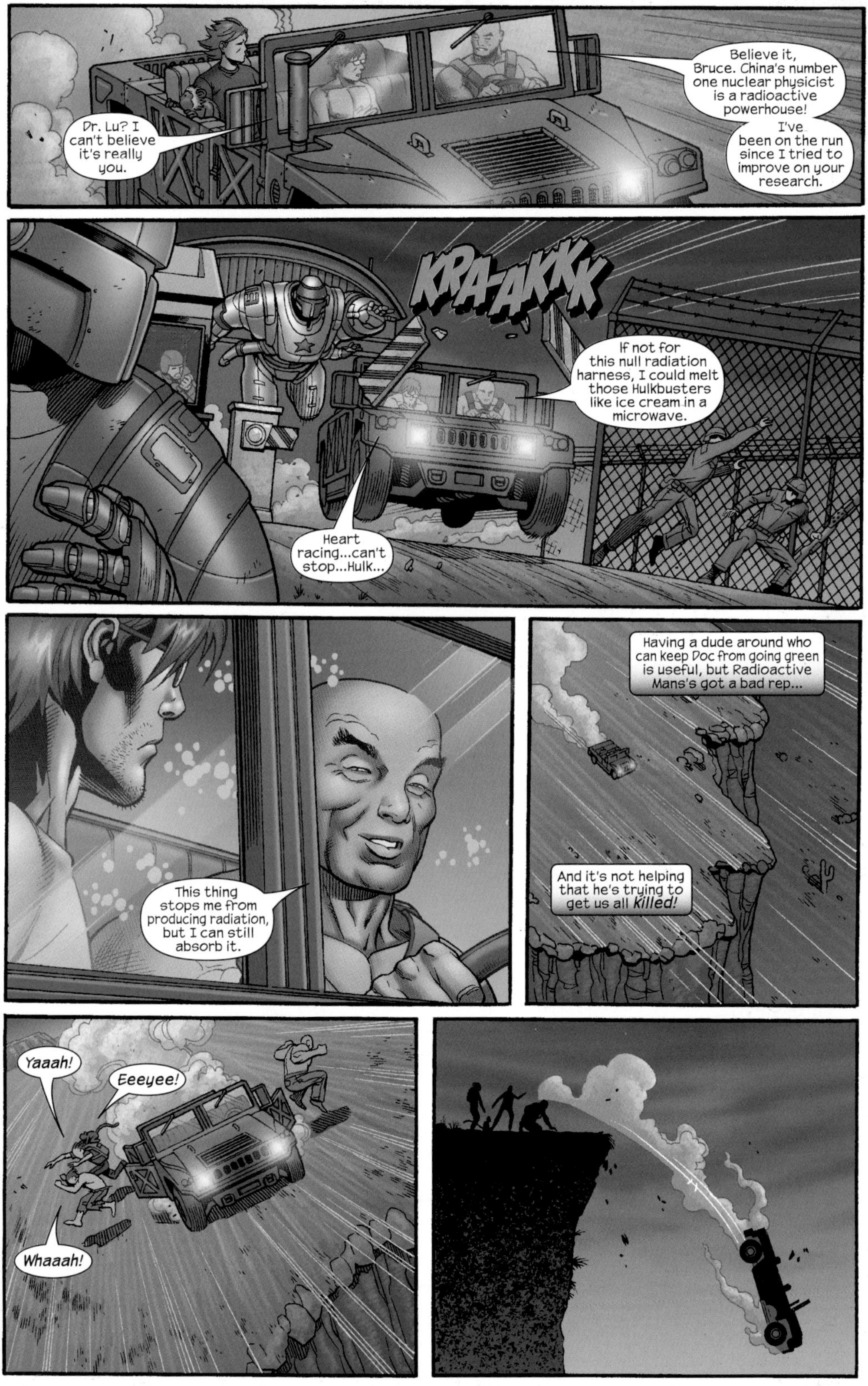
Dr. Lu? I can't believe it's really you.
Believe it, Bruce. China's number one nuclear physicist is a radioactive powerhouse!
I've been on the run since I tried to improve on your research.
KRA-AKKK
If not for this null radiation harness, I could melt those Hulkbusters like ice cream in a microwave.
Heart racing...can't stop...Hulk...
This thing stops me from producing radiation, but I can still absorb it.
Having a dude around who can keep Doc from going green is useful, but Radioactive Mans's got a bad rep...
And it's not helping that he's trying to get us all *killed!*
Yaaah!
Eeeyee!
Whaaah!

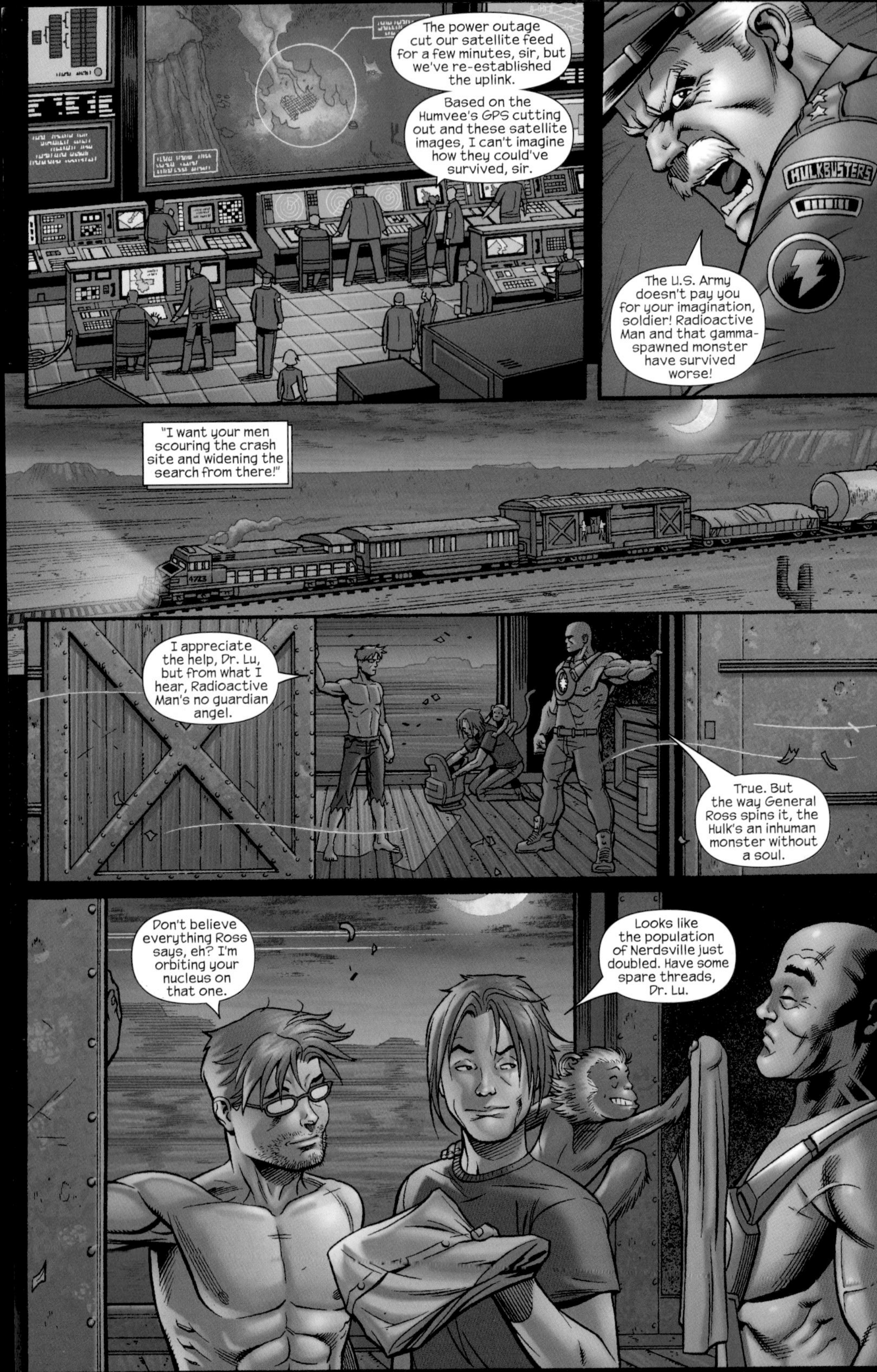
The power outage cut our satellite feed for a few minutes, sir, but we've re-established the uplink.
Based on the Humvee's GPS cutting out and these satellite images, I can't imagine how they could've survived, sir.
HULKBUSTERS
The U.S. Army doesn't pay you for your imagination, soldier! Radioactive Man and that gamma-spawned monster have survived worse!
"I want your men scouring the crash site and widening the search from there!"
4723
I appreciate the help, Dr. Lu, but from what I hear, Radioactive Man's no guardian angel.
True. But the way General Ross spins it, the Hulk's an inhuman monster without a soul.
Don't believe everything Ross says, eh? I'm orbiting your nucleus on that one.
Looks like the population of Nerdsville just doubled. Have some spare threads, Dr. Lu.

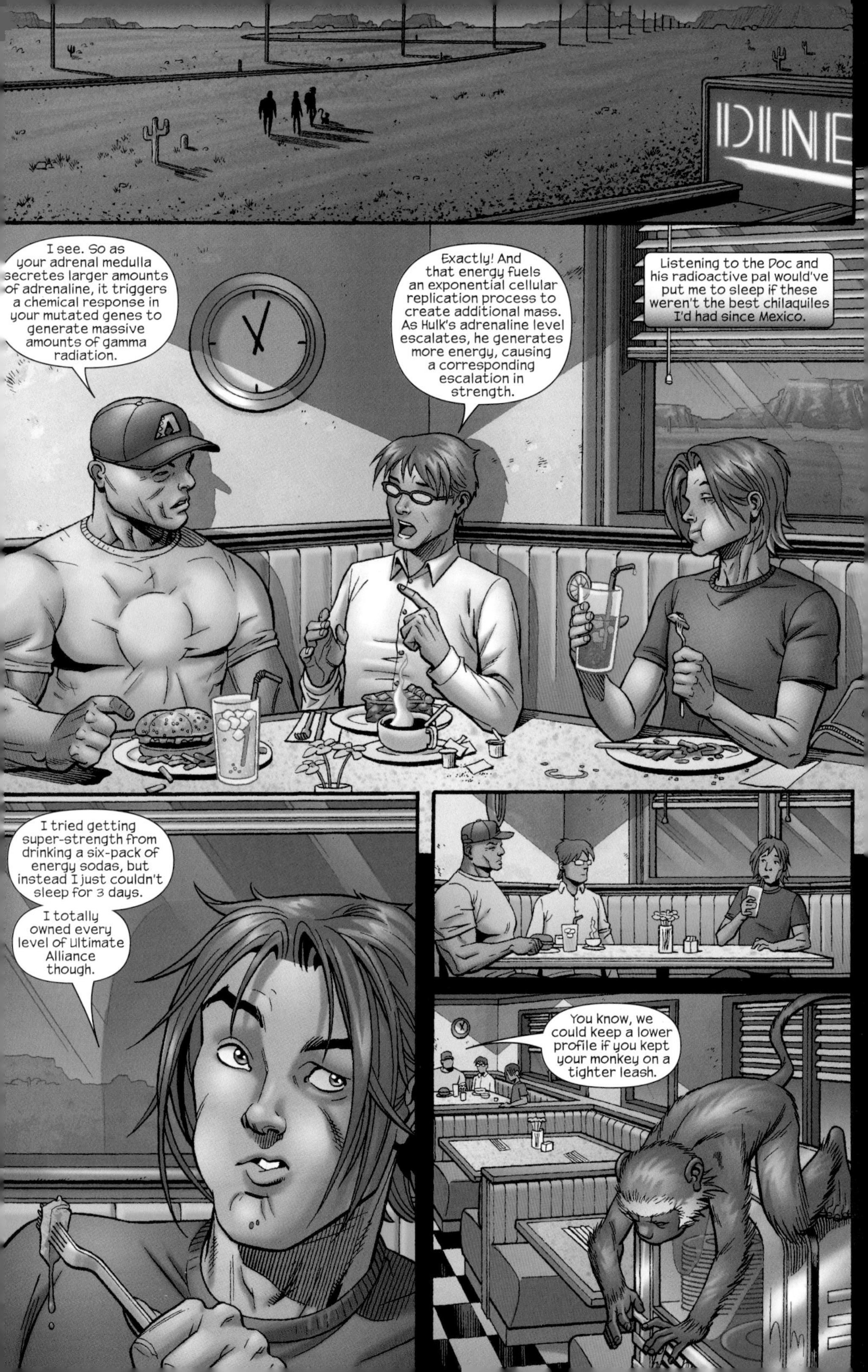

DINE
I see. So as your adrenal medulla secretes larger amounts of adrenaline, it triggers a chemical response in your mutated genes to generate massive amounts of gamma radiation.
Exactly! And that energy fuels an exponential cellular replication process to create additional mass. As Hulk's adrenaline level escalates, he generates more energy, causing a corresponding escalation in strength.
Listening to the Doc and his radioactive pal would've put me to sleep if these weren't the best chilaquiles I'd had since Mexico.
I tried getting super-strength from drinking a six-pack of energy sodas, but instead I just couldn't sleep for 3 days.
I totally owned every level of Ultimate Alliance though.
You know, we could keep a lower profile if you kept your monkey on a tighter leash.

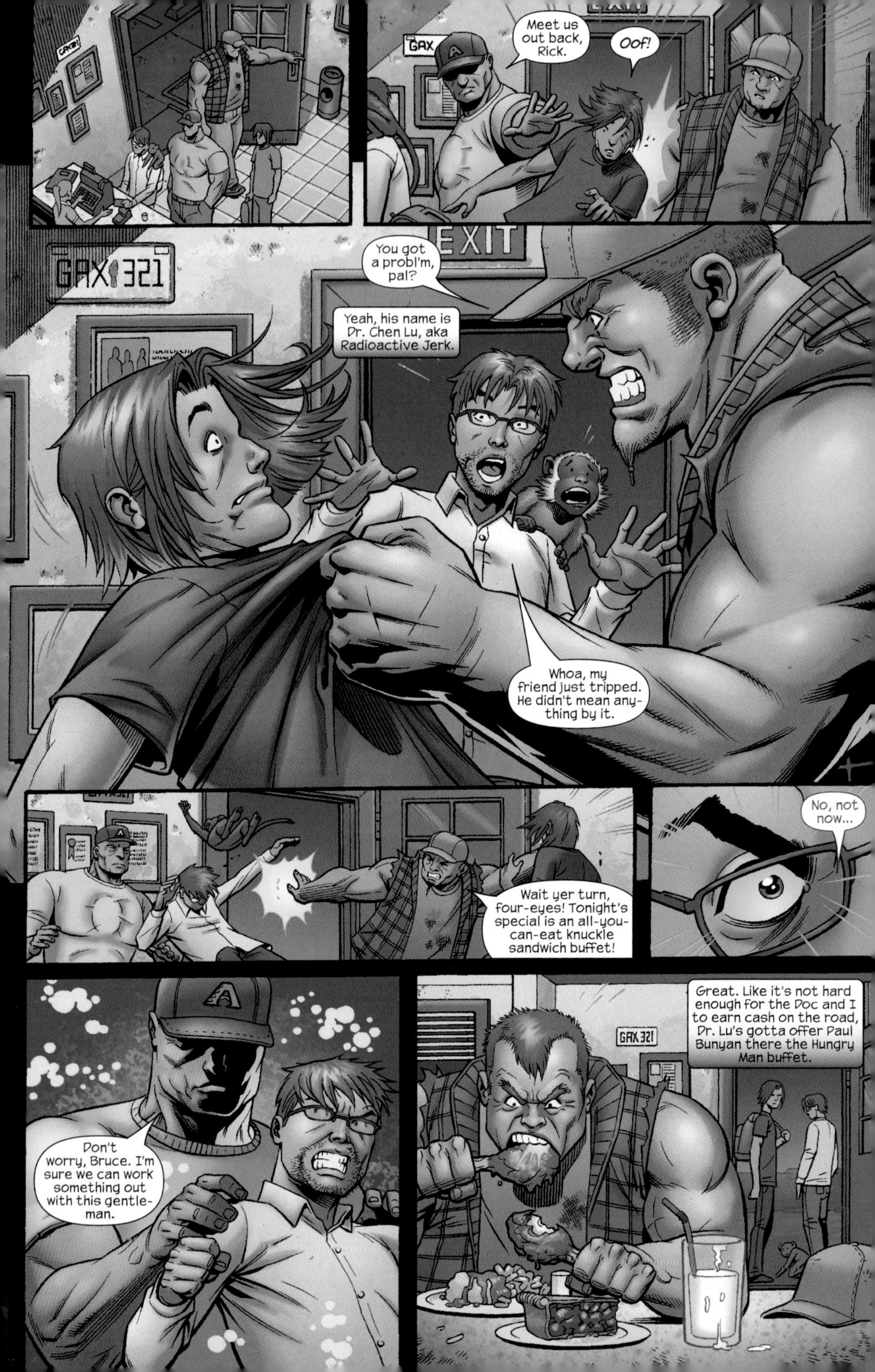
GAX
Meet us out back, Rick.
Oof!
GAX 321
EXIT
You got a probl'm, pal?
Yeah, his name is Dr. Chen Lu, aka Radioactive Jerk.
Whoa, my friend just tripped. He didn't mean any-thing by it.
Wait yer turn, four-eyes! Tonight's special is an all-you-can-eat knuckle sandwich buffet!
No, not now...
Don't worry, Bruce. I'm sure we can work something out with this gentle-man.
GAX 321
Great. Like it's not hard enough for the Doc and I to earn cash on the road, Dr. Lu's gotta offer Paul Bunyan there the Hungry Man buffet.

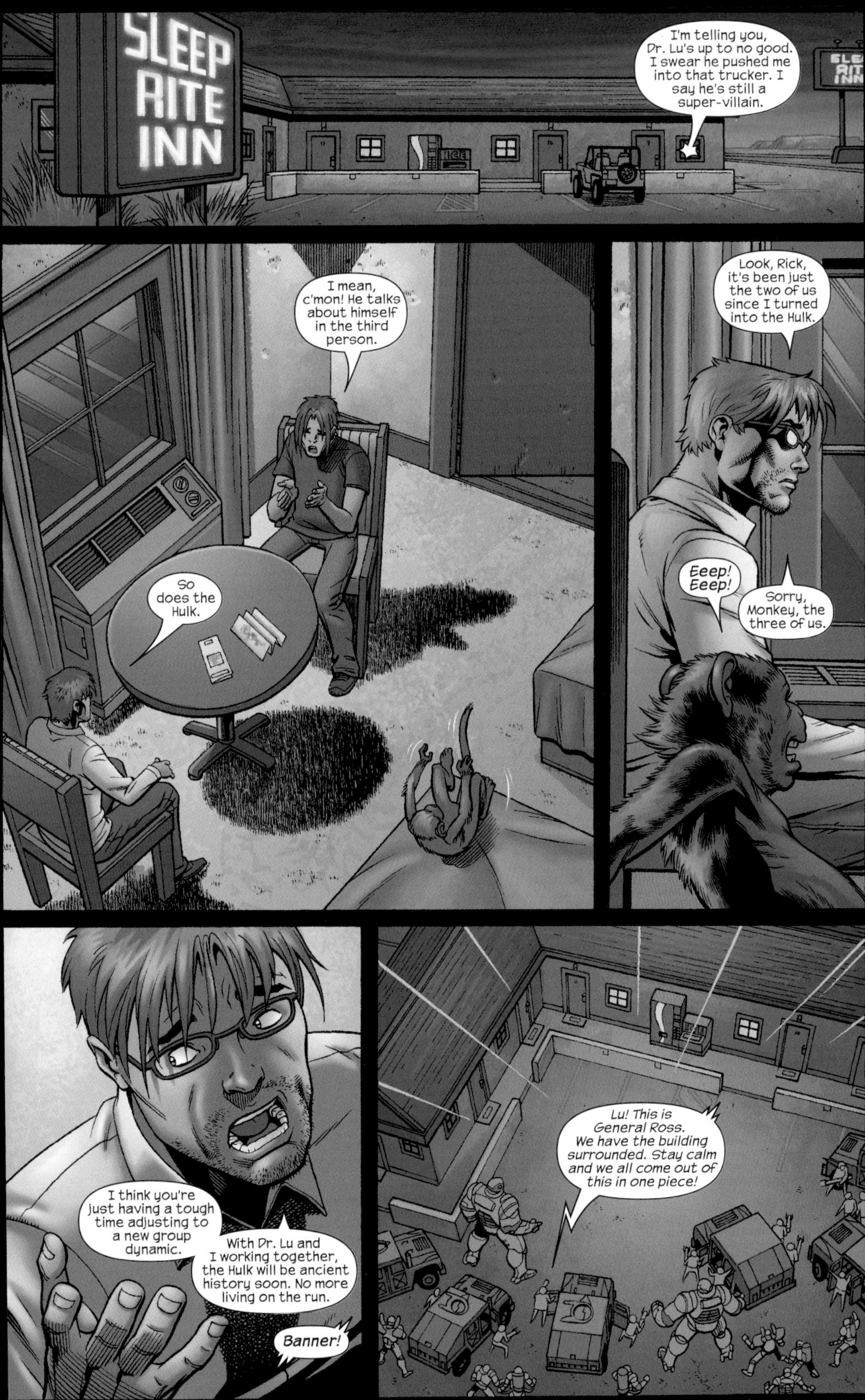
SLEEP RITE INN
I'm telling you, Dr. Lu's up to no good. I swear he pushed me into that trucker. I say he's still a super-villain.
I mean, c'mon! He talks about himself in the third person.
So does the Hulk.
Look, Rick, it's been just the two of us since I turned into the Hulk.
Eeep! Eeep!
Sorry, Monkey, the three of us.
I think you're just having a tough time adjusting to a new group dynamic.
With Dr. Lu and I working together, the Hulk will be ancient history soon. No more living on the run.
Banner!
Lu! This is General Ross. We have the building surrounded. Stay calm and we all come out of this in one piece!

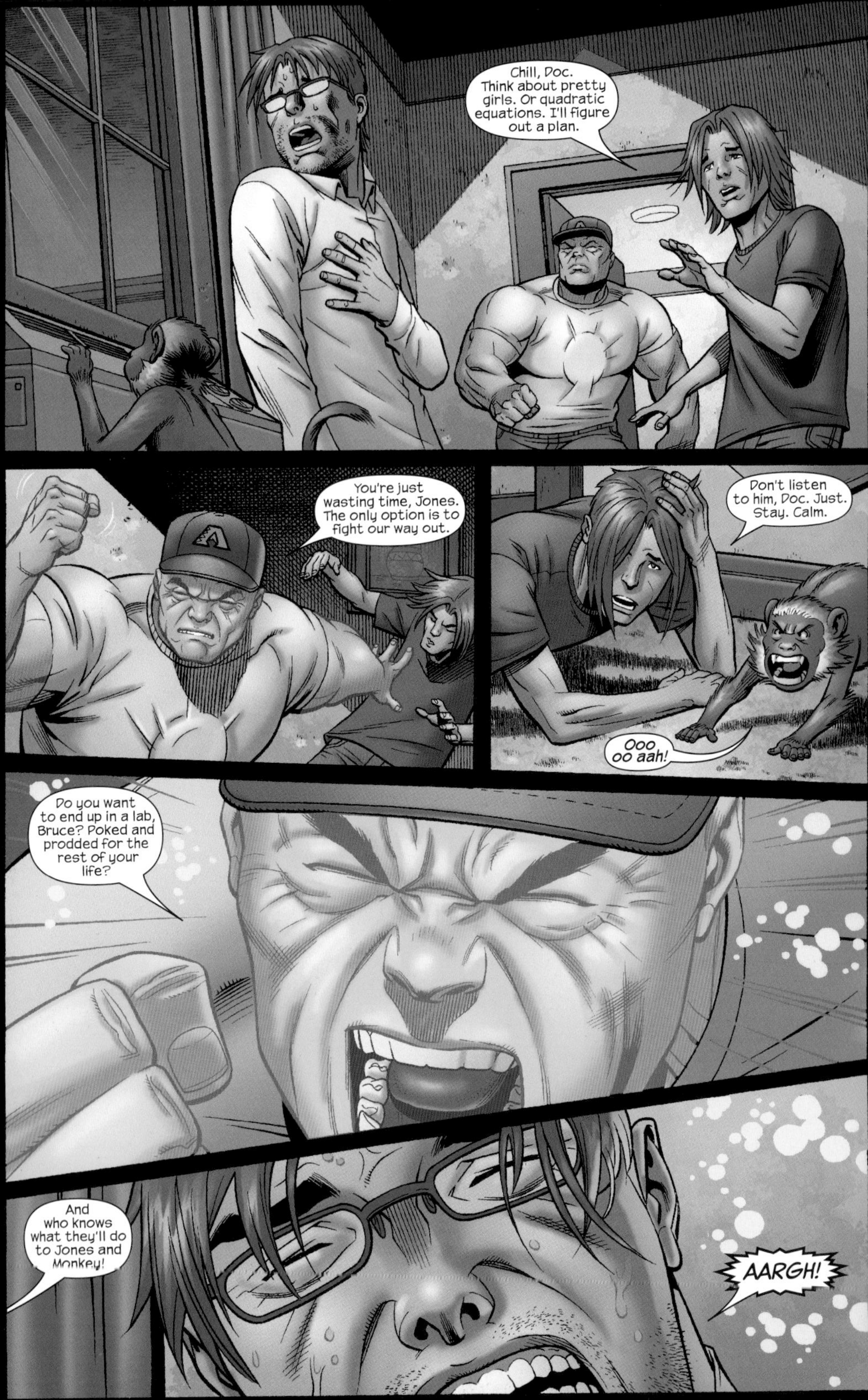
Chill, Doc. Think about pretty girls. Or quadratic equations. I'll figure out a plan.
You're just wasting time, Jones. The only option is to fight our way out.
Don't listen to him, Doc. Just. Stay. Calm.
Ooo oo aah!
Do you want to end up in a lab, Bruce? Poked and prodded for the rest of your life?
And who knows what they'll do to Jones and Monkey!
AARGH!

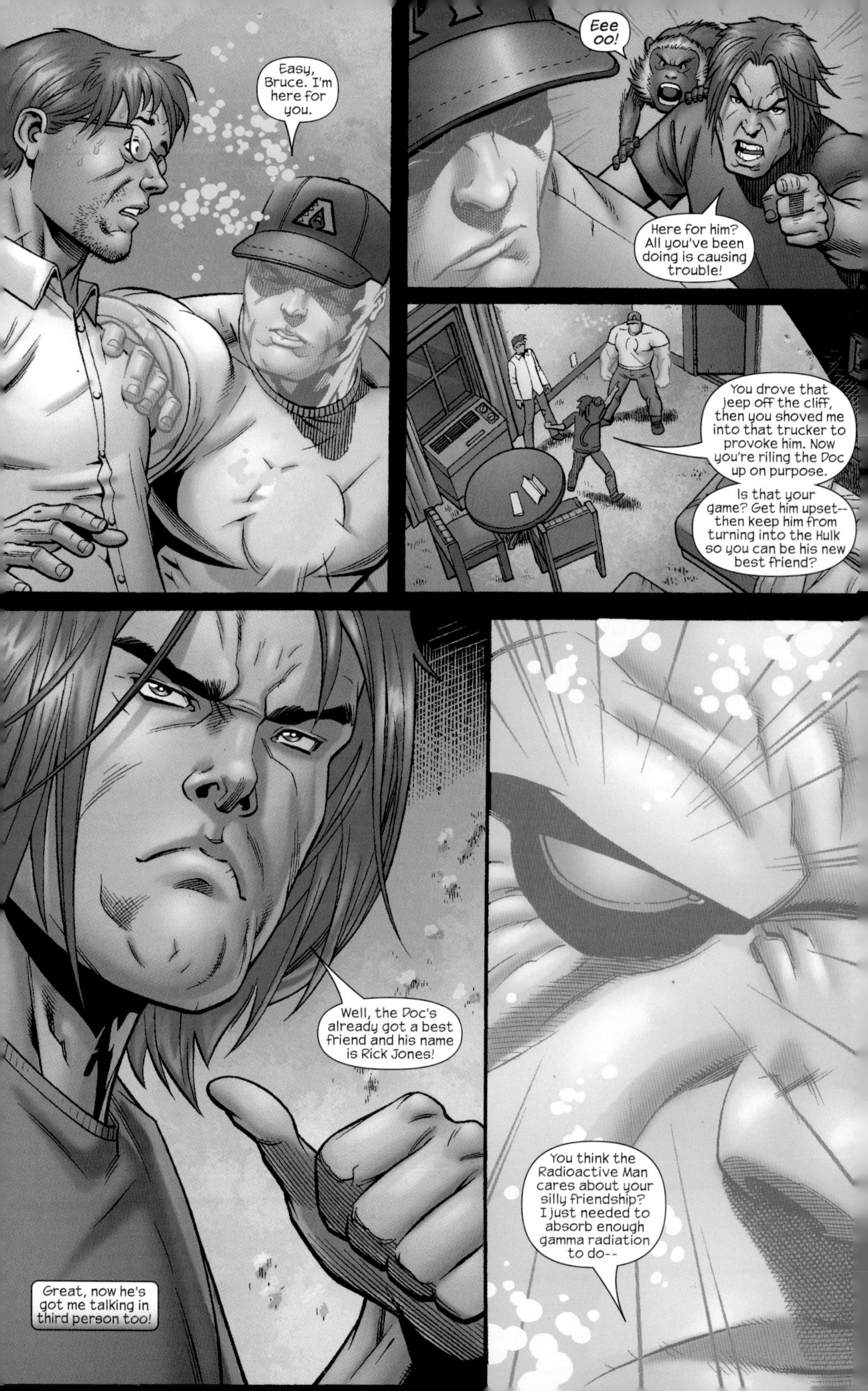
Easy, Bruce. I'm here for you.
Eee oo!
Here for him? All you've been doing is causing trouble!
You drove that jeep off the cliff, then you shoved me into that trucker to provoke him. Now you're riling the Doc up on purpose.
Is that your game? Get him upset-- then keep him from turning into the Hulk so you can be his new best friend?
Well, the Doc's already got a best friend and his name is Rick Jones!
Great, now he's got me talking in third person too!
You think the Radioactive Man cares about your silly friendship? I just needed to absorb enough gamma radiation to do--

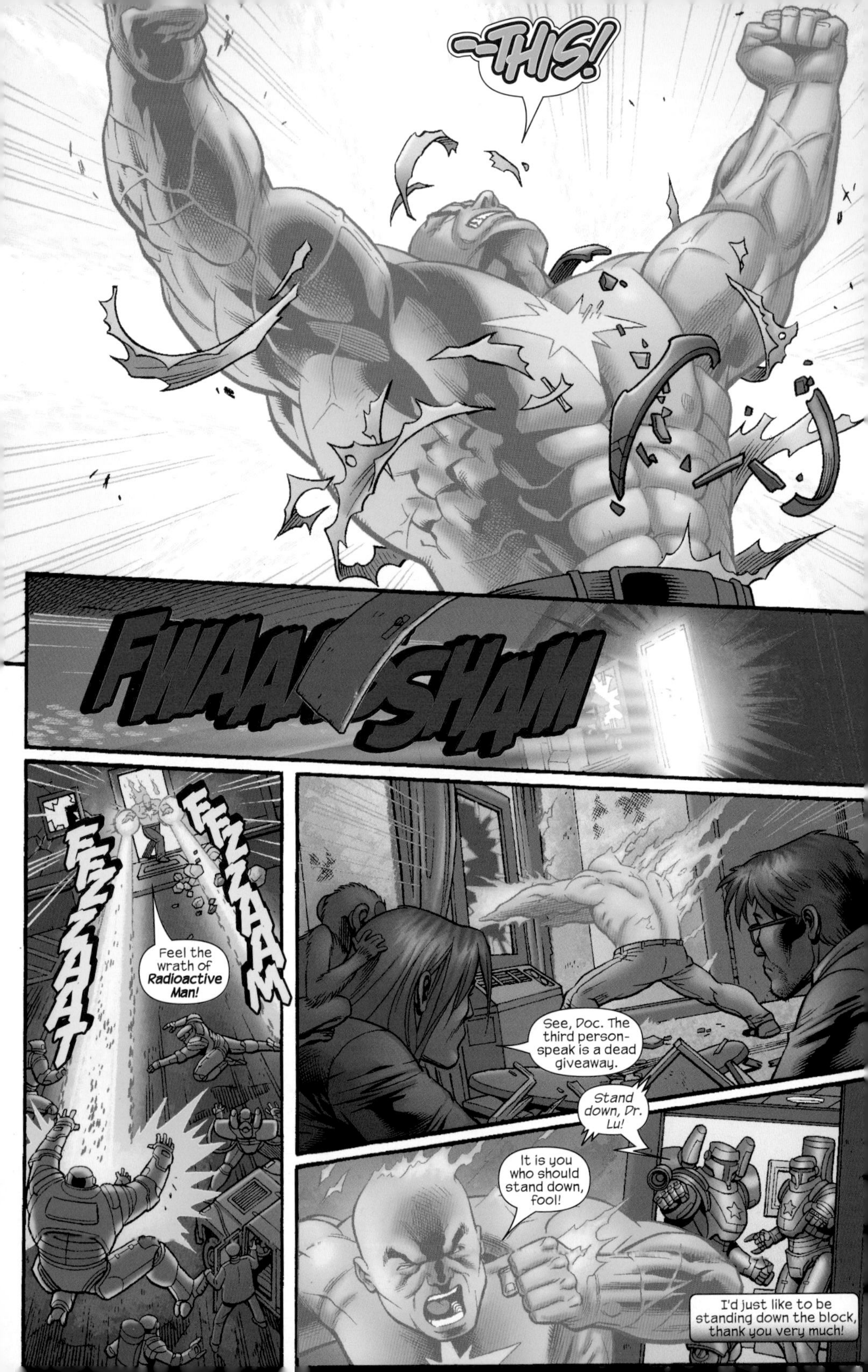
--THIS!
FWAAAKSHAM
FEZZAAT
FEZZAAM
Feel the wrath of Radioactive Man!
See, Doc. The third person-speak is a dead giveaway.
Stand down, Dr. Lu!
It is you who should stand down, fool!
I'd just like to be standing down the block, thank you very much!

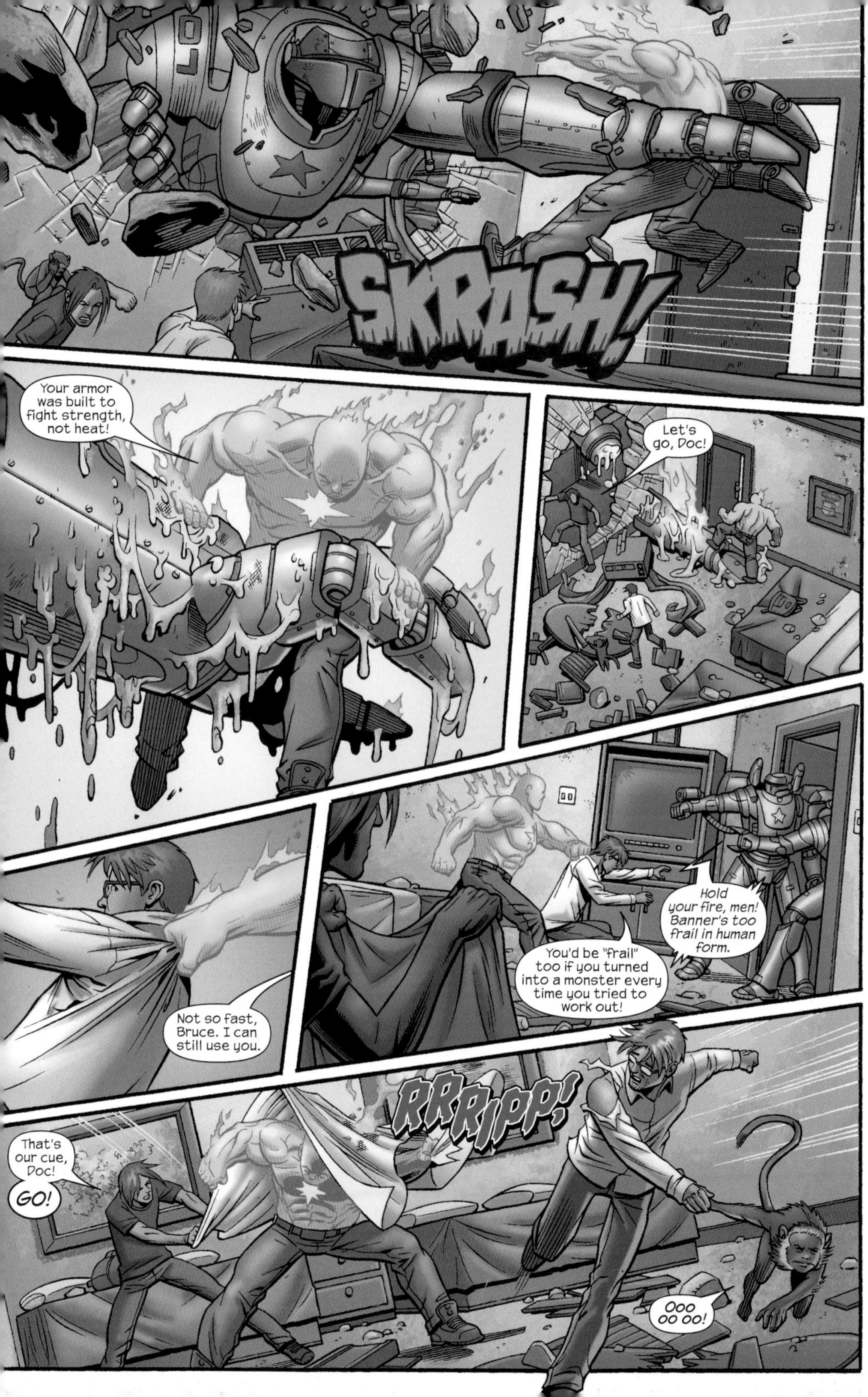
SKRASH!
Your armor was built to fight strength, not heat!
Let's go, Doc!
Hold your fire, men! Banner's too frail in human form.
You'd be "frail" too if you turned into a monster every time you tried to work out!
Not so fast, Bruce. I can still use you.
RRRIPP!
That's our cue, Doc!
GO!
Ooo oo oo!

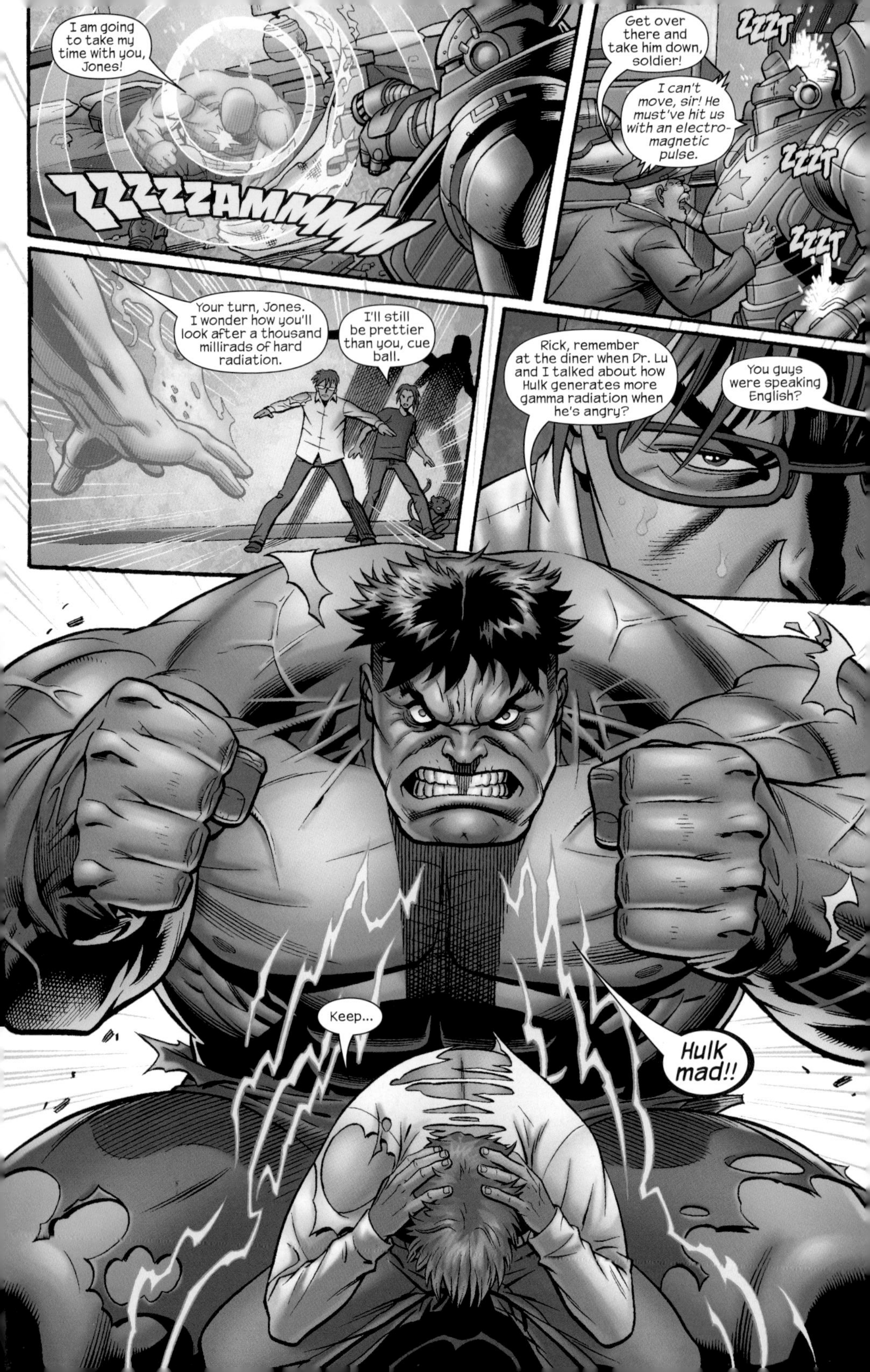
I am going to take my time with you, Jones!
ZZZZZAMMMMMM
Get over there and take him down, soldier!
ZZZT
I can't move, sir! He must've hit us with an electro-magnetic pulse.
ZZZT
ZZZT
Your turn, Jones. I wonder how you'll look after a thousand millirads of hard radiation.
I'll still be prettier than you, cue ball.
Rick, remember at the diner when Dr. Lu and I talked about how Hulk generates more gamma radiation when he's angry?
You guys were speaking English?
Keep...
Hulk mad!!

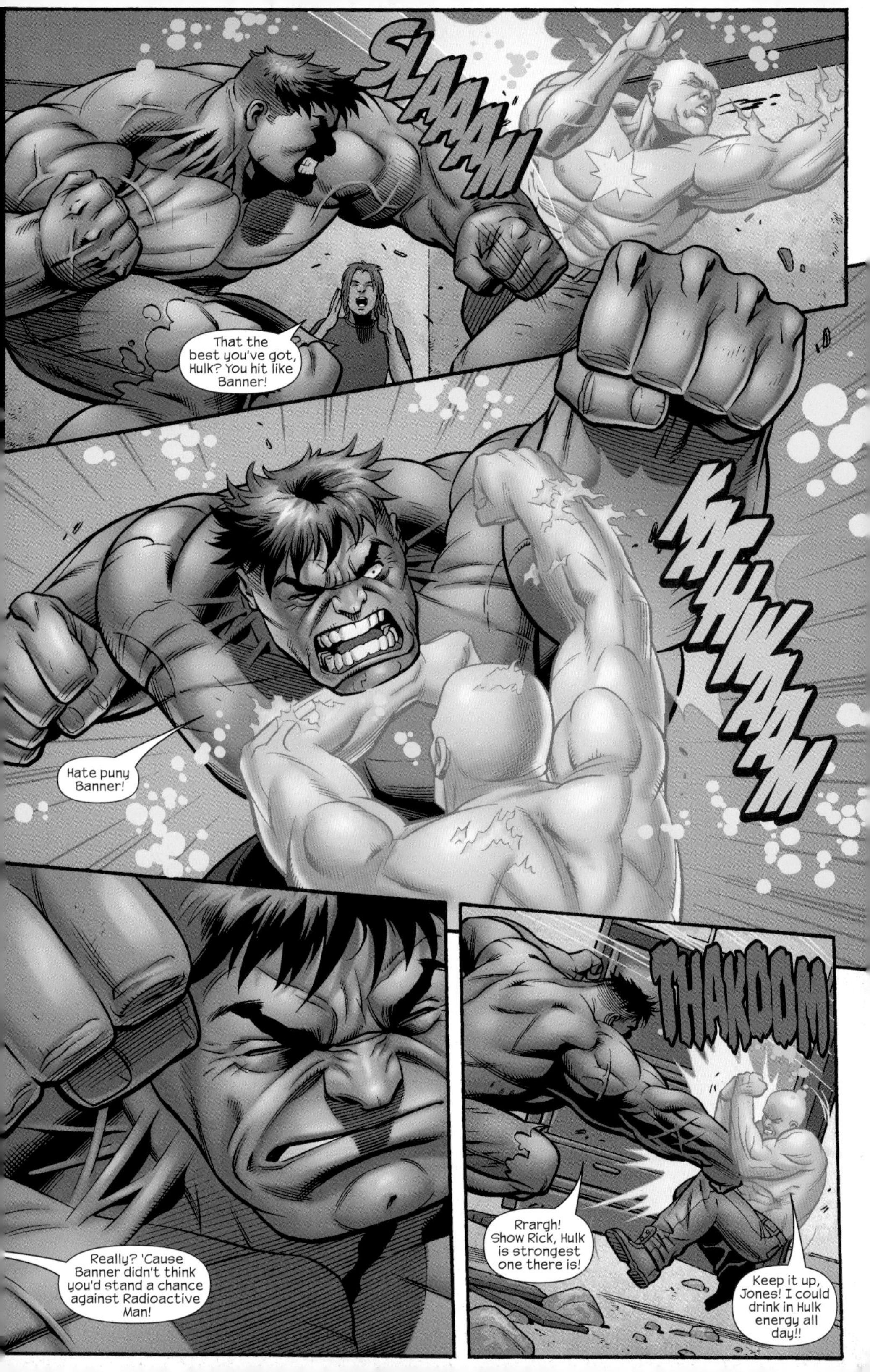
SLAAAAM
That the best you've got, Hulk? You hit like Banner!
Hate puny Banner!
KATHUNKAAAM
Really? 'Cause Banner didn't think you'd stand a chance against Radioactive Man!
THAKOOM
Rrargh! Show Rick, Hulk is strongest one there is!
Keep it up, Jones! I could drink in Hulk energy all day!!

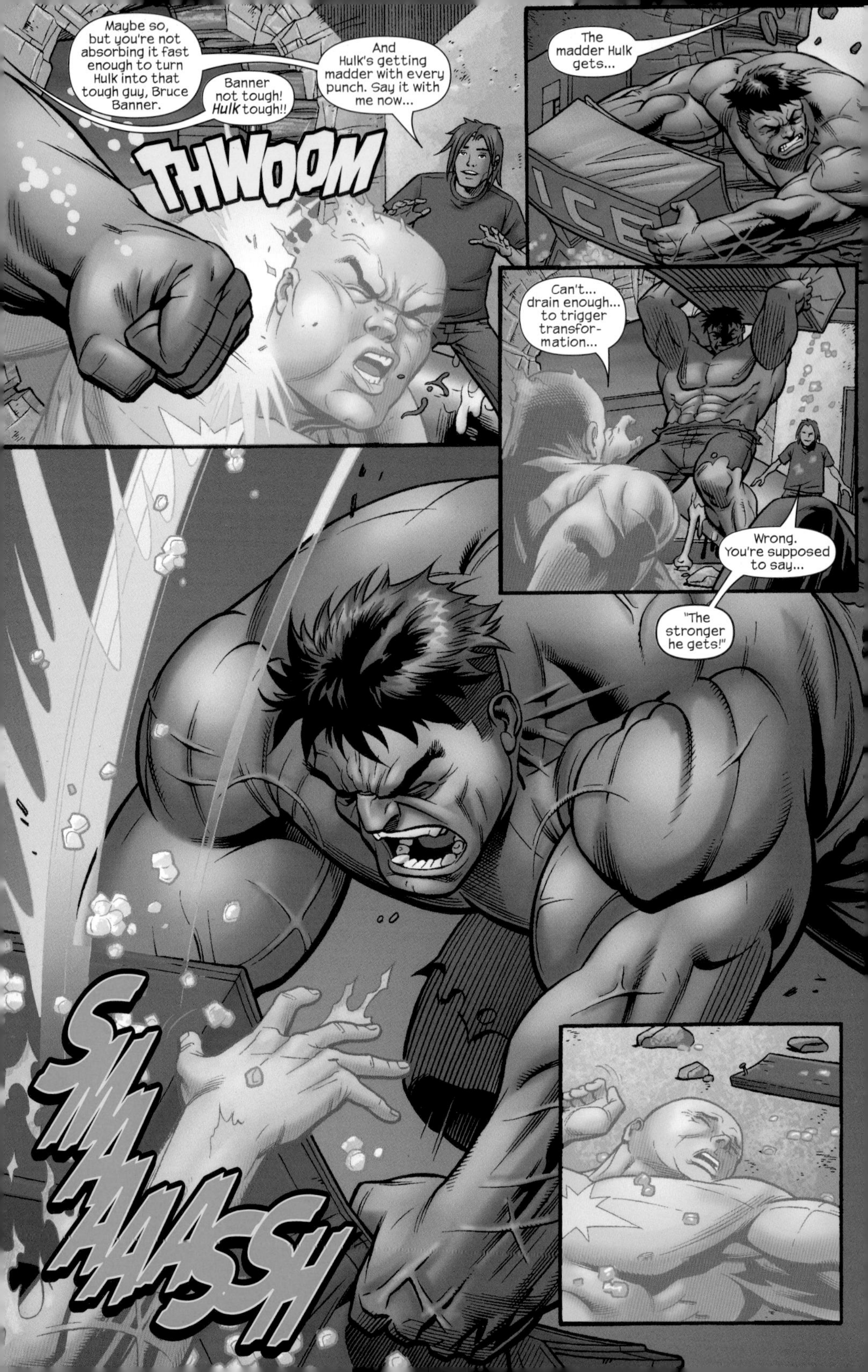
Maybe so, but you're not absorbing it fast enough to turn Hulk into that tough guy, Bruce Banner.
Banner not tough! Hulk tough!!
And Hulk's getting madder with every punch. Say it with me now...
THWOOM
The madder Hulk gets...
Can't... drain enough... to trigger transfor-mation...
Wrong. You're supposed to say...
"The stronger he gets!"
SMAASH

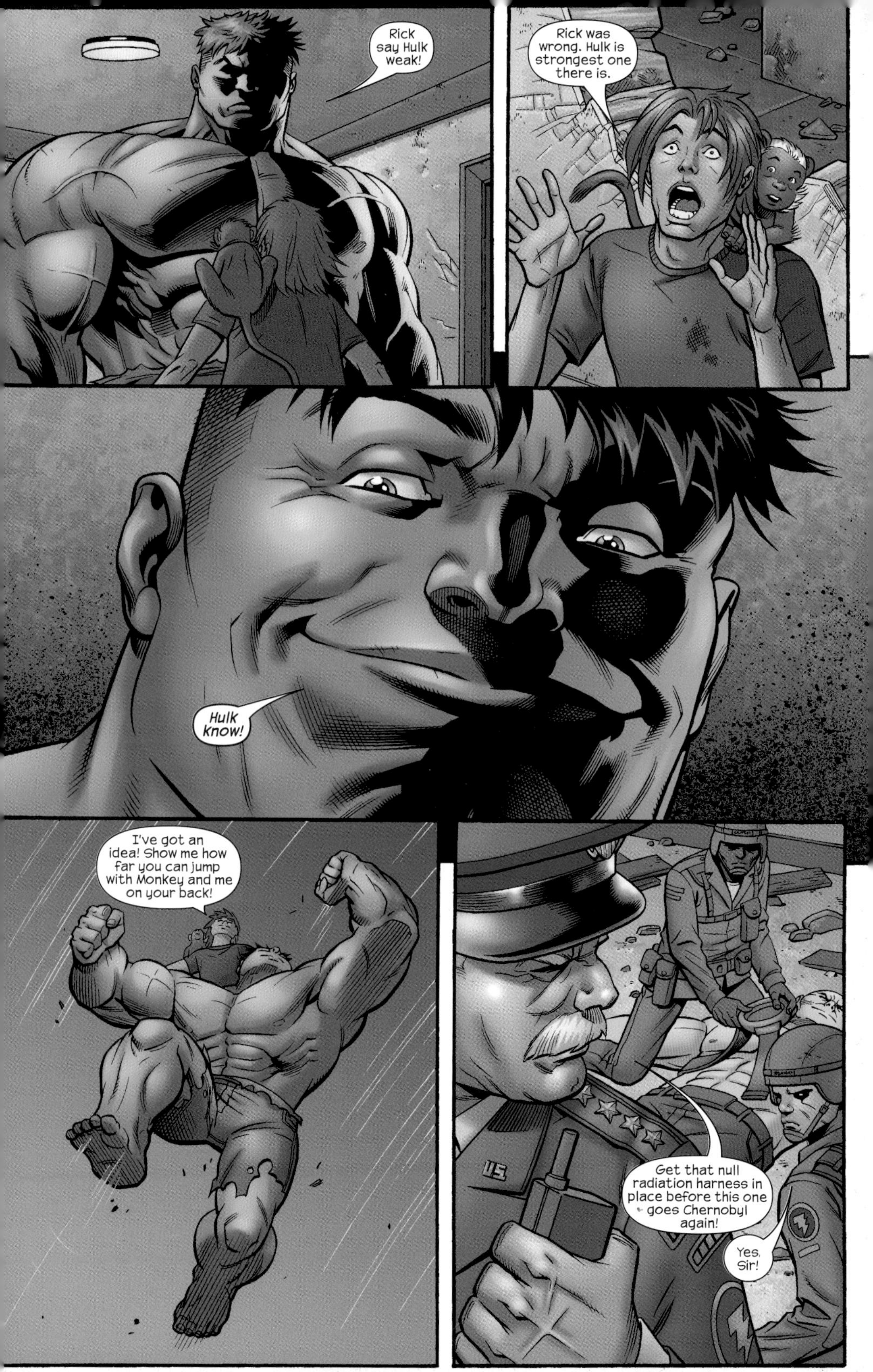
Rick say Hulk weak!
Rick was wrong. Hulk is strongest one there is.
Hulk know!
I've got an idea! Show me how far you can jump with Monkey and me on your back!
Get that null radiation harness in place before this one goes Chernobyl again!
Yes, Sir!

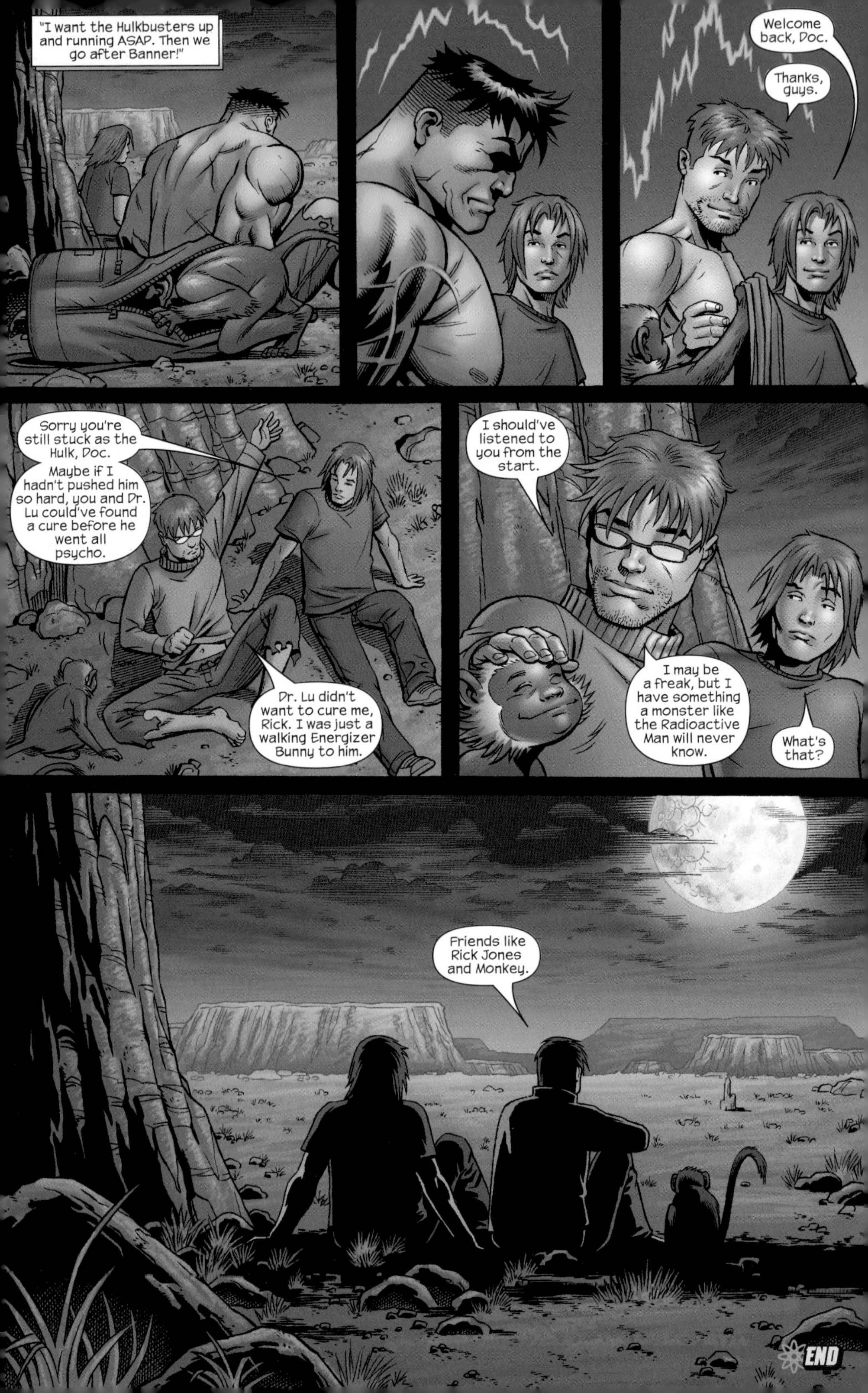
"I want the Hulkbusters up and running ASAP. Then we go after Banner!"
Welcome back, Doc.
Thanks, guys.
Sorry you're still stuck as the Hulk, Doc.
Maybe if I hadn't pushed him so hard, you and Dr. Lu could've found a cure before he went all psycho.
Dr. Lu didn't want to cure me, Rick. I was just a walking Energizer Bunny to him.
I should've listened to you from the start.
I may be a freak, but I have something a monster like the Radioactive Man will never know.
What's that?
Friends like Rick Jones and Monkey.
END

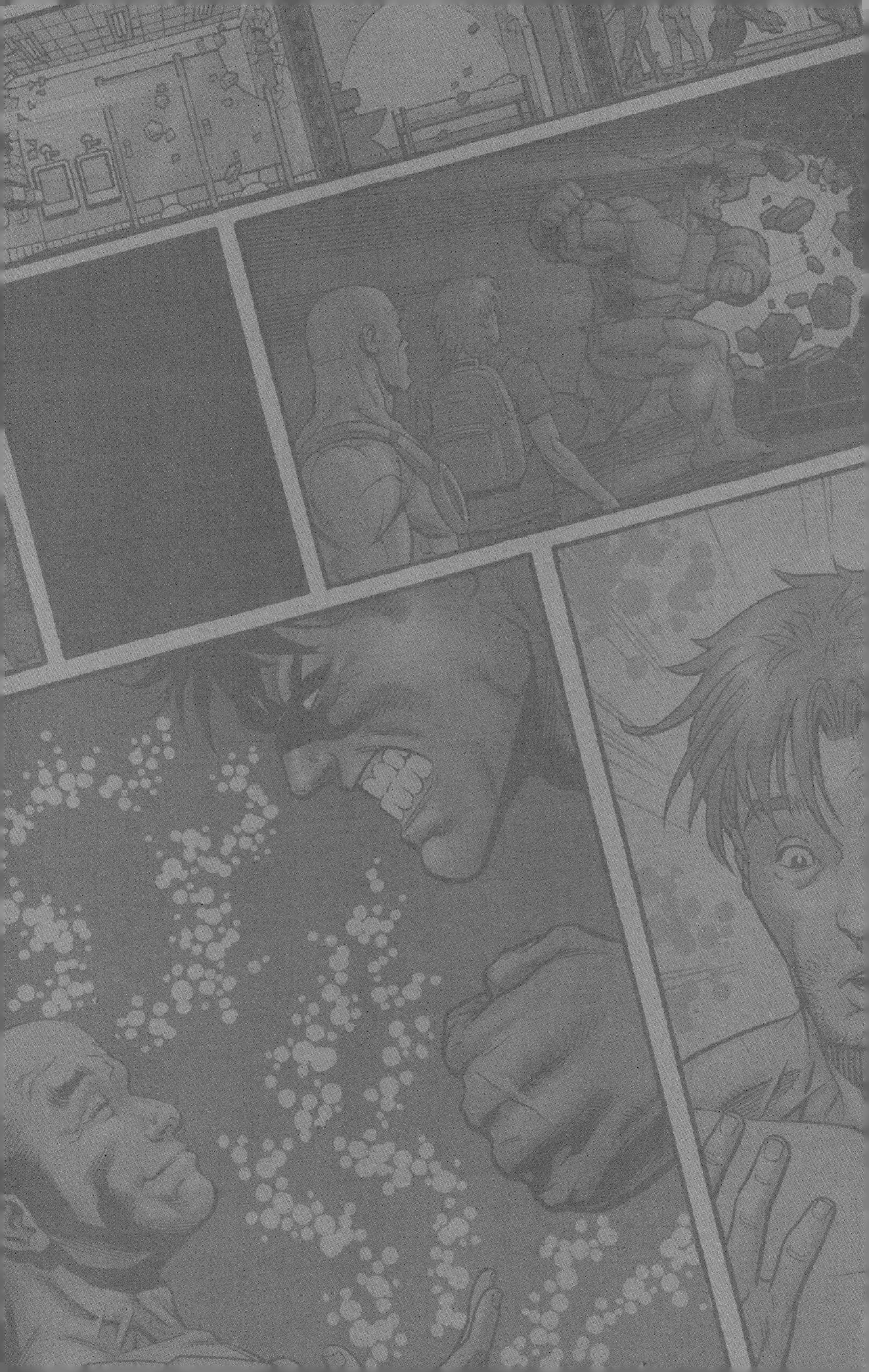

04

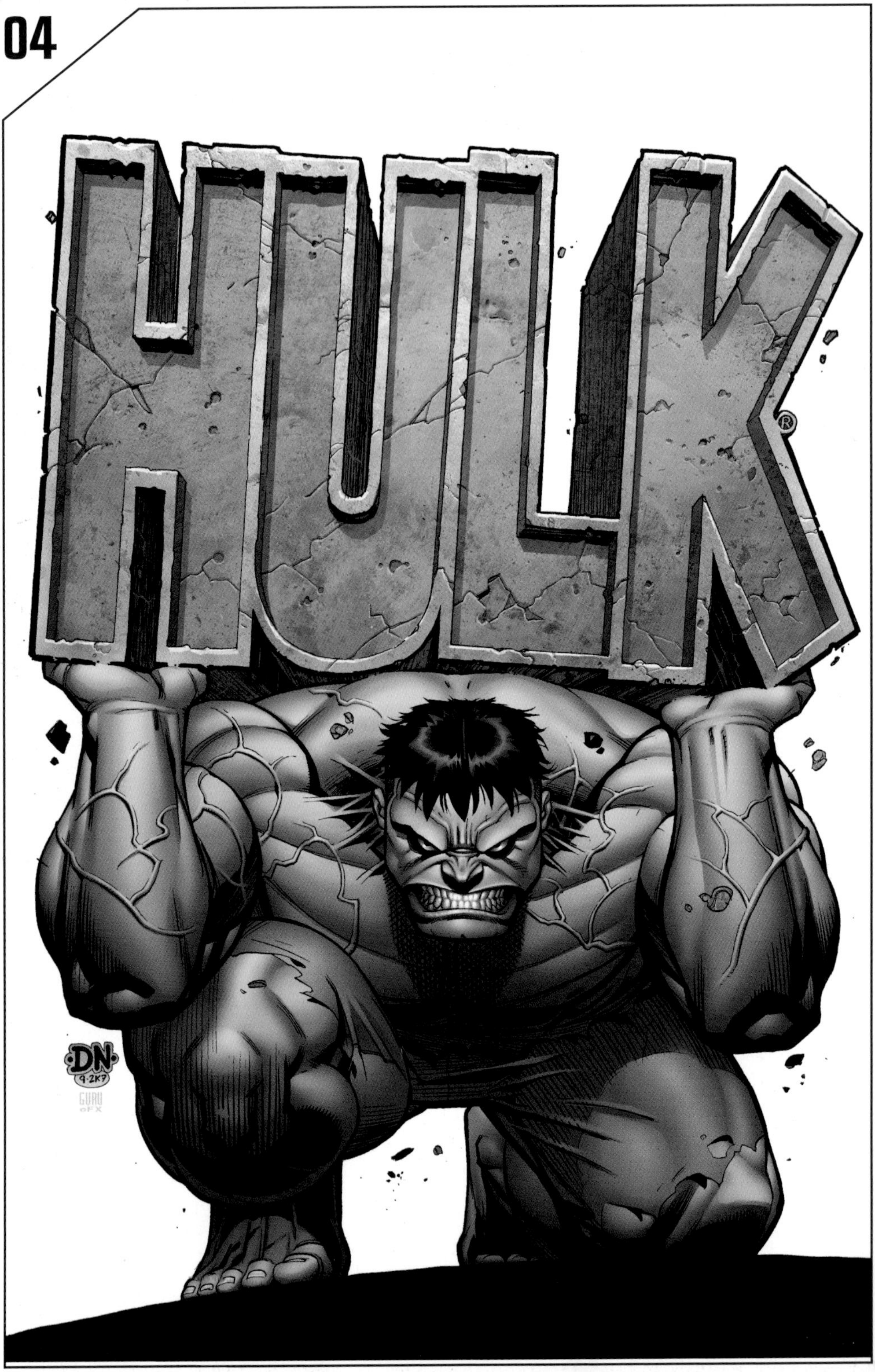
HULK

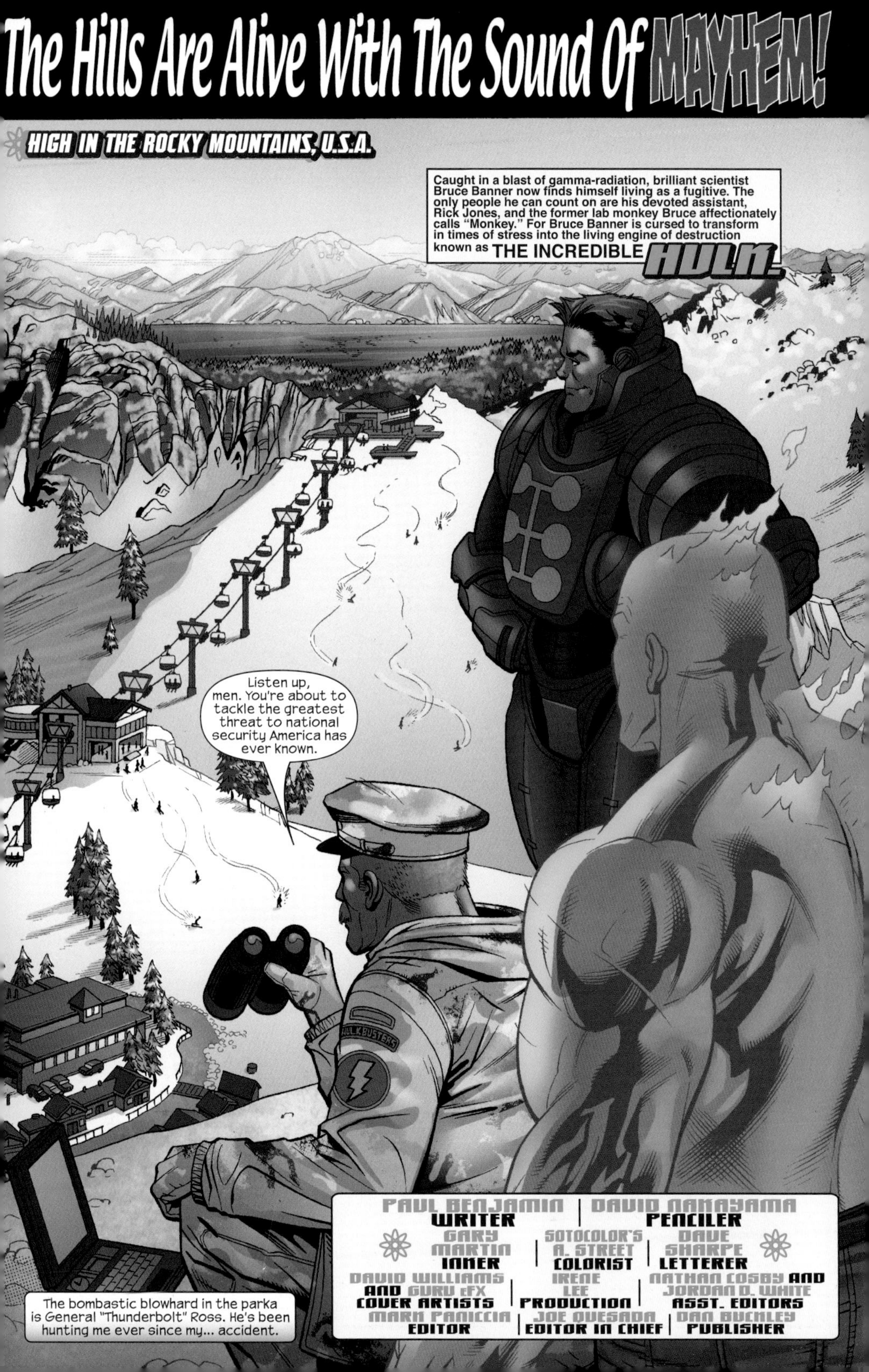
The Hills Are Alive With The Sound Of MAYHEM!
HIGH IN THE ROCKY MOUNTAINS, U.S.A.
Caught in a blast of gamma-radiation, brilliant scientist Bruce Banner now finds himself living as a fugitive. The only people he can count on are his devoted assistant, Rick Jones, and the former lab monkey Bruce affectionately calls "Monkey." For Bruce Banner is cursed to transform in times of stress into the living engine of destruction known as THE INCREDIBLE HULK.
Listen up, men. You're about to tackle the greatest threat to national security America has ever known.
HULKBUSTERS
The bombastic blowhard in the parka is General "Thunderbolt" Ross. He's been hunting me ever since my... accident.
PAUL BENJAMIN WRITER | DAVID NAKAYAMA PENCILER
GARY MARTIN INKER | SOTOCOLOR'S A. STREET COLORIST | DAVE SHARPE LETTERER
DAVID WILLIAMS AND GURU eFX COVER ARTISTS | IRENE LEE PRODUCTION | NATHAN COSBY AND JORDAN D. WHITE ASST. EDITORS
MARK PANICCIA EDITOR | JOE QUESADA EDITOR IN CHIEF | DAN BUCKLEY PUBLISHER

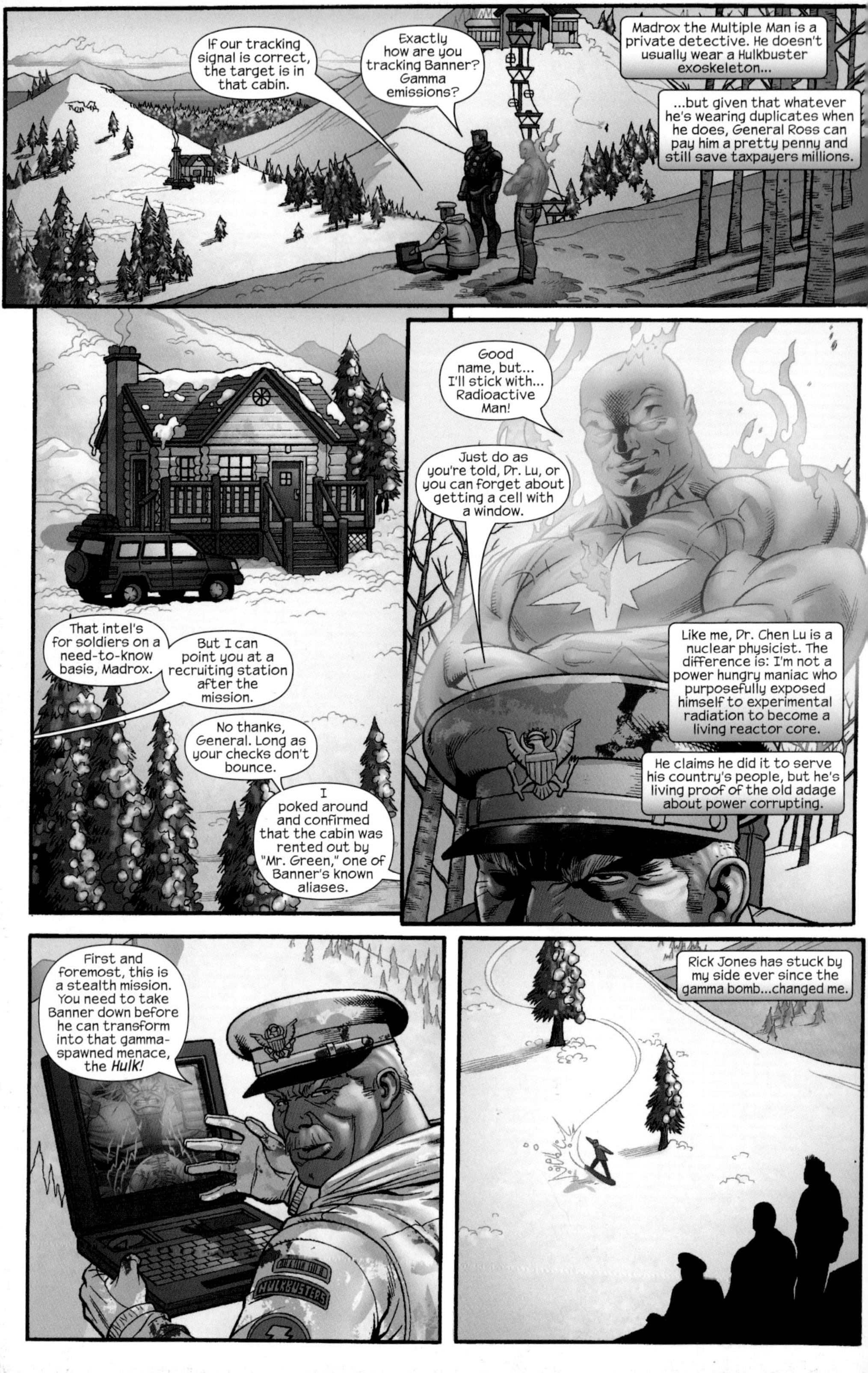
Madrox the Multiple Man is a private detective. He doesn't usually wear a Hulkbuster exoskeleton...
...but given that whatever he's wearing duplicates when he does, General Ross can pay him a pretty penny and still save taxpayers millions.
If our tracking signal is correct, the target is in that cabin.
Exactly how are you tracking Banner? Gamma emissions?
That intel's for soldiers on a need-to-know basis, Madrox.
But I can point you at a recruiting station after the mission.
No thanks, General. Long as your checks don't bounce.
I poked around and confirmed that the cabin was rented out by "Mr. Green," one of Banner's known aliases.
Good name, but... I'll stick with... Radioactive Man!
Just do as you're told, Dr. Lu, or you can forget about getting a cell with a window.
Like me, Dr. Chen Lu is a nuclear physicist. The difference is: I'm not a power hungry maniac who purposefully exposed himself to experimental radiation to become a living reactor core.
He claims he did it to serve his country's people, but he's living proof of the old adage about power corrupting.
First and foremost, this is a stealth mission. You need to take Banner down before he can transform into that gamma-spawned menace, the *Hulk!*
HULKBUSTERS
Rick Jones has stuck by my side ever since the gamma bomb...changed me.

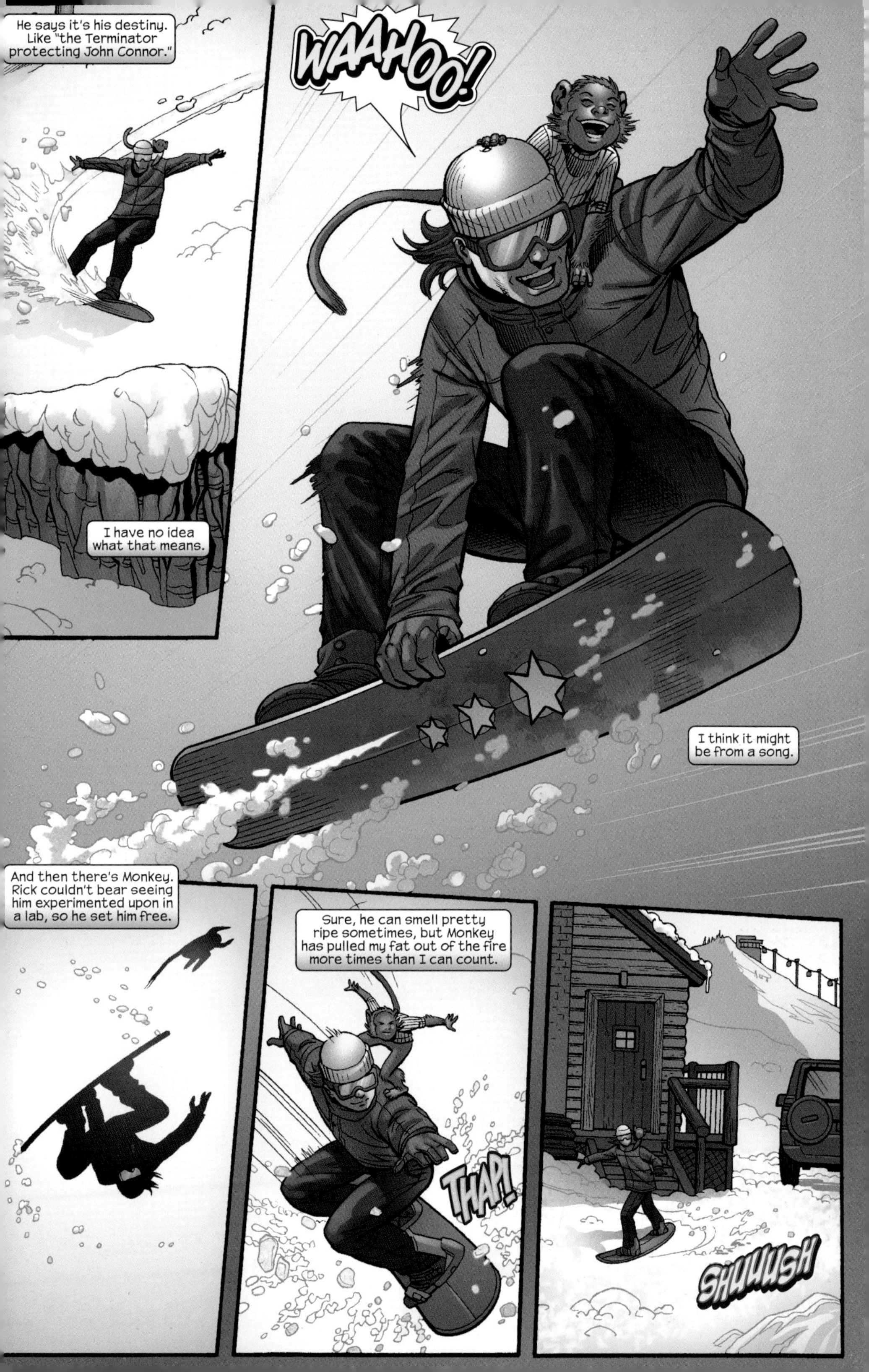
He says it's his destiny. Like "the Terminator protecting John Connor."
WAAHOO!
I have no idea what that means.
I think it might be from a song.
And then there's Monkey. Rick couldn't bear seeing him experimented upon in a lab, so he set him free.
Sure, he can smell pretty ripe sometimes, but Monkey has pulled my fat out of the fire more times than I can count.
THAP!
SHUUUSH

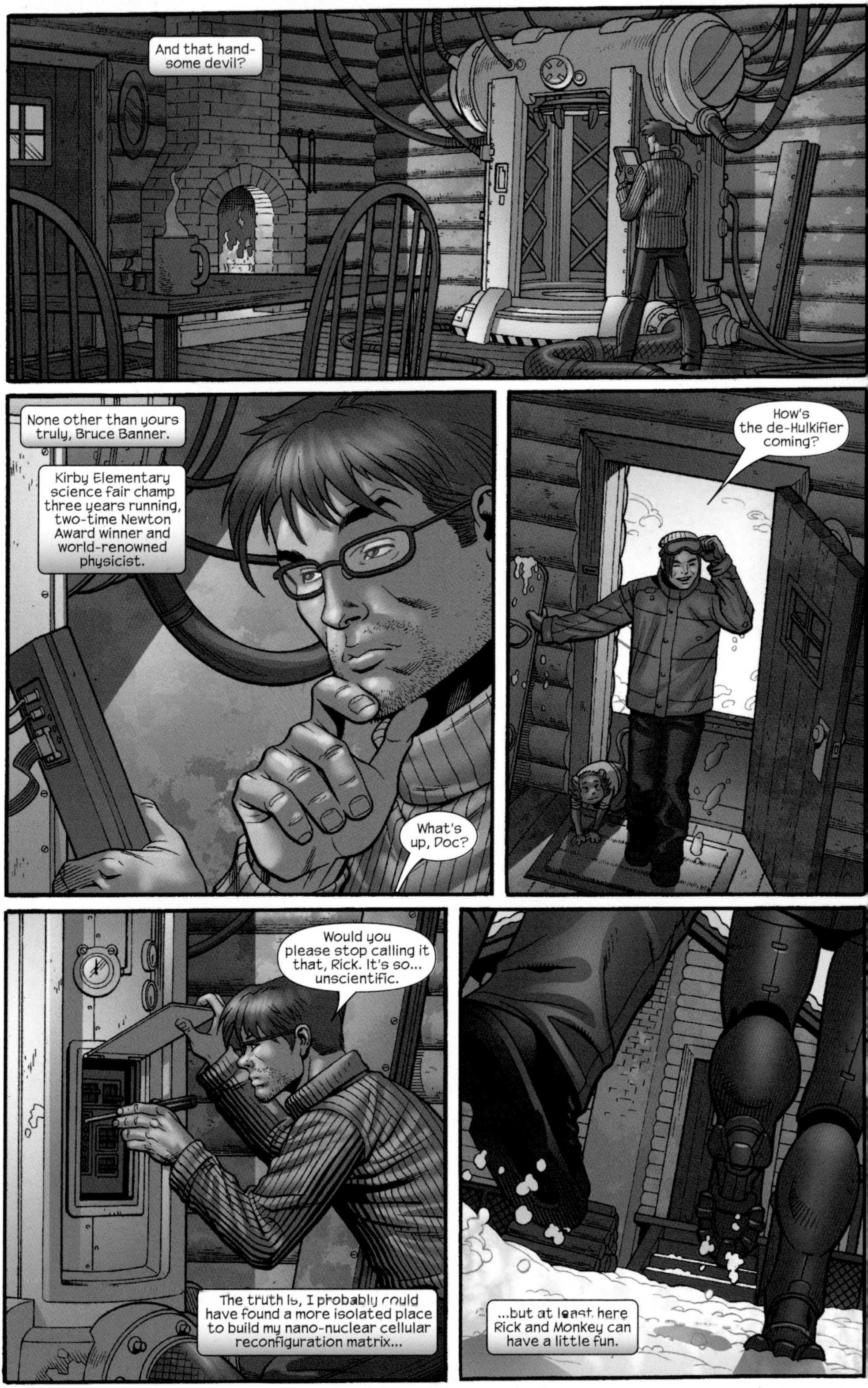
And that hand-some devil?
None other than yours truly, Bruce Banner.
Kirby Elementary science fair champ three years running, two-time Newton Award winner and world-renowned physicist.
What's up, Doc?
How's the de-Hulkifier coming?
Would you please stop calling it that, Rick. It's so... unscientific.
The truth is, I probably could have found a more isolated place to build my nano-nuclear cellular reconfiguration matrix...
...but at least here Rick and Monkey can have a little fun.

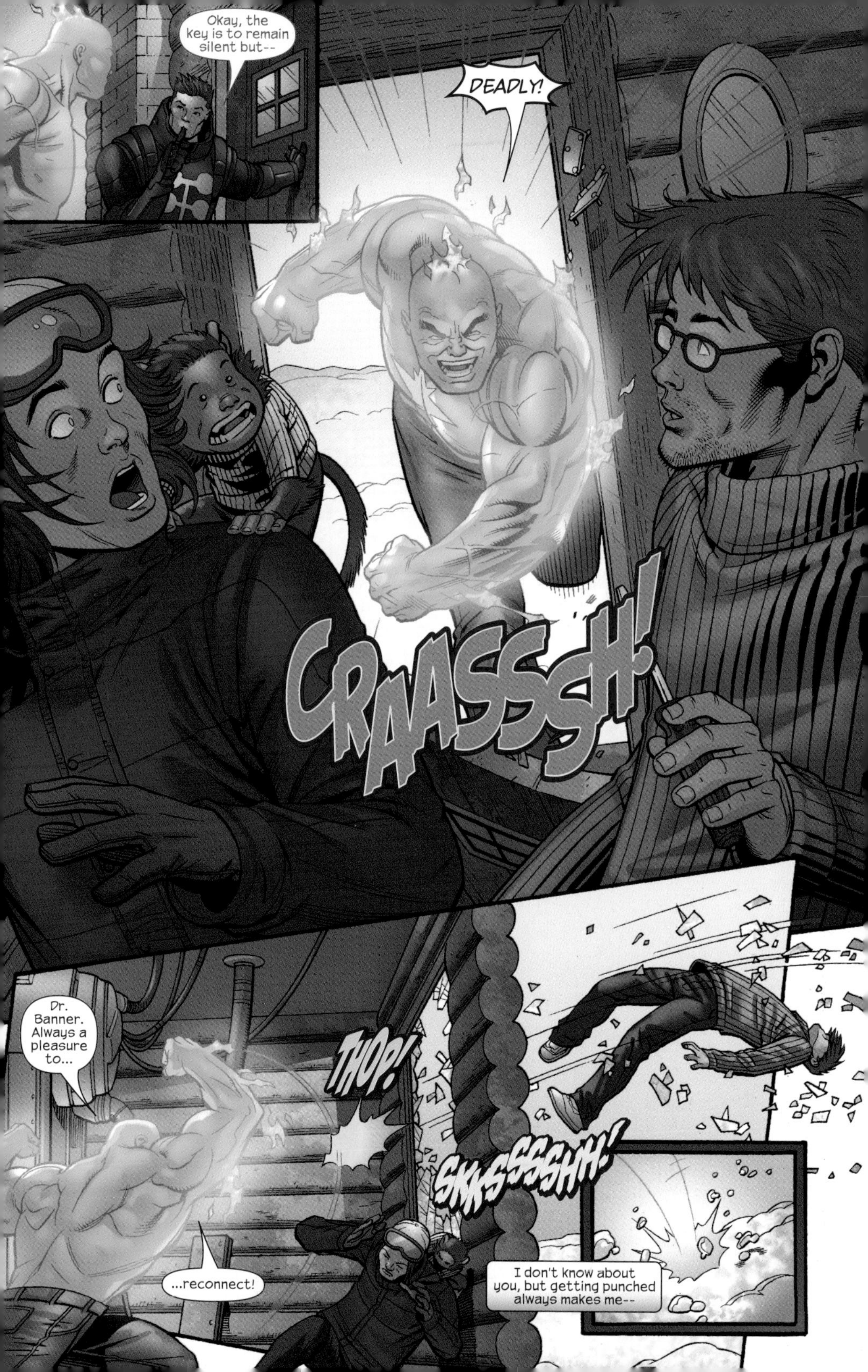
Okay, the key is to remain silent but--
DEADLY!
CRAASSSH!
Dr. Banner. Always a pleasure to...
THOP!
...reconnect!
SKKSSSSHH!
I don't know about you, but getting punched always makes me--

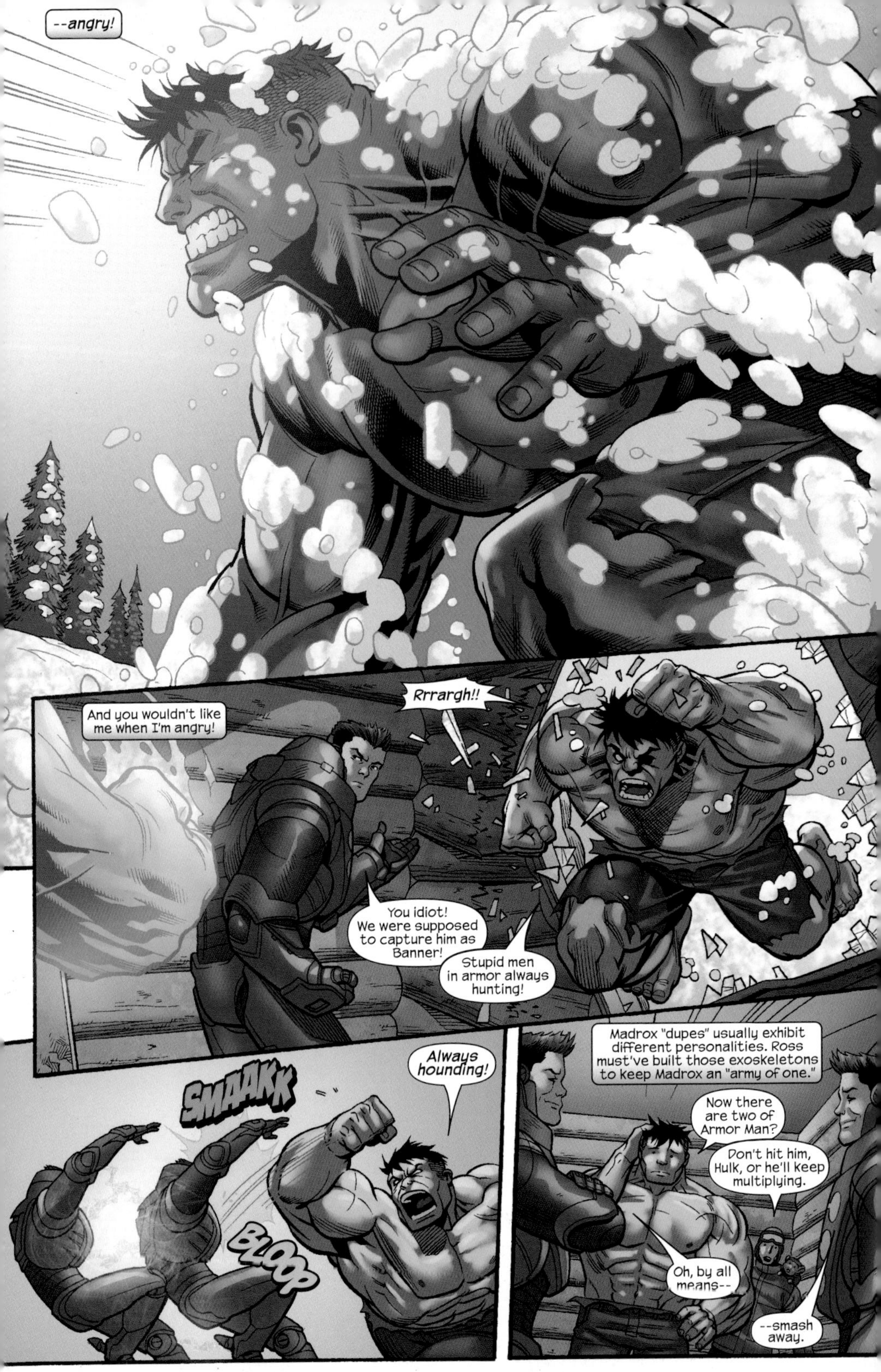
--angry!
And you wouldn't like me when I'm angry!
Rrrargh!!
You idiot! We were supposed to capture him as Banner!
Stupid men in armor always hunting!
SMAAKK
Always hounding!
BLOOP
Madrox "dupes" usually exhibit different personalities. Ross must've built those exoskeletons to keep Madrox an "army of one."
Now there are two of Armor Man?
Don't hit him, Hulk, or he'll keep multiplying.
Oh, by all means--
--smash away.

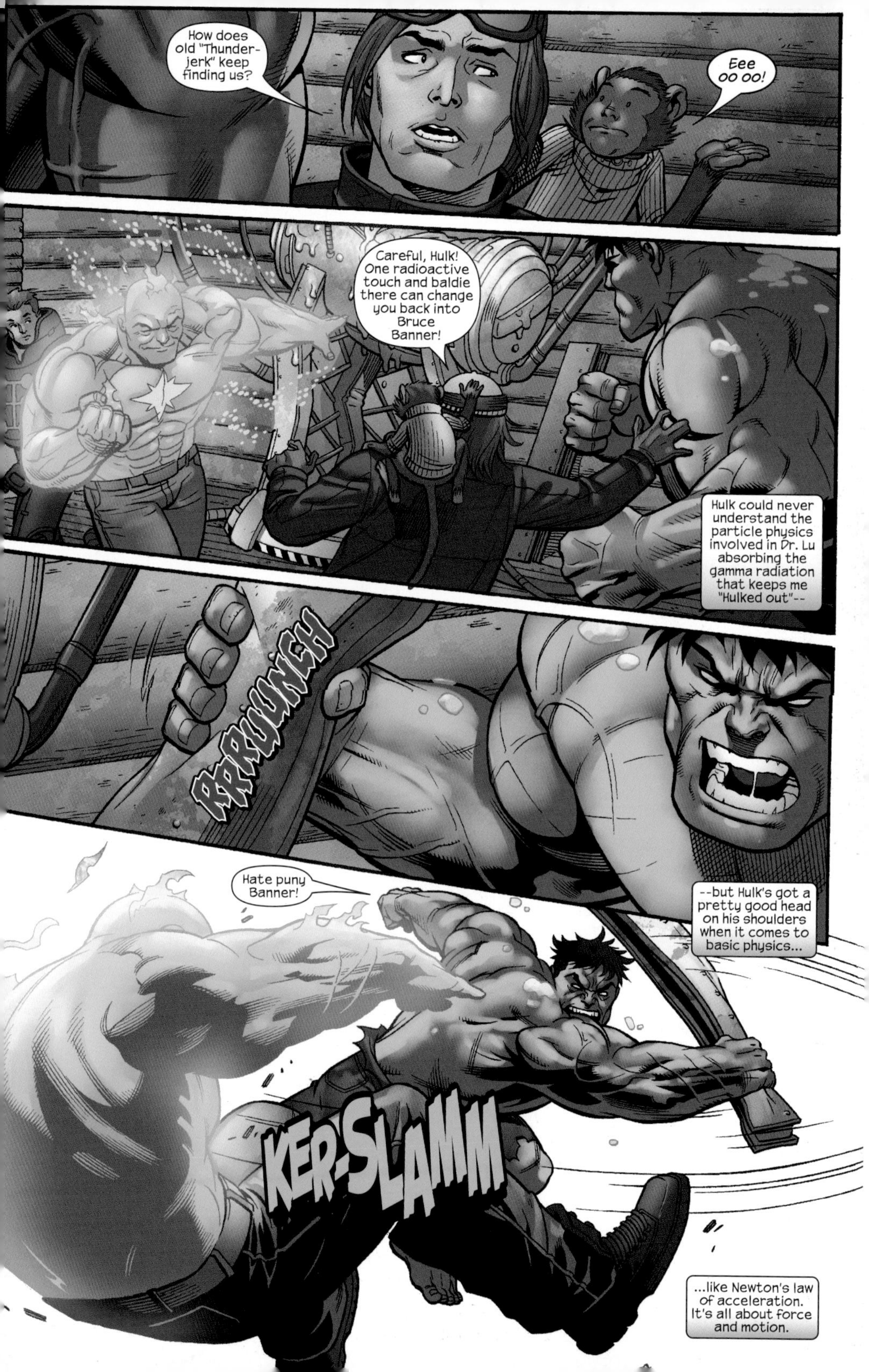
How does old "Thunder-jerk" keep finding us?
Eee oo oo!
Careful, Hulk! One radioactive touch and baldie there can change you back into Bruce Banner!
Hulk could never understand the particle physics involved in Dr. Lu absorbing the gamma radiation that keeps me "Hulked out"--
RRRUUNCH
Hate puny Banner!
--but Hulk's got a pretty good head on his shoulders when it comes to basic physics...
KER-SLAMM
...like Newton's law of acceleration. It's all about force and motion.

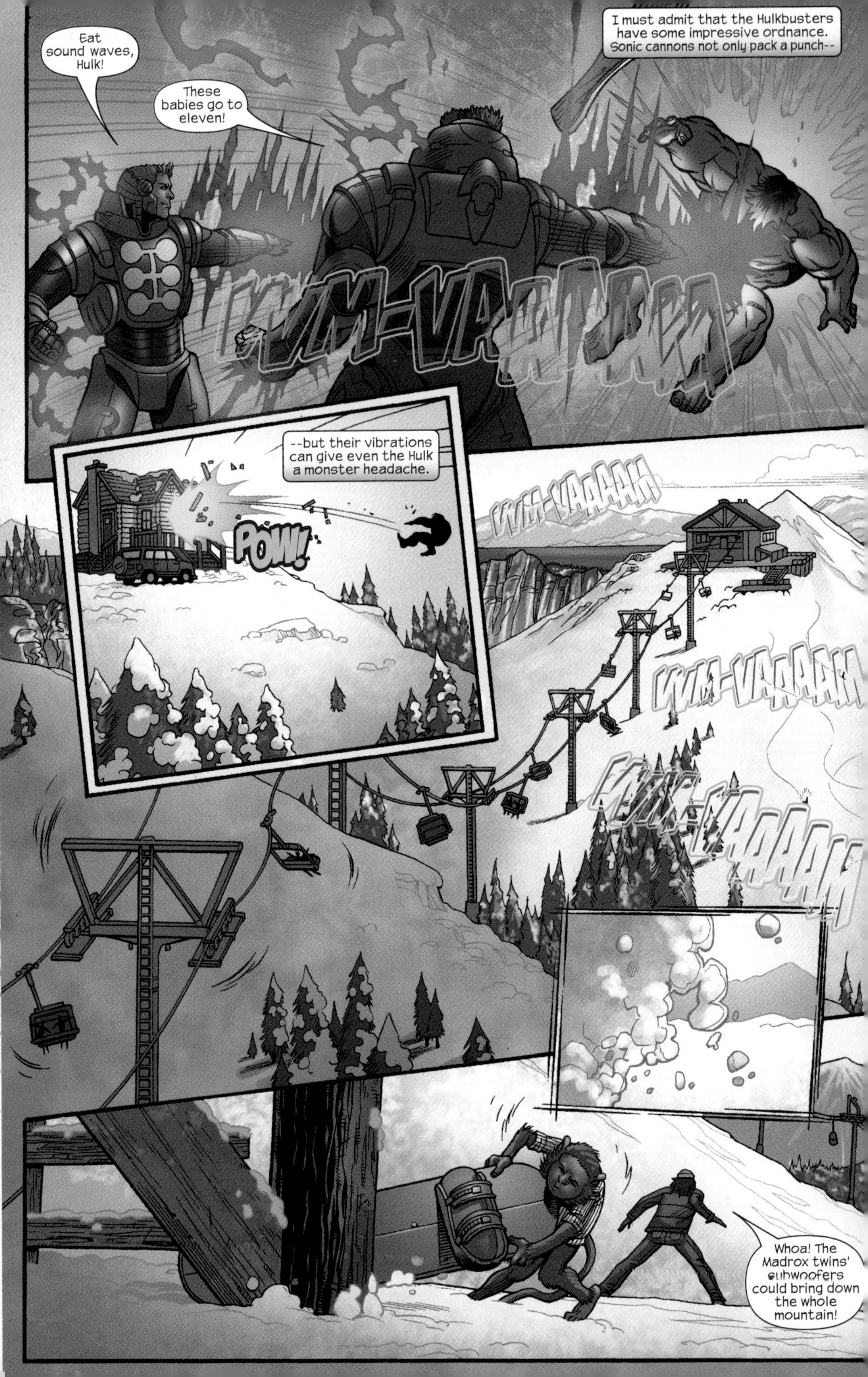

Eat sound waves, Hulk!
These babies go to eleven!
I must admit that the Hulkbusters have some impressive ordnance. Sonic cannons not only pack a punch--
--but their vibrations can give even the Hulk a monster headache.
POW!
VVM-VAAAAM
VVM-VAAAAM
Whoa! The Madrox twins' subwoofers could bring down the whole mountain!

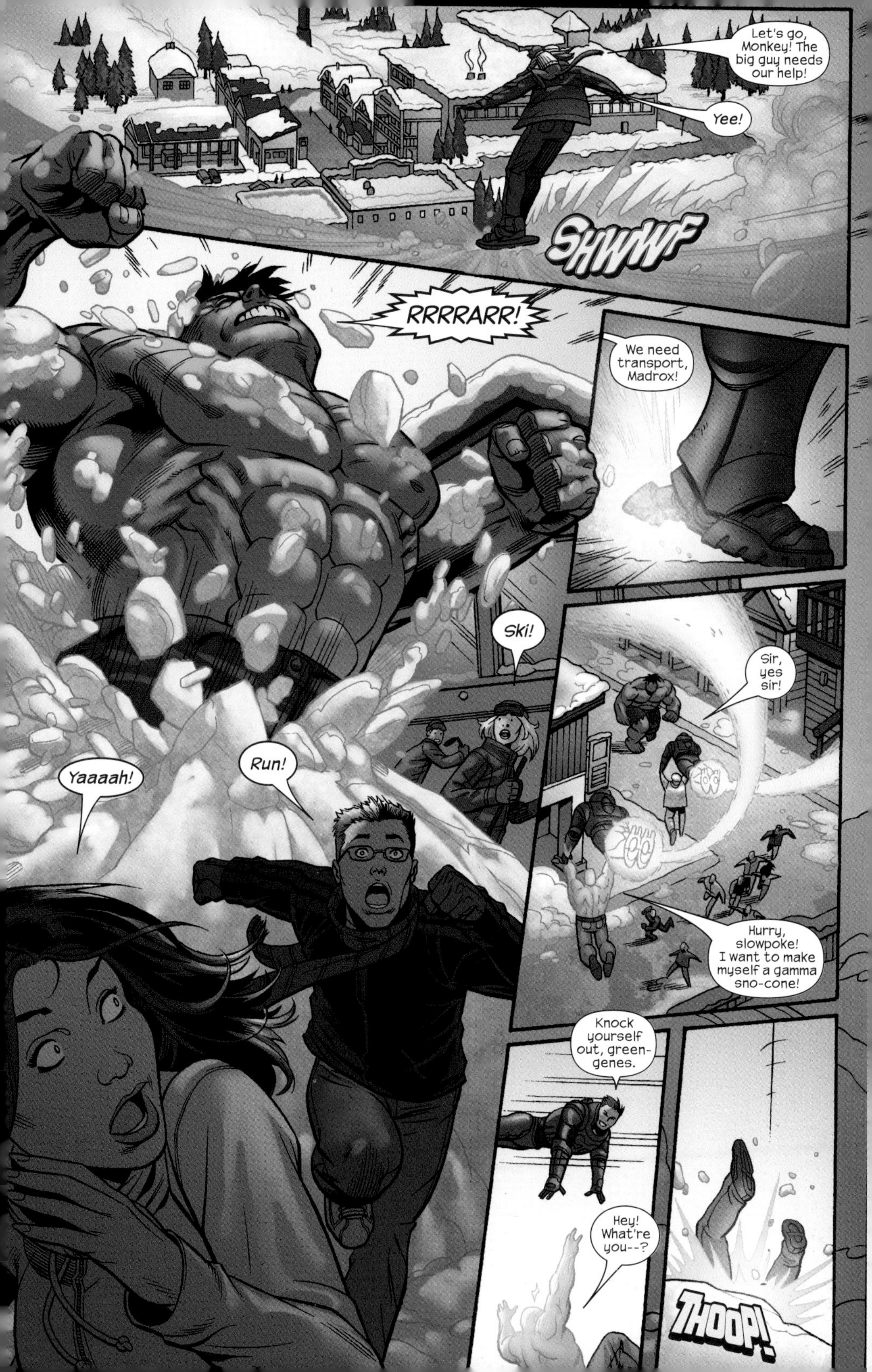
Let's go, Monkey! The big guy needs our help!
Yee!
SHWWF
RRRRARR!
We need transport, Madrox!
Ski!
Sir, yes sir!
Yaaaah!
Run!
Hurry, slowpoke! I want to make myself a gamma sno-cone!
Knock yourself out, green-genes.
Hey! What're you--?
THOOP!

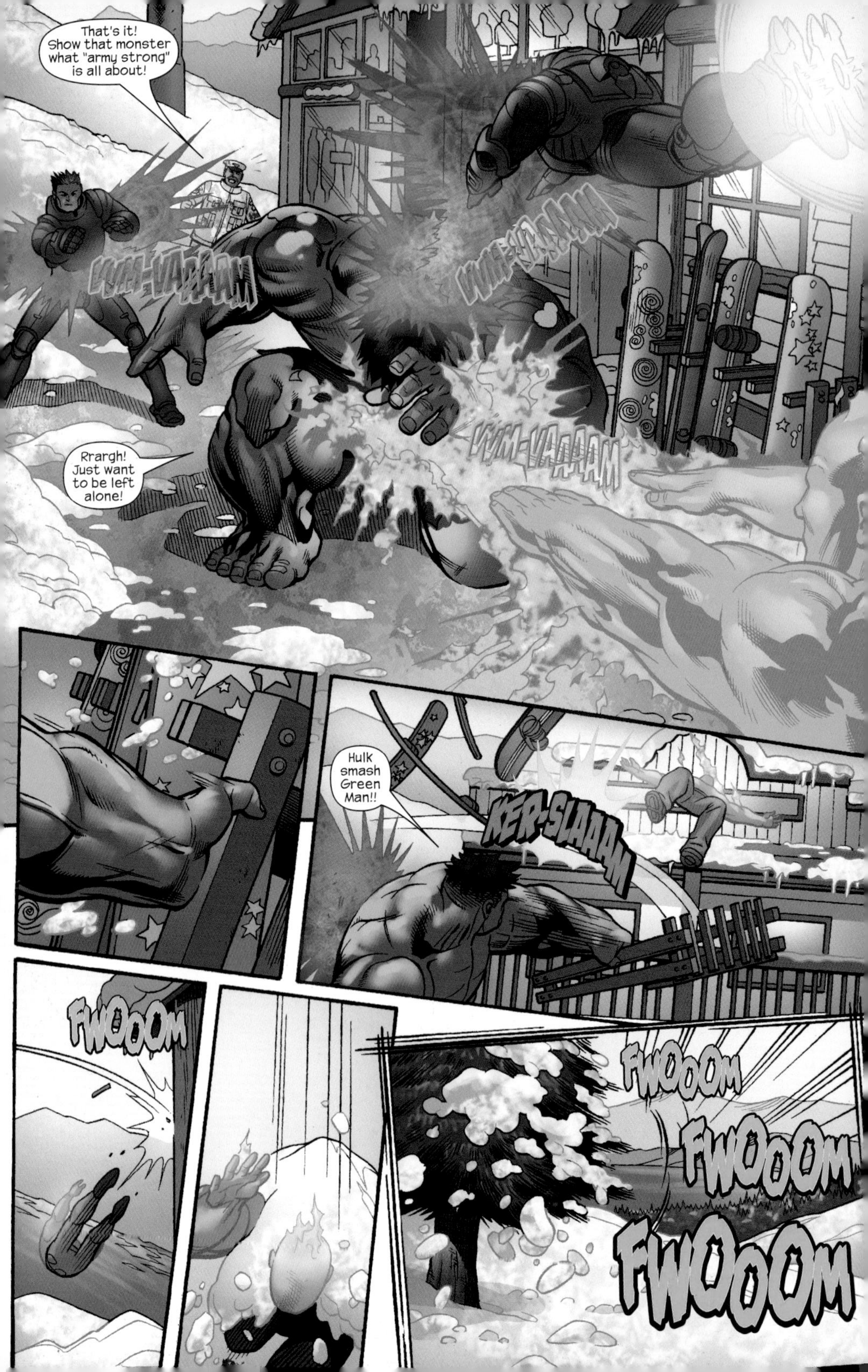

That's it! Show that monster what "army strong" is all about!
VVM-VAAAAM
VVM-VAAAAM
Rrargh! Just want to be left alone!
VVM-VAAAAM
Hulk smash Green Man!!
KER-SLAAAM
FWOOOM
FWOOOM
FWOOOM
FWOOOM

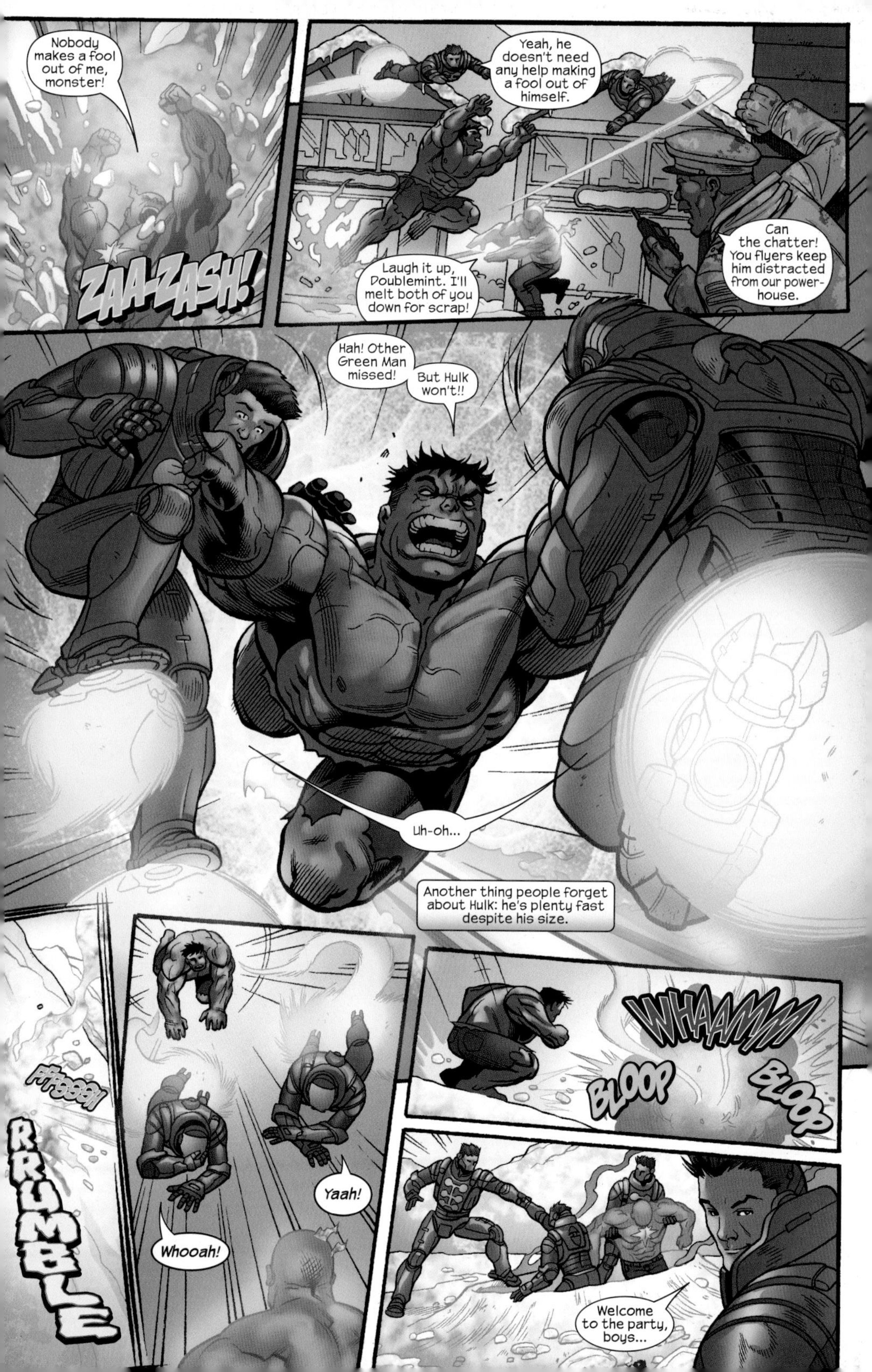

Nobody makes a fool out of me, monster!
ZAA-ZASH!
Yeah, he doesn't need any help making a fool out of himself.
Laugh it up, Doublemint. I'll melt both of you down for scrap!
Can the chatter! You flyers keep him distracted from our power-house.
Hah! Other Green Man missed!
But Hulk won't!!
Uh-oh...
Another thing people forget about Hulk: he's plenty fast despite his size.
RRUMBLE
Whooah!
Yaah!
WHAAMM
BLOOP
BLOOP
Welcome to the party, boys...

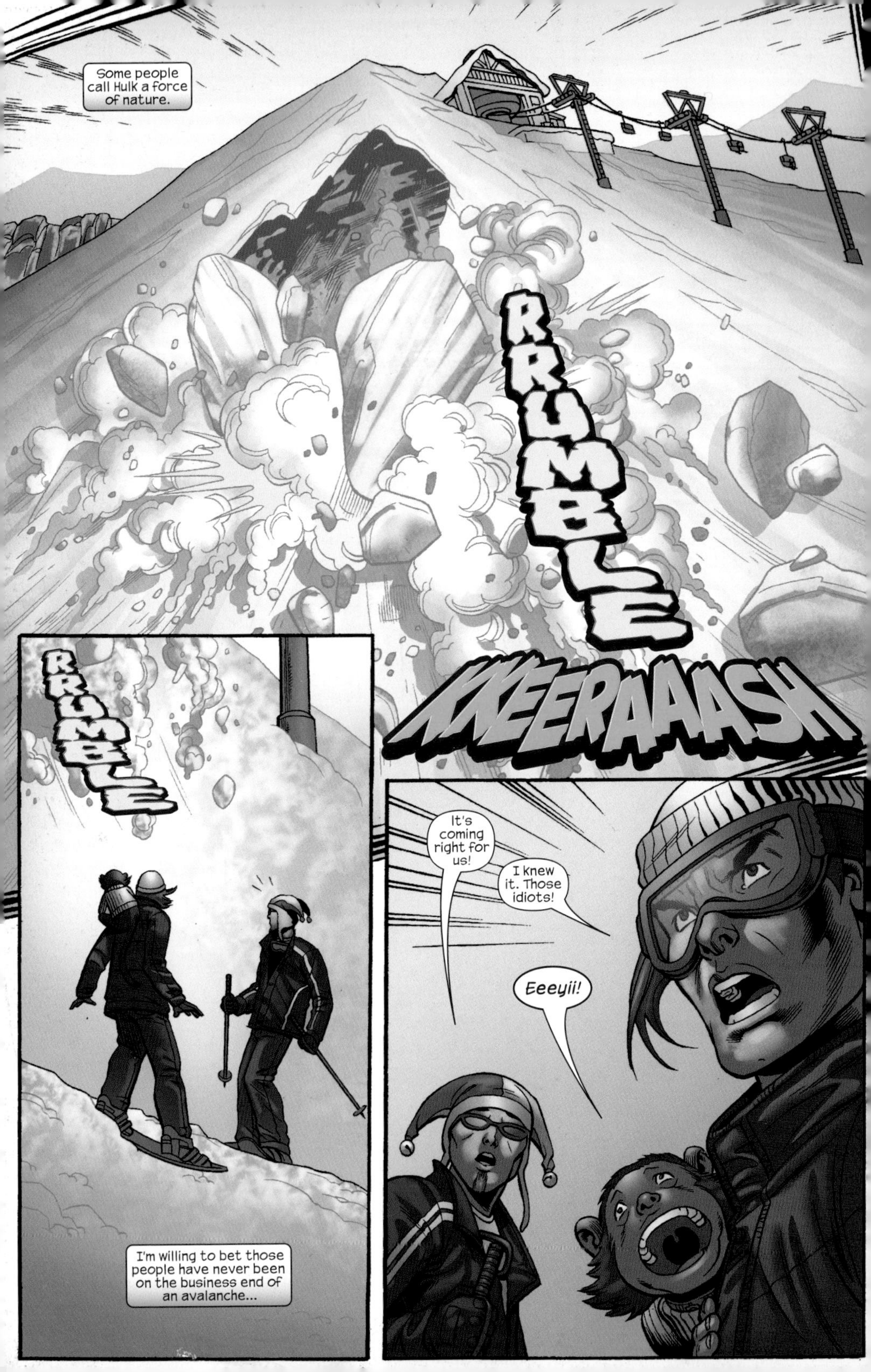
Some people call Hulk a force of nature.
RRUMBLE
KKEERAAASH
RRUMBLE
I'm willing to bet those people have never been on the business end of an avalanche...
It's coming right for us!
I knew it. Those idiots!
Eeeyii!

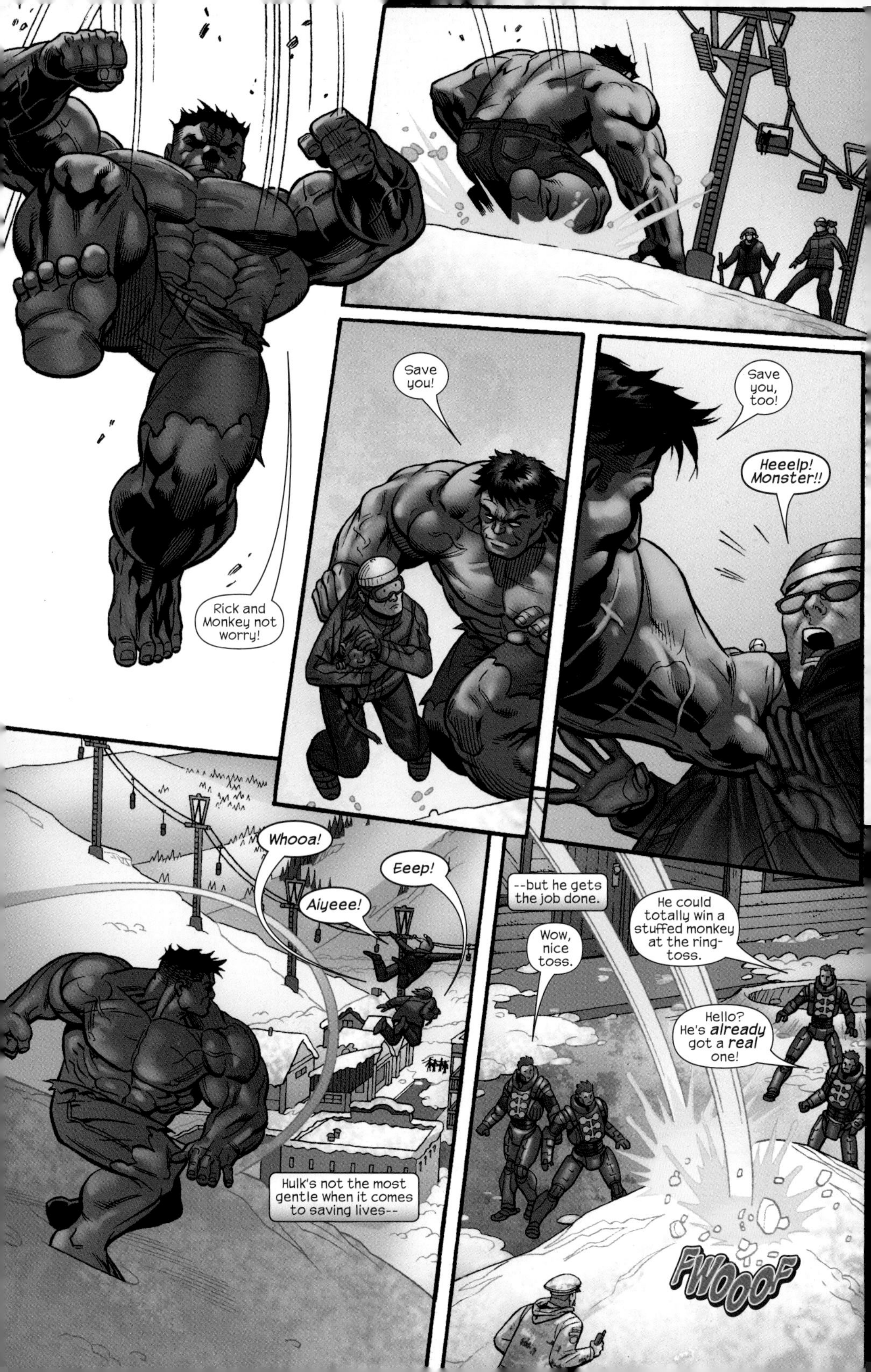
Rick and Monkey not worry!
Save you!
Save you, too!
Heeelp! Monster!!
Whooa!
Eeep!
Aiyeee!
Hulk's not the most gentle when it comes to saving lives--
--but he gets the job done.
Wow, nice toss.
He could totally win a stuffed monkey at the ring-toss.
Hello? He's already got a real one!
FWOOOF

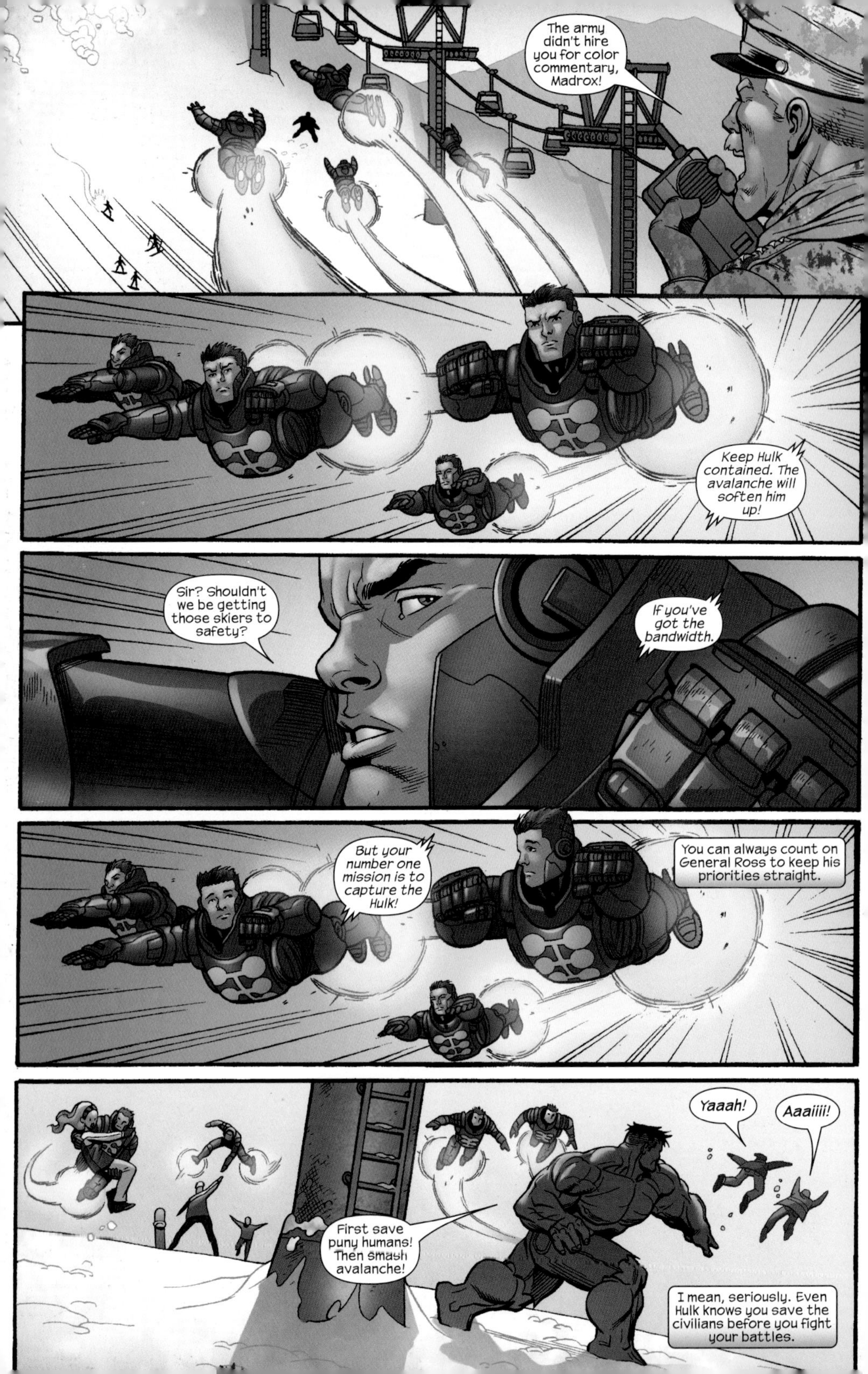
The army didn't hire you for color commentary, Madrox!
Keep Hulk contained. The avalanche will soften him up!
Sir? Shouldn't we be getting those skiers to safety?
If you've got the bandwidth.
But your number one mission is to capture the Hulk!
You can always count on General Ross to keep his priorities straight.
Yaaah!
Aaaiiii!
First save puny humans! Then smash avalanche!
I mean, seriously. Even Hulk knows you save the civilians before you fight your battles.

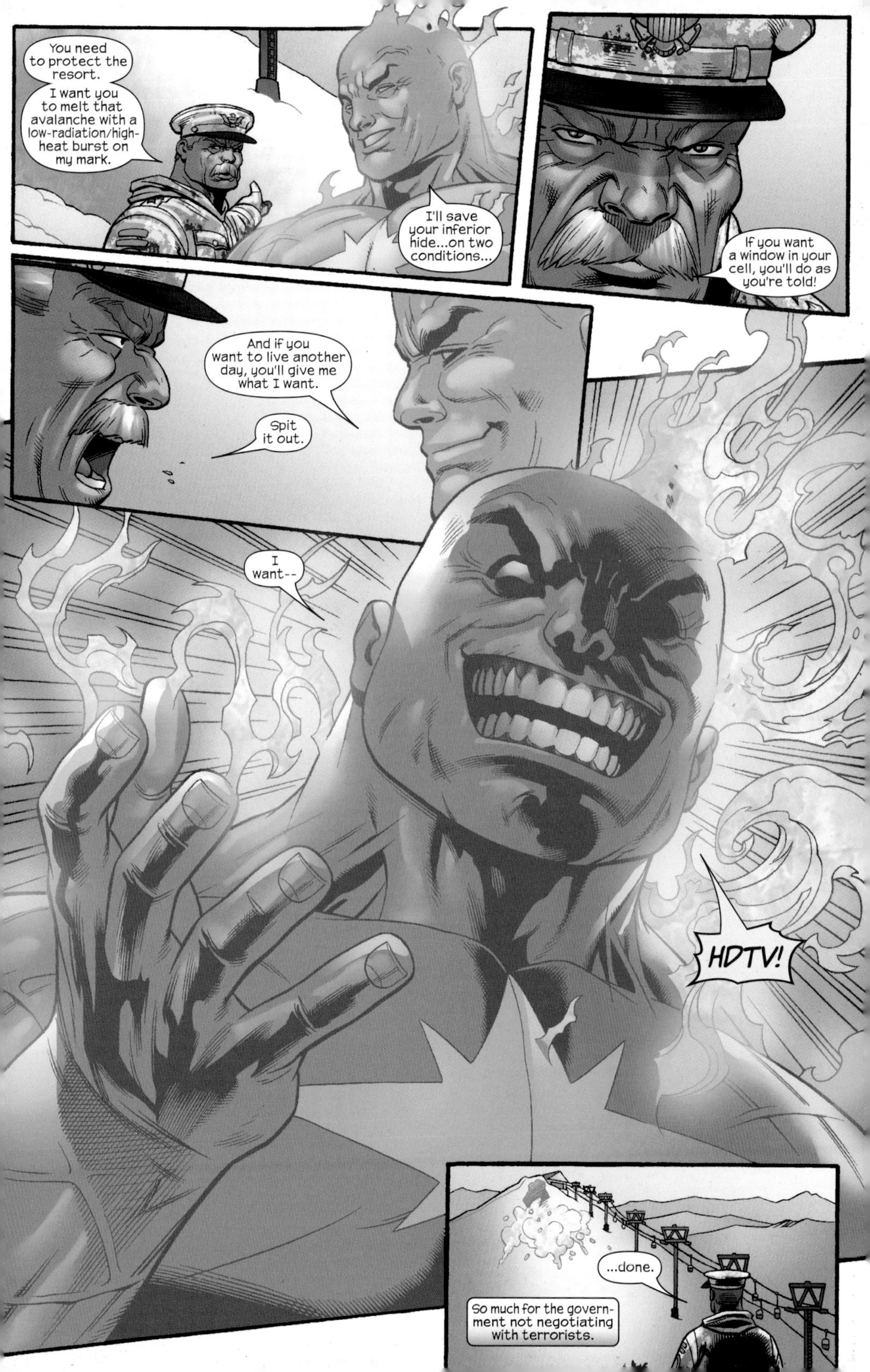

You need to protect the resort.
I want you to melt that avalanche with a low-radiation/high-heat burst on my mark.
I'll save your inferior hide...on two conditions...
If you want a window in your cell, you'll do as you're told!
And if you want to live another day, you'll give me what I want.
Spit it out.
I want--
HDTV!
...done.
So much for the government not negotiating with terrorists.

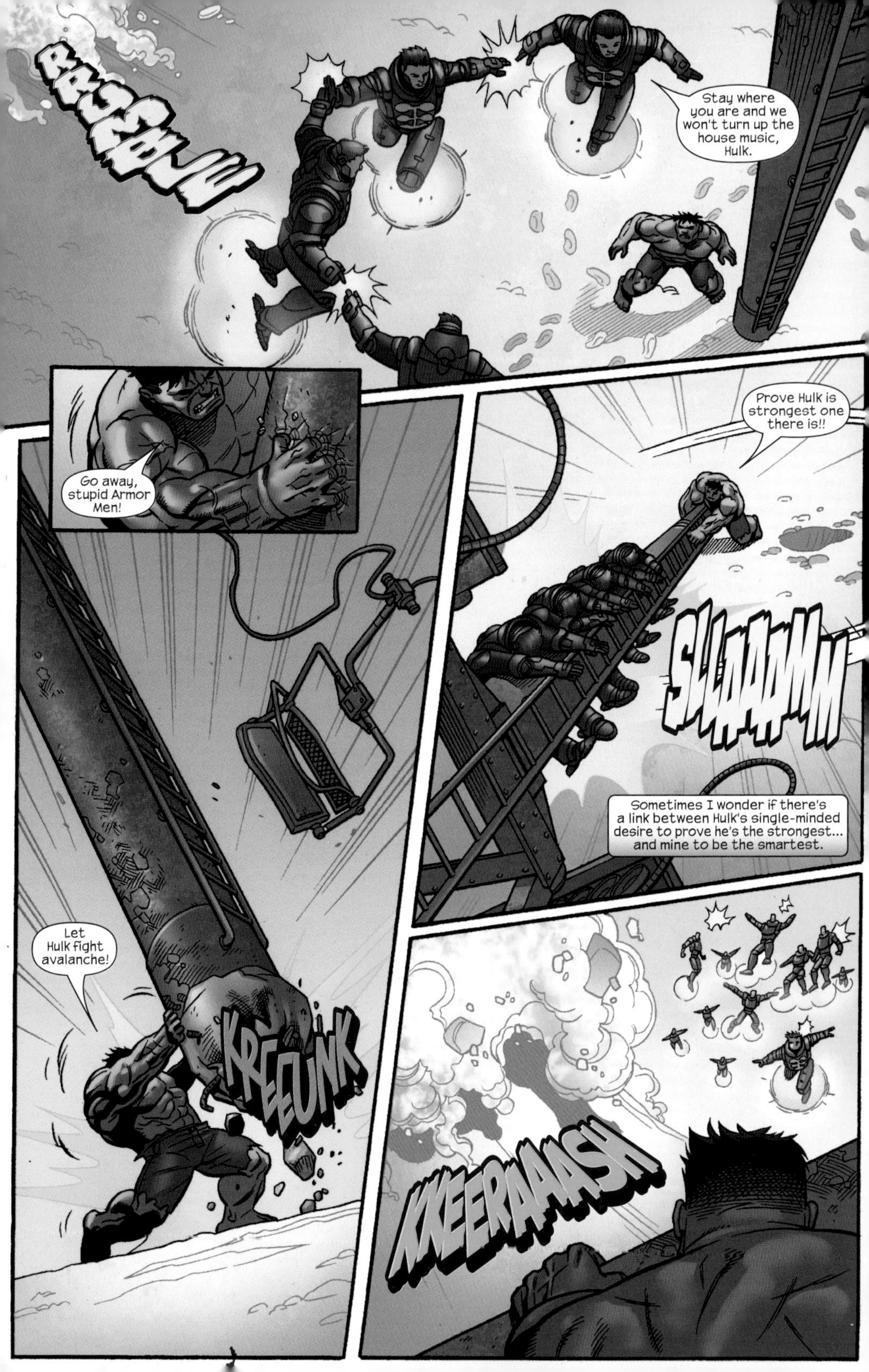
RRUMBLE
Stay where you are and we won't turn up the house music, Hulk.
Go away, stupid Armor Men!
Prove Hulk is strongest one there is!!
SLAAAMM
Sometimes I wonder if there's a link between Hulk's single-minded desire to prove he's the strongest... and mine to be the smartest.
Let Hulk fight avalanche!
KREEUNK
KKEERAAASH

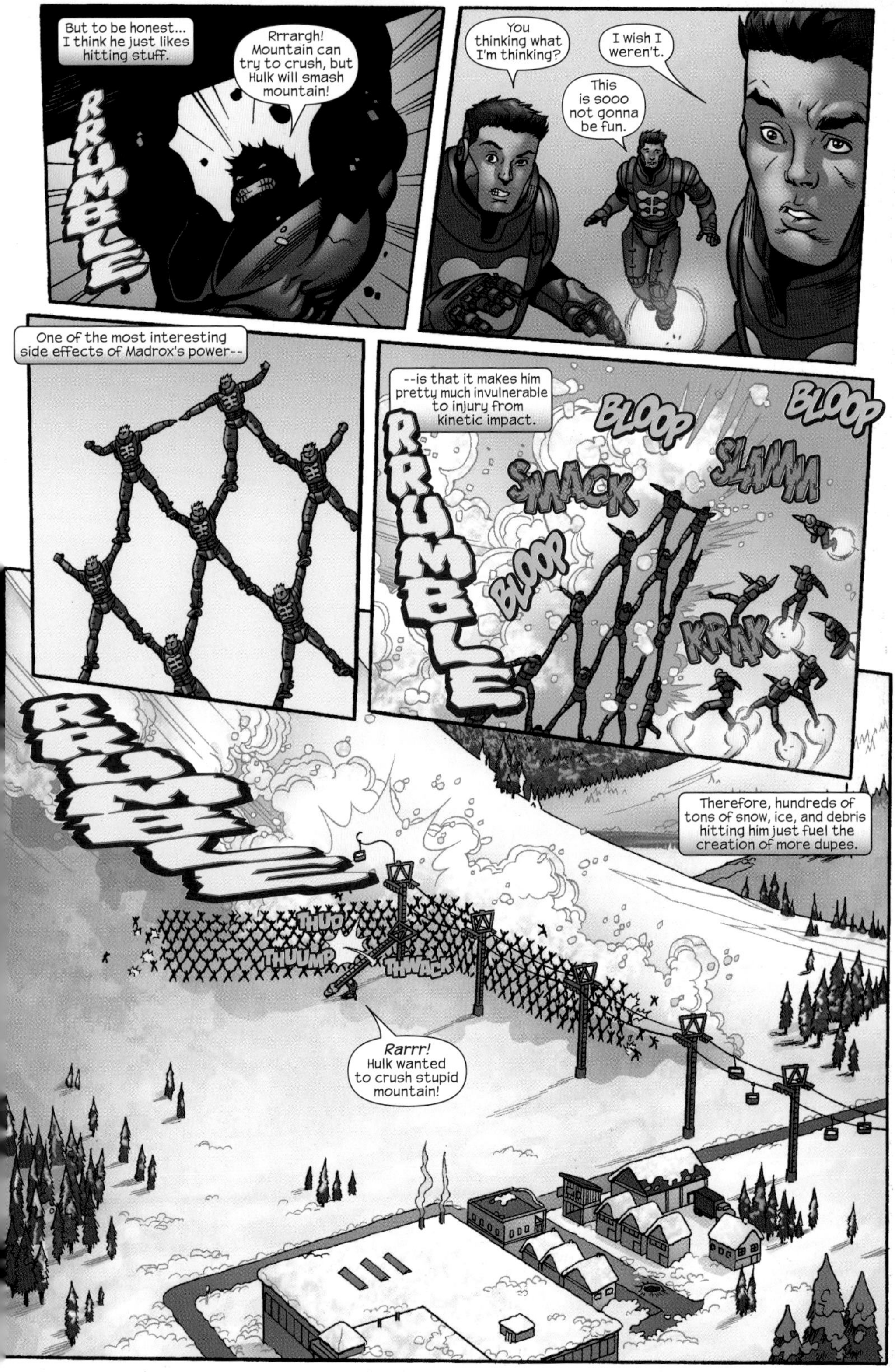
But to be honest... I think he just likes hitting stuff.
Rrrargh! Mountain can try to crush, but Hulk will smash mountain!
RRUMBLE
You thinking what I'm thinking?
I wish I weren't.
This is sooo not gonna be fun.
One of the most interesting side effects of Madrox's power--
--is that it makes him pretty much invulnerable to injury from kinetic impact.
RRUMBLE
BLOOP
BLOOP
SMACK
SLAMM
BLOOP
KRAK
Therefore, hundreds of tons of snow, ice, and debris hitting him just fuel the creation of more dupes.
THUD
THUUMP
THWACK
Rarrr! Hulk wanted to crush stupid mountain!

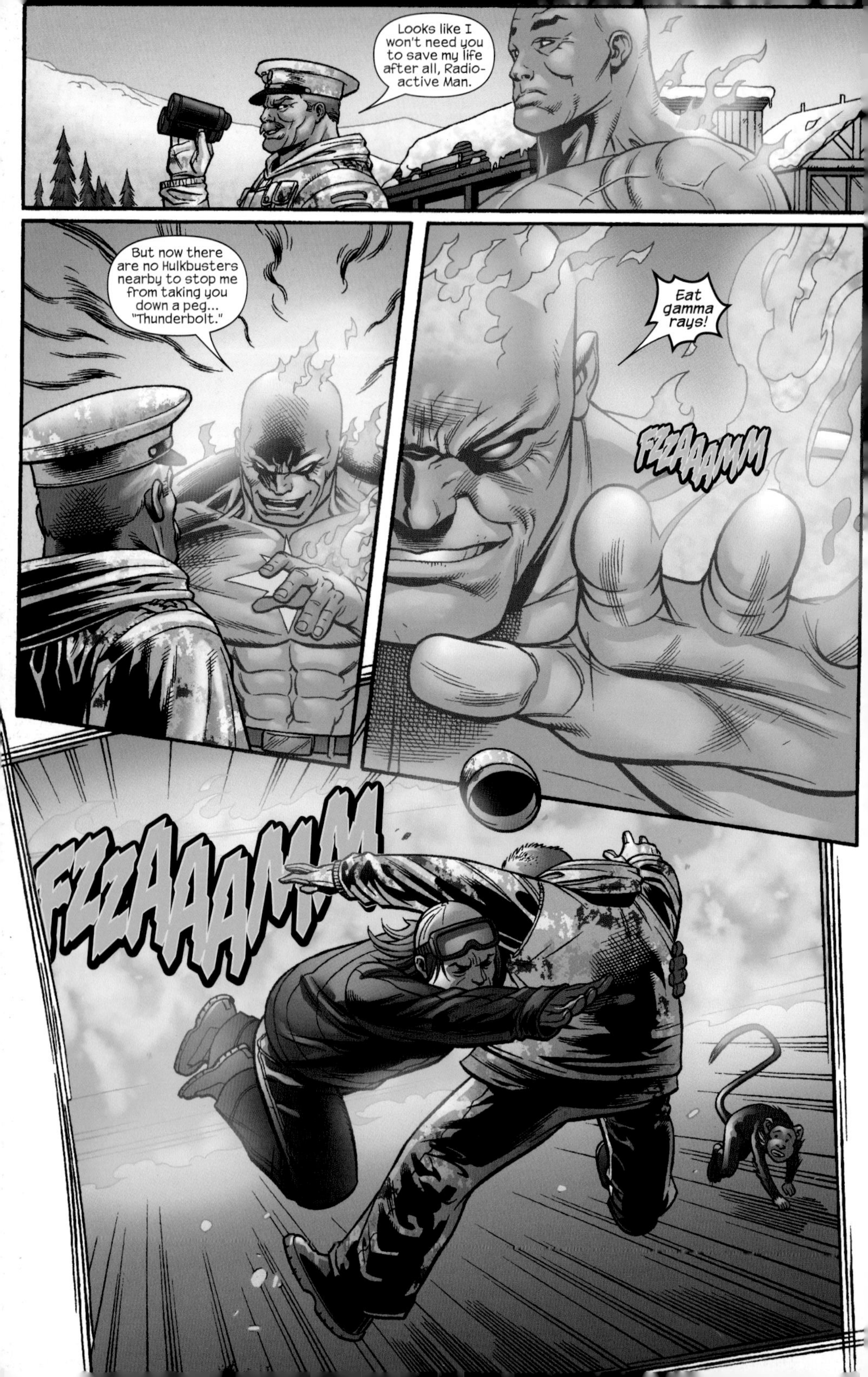
Looks like I won't need you to save my life after all, Radio-active Man.
But now there are no Hulkbusters nearby to stop me from taking you down a peg... "Thunderbolt."
Eat gamma rays!
FZZAAAMM
FZZAAAMM

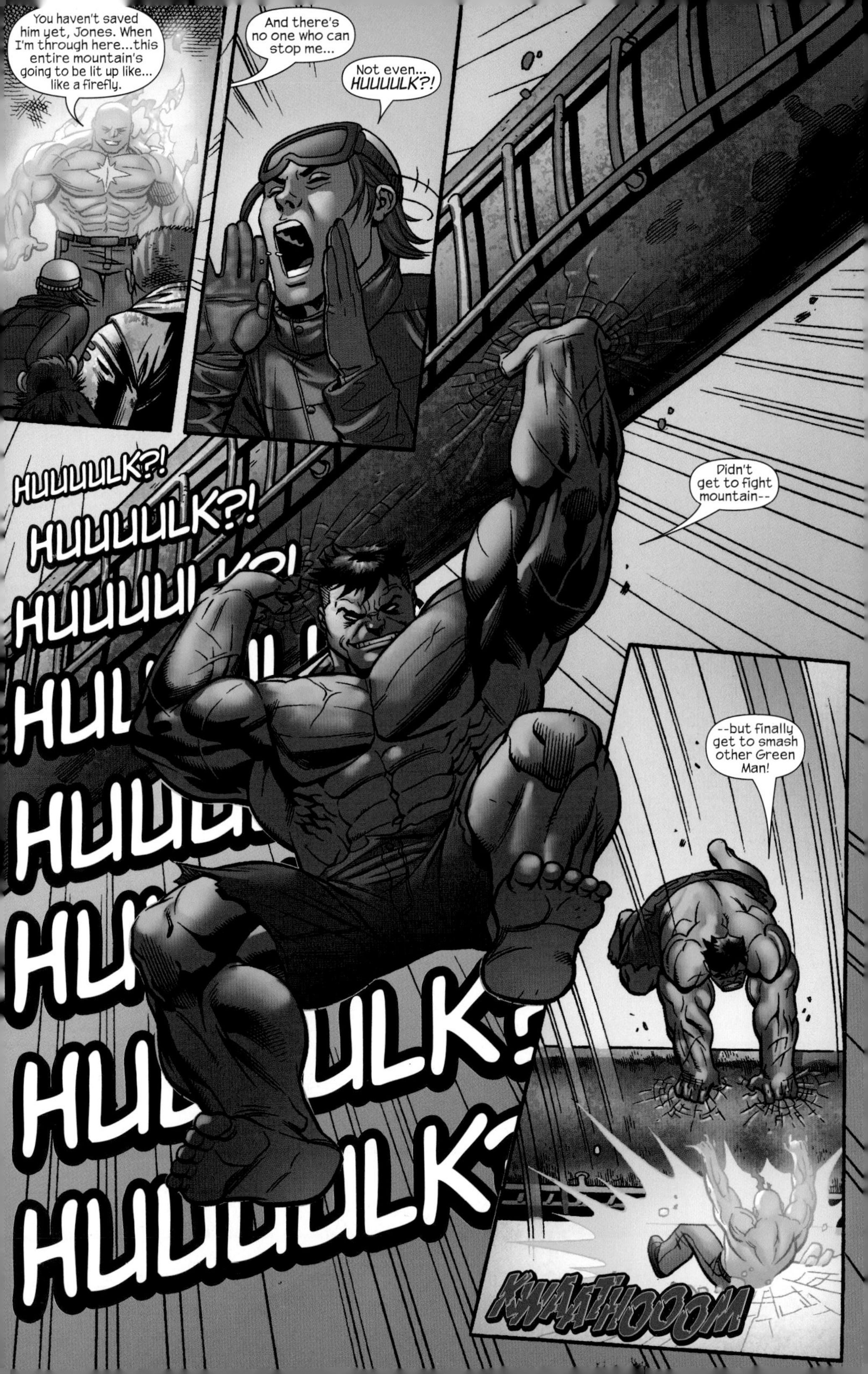

You haven't saved him yet, Jones. When I'm through here...this entire mountain's going to be lit up like... like a firefly.
And there's no one who can stop me...
Not even... HUUUULK?!
HUUUULK?!
HUUUULK?!
Didn't get to fight mountain--
--but finally get to smash other Green Man!
KWAATHOOOM

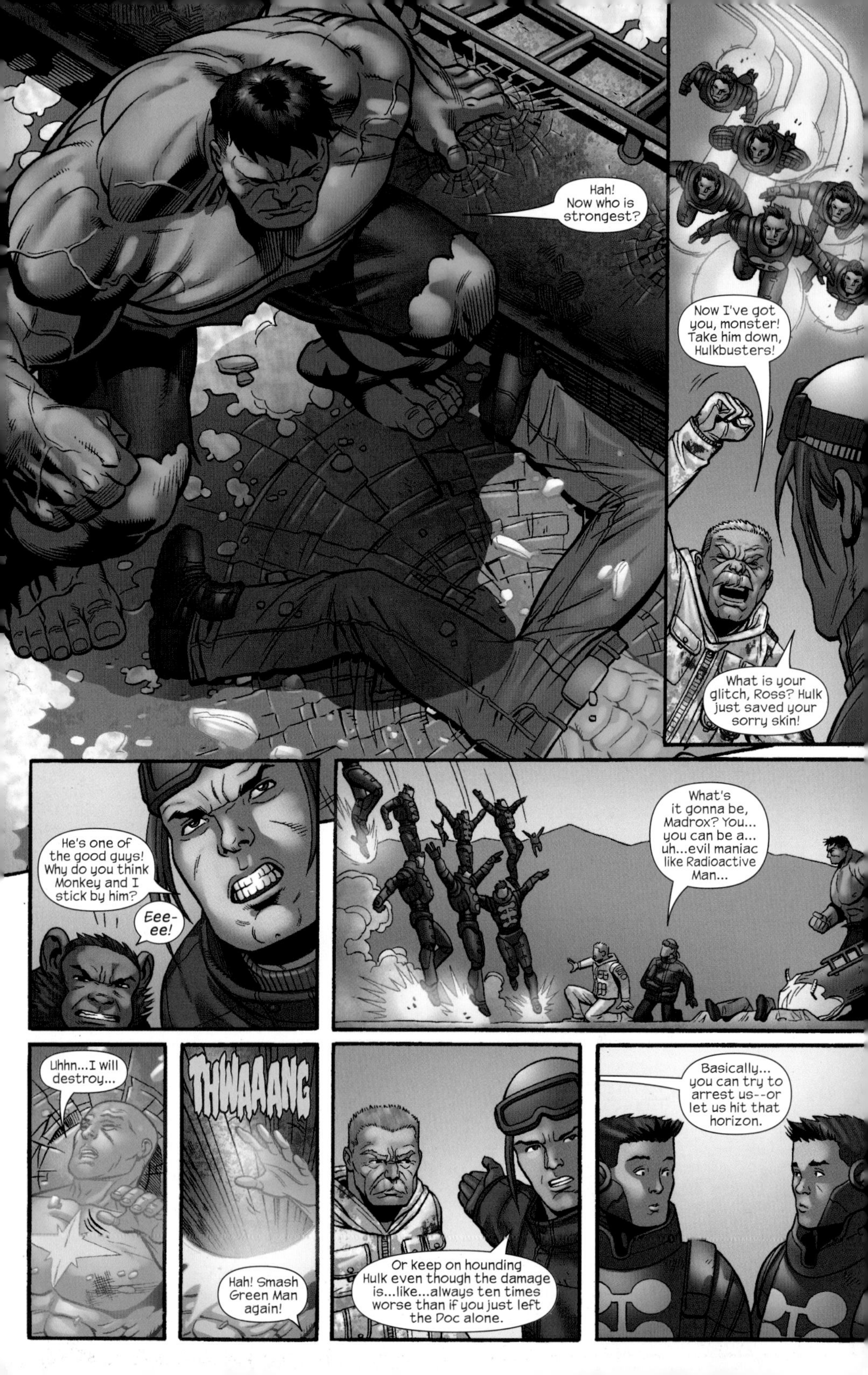
Hah! Now who is strongest?
Now I've got you, monster! Take him down, Hulkbusters!
What is your glitch, Ross? Hulk just saved your sorry skin!
He's one of the good guys! Why do you think Monkey and I stick by him?
Eeee-ee!
What's it gonna be, Madrox? You... you can be a... uh...evil maniac like Radioactive Man...
Uhhn...I will destroy...
THWAAANG
Hah! Smash Green Man again!
Or keep on hounding Hulk even though the damage is...like...always ten times worse than if you just left the Doc alone.
Basically... you can try to arrest us--or let us hit that horizon.

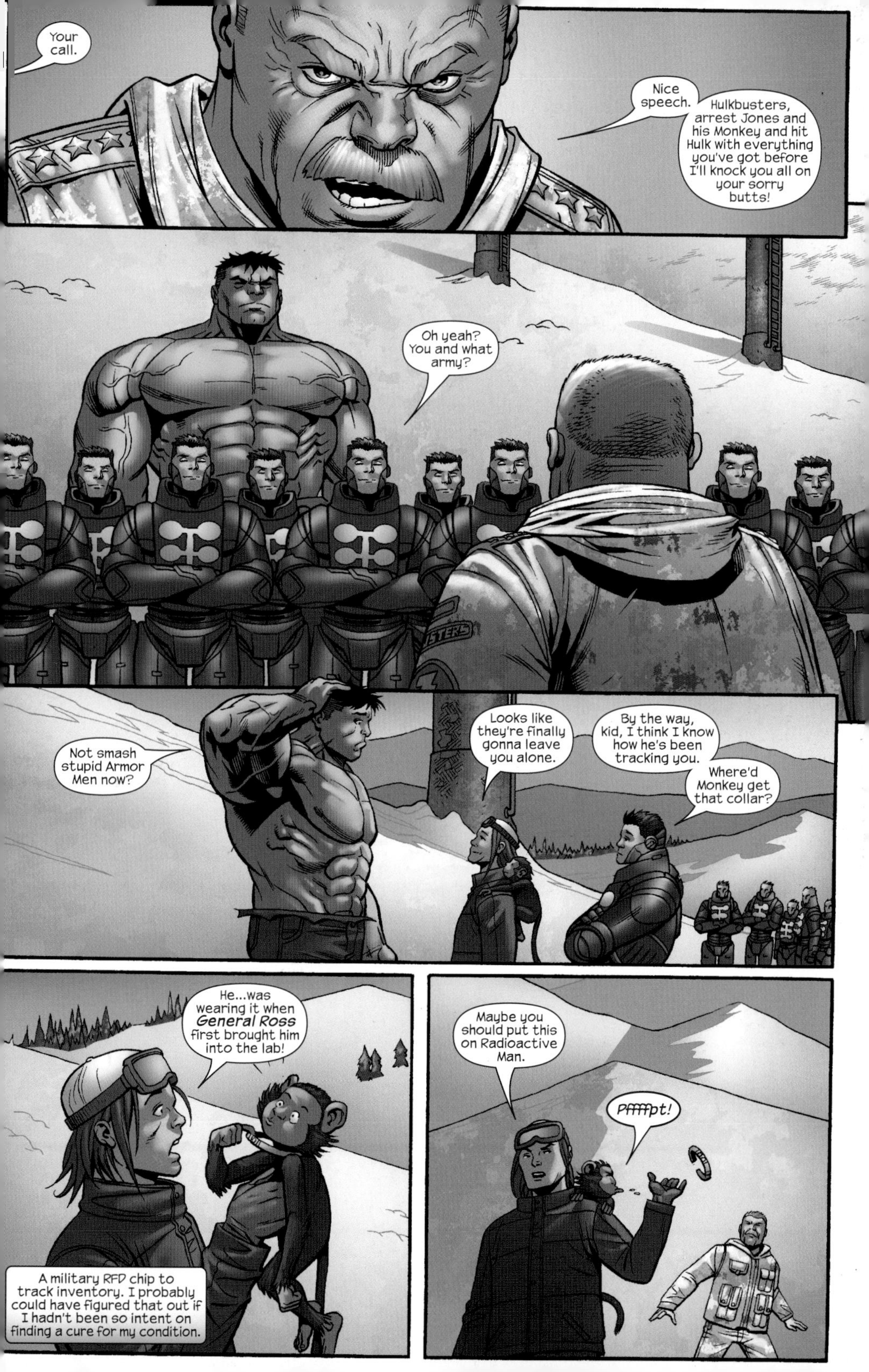
Your call.
Nice speech.
Hulkbusters, arrest Jones and his Monkey and hit Hulk with everything you've got before I'll knock you all on your sorry butts!
Oh yeah? You and what army?
Not smash stupid Armor Men now?
Looks like they're finally gonna leave you alone.
By the way, kid, I think I know how he's been tracking you.
Where'd Monkey get that collar?
He...was wearing it when *General Ross* first brought him into the lab!
A military RFD chip to track inventory. I probably could have figured that out if I hadn't been so intent on finding a cure for my condition.
Maybe you should put this on Radioactive Man.
Pffffpt!

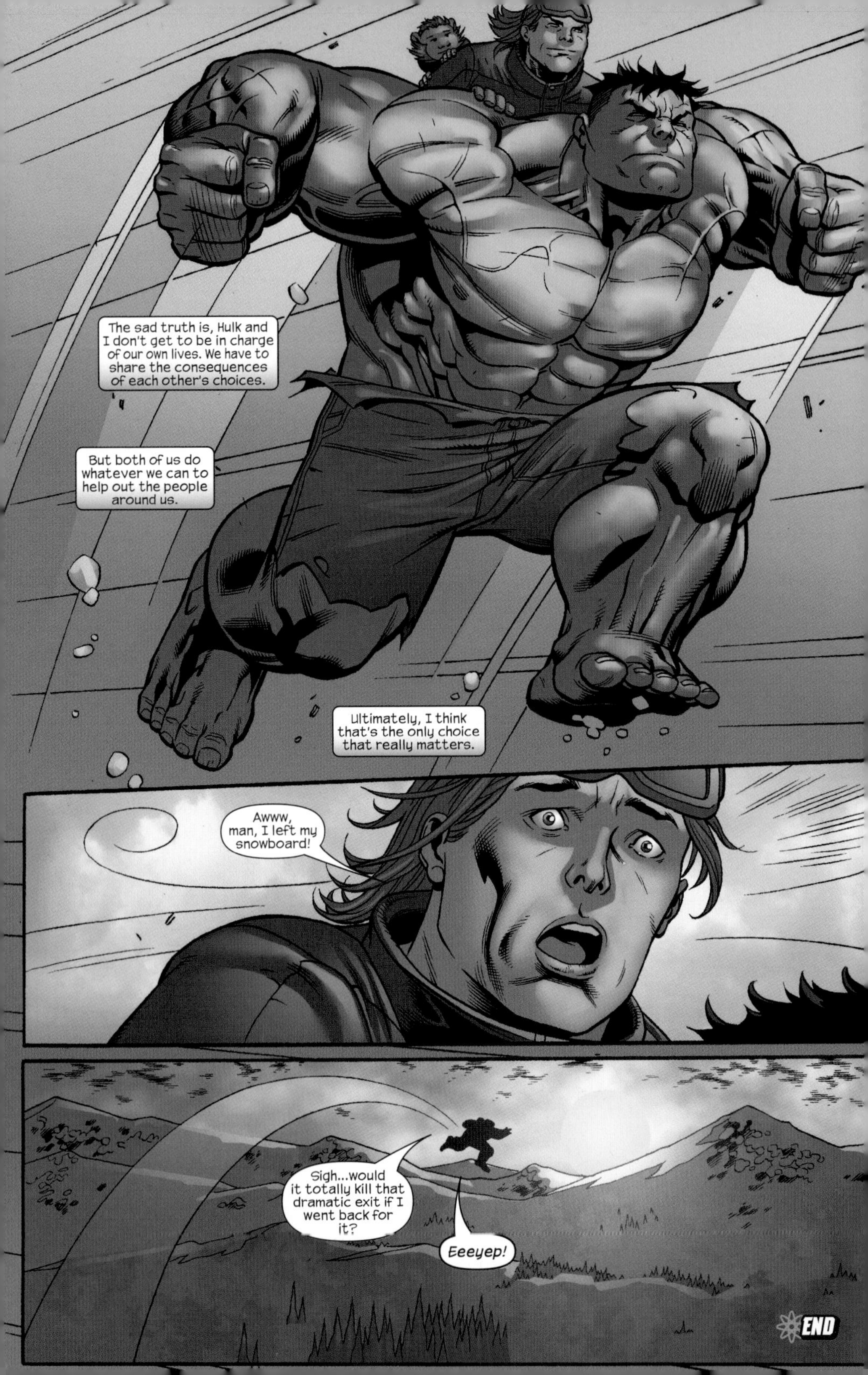
The sad truth is, Hulk and I don't get to be in charge of our own lives. We have to share the consequences of each other's choices.
But both of us do whatever we can to help out the people around us.
Ultimately, I think that's the only choice that really matters.
Awww, man, I left my snowboard!
Sigh...would it totally kill that dramatic exit if I went back for it?
Eeeyep!
END

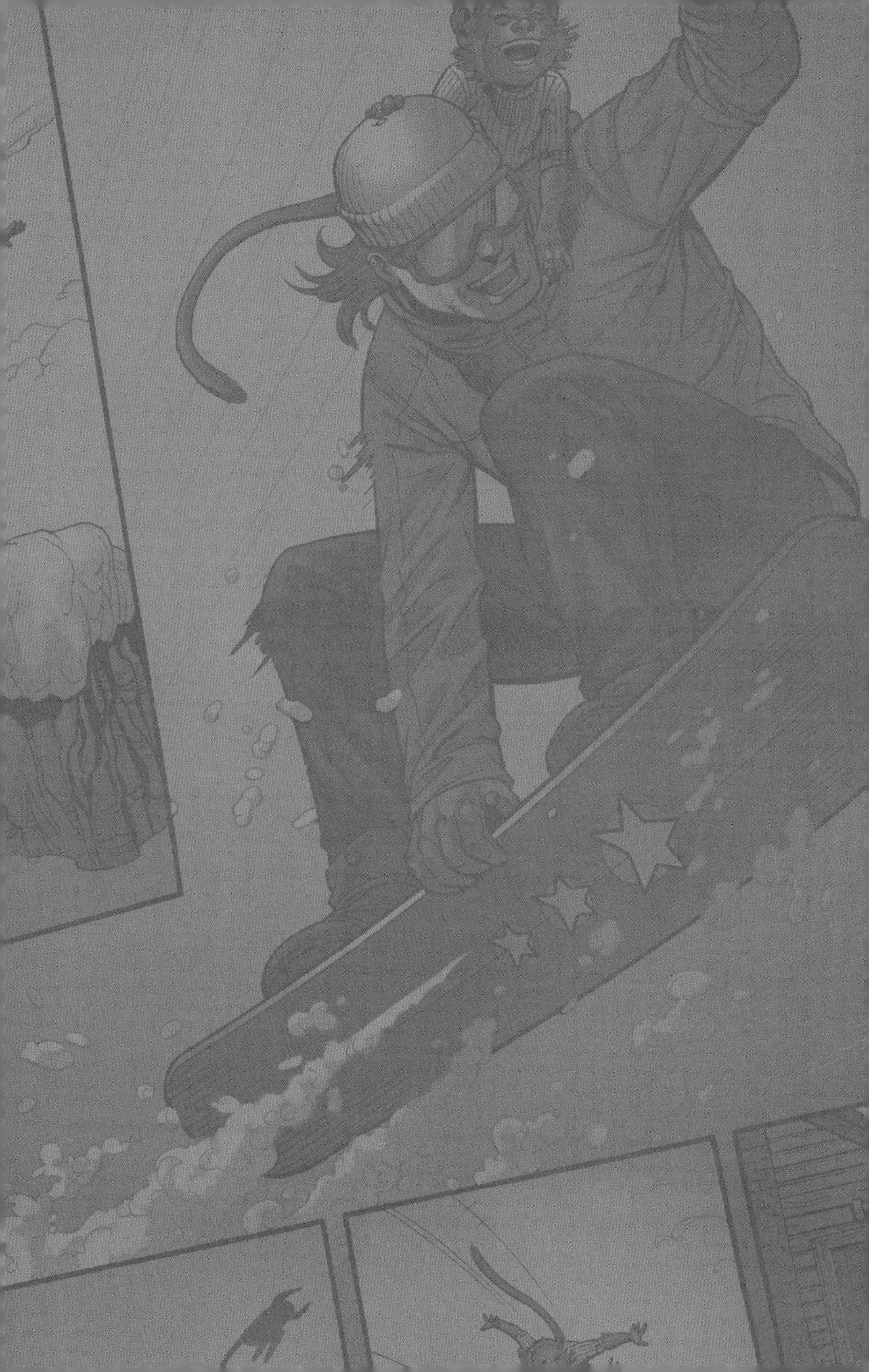

05

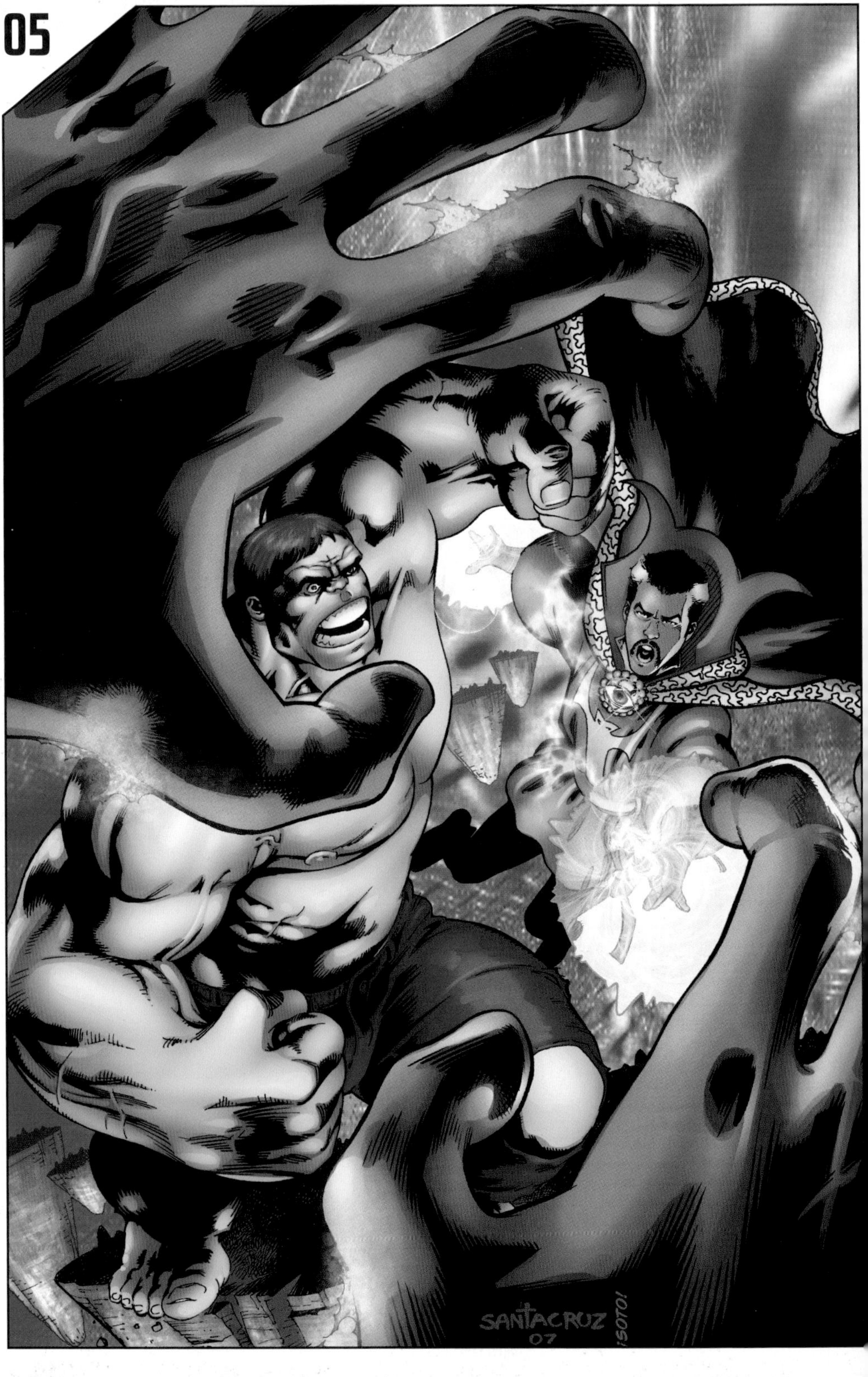
SANTACRUZ
07
¡SOTO!

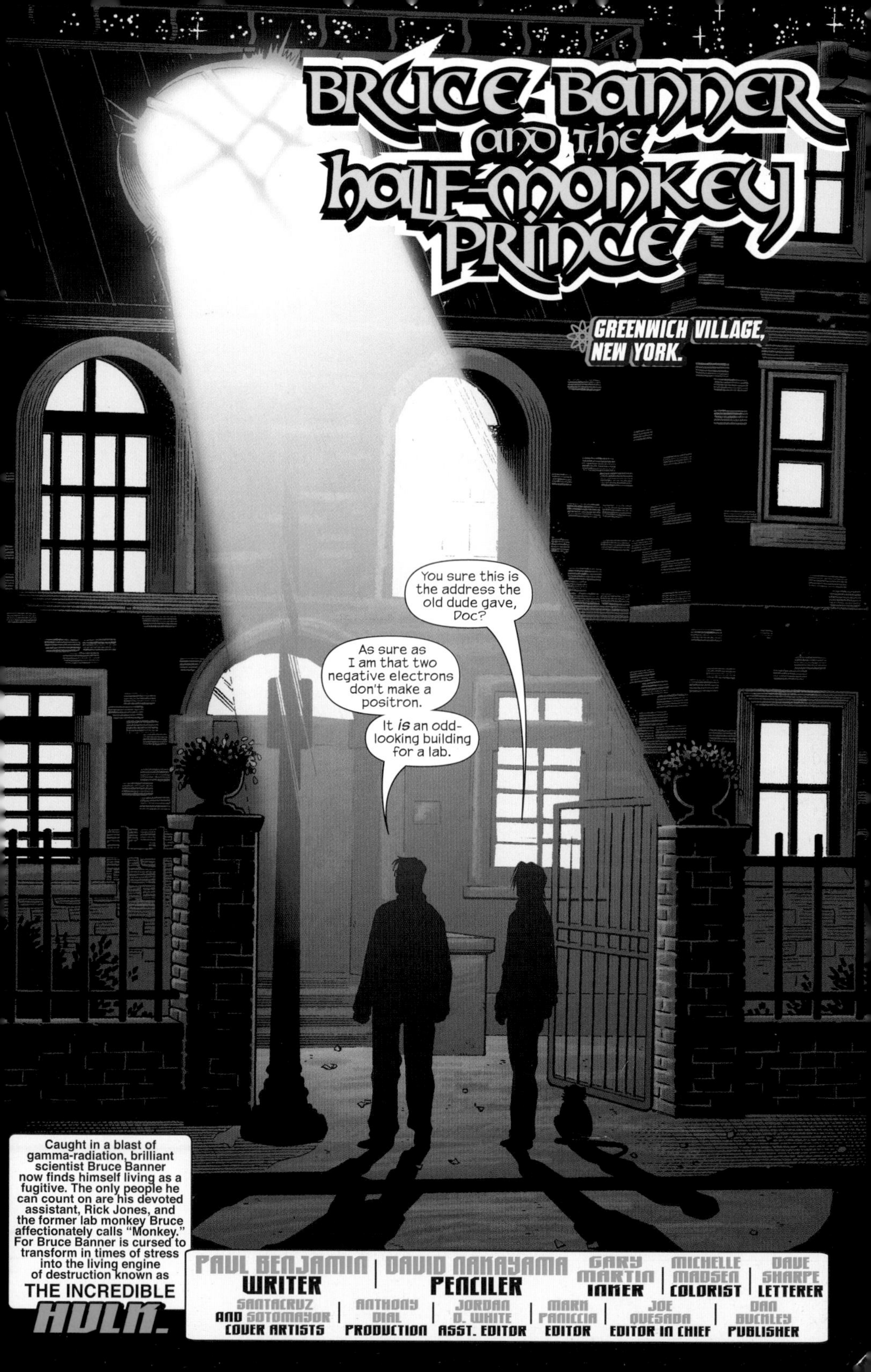

BRUCE BANNER AND THE HALF-MONKEY PRINCE
GREENWICH VILLAGE, NEW YORK.
You sure this is the address the old dude gave, Doc?
As sure as I am that two negative electrons don't make a positron.
It *is* an odd-looking building for a lab.
Caught in a blast of gamma-radiation, brilliant scientist Bruce Banner now finds himself living as a fugitive. The only people he can count on are his devoted assistant, Rick Jones, and the former lab monkey Bruce affectionately calls "Monkey." For Bruce Banner is cursed to transform in times of stress into the living engine of destruction known as THE INCREDIBLE HULK.
PAUL BENJAMIN WRITER
DAVID NAKAYAMA PENCILER
GARY MARTIN INKER
MICHELLE MADSEN COLORIST
DAVE SHARPE LETTERER
SANTACRUZ AND SOTOMAYOR COVER ARTISTS
ANTHONY DIAL PRODUCTION
JORDAN D. WHITE ASST. EDITOR
MARK PANICCIA EDITOR
JOE QUESADA EDITOR IN CHIEF
DAN BUCKLEY PUBLISHER

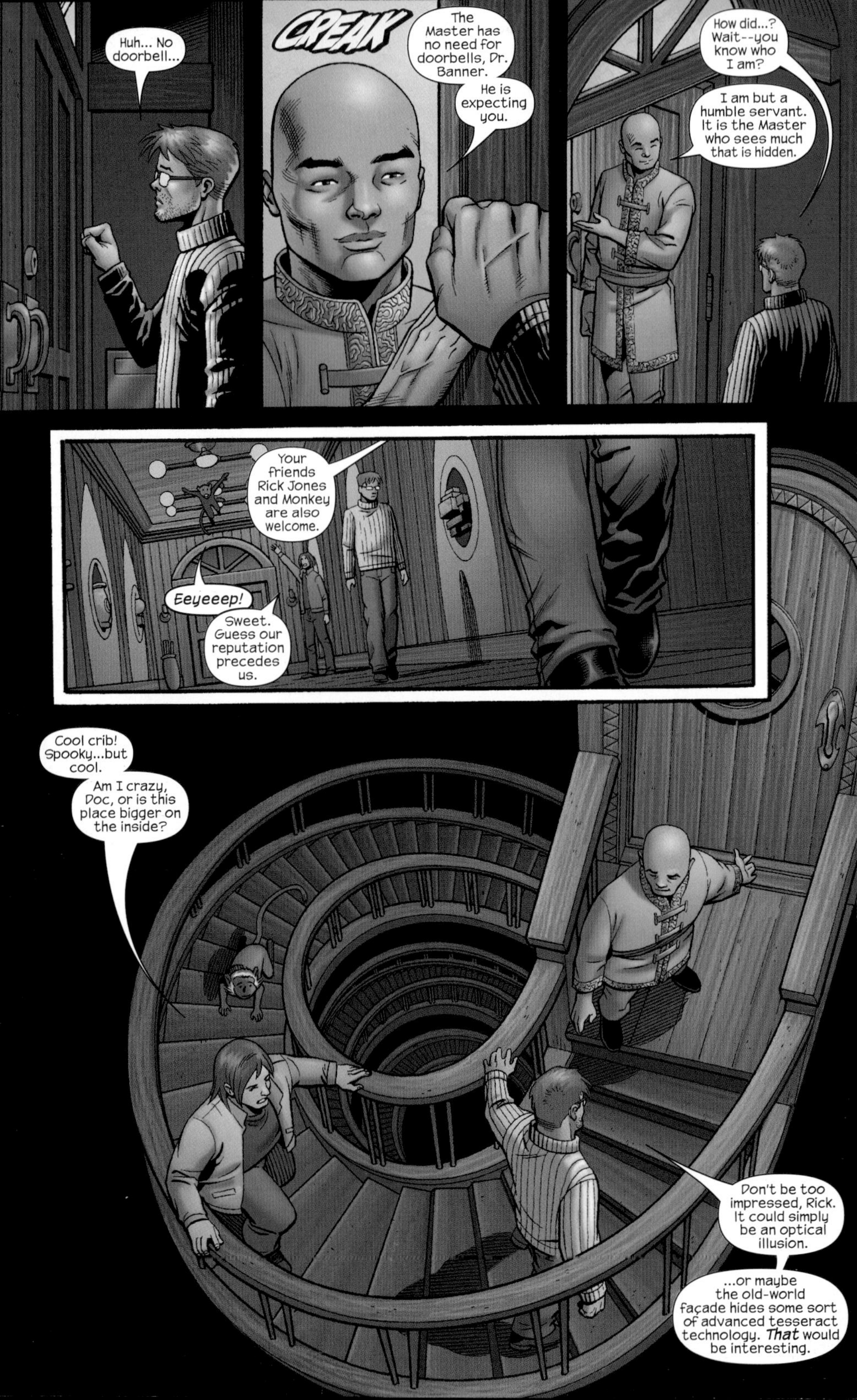
Huh... No doorbell...
CREAK
The Master has no need for doorbells, Dr. Banner.
He is expecting you.
How did...? Wait--you know who I am?
I am but a humble servant. It is the Master who sees much that is hidden.
Your friends Rick Jones and Monkey are also welcome.
Eeyeeep!
Sweet. Guess our reputation precedes us.
Cool crib! Spooky...but cool.
Am I crazy, Doc, or is this place bigger on the inside?
Don't be too impressed, Rick. It could simply be an optical illusion.
...or maybe the old-world façade hides some sort of advanced tesseract technology. *That* would be interesting.

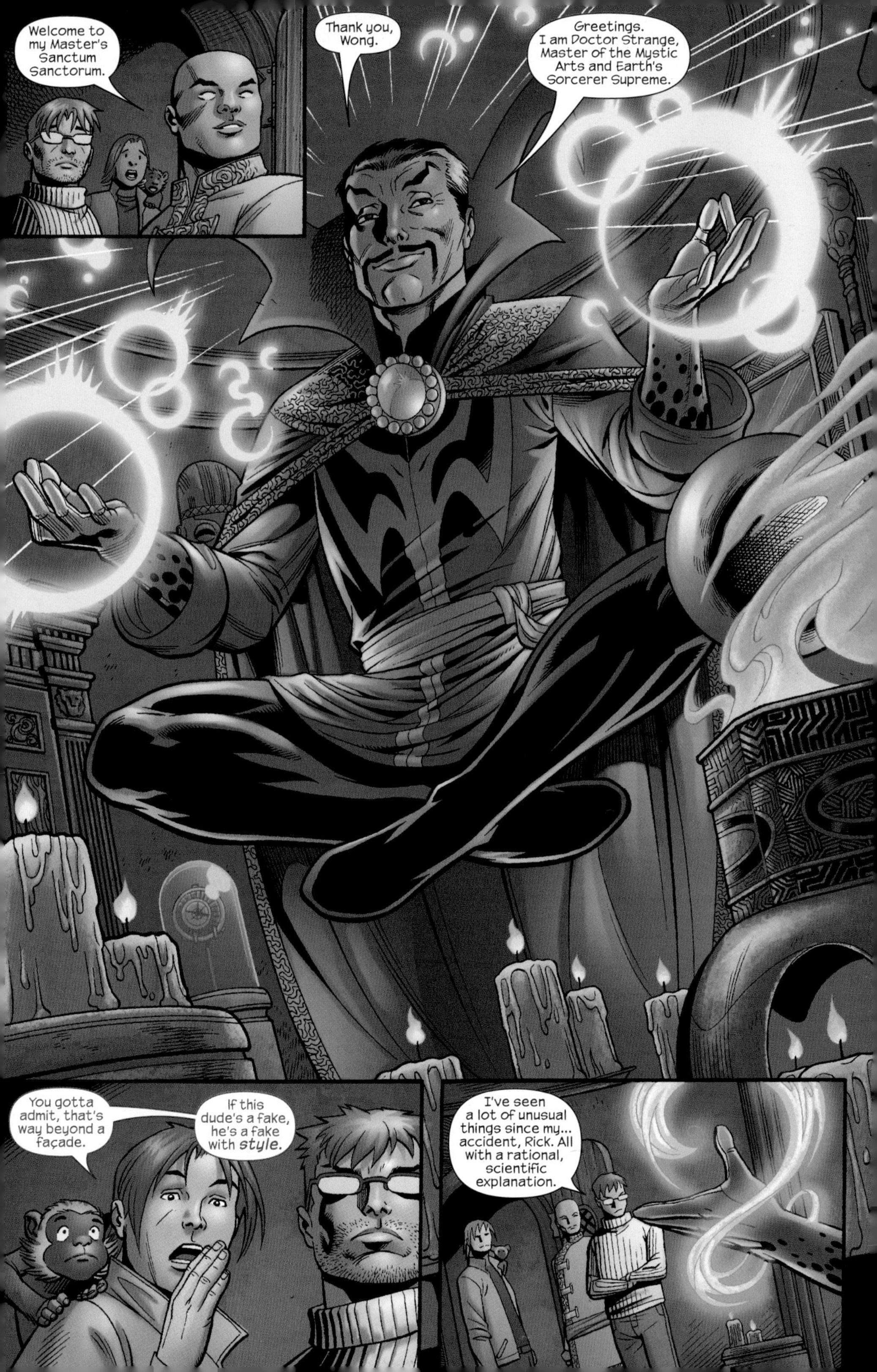
Welcome to my Master's Sanctum Sanctorum.
Thank you, Wong.
Greetings. I am Doctor Strange, Master of the Mystic Arts and Earth's Sorcerer Supreme.
You gotta admit, that's way beyond a façade.
If this dude's a fake, he's a fake with *style*.
I've seen a lot of unusual things since my... accident, Rick. All with a rational, scientific explanation.

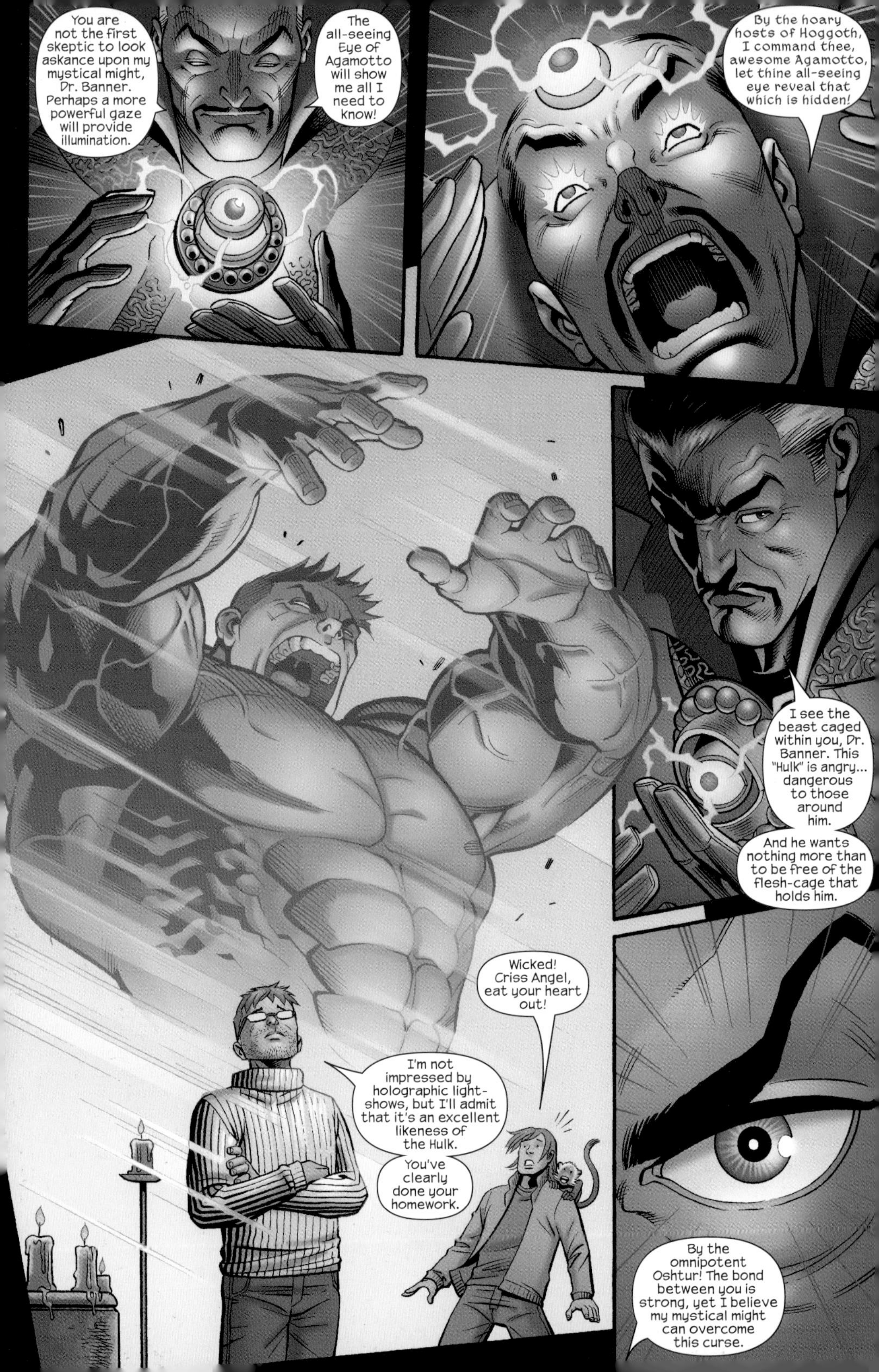
You are not the first skeptic to look askance upon my mystical might, Dr. Banner. Perhaps a more powerful gaze will provide illumination.
The all-seeing Eye of Agamotto will show me all I need to know!
By the hoary hosts of Hoggoth, I command thee, awesome Agamotto, let thine all-seeing eye reveal that which is hidden!
I see the beast caged within you, Dr. Banner. This "Hulk" is angry... dangerous to those around him.
And he wants nothing more than to be free of the flesh-cage that holds him.
I'm not impressed by holographic light-shows, but I'll admit that it's an excellent likeness of the Hulk.
You've clearly done your homework.
Wicked! Criss Angel, eat your heart out!
By the omnipotent Oshtur! The bond between you is strong, yet I believe my mystical might can overcome this curse.

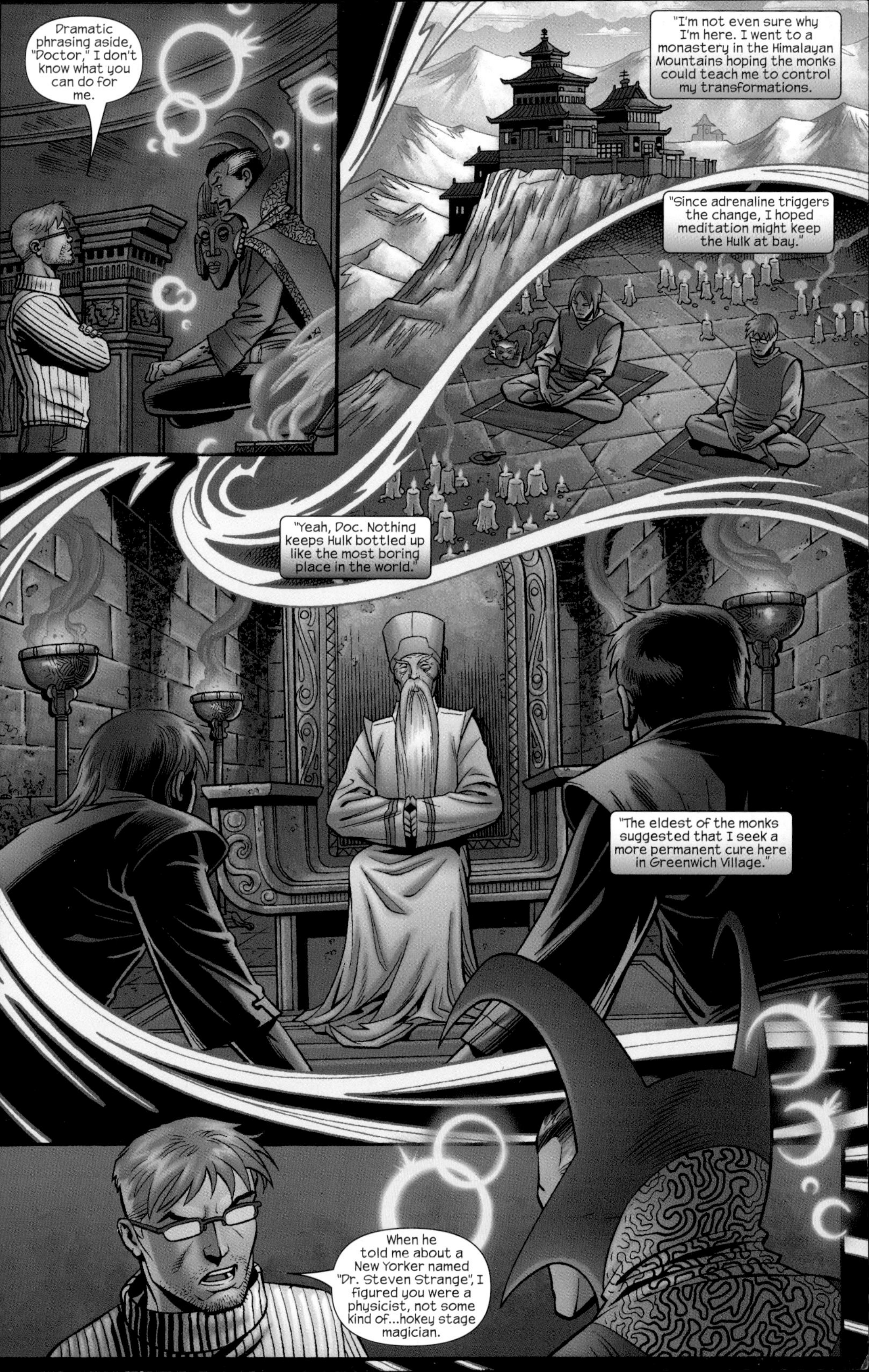
Dramatic phrasing aside, "Doctor," I don't know what you can do for me.
"I'm not even sure why I'm here. I went to a monastery in the Himalayan Mountains hoping the monks could teach me to control my transformations.
"Since adrenaline triggers the change, I hoped meditation might keep the Hulk at bay."
"Yeah, Doc. Nothing keeps Hulk bottled up like the most boring place in the world."
"The eldest of the monks suggested that I seek a more permanent cure here in Greenwich Village."
When he told me about a New Yorker named "Dr. Steven Strange", I figured you were a physicist, not some kind of...hokey stage magician.

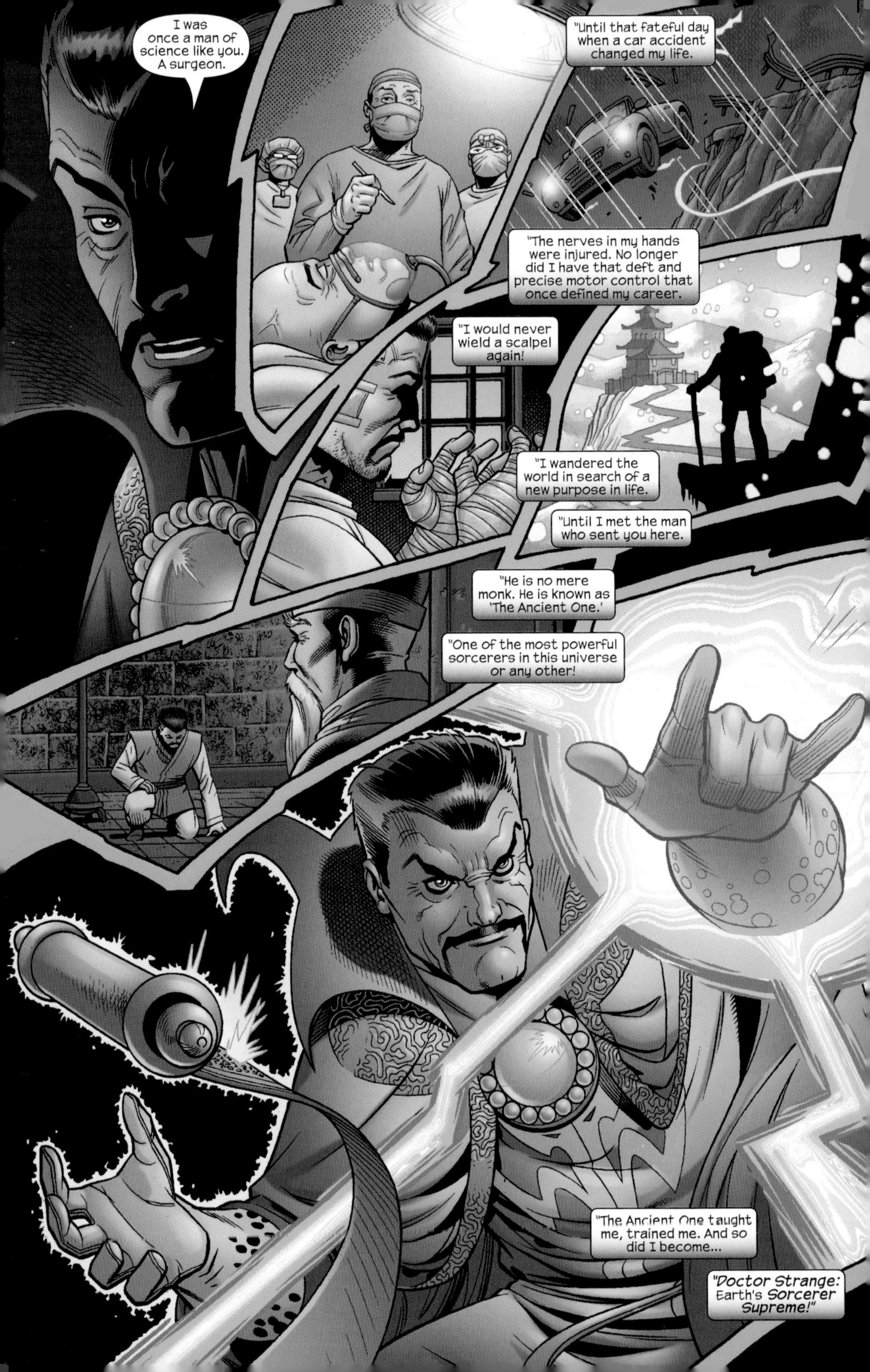
I was once a man of science like you. A surgeon.
"Until that fateful day when a car accident changed my life.
"The nerves in my hands were injured. No longer did I have that deft and precise motor control that once defined my career.
"I would never wield a scalpel again!
"I wandered the world in search of a new purpose in life.
"Until I met the man who sent you here.
"He is no mere monk. He is known as 'The Ancient One.'
"One of the most powerful sorcerers in this universe or any other!
"The Ancient One taught me, trained me. And so did I become...
"Doctor Strange: Earth's Sorcerer Supreme!"

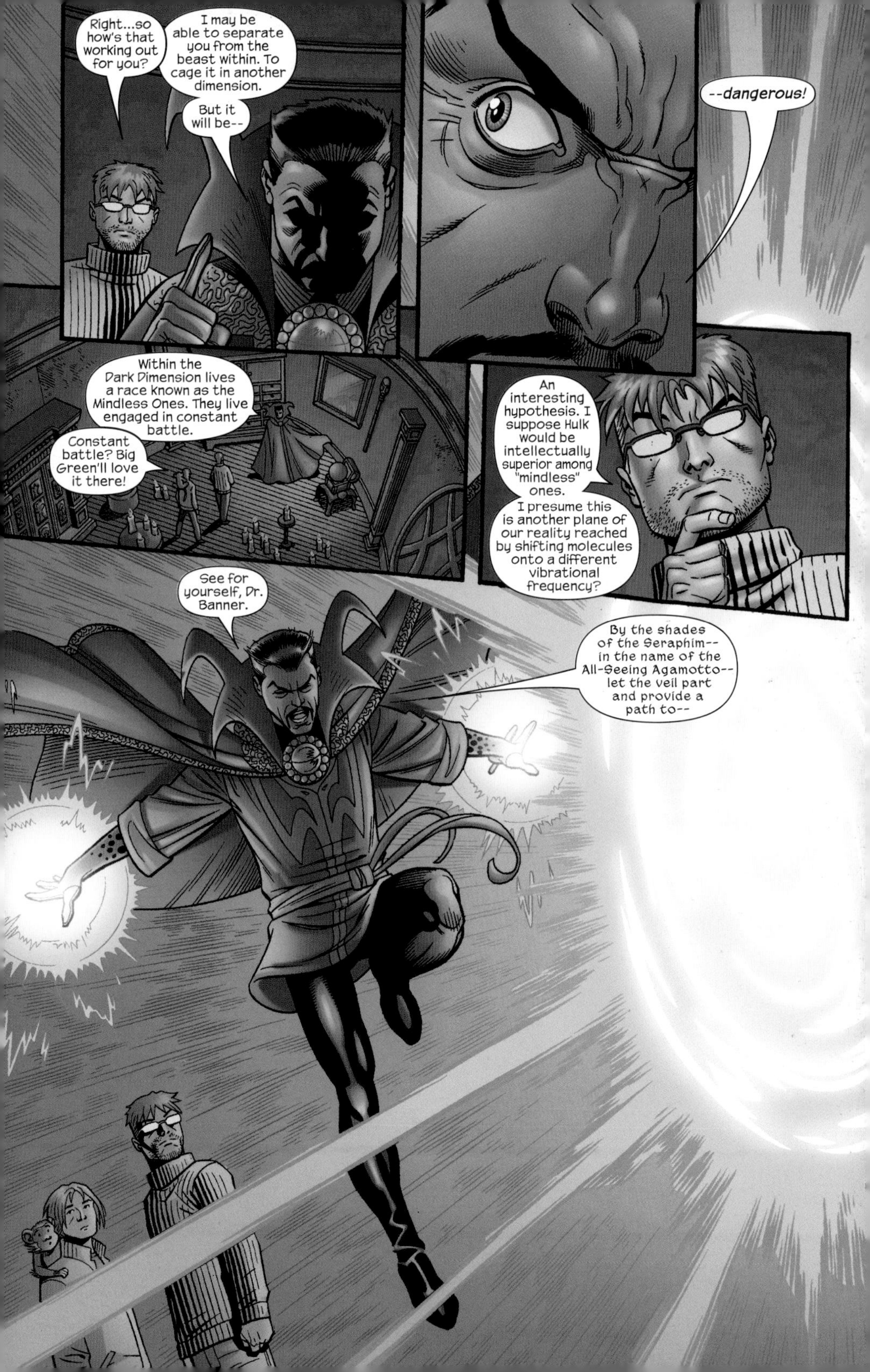
Right...so how's that working out for you?
I may be able to separate you from the beast within. To cage it in another dimension.
But it will be--
--dangerous!
Within the Dark Dimension lives a race known as the Mindless Ones. They live engaged in constant battle.
Constant battle? Big Green'll love it there!
An interesting hypothesis. I suppose Hulk would be intellectually superior among "mindless" ones.
I presume this is another plane of our reality reached by shifting molecules onto a different vibrational frequency?
See for yourself, Dr. Banner.
By the shades of the Seraphim-- in the name of the All-Seeing Agamotto-- let the veil part and provide a path to--

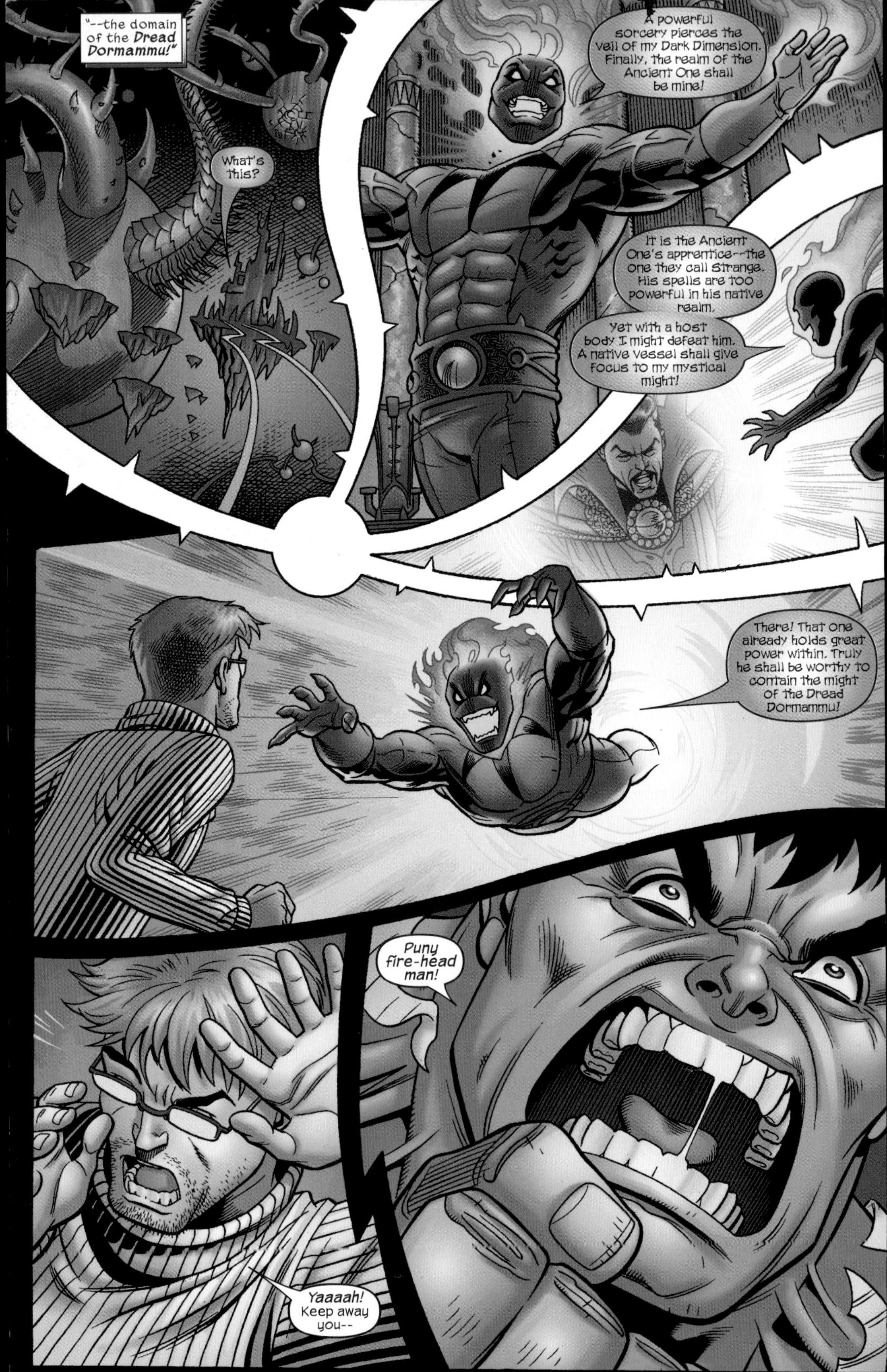
"--the domain of the *Dread Dormammu!*"
A powerful sorcery pierces the veil of my Dark Dimension. Finally, the realm of the Ancient One shall be mine!
What's this?
It is the Ancient One's apprentice--the one they call Strange. His spells are too powerful in his native realm.
Yet with a host body I might defeat him. A native vessel shall give focus to my mystical might!
There! That one already holds great power within. Truly he shall be worthy to contain the might of the Dread Dormammu!
Puny fire-head man!
Yaaaah! Keep away you--

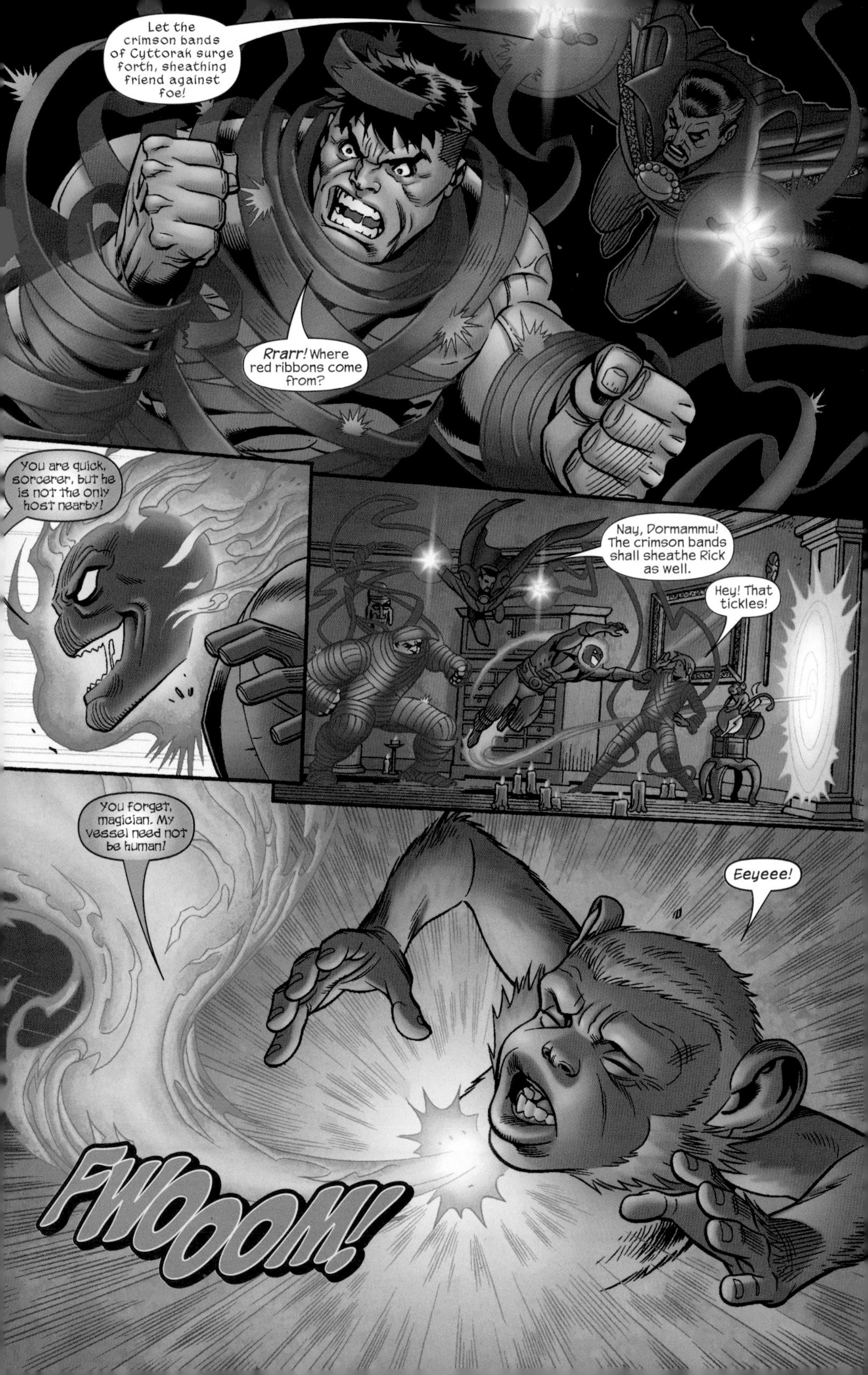
Let the crimson bands of Cyttorak surge forth, sheathing friend against foe!
Rrarr! Where red ribbons come from?
You are quick, sorcerer, but he is not the only host nearby!
Nay, Dormammu! The crimson bands shall sheathe the Rick as well.
Hey! That tickles!
You forget, magician. My vessel need not be human!
Eeyeee!
FWOOOM!

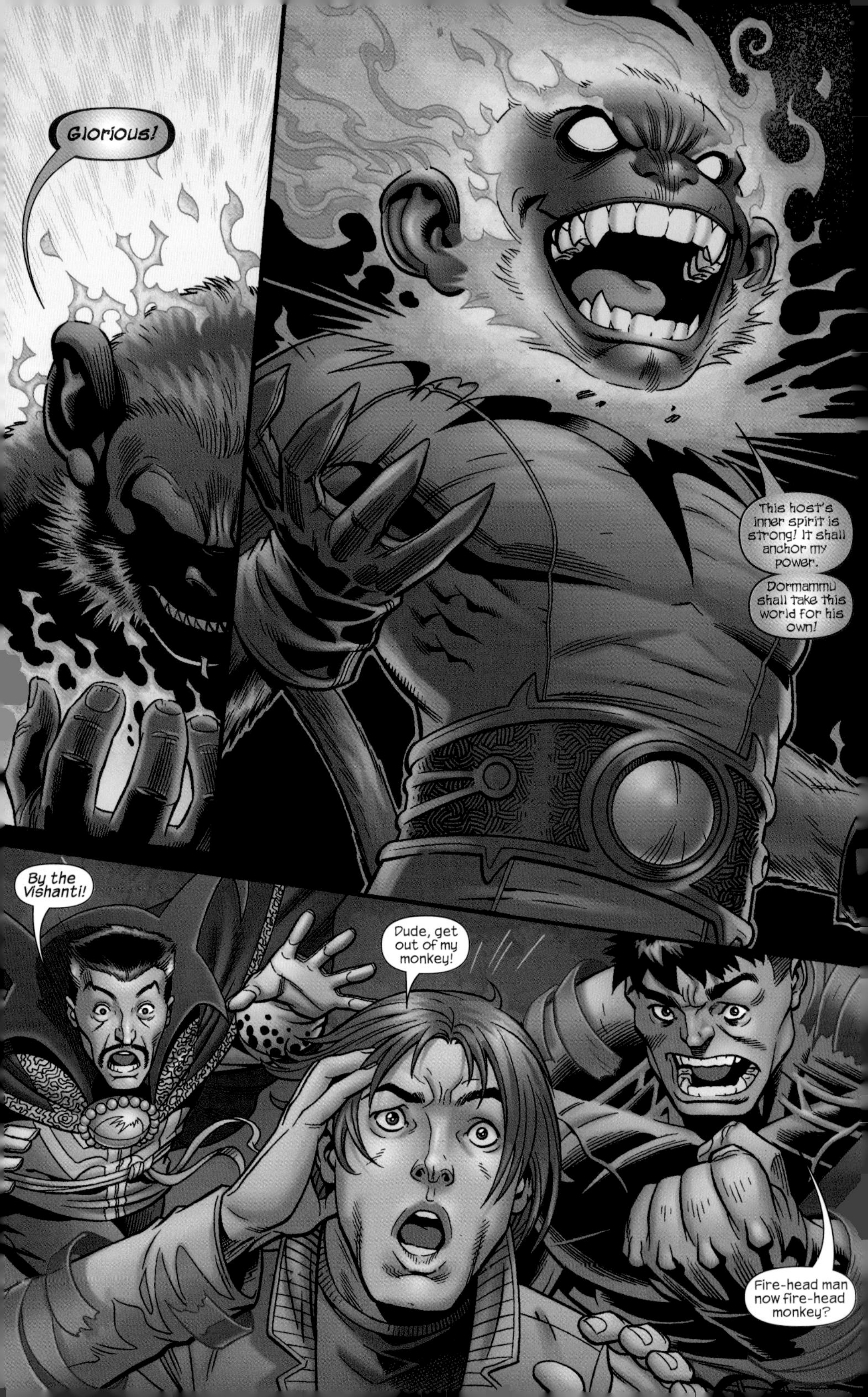
Glorious!
This host's inner spirit is strong! It shall anchor my power.
Dormammu shall take this world for his own!
By the Vishanti!
Dude, get out of my monkey!
Fire-head man now fire-head monkey?

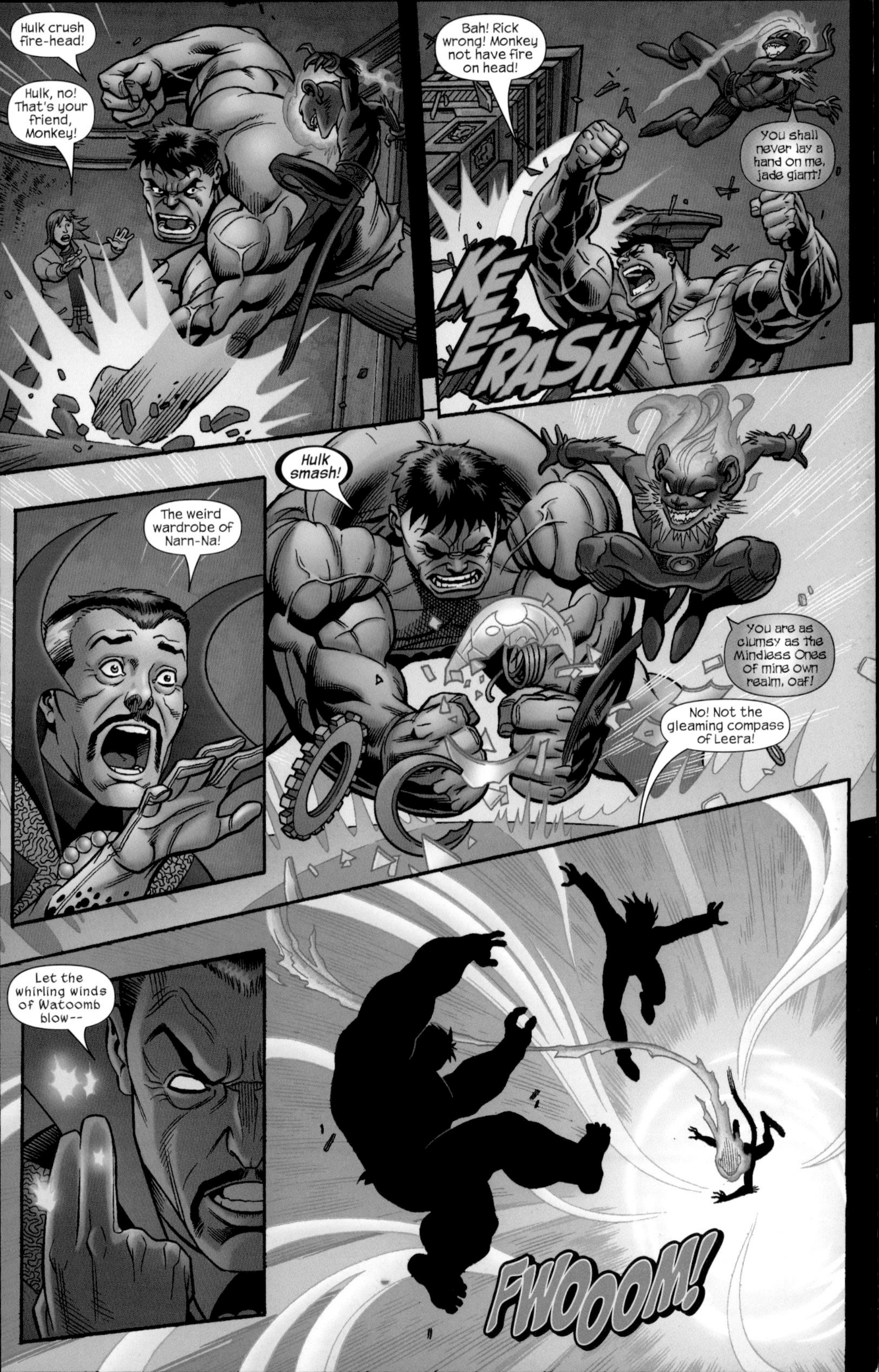
Hulk crush fire-head!
Hulk, no! That's your friend, Monkey!
Bah! Rick wrong! Monkey not have fire on head!
You shall never lay a hand on me, jade giant!
KE-E-RASH
Hulk smash!
The weird wardrobe of Narn-Na!
You are as clumsy as the Mindless Ones of mine own realm, oaf!
No! Not the gleaming compass of Leera!
Let the whirling winds of Watoomb blow--
FWOOOM!

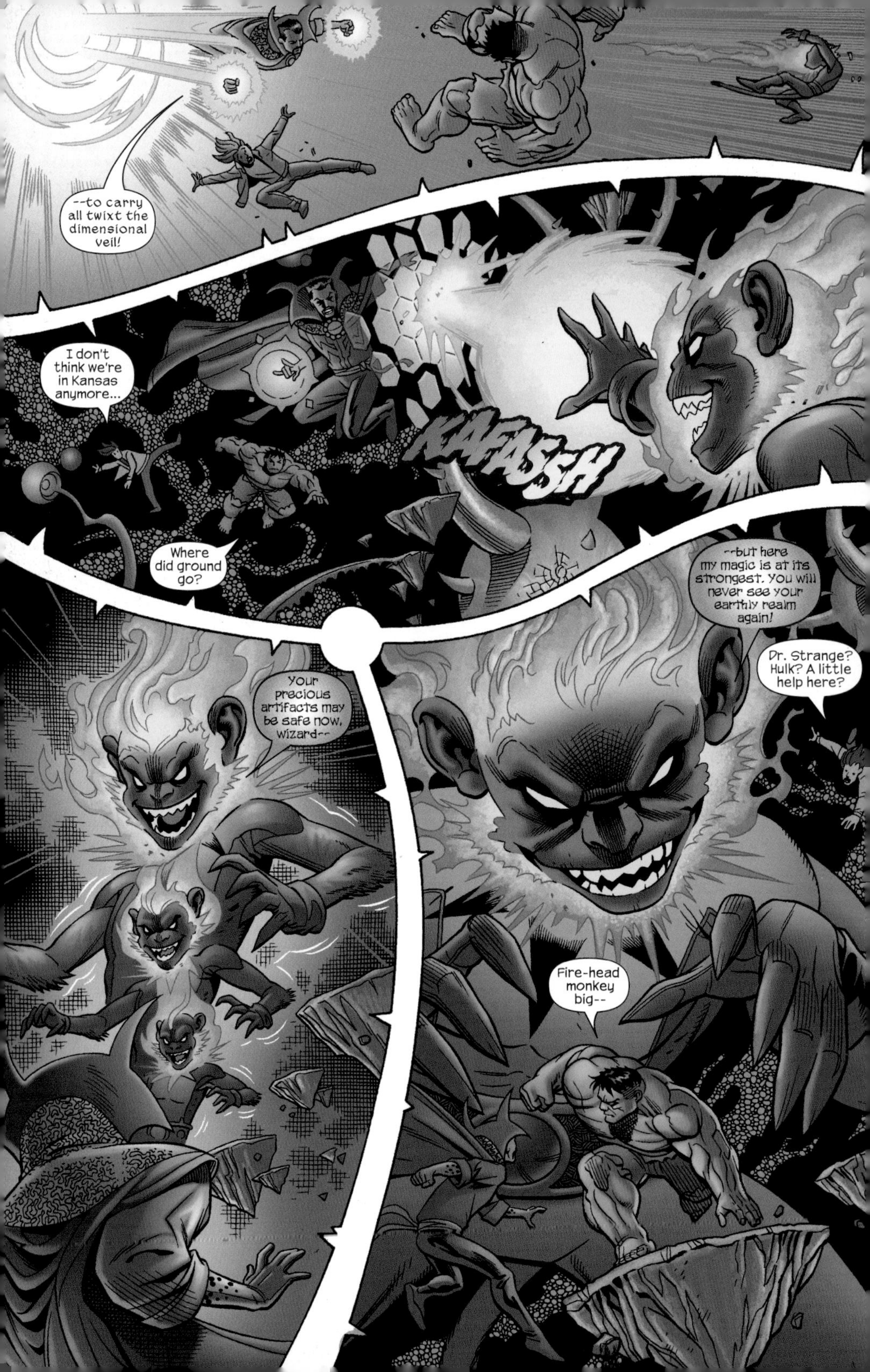
--to carry all twixt the dimensional veil!
I don't think we're in Kansas anymore...
KAFASH
Where did ground go?
Your precious artifacts may be safe now, wizard--
--but here my magic is at its strongest. You will never see your earthly realm again!
Dr. Strange? Hulk? A little help here?
Fire-head monkey big--

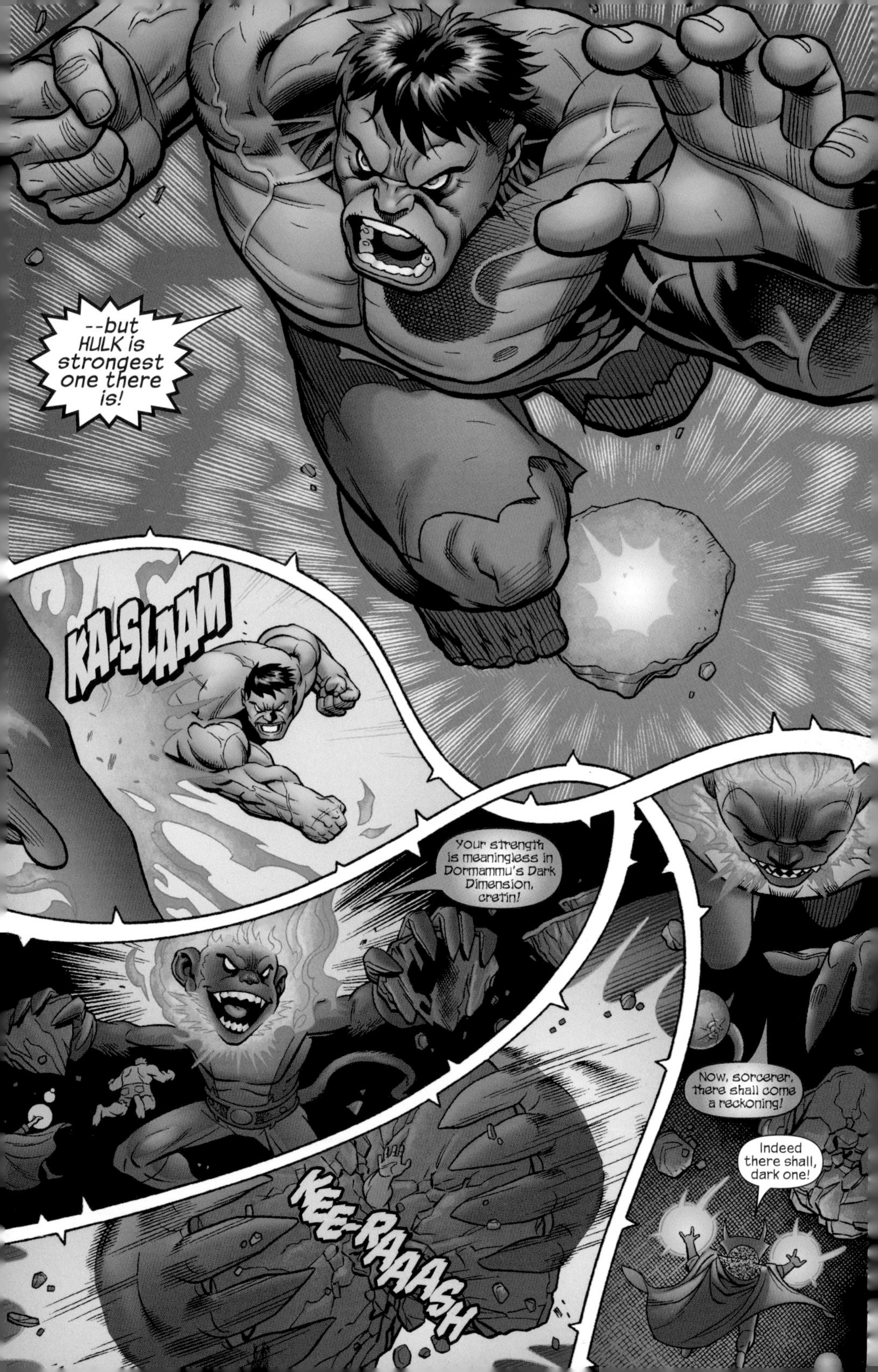
--but HULK is strongest one there is!
KA-SLAAM
Your strength is meaningless in Dormammu's Dark Dimension, cretin!
KEE-RAAASH
Now, sorcerer, there shall come a reckoning!
Indeed there shall, dark one!

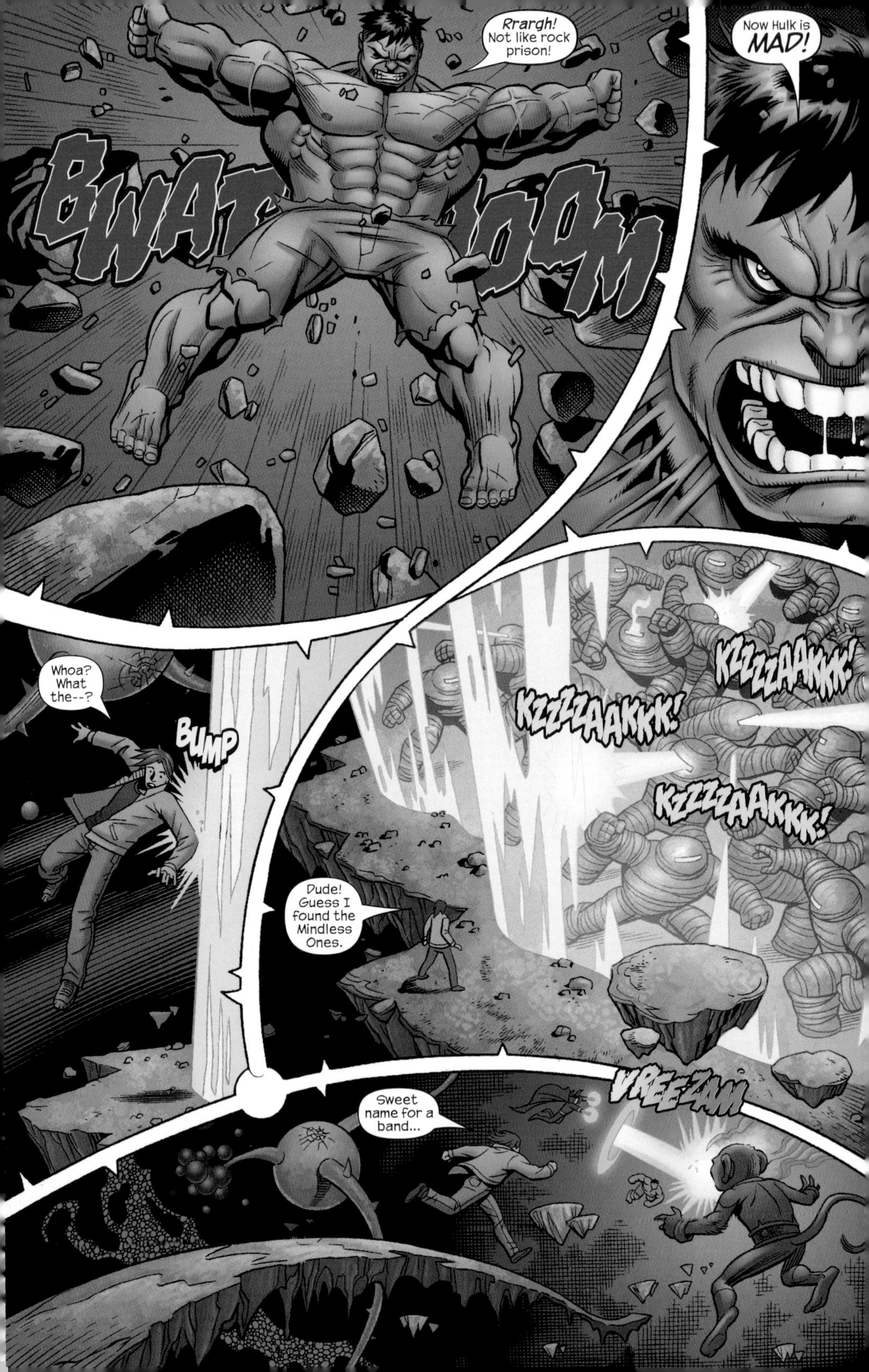
BWATHOOOM
Rrargh! Not like rock prison!
Now Hulk is MAD!
Whoa? What the--?
BUMP
KZZZZAAKKK!
KZZZZAAKKK!
KZZZZAAKKK!
Dude! Guess I found the Mindless Ones.
Sweet name for a band...
VREEZAM

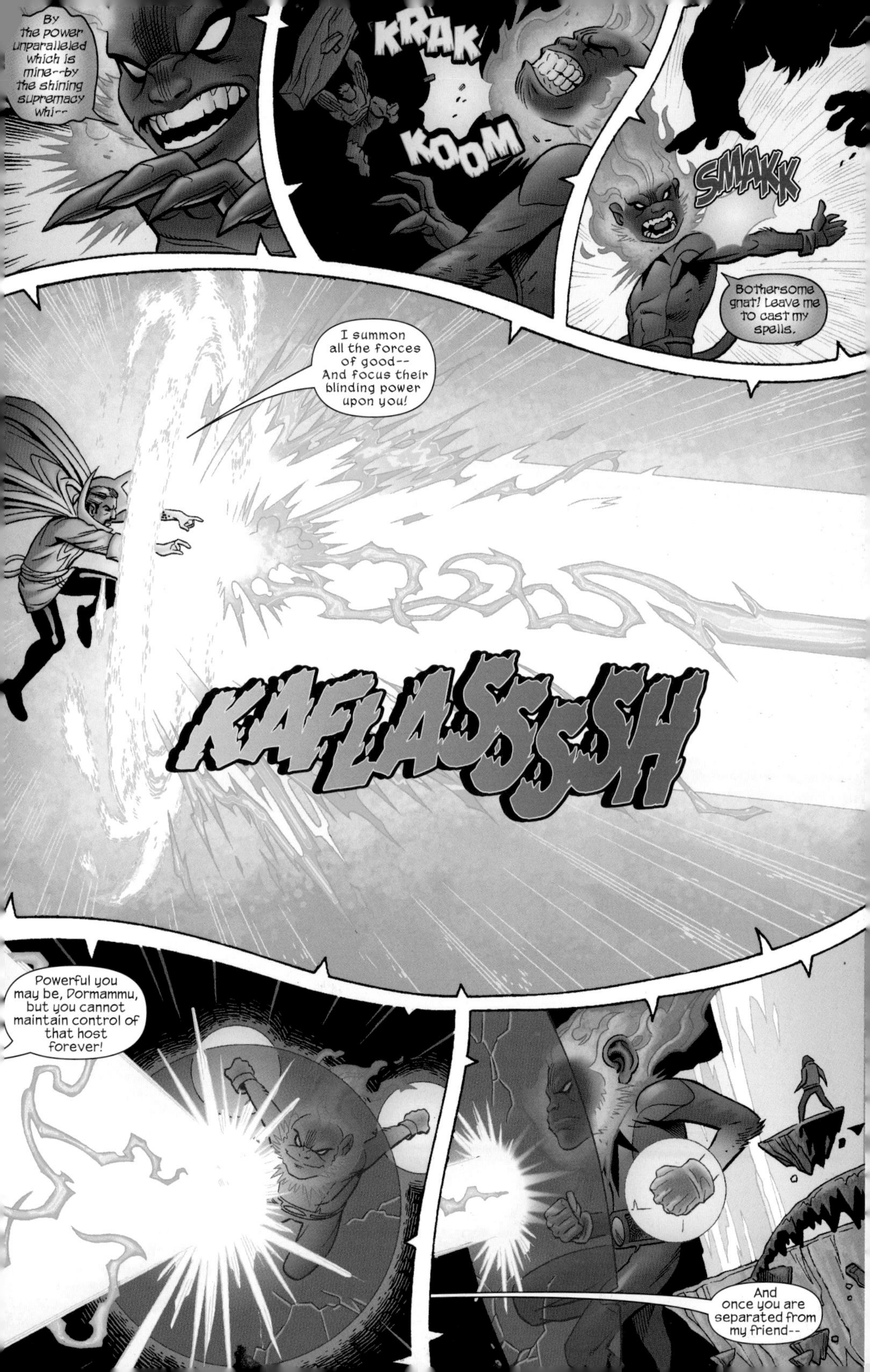

By the power unparalleled which is mine--by the shining supremacy whi--
KRAK
KOOM
SMAKK
Bothersome gnat! Leave me to cast my spells.
I summon all the forces of good--
And focus their blinding power upon you!
KAFLASSSH
Powerful you may be, Dormammu, but you cannot maintain control of that host forever!
And once you are separated from my friend--

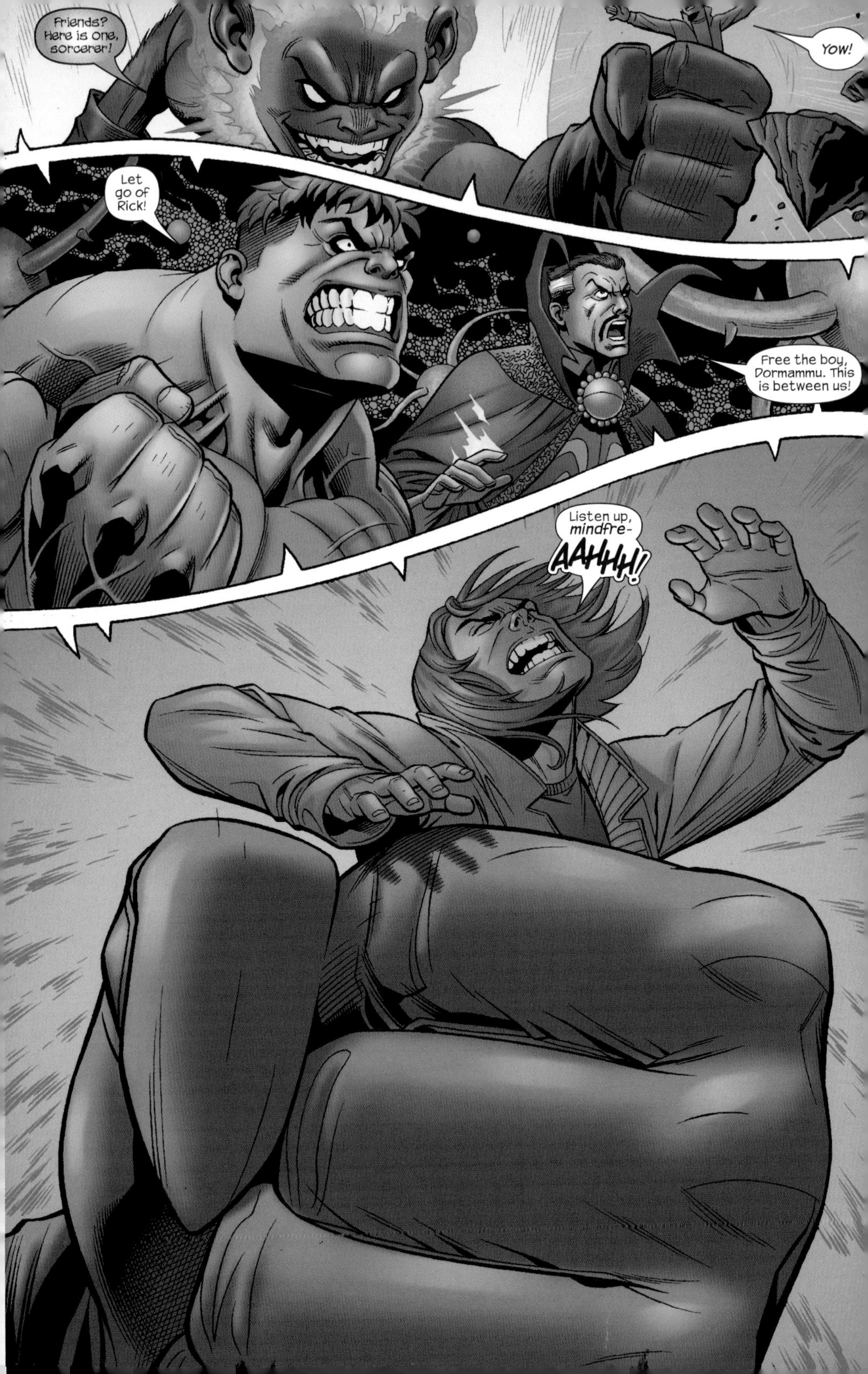
Friends? Here is one, sorcerer!
YOW!
Let go of Rick!
Free the boy, Dormammu. This is between us!
Listen up, mindfre-
AAHHH!

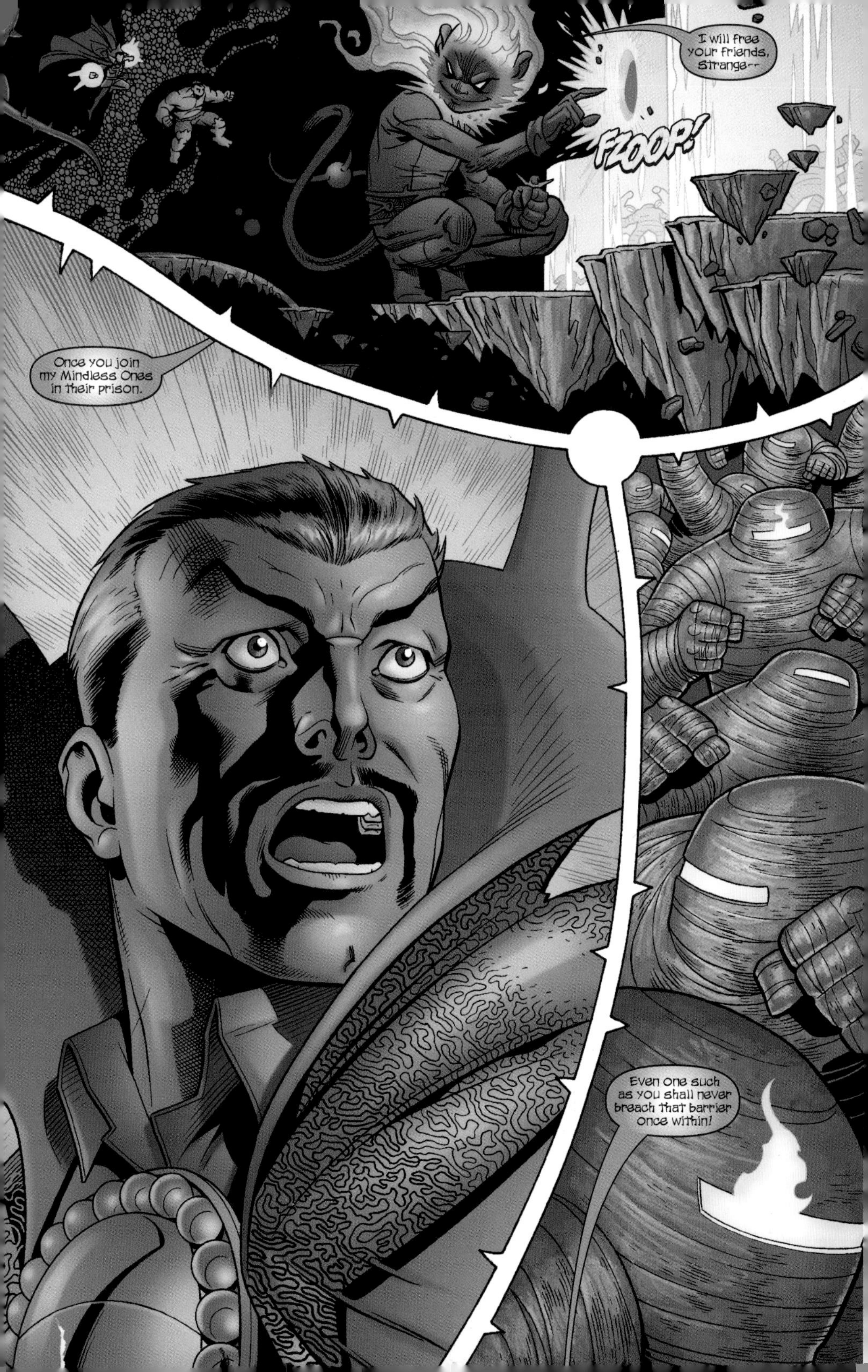
I will free your friends, Strange--
FZOOP!
Once you join my Mindless Ones in their prison.
Even one such as you shall never breach that barrier once within!

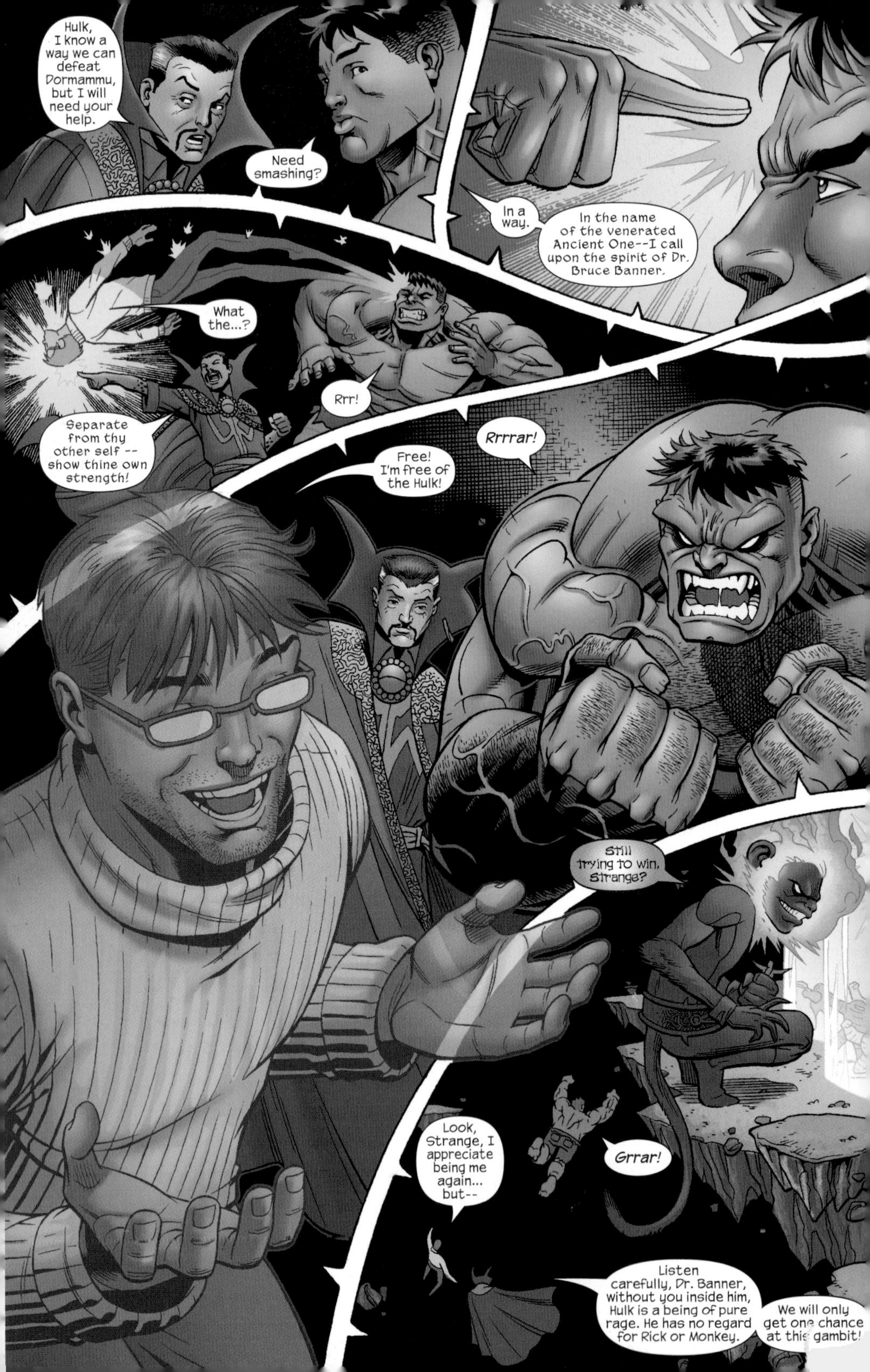

Hulk, I know a way we can defeat Dormammu, but I will need your help.
Need smashing?
In a way.
In the name of the venerated Ancient One--I call upon the spirit of Dr. Bruce Banner.
What the...?
Rrr!
Separate from thy other self -- show thine own strength!
Rrrrar!
Free! I'm free of the Hulk!
Still trying to win, Strange?
Look, Strange, I appreciate being me again... but--
Grrar!
Listen carefully, Dr. Banner, without you inside him, Hulk is a being of pure rage. He has no regard for Rick or Monkey.
We will only get one chance at this gambit!

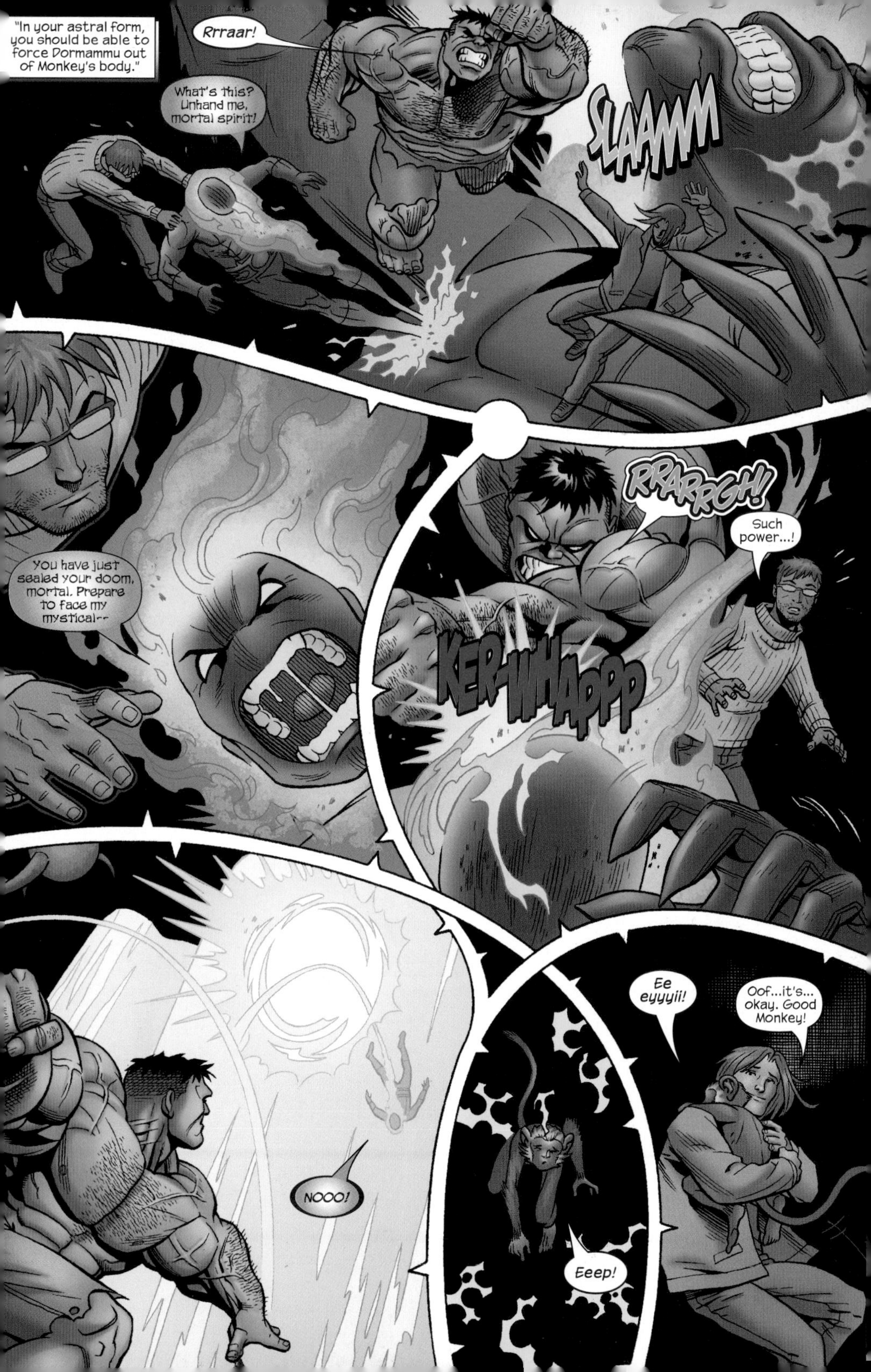
"In your astral form, you should be able to force Dormammu out of Monkey's body."
Rrraar!
What's this? Unhand me, mortal spirit!
SLAAMM
You have just sealed your doom, mortal. Prepare to face my mystical--
RRARRGH!
Such power...!
KER-WHAPPP
NOOO!
Ee eyyyii!
Oof...it's... okay. Good Monkey!
Eeep!

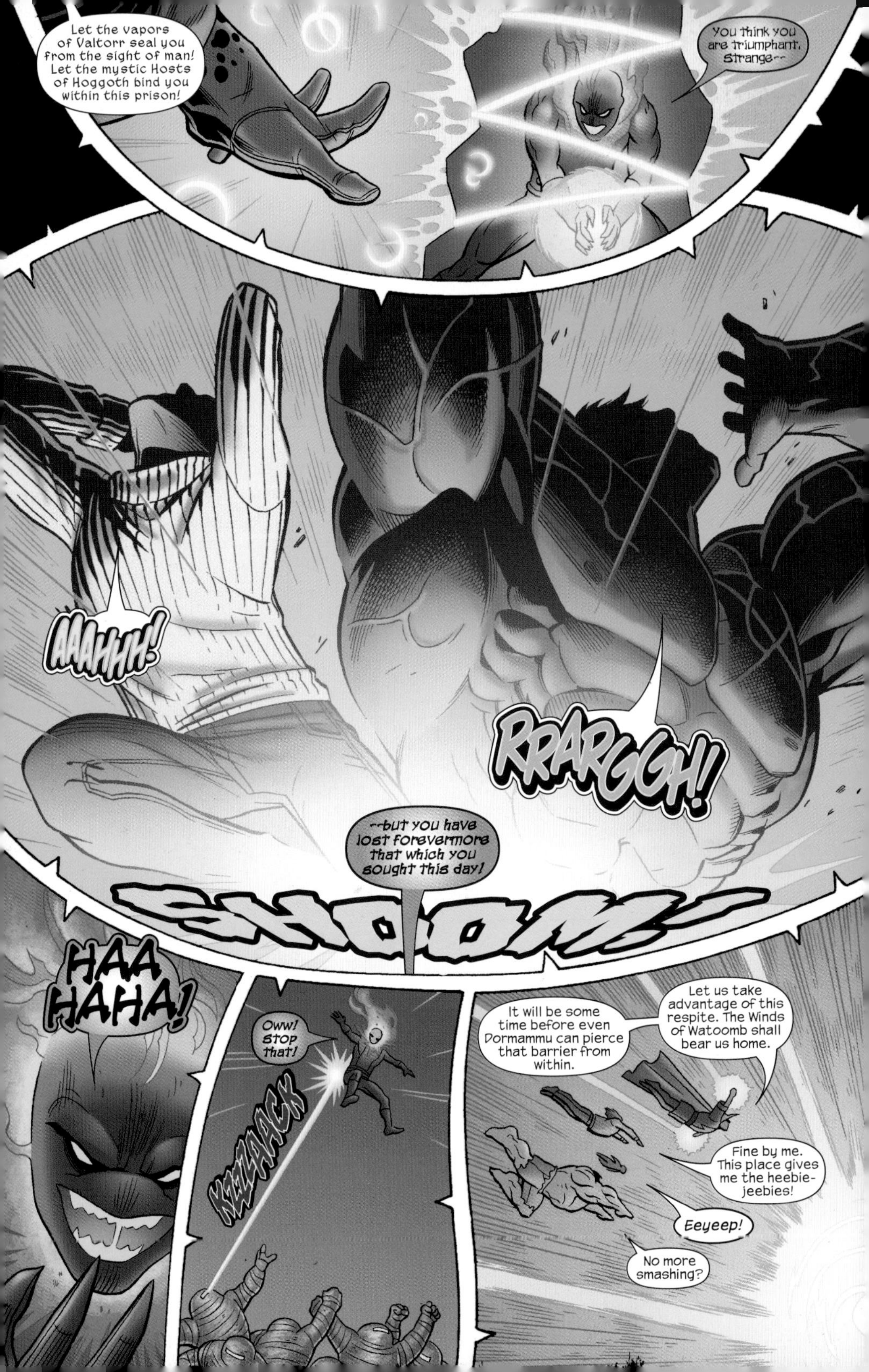
Let the vapors of Valtorr seal you from the sight of man! Let the mystic Hosts of Hoggoth bind you within this prison!
You think you are triumphant, Strange--
AAAHHH!
RRARGGH!
--but you have lost forevermore that which you sought this day!
SHOOM!
HAA HAHA!
Oww! Stop that!
KZZZACK
It will be some time before even Dormammu can pierce that barrier from within.
Let us take advantage of this respite. The Winds of Watoomb shall bear us home.
Fine by me. This place gives me the heebie-jeebies!
Eeyeep!
No more smashing?

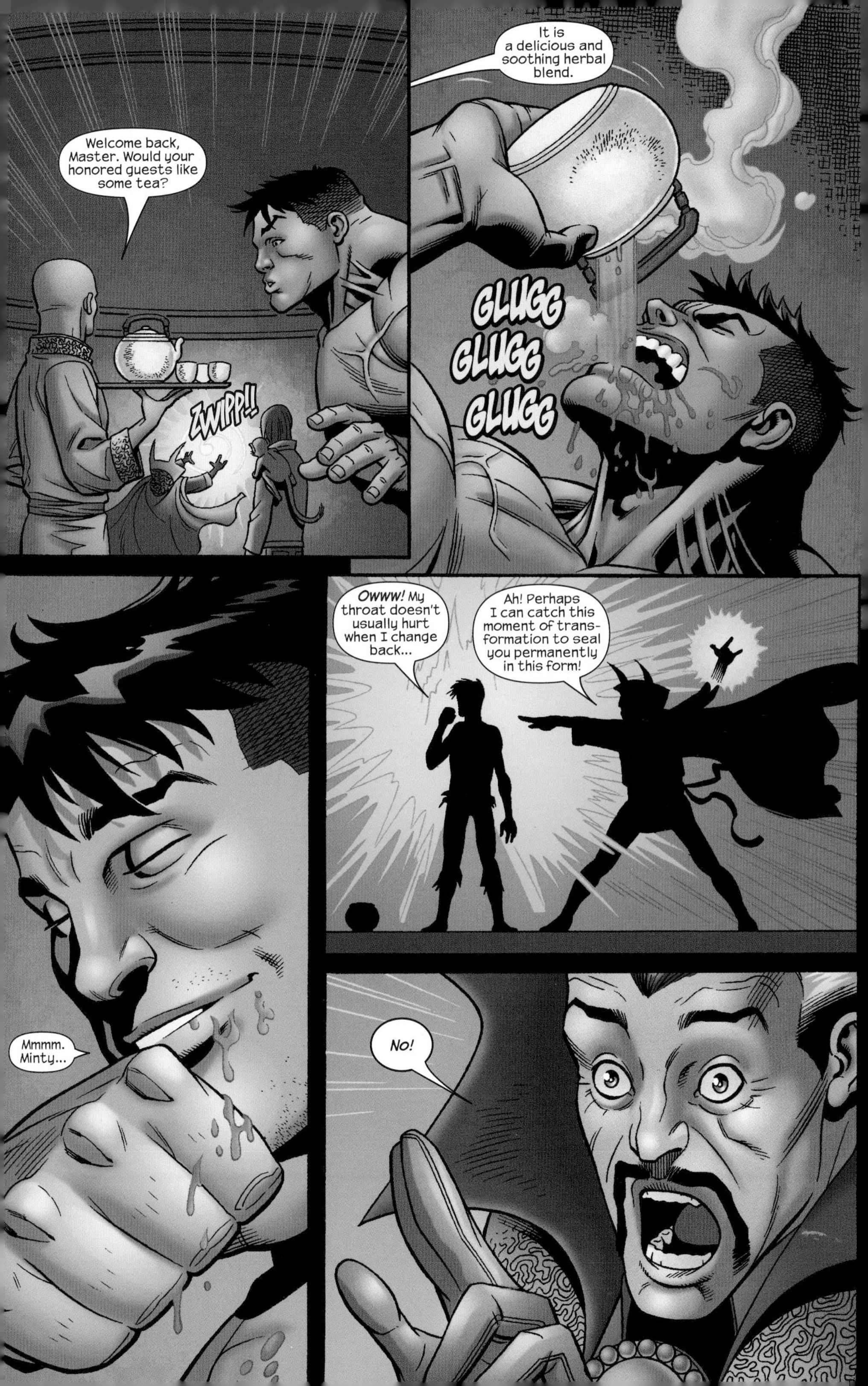
Welcome back, Master. Would your honored guests like some tea?
ZWIPP!!
It is a delicious and soothing herbal blend.
GLUGG GLUGG GLUGG
Mmmm. Minty...
Owww! My throat doesn't usually hurt when I change back...
Ah! Perhaps I can catch this moment of trans-formation to seal you permanently in this form!
No!

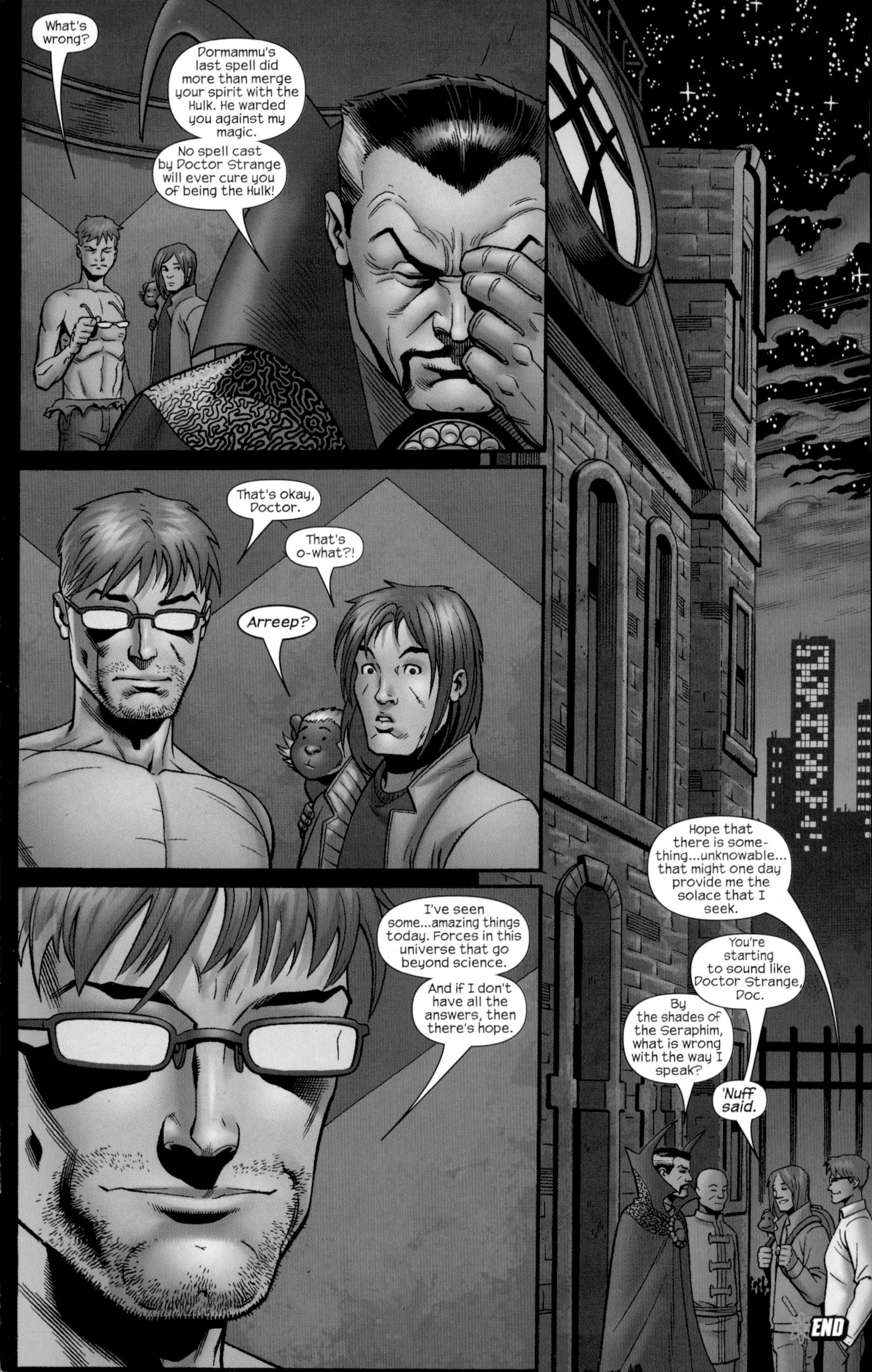
What's wrong?
Dormammu's last spell did more than merge your spirit with the Hulk. He warded you against my magic.
No spell cast by Doctor Strange will ever cure you of being the Hulk!
That's okay, Doctor.
That's o-what?!
Arreep?
I've seen some...amazing things today. Forces in this universe that go beyond science.
And if I don't have all the answers, then there's hope.
Hope that there is some-thing...unknowable... that might one day provide me the solace that I seek.
You're starting to sound like Doctor Strange, Doc.
By the shades of the Seraphim, what is wrong with the way I speak?
'Nuff said.
END

06

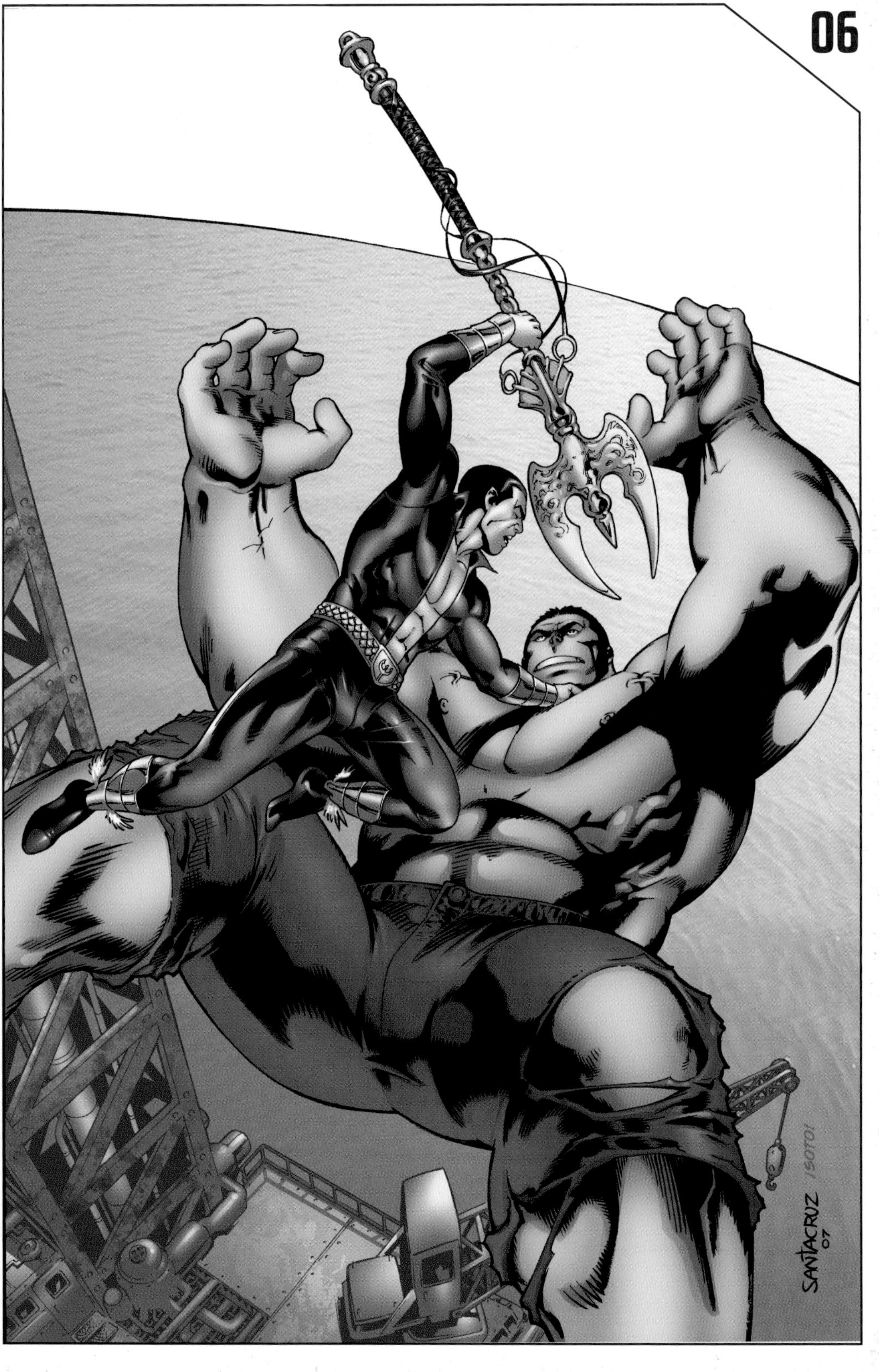
SANTACRUZ 07
¡SOTO!

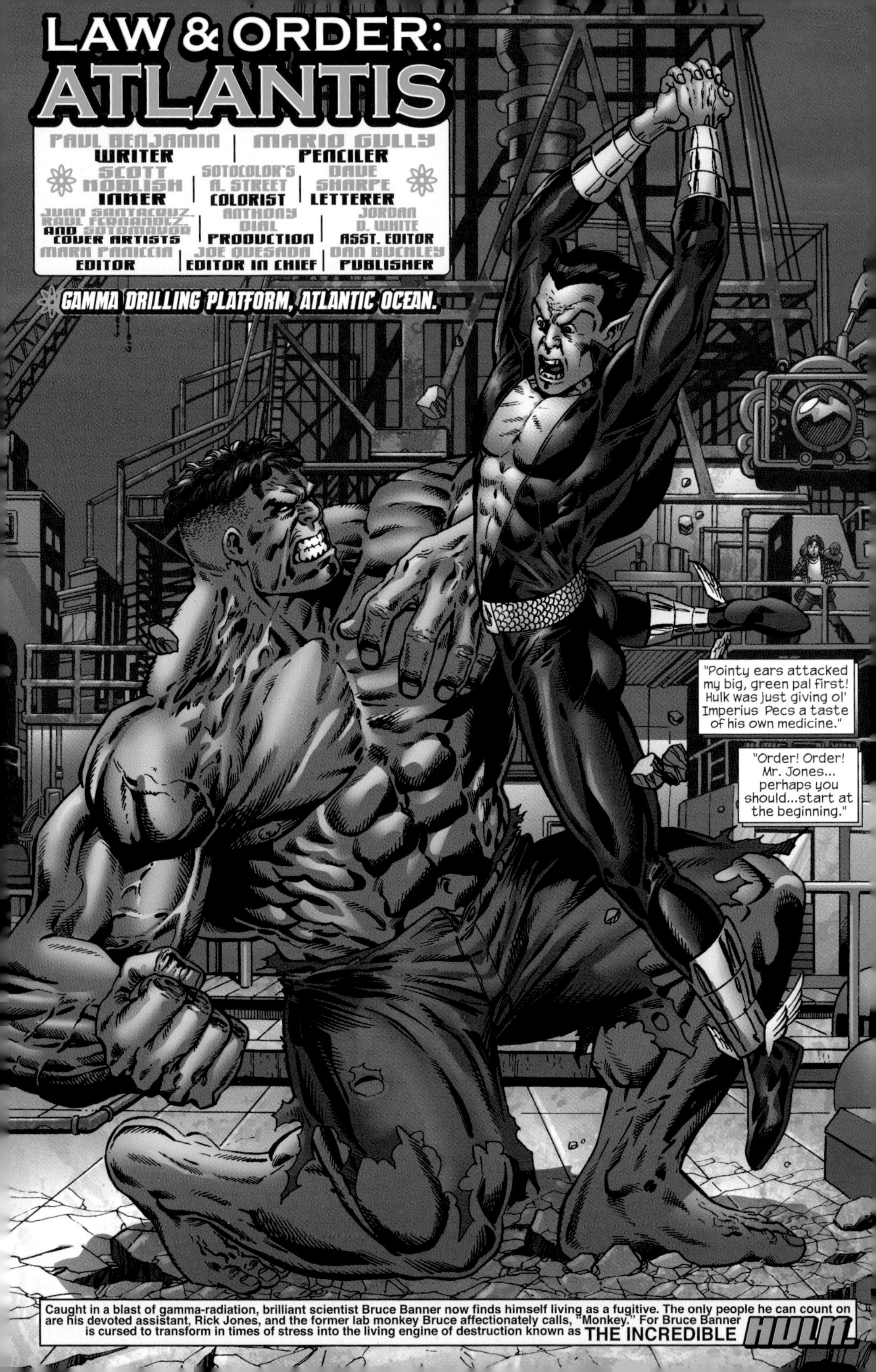
LAW & ORDER:
ATLANTIS
PAUL BENJAMIN WRITER
MARIO GULLY PENCILER
SCOTT KOBLISH INKER
SOTOCOLOR'S A. STREET COLORIST
DAVE SHARPE LETTERER
JUAN SANTACRUZ, RAUL FERNANDEZ, AND SOTOMAYOR COVER ARTISTS
ANTHONY DIAL PRODUCTION
JORDAN D. WHITE ASST. EDITOR
MARK PANICCIA EDITOR
JOE QUESADA EDITOR IN CHIEF
DAN BUCKLEY PUBLISHER
GAMMA DRILLING PLATFORM, ATLANTIC OCEAN.
"Pointy ears attacked my big, green pal first! Hulk was just giving ol' Imperius Pecs a taste of his own medicine."
"Order! Order! Mr. Jones... perhaps you should...start at the beginning."
Caught in a blast of gamma-radiation, brilliant scientist Bruce Banner now finds himself living as a fugitive. The only people he can count on are his devoted assistant, Rick Jones, and the former lab monkey Bruce affectionately calls, "Monkey." For Bruce Banner is cursed to transform in times of stress into the living engine of destruction known as THE INCREDIBLE HULK.

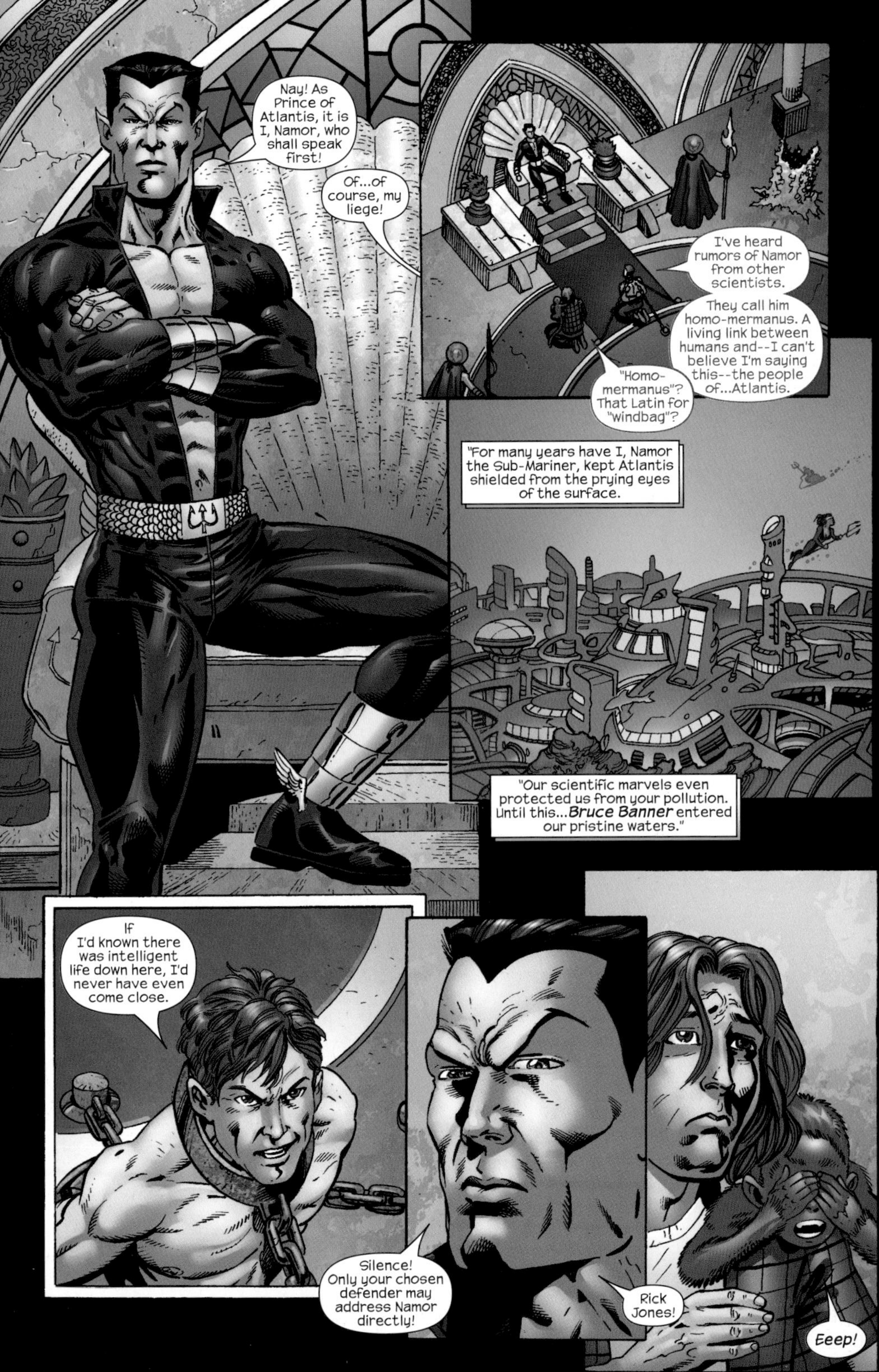
Nay! As Prince of Atlantis, it is I, Namor, who shall speak first!
Of...of course, my liege!
I've heard rumors of Namor from other scientists.
They call him homo-mermanus. A living link between humans and--I can't believe I'm saying this--the people of...Atlantis.
"Homo-mermanus"? That Latin for "windbag"?
"For many years have I, Namor the Sub-Mariner, kept Atlantis shielded from the prying eyes of the surface.
"Our scientific marvels even protected us from your pollution. Until this...Bruce Banner entered our pristine waters."
If I'd known there was intelligent life down here, I'd never have even come close.
Silence! Only your chosen defender may address Namor directly!
Rick Jones!
Eeep!

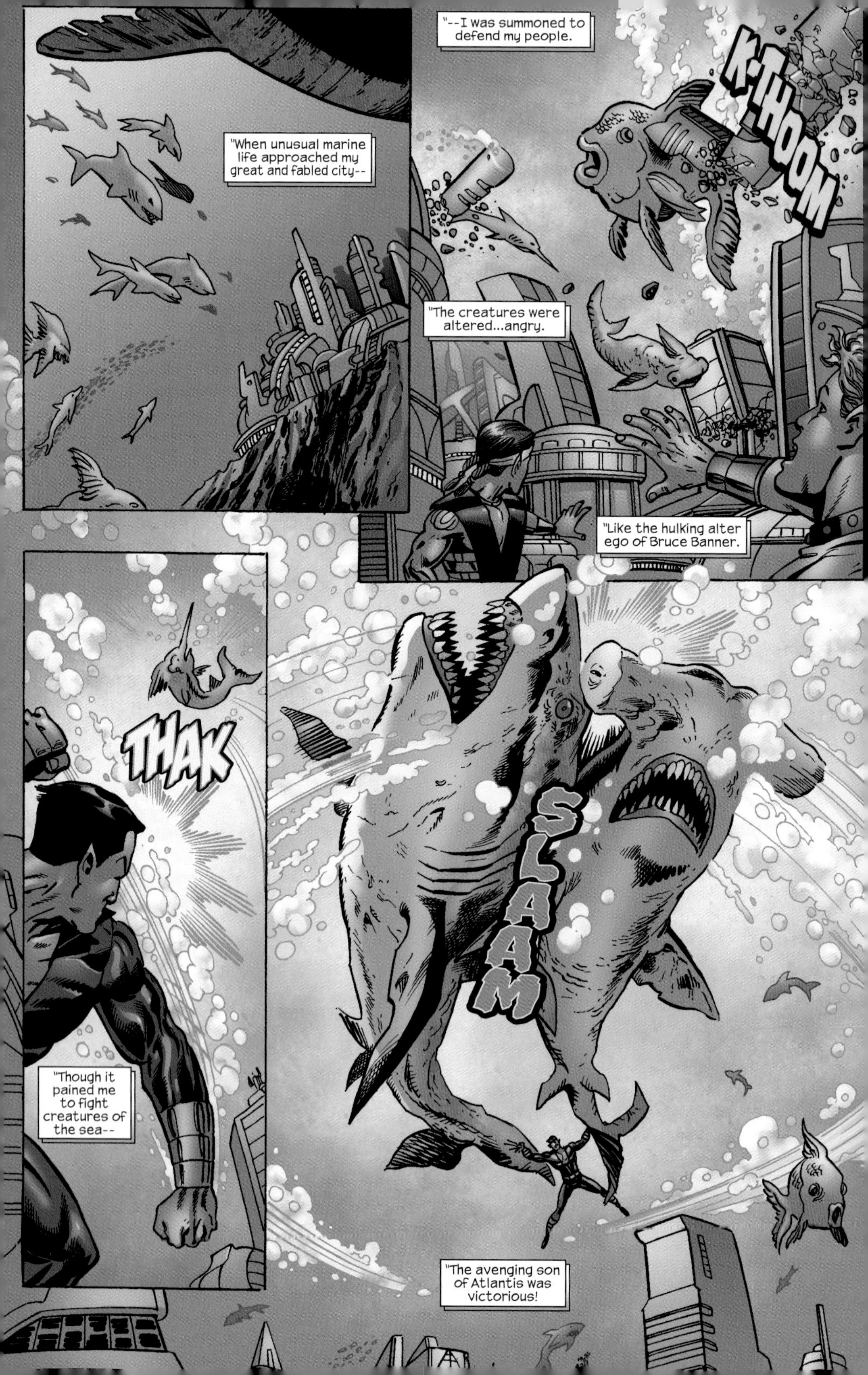
"When unusual marine life approached my great and fabled city--
"--I was summoned to defend my people.
K-THOOM
"The creatures were altered...angry.
"Like the hulking alter ego of Bruce Banner.
THAK
SLAAM
"Though it pained me to fight creatures of the sea--
"The avenging son of Atlantis was victorious!

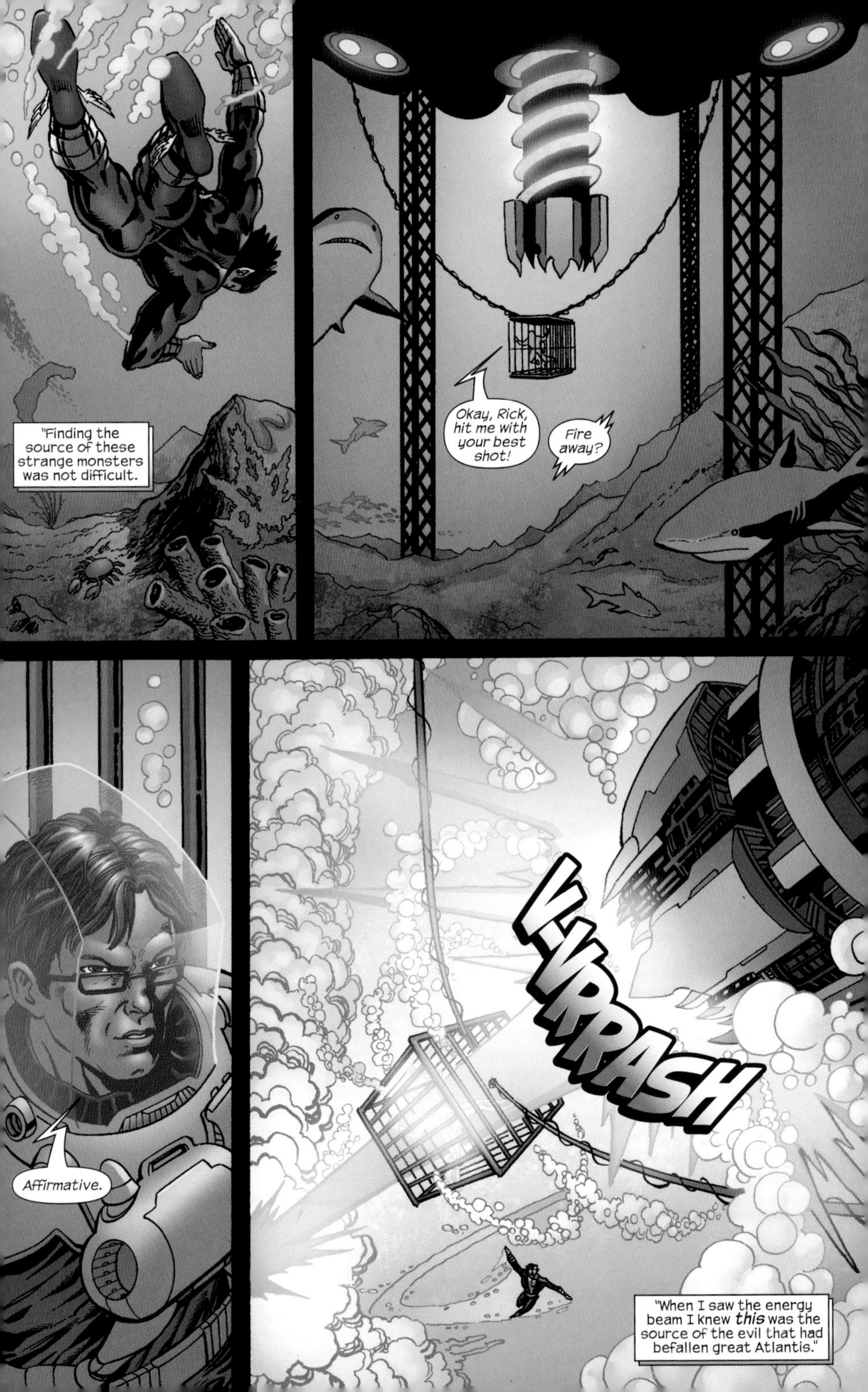
"Finding the source of these strange monsters was not difficult.
Okay, Rick, hit me with your best shot!
Fire away?
Affirmative.
V-VRASH
"When I saw the energy beam I knew *this* was the source of the evil that had befallen great Atlantis."

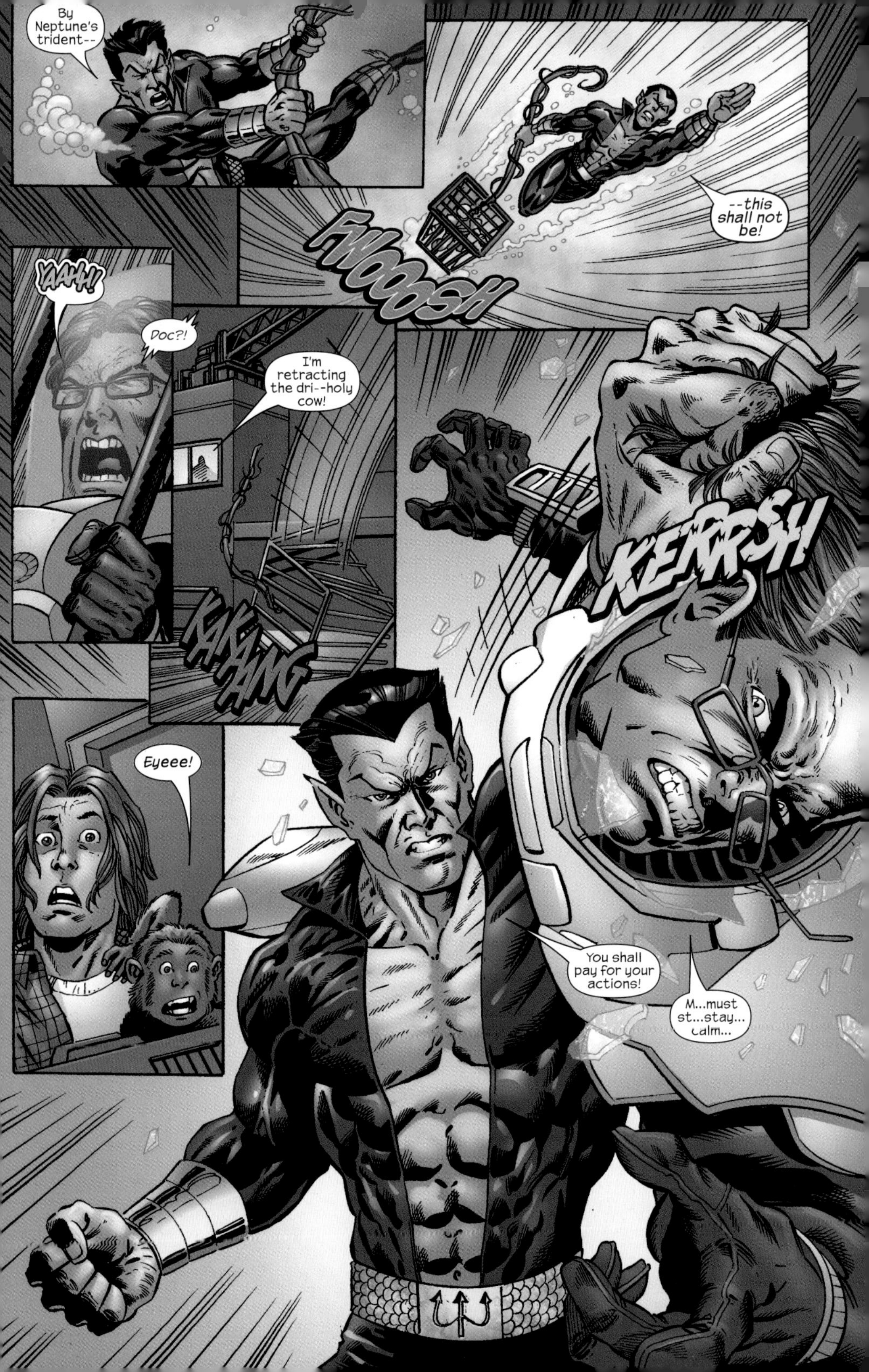

By Neptune's trident--
--this shall not be!
FWOOOSH
YAAHH!
Doc?!
I'm retracting the dri--holy cow!
KAKANG
KERRSH!
Eyeee!
You shall pay for your actions!
M...must st...stay... calm...

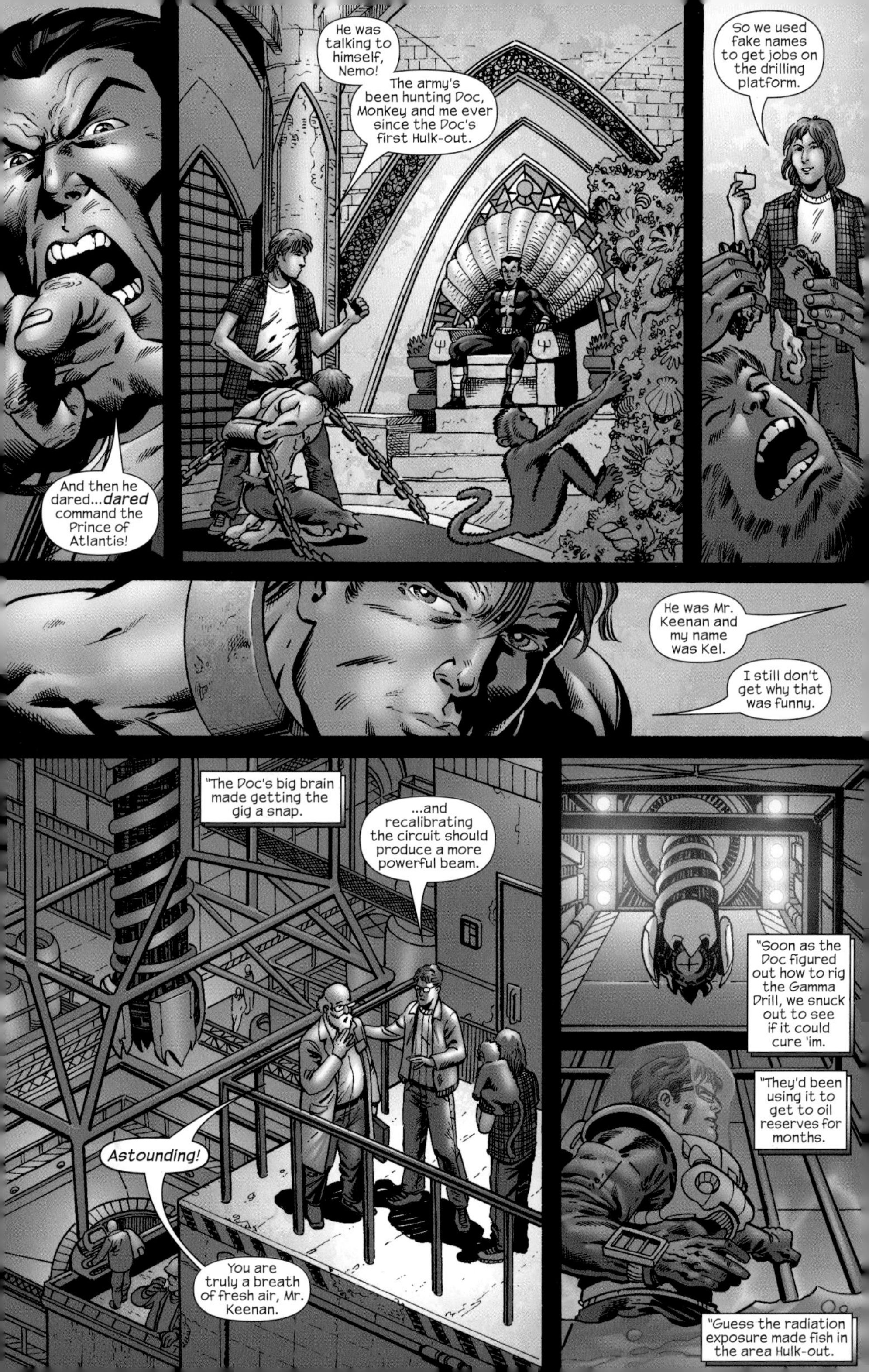
And then he dared...*dared* command the Prince of Atlantis!
He was talking to himself, Nemo!
The army's been hunting Doc, Monkey and me ever since the Doc's first Hulk-out.
So we used fake names to get jobs on the drilling platform.
He was Mr. Keenan and my name was Kel.
I still don't get why that was funny.
"The Doc's big brain made getting the gig a snap.
...and recalibrating the circuit should produce a more powerful beam.
Astounding!
You are truly a breath of fresh air, Mr. Keenan.
"Soon as the Doc figured out how to rig the Gamma Drill, we snuck out to see if it could cure 'im.
"They'd been using it to get to oil reserves for months.
"Guess the radiation exposure made fish in the area Hulk-out.

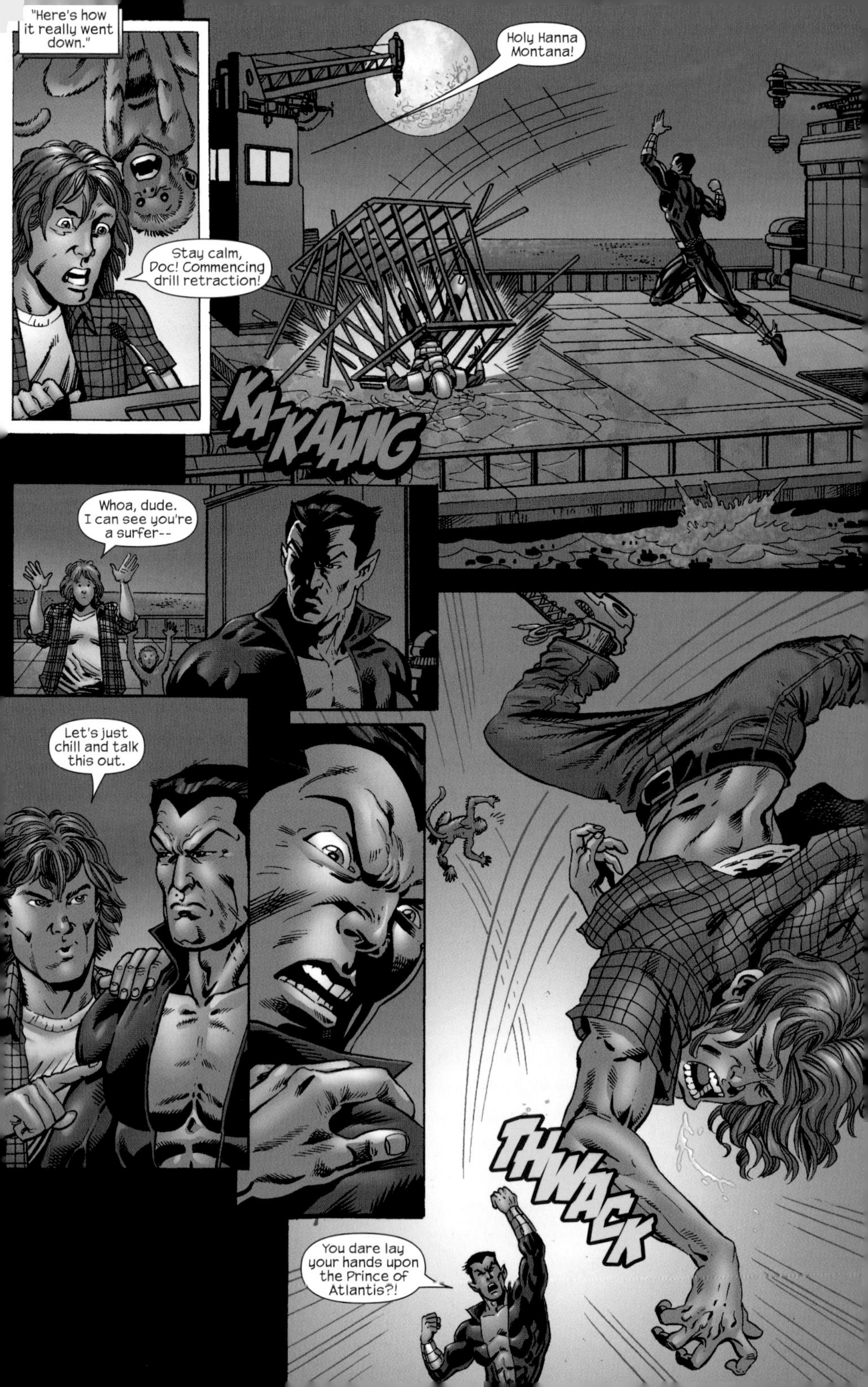
"Here's how it really went down."
Stay calm, Doc! Commencing drill retraction!
Holy Hanna Montana!
KA-KAANG
Whoa, dude. I can see you're a surfer--
Let's just chill and talk this out.
THWACK
You dare lay your hands upon the Prince of Atlantis?!

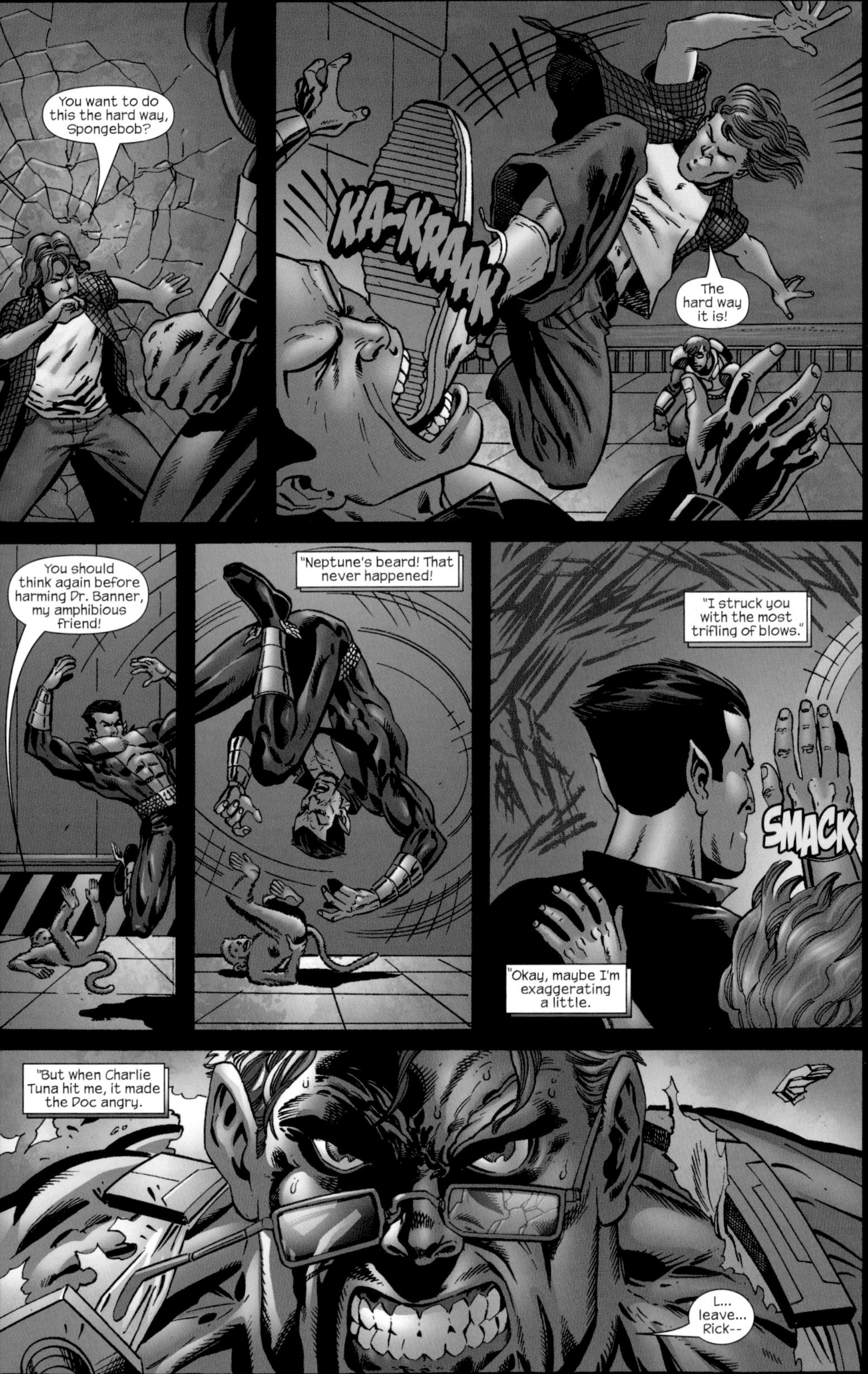

You want to do this the hard way, Spongebob?
KA-KRAAAK
The hard way it is!
You should think again before harming Dr. Banner, my amphibious friend!
"Neptune's beard! That never happened!
"I struck you with the most trifling of blows."
SMACK
"Okay, maybe I'm exaggerating a little.
"But when Charlie Tuna hit me, it made the Doc angry.
L... leave... Rick--

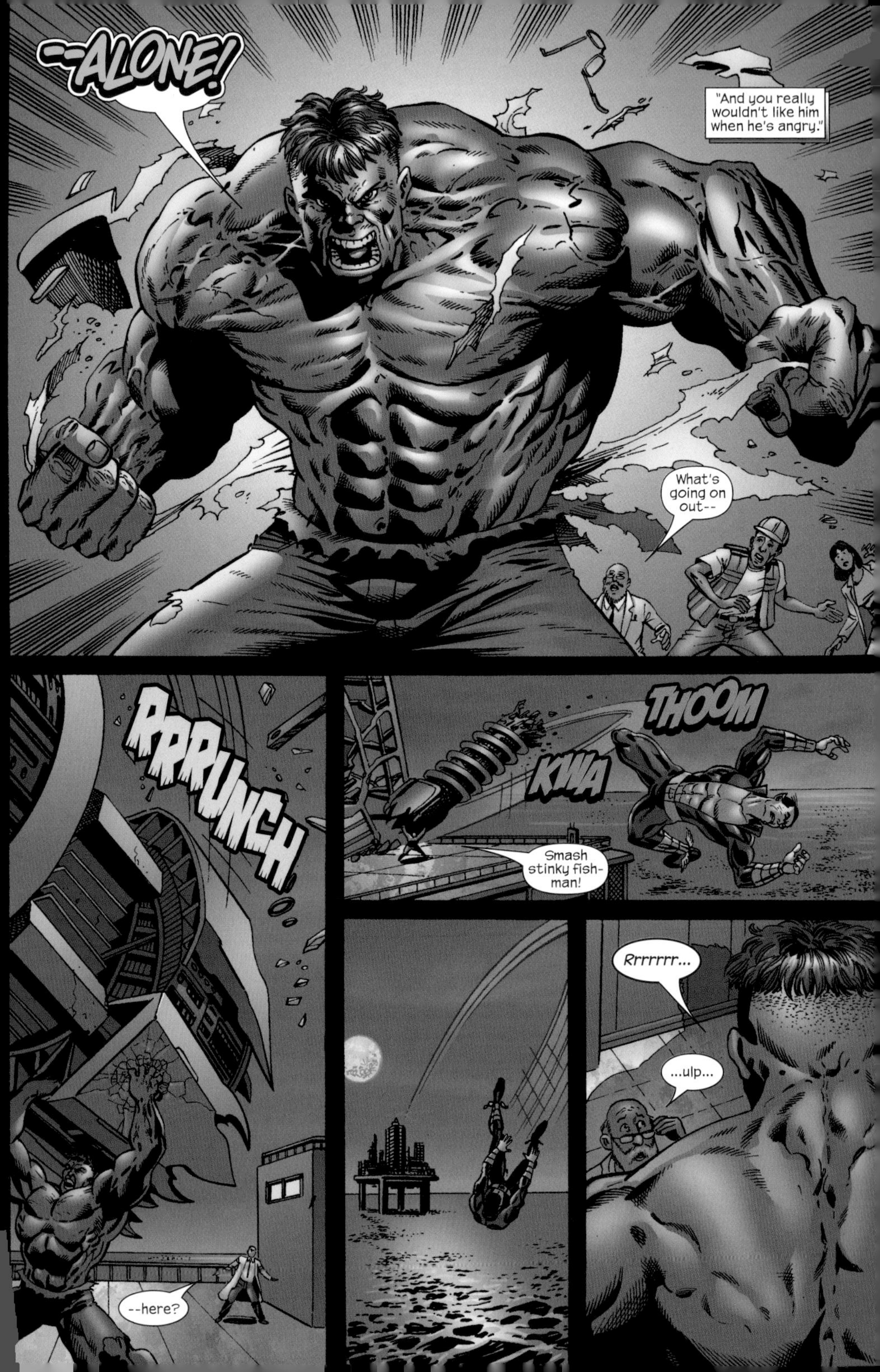
--ALONE!
"And you really wouldn't like him when he's angry."
What's going on out--
RRRUNCH
--here?
THOOM
KWA
Smash stinky fish-man!
Rrrrrrr...
...ulp...

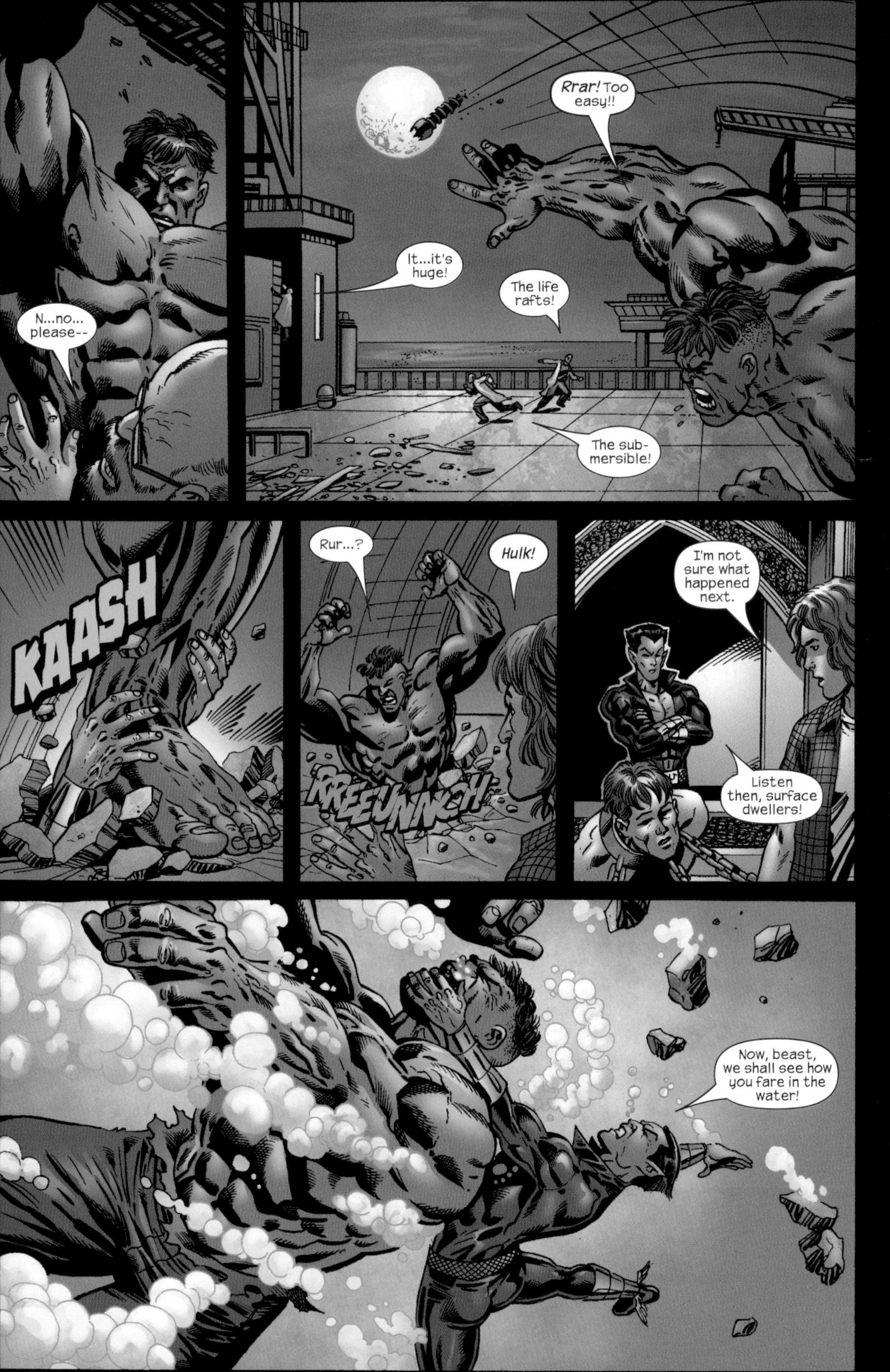

N...no... please--
Rrar! Too easy!!
It...it's huge!
The life rafts!
The sub-mersible!
KAASH
Rur...?
Hulk!
KREEUNNCH
I'm not sure what happened next.
Listen then, surface dwellers!
Now, beast, we shall see how you fare in the water!

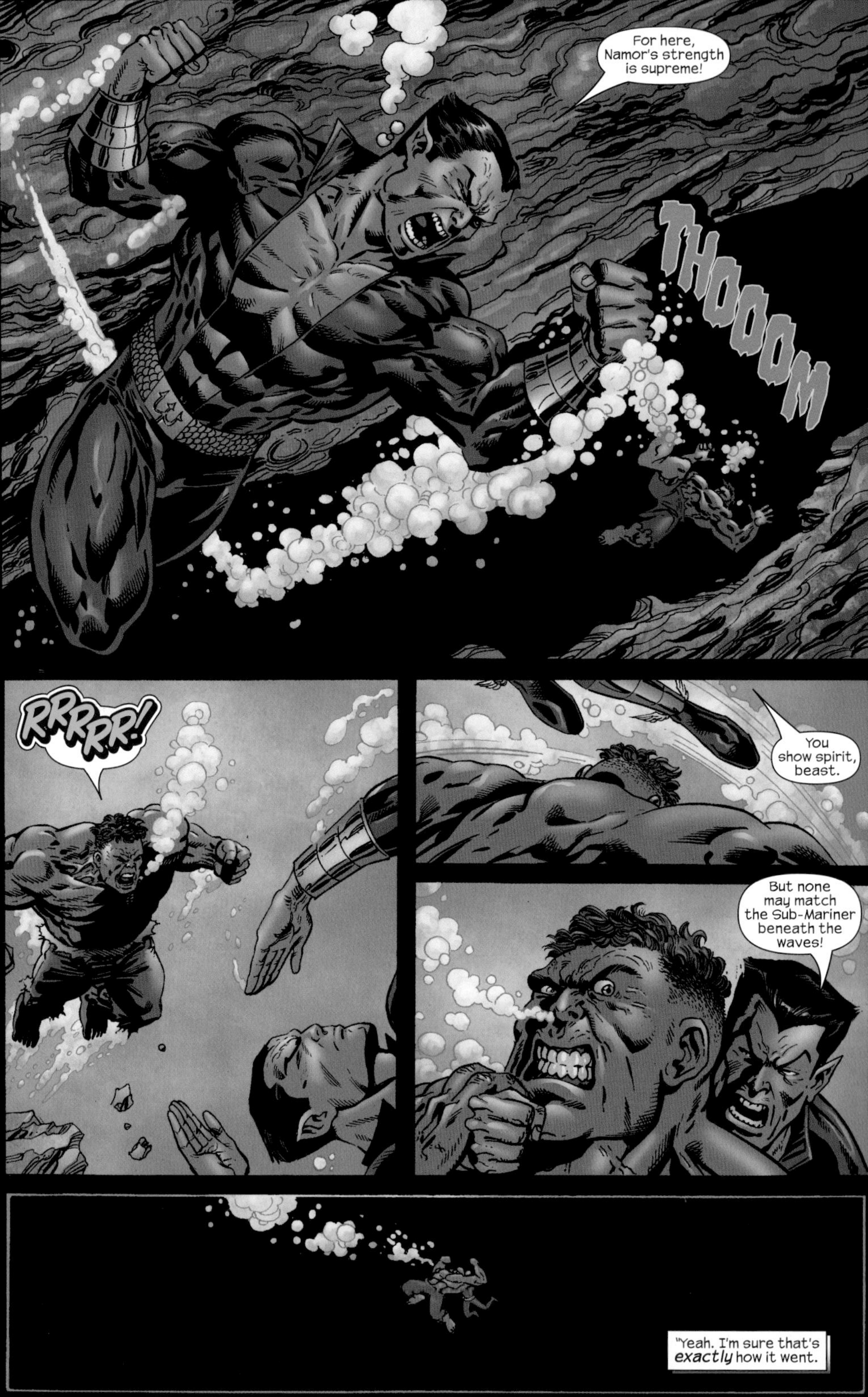
For here, Namor's strength is supreme!
THOOOM
RRRRR!
You show spirit, beast.
But none may match the Sub-Mariner beneath the waves!
"Yeah. I'm sure that's *exactly* how it went.

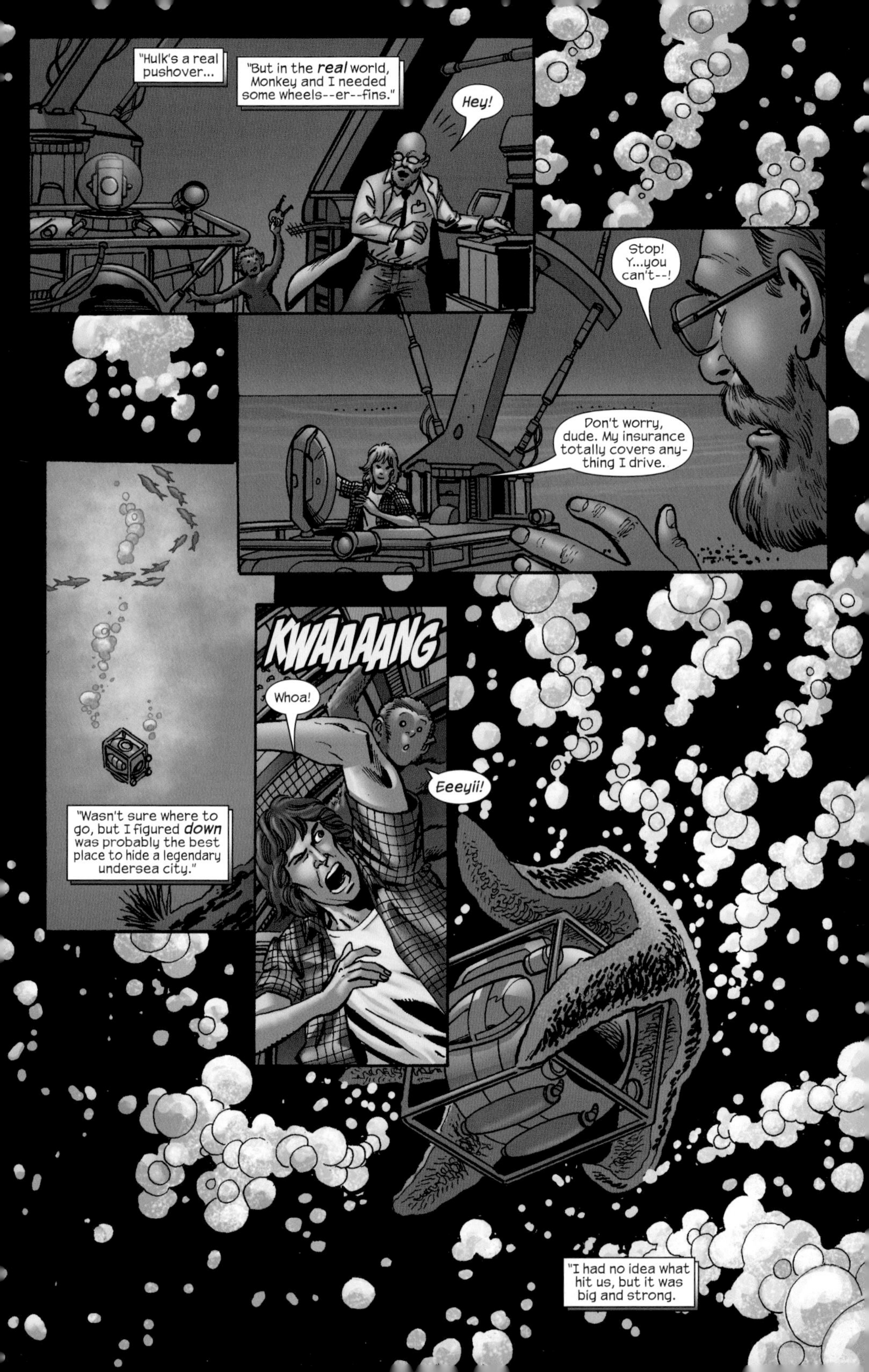
"Hulk's a real pushover...
"But in the real world, Monkey and I needed some wheels--er--fins."
Hey!
Stop! Y...you can't--!
Don't worry, dude. My insurance totally covers anything I drive.
"Wasn't sure where to go, but I figured down was probably the best place to hide a legendary undersea city."
KWAAAANG
Whoa!
Eeeyii!
"I had no idea what hit us, but it was big and strong.

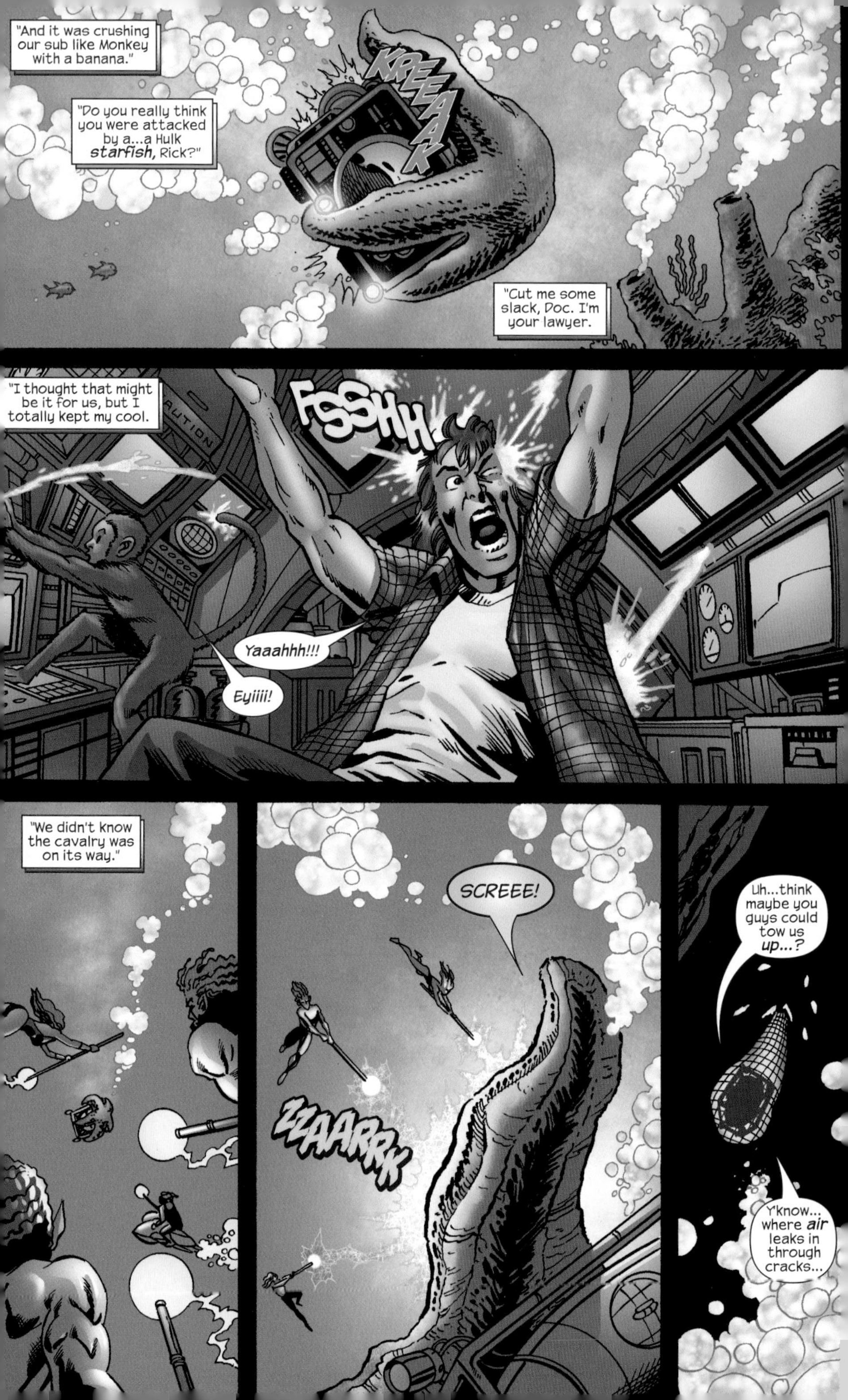
"And it was crushing our sub like Monkey with a banana."
"Do you really think you were attacked by a...a Hulk *starfish*, Rick?"
KREEAAK
"Cut me some slack, Doc. I'm your lawyer.
"I thought that might be it for us, but I totally kept my cool.
FSSHH
Yaaahhh!!!
Eyiiii!
"We didn't know the cavalry was on its way."
SCREEE!
ZZAARRK
Uh...think maybe you guys could tow us *up*...?
Y'know... where *air* leaks in through cracks...

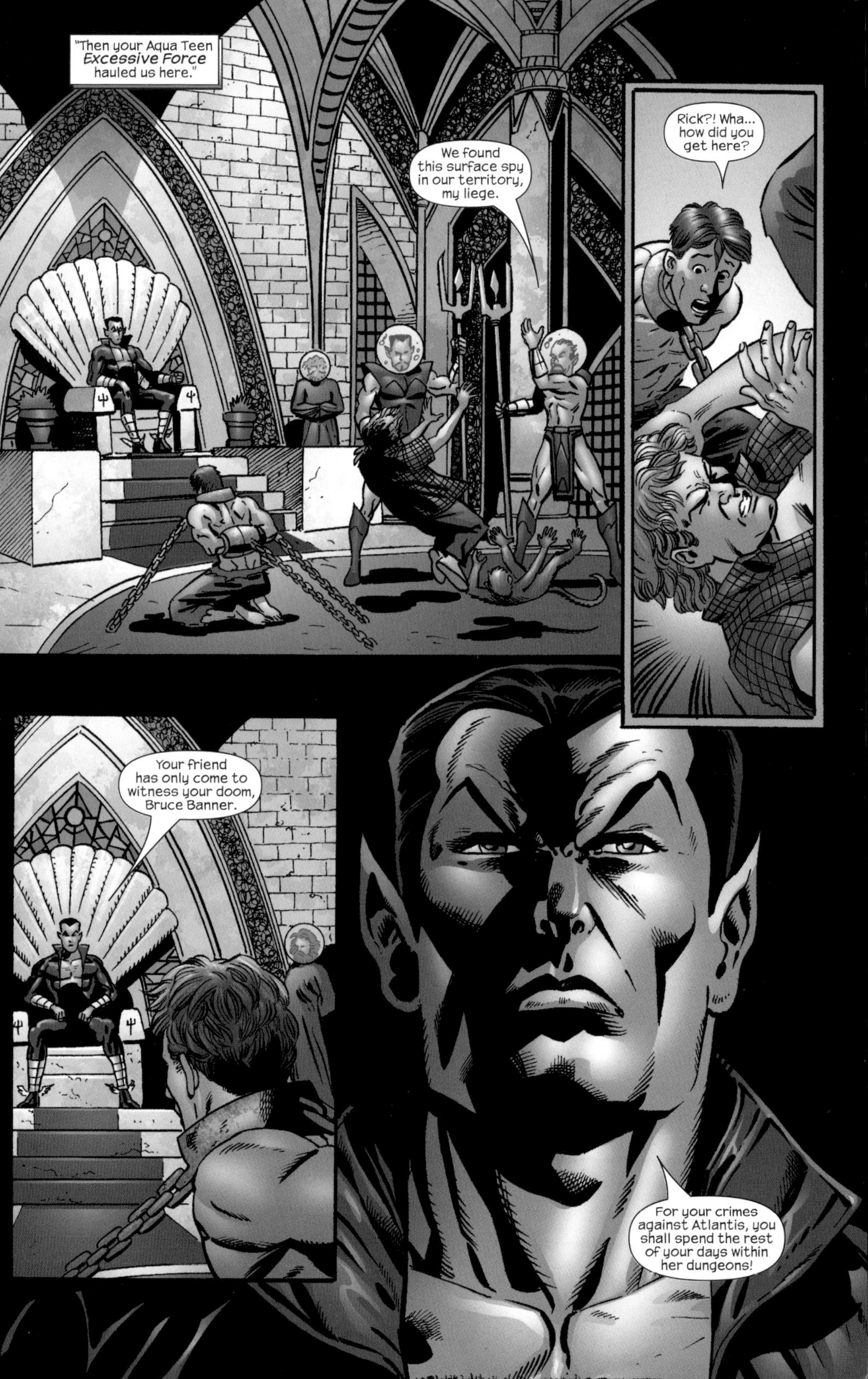
"Then your Aqua Teen *Excessive Force* hauled us here."
We found this surface spy in our territory, my liege.
Rick?! Wha... how did you get here?
Your friend has only come to witness your doom, Bruce Banner.
For your crimes against Atlantis, you shall spend the rest of your days within her dungeons!

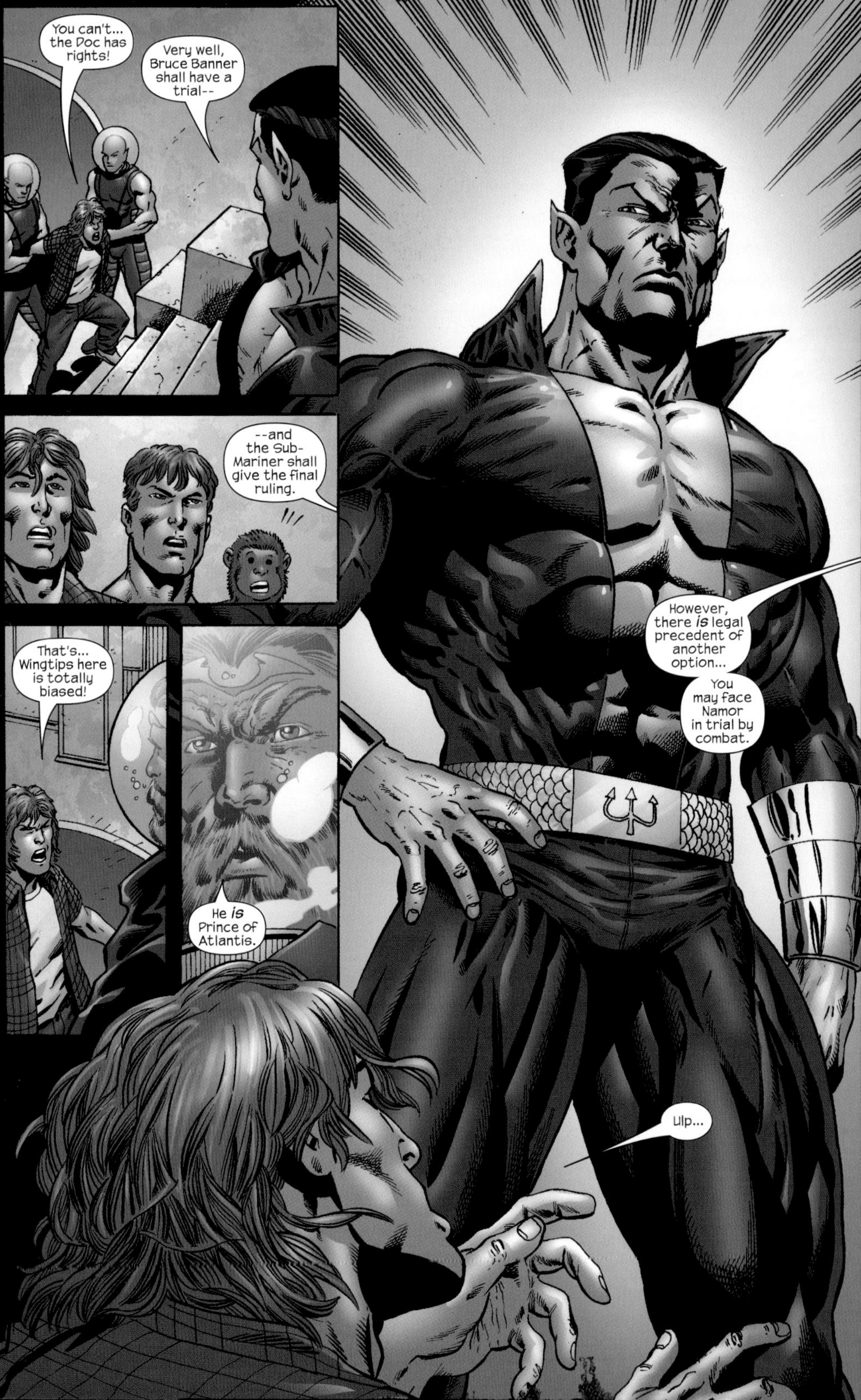
You can't... the Doc has rights!
Very well, Bruce Banner shall have a trial--
--and the Sub-Mariner shall give the final ruling.
!!
That's... Wingtips here is totally biased!
He *is* Prince of Atlantis.
However, there *is* legal precedent of another option...
You may face Namor in trial by combat.
Ulp...

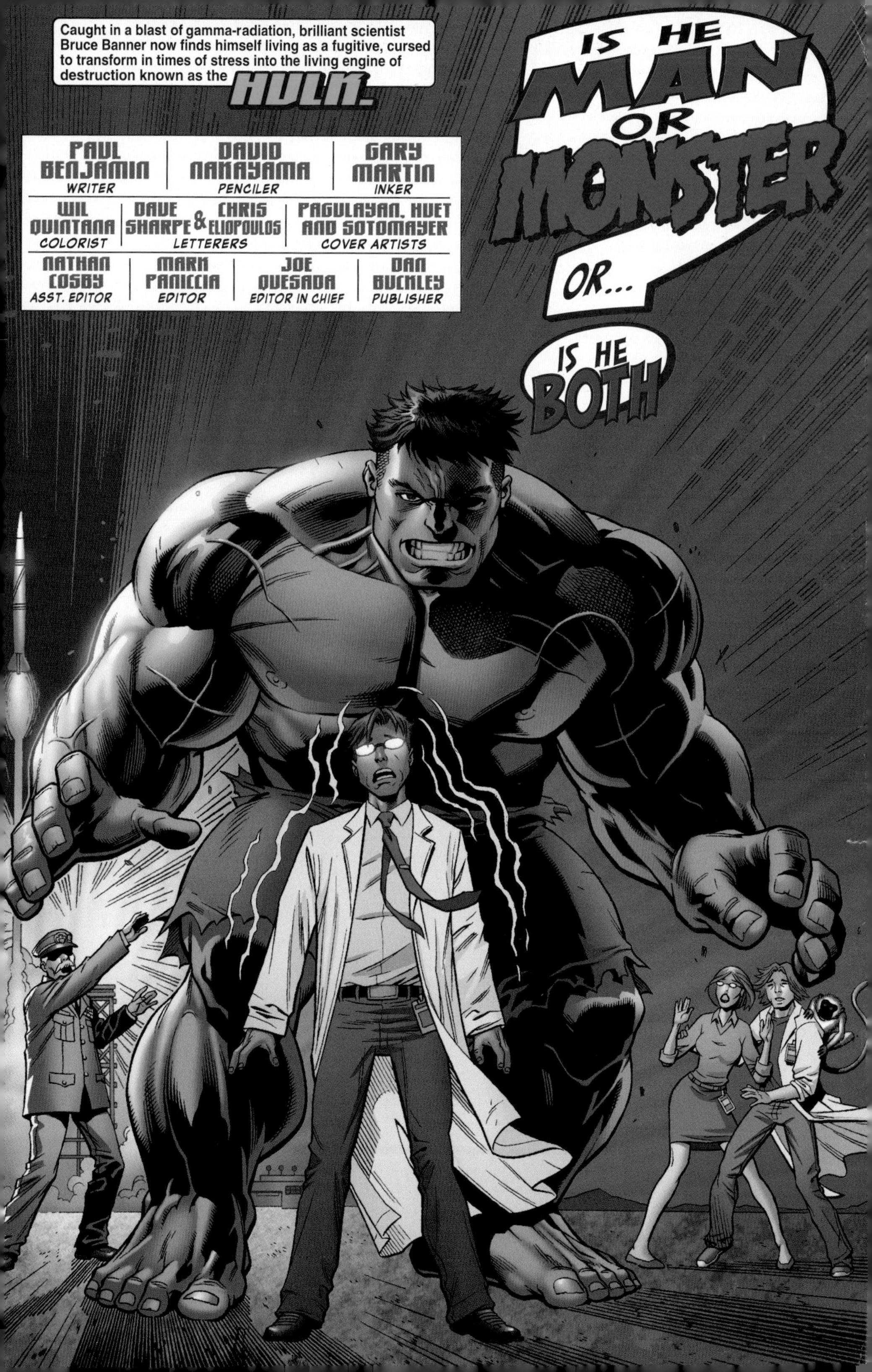

Caught in a blast of gamma-radiation, brilliant scientist Bruce Banner now finds himself living as a fugitive, cursed to transform in times of stress into the living engine of destruction known as the HULK.
PAUL BENJAMIN WRITER
DAVID NAKAYAMA PENCILER
GARY MARTIN INKER
WIL QUINTANA COLORIST
DAVE SHARPE & CHRIS ELIOPOULOS LETTERERS
PAGULAYAN, HUET AND SOTOMAYER COVER ARTISTS
NATHAN COSBY ASST. EDITOR
MARK PANICCIA EDITOR
JOE QUESADA EDITOR IN CHIEF
DAN BUCKLEY PUBLISHER
IS HE MAN OR MONSTER
OR...
IS HE BOTH

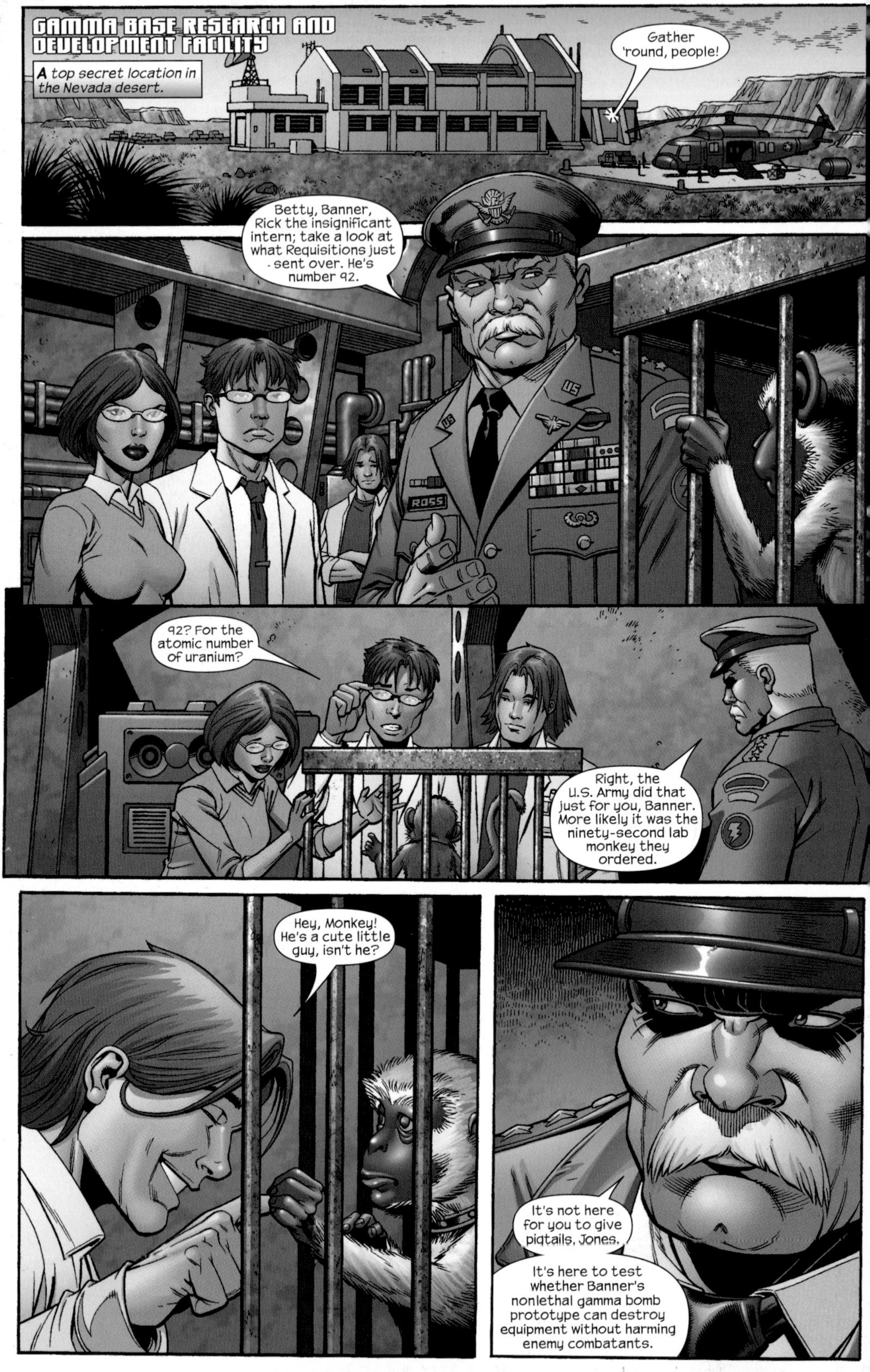
GAMMA BASE RESEARCH AND DEVELOPMENT FACILITY
A top secret location in the Nevada desert.
Gather 'round, people!
Betty, Banner, Rick the insignificant intern; take a look at what Requisitions just sent over. He's number 92.
92? For the atomic number of uranium?
Right, the U.S. Army did that just for you, Banner. More likely it was the ninety-second lab monkey they ordered.
Hey, Monkey! He's a cute little guy, isn't he?
It's not here for you to give pigtails, Jones.
It's here to test whether Banner's nonlethal gamma bomb prototype can destroy equipment without harming enemy combatants.

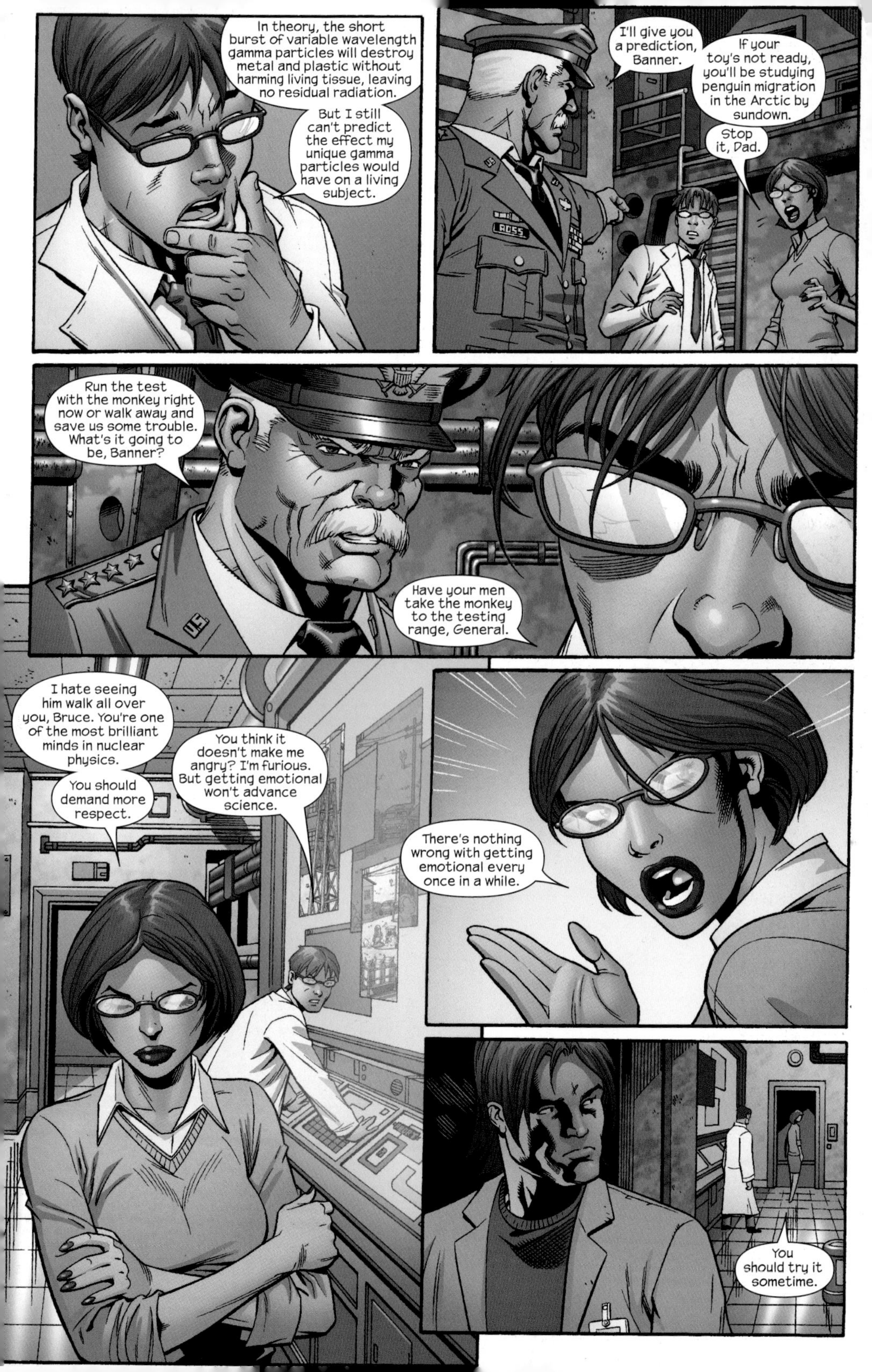
In theory, the short burst of variable wavelength gamma particles will destroy metal and plastic without harming living tissue, leaving no residual radiation.
But I still can't predict the effect my unique gamma particles would have on a living subject.
I'll give you a prediction, Banner.
If your toy's not ready, you'll be studying penguin migration in the Arctic by sundown.
Stop it, Dad.
ROSS
Run the test with the monkey right now or walk away and save us some trouble. What's it going to be, Banner?
Have your men take the monkey to the testing range, General.
I hate seeing him walk all over you, Bruce. You're one of the most brilliant minds in nuclear physics.
You should demand more respect.
You think it doesn't make me angry? I'm furious. But getting emotional won't advance science.
There's nothing wrong with getting emotional every once in a while.
You should try it sometime.

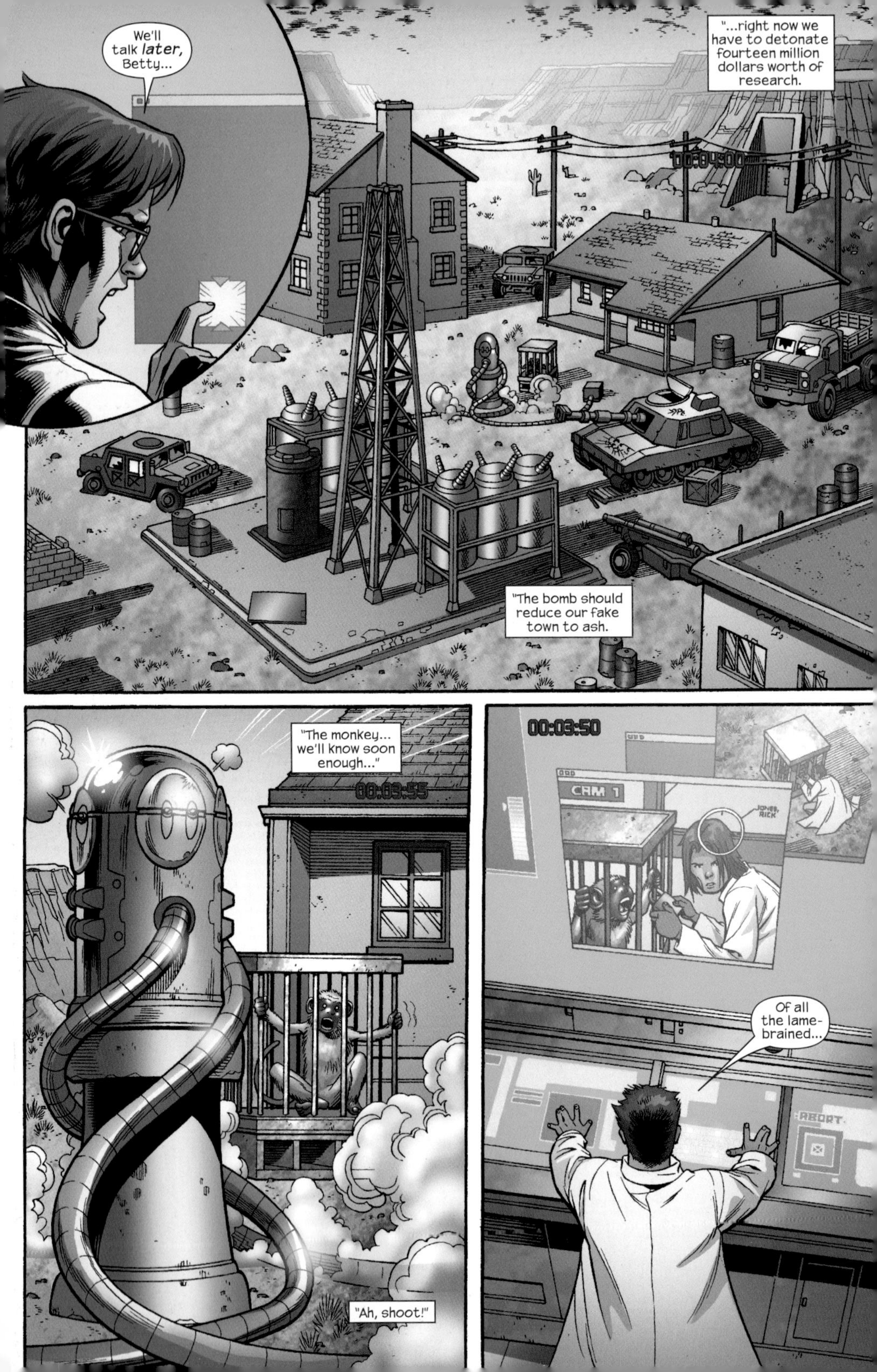
We'll talk *later,* Betty...
"...right now we have to detonate fourteen million dollars worth of research.
00:04:00
"The bomb should reduce our fake town to ash.
"The monkey... we'll know soon enough..."
00:03:55
"Ah, shoot!"
00:03:50
CAM 1
JONES, RICK
Of all the lame-brained...
ABORT

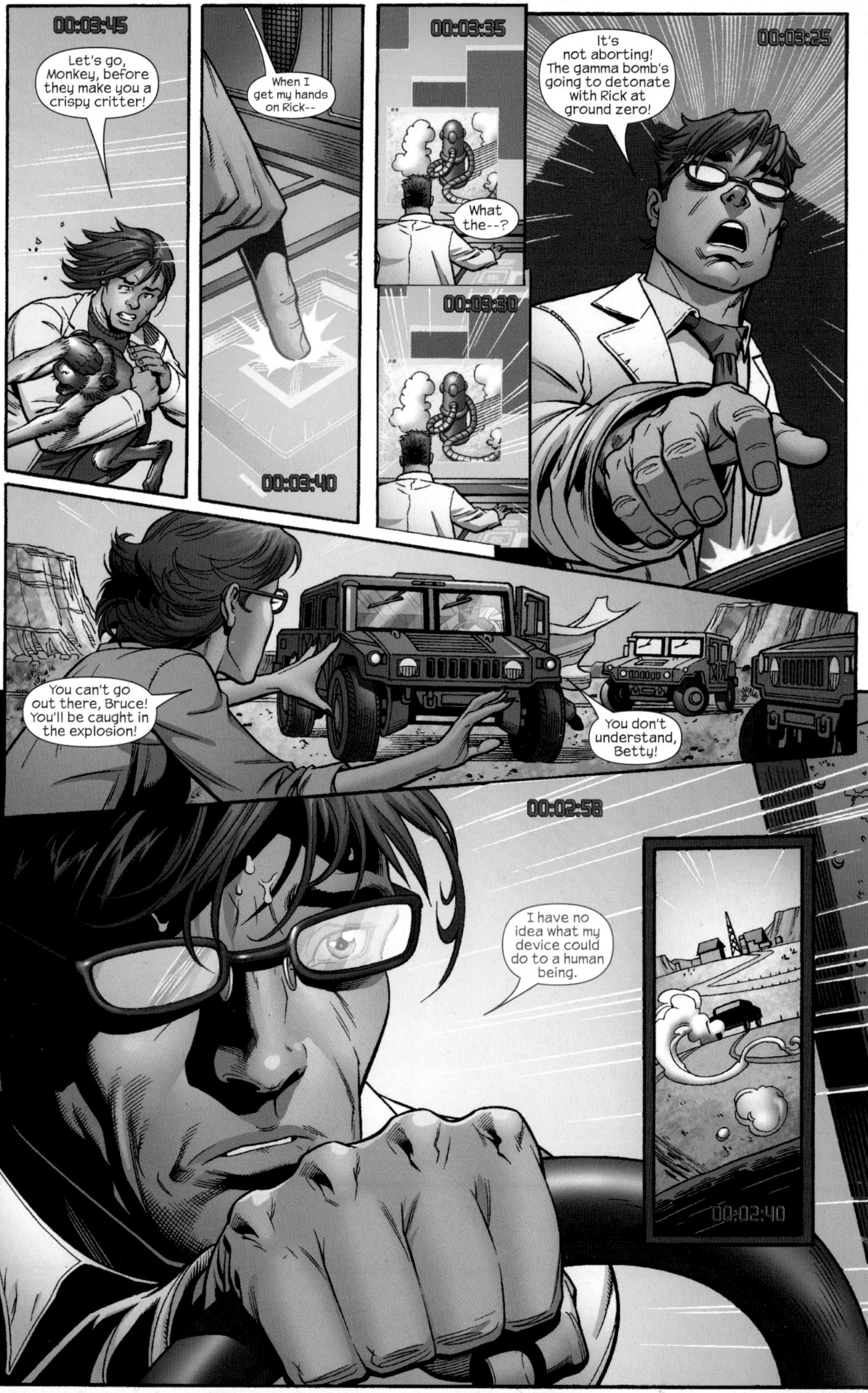
00:03:45
Let's go, Monkey, before they make you a crispy critter!
When I get my hands on Rick--
00:03:40
00:03:35
What the--?
00:03:30
It's not aborting! The gamma bomb's going to detonate with Rick at ground zero!
00:03:25
You can't go out there, Bruce! You'll be caught in the explosion!
You don't understand, Betty!
00:02:58
I have no idea what my device could do to a human being.
00:02:40

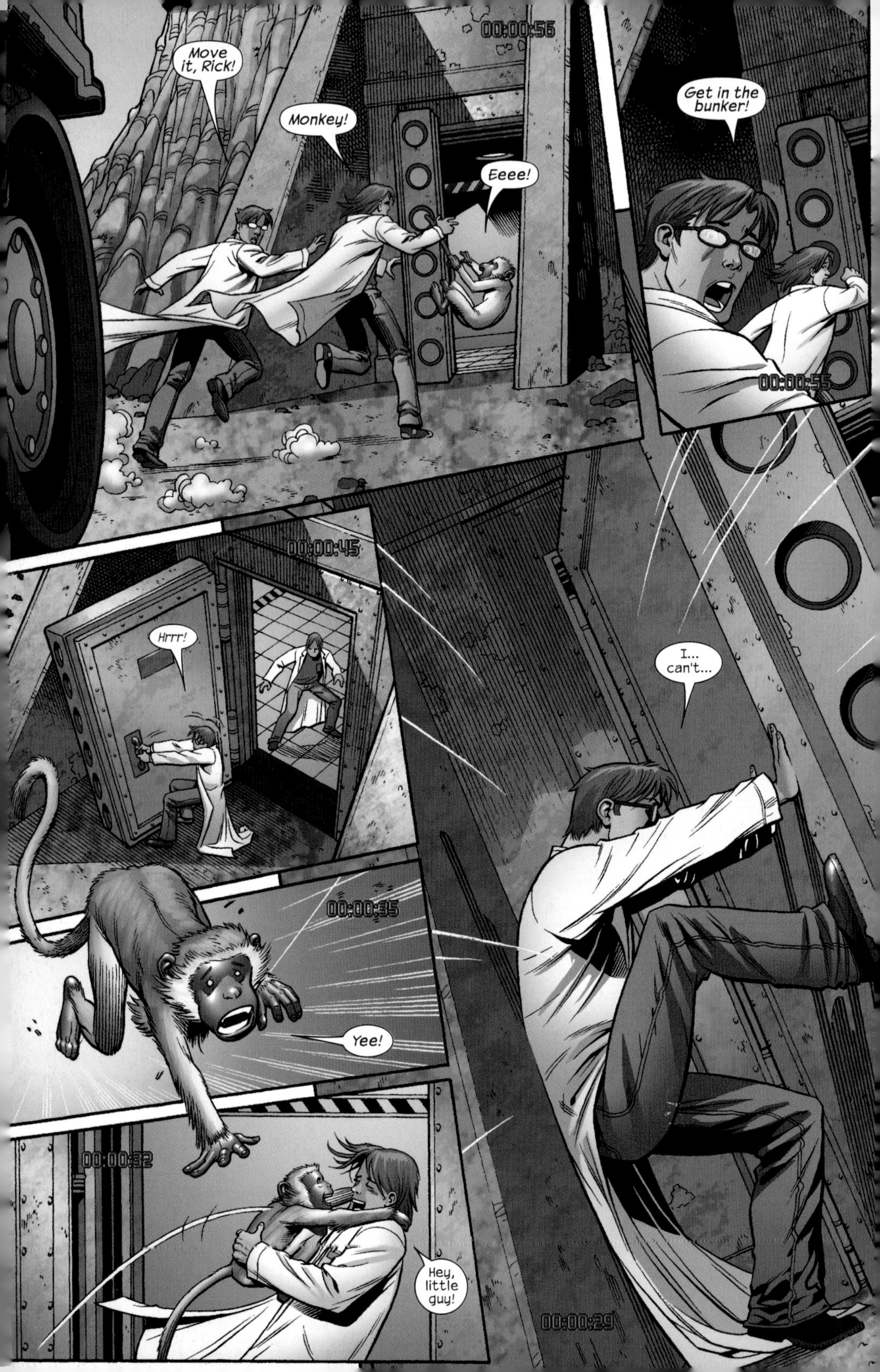
00:00:56
Move it, Rick!
Monkey!
Eeee!
Get in the bunker!
00:00:55
00:00:45
Hrrr!
00:00:35
Yee!
00:00:32
Hey, little guy!
I... can't...
00:00:29

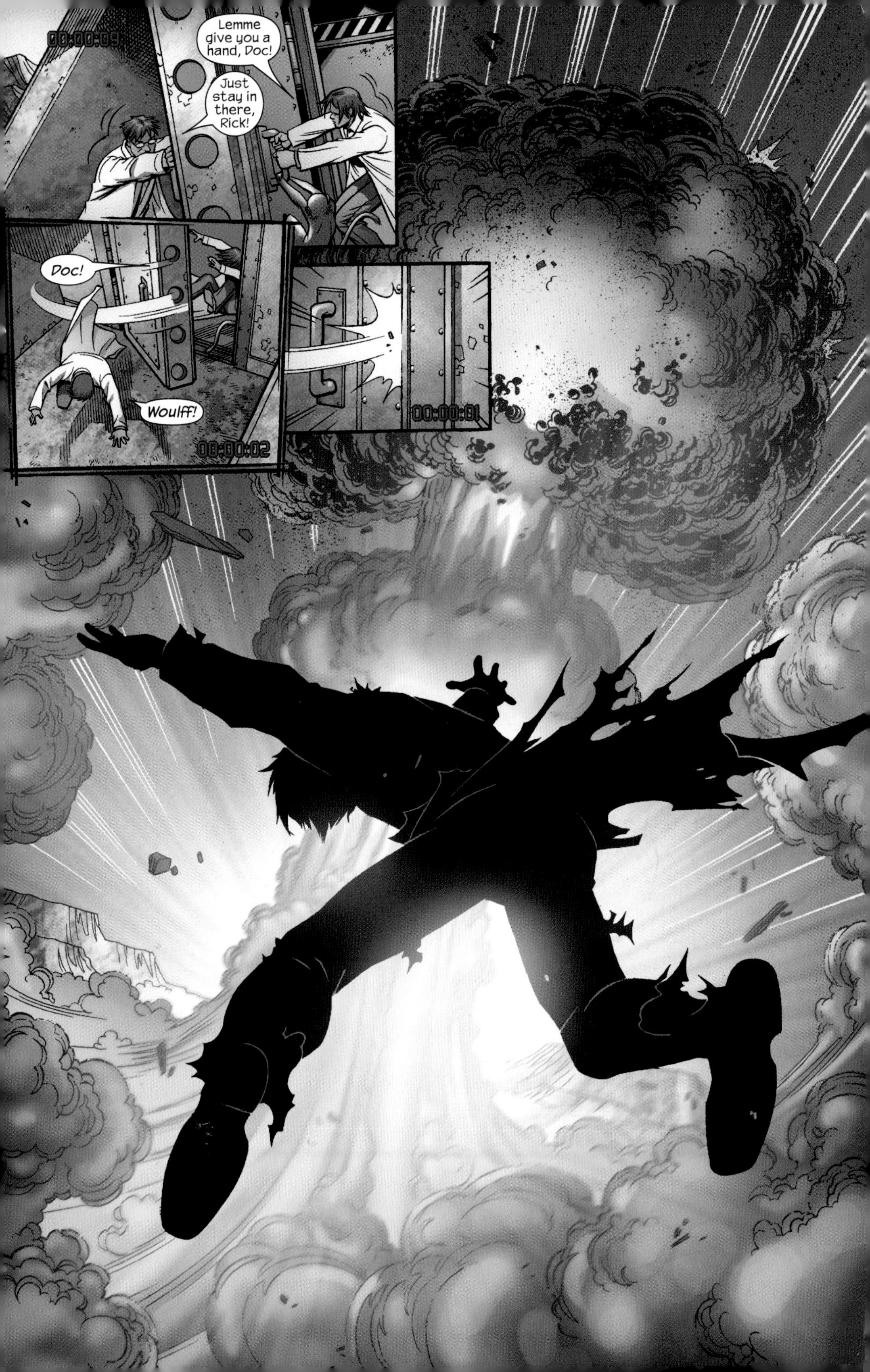
00:00:09
Lemme give you a hand, Doc!
Just stay in there, Rick!
Doc!
Woulff!
00:00:02
00:00:01

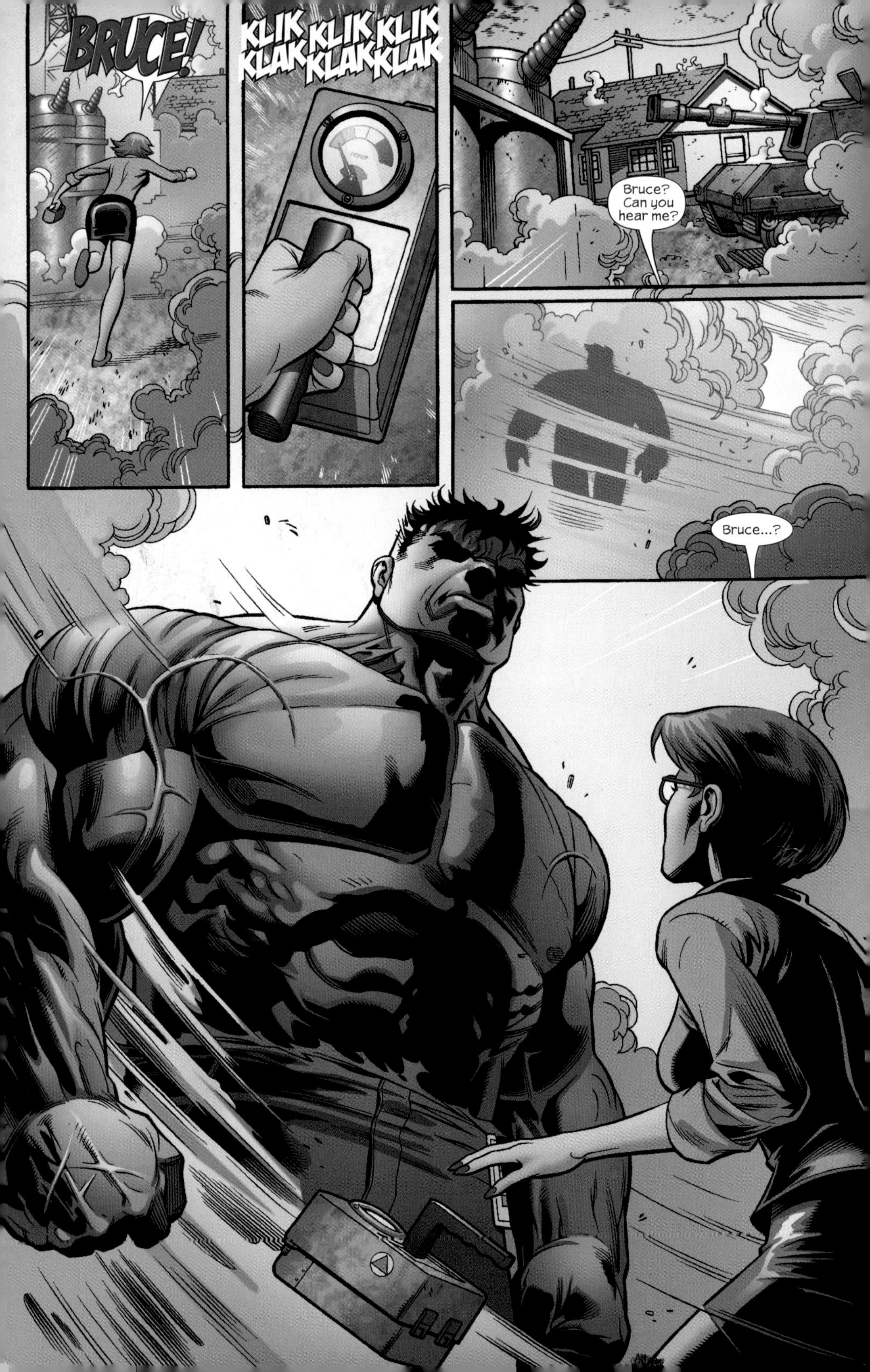

BRUCE!
KLIK KLAK KLIK KLAK KLIK KLAK
Bruce? Can you hear me?
Bruce...?

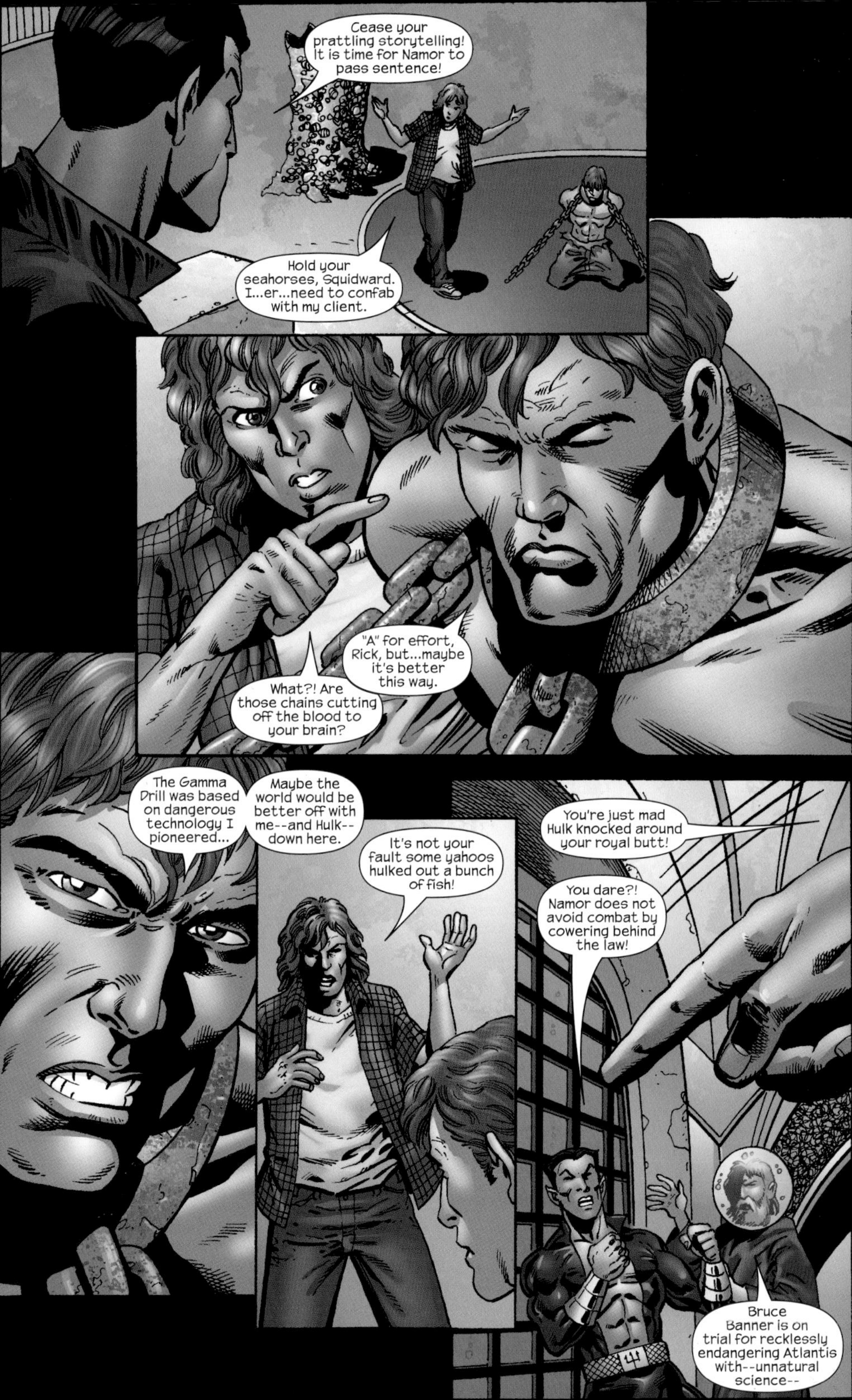
Cease your prattling storytelling! It is time for Namor to pass sentence!
Hold your seahorses, Squidward. I...er...need to confab with my client.
"A" for effort, Rick, but...maybe it's better this way.
What?! Are those chains cutting off the blood to your brain?
The Gamma Drill was based on dangerous technology I pioneered...
Maybe the world would be better off with me--and Hulk--down here.
It's not your fault some yahoos hulked out a bunch of fish!
You're just mad Hulk knocked around your royal butt!
You dare?! Namor does not avoid combat by cowering behind the law!
Bruce Banner is on trial for recklessly endangering Atlantis with--unnatural science--

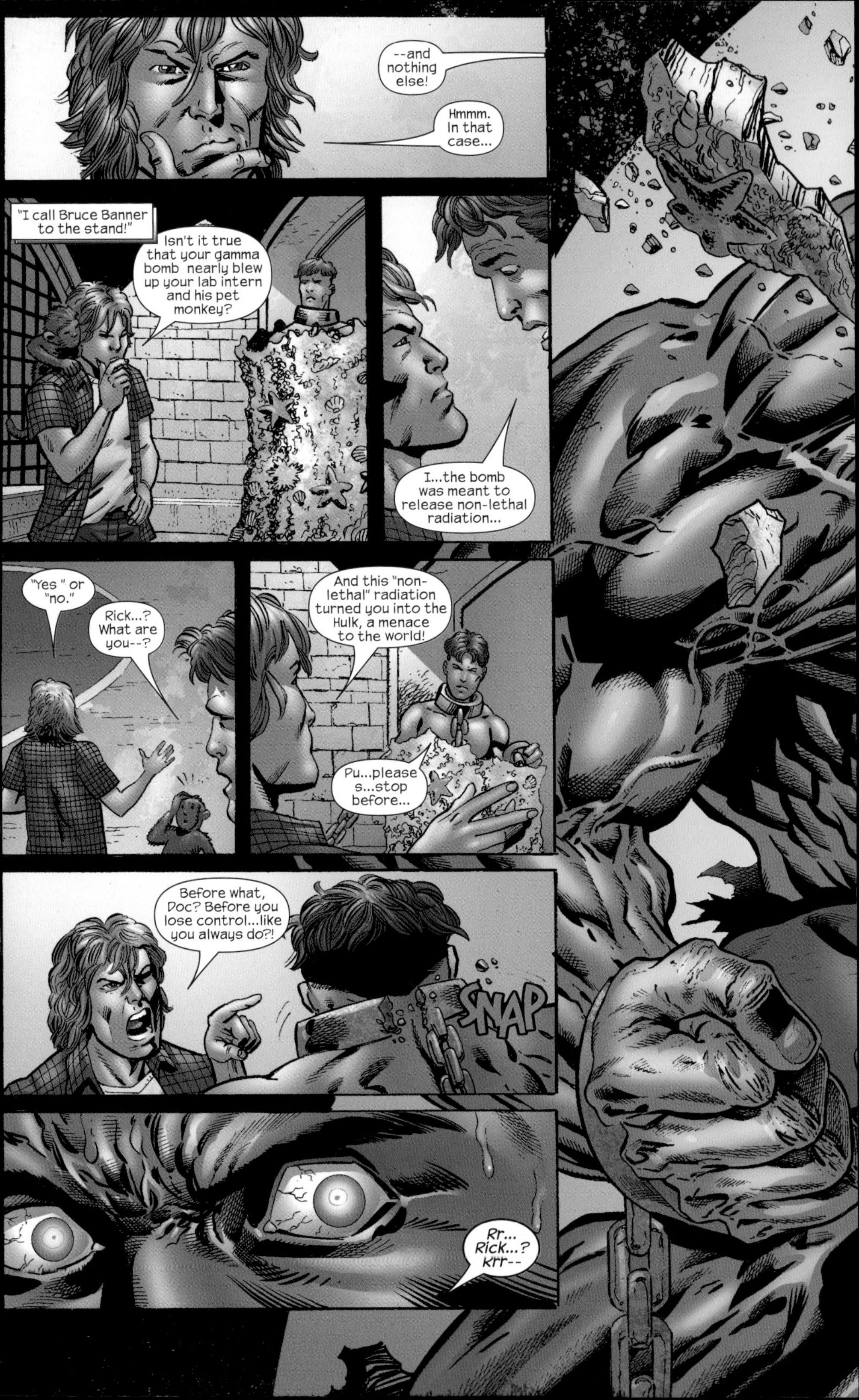
--and nothing else!
Hmmm. In that case...
"I call Bruce Banner to the stand!"
Isn't it true that your gamma bomb nearly blew up your lab intern and his pet monkey?
I...the bomb was meant to release non-lethal radiation...
"Yes" or "no."
Rick...? What are you--?
And this "non-lethal" radiation turned you into the Hulk, a menace to the world!
Pu...please s...stop before...
Before what, Doc? Before you lose control...like you always do?!
SNAP
Rr... Rick...? krr--

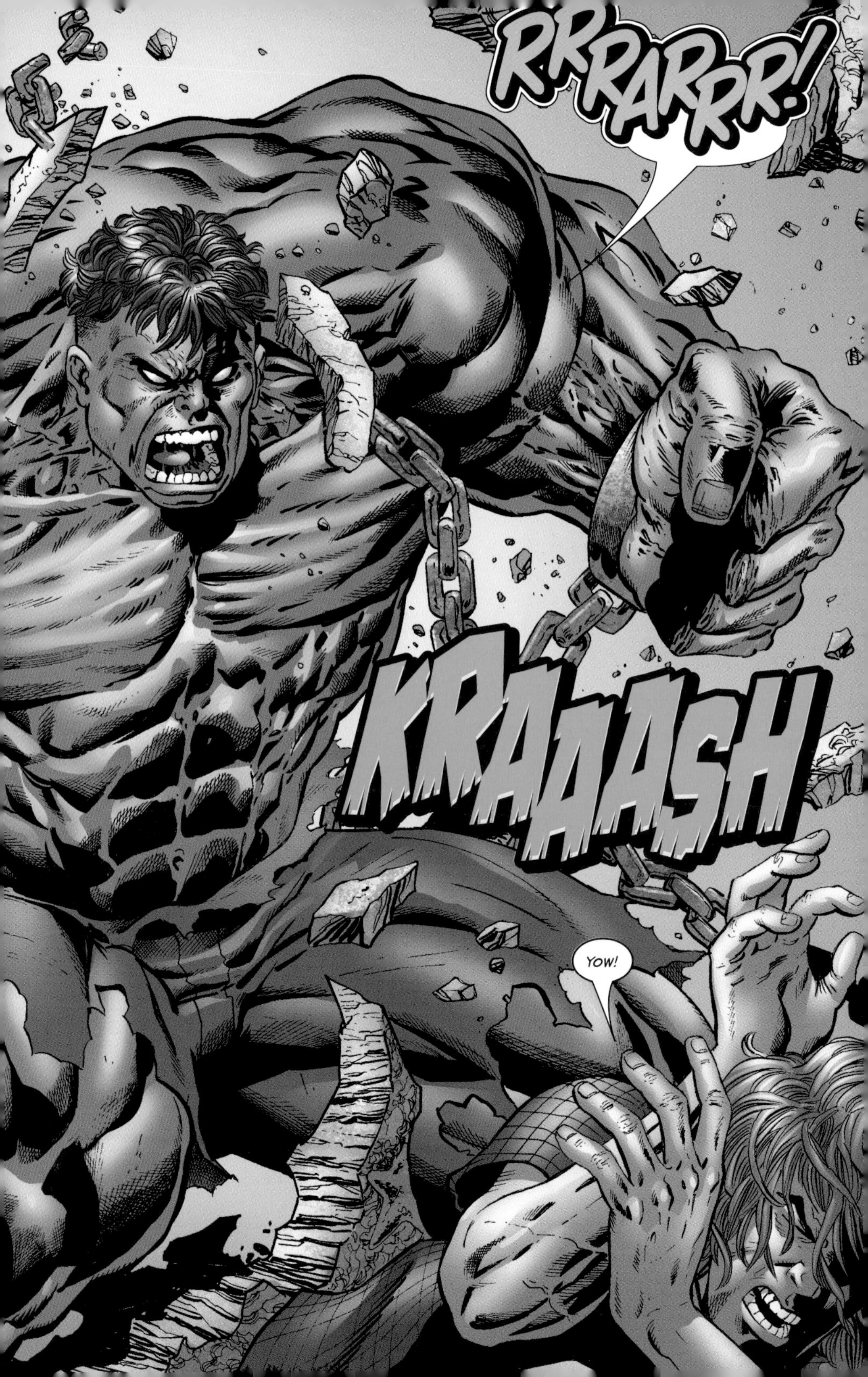
RRRARRR!
KRAAAASH
YOW!

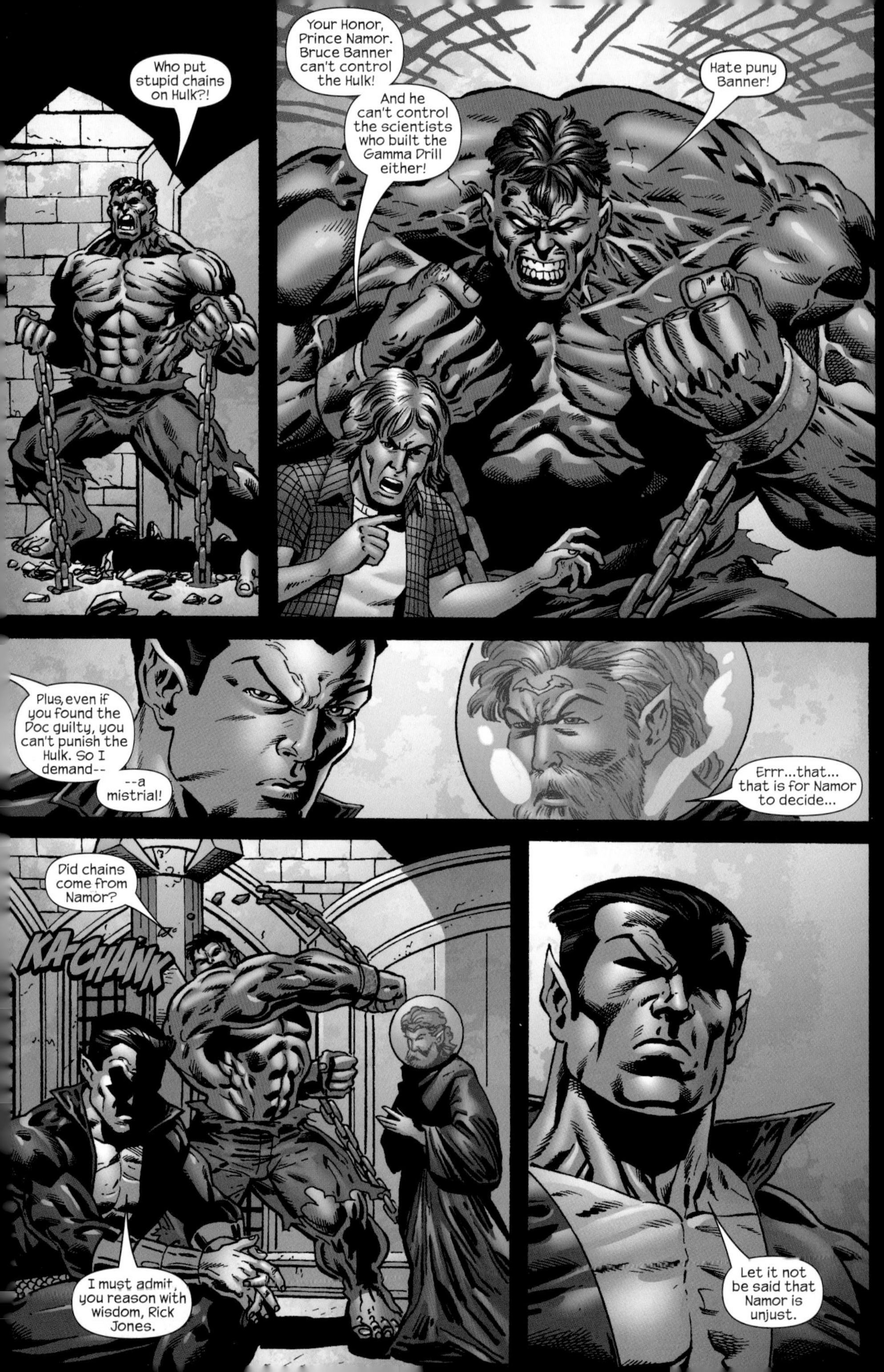
Who put stupid chains on Hulk?!
Your Honor, Prince Namor. Bruce Banner can't control the Hulk!
And he can't control the scientists who built the Gamma Drill either!
Hate puny Banner!
Plus, even if you found the Doc guilty, you can't punish the Hulk. So I demand--
--a mistrial!
Errr...that... that is for Namor to decide...
Did chains come from Namor?
KA-CHANK
I must admit, you reason with wisdom, Rick Jones.
Let it not be said that Namor is unjust.

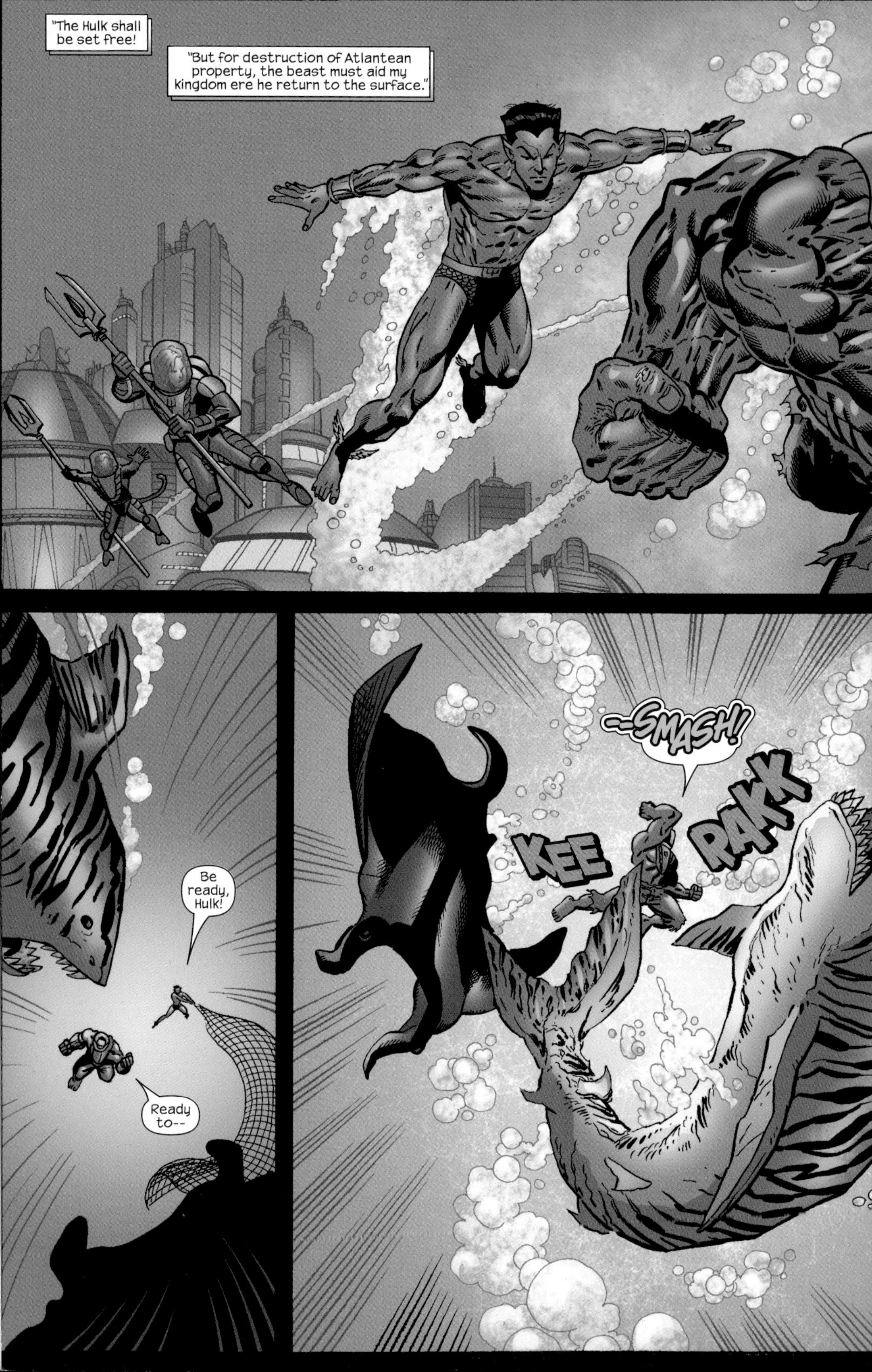
"The Hulk shall be set free!
"But for destruction of Atlantean property, the beast must aid my kingdom ere he return to the surface."
Be ready, Hulk!
Ready to--
--SMASH!
KEE RAKK

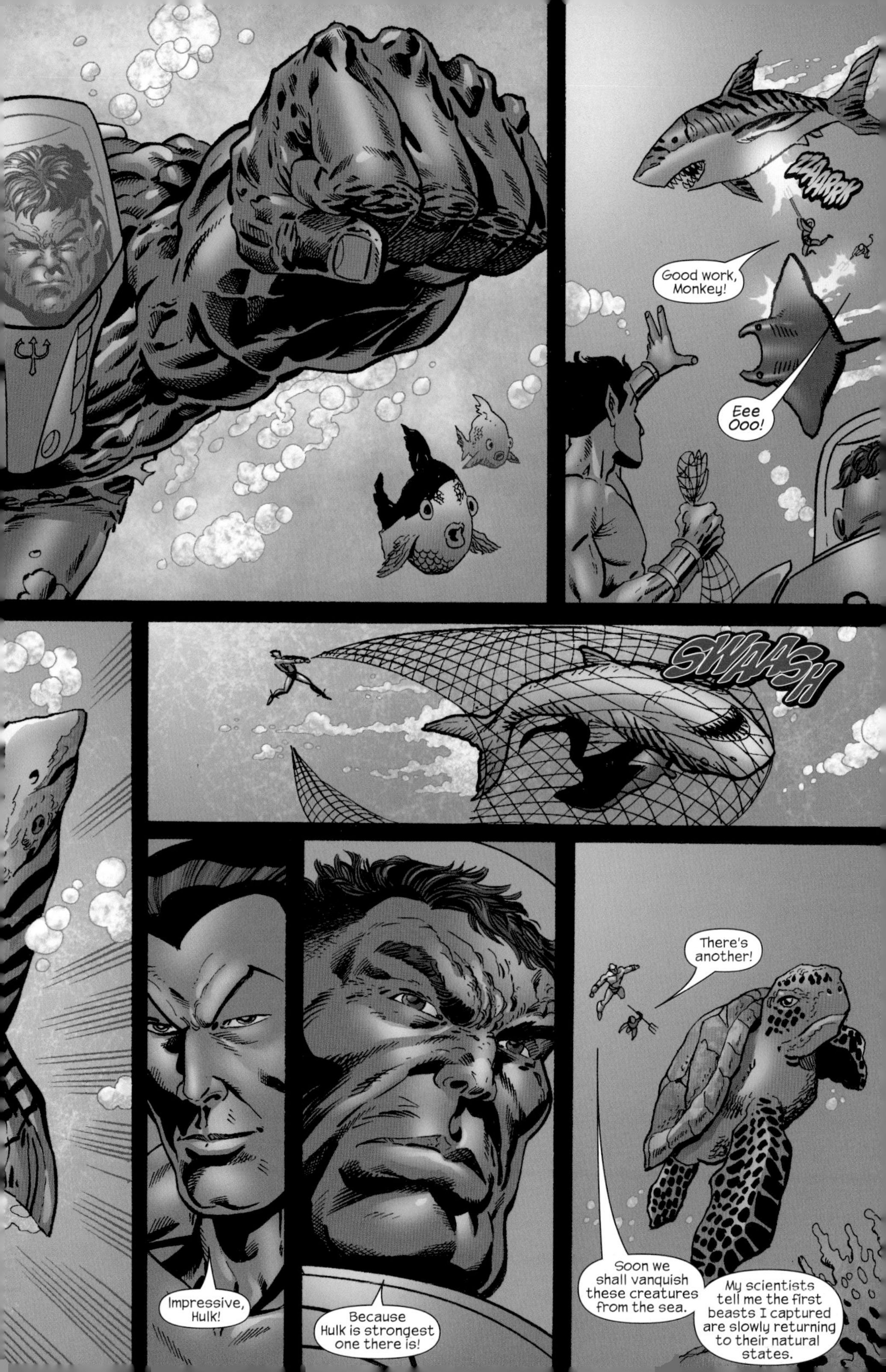

ZAARK
Good work, Monkey!
Eee Ooo!
SWAASH
Impressive, Hulk!
Because Hulk is strongest one there is!
There's another!
Soon we shall vanquish these creatures from the sea.
My scientists tell me the first beasts I captured are slowly returning to their natural states.

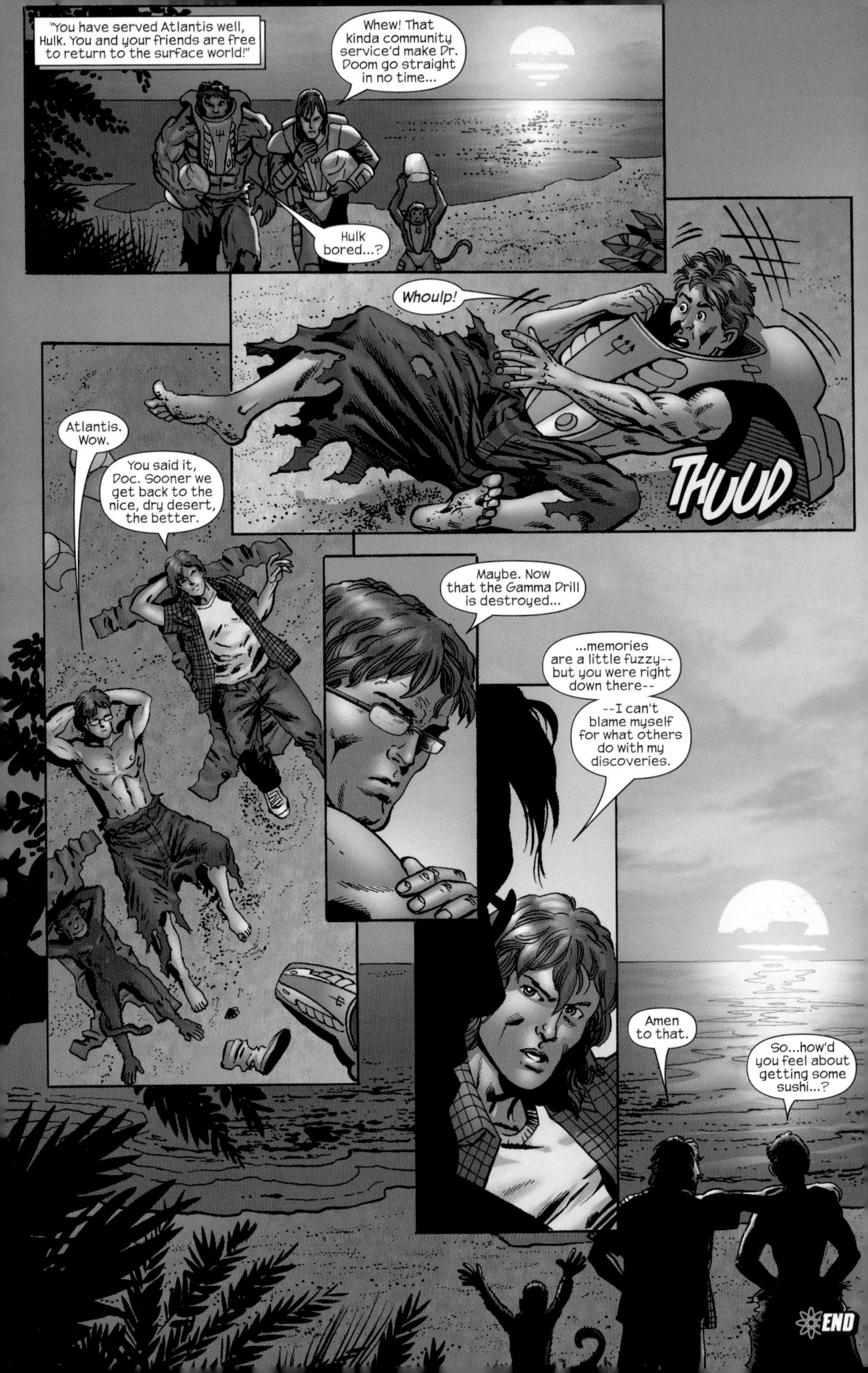
"You have served Atlantis well, Hulk. You and your friends are free to return to the surface world!"
Whew! That kinda community service'd make Dr. Doom go straight in no time...
Hulk bored...?
Whoulp!
THUUD
Atlantis. Wow.
You said it, Doc. Sooner we get back to the nice, dry desert, the better.
Maybe. Now that the Gamma Drill is destroyed...
...memories are a little fuzzy--but you were right down there--
--I can't blame myself for what others do with my discoveries.
Amen to that.
So...how'd you feel about getting some sushi...?
END

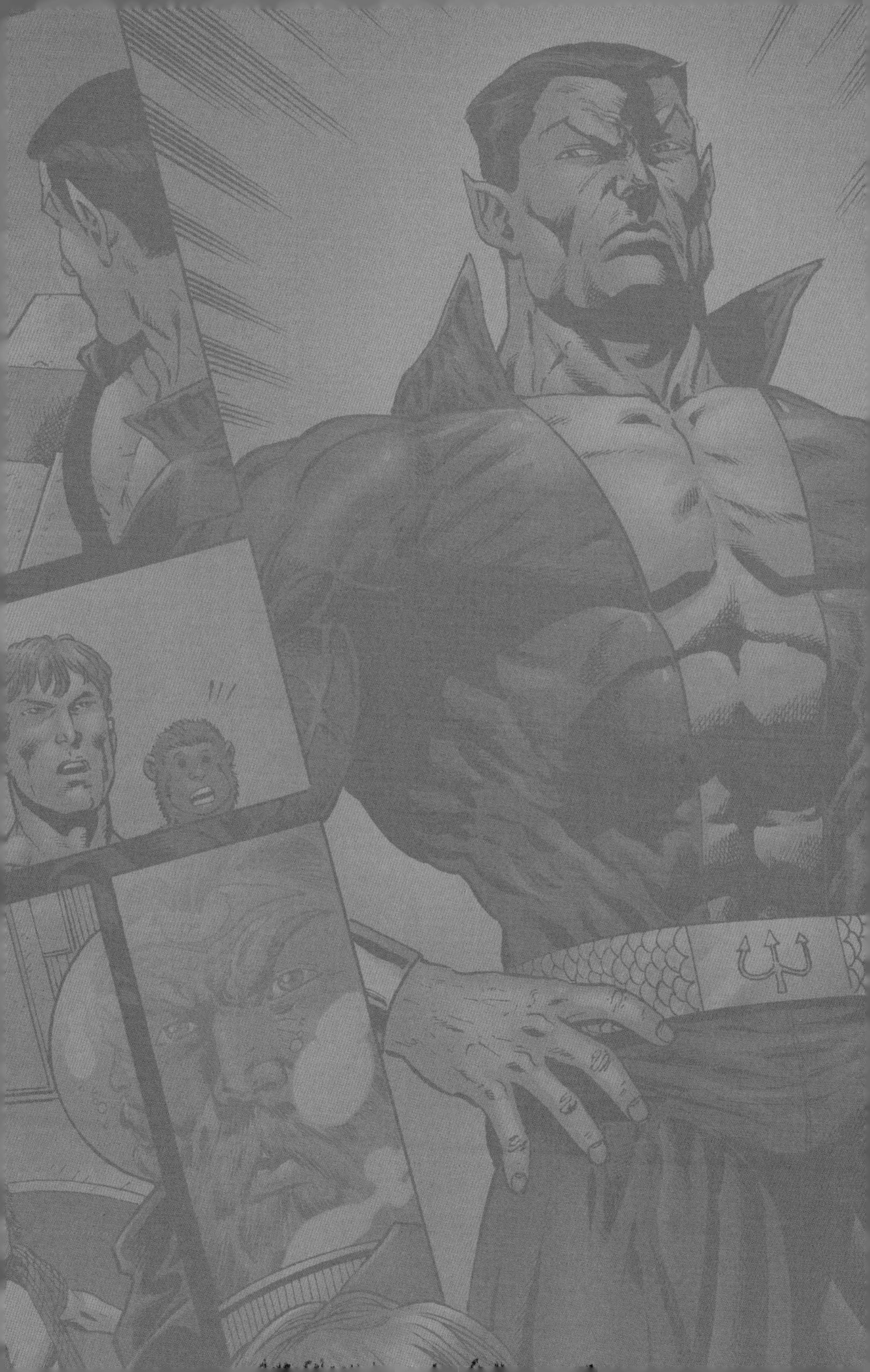

07

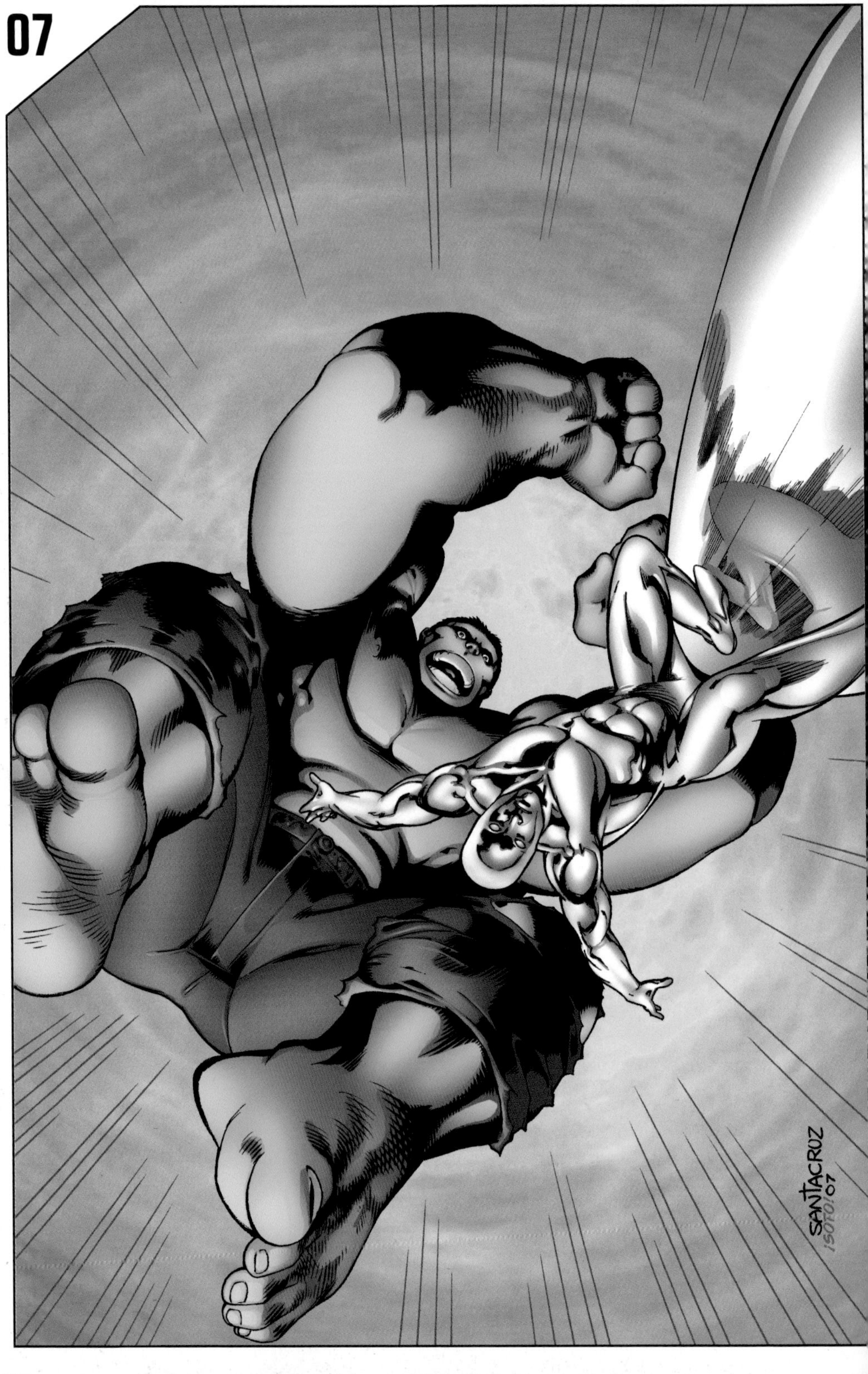
SANTACRUZ

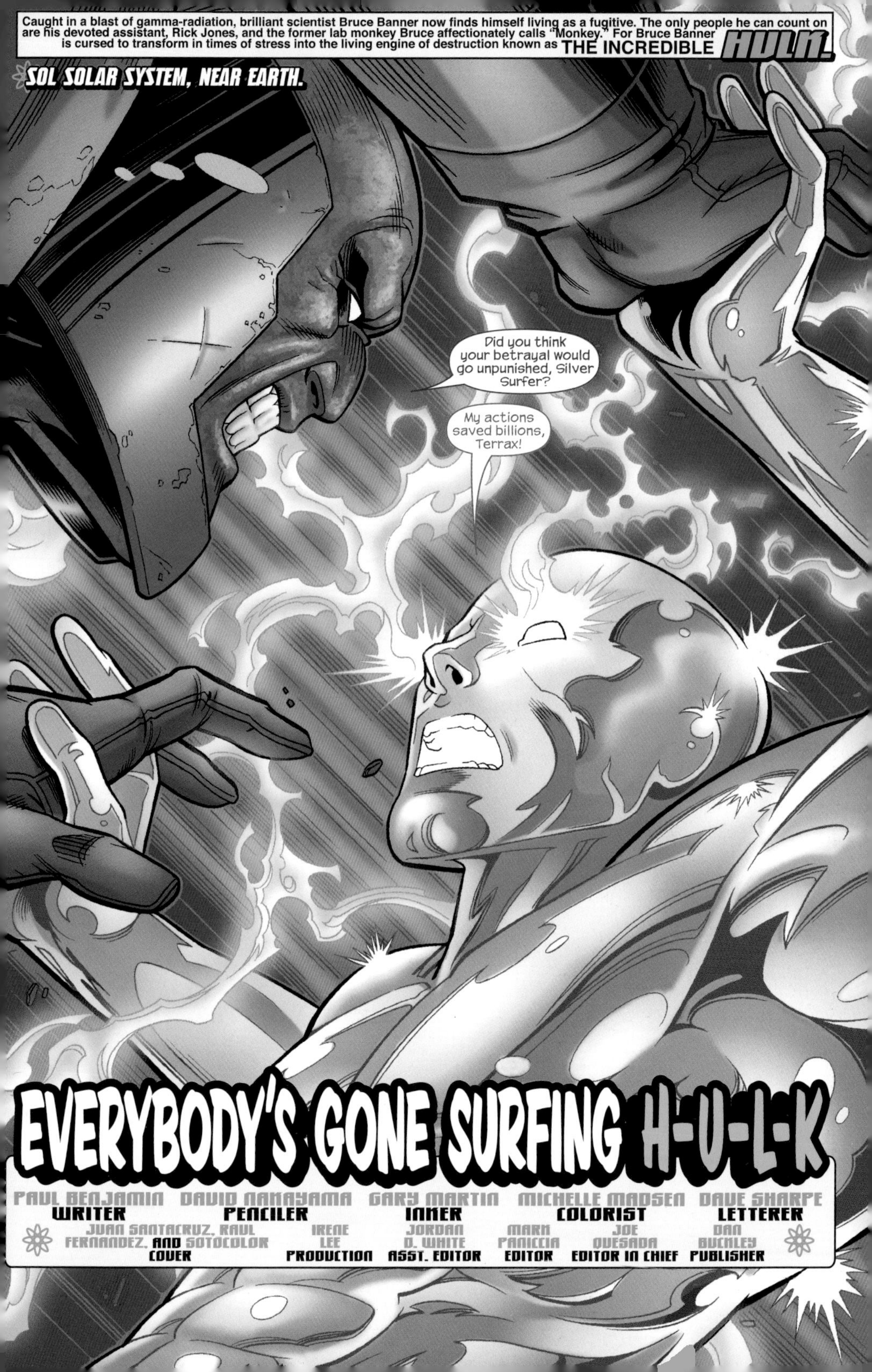
Caught in a blast of gamma-radiation, brilliant scientist Bruce Banner now finds himself living as a fugitive. The only people he can count on are his devoted assistant, Rick Jones, and the former lab monkey Bruce affectionately calls "Monkey." For Bruce Banner is cursed to transform in times of stress into the living engine of destruction known as THE INCREDIBLE HULK.
SOL SOLAR SYSTEM, NEAR EARTH.
Did you think your betrayal would go unpunished, Silver Surfer?
My actions saved billions, Terrax!
EVERYBODY'S GONE SURFING H-U-L-K
PAUL BENJAMIN WRITER
DAVID NAKAYAMA PENCILER
GARY MARTIN INKER
MICHELLE MADSEN COLORIST
DAVE SHARPE LETTERER
JUAN SANTACRUZ, RAUL FERNANDEZ, AND SOTOCOLOR COVER
IRENE LEE PRODUCTION
JORDAN D. WHITE ASST. EDITOR
MARK PANICCIA EDITOR
JOE QUESADA EDITOR IN CHIEF
DAN BUCKLEY PUBLISHER

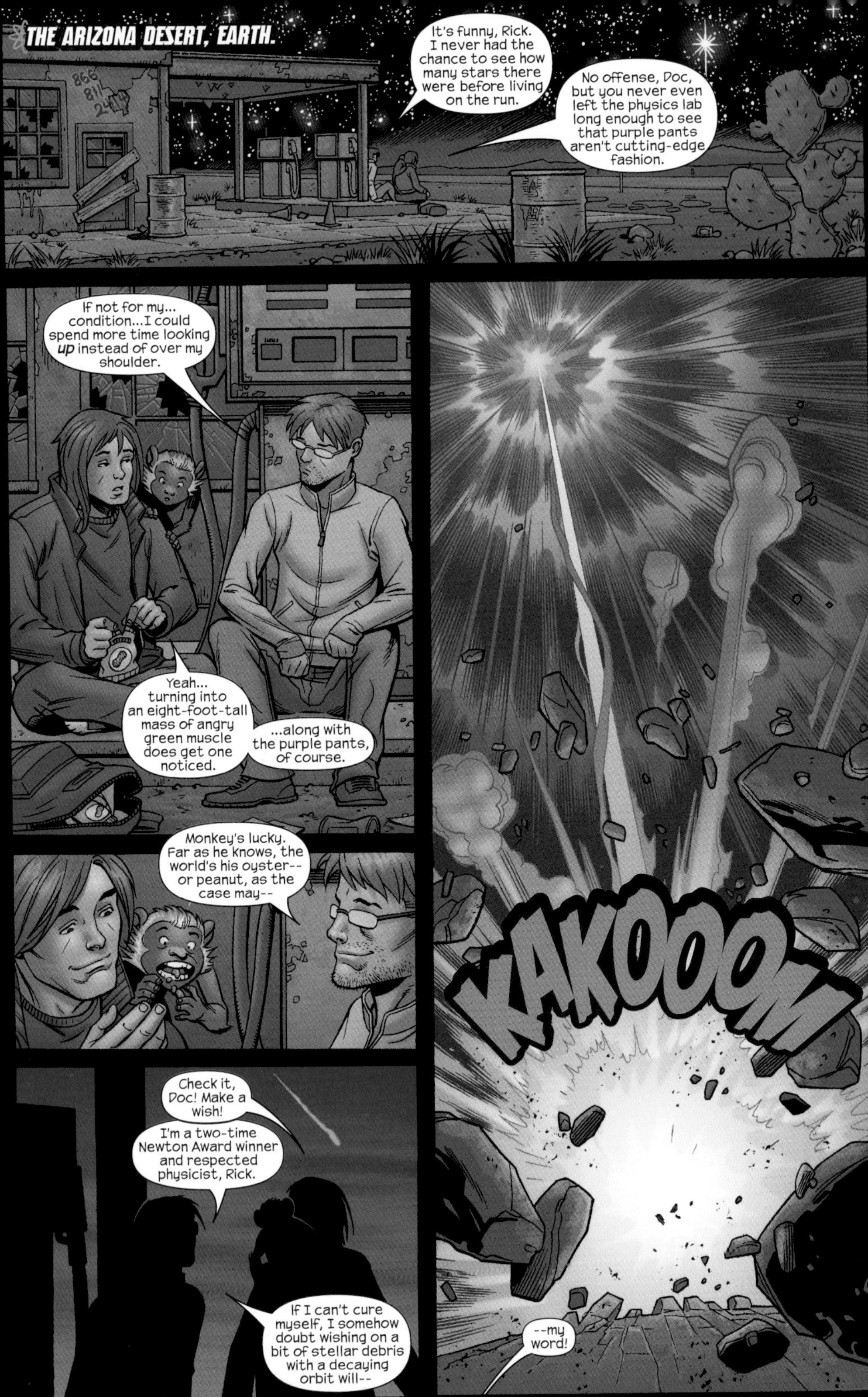
THE ARIZONA DESERT, EARTH.
866 811 2414
It's funny, Rick. I never had the chance to see how many stars there were before living on the run.
No offense, Doc, but you never even left the physics lab long enough to see that purple pants aren't cutting-edge fashion.
If not for my... condition...I could spend more time looking up instead of over my shoulder.
Yeah... turning into an eight-foot-tall mass of angry green muscle does get one noticed.
...along with the purple pants, of course.
Monkey's lucky. Far as he knows, the world's his oyster-- or peanut, as the case may--
KAKOOOM
Check it, Doc! Make a wish!
I'm a two-time Newton Award winner and respected physicist, Rick.
If I can't cure myself, I somehow doubt wishing on a bit of stellar debris with a decaying orbit will--
--my word!

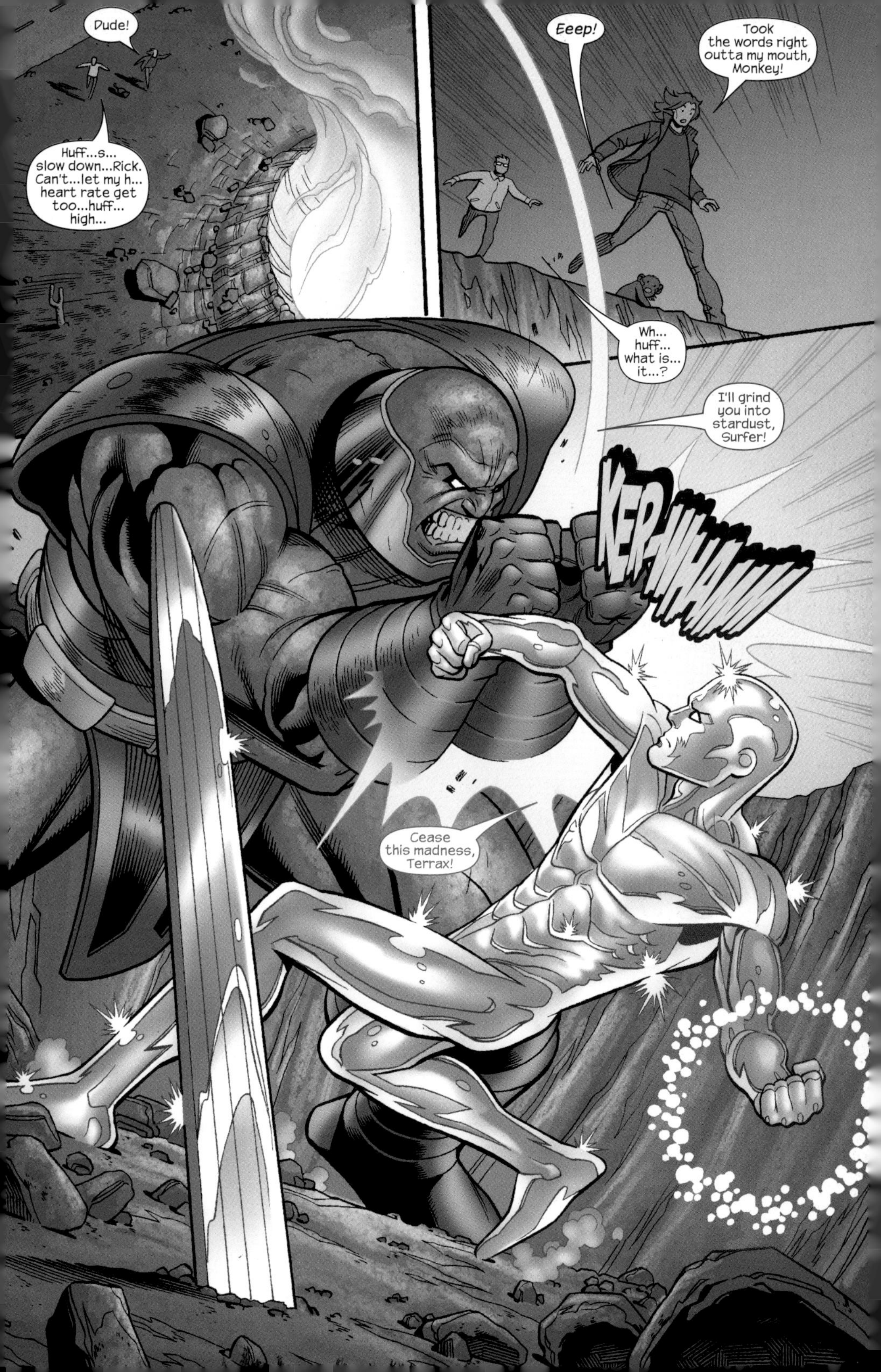
Dude!
Huff...s... slow down...Rick. Can't...let my h... heart rate get too...huff... high...
Eeep!
Took the words right outta my mouth, Monkey!
Wh... huff... what is... it...?
I'll grind you into stardust, Surfer!
KER-WHAMM!
Cease this madness, Terrax!

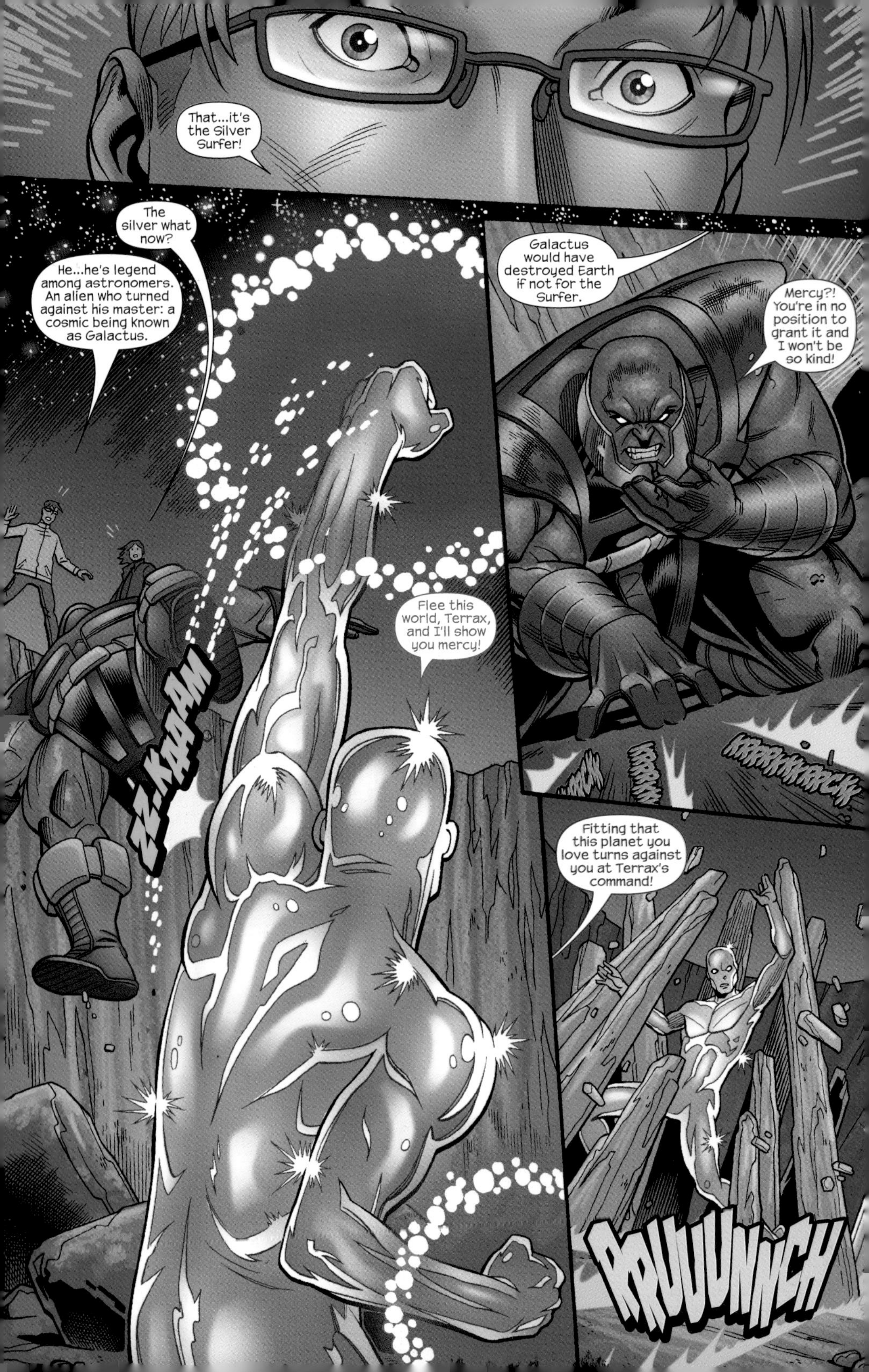
That...it's the Silver Surfer!
The silver what now?
He...he's legend among astronomers. An alien who turned against his master: a cosmic being known as Galactus.
Galactus would have destroyed Earth if not for the Surfer.
Mercy?! You're in no position to grant it and I won't be so kind!
Flee this world, Terrax, and I'll show you mercy!
ZZ-KAAAM
KRRRKKRRCK
Fitting that this planet you love turns against you at Terrax's command!
BRRUUUNNCH

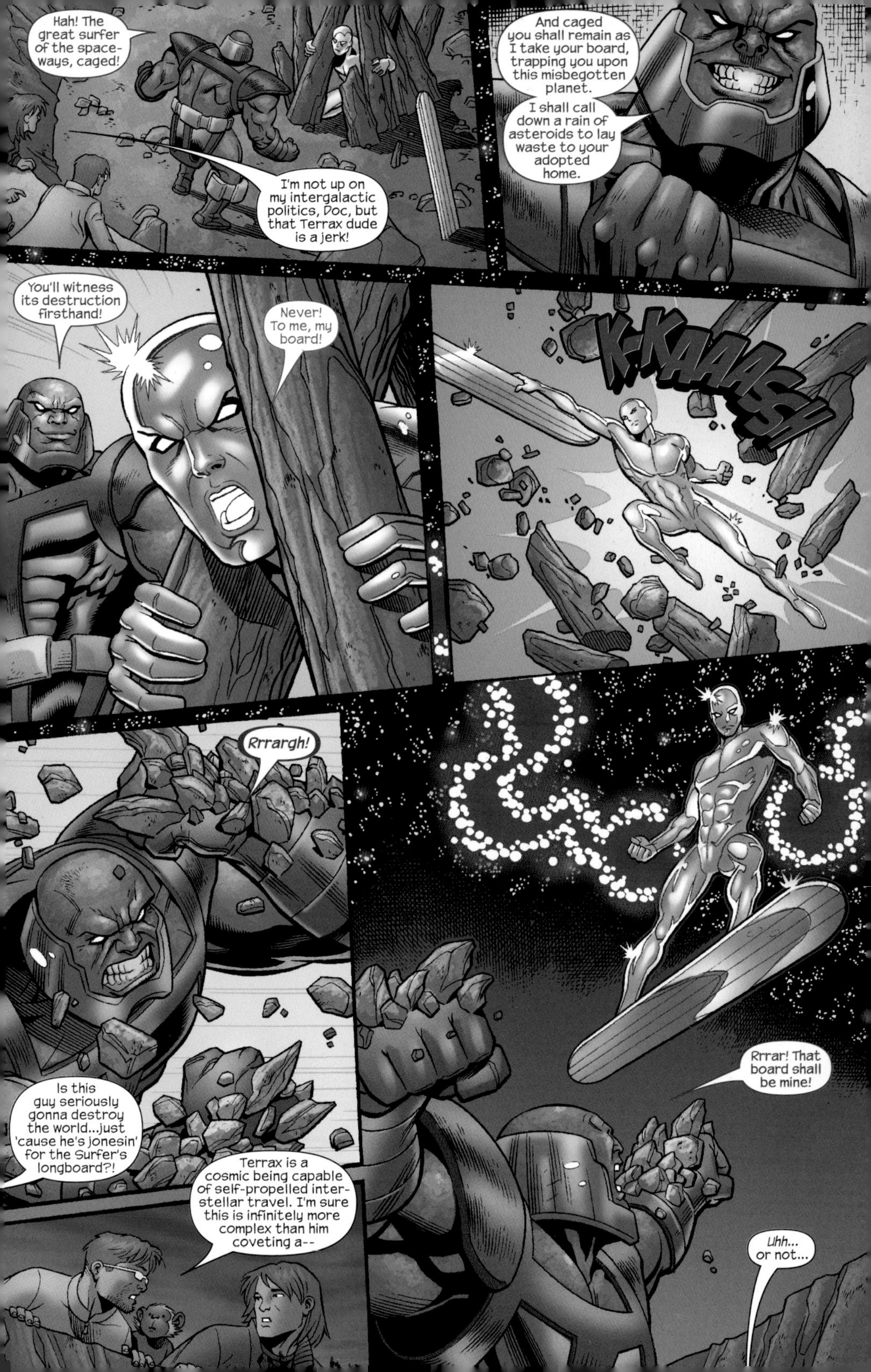
Hah! The great surfer of the space-ways, caged!
I'm not up on my intergalactic politics, Doc, but that Terrax dude is a jerk!
And caged you shall remain as I take your board, trapping you upon this misbegotten planet.
I shall call down a rain of asteroids to lay waste to your adopted home.
You'll witness its destruction firsthand!
Never! To me, my board!
K-KAAAASH
Rrrargh!
Rrrar! That board shall be mine!
Is this guy seriously gonna destroy the world...just 'cause he's jonesin' for the Surfer's longboard?!
Terrax is a cosmic being capable of self-propelled inter-stellar travel. I'm sure this is infinitely more complex than him coveting a--
Uhh... or not...

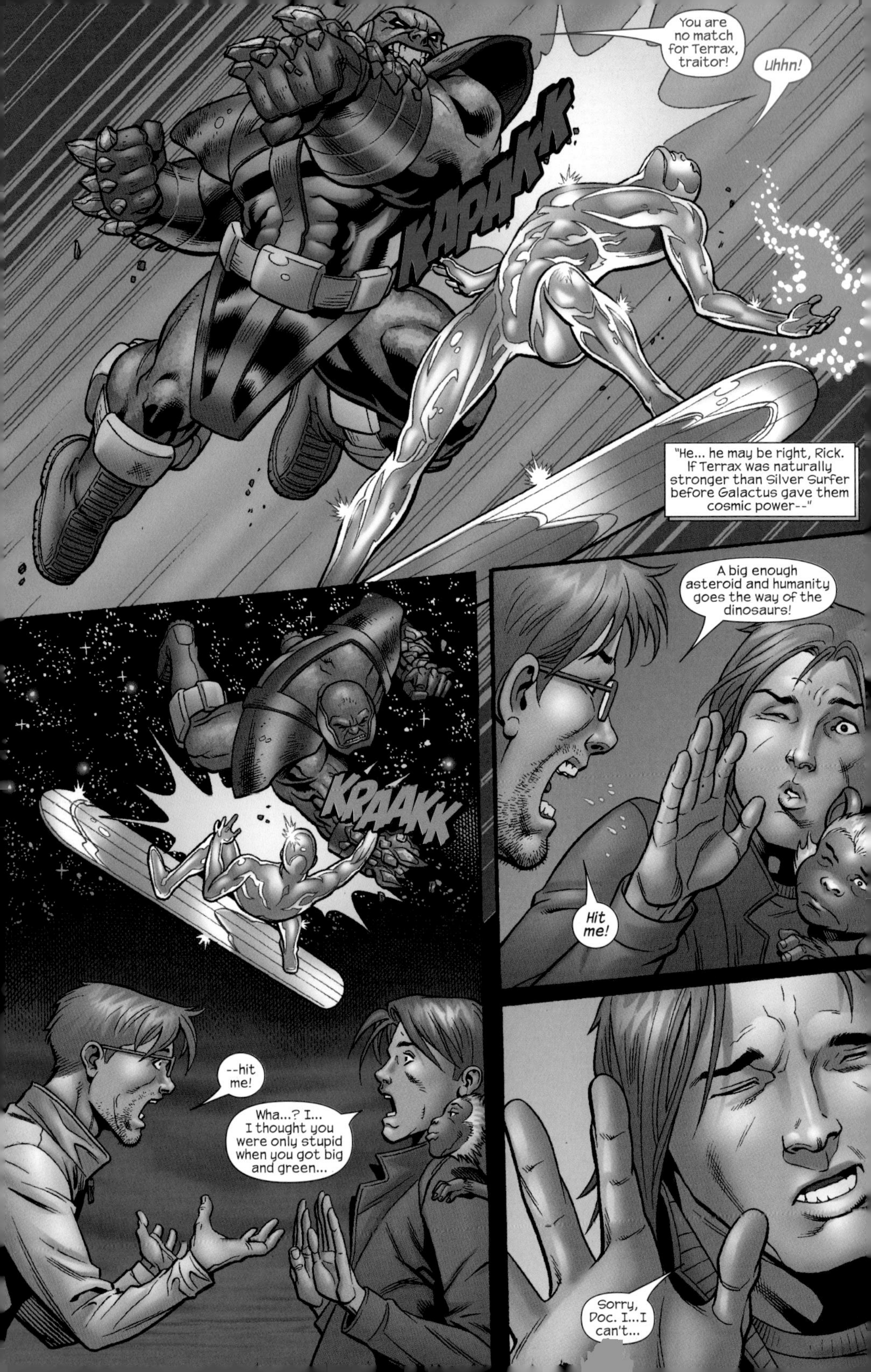
You are no match for Terrax, traitor!
Uhhn!
KAPAKK
"He... he may be right, Rick. If Terrax was naturally stronger than Silver Surfer before Galactus gave them cosmic power--"
KRAAKK
A big enough asteroid and humanity goes the way of the dinosaurs!
Hit me!
--hit me!
Wha...? I... I thought you were only stupid when you got big and green...
Sorry, Doc. I...I can't...

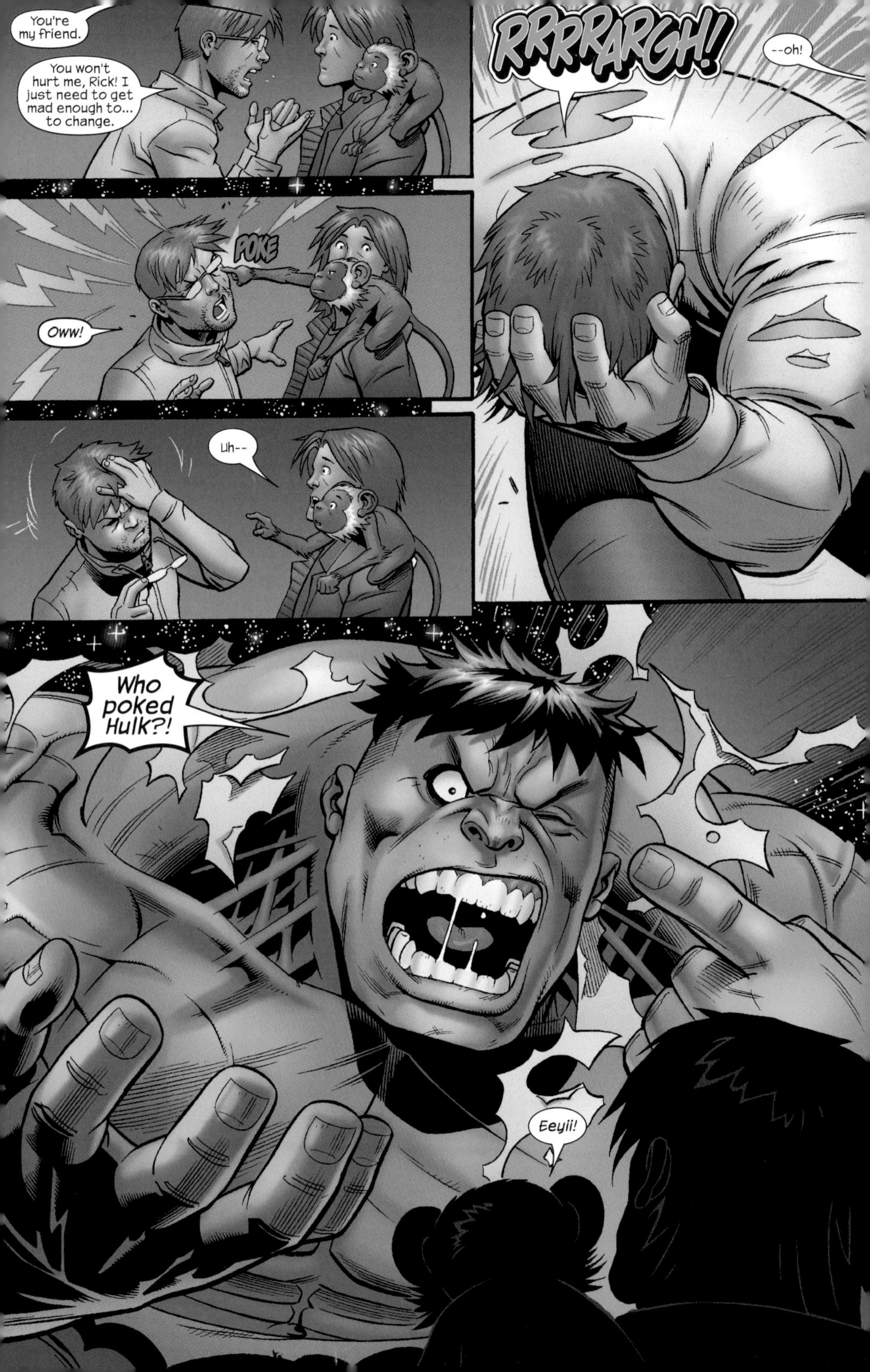
You're my friend.
You won't hurt me, Rick! I just need to get mad enough to... to change.
POKE
Oww!
Uh--
RRRRARGH!
--oh!
Who poked Hulk?!
Eeyii!

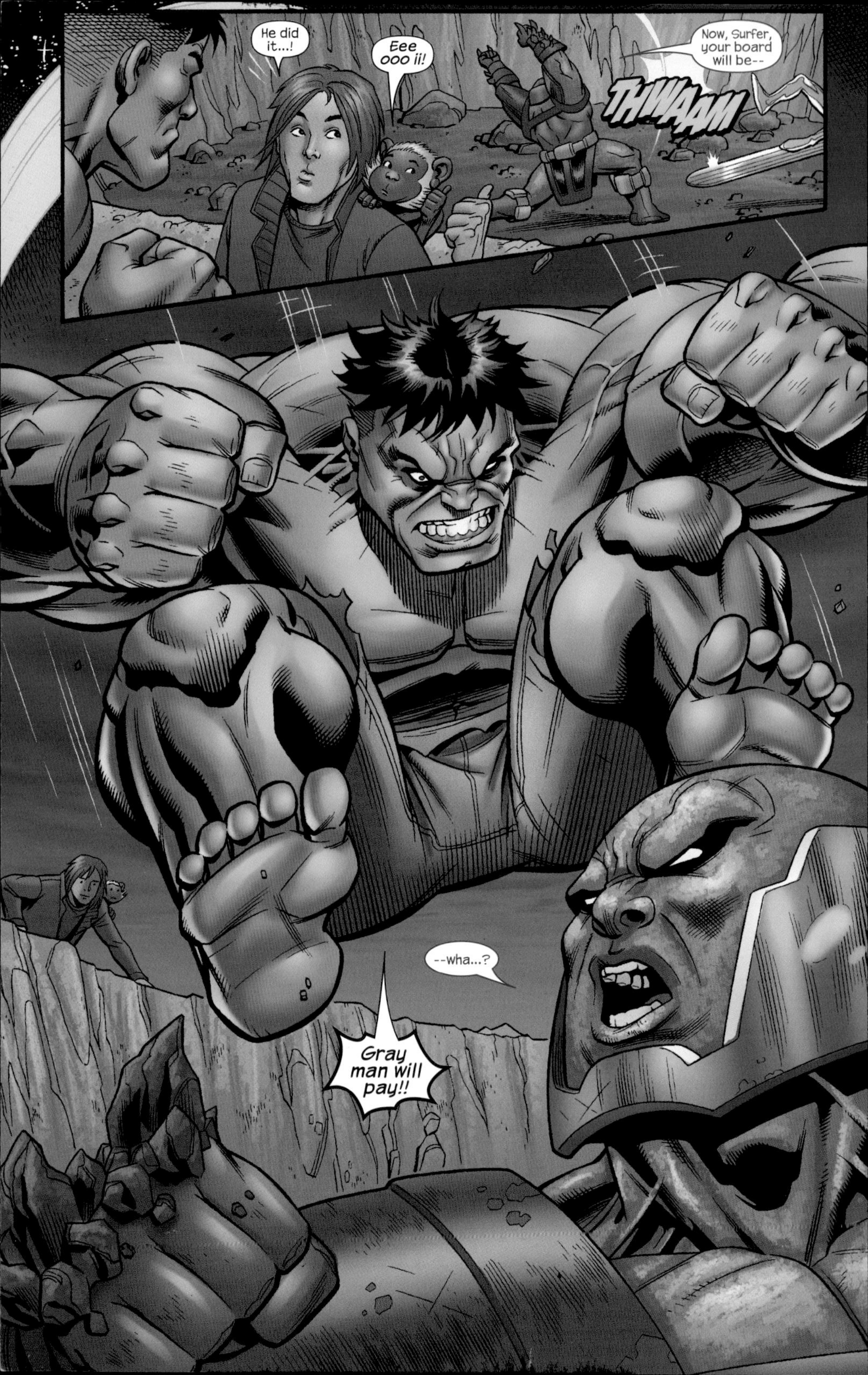
He did it...!
Eee ooo ii!
Now, Surfer, your board will be--
THWAAM
--wha...?
Gray man will pay!!

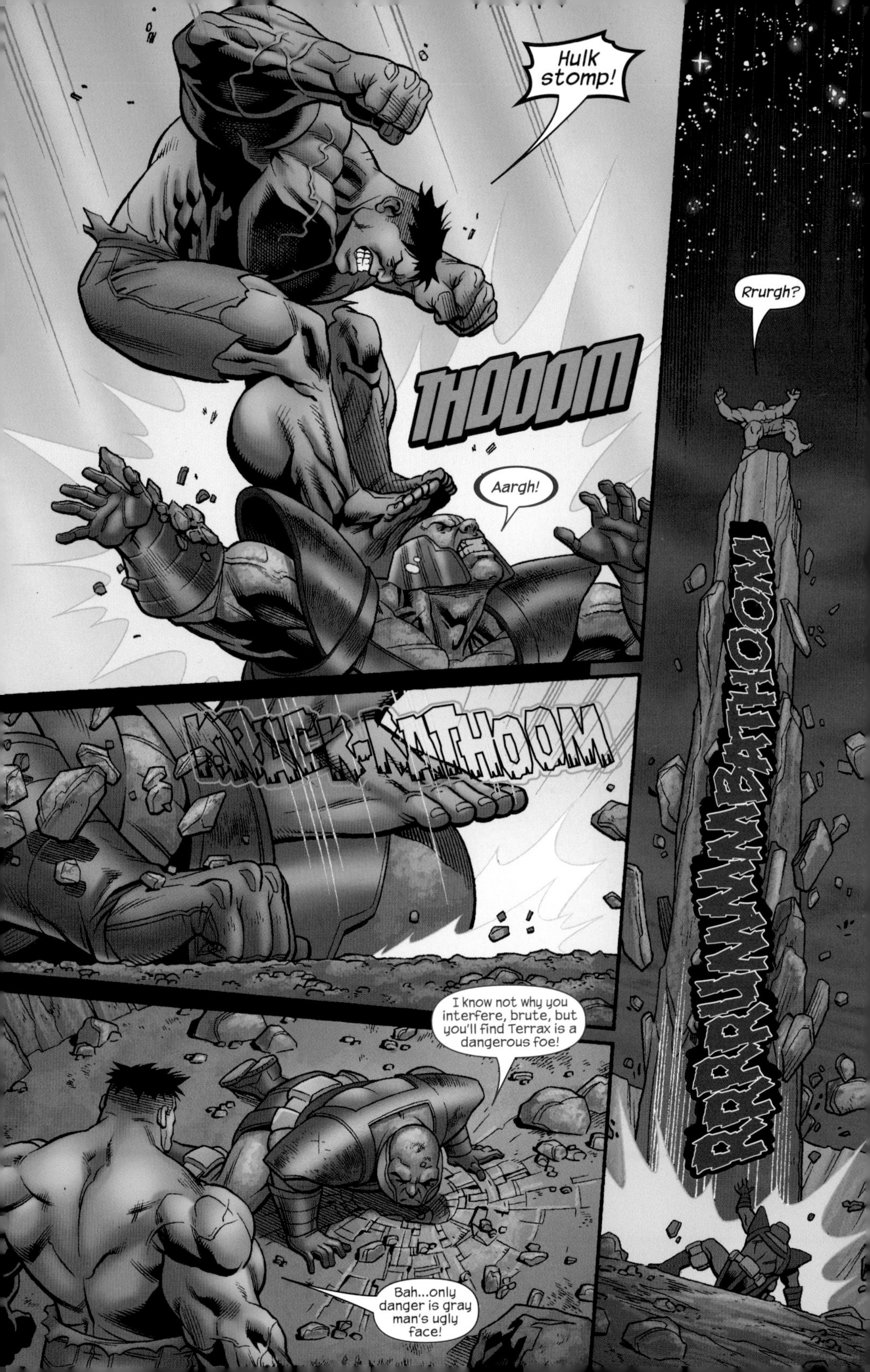
Hulk stomp!
THOOM
Aargh!
Rrurgh?
I know not why you interfere, brute, but you'll find Terrax is a dangerous foe!
Bah...only danger is gray man's ugly face!

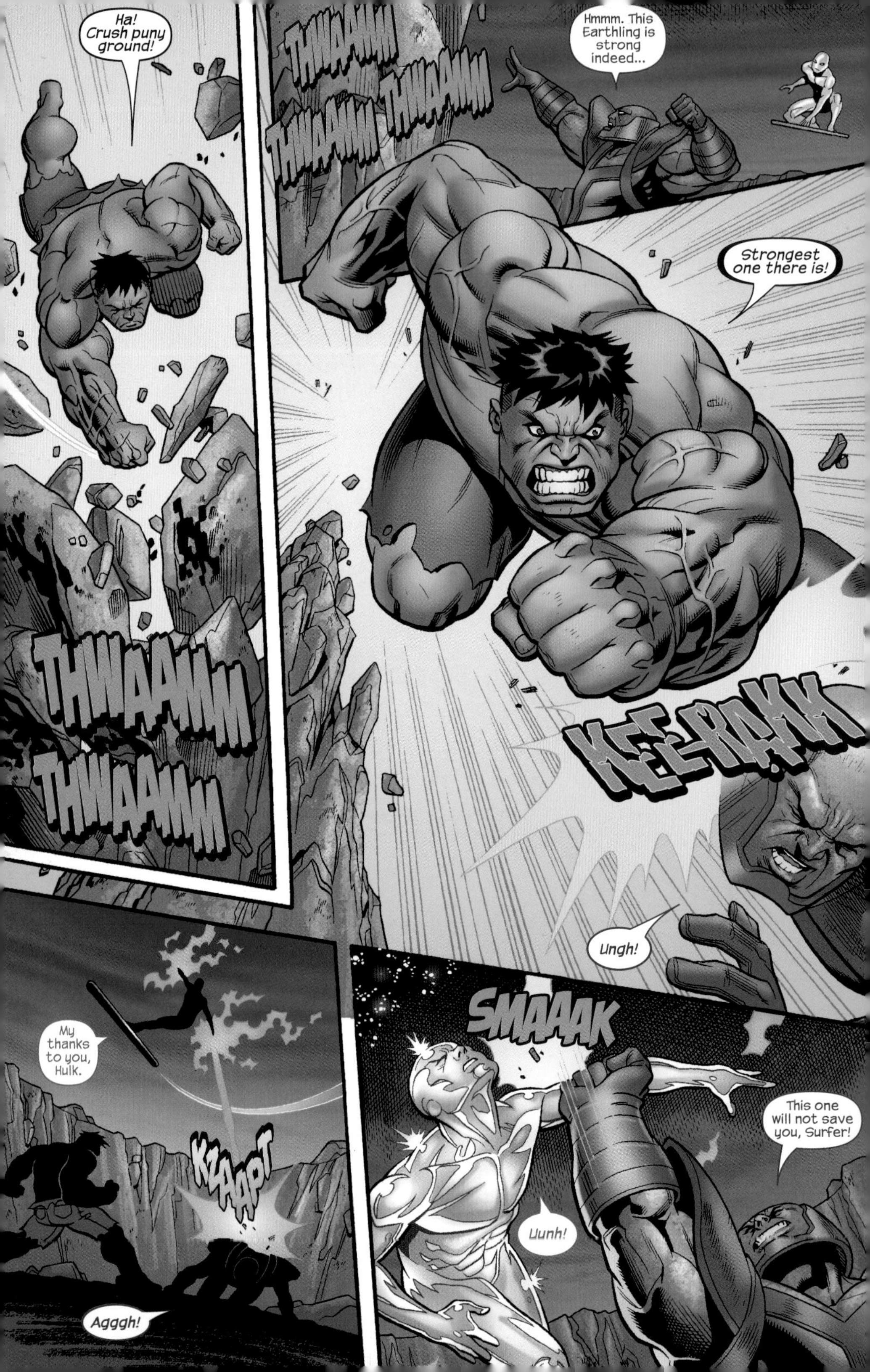
Ha! Crush puny ground!
THWAAMM
THWAAMM
THWAAMM
THWAAMM
THWAAMM
THWAAMM
Hmmm. This Earthling is strong indeed...
Strongest one there is!
KEE-RAKK
Ungh!
My thanks to you, Hulk.
KZAAPT
Agggh!
SMAAAK
This one will not save you, Surfer!
Uunh!

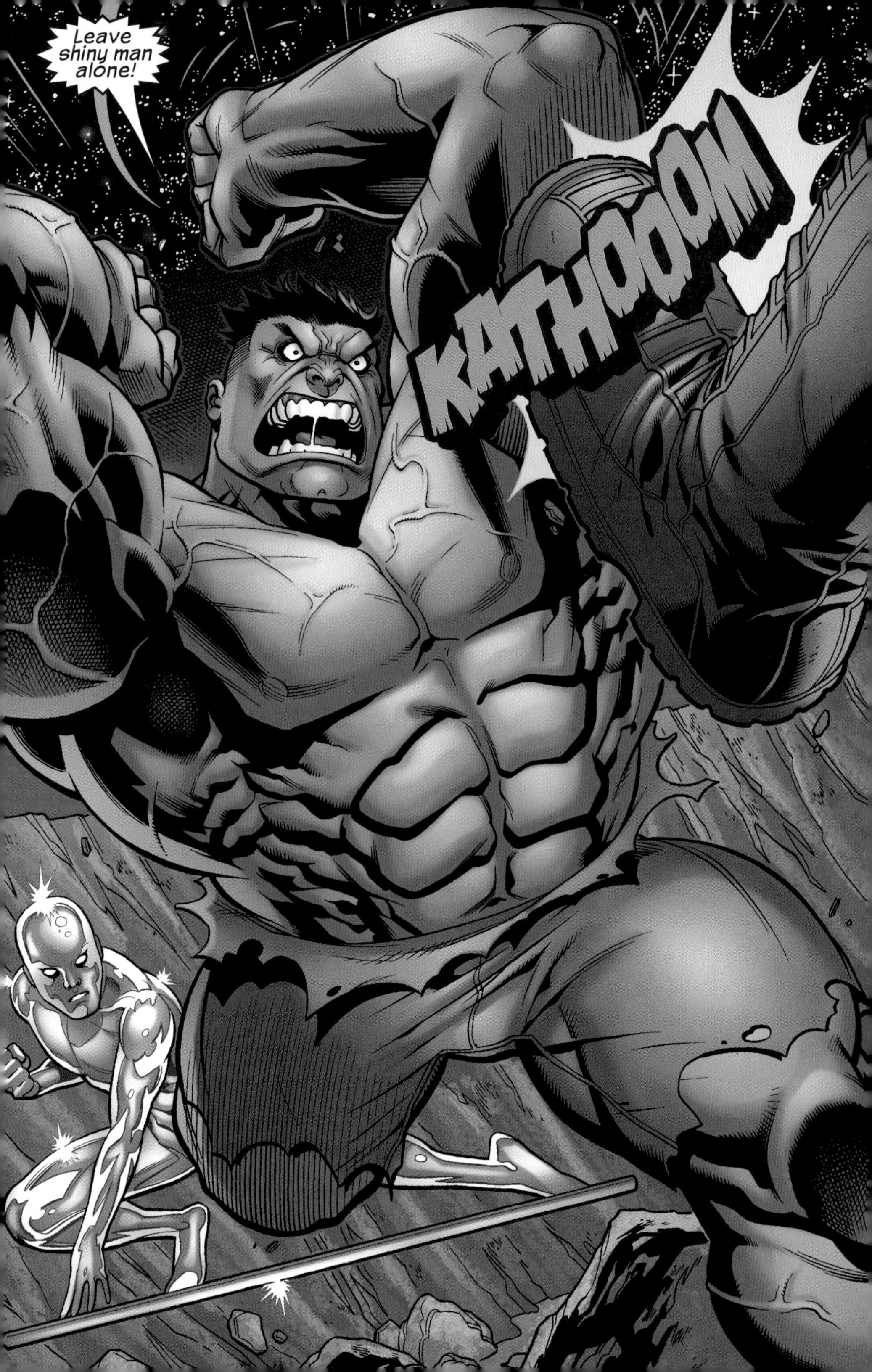
Leave shiny man alone!
KATHOOOM

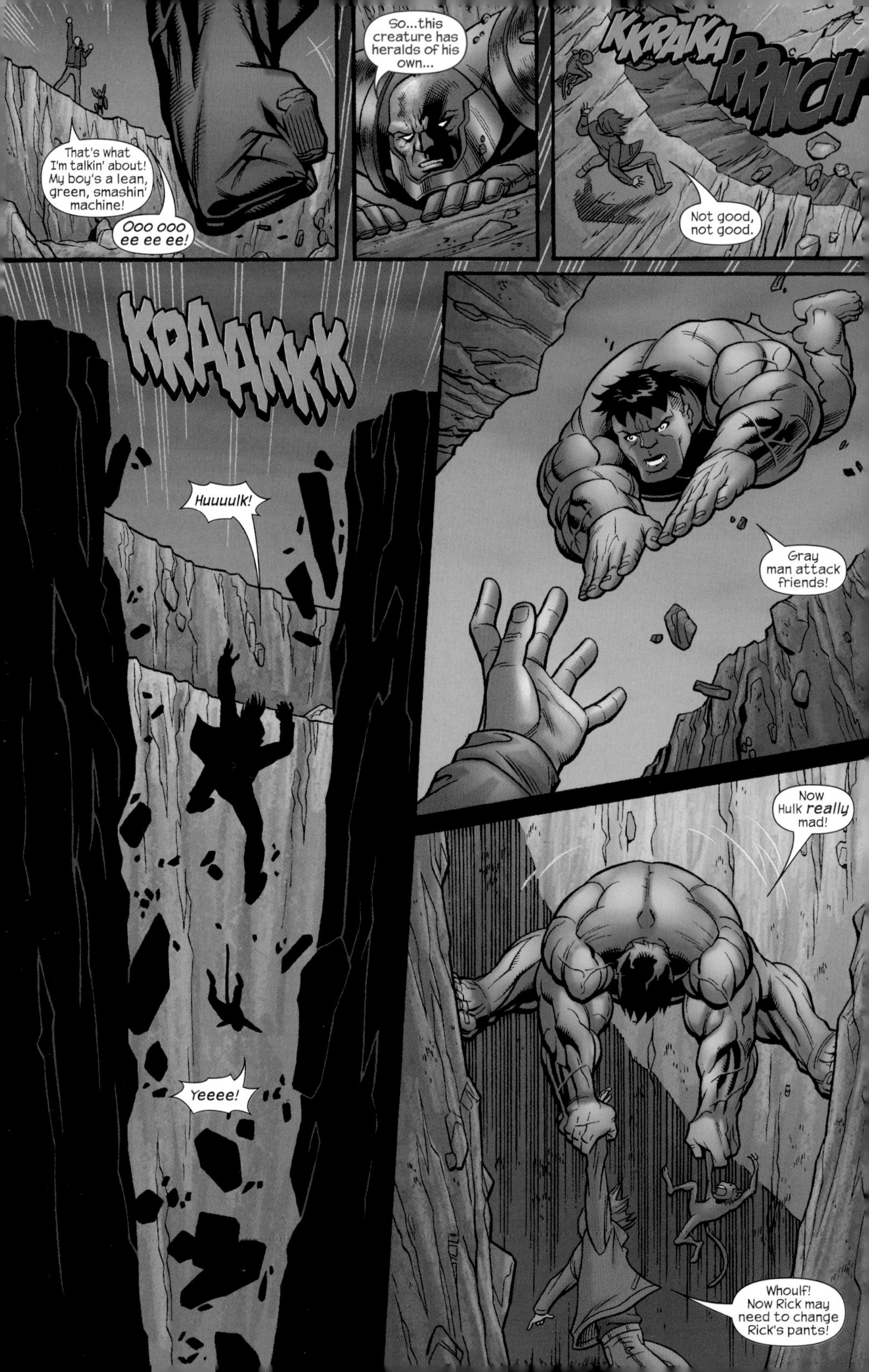
That's what I'm talkin' about! My boy's a lean, green, smashin' machine!
Ooo ooo ee ee ee!
So...this creature has heralds of his own...
KKRAKA RRNCH
Not good, not good.
KRAAKKK
Huuuulk!
Yeeee!
Gray man attack friends!
Now Hulk *really* mad!
Whoulf! Now Rick may need to change Rick's pants!

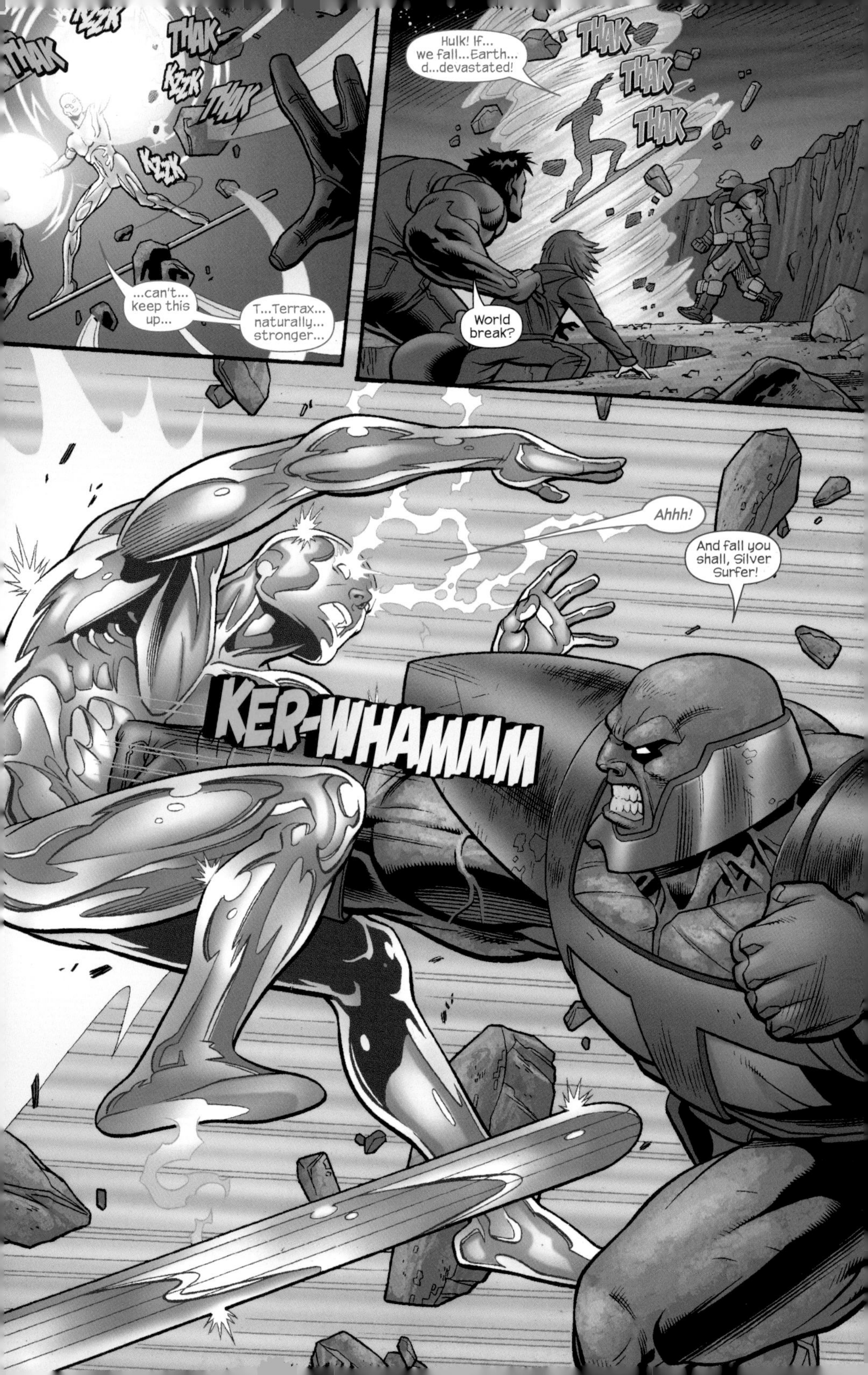
THAK
KZZK
THAK
KZZK
THAK
KZZK
...can't... keep this up...
T...Terrax... naturally... stronger...
Hulk! If... we fall...Earth... d...devastated!
THAK
THAK
THAK
World break?
Ahhh!
And fall you shall, Silver Surfer!
KER-WHAMMMM

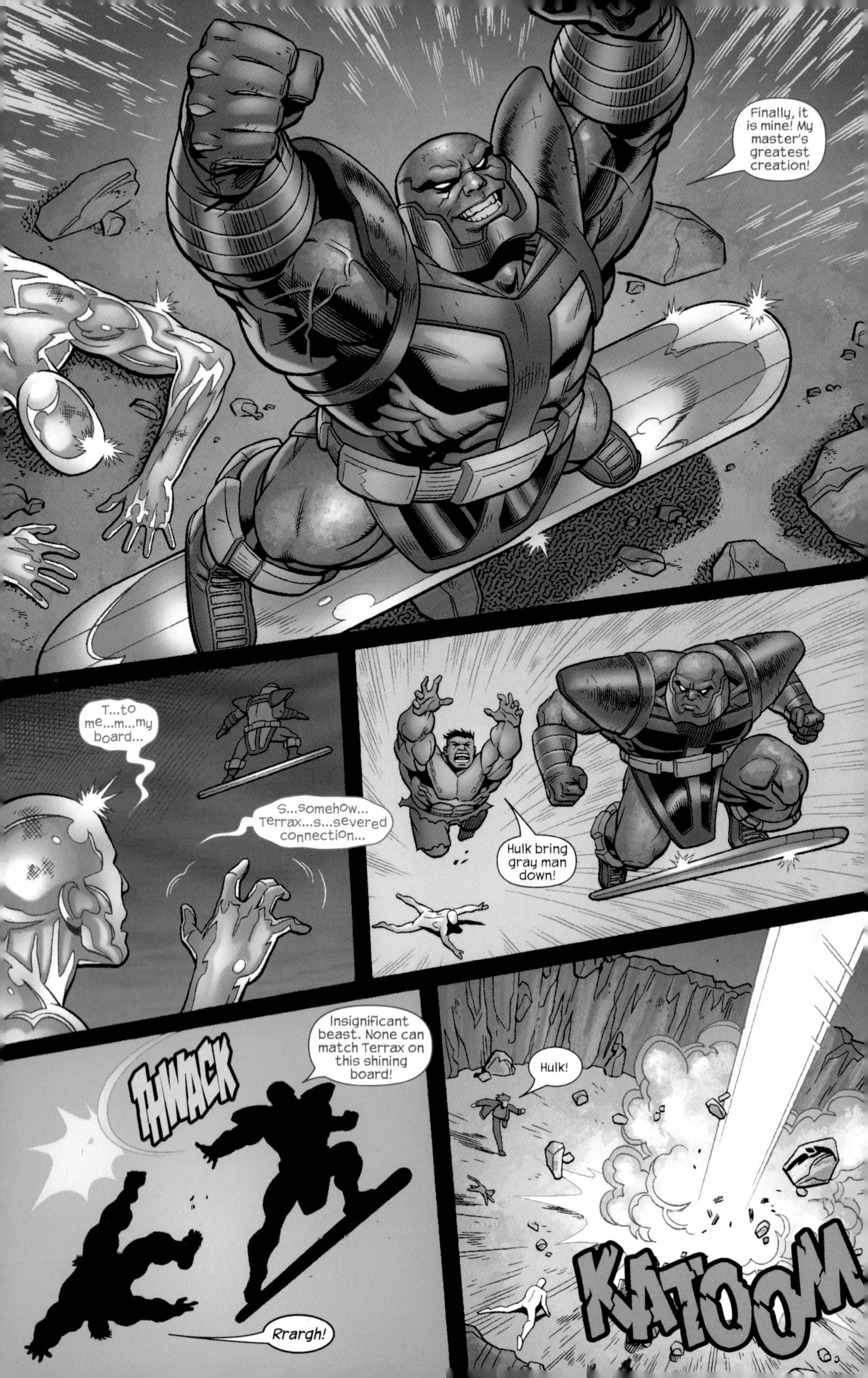
Finally, it is mine! My master's greatest creation!
T...to me...m...my board...
S...somehow... Terrax...s...severed connection...
Hulk bring gray man down!
THWACK
Insignificant beast. None can match Terrax on this shining board!
Rrargh!
Hulk!
KATOOM

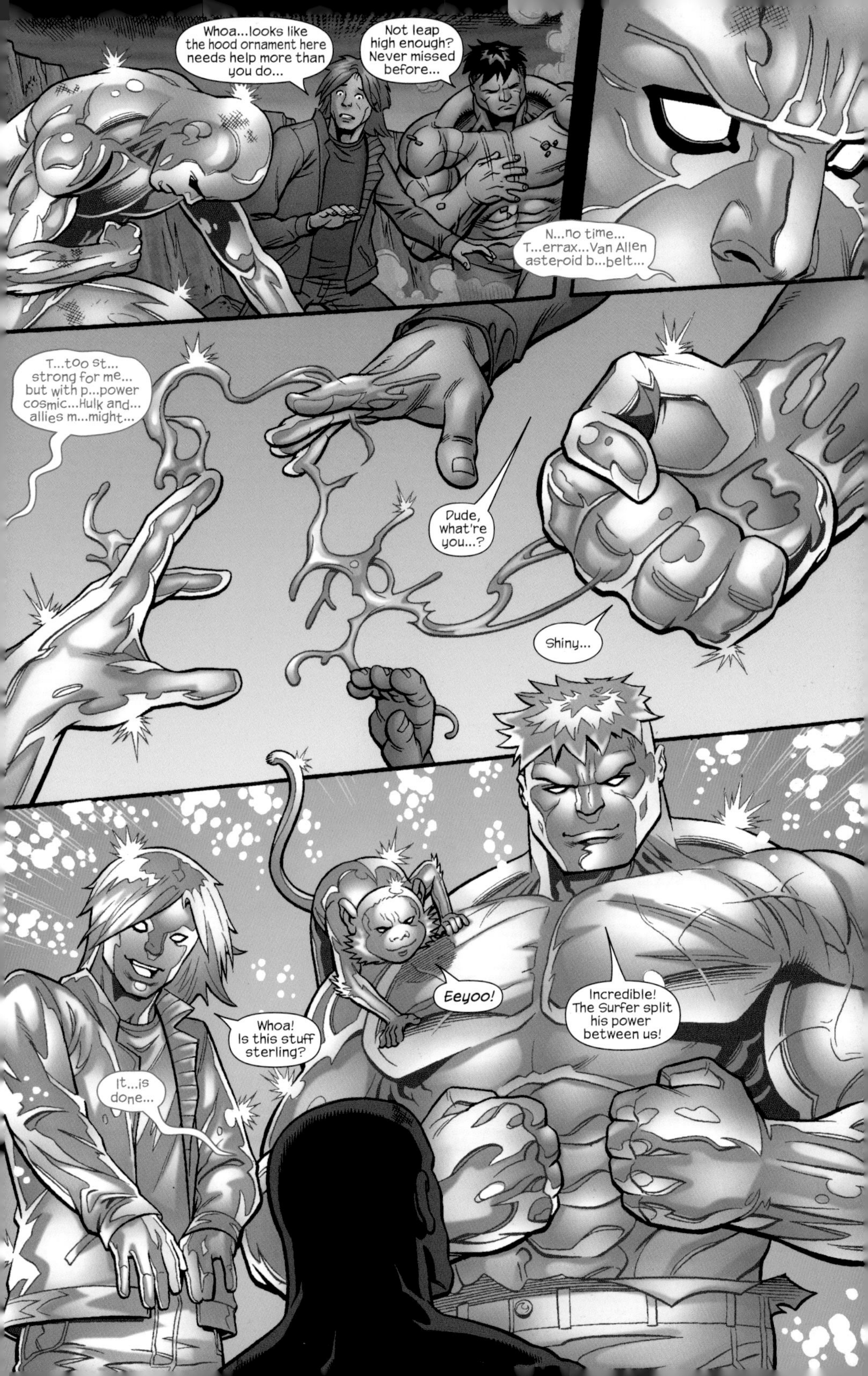
Whoa...looks like the hood ornament here needs help more than you do...
Not leap high enough? Never missed before...
N...no time... T...errax...Van Allen asteroid b...belt...
T...too st... strong for me... but with p...power cosmic...Hulk and... allies m...might...
Dude, what're you...?
Shiny...
It...is done...
Whoa! Is this stuff sterling?
Eeyoo!
Incredible! The Surfer split his power between us!

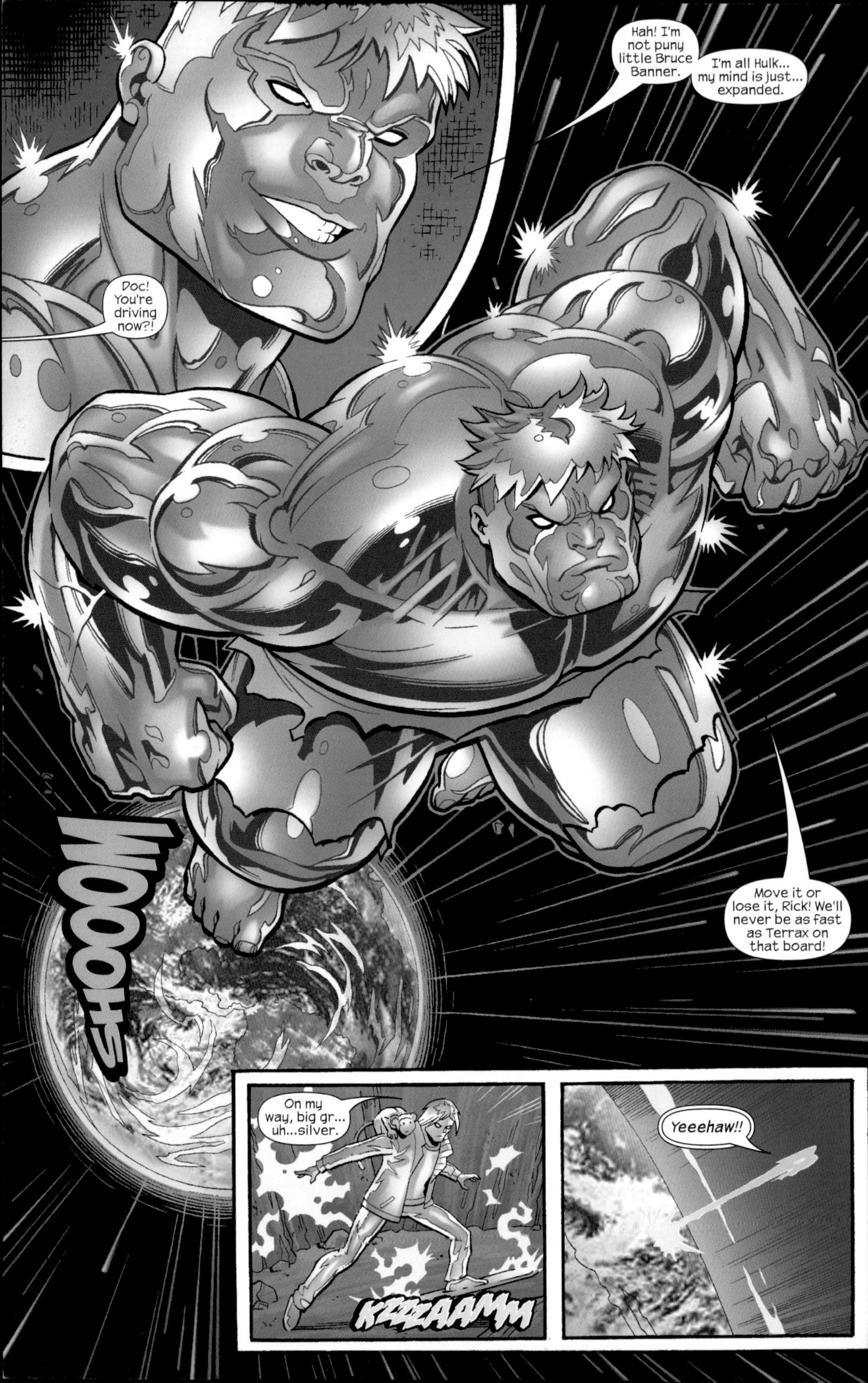
Hah! I'm not puny little Bruce Banner.
I'm all Hulk... my mind is just... expanded.
Doc! You're driving now?!
Move it or lose it, Rick! We'll never be as fast as Terrax on that board!
SHOOOOW
On my way, big gr... uh...silver.
KZZZAAMM
Yeeehaw!!

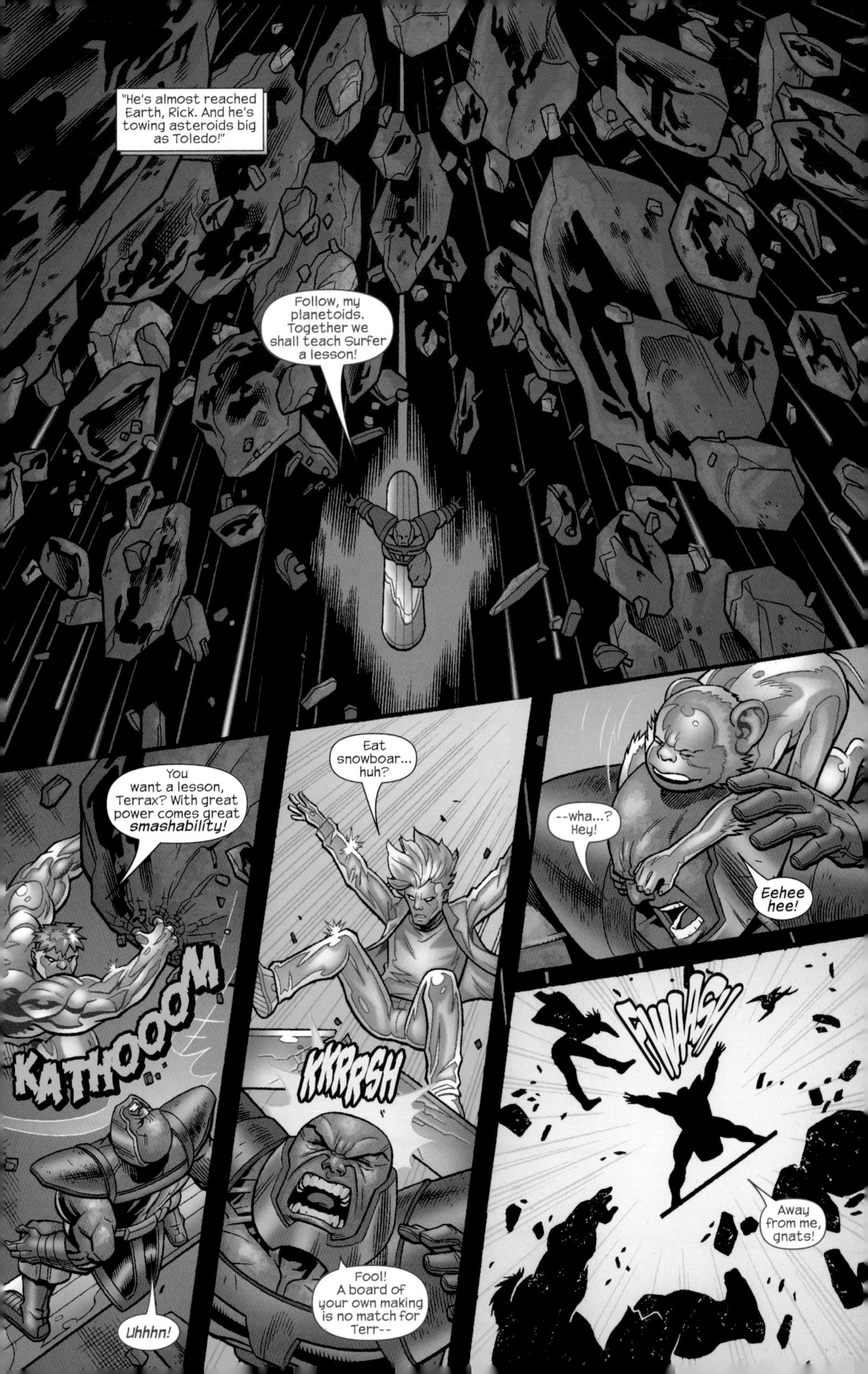
"He's almost reached Earth, Rick. And he's towing asteroids big as Toledo!"
Follow, my planetoids. Together we shall teach Surfer a lesson!
You want a lesson, Terrax? With great power comes great *smashability!*
KATHOOOOM
Uhhhn!
Eat snowboar... huh?
KKRRSH
Fool! A board of your own making is no match for Terr--
--Wha...? Hey!
Eehee hee!
FWASH
Away from me, gnats!

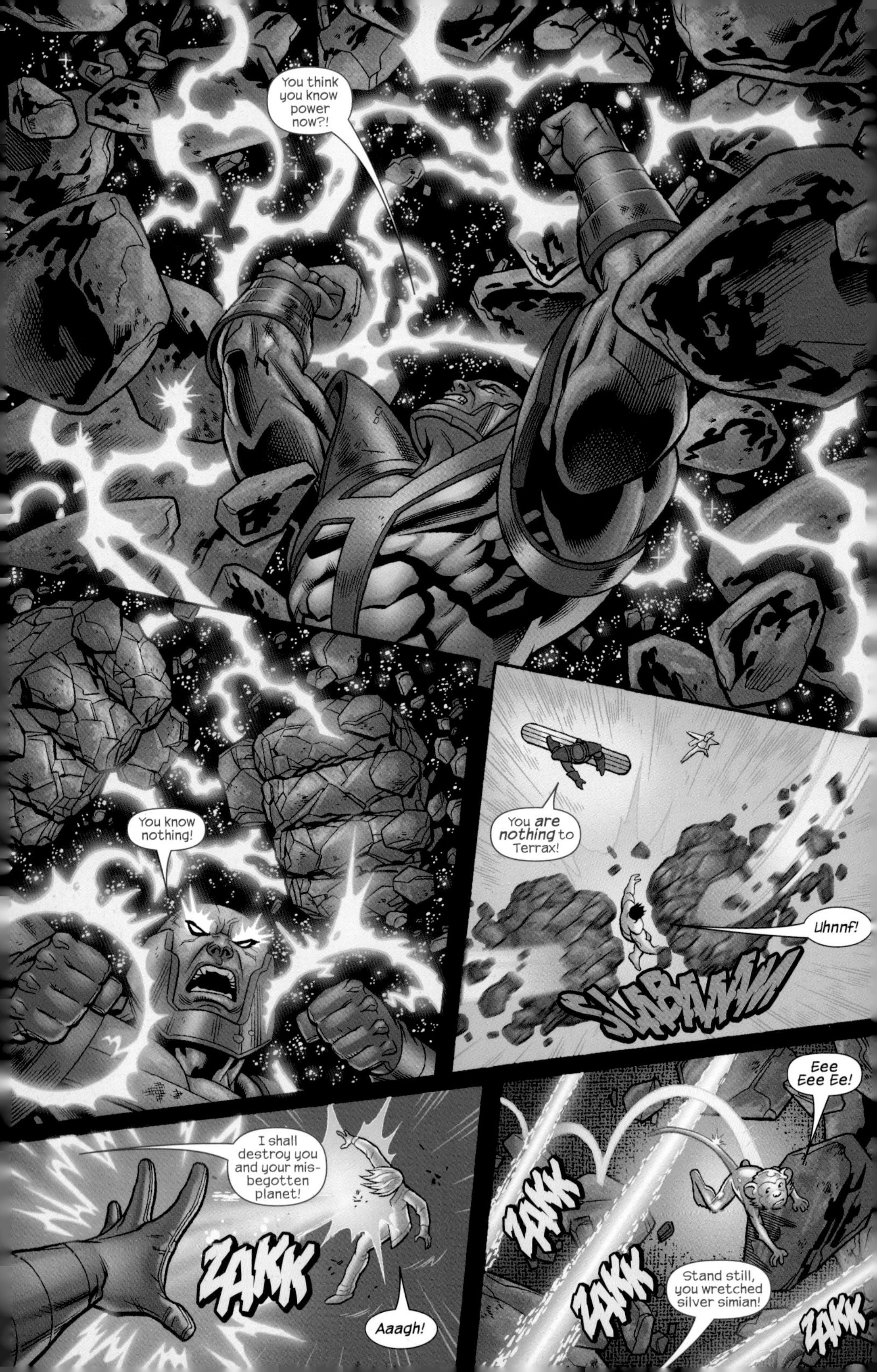
You think you know power now?!
You know nothing!
You are nothing to Terrax!
Uhnnf!
SLABAAAM
I shall destroy you and your mis-begotten planet!
ZAKK
Aaagh!
Eee Eee Ee!
ZAKK
ZAKK
Stand still, you wretched silver simian!
ZAKK

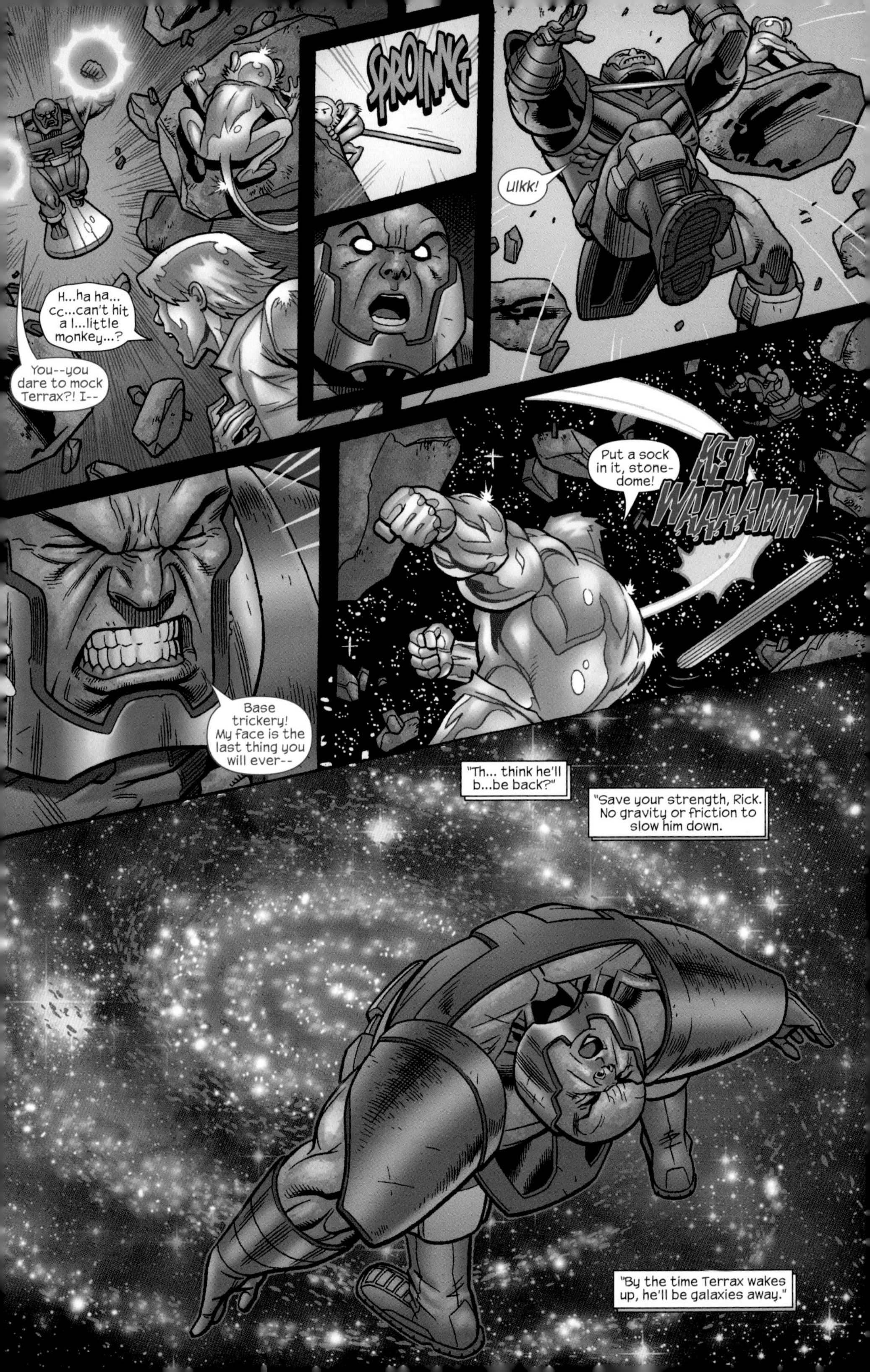
SPROINNG
ULKK!
H...ha ha... cc...can't hit a l...little monkey...?
You--you dare to mock Terrax?! I--
Base trickery! My face is the last thing you will ever--
Put a sock in it, stone-dome!
KER WAAAAMM
"Th... think he'll b...be back?"
"Save your strength, Rick. No gravity or friction to slow him down.
"By the time Terrax wakes up, he'll be galaxies away."

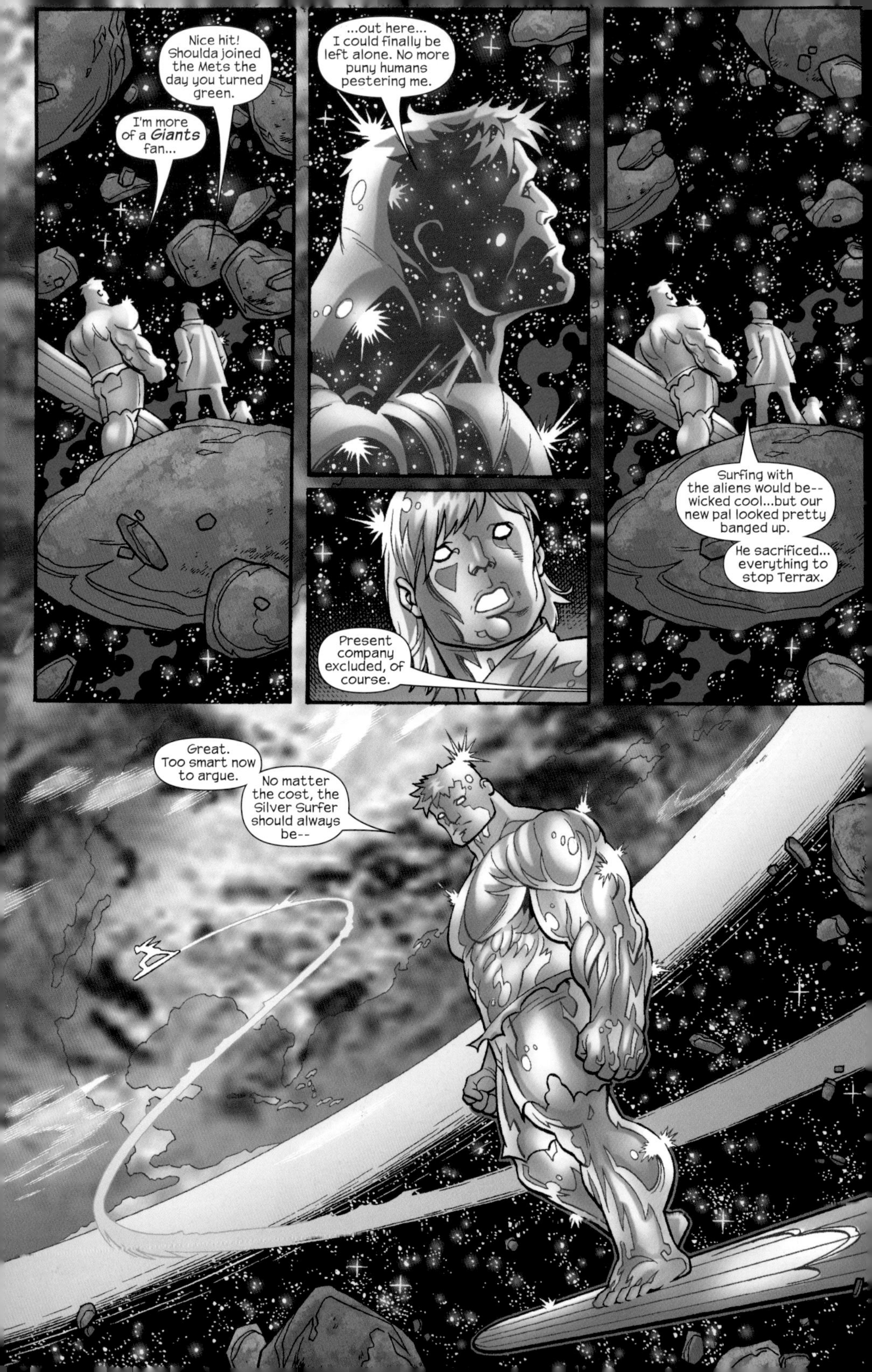
Nice hit! Shoulda joined the Mets the day you turned green.
I'm more of a *Giants* fan...
...out here... I could finally be left alone. No more puny humans pestering me.
Present company excluded, of course.
Surfing with the aliens would be-- wicked cool...but our new pal looked pretty banged up.
He sacrificed... everything to stop Terrax.
Great. Too smart now to argue.
No matter the cost, the Silver Surfer should always be--

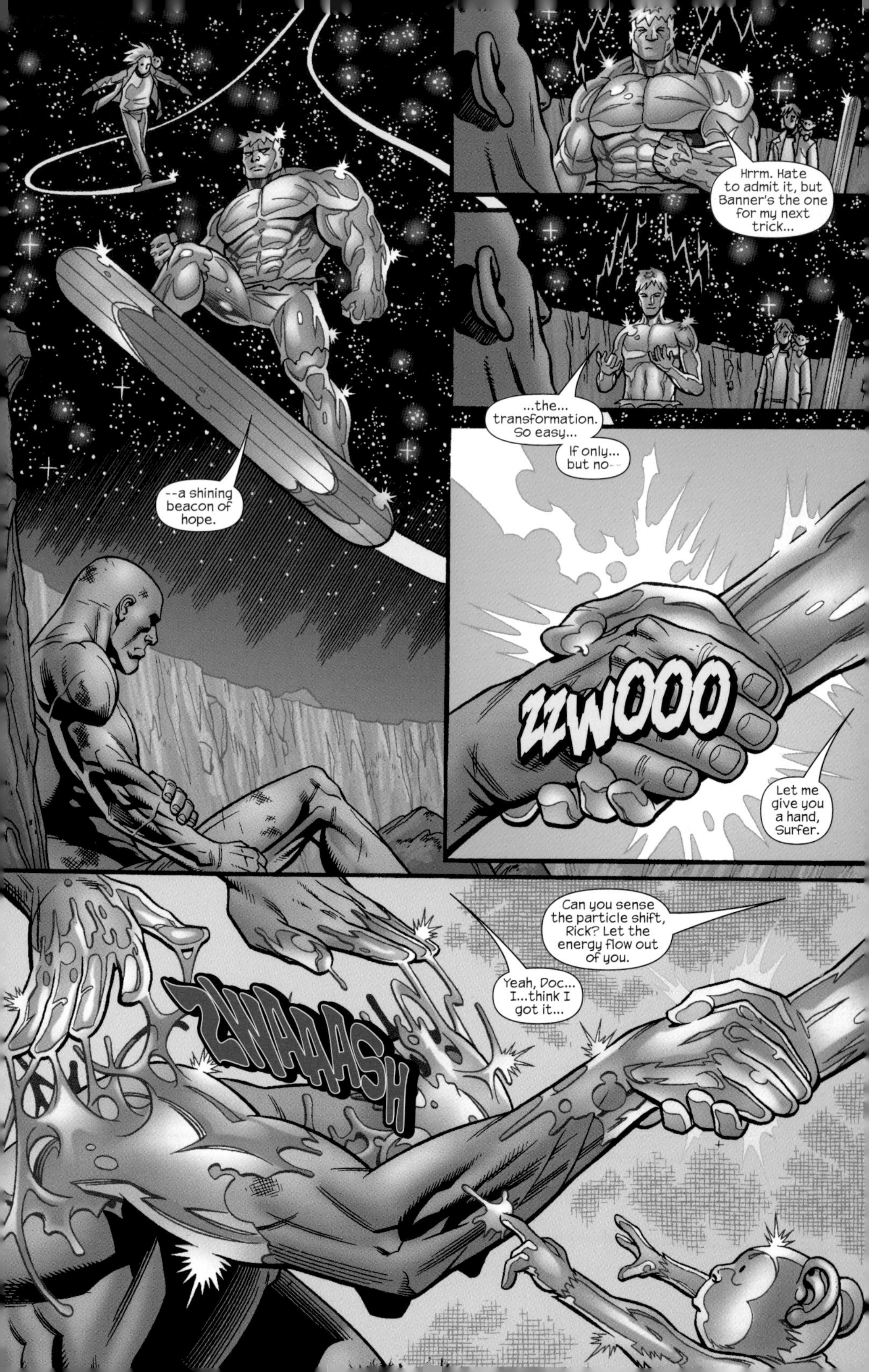
--a shining beacon of hope.
Hrrm. Hate to admit it, but Banner's the one for my next trick...
...the... transformation. So easy...
If only... but no--
ZZWOOO
Let me give you a hand, Surfer.
Can you sense the particle shift, Rick? Let the energy flow out of you.
Yeah, Doc... I...think I got it...
ZWAAASH

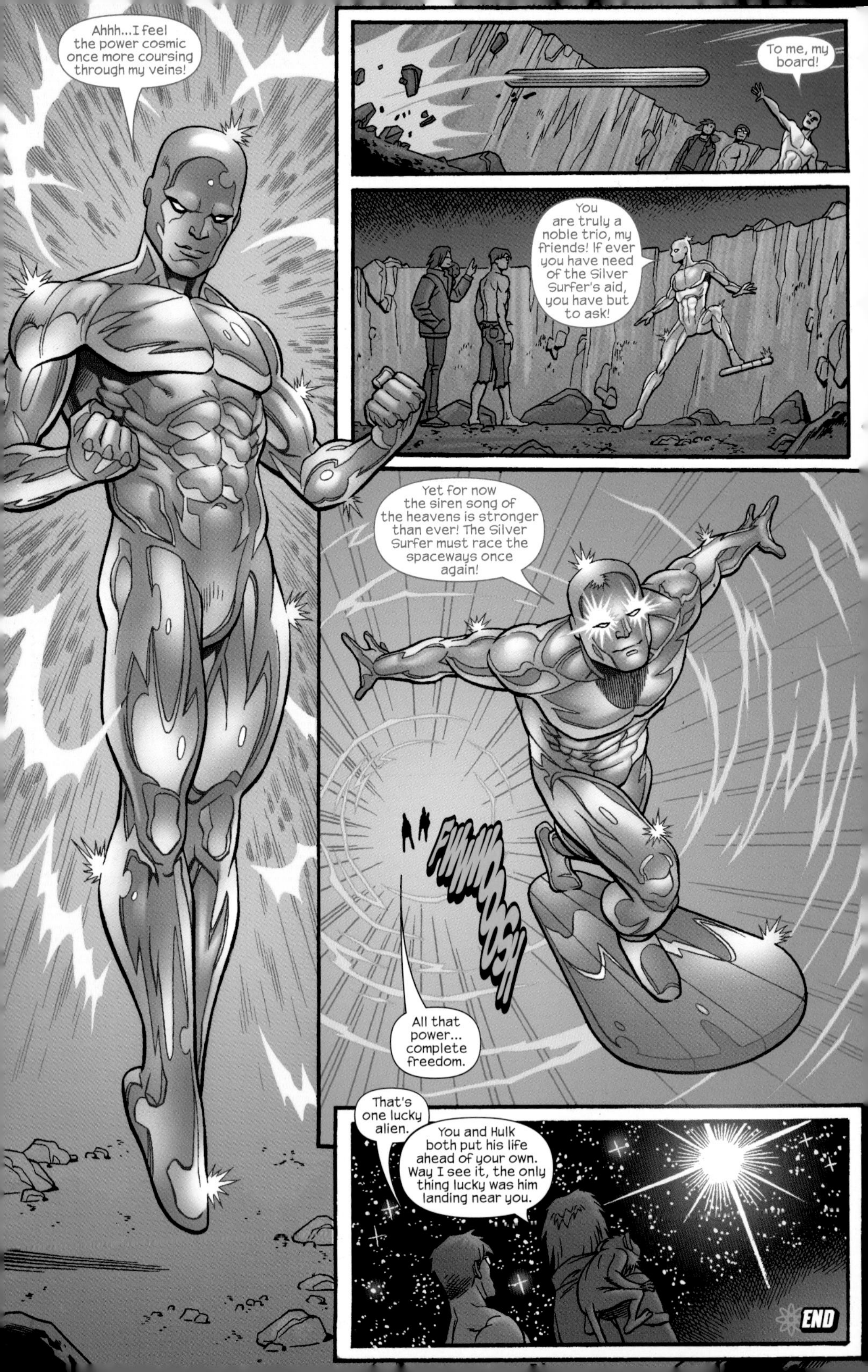
Ahhh...I feel the power cosmic once more coursing through my veins!
To me, my board!
You are truly a noble trio, my friends! If ever you have need of the Silver Surfer's aid, you have but to ask!
Yet for now the siren song of the heavens is stronger than ever! The Silver Surfer must race the spaceways once again!
FWHOOOSH
All that power... complete freedom.
That's one lucky alien.
You and Hulk both put his life ahead of your own. Way I see it, the only thing lucky was him landing near you.
END

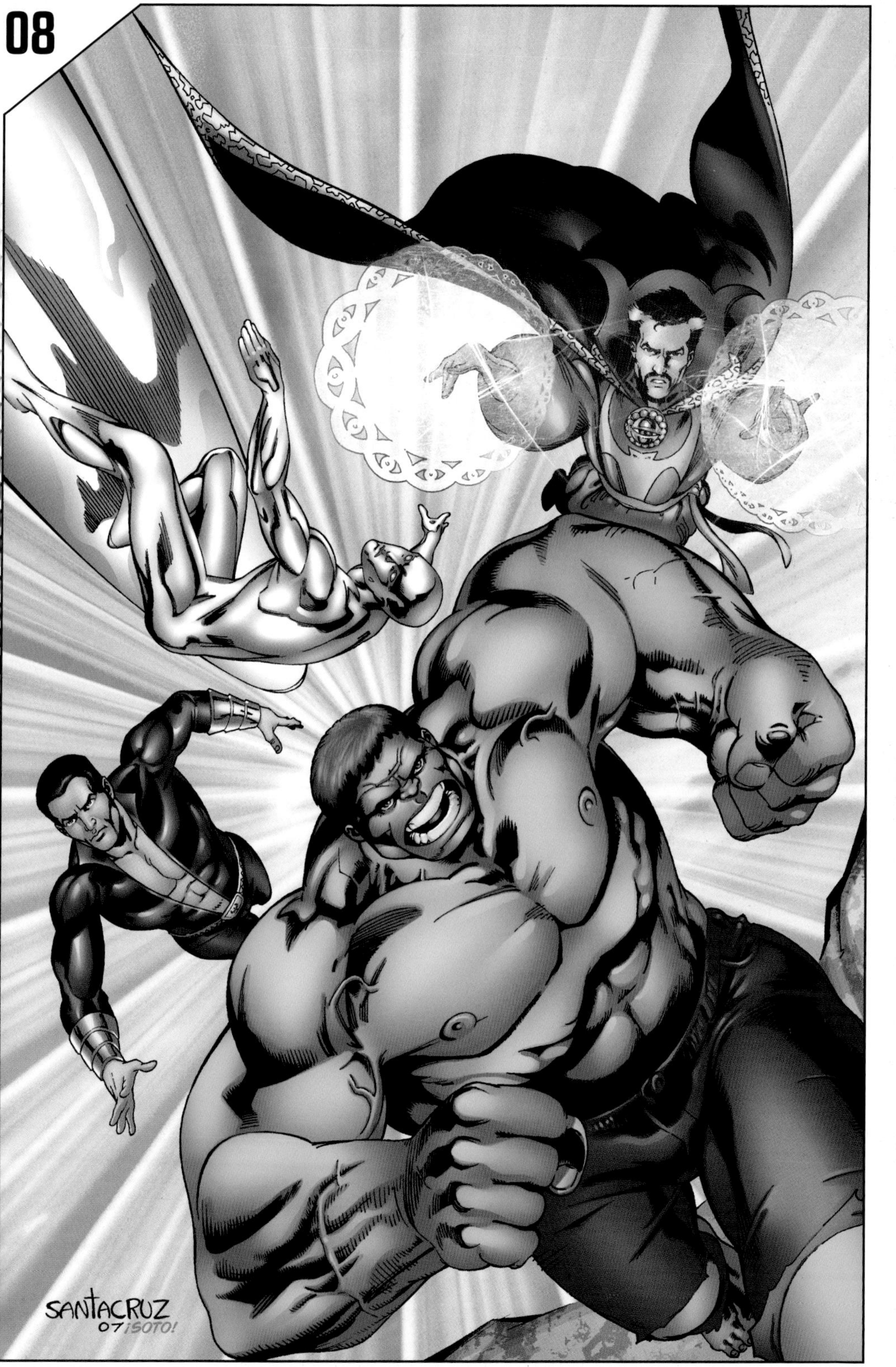
SANTACRUZ
07 ¡SOTO!

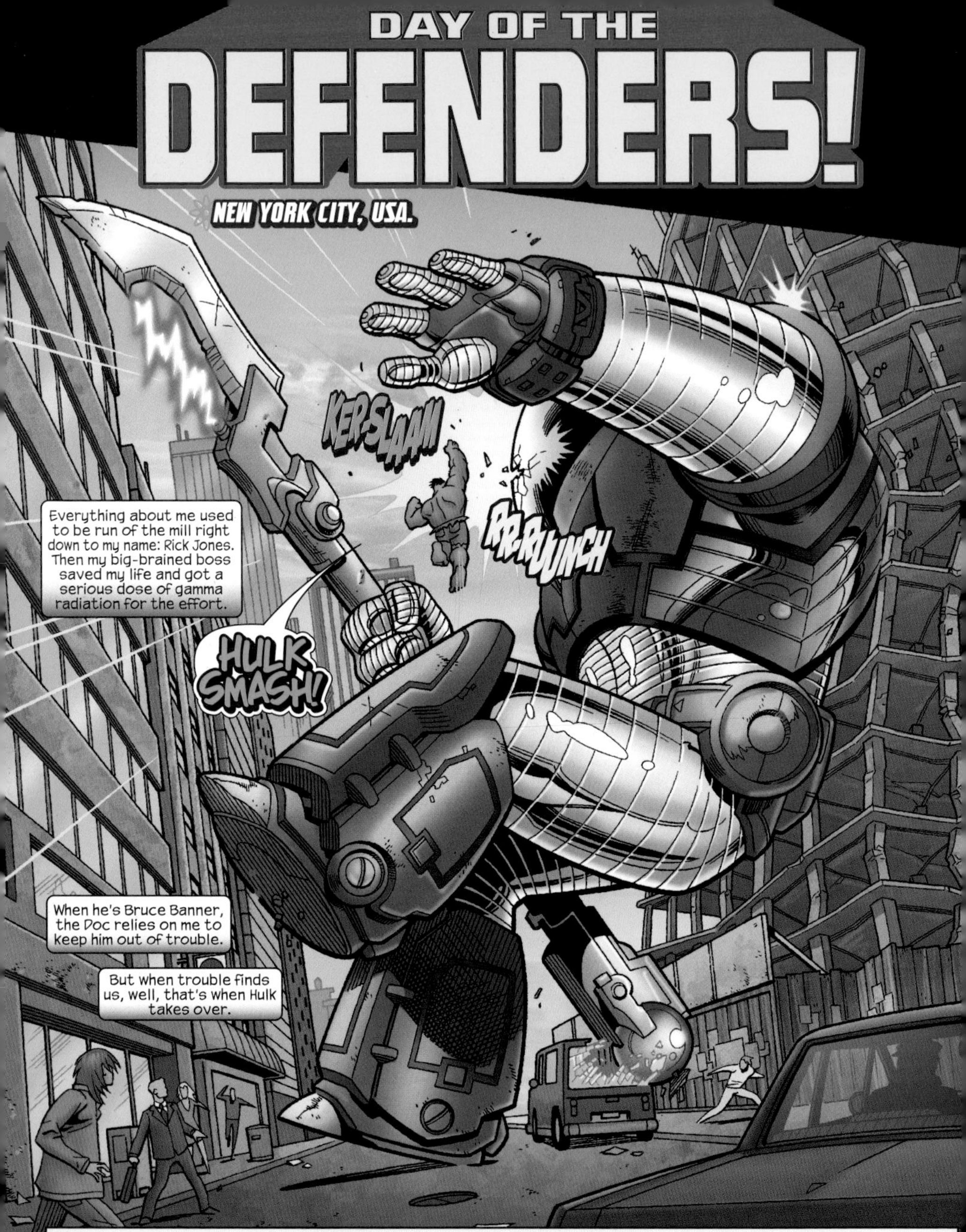

DAY OF THE
DEFENDERS!
NEW YORK CITY, USA.
Everything about me used to be run of the mill right down to my name: Rick Jones. Then my big-brained boss saved my life and got a serious dose of gamma radiation for the effort.
KER-SLAAM
RR-RUUNCH
HULK SMASH!
When he's Bruce Banner, the Doc relies on me to keep him out of trouble.
But when trouble finds us, well, that's when Hulk takes over.

Caught in a blast of gamma radiation, brilliant scientist Bruce Banner now finds himself living as a fugitive. The only people he can count on are his devoted assistant, Rick Jones, and the former lab monkey Bruce affectionately calls "Monkey." For Bruce Banner is cursed to transform in times of stress into the living engine of destruction known as THE INCREDIBLE HULK.

PAUL BENJAMIN WRITER
DAVID NAKAYAMA PENCILER
GARY MARTIN INKER
MICHELLE MADSEN COLORIST
DAVE SHARPE LETTERER
SANTACRUZ, FERNANDEZ AND SOTOCOLOR COVER ARTISTS
RICH GINTER PRODUCTION
JORDAN D. WHITE ASST. EDITOR
MARK PANICCIA EDITOR
JOE QUESADA EDITOR IN CHIEF
DAN BUCKLEY PUBLISHER

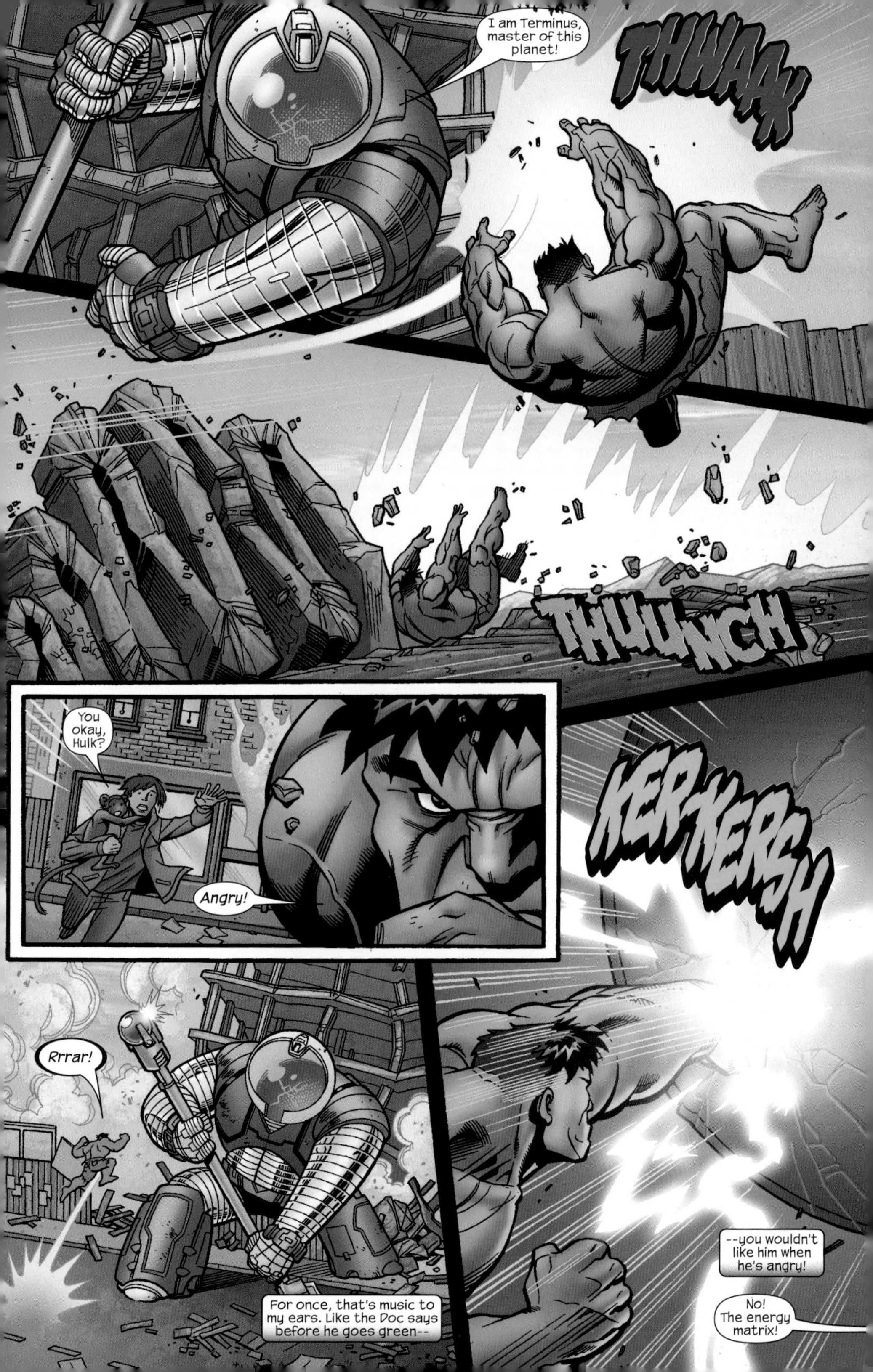
I am Terminus, master of this planet!
THWAAK
THUUNCH
You okay, Hulk?
Angry!
KER-KERSH
Rrrar!
For once, that's music to my ears. Like the Doc says before he goes green--
--you wouldn't like him when he's angry!
No! The energy matrix!

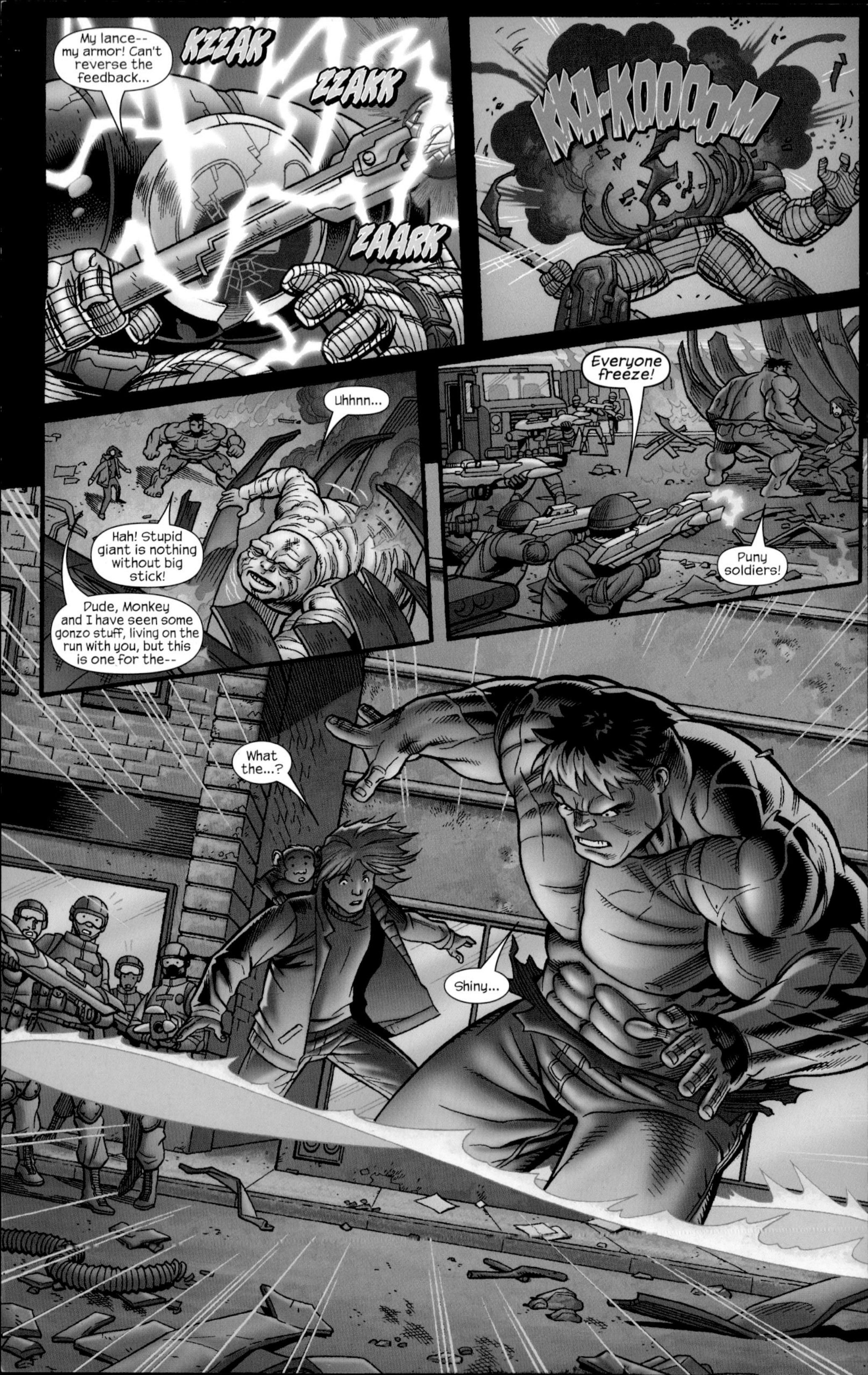
My lance-- my armor! Can't reverse the feedback...
KZZAK
ZZAKK
ZAARK
KKA-KOOOOM
Uhhnn...
Hah! Stupid giant is nothing without big stick!
Dude, Monkey and I have seen some gonzo stuff, living on the run with you, but this is one for the--
Everyone freeze!
Puny soldiers!
What the...?
Shiny...

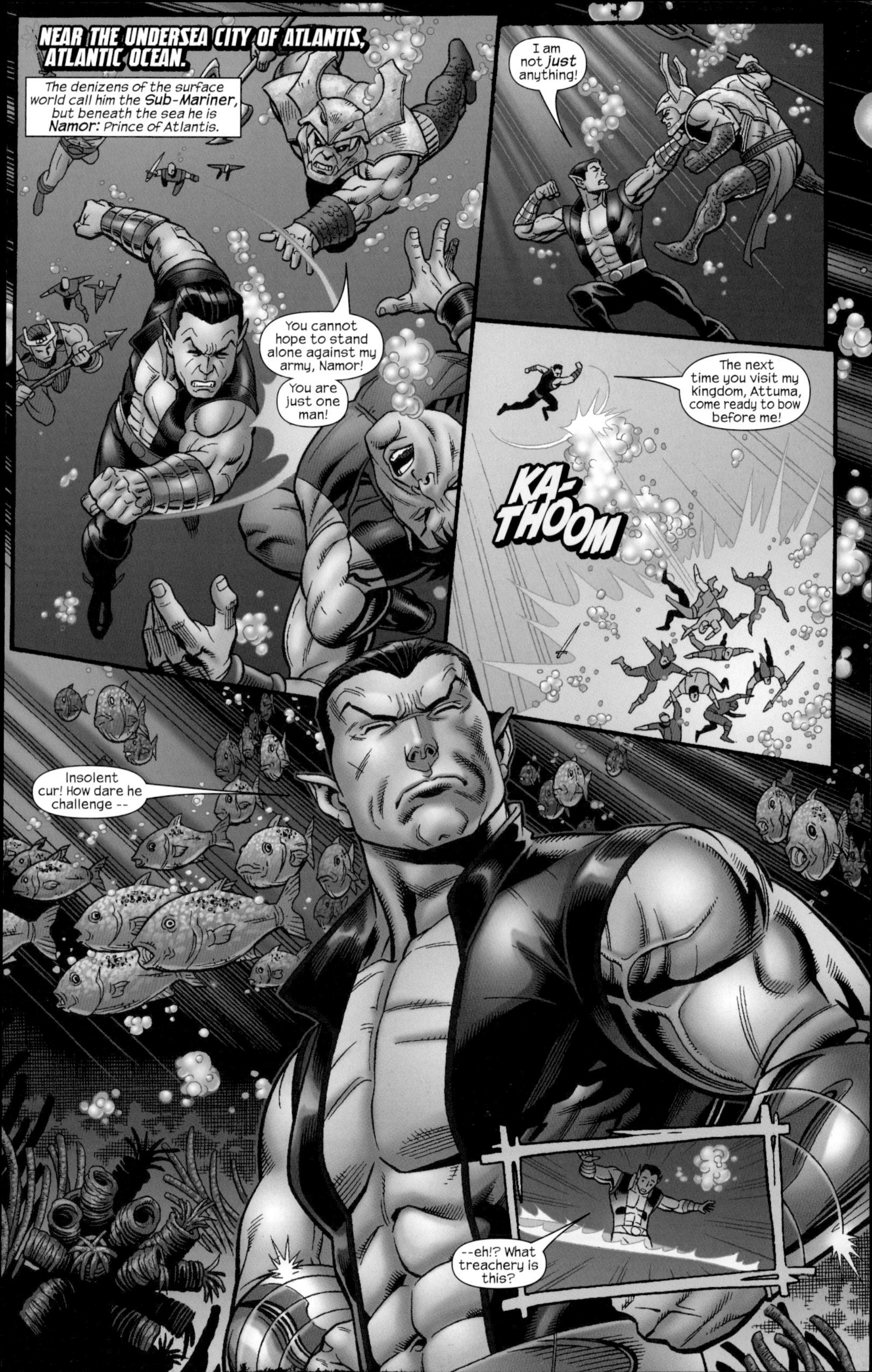
NEAR THE UNDERSEA CITY OF ATLANTIS, ATLANTIC OCEAN.
The denizens of the surface world call him the Sub-Mariner, but beneath the sea he is Namor: Prince of Atlantis.
You cannot hope to stand alone against my army, Namor!
You are just one man!
I am not just anything!
The next time you visit my Kingdom, Attuma, come ready to bow before me!
KA-THOOM
Insolent cur! How dare he challenge --
--eh!? What treachery is this?

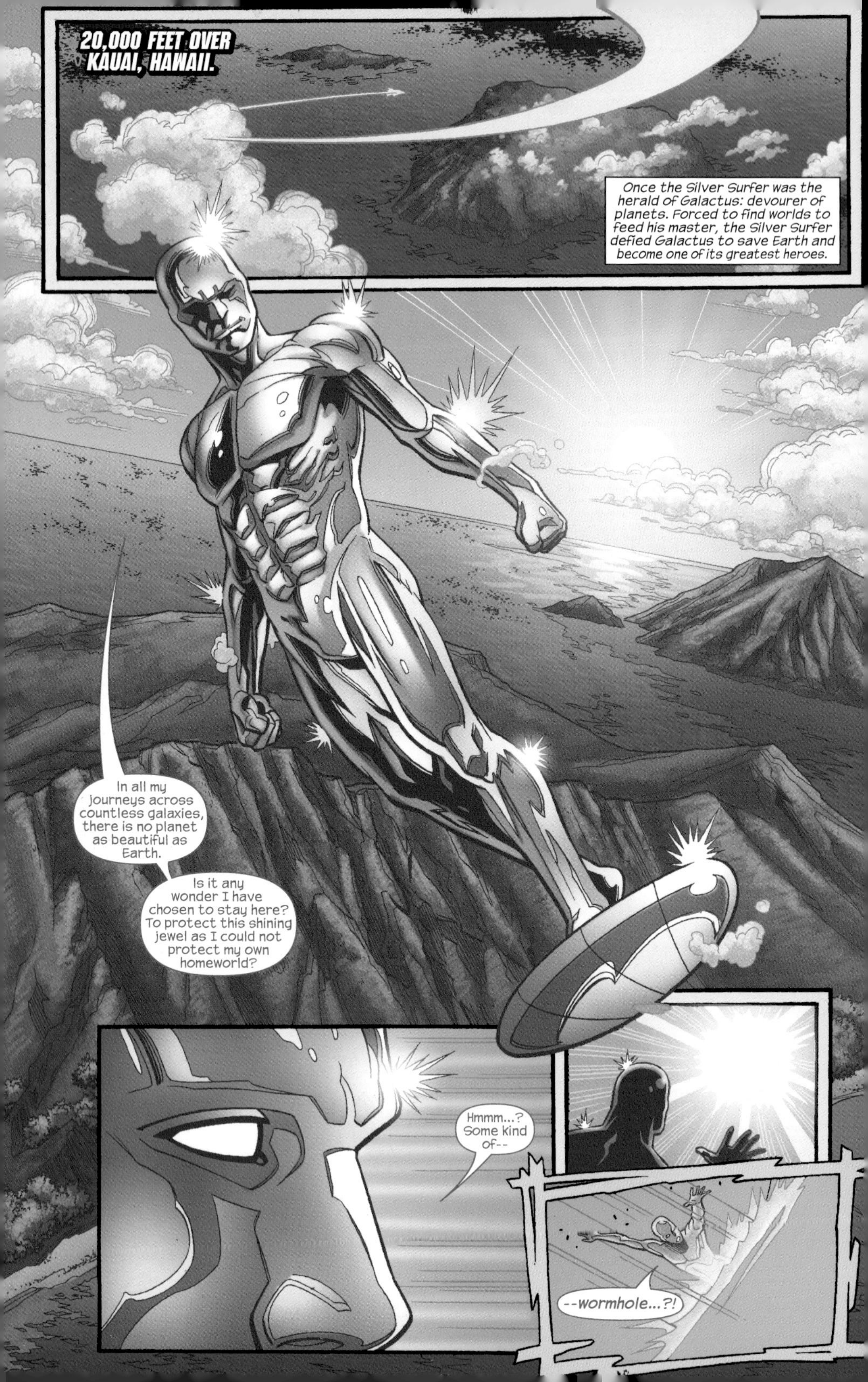
20,000 FEET OVER KAUAI, HAWAII.
Once the Silver Surfer was the herald of Galactus: devourer of planets. Forced to find worlds to feed his master, the Silver Surfer defied Galactus to save Earth and become one of its greatest heroes.
In all my journeys across countless galaxies, there is no planet as beautiful as Earth.
Is it any wonder I have chosen to stay here? To protect this shining jewel as I could not protect my own homeworld?
Hmmm...? Some kind of--
--wormhole...?!

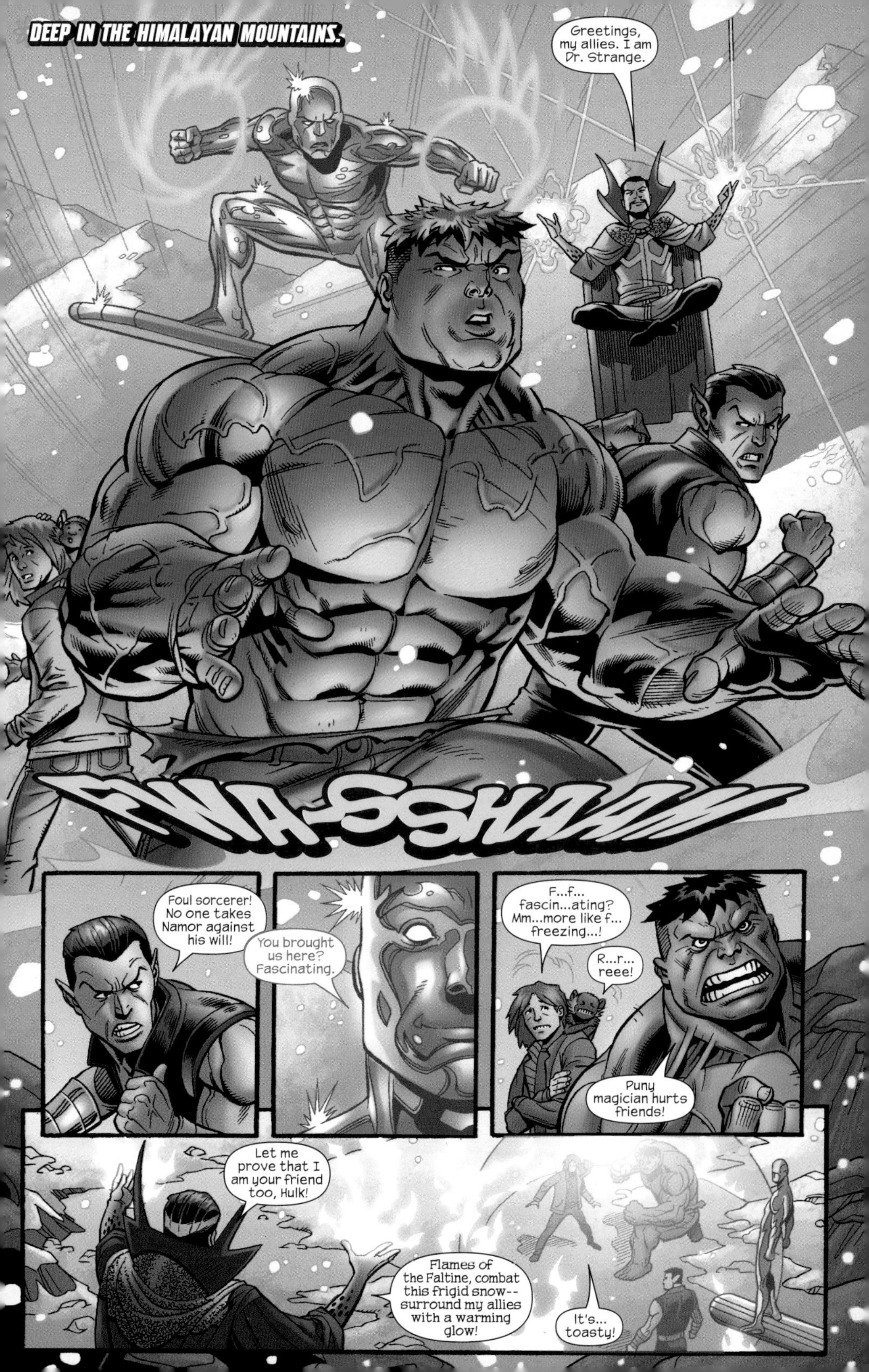
DEEP IN THE HIMALAYAN MOUNTAINS.
Greetings, my allies. I am Dr. Strange.
Foul sorcerer! No one takes Namor against his will!
You brought us here? Fascinating.
F...f... fascin...ating? Mm...more like f... freezing...!
R...r... reee!
Puny magician hurts friends!
Let me prove that I am your friend too, Hulk!
Flames of the Faltine, combat this frigid snow-- surround my allies with a warming glow!
It's... toasty!

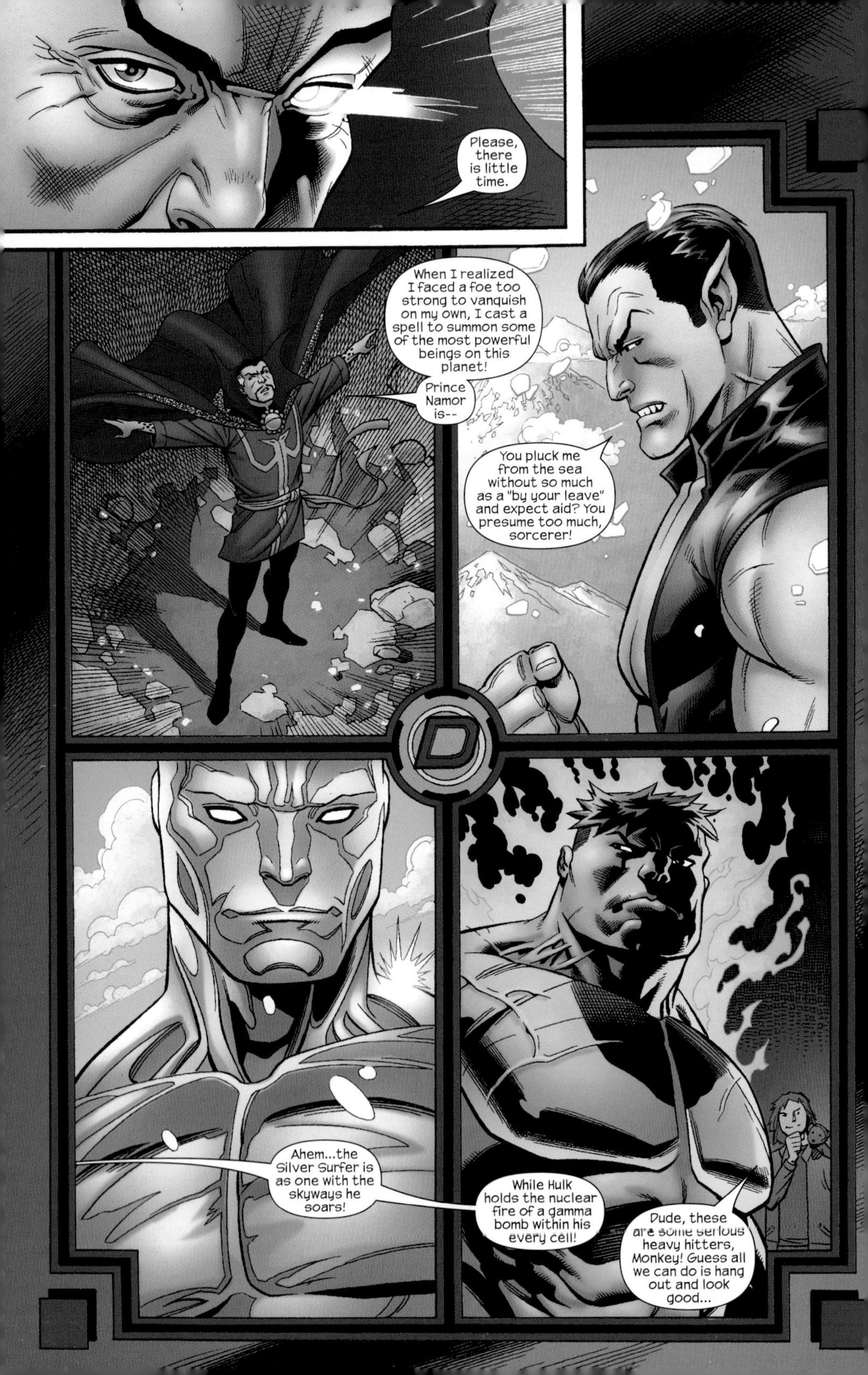

Please, there is little time.
When I realized I faced a foe too strong to vanquish on my own, I cast a spell to summon some of the most powerful beings on this planet!
Prince Namor is--
You pluck me from the sea without so much as a "by your leave" and expect aid? You presume too much, sorcerer!
Ahem...the Silver Surfer is as one with the skyways he soars!
While Hulk holds the nuclear fire of a gamma bomb within his every cell!
Dude, these are some serious heavy hitters, Monkey! Guess all we can do is hang out and look good...

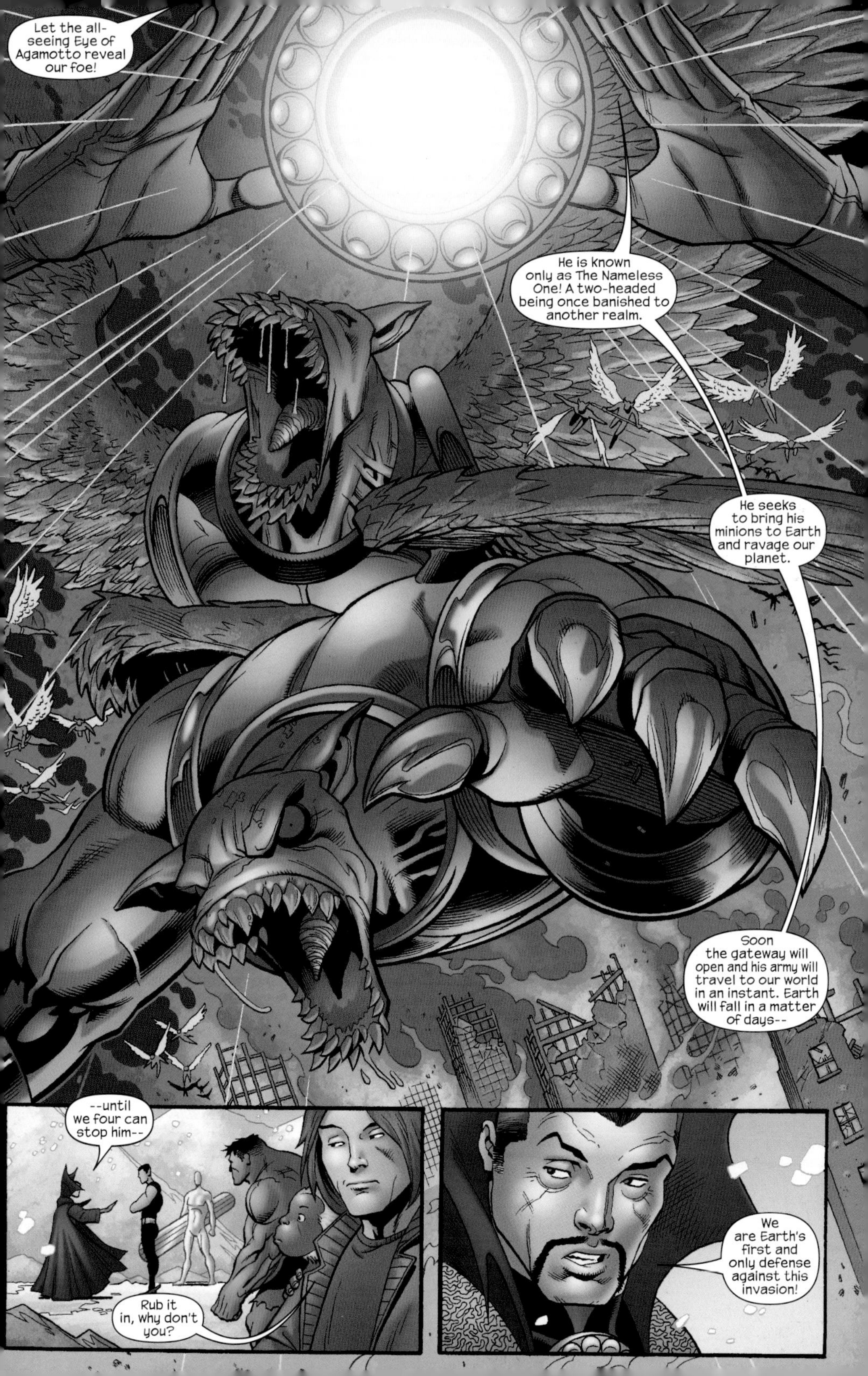

Let the all-seeing Eye of Agamotto reveal our foe!
He is known only as The Nameless One! A two-headed being once banished to another realm.
He seeks to bring his minions to Earth and ravage our planet.
Soon the gateway will open and his army will travel to our world in an instant. Earth will fall in a matter of days--
--until we four can stop him--
Rub it in, why don't you?
We are Earth's first and only defense against this invasion!

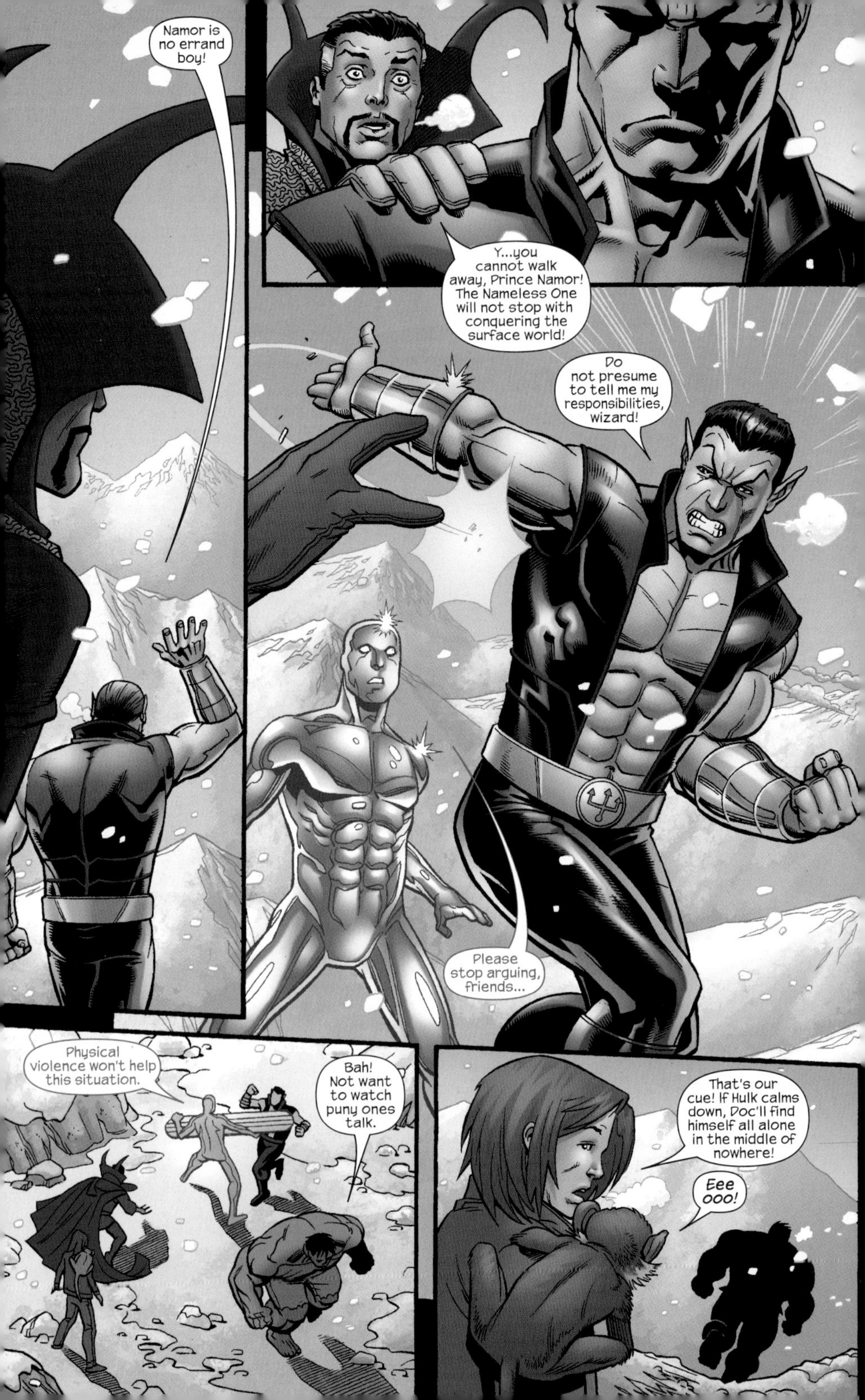
Namor is no errand boy!
Y...you cannot walk away, Prince Namor! The Nameless One will not stop with conquering the surface world!
Do not presume to tell me my responsibilities, wizard!
Please stop arguing, friends...
Physical violence won't help this situation.
Bah! Not want to watch puny ones talk.
That's our cue! If Hulk calms down, Doc'll find himself all alone in the middle of nowhere!
Eee ooo!

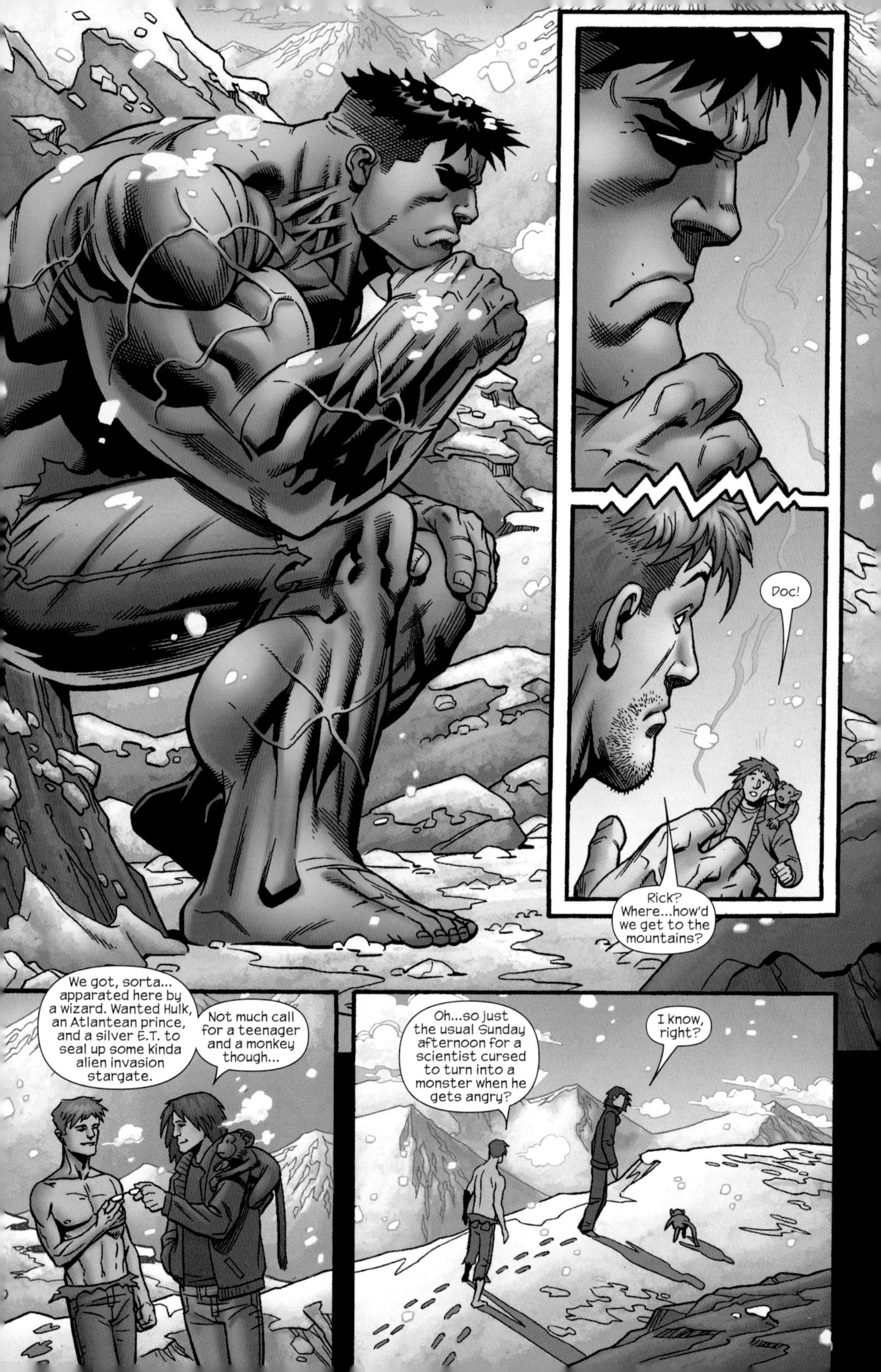

Doc!
Rick? Where...how'd we get to the mountains?
We got, sorta... apparated here by a wizard. Wanted Hulk, an Atlantean prince, and a silver E.T. to seal up some kinda alien invasion stargate.
Not much call for a teenager and a monkey though...
Oh...so just the usual Sunday afternoon for a scientist cursed to turn into a monster when he gets angry?
I know, right?

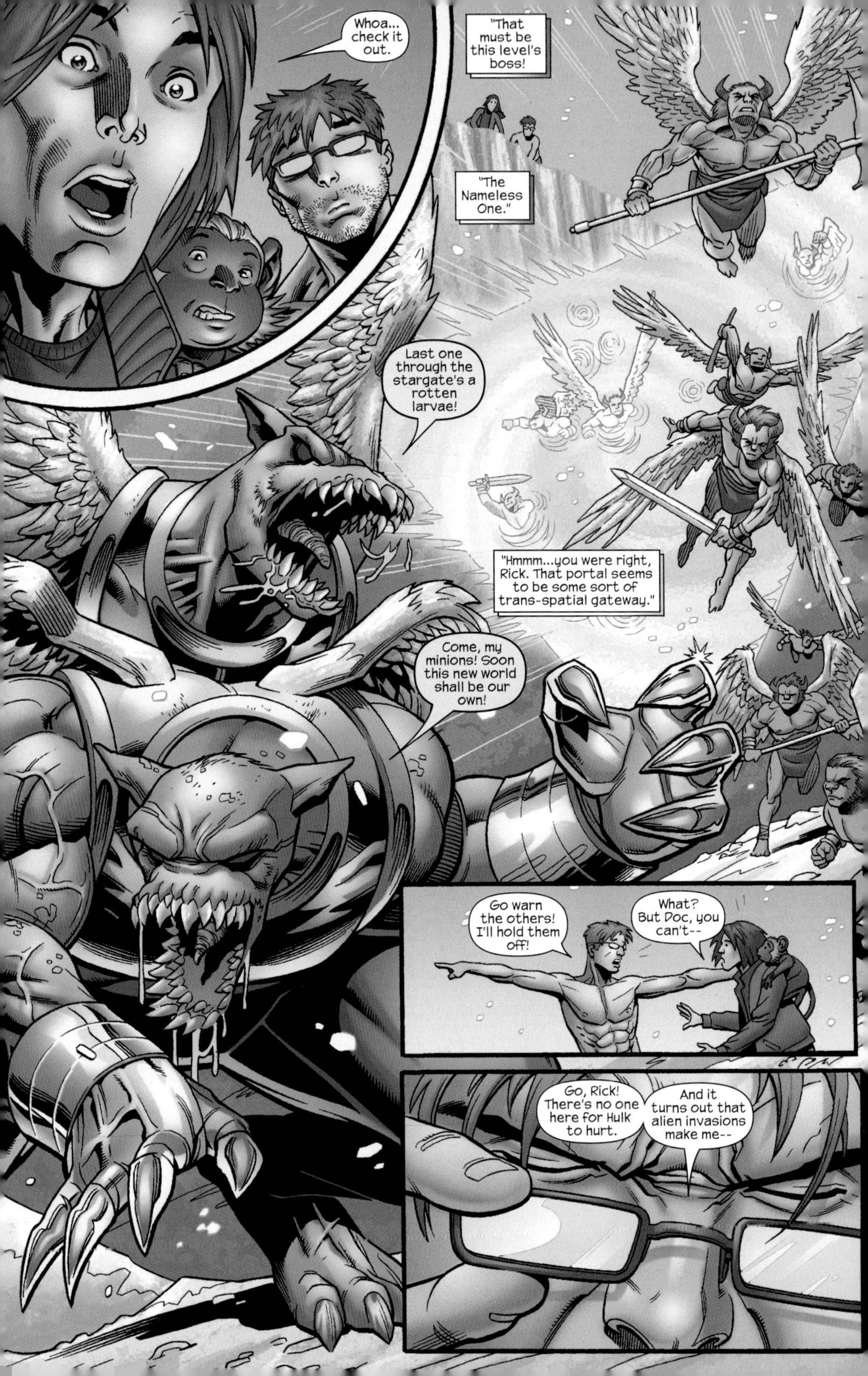
Whoa... check it out.
"That must be this level's boss!
"The Nameless One."
Last one through the stargate's a rotten larvae!
"Hmmm...you were right, Rick. That portal seems to be some sort of trans-spatial gateway."
Come, my minions! Soon this new world shall be our own!
Go warn the others! I'll hold them off!
What? But Doc, you can't--
Go, Rick! There's no one here for Hulk to hurt.
And it turns out that alien invasions make me--

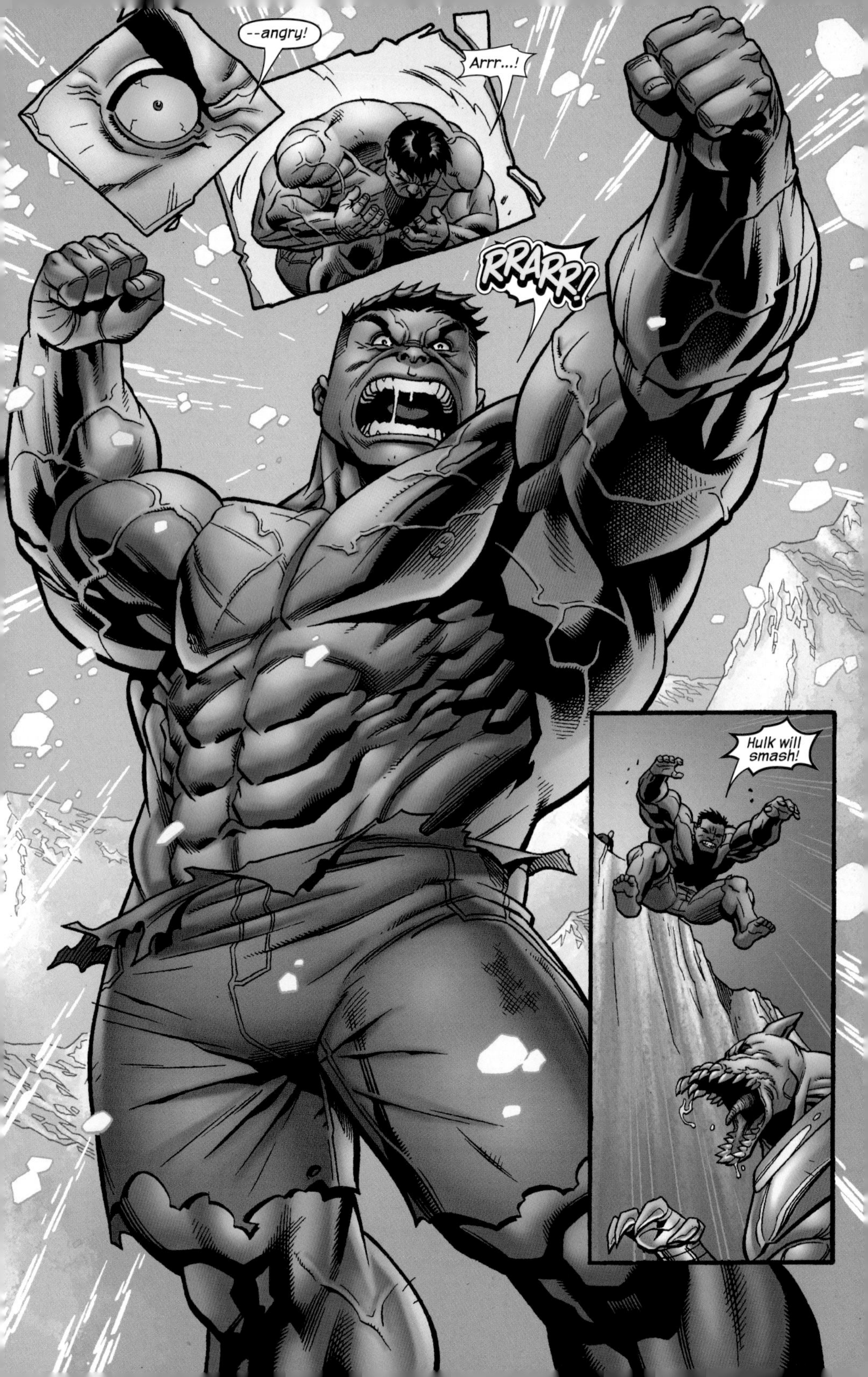
--angry!
Arrr...!
RRARR!
Hulk will smash!

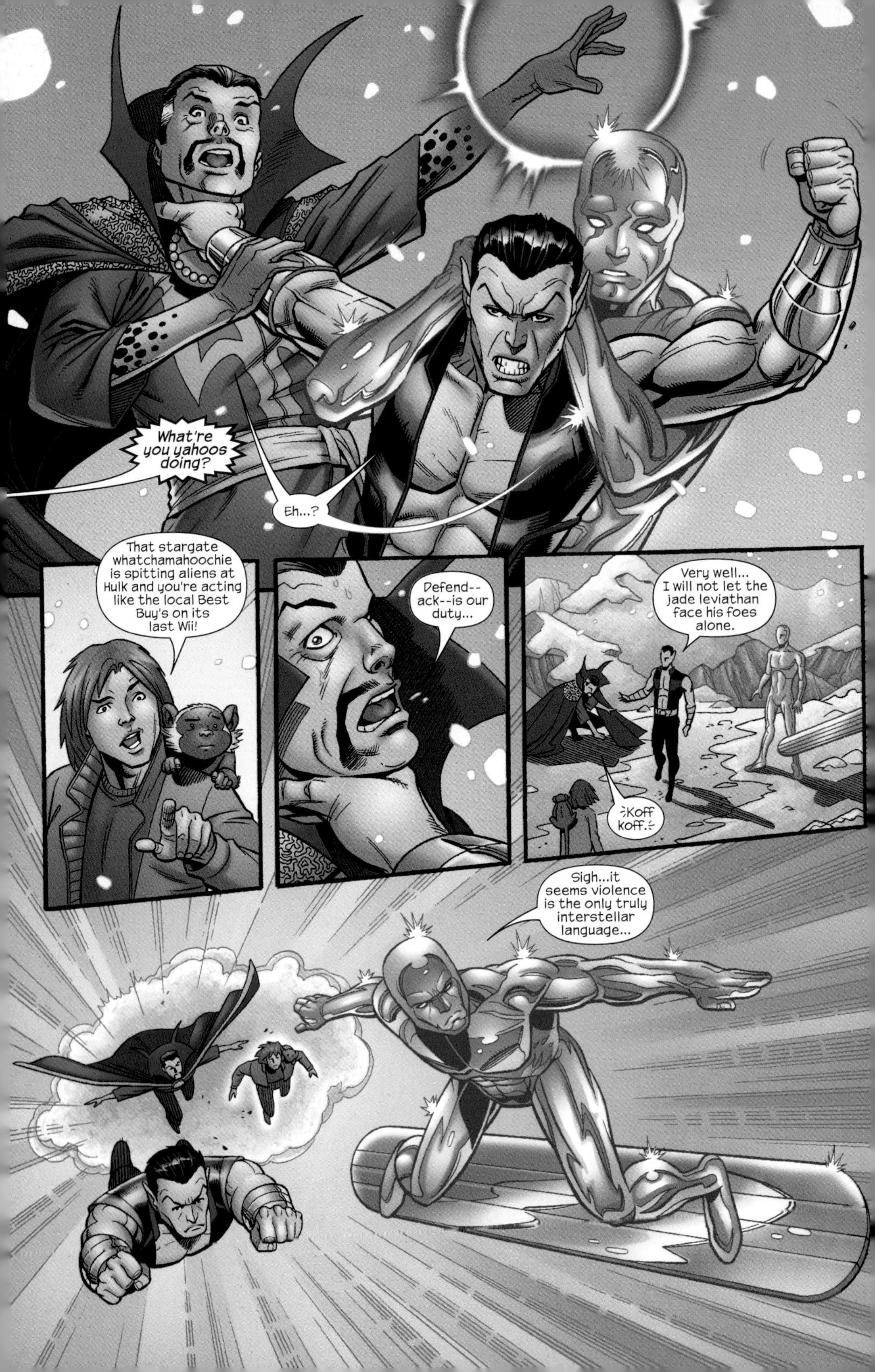
What're you yahoos doing?
Eh...?
That stargate whatchamahoochie is spitting aliens at Hulk and you're acting like the local Best Buy's on its last Wii!
Defend-- ack--is our duty...
Very well... I will not let the jade leviathan face his foes alone.
Koff koff.
Sigh...it seems violence is the only truly interstellar language...

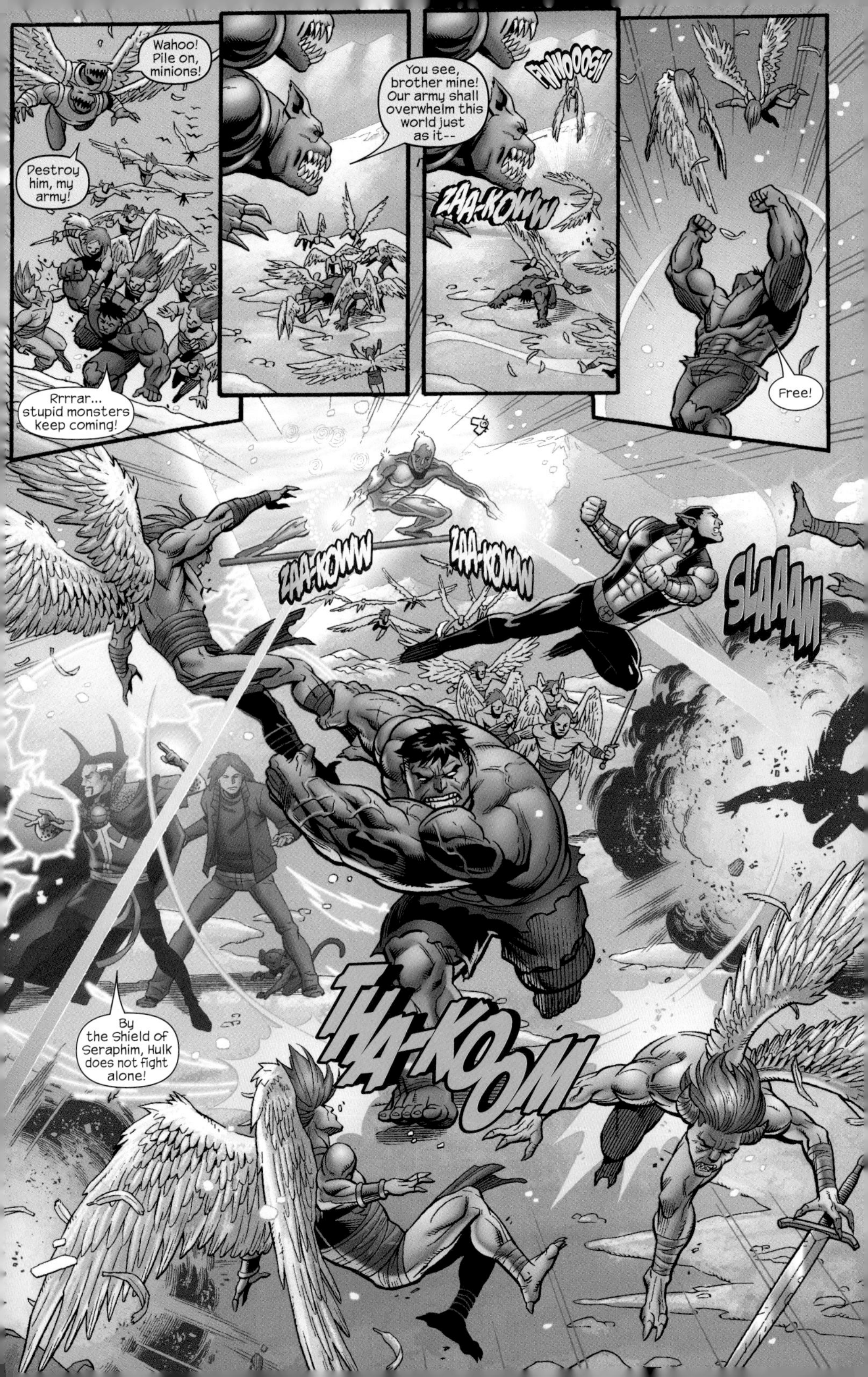

Wahoo! Pile on, minions!
Destroy him, my army!
Rrrrar... stupid monsters keep coming!
You see, brother mine! Our army shall overwhelm this world just as it--
FWWOOOSH
ZAA-KOWW
Free!
ZAA-KOWW
ZAA-KOWW
SLAAAM
By the Shield of Seraphim, Hulk does not fight alone!
THA-KOOOM

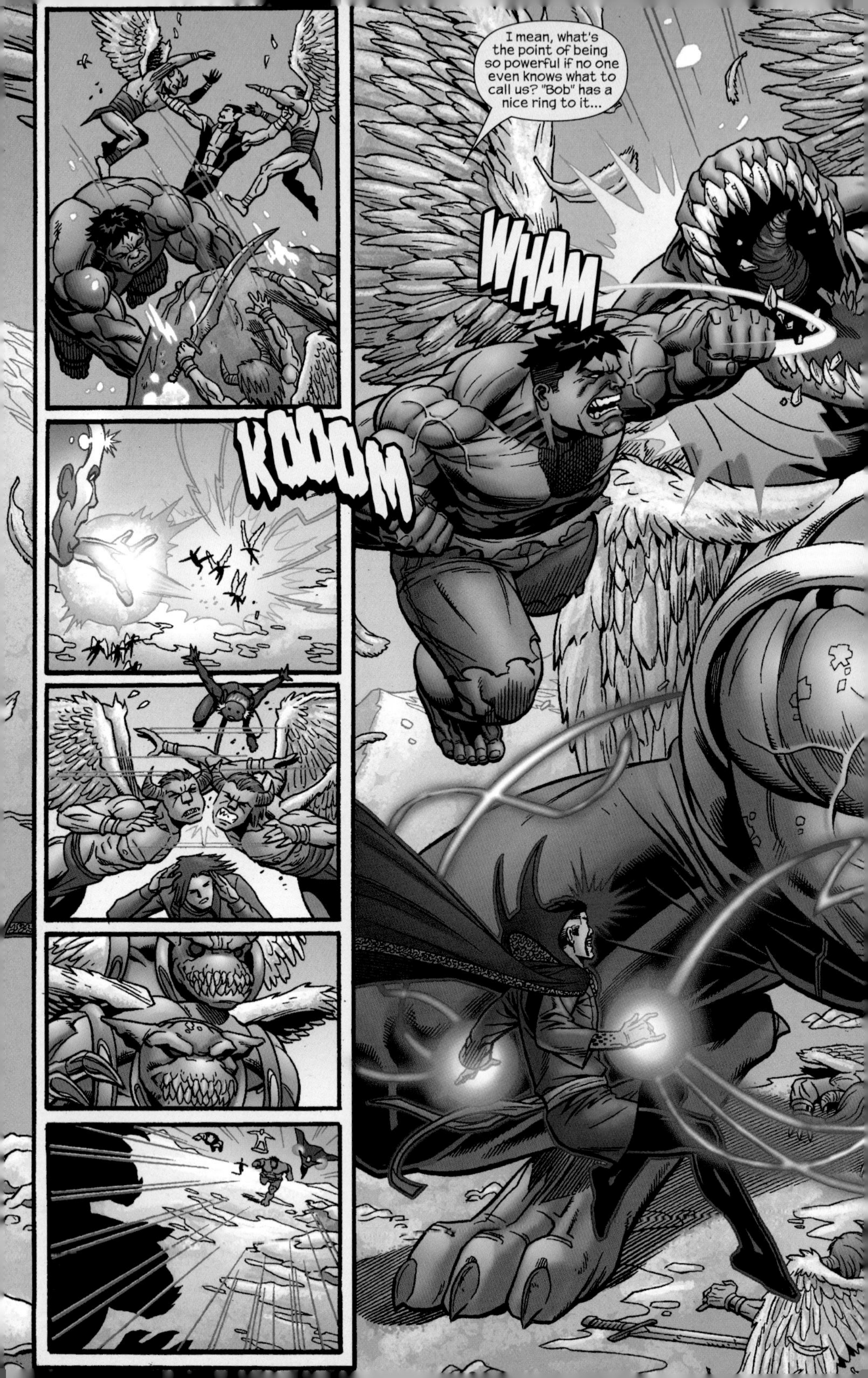

I mean, what's the point of being so powerful if no one even knows what to call us? "Bob" has a nice ring to it...
WHAM
KOOOM

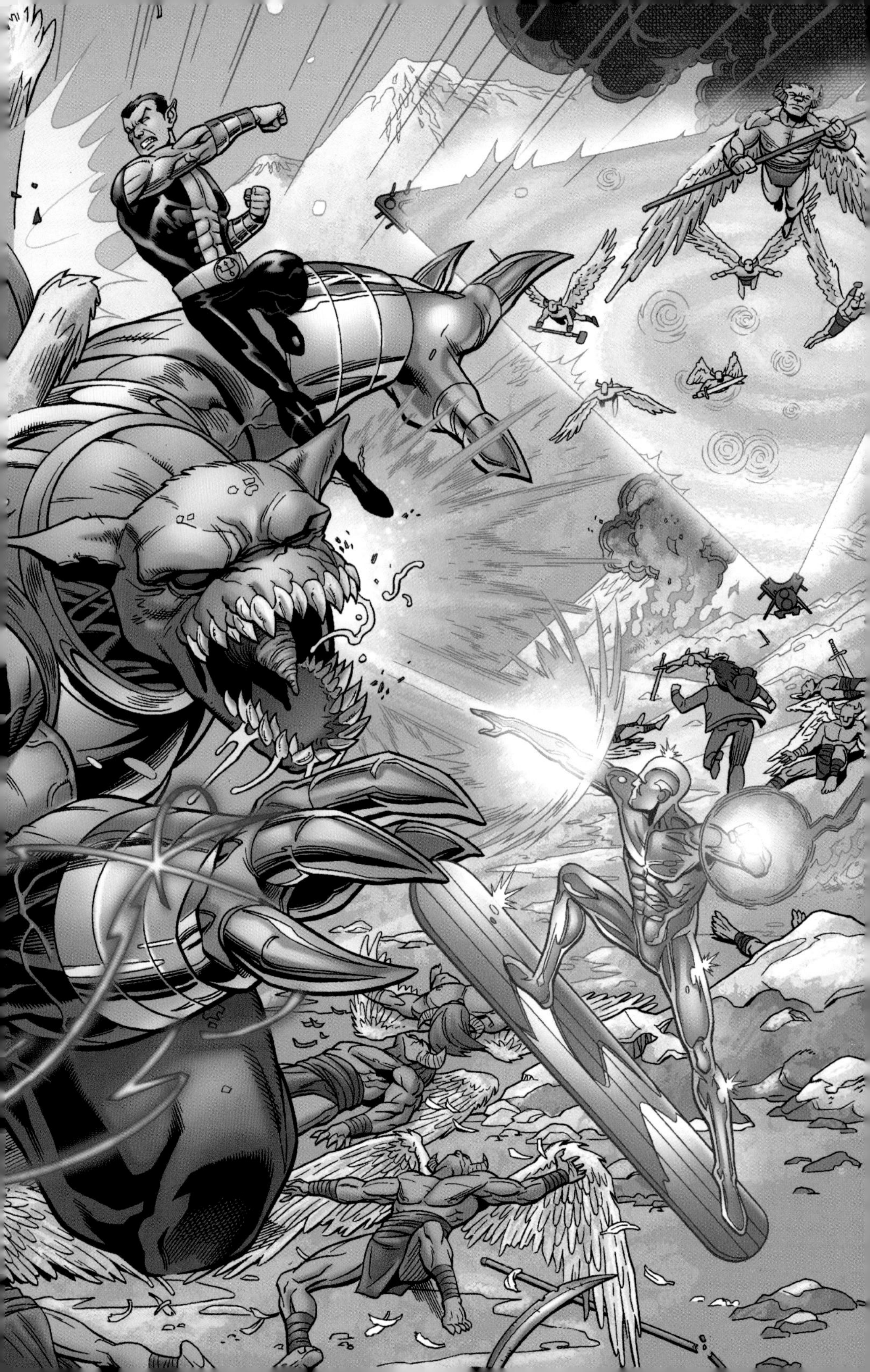

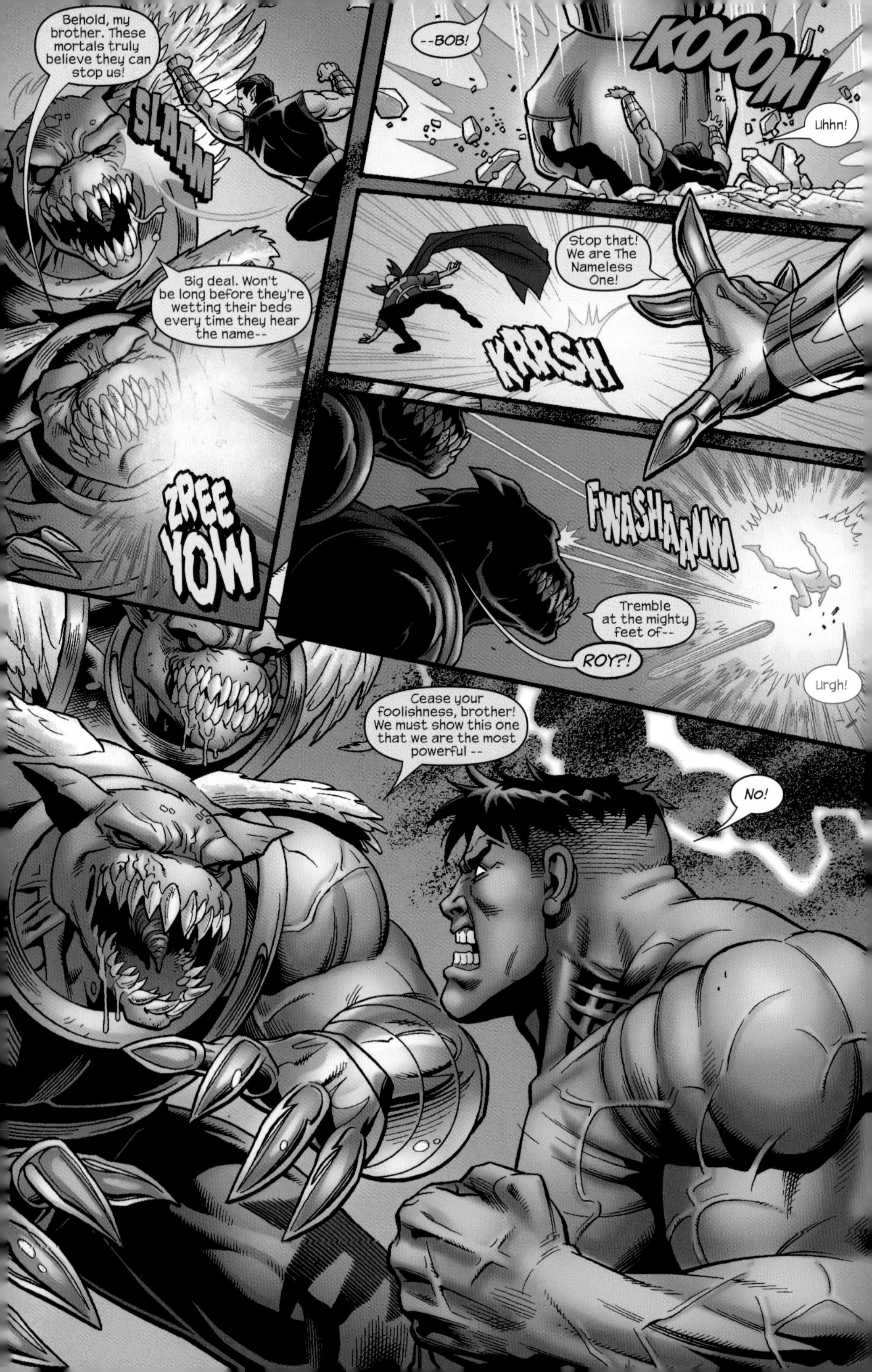
Behold, my brother. These mortals truly believe they can stop us!
SLAAM
Big deal. Won't be long before they're wetting their beds every time they hear the name--
ZREE YOW
--BOB!
KOOOM
Uhhn!
Stop that! We are The Nameless One!
KRRSH
FWASHAAMM
Tremble at the mighty feet of--
ROY?!
Urgh!
Cease your foolishness, brother! We must show this one that we are the most powerful --
No!

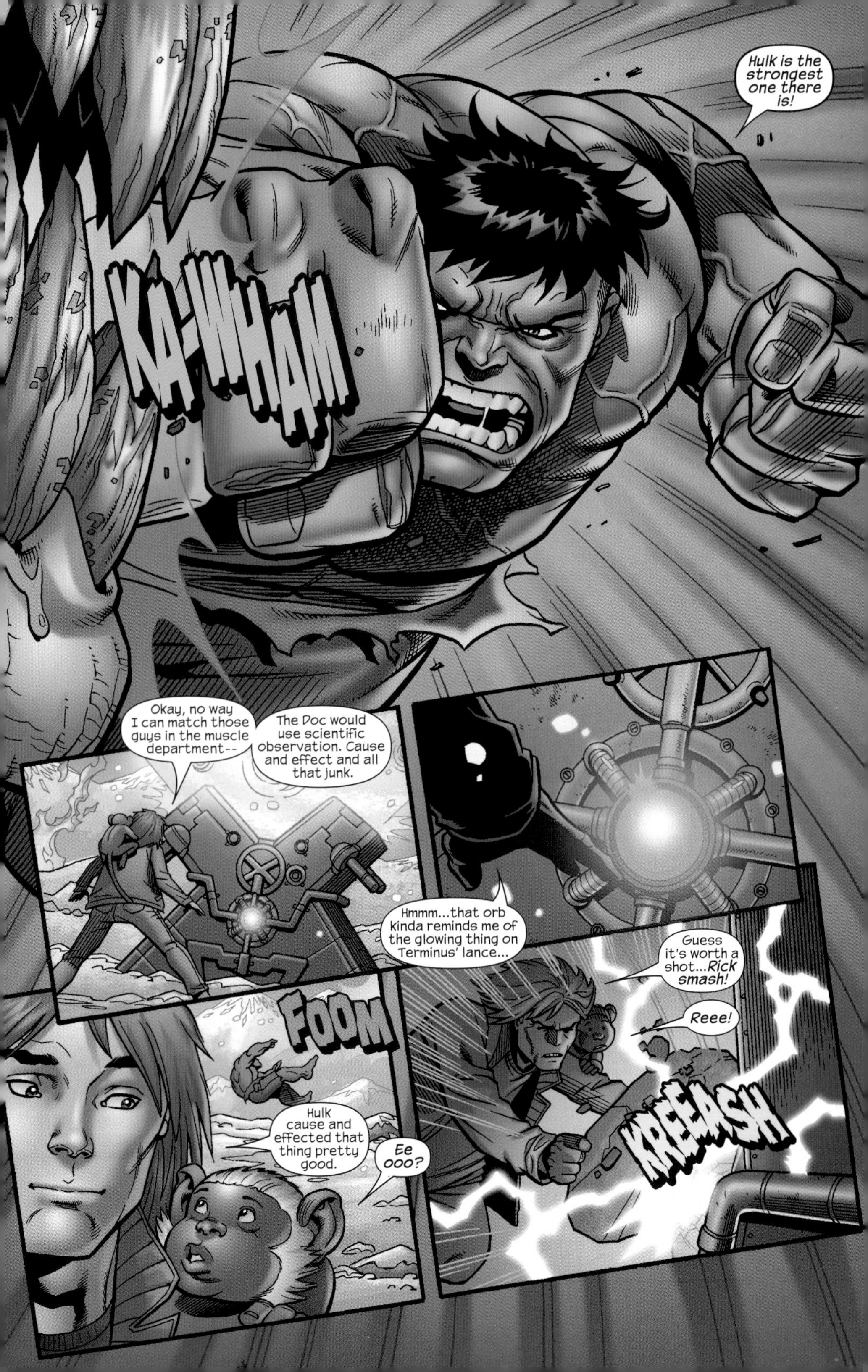
Hulk is the strongest one there is!
KA-WHAM
Okay, no way I can match those guys in the muscle department--
The Doc would use scientific observation. Cause and effect and all that junk.
Hmmm...that orb kinda reminds me of the glowing thing on Terminus' lance...
Guess it's worth a shot...Rick smash!
Reee!
KREEASH
FOOM
Hulk cause and effected that thing pretty good.
Ee ooo?

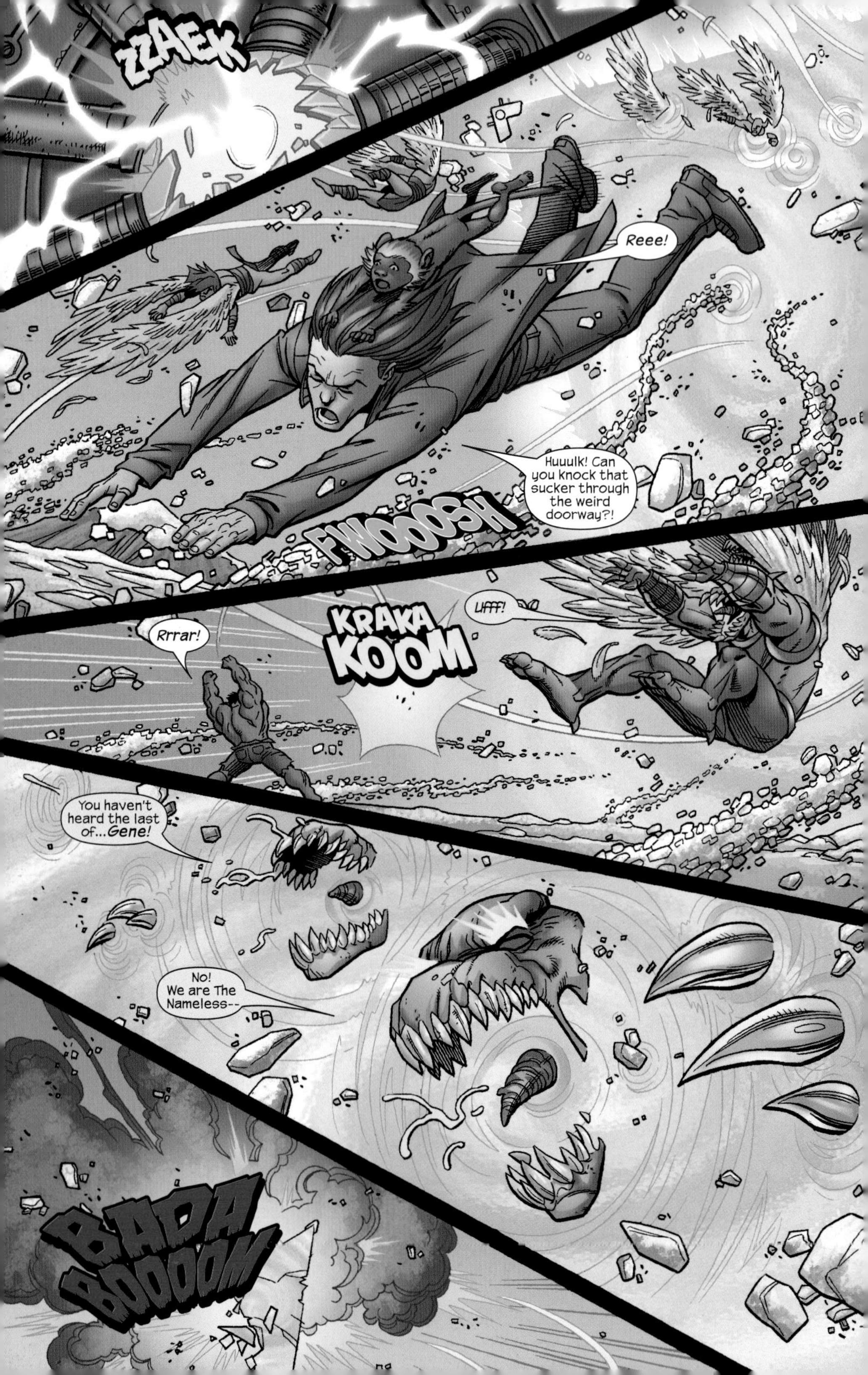
ZZAEK
Reee!
Huuulk! Can you knock that sucker through the weird doorway?!
FWOOOSH
Rrrar!
KRAKA KOOM
UFFF!
You haven't heard the last of...Gene!
No! We are The Nameless--
BADA BOOOOM

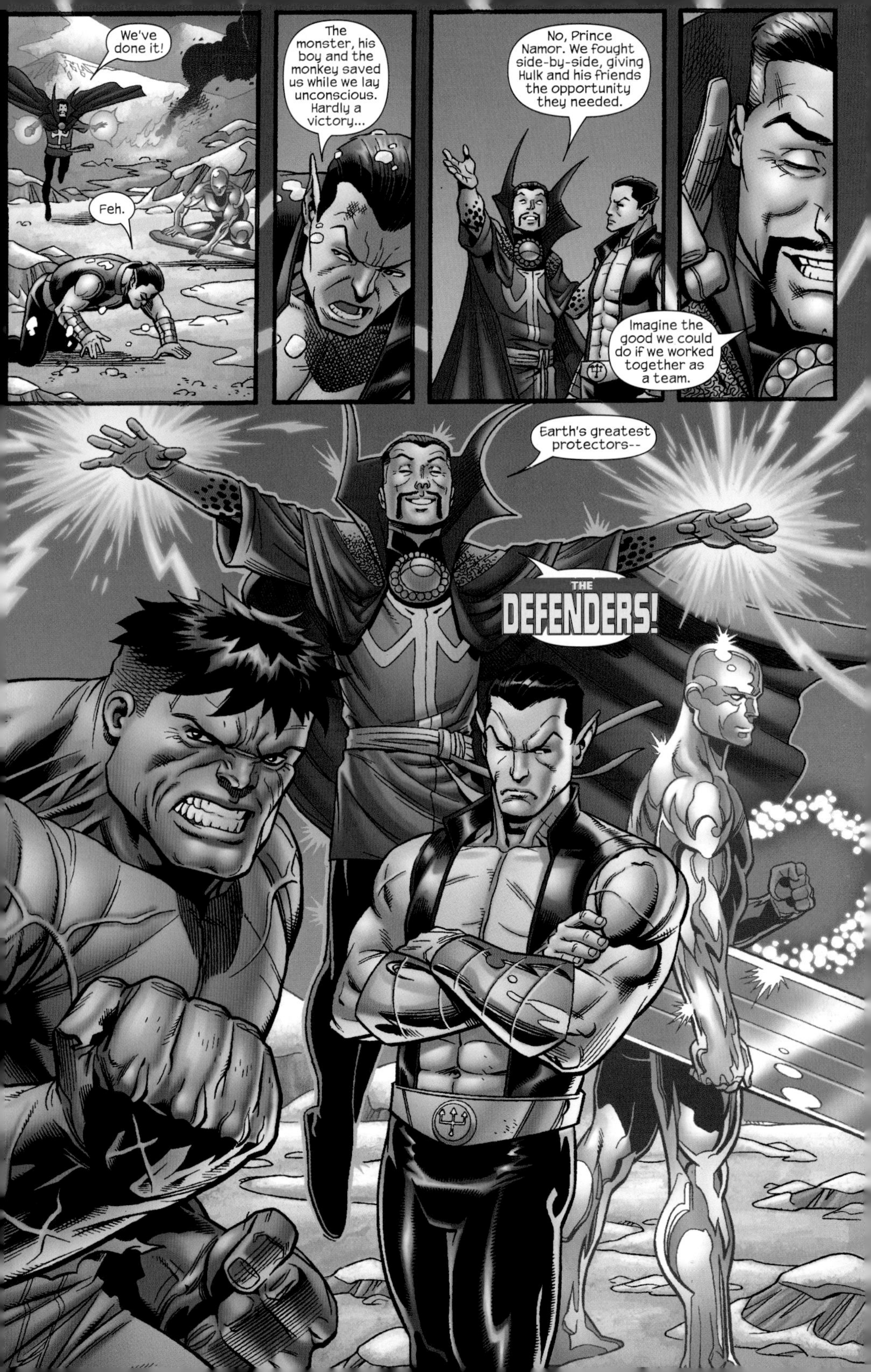
We've done it!
Feh.
The monster, his boy and the monkey saved us while we lay unconscious. Hardly a victory...
No, Prince Namor. We fought side-by-side, giving Hulk and his friends the opportunity they needed.
Imagine the good we could do if we worked together as a team.
Earth's greatest protectors--
THE DEFENDERS!

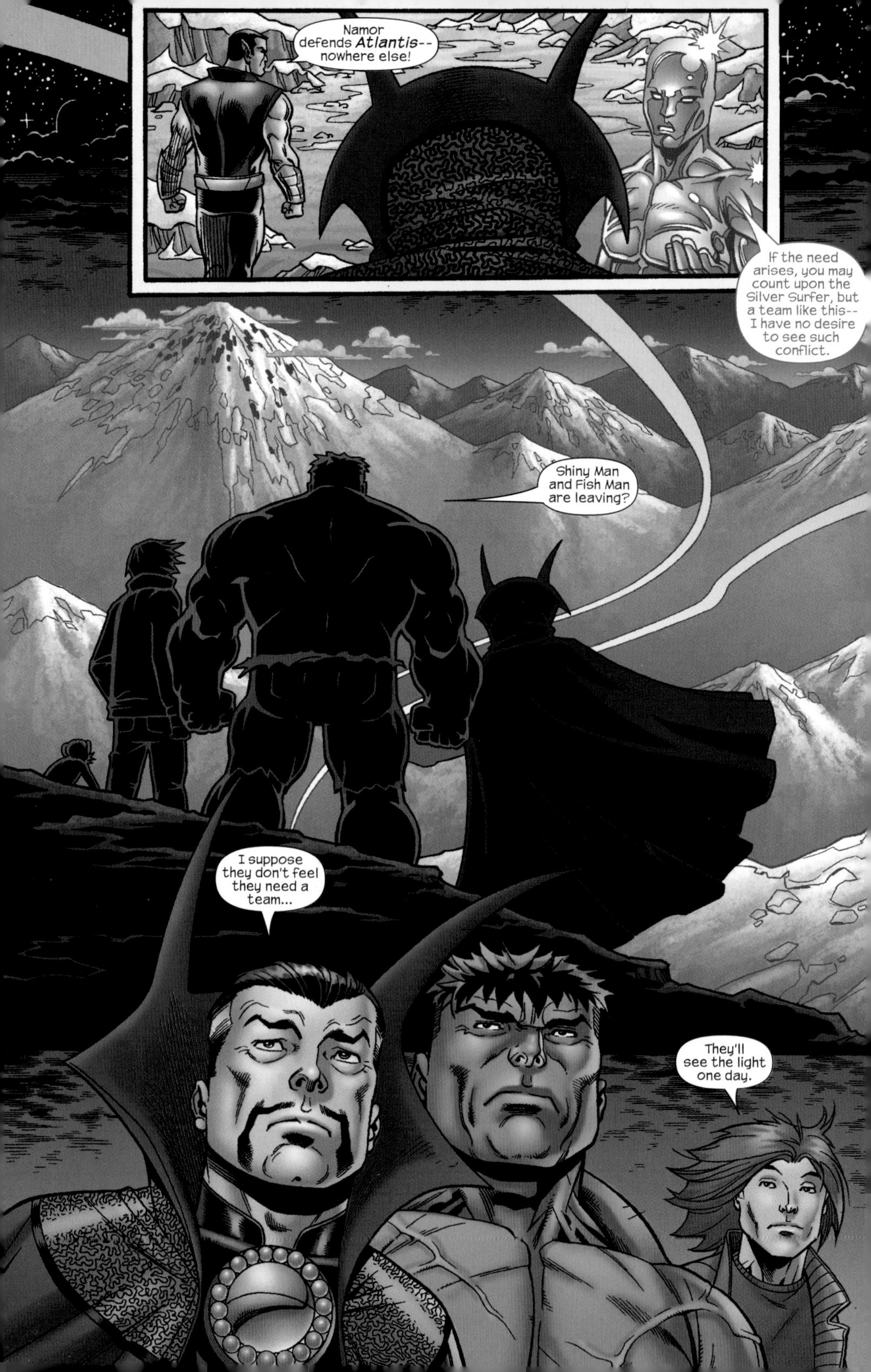
Namor defends Atlantis-- nowhere else!
If the need arises, you may count upon the Silver Surfer, but a team like this-- I have no desire to see such conflict.
Shiny Man and Fish Man are leaving?
I suppose they don't feel they need a team...
They'll see the light one day.

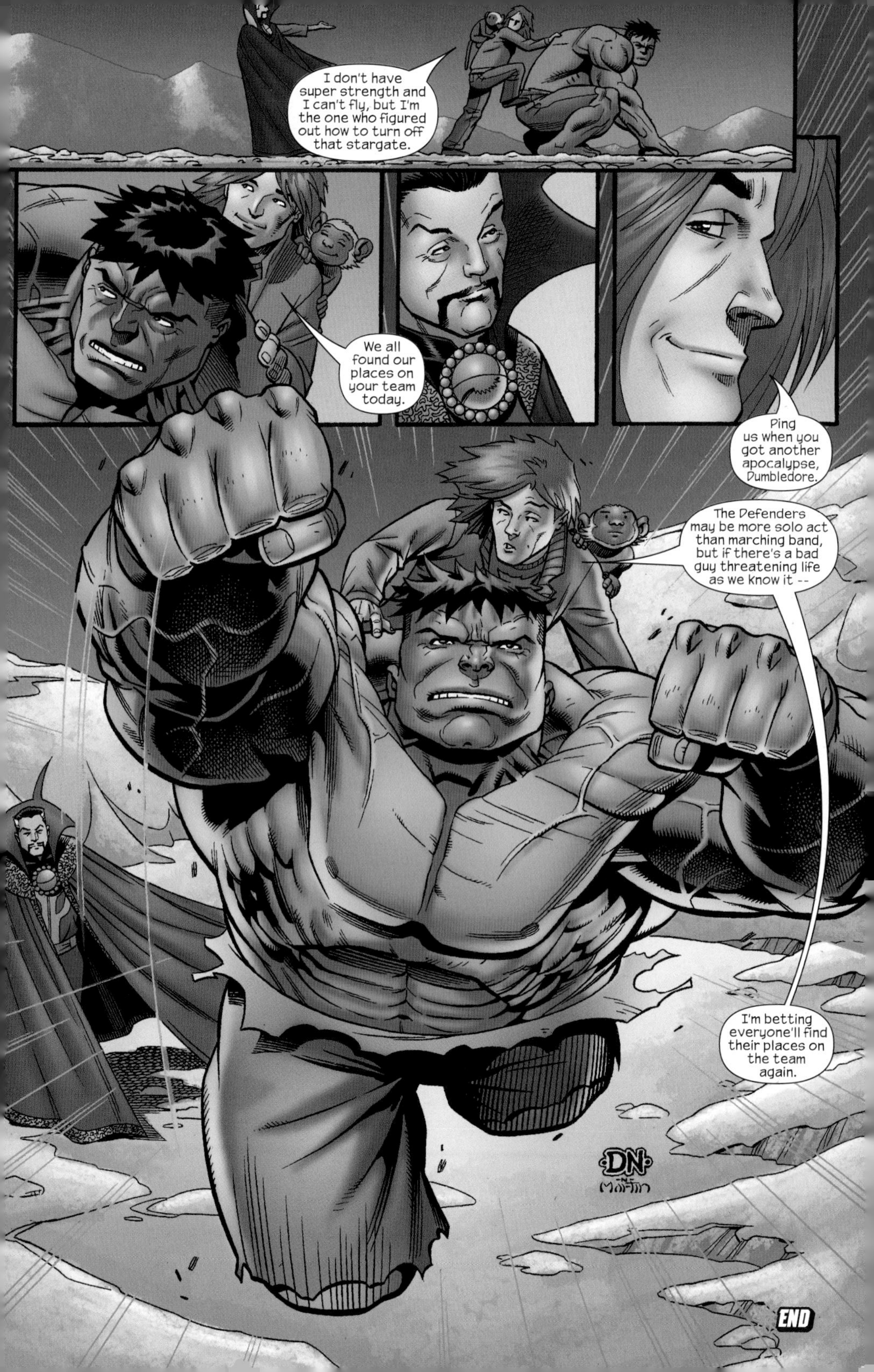

I don't have super strength and I can't fly, but I'm the one who figured out how to turn off that stargate.
We all found our places on your team today.
Ping us when you got another apocalypse, Dumbledore.
The Defenders may be more solo act than marching band, but if there's a bad guy threatening life as we know it --
I'm betting everyone'll find their places on the team again.
END

09

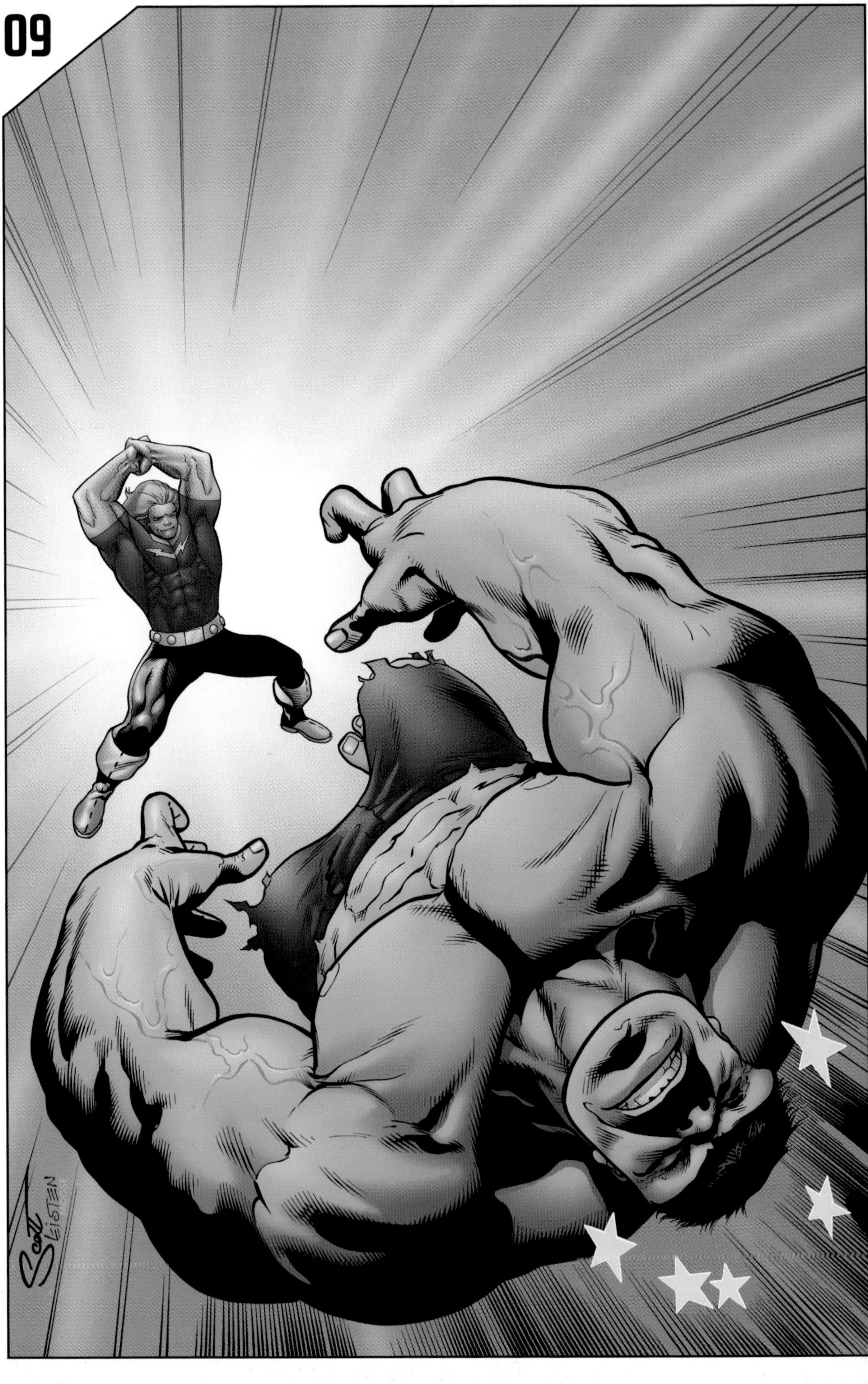

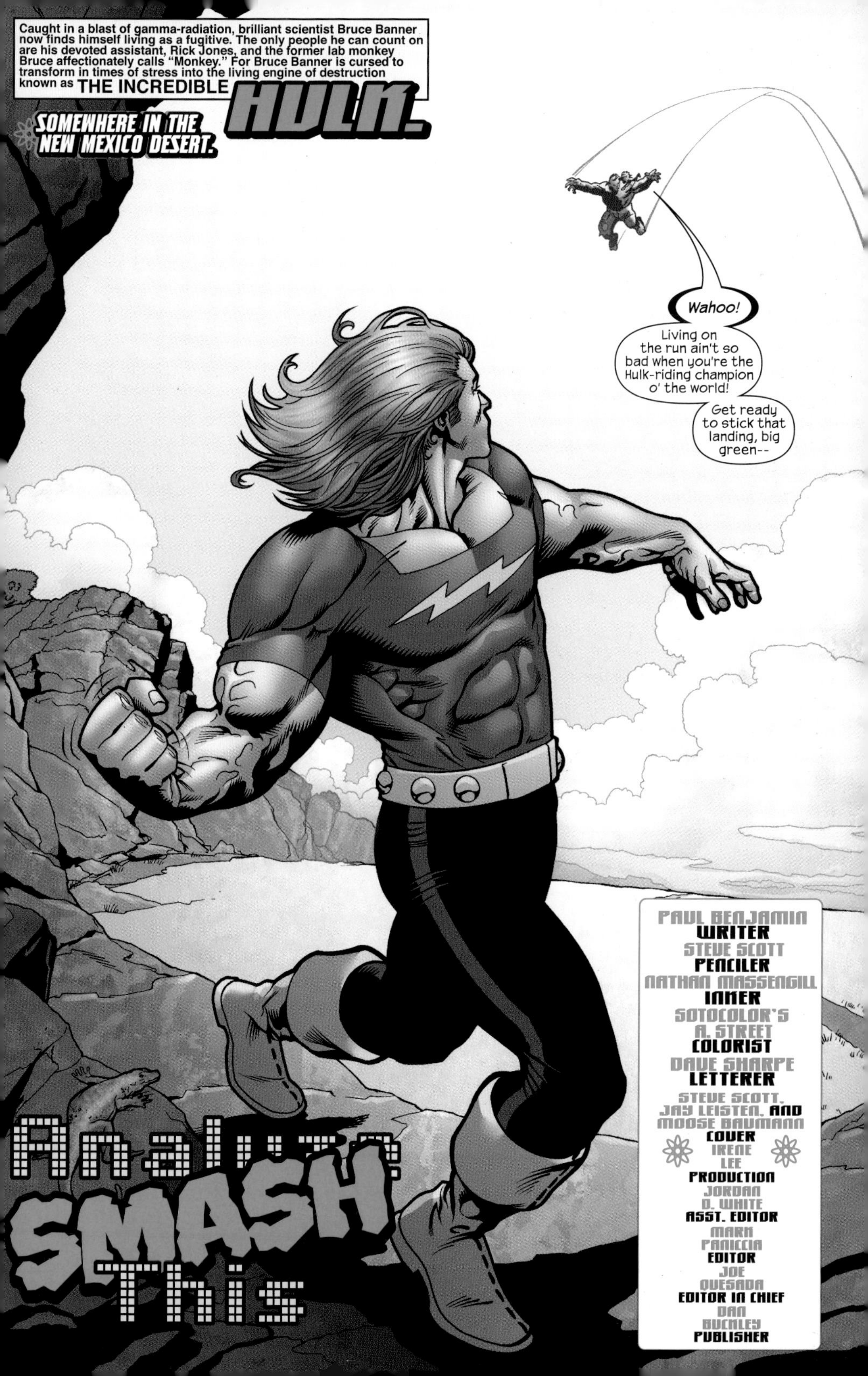

Caught in a blast of gamma-radiation, brilliant scientist Bruce Banner now finds himself living as a fugitive. The only people he can count on are his devoted assistant, Rick Jones, and the former lab monkey Bruce affectionately calls "Monkey." For Bruce Banner is cursed to transform in times of stress into the living engine of destruction known as THE INCREDIBLE HULK.
SOMEWHERE IN THE NEW MEXICO DESERT.
Wahoo!
Living on the run ain't so bad when you're the Hulk-riding champion o' the world!
Get ready to stick that landing, big green--
Analyze SMASH This
PAUL BENJAMIN WRITER
STEVE SCOTT PENCILER
NATHAN MASSENGILL INKER
SOTOCOLOR'S A. STREET COLORIST
DAVE SHARPE LETTERER
STEVE SCOTT, JAY LEISTEN, AND MOOSE BAUMANN COVER
IRENE LEE PRODUCTION
JORDAN D. WHITE ASST. EDITOR
MARK PANICCIA EDITOR
JOE QUESADA EDITOR IN CHIEF
DAN BUCKLEY PUBLISHER

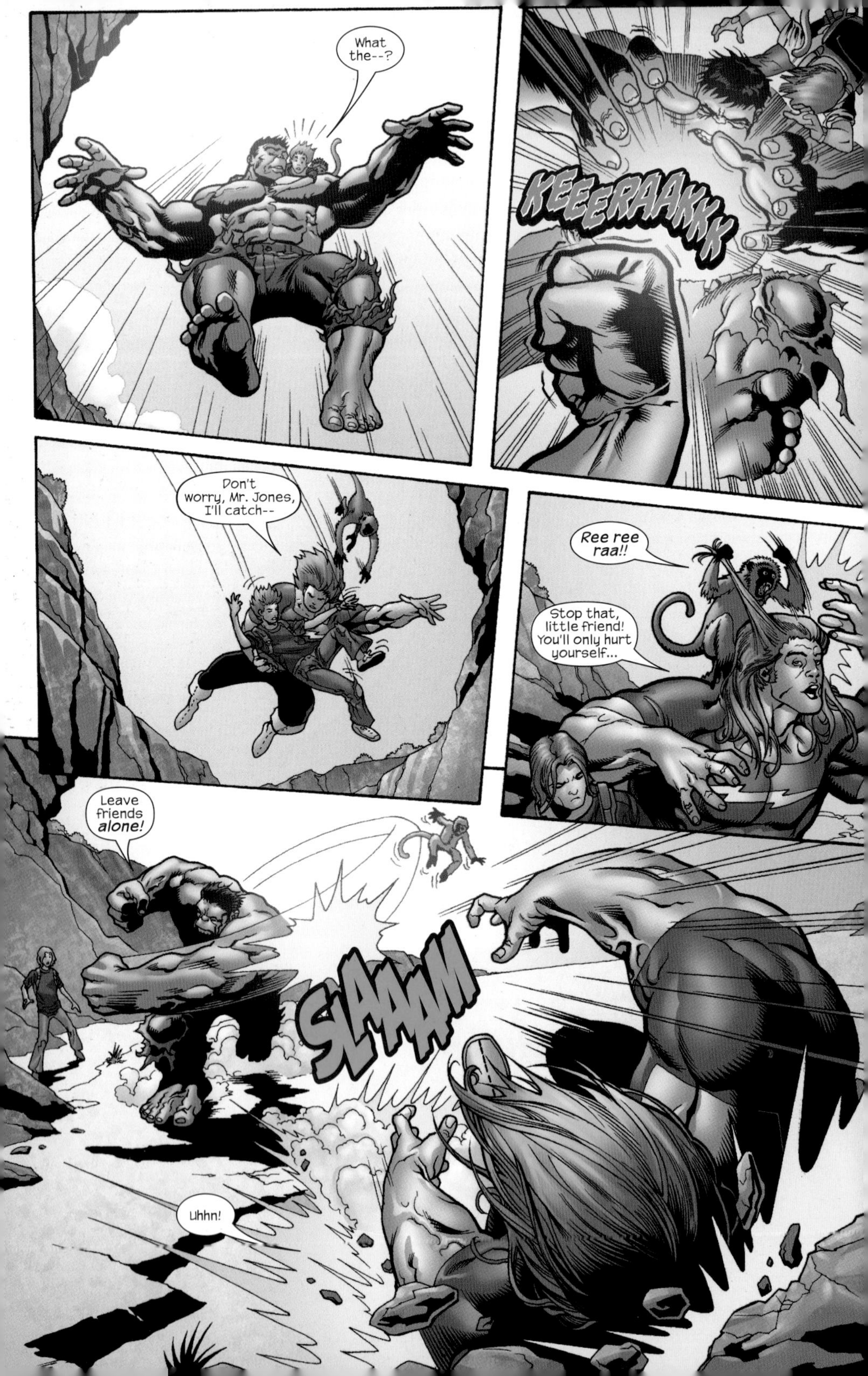
What the--?
KEEERAAKKK
Don't worry, Mr. Jones, I'll catch--
Ree ree raa!!
Stop that, little friend! You'll only hurt yourself...
Leave friends alone!
SLAAAM
Uhhn!

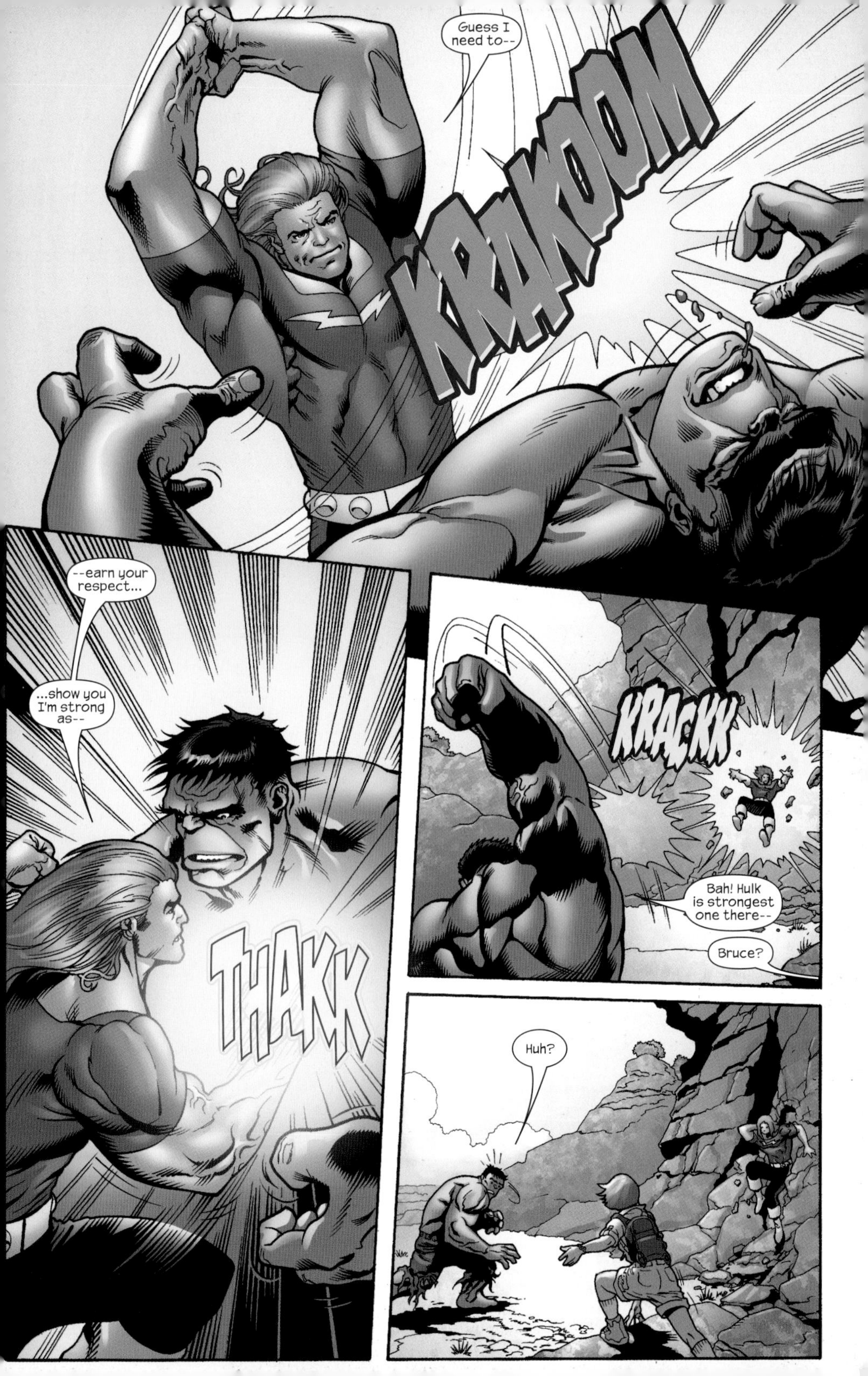
Guess I need to--
KRAKOOM
--earn your respect...
...show you I'm strong as--
THAKK
KRACKK
Bah! Hulk is strongest one there--
Bruce?
Huh?

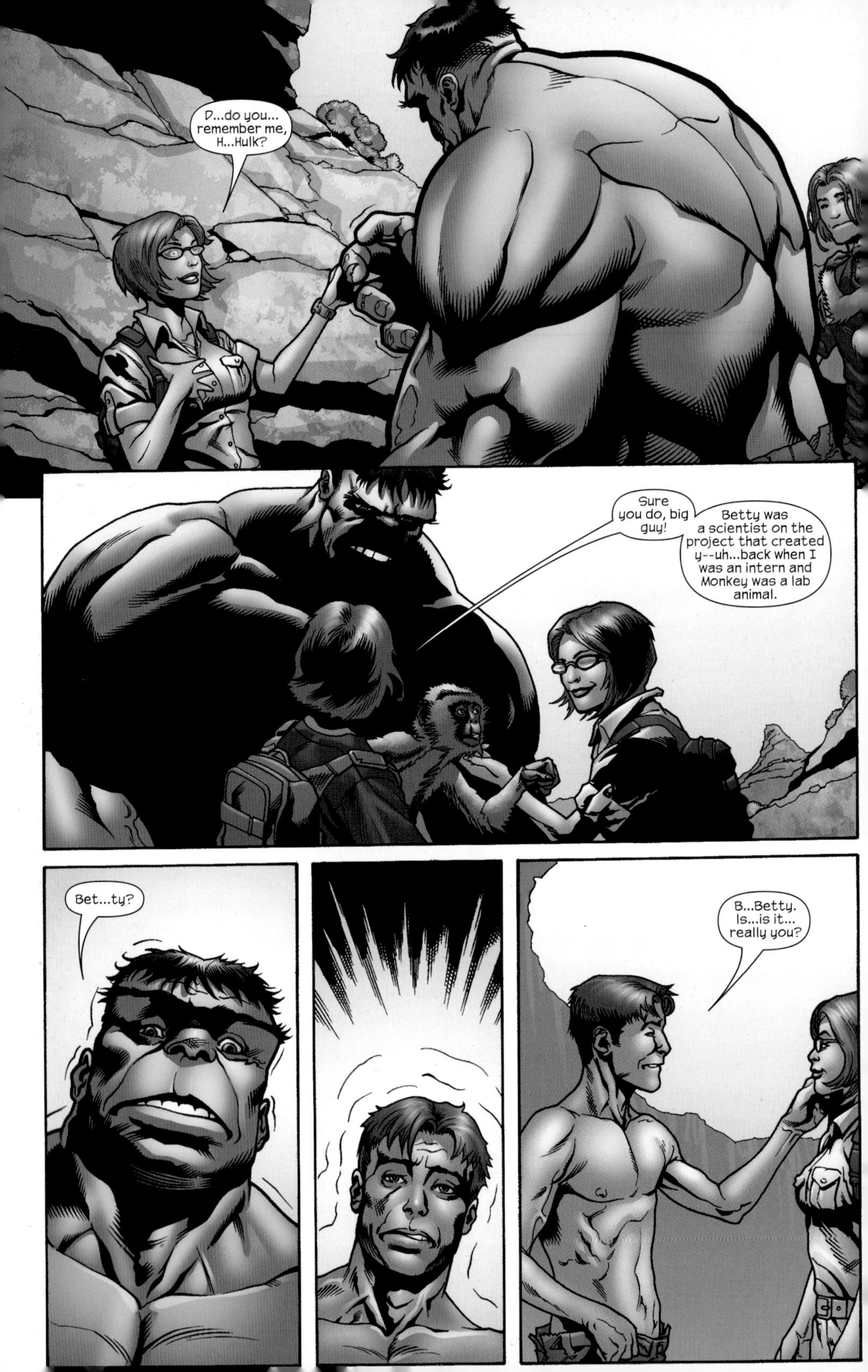
D...do you... remember me, H...Hulk?
Sure you do, big guy!
Betty was a scientist on the project that created y--uh...back when I was an intern and Monkey was a lab animal.
Bet...ty?
B...Betty. Is...is it... really you?

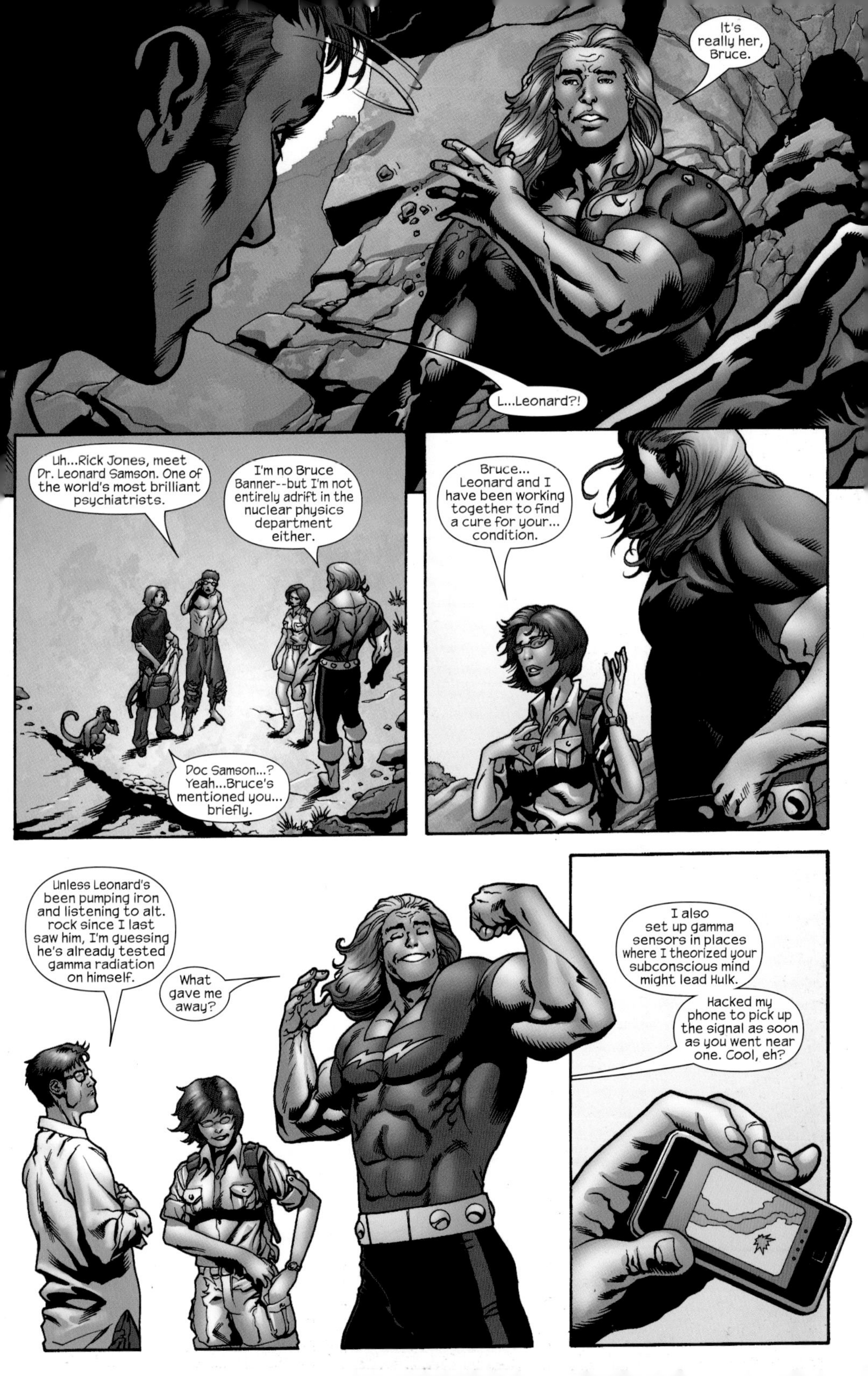
It's really her, Bruce.
L...Leonard?!
Uh...Rick Jones, meet Dr. Leonard Samson. One of the world's most brilliant psychiatrists.
I'm no Bruce Banner--but I'm not entirely adrift in the nuclear physics department either.
Doc Samson...? Yeah...Bruce's mentioned you... briefly.
Bruce... Leonard and I have been working together to find a cure for your... condition.
Unless Leonard's been pumping iron and listening to alt. rock since I last saw him, I'm guessing he's already tested gamma radiation on himself.
What gave me away?
I also set up gamma sensors in places where I theorized your subconscious mind might lead Hulk.
Hacked my phone to pick up the signal as soon as you went near one. Cool, eh?

"Betty and I have designed a combination of psychotherapy and low-dosage radiation treatments to suppress the triggers that cause your transformation."

General Ross gave Betty carte blanche to continue your work after the... accident.

First time I was ever glad to be a military brat...

Betty's father has no clue that we've been using this facility to find a cure.

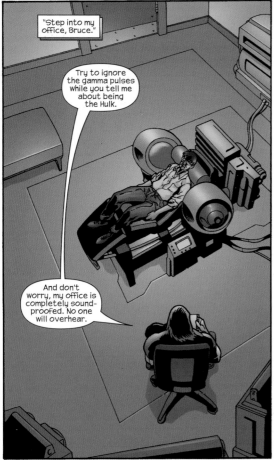

"Step into my office, Bruce."

Try to ignore the gamma pulses while you tell me about being the Hulk.

And don't worry, my office is completely sound-proofed. No one will overhear.

Okay... ummm...think about your own gamma-boosted strength.

You could punch a man through a brick wall, right?

This isn't about me, Bruce.

Now imagine being constantly afraid you'll lose control of those fists...getting angry and waking up to find out you've leveled a small town.

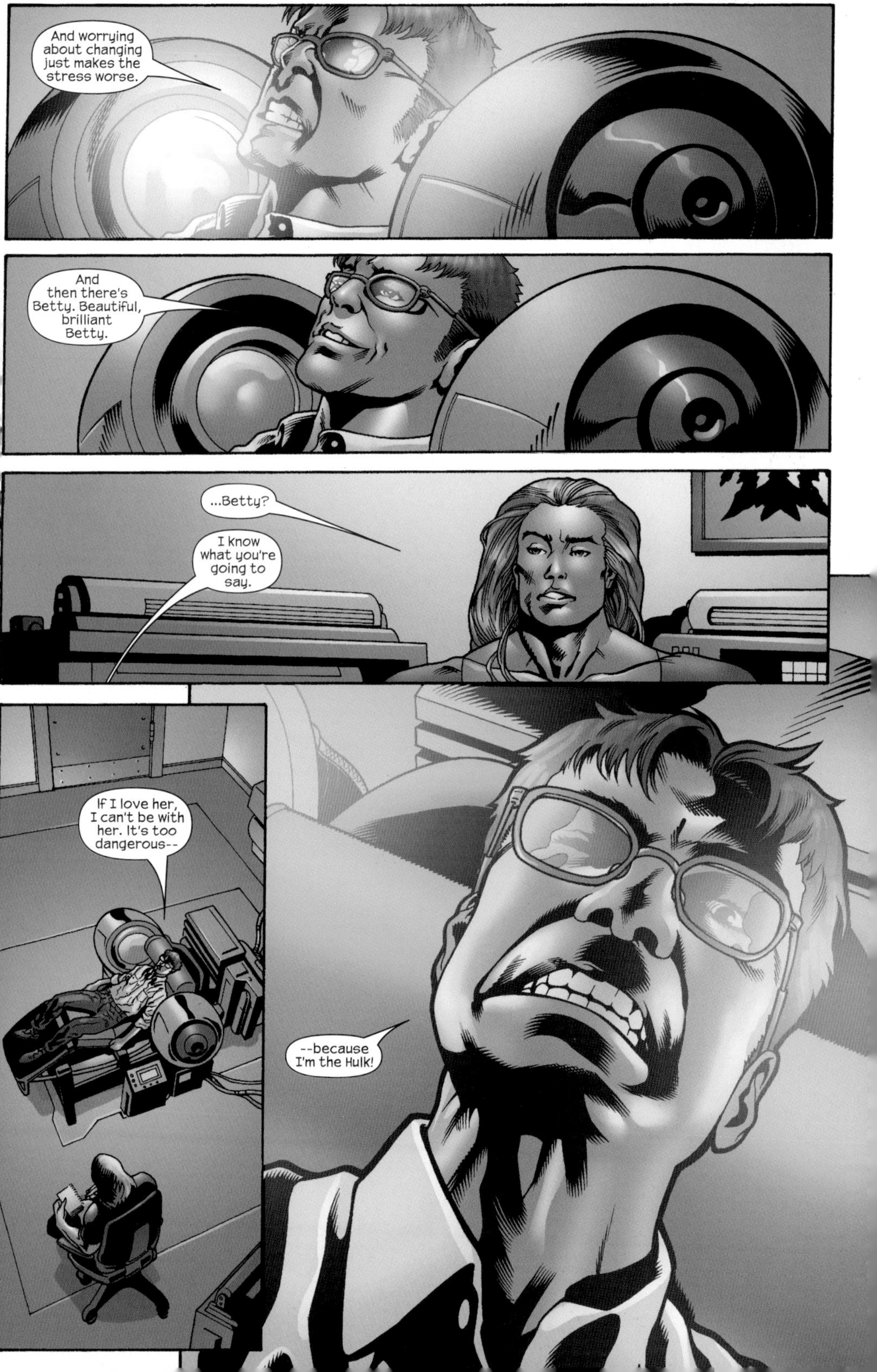
And worrying about changing just makes the stress worse.
And then there's Betty. Beautiful, brilliant Betty.
...Betty?
I know what you're going to say.
If I love her, I can't be with her. It's too dangerous--
--because I'm the Hulk!

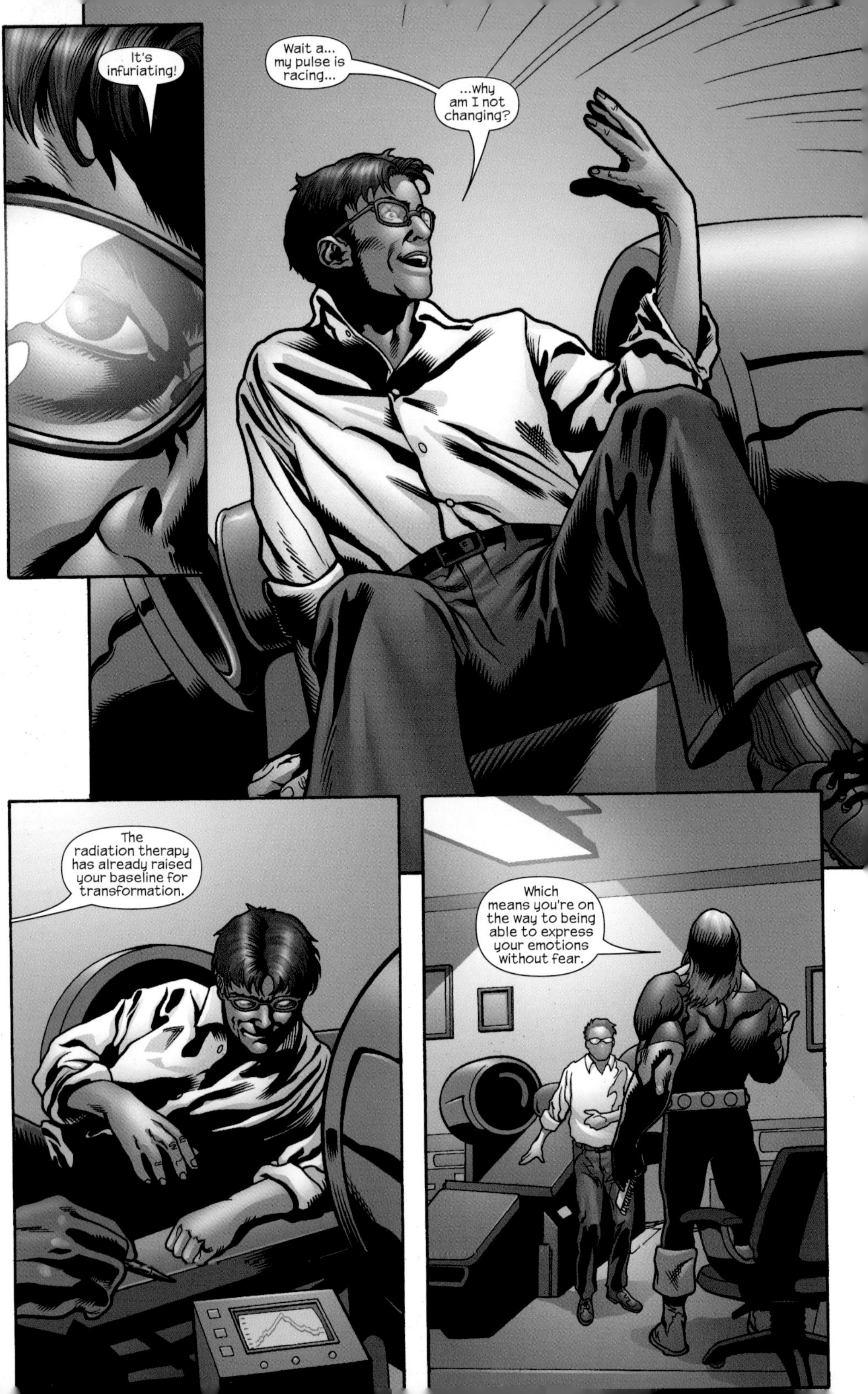
It's infuriating!
Wait a... my pulse is racing...
...why am I not changing?
The radiation therapy has already raised your baseline for transformation.
Which means you're on the way to being able to express your emotions without fear.

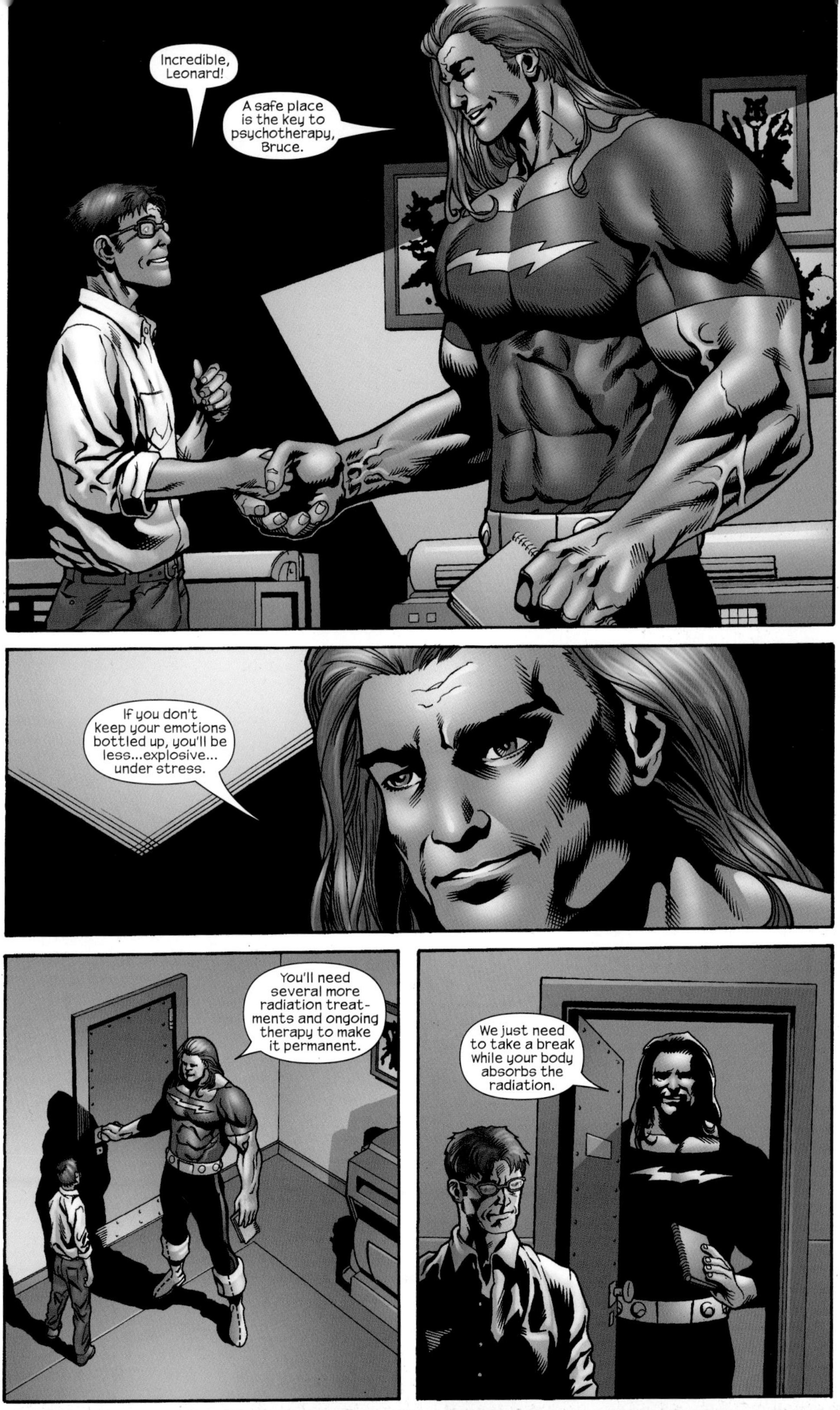
Incredible, Leonard!
A safe place is the key to psychotherapy, Bruce.
If you don't keep your emotions bottled up, you'll be less...explosive... under stress.
You'll need several more radiation treat-ments and ongoing therapy to make it permanent.
We just need to take a break while your body absorbs the radiation.

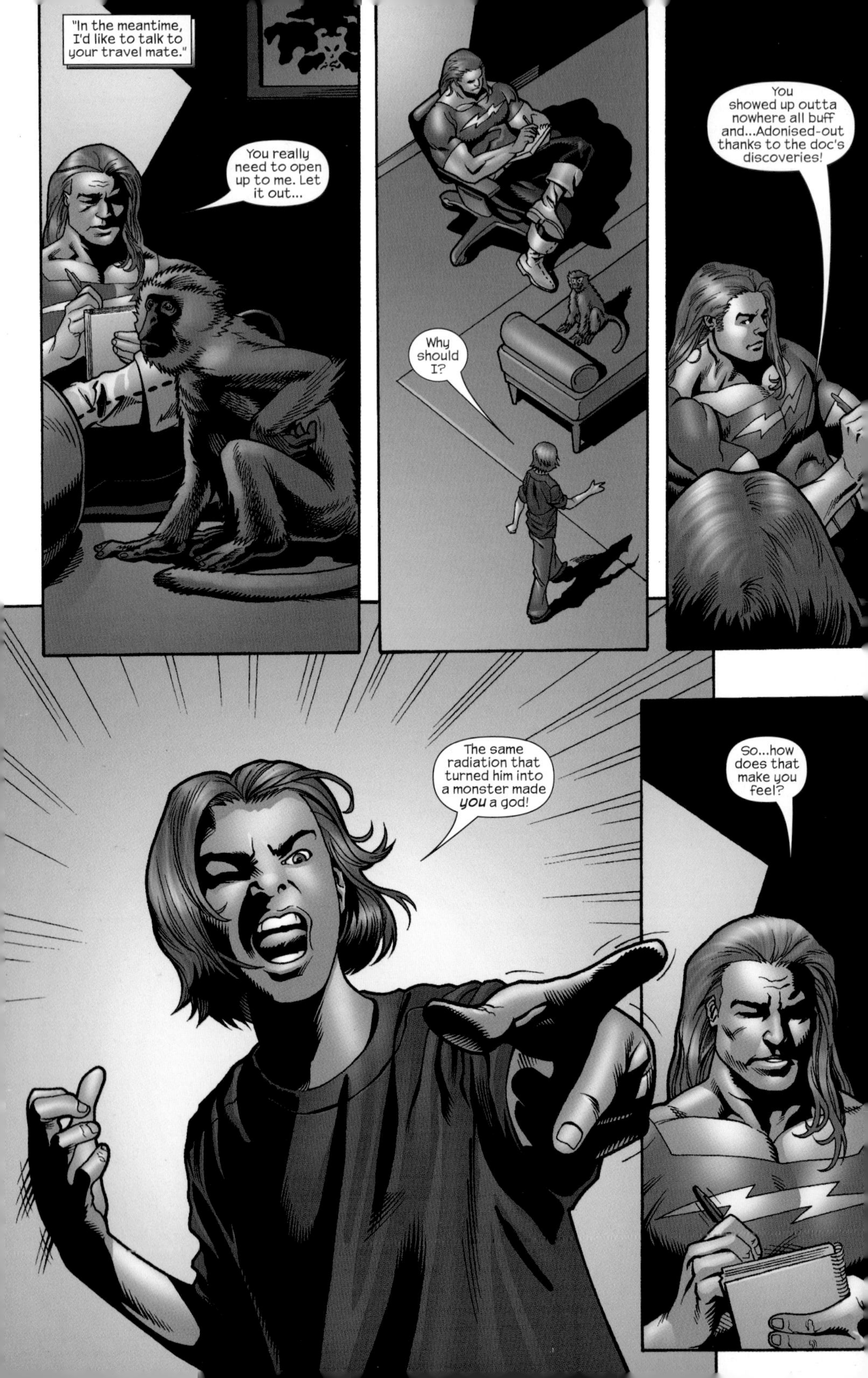
"In the meantime, I'd like to talk to your travel mate."
You really need to open up to me. Let it out...
Why should I?
You showed up outta nowhere all buff and...Adonised-out thanks to the doc's discoveries!
The same radiation that turned him into a monster made YOU a god!
So...how does that make you feel?

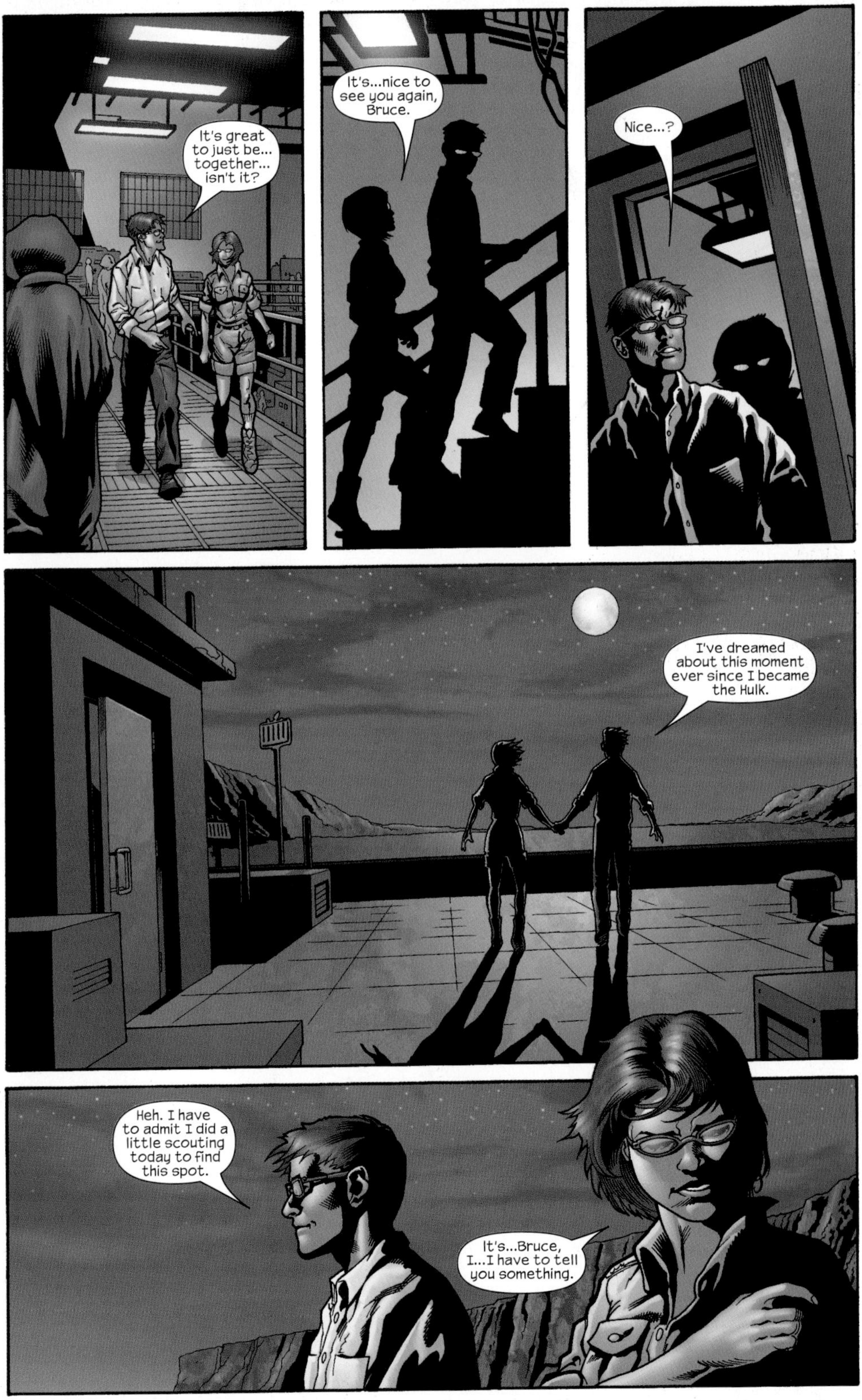

It's great to just be... together... isn't it?
It's...nice to see you again, Bruce.
Nice...?
I've dreamed about this moment ever since I became the Hulk.
Heh. I have to admit I did a little scouting today to find this spot.
It's...Bruce, I...I have to tell you something.

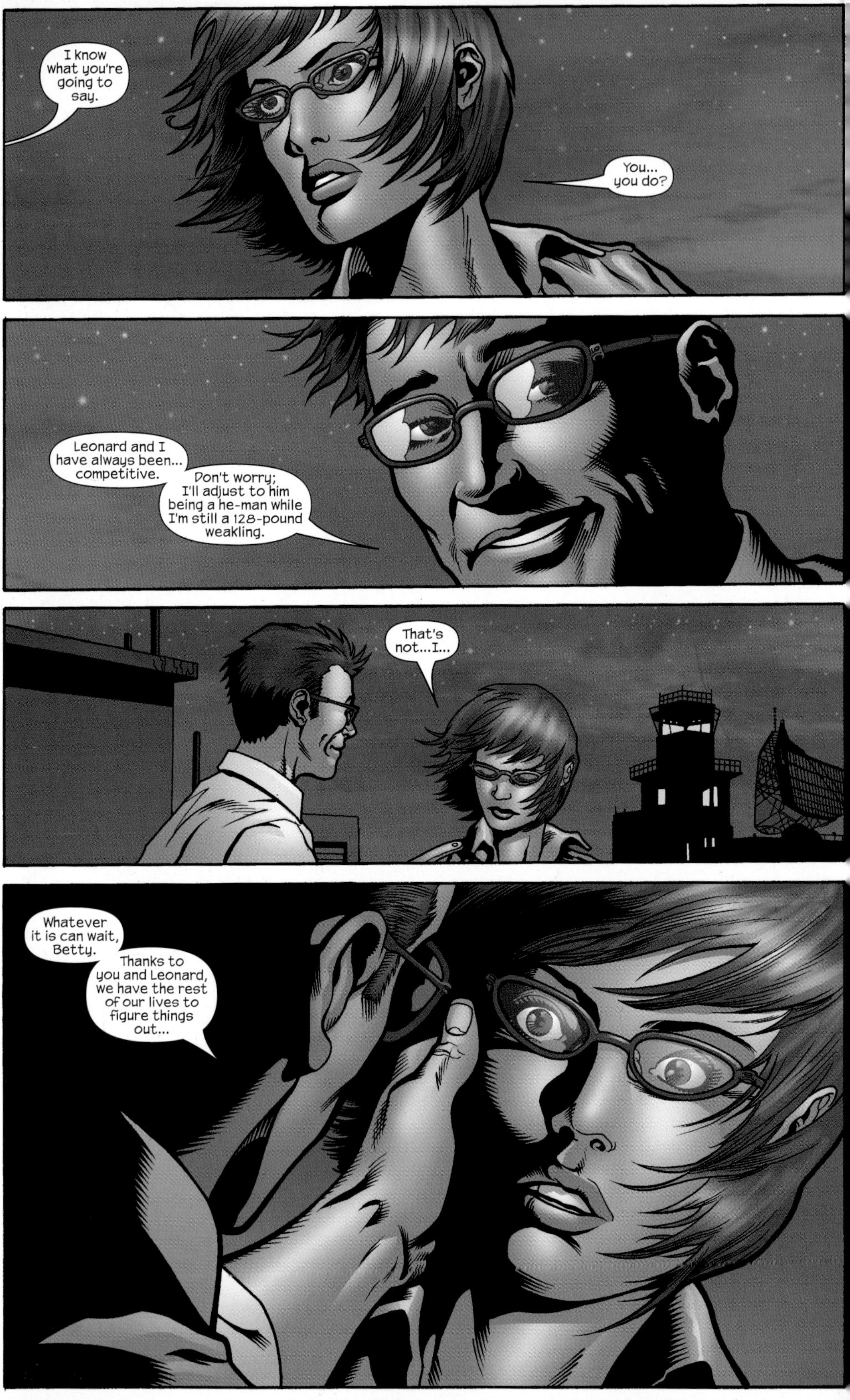
I know what you're going to say.
You... you do?
Leonard and I have always been... competitive.
Don't worry; I'll adjust to him being a he-man while I'm still a 128-pound weakling.
That's not...I...
Whatever it is can wait, Betty.
Thanks to you and Leonard, we have the rest of our lives to figure things out...

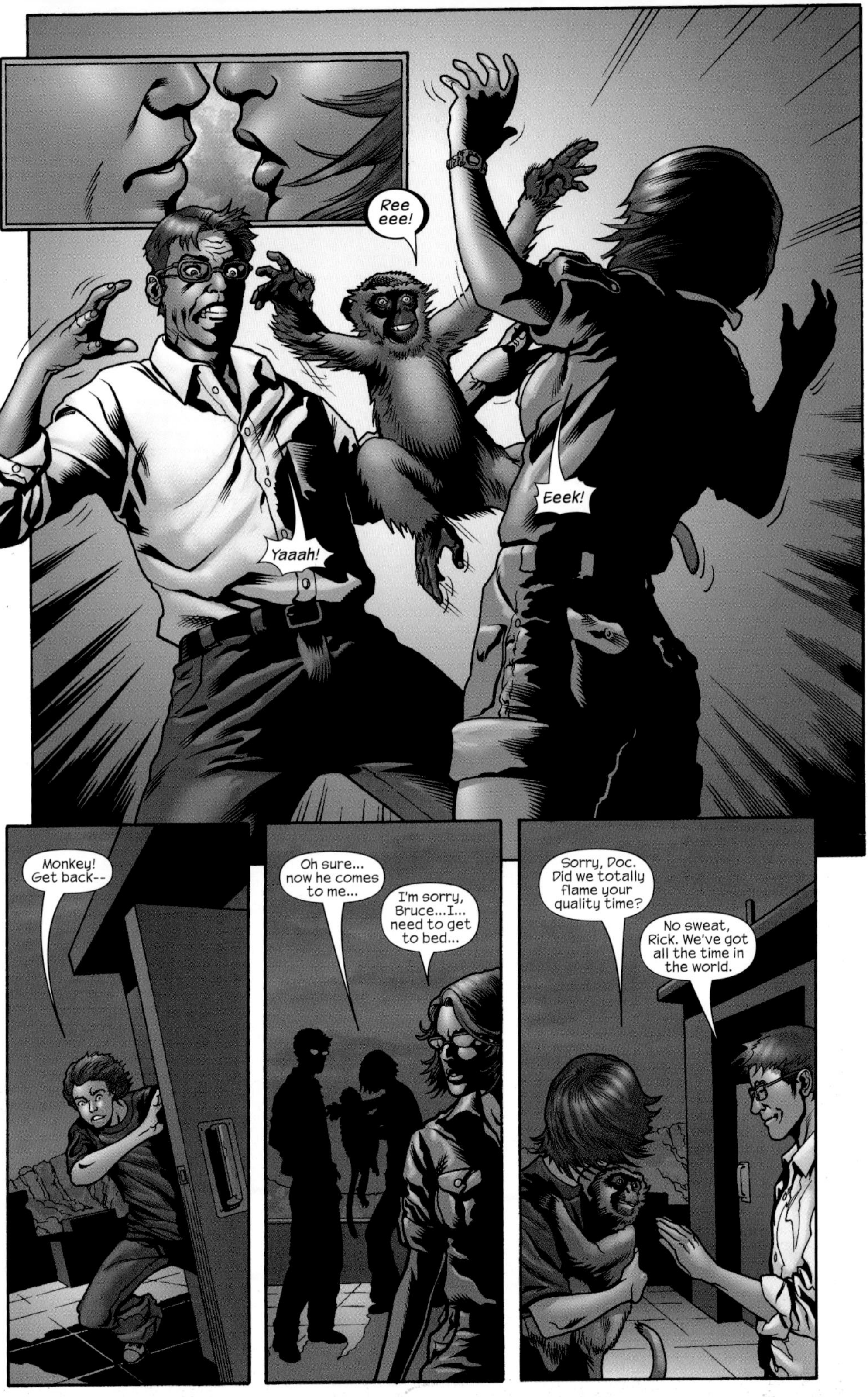
Ree eee!
Yaaah!
Eeek!
Monkey! Get back--
Oh sure... now he comes to me...
I'm sorry, Bruce...I... need to get to bed...
Sorry, Doc. Did we totally flame your quality time?
No sweat, Rick. We've got all the time in the world.

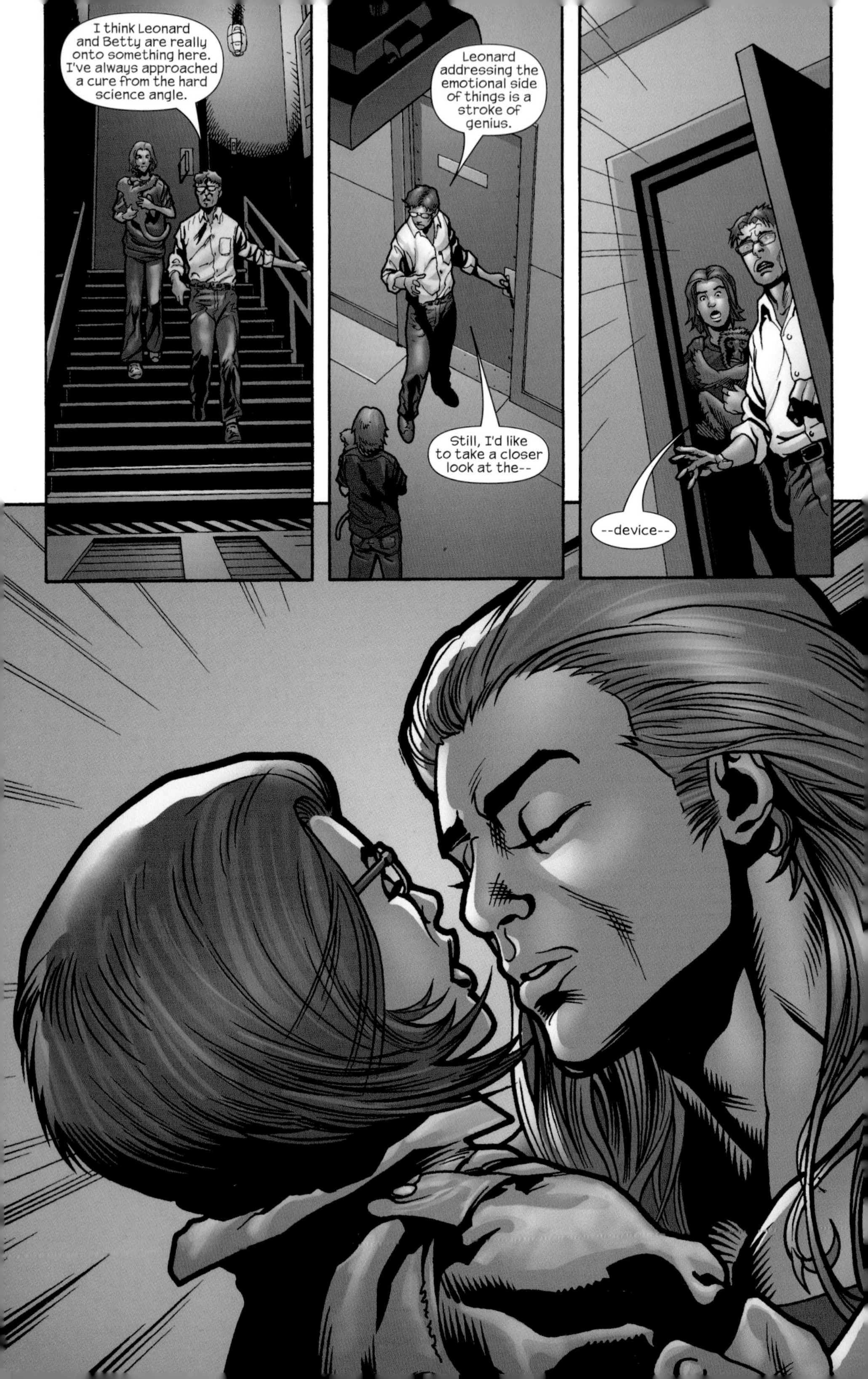
I think Leonard and Betty are really onto something here. I've always approached a cure from the hard science angle.
Leonard addressing the emotional side of things is a stroke of genius.
Still, I'd like to take a closer look at the--
--device--

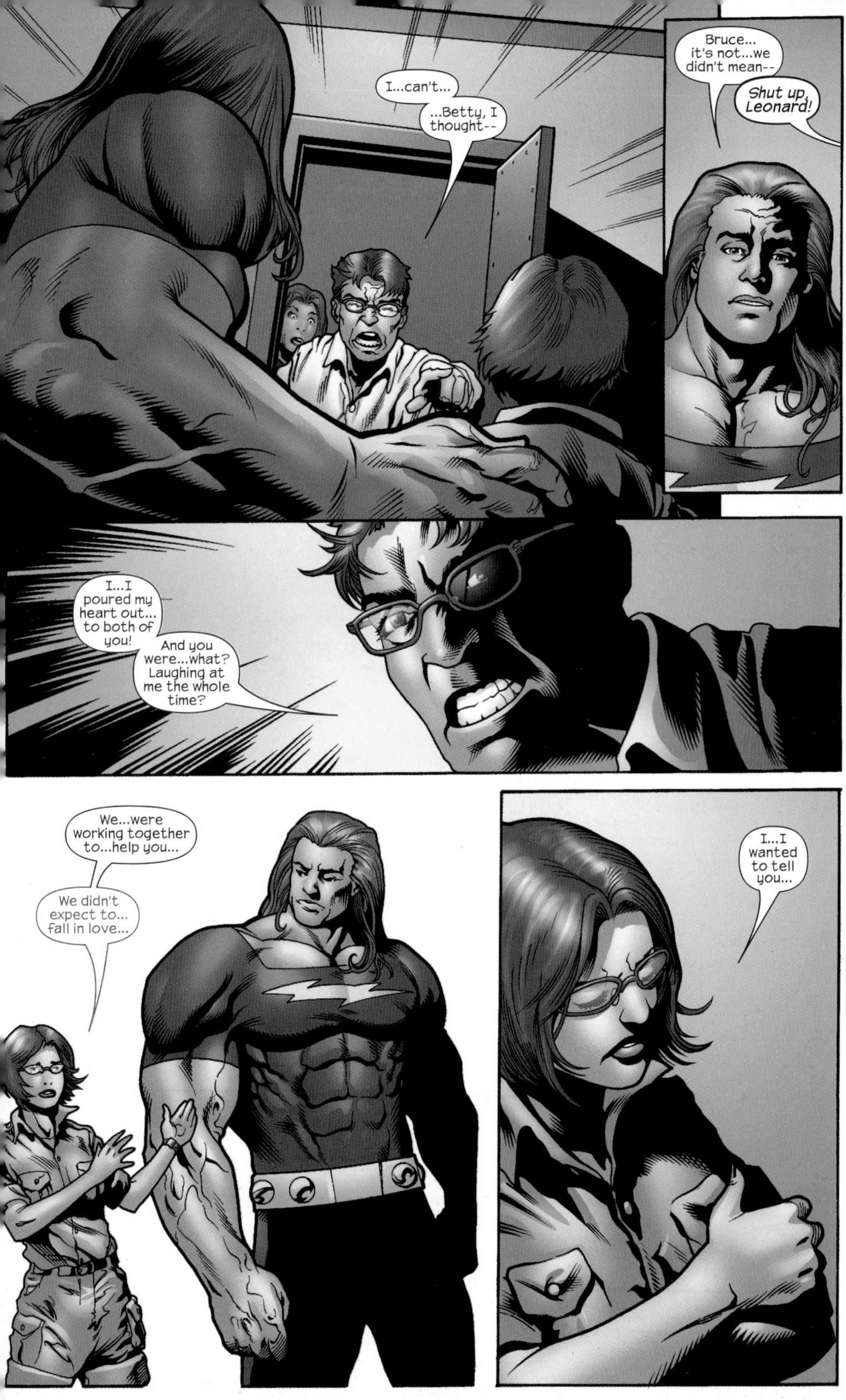
I...can't...
...Betty, I thought--
Bruce... it's not...we didn't mean--
Shut up, Leonard!
I...I poured my heart out... to both of you!
And you were...what? Laughing at me the whole time?
We...were working together to...help you...
We didn't expect to... fall in love...
I...I wanted to tell you...

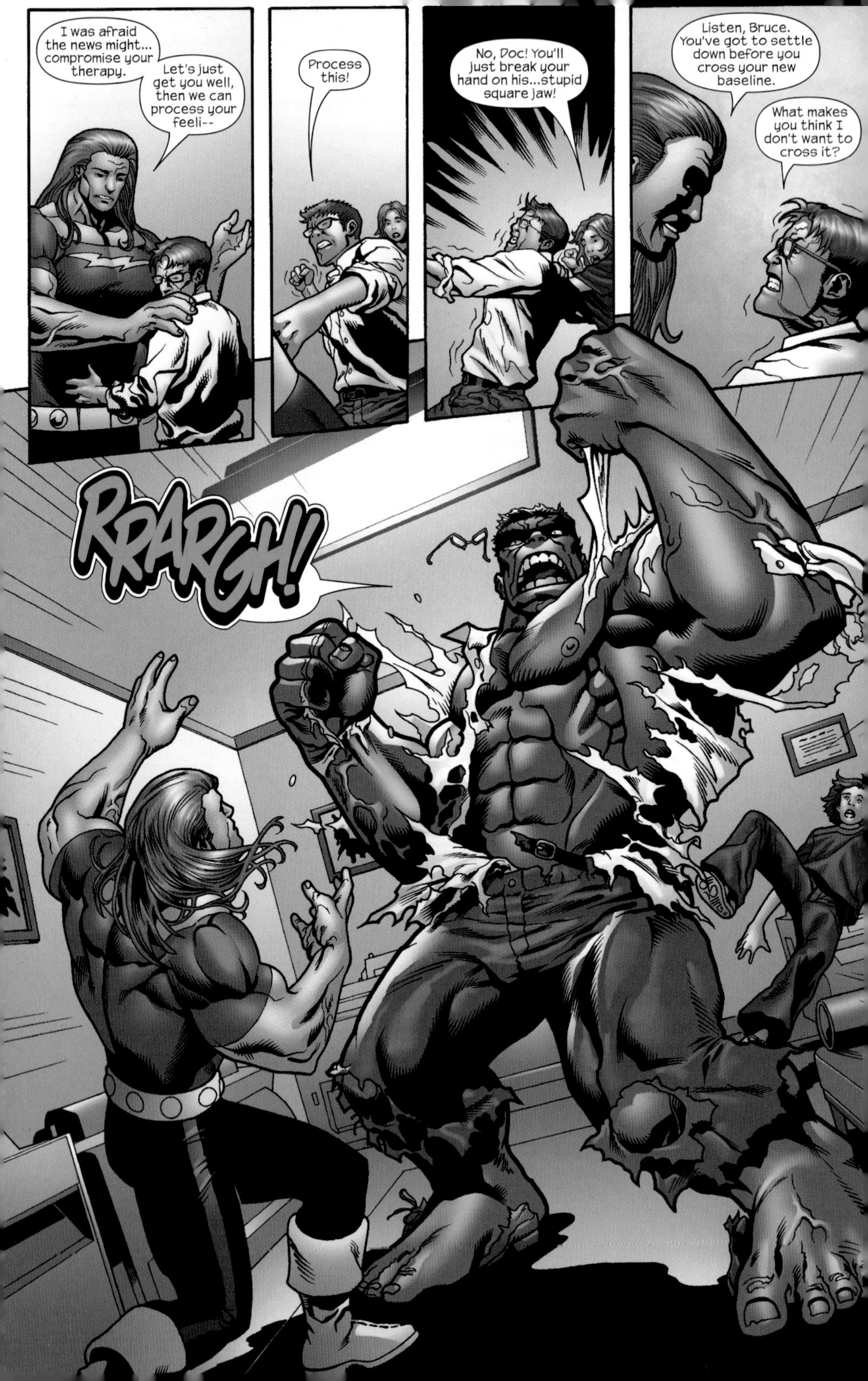
I was afraid the news might... compromise your therapy.
Let's just get you well, then we can process your feeli--
Process this!
No, Doc! You'll just break your hand on his...stupid square jaw!
Listen, Bruce. You've got to settle down before you cross your new baseline.
What makes you think I don't want to cross it?
RRARGH!

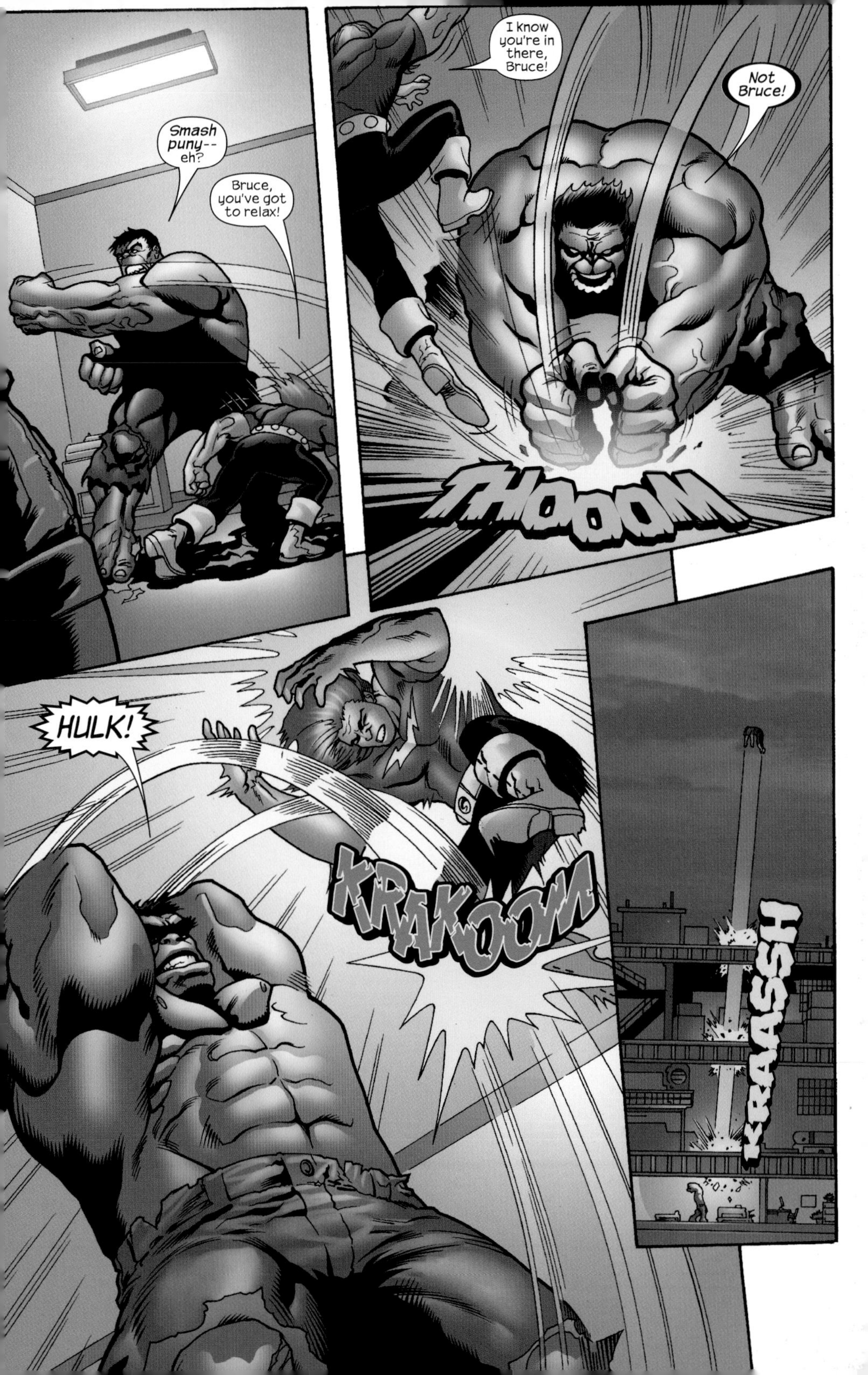
Smash puny-- eh?
Bruce, you've got to relax!
I know you're in there, Bruce!
Not Bruce!
THOOOM
HULK!
KRAKOOM
KRAASSH

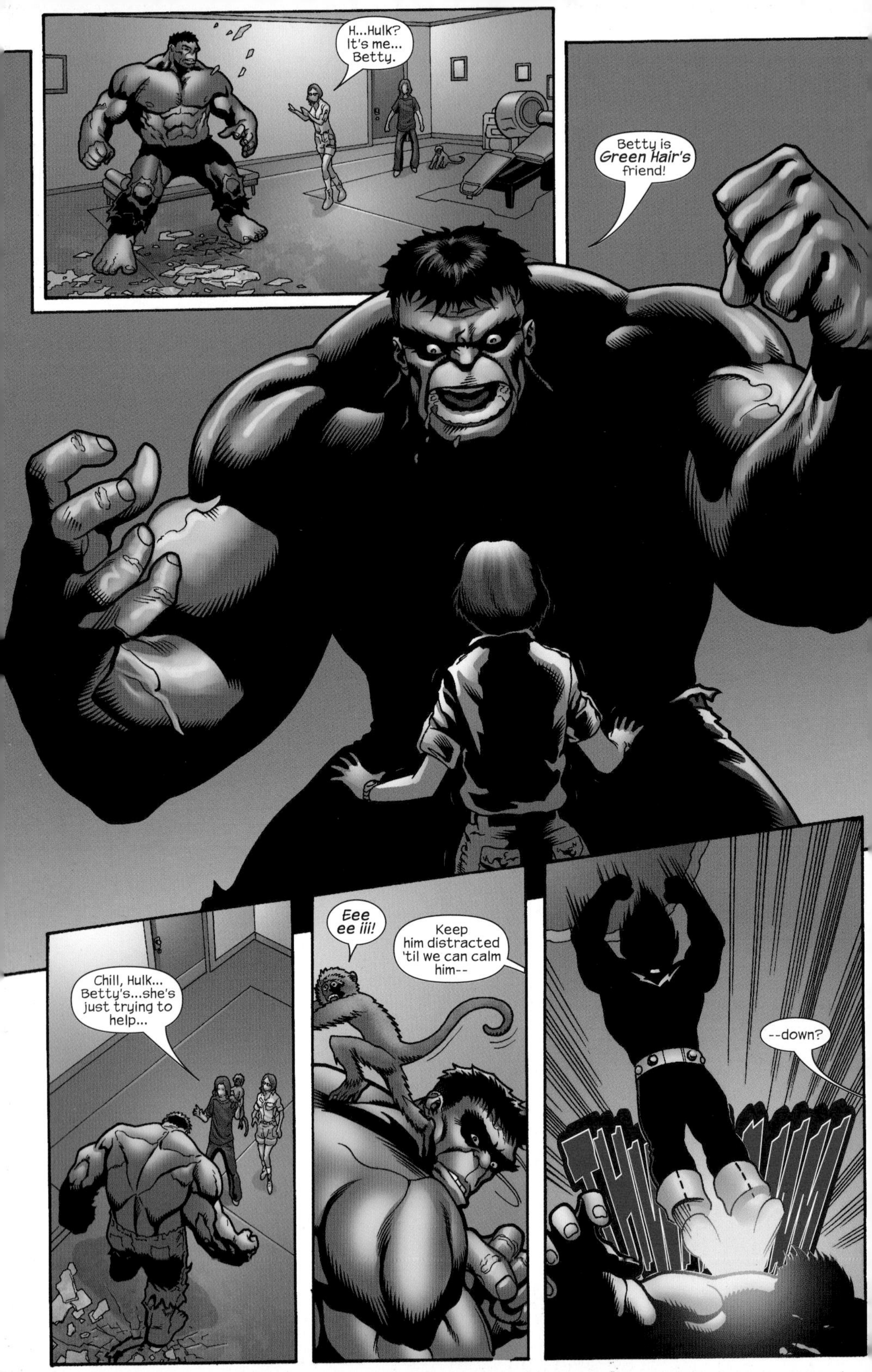
H...Hulk? It's me... Betty.
Betty is Green Hair's friend!
Chill, Hulk... Betty's...she's just trying to help...
Eee ee iii!
Keep him distracted 'til we can calm him--
--down?
THWUMM

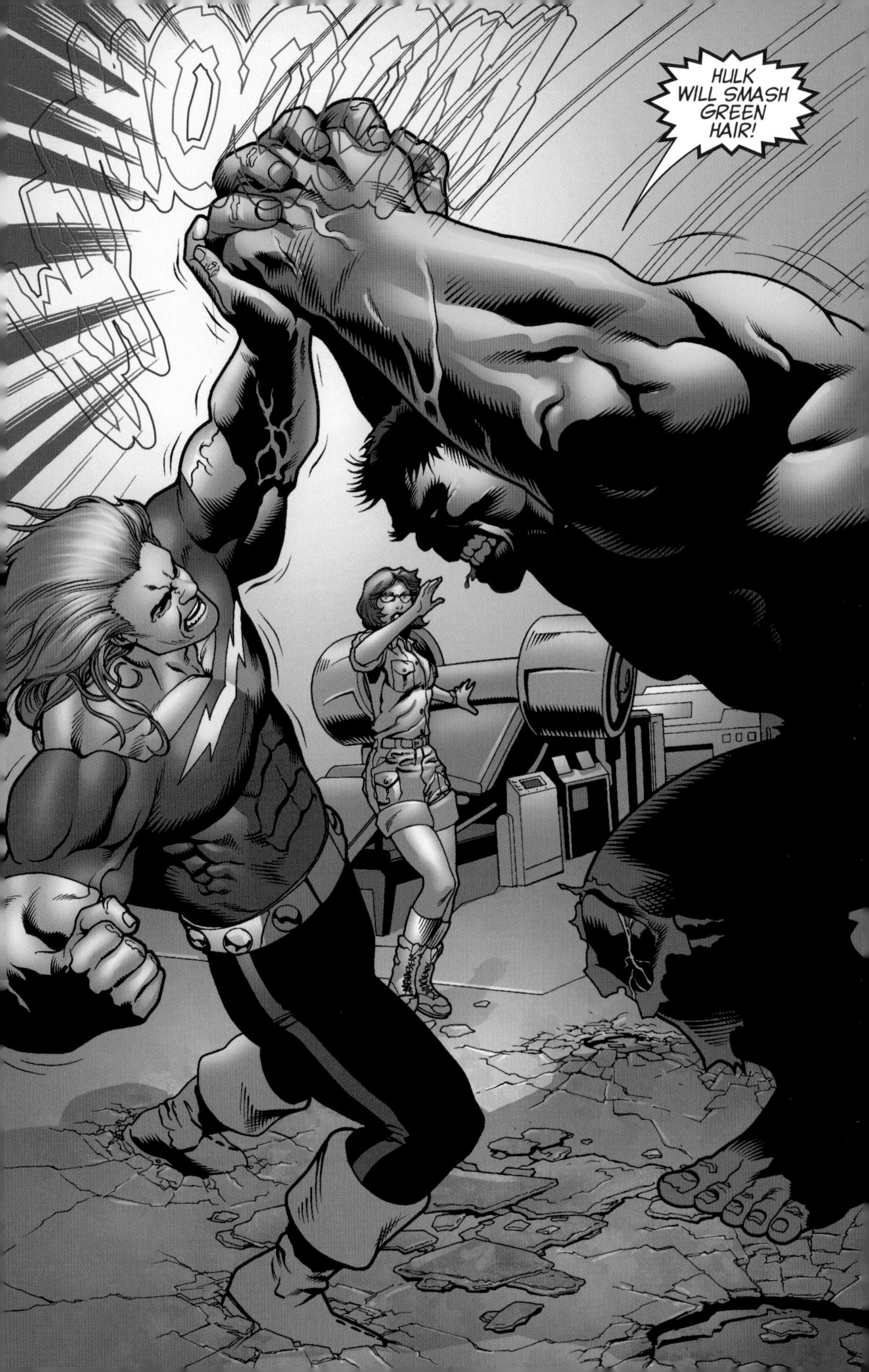
HULK WILL SMASH GREEN HAIR!

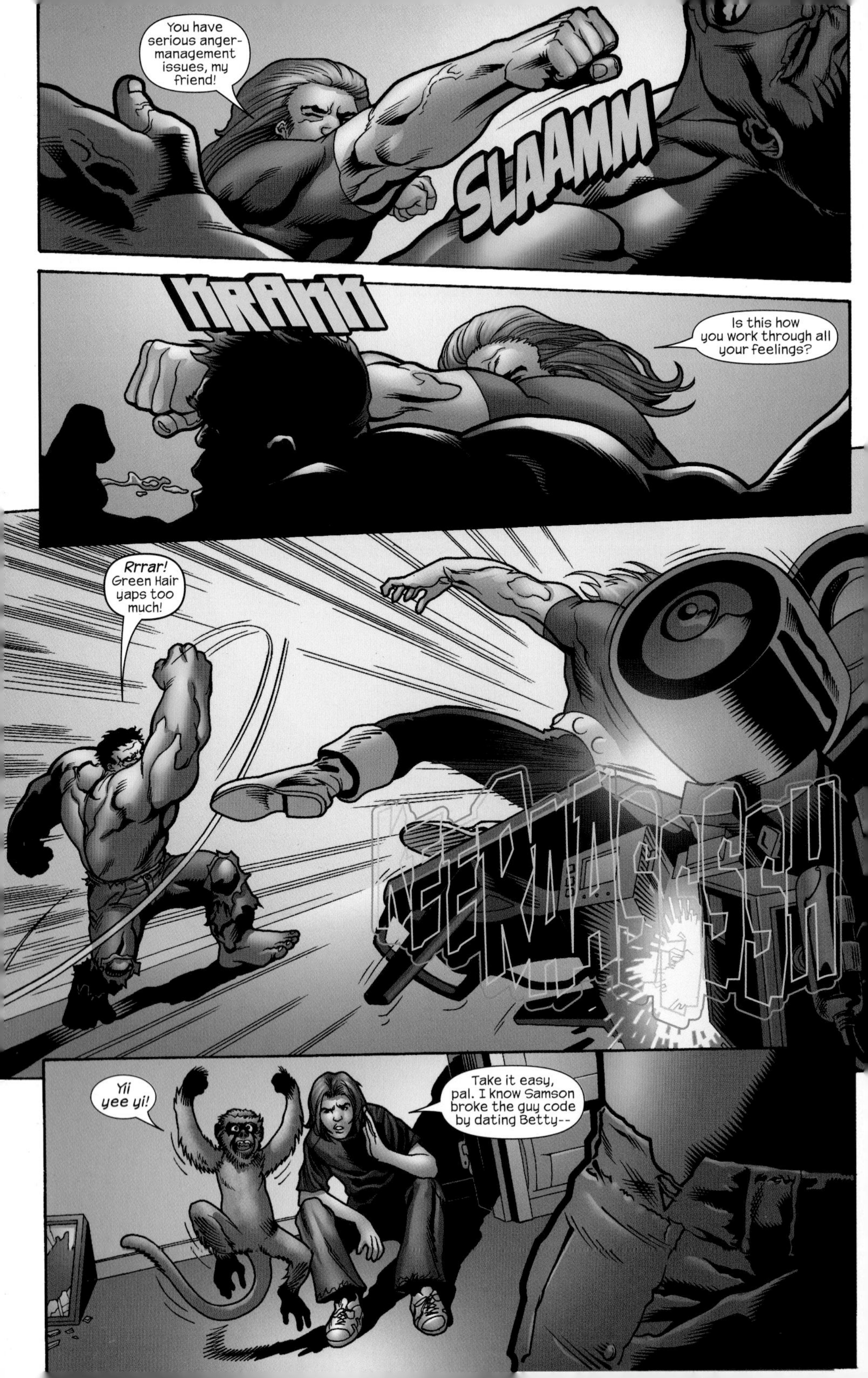
You have serious anger-management issues, my friend!
SLAAMM
KRAKK
Is this how you work through all your feelings?
Rrrar! Green Hair yaps too much!
Yii yee yi!
Take it easy, pal. I know Samson broke the guy code by dating Betty--

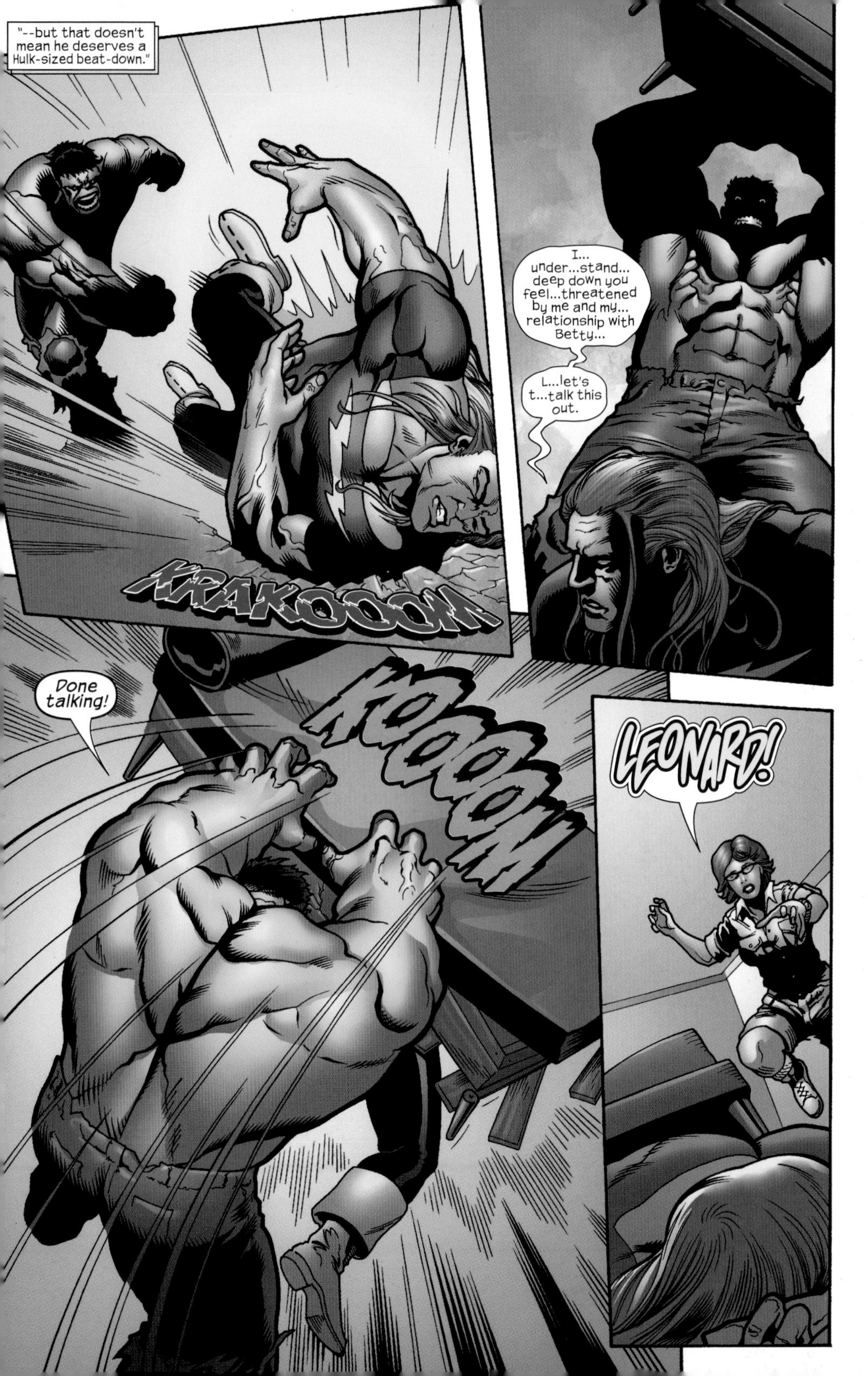
"--but that doesn't mean he deserves a Hulk-sized beat-down."
KRAKOOOM
I... under...stand... deep down you feel...threatened by me and my... relationship with Betty...
L...let's t...talk this out.
Done talking!
KOOOOM
LEONARD!

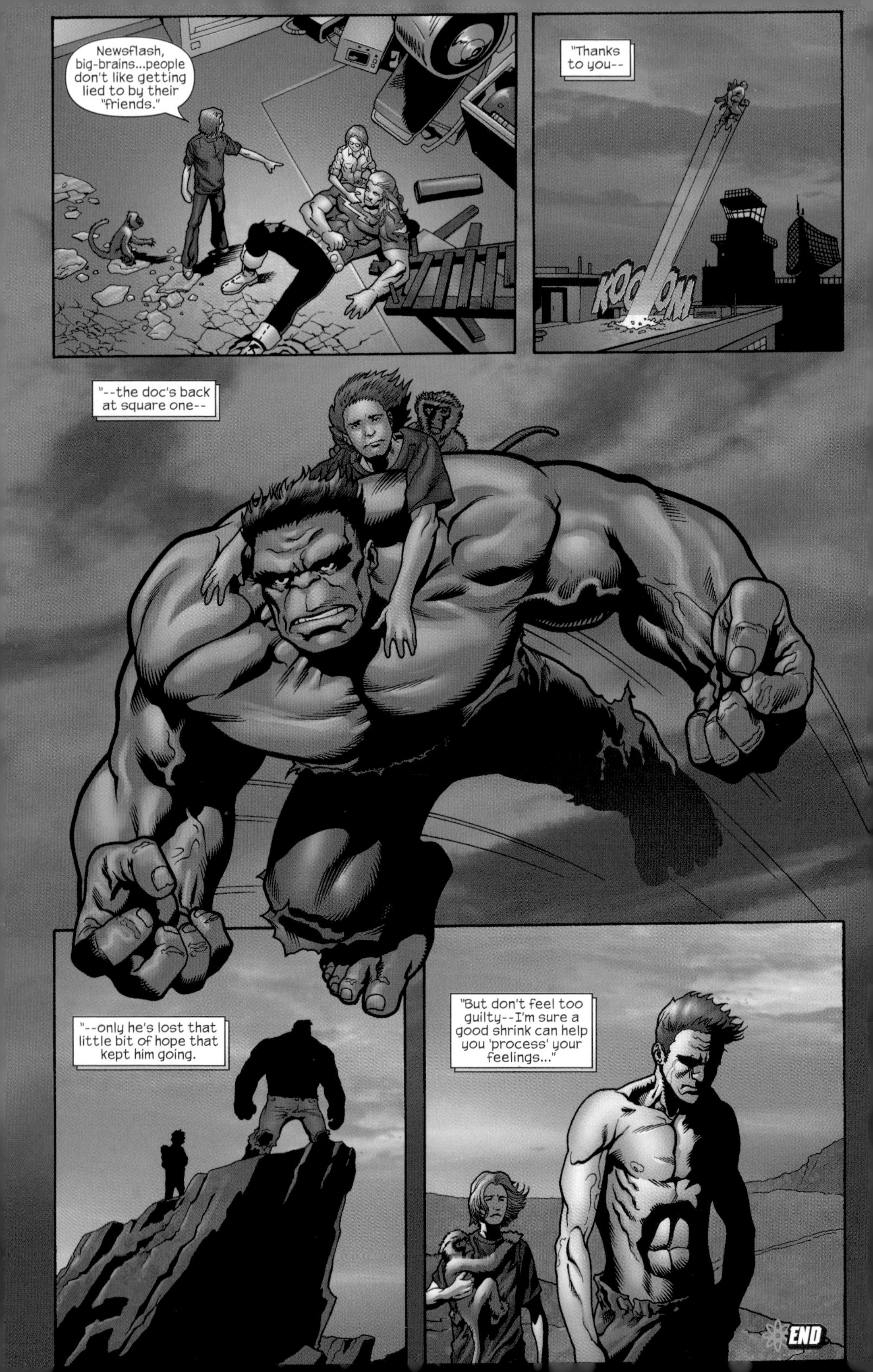
Newsflash, big-brains...people don't like getting lied to by their "friends."
"Thanks to you--
KOOOOM
"--the doc's back at square one--
"--only he's lost that little bit of hope that kept him going.
"But don't feel too guilty--I'm sure a good shrink can help you 'process' your feelings..."
END

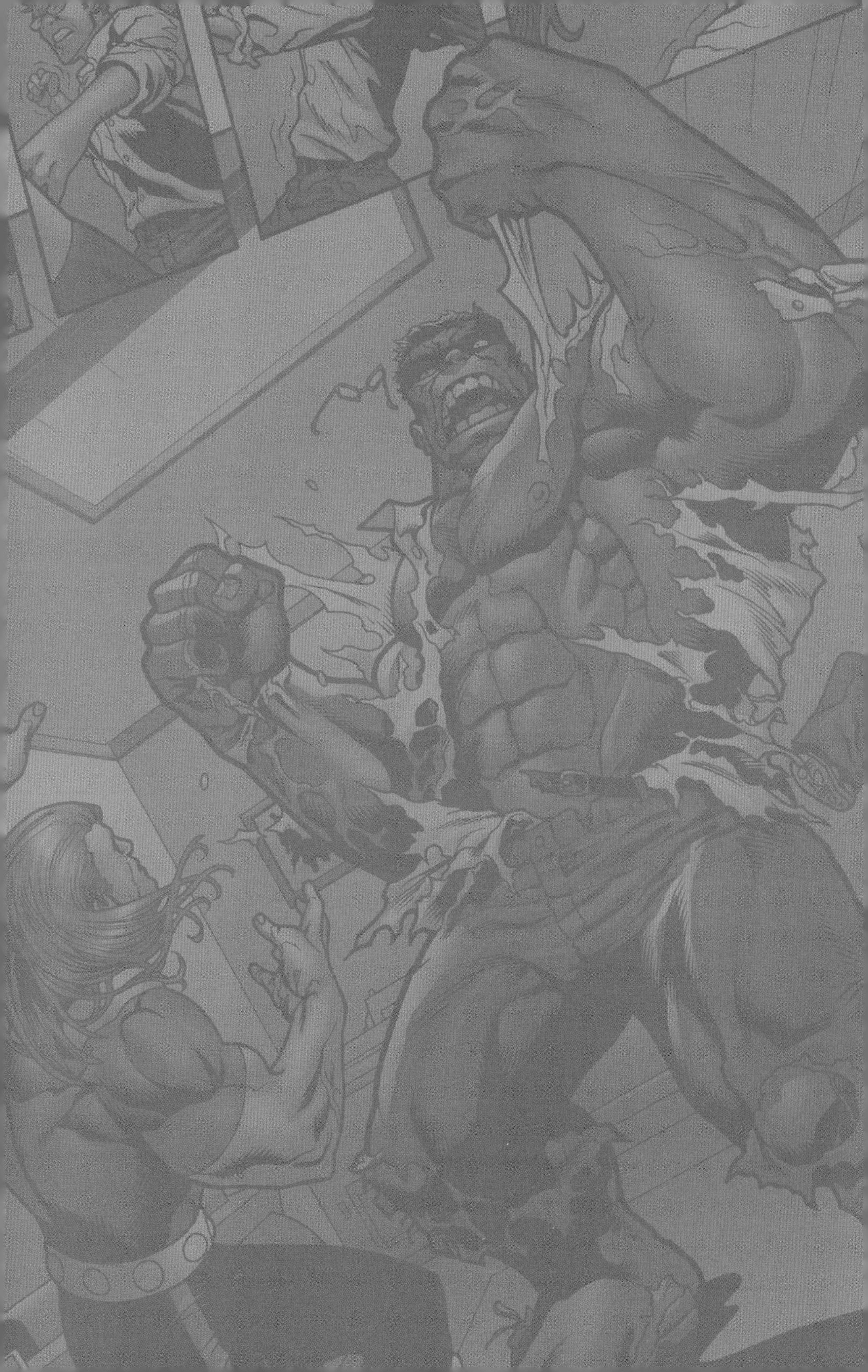

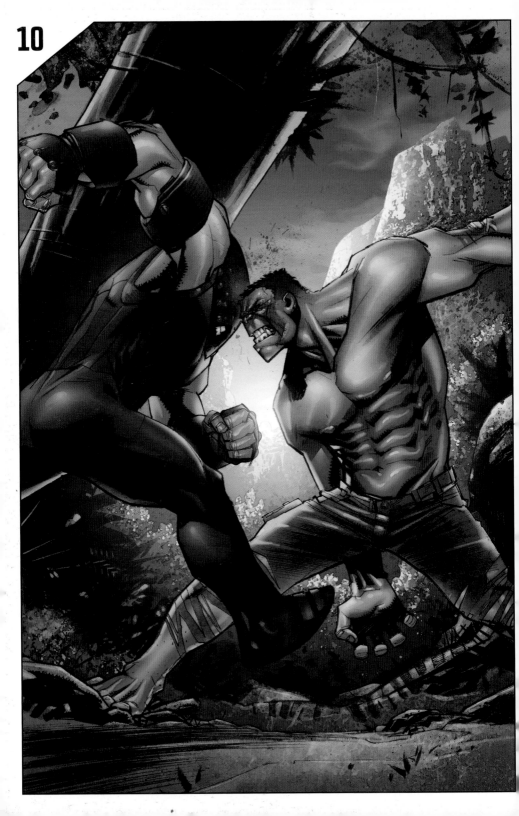

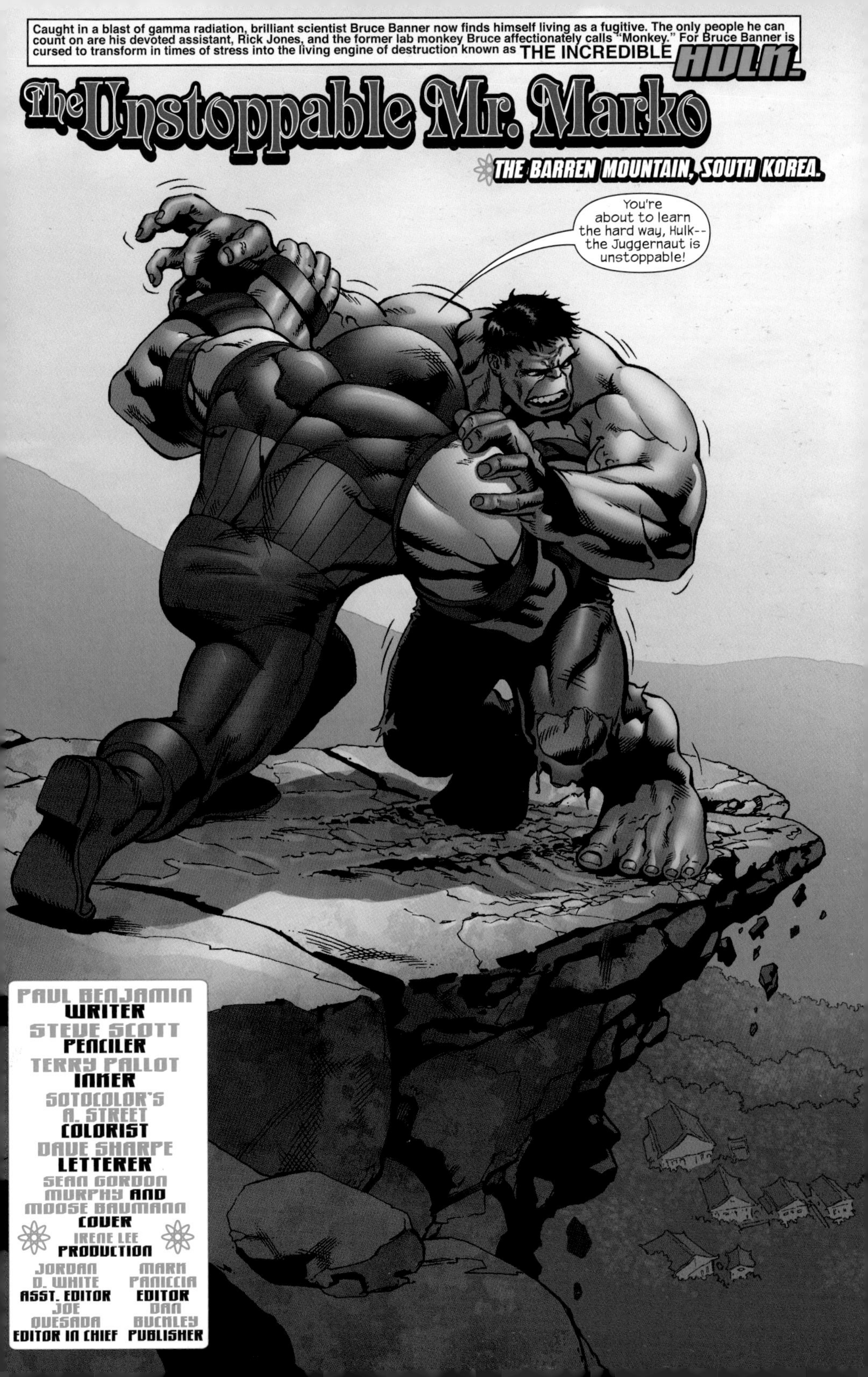

Caught in a blast of gamma radiation, brilliant scientist Bruce Banner now finds himself living as a fugitive. The only people he can count on are his devoted assistant, Rick Jones, and the former lab monkey Bruce affectionately calls "Monkey." For Bruce Banner is cursed to transform in times of stress into the living engine of destruction known as THE INCREDIBLE HULK.
The Unstoppable Mr. Marko
THE BARREN MOUNTAIN, SOUTH KOREA.
You're about to learn the hard way, Hulk-- the Juggernaut is unstoppable!
PAUL BENJAMIN WRITER
STEVE SCOTT PENCILER
TERRY PALLOT INKER
SOTOCOLOR'S A. STREET COLORIST
DAVE SHARPE LETTERER
SEAN GORDON MURPHY AND MOOSE BAUMANN COVER
IRENE LEE PRODUCTION
JORDAN D. WHITE ASST. EDITOR
MARK PANICCIA EDITOR
JOE QUESADA EDITOR IN CHIEF
DAN BUCKLEY PUBLISHER

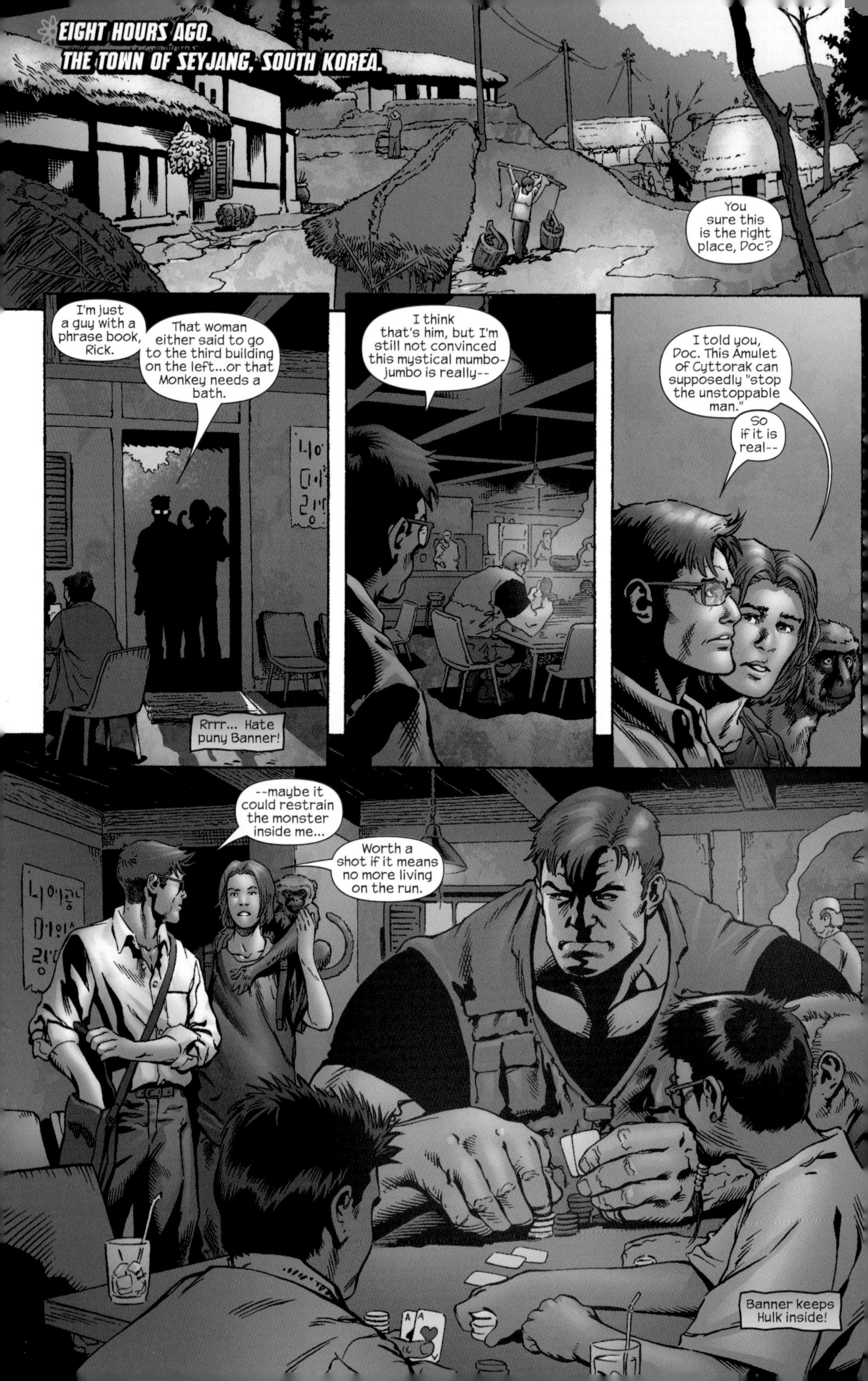
EIGHT HOURS AGO.
THE TOWN OF SEYJANG, SOUTH KOREA.
You sure this is the right place, Doc?
I'm just a guy with a phrase book, Rick.
That woman either said to go to the third building on the left...or that Monkey needs a bath.
Rrrr... Hate puny Banner!
I think that's him, but I'm still not convinced this mystical mumbo-jumbo is really--
I told you, Doc. This Amulet of Cyttorak can supposedly "stop the unstoppable man."
So if it is real--
--maybe it could restrain the monster inside me...
Worth a shot if it means no more living on the run.
Banner keeps Hulk inside!

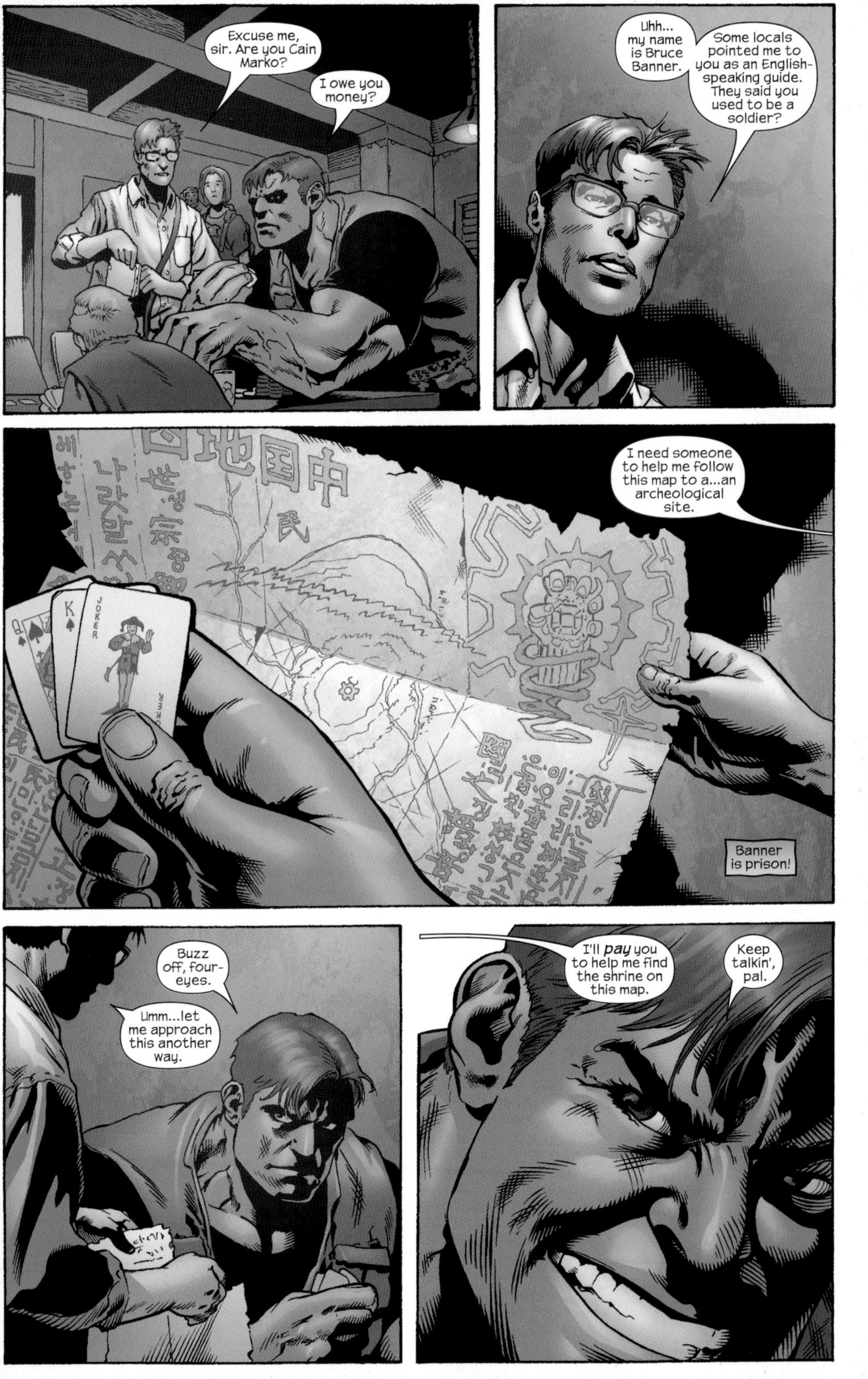
Excuse me, sir. Are you Cain Marko?
I owe you money?
Uhh... my name is Bruce Banner.
Some locals pointed me to you as an English-speaking guide. They said you used to be a soldier?
I need someone to help me follow this map to a...an archeological site.
Banner is prison!
Buzz off, four-eyes.
Umm...let me approach this another way.
I'll *pay* you to help me find the shrine on this map.
Keep talkin', pal.

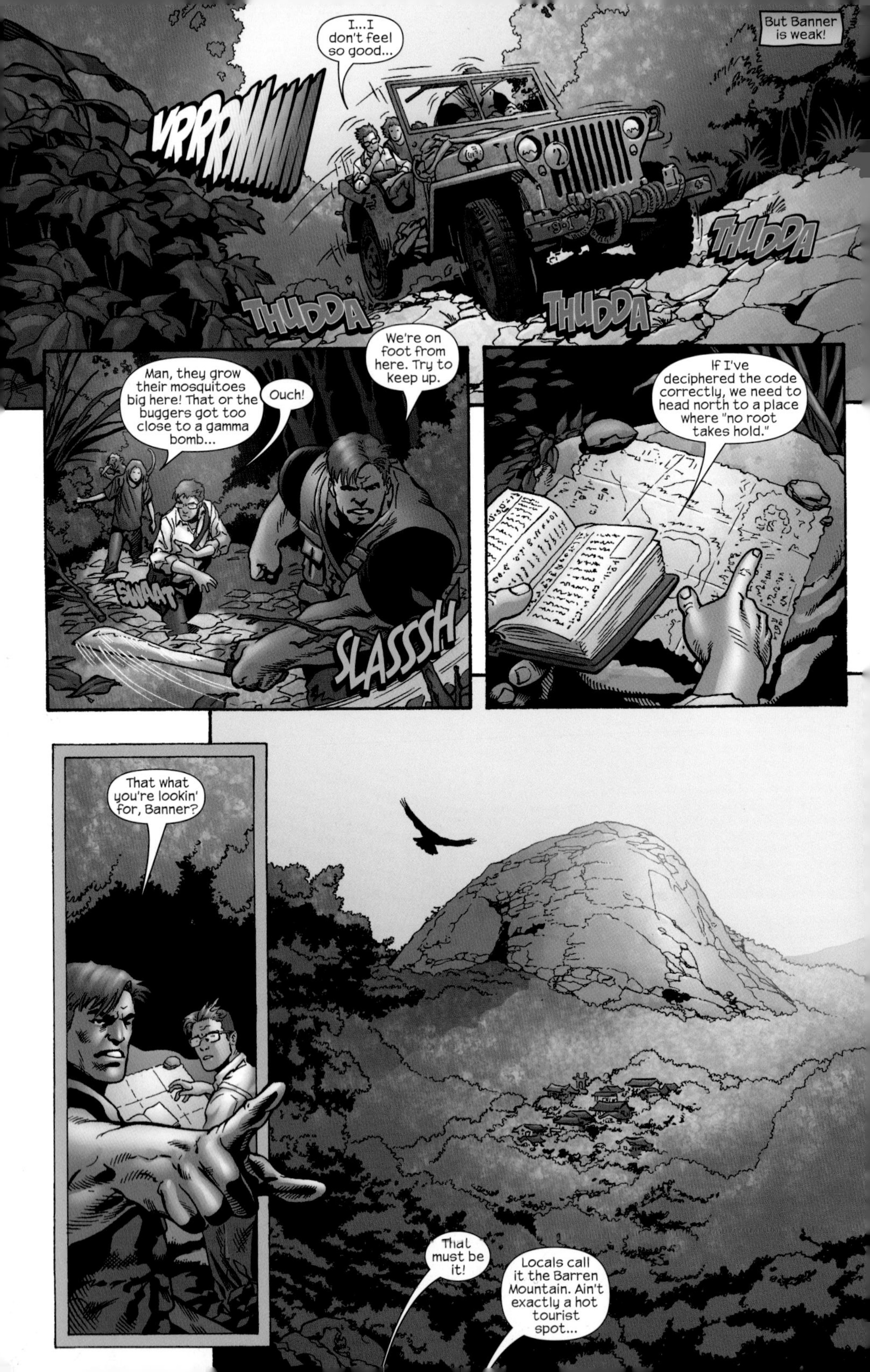
But Banner is weak!
I...I don't feel so good...
VRRRMMMM
THUDDA
THUDDA
THUDDA
Man, they grow their mosquitoes big here! That or the buggers got too close to a gamma bomb...
Ouch!
SWAAT
We're on foot from here. Try to keep up.
SLASSSH
If I've deciphered the code correctly, we need to head north to a place where "no root takes hold."
That what you're lookin' for, Banner?
That must be it!
Locals call it the Barren Mountain. Ain't exactly a hot tourist spot...

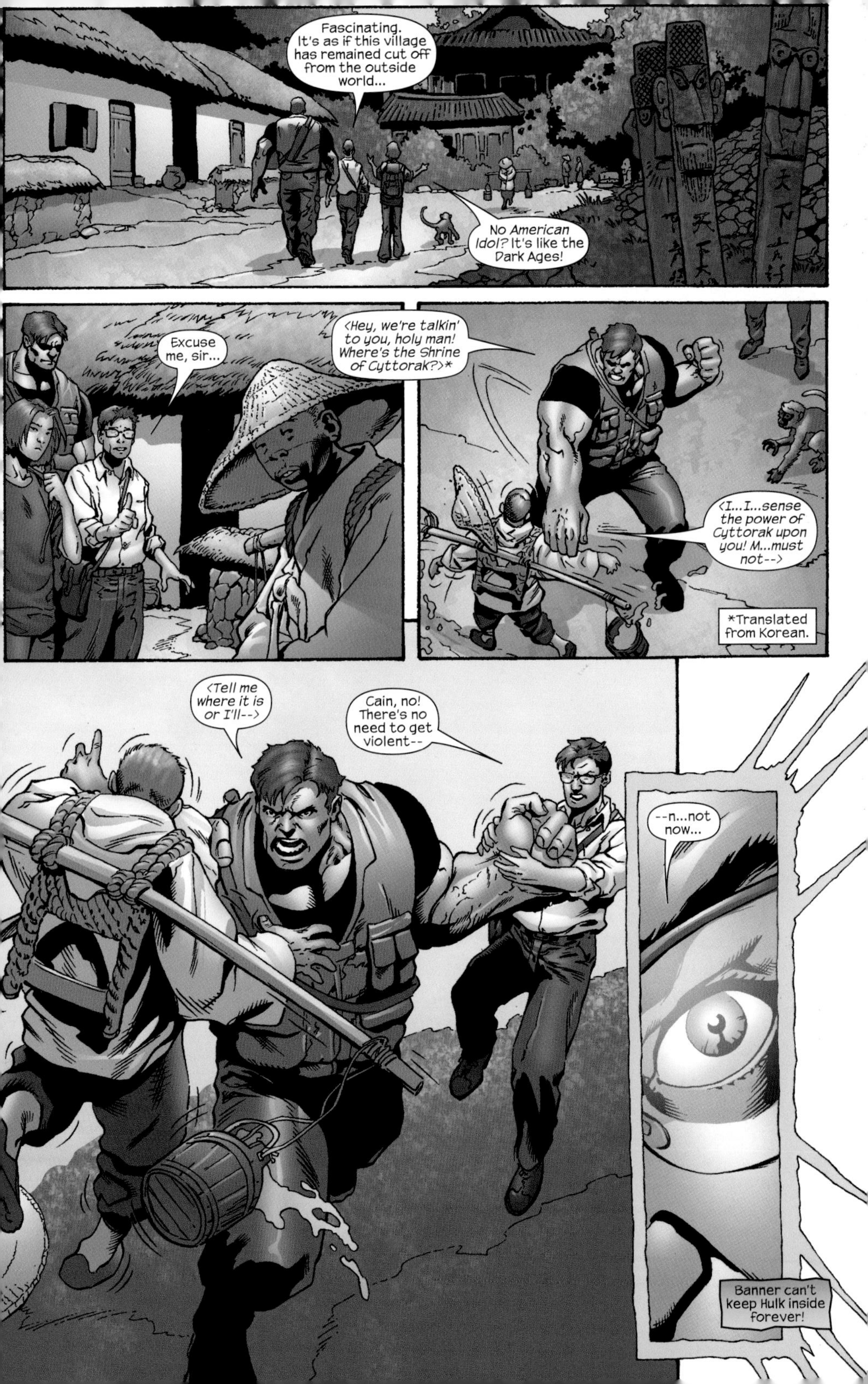
Fascinating. It's as if this village has remained cut off from the outside world...
No *American Idol*? It's like the Dark Ages!
Excuse me, sir...
<Hey, we're talkin' to you, holy man! Where's the Shrine of Cyttorak?>*
<I...I...sense the power of Cyttorak upon you! M...must not-->
*Translated from Korean.
<Tell me where it is or I'll-->
Cain, no! There's no need to get violent--
--n...not now...
Banner can't keep Hulk inside forever!

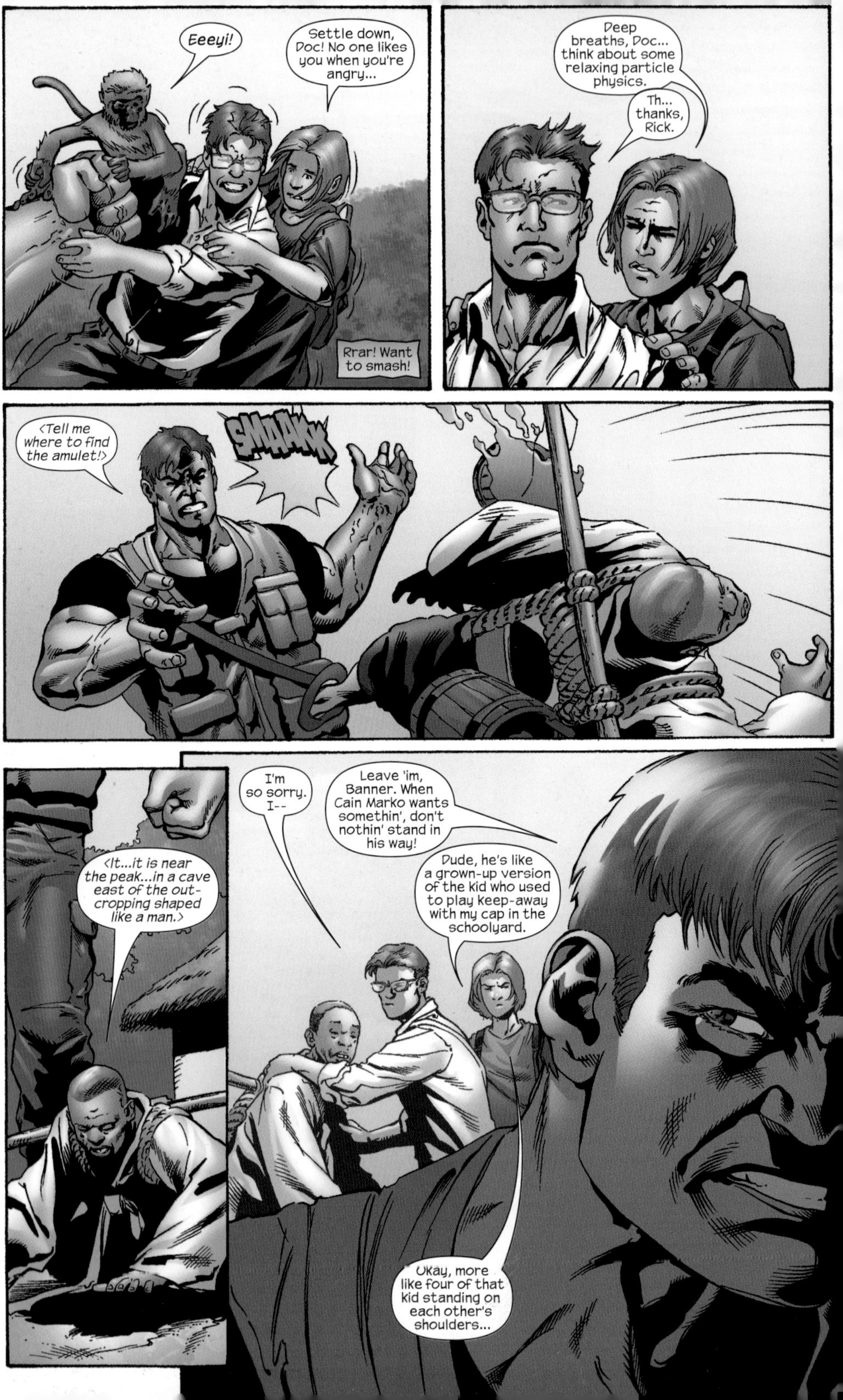

Eeeyi!
Settle down, Doc! No one likes you when you're angry...
Rrar! Want to smash!
Deep breaths, Doc... think about some relaxing particle physics.
Th... thanks, Rick.
<Tell me where to find the amulet!>
SMAAKK
<It...it is near the peak...in a cave east of the out-cropping shaped like a man.>
I'm so sorry. I--
Leave 'im, Banner. When Cain Marko wants somethin', don't nothin' stand in his way!
Dude, he's like a grown-up version of the kid who used to play keep-away with my cap in the schoolyard.
Okay, more like four of that kid standing on each other's shoulders...

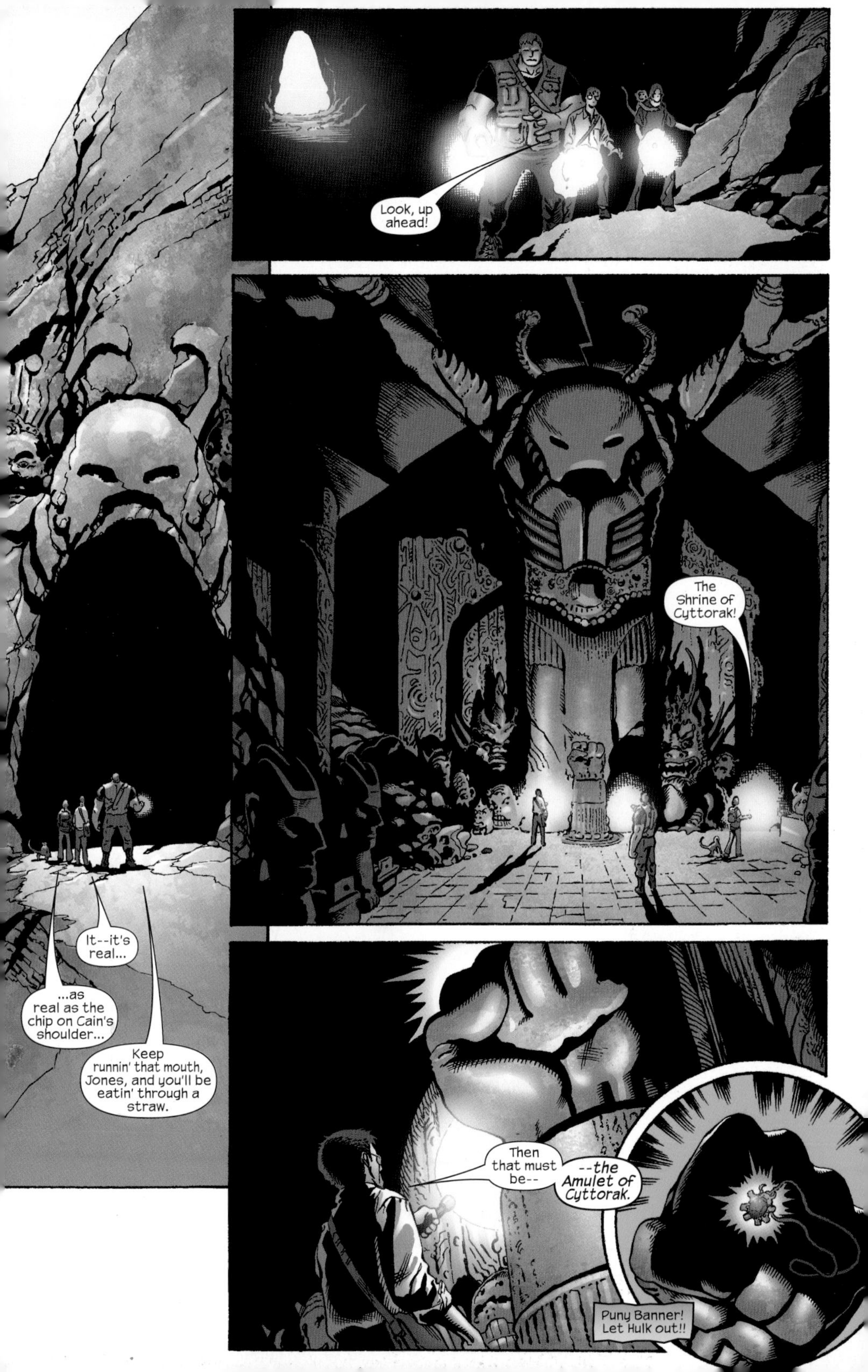
Look, up ahead!
The Shrine of Cyttorak!
It--it's real...
...as real as the chip on Cain's shoulder...
Keep runnin' that mouth, Jones, and you'll be eatin' through a straw.
Then that must be--
--the Amulet of Cyttorak.
Puny Banner! Let Hulk out!!

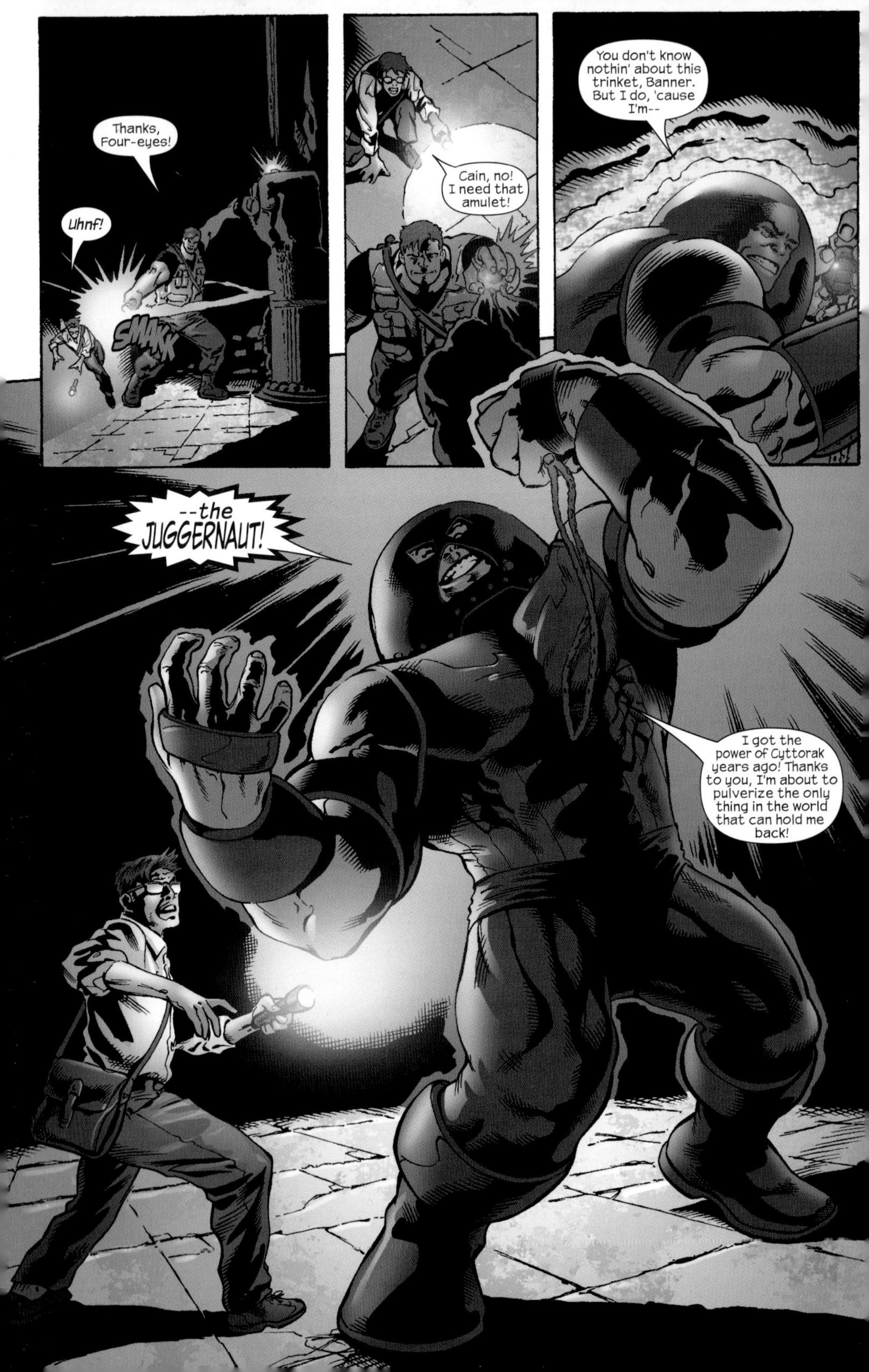
Thanks, Four-eyes!
Uhnf!
SMAKK
Cain, no! I need that amulet!
You don't know nothin' about this trinket, Banner. But I do, 'cause I'm--
--the JUGGERNAUT!
I got the power of Cyttorak years ago! Thanks to you, I'm about to pulverize the only thing in the world that can hold me back!

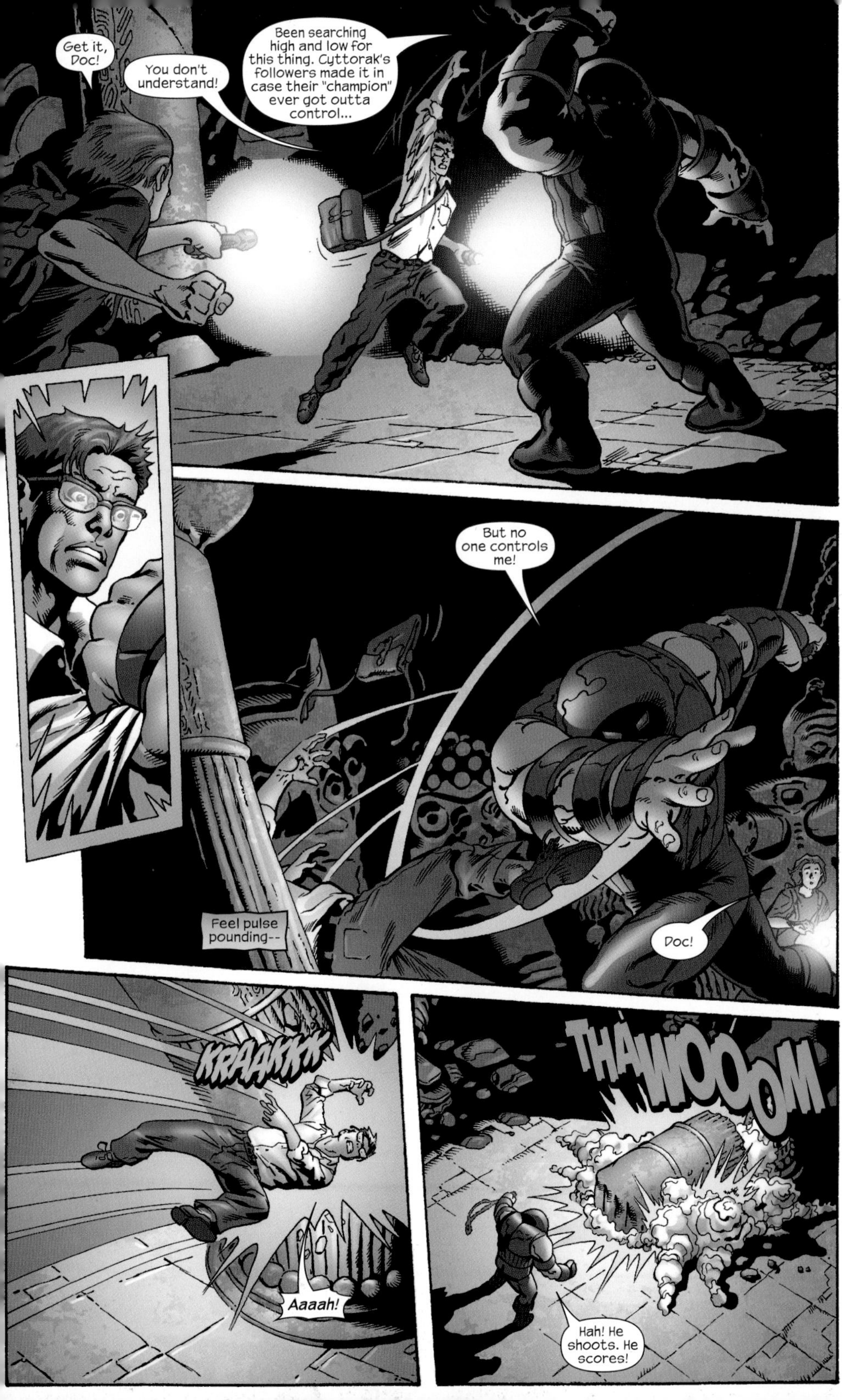

Get it, Doc!
You don't understand!
Been searching high and low for this thing. Cyttorak's followers made it in case their "champion" ever got outta control...
But no one controls me!
Feel pulse pounding--
Doc!
KRAAKKK
Aaaah!
THAWOOOM
Hah! He shoots. He scores!

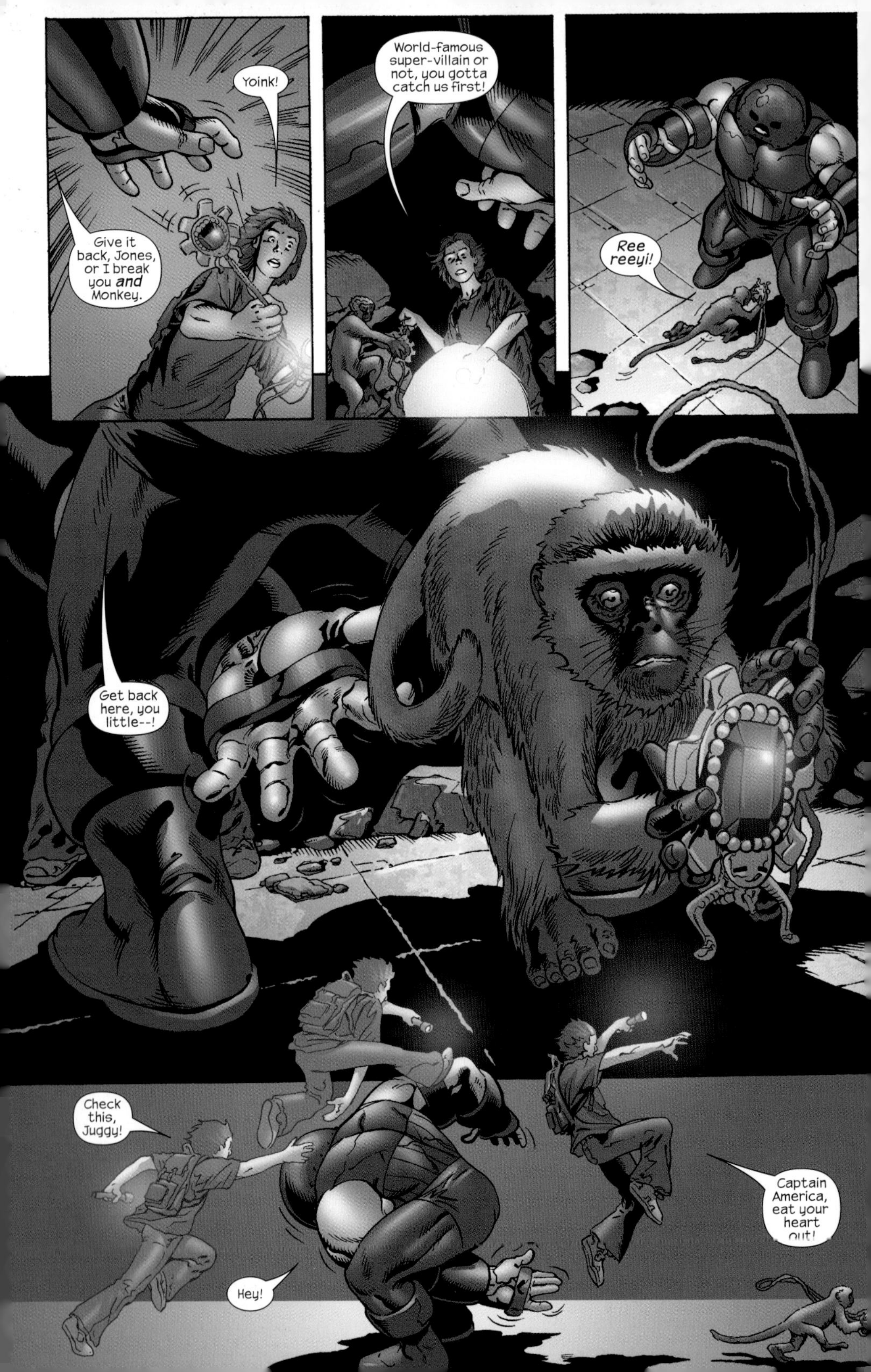
Yoink!
Give it back, Jones, or I break you *and* Monkey.
World-famous super-villain or not, you gotta catch us first!
Ree reeyi!
Get back here, you little--!
Check this, Juggy!
Captain America, eat your heart out!
Hey!

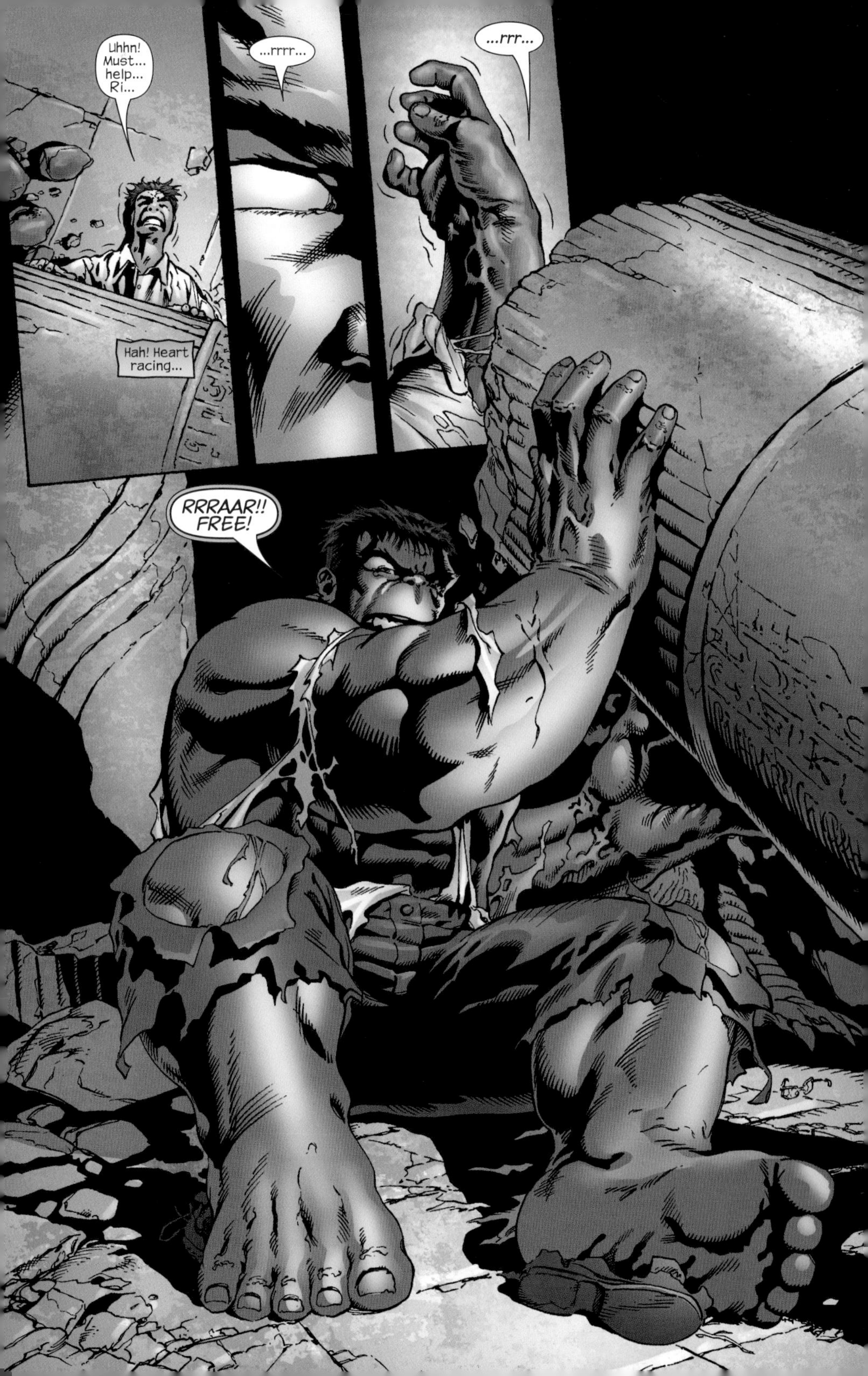
Uhhn! Must... help... Ri...
Hah! Heart racing...
...rrrr...
...rrr...
RRRAAR!! FREE!

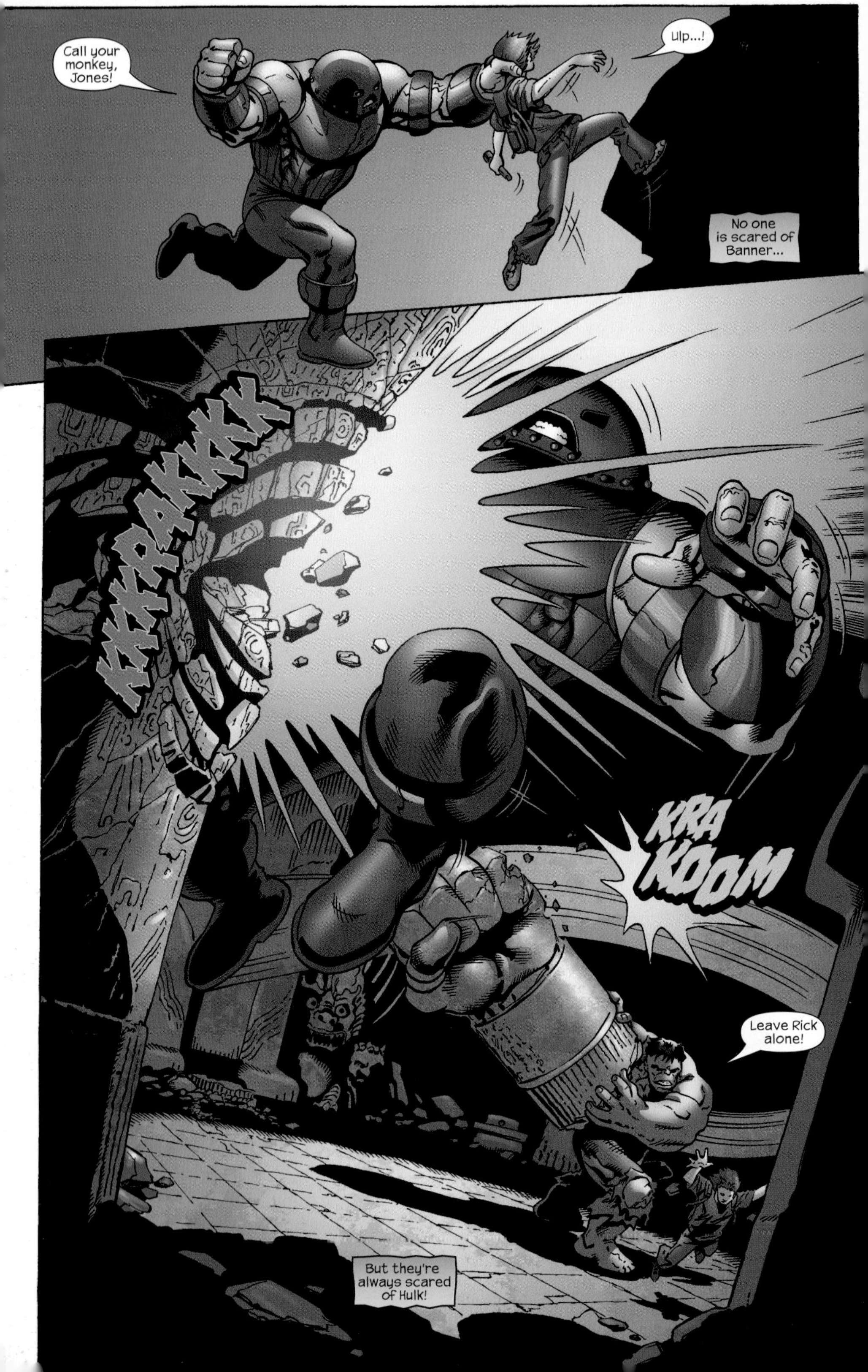
Call your monkey, Jones!
Ulp...!
No one is scared of Banner...
KKRAKKKK
KRA KOOM
Leave Rick alone!
But they're always scared of Hulk!

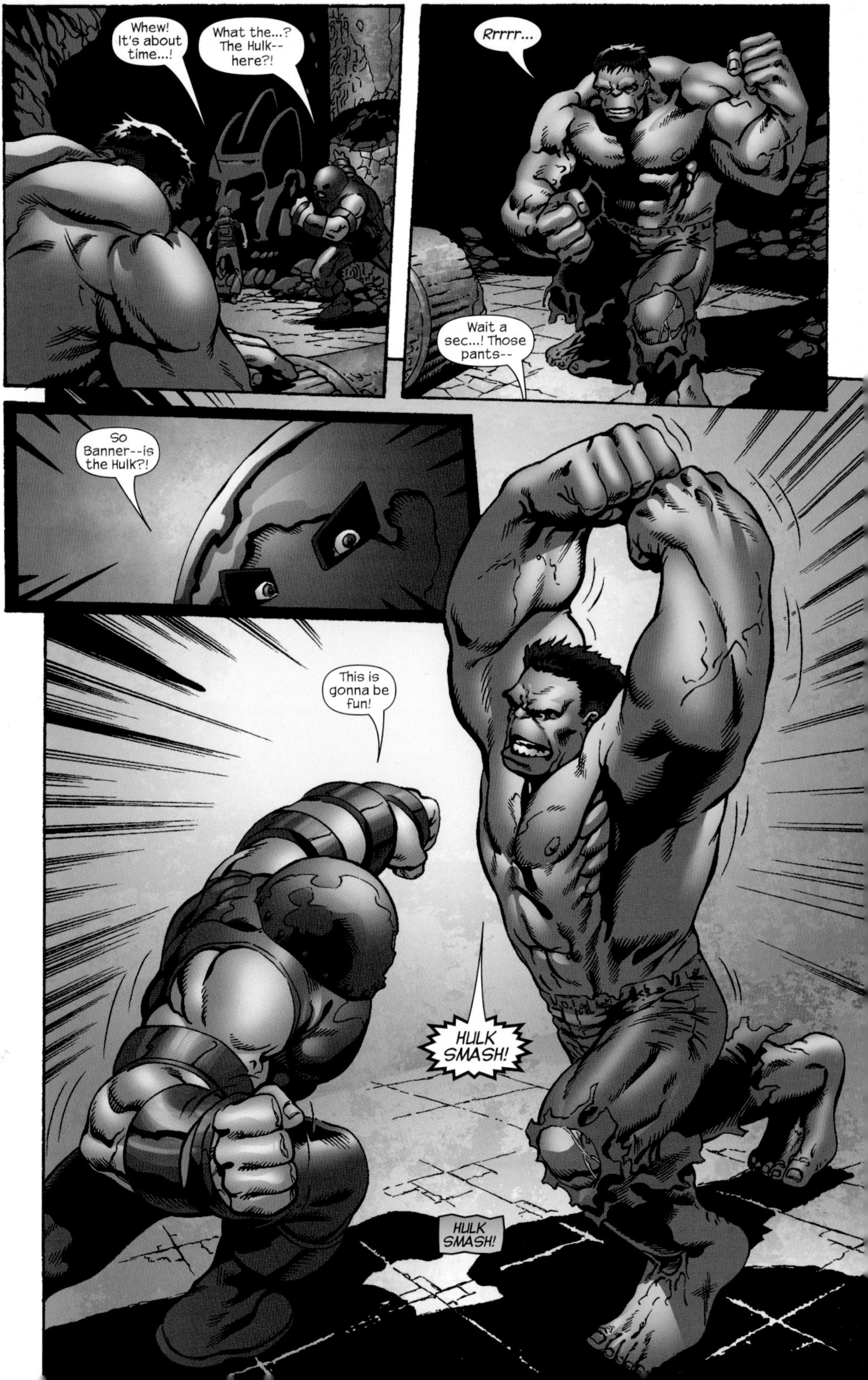
Whew! It's about time...!
What the...? The Hulk-- here?!
Rrrrr...
Wait a sec...! Those pants--
So Banner--is the Hulk?!
This is gonna be fun!
HULK SMASH!
HULK SMASH!

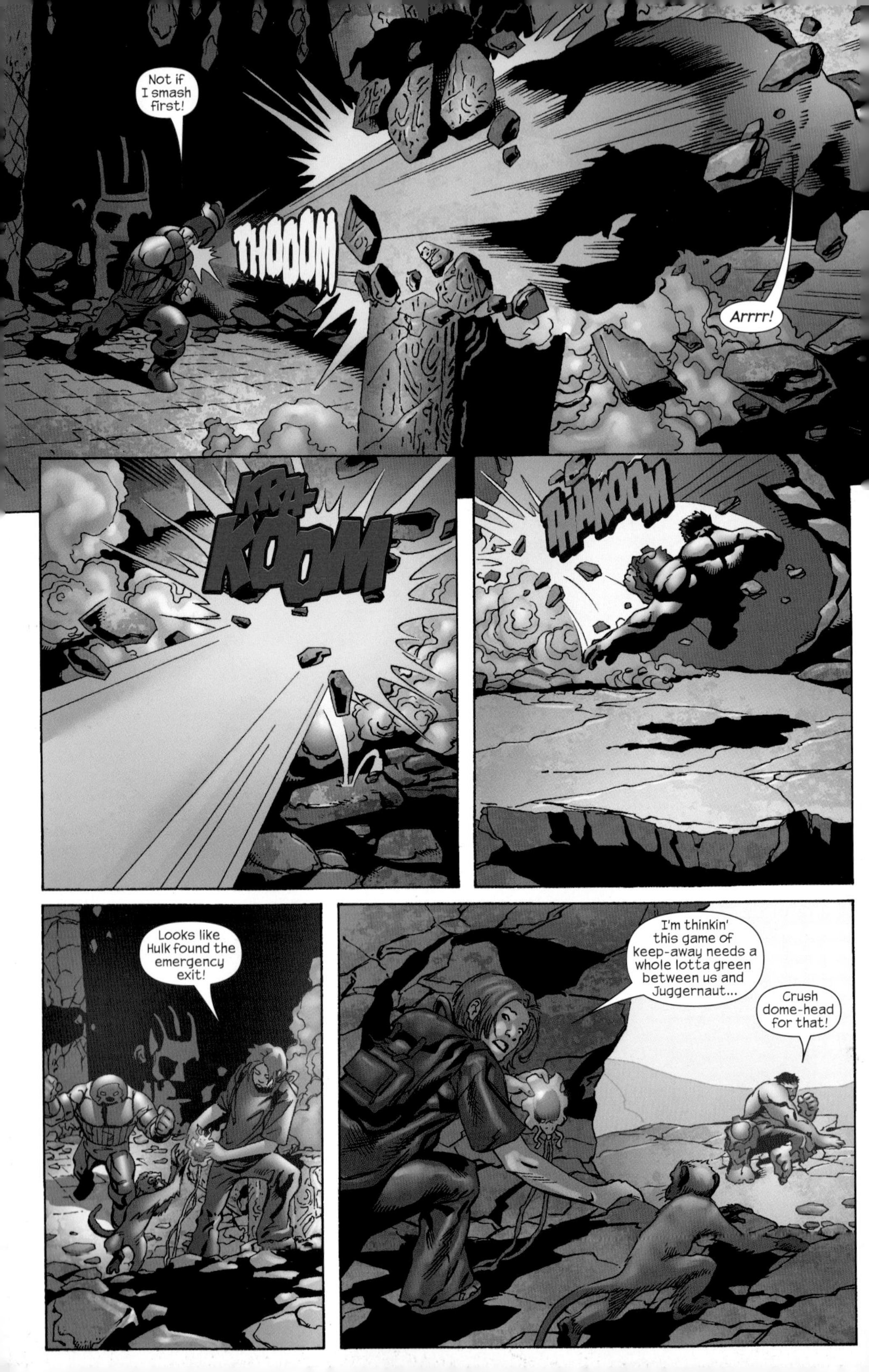
Not if I smash first!
THOOOM
Arrrr!
KRA-KOOM
THAKOOM
Looks like Hulk found the emergency exit!
I'm thinkin' this game of keep-away needs a whole lotta green between us and Juggernaut...
Crush dome-head for that!

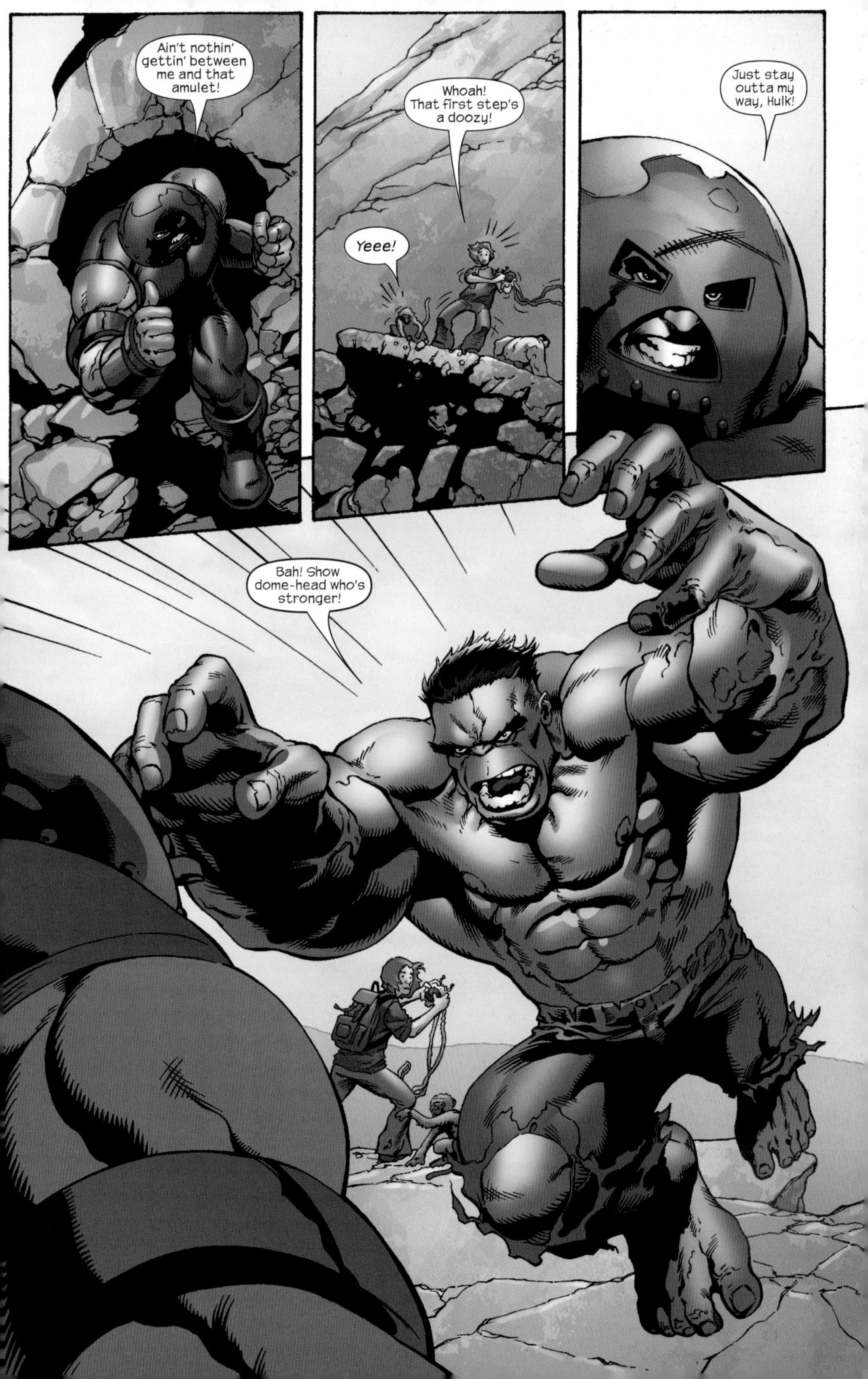
Ain't nothin' gettin' between me and that amulet!
Whoah! That first step's a doozy!
Yeee!
Just stay outta my way, Hulk!
Bah! Show dome-head who's stronger!

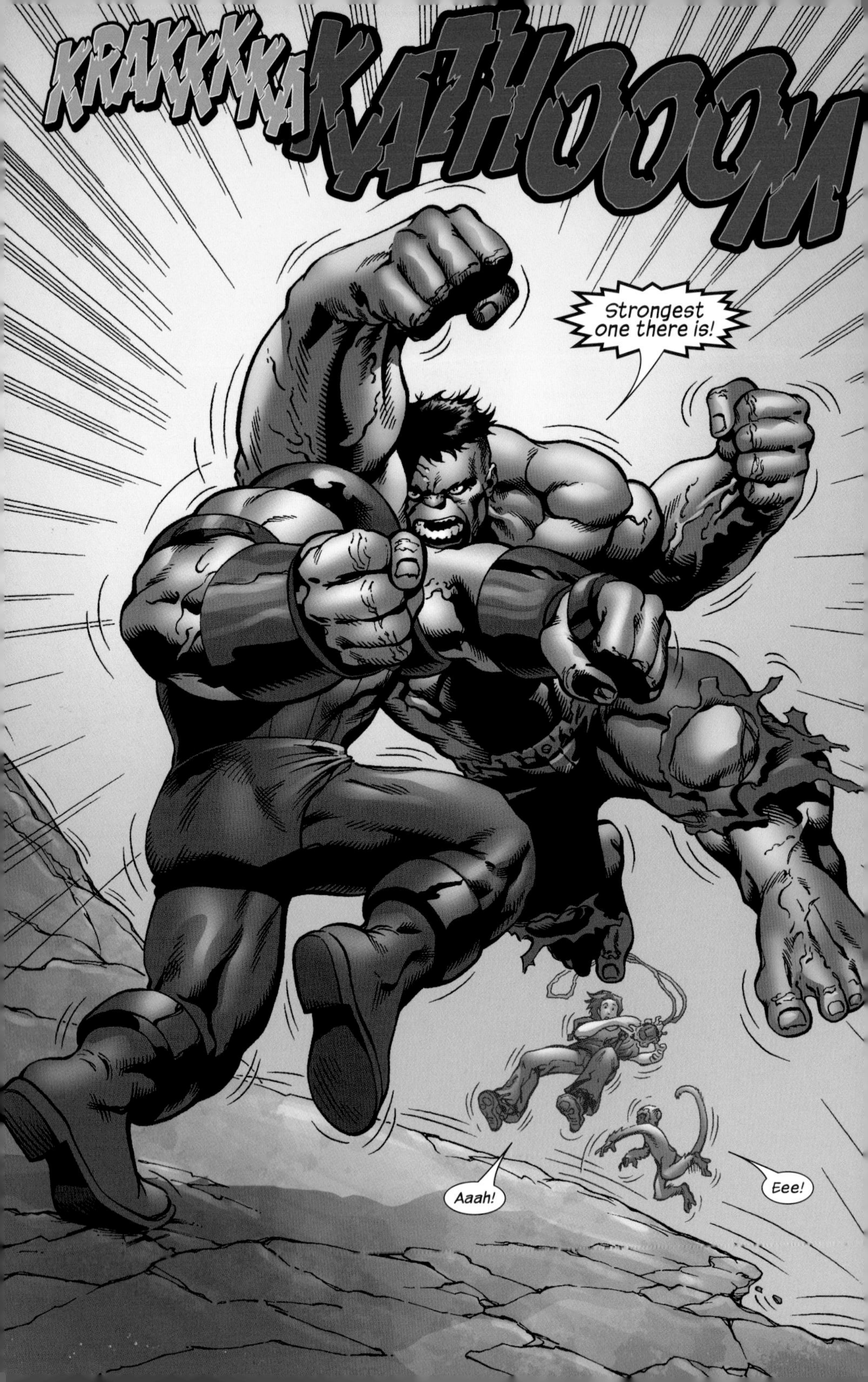
KRAKKKKA
KATHOOOM
Strongest one there is!
Aaah!
Eee!

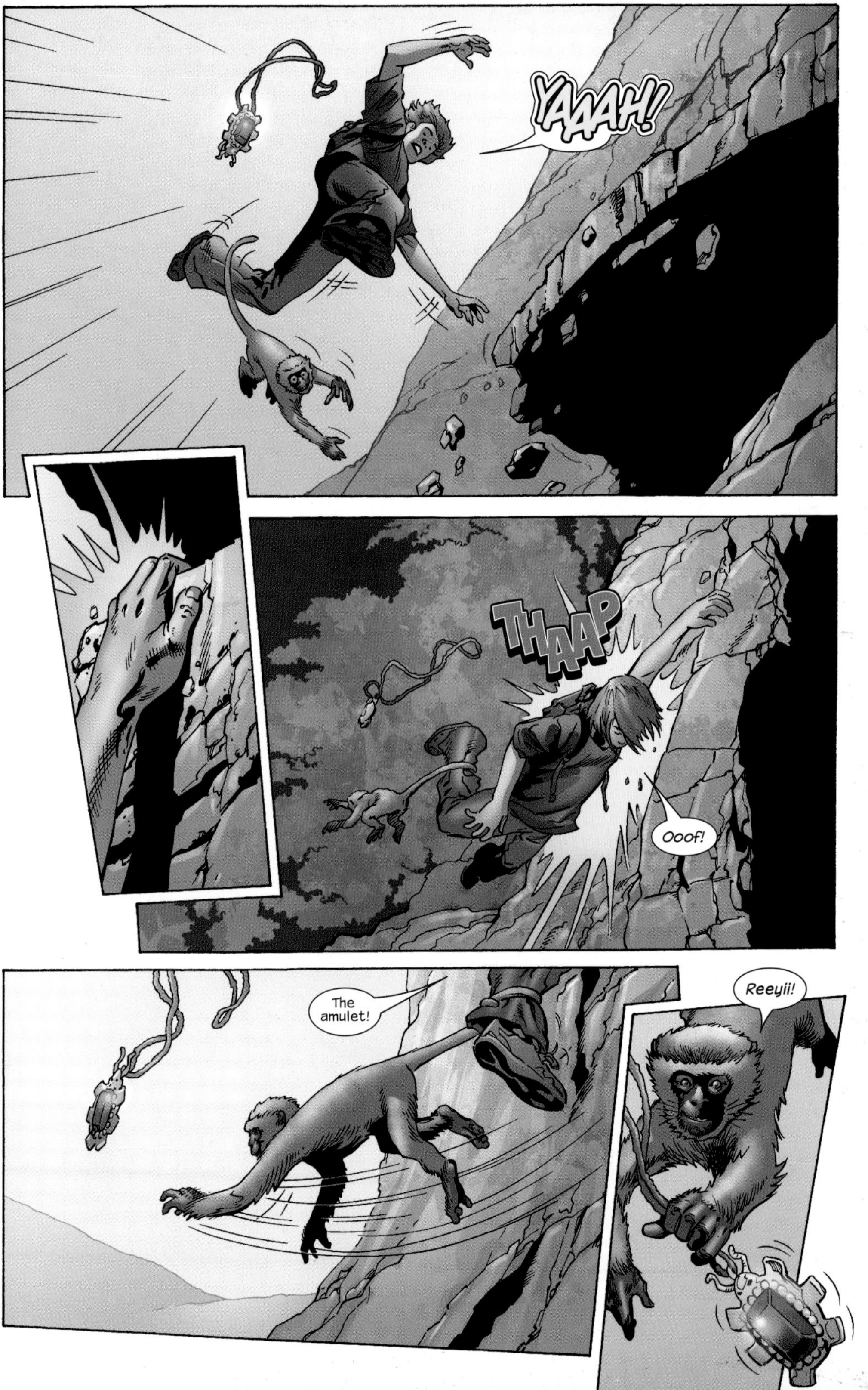
YAAAH!
THAAP
Ooof!
The amulet!
Reeyii!

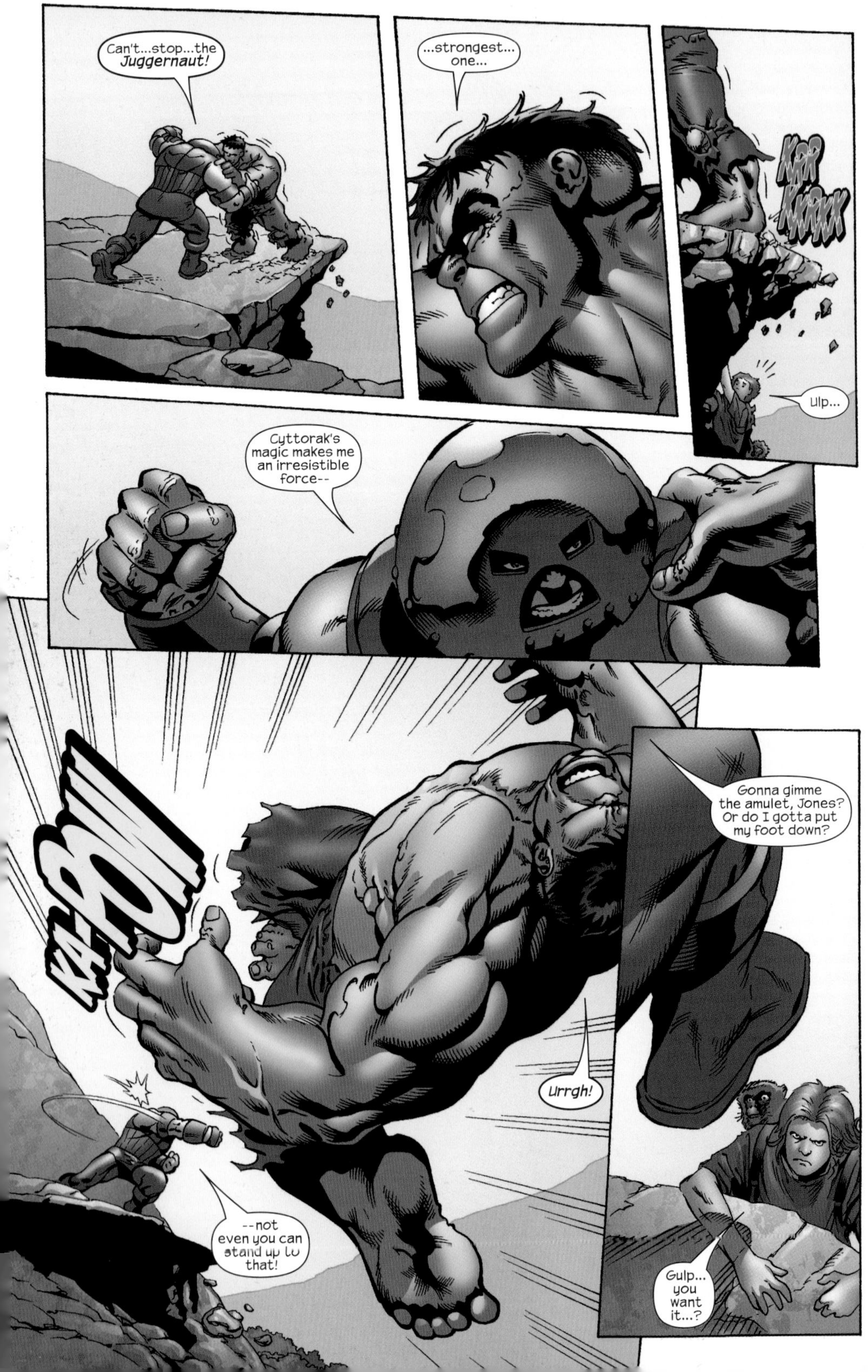

Can't...stop...the *Juggernaut!*
...strongest... one...
KRR KKRKK
Ulp...
Cyttorak's magic makes me an irresistible force--
KA-BUM
--not even you can stand up to that!
Urrgh!
Gonna gimme the amulet, Jones? Or do I gotta put my foot down?
Gulp... you want it...?

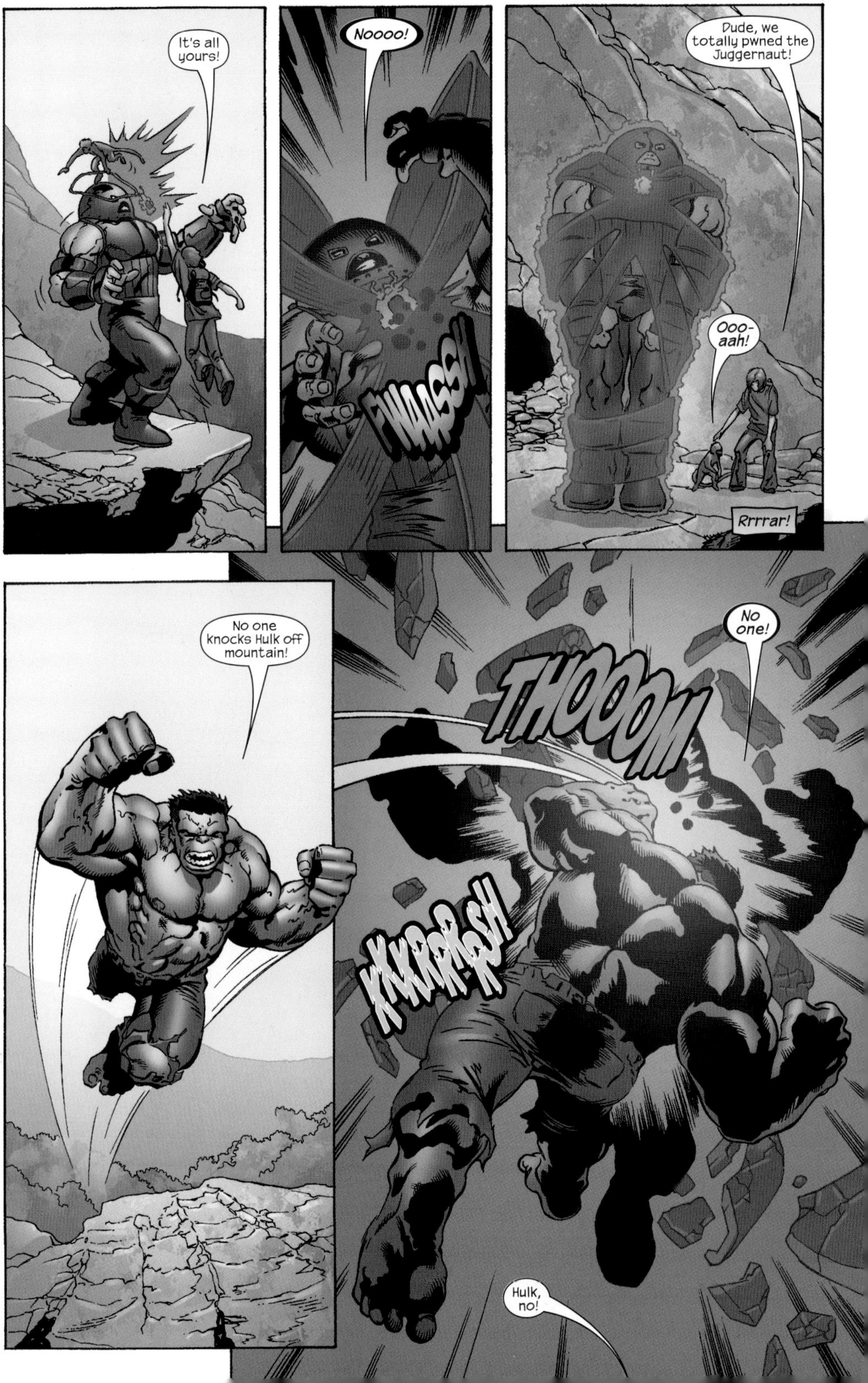
It's all yours!
Noooo!
FWAASSH
Dude, we totally pwned the Juggernaut!
Ooo-aah!
Rrrrar!
No one knocks Hulk off mountain!
No one!
THOOOM
KKKRRRSH
Hulk, no!

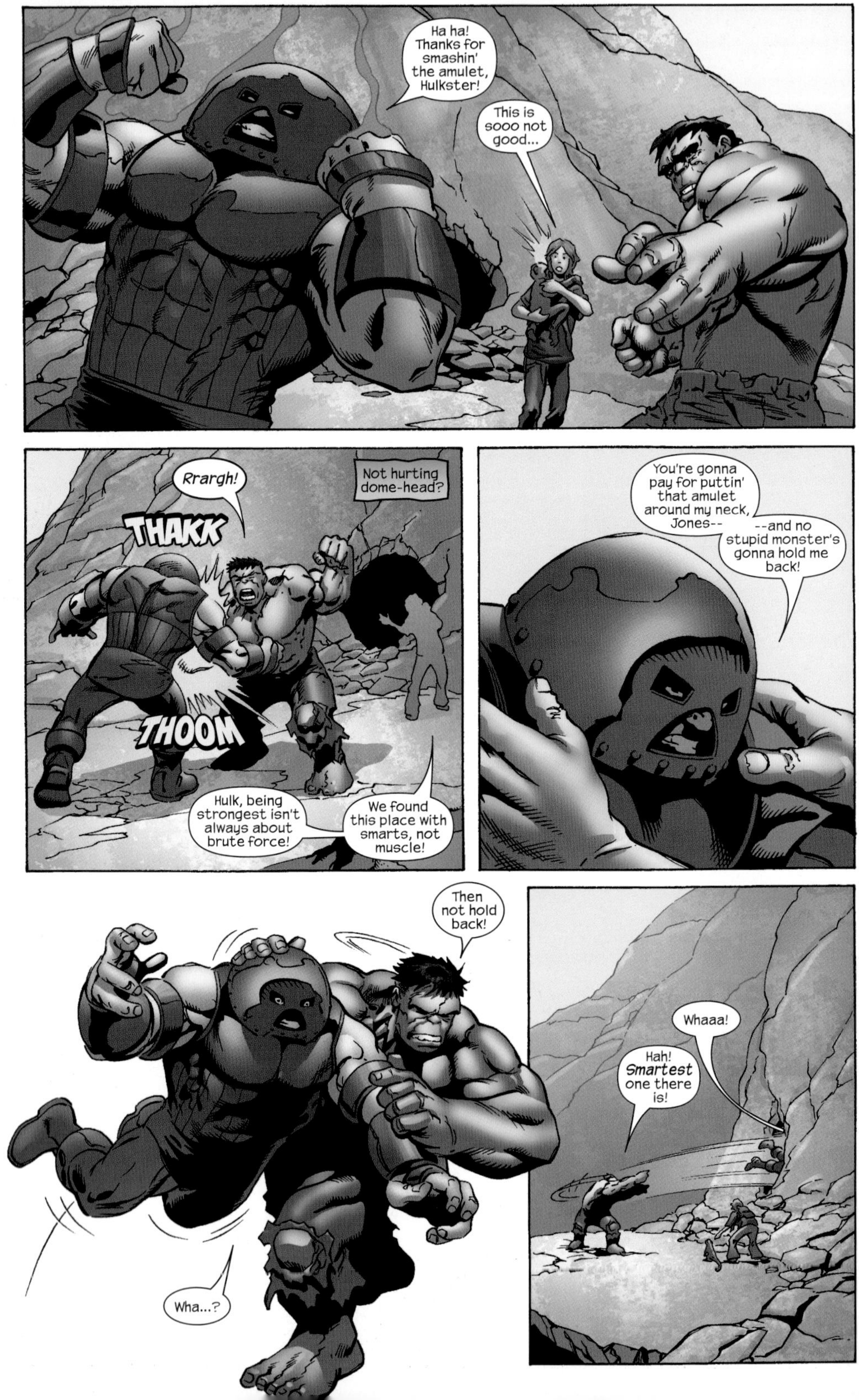
Ha ha! Thanks for smashin' the amulet, Hulkster!
This is sooo not good...
Rrargh!
Not hurting dome-head?
THAKK
THOOM
Hulk, being strongest isn't always about brute force!
We found this place with smarts, not muscle!
You're gonna pay for puttin' that amulet around my neck, Jones--
--and no stupid monster's gonna hold me back!
Then not hold back!
Wha...?
Whaaa!
Hah! Smartest one there is!

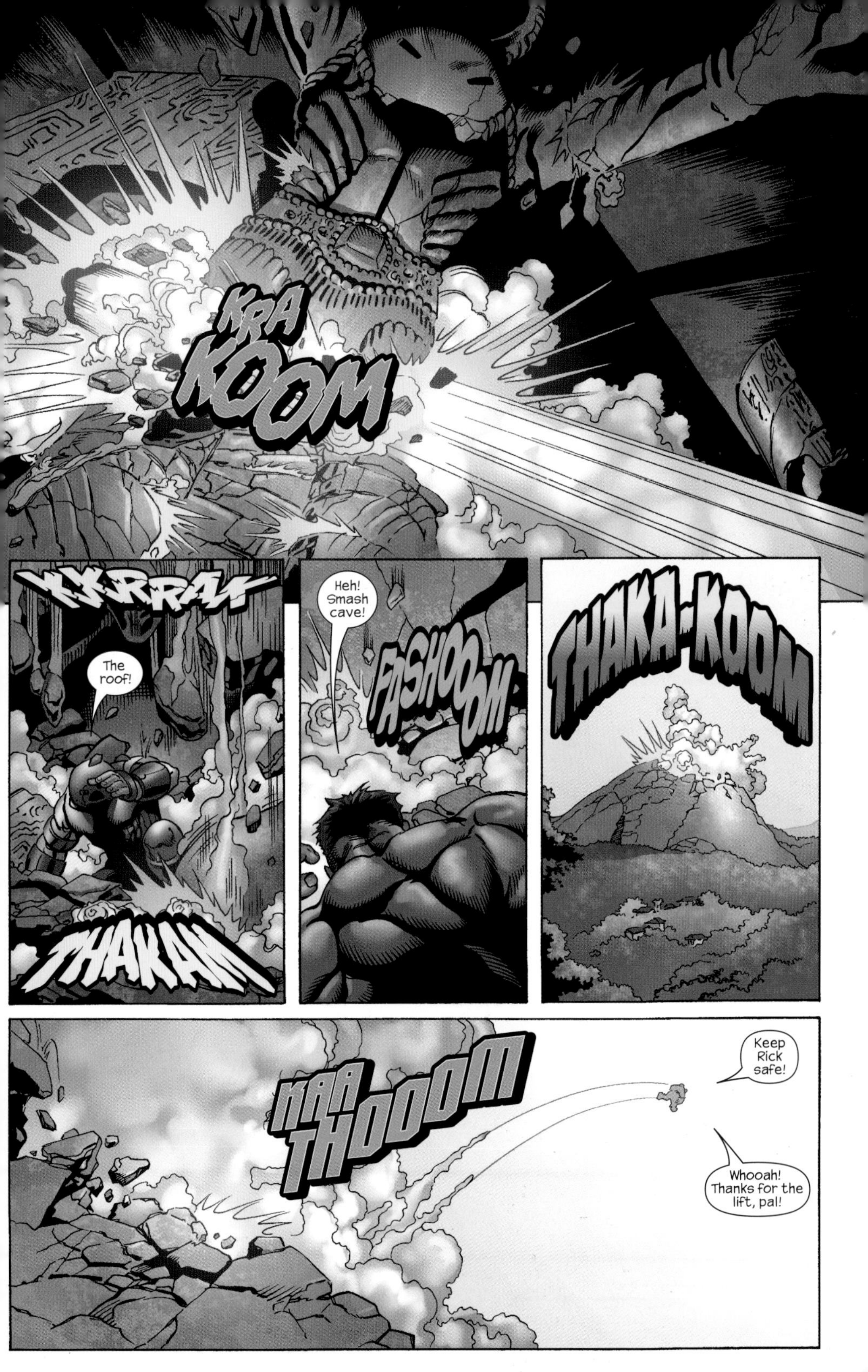
KRA KOOM
KKRRAK
The roof!
THAKAM
Heh! Smash cave!
FASHOOOOM
THAKA-KOOM
KAA THOOOM
Keep Rick safe!
Whooah! Thanks for the lift, pal!

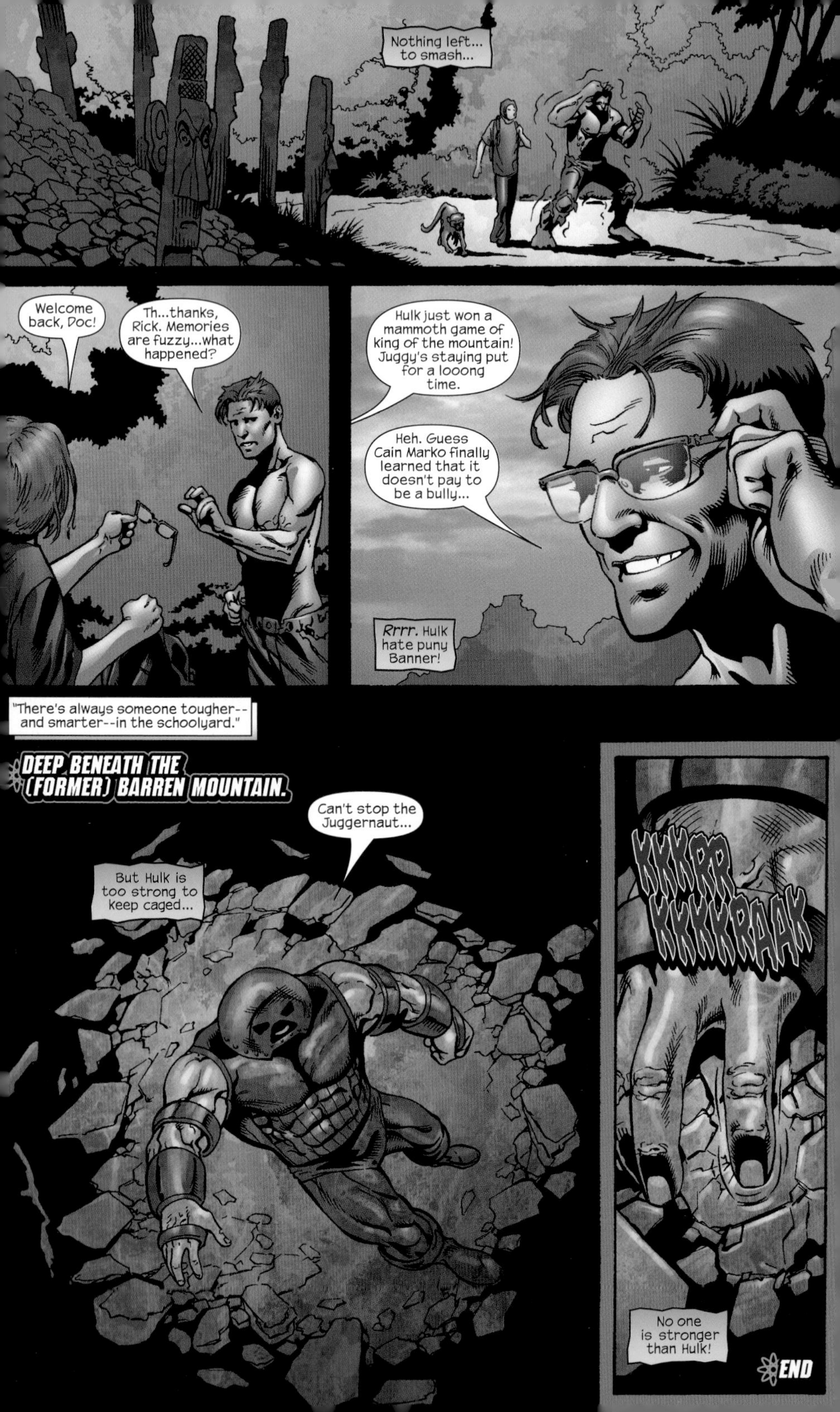
Nothing left... to smash...
Welcome back, Doc!
Th...thanks, Rick. Memories are fuzzy...what happened?
Hulk just won a mammoth game of king of the mountain! Juggy's staying put for a looong time.
Heh. Guess Cain Marko finally learned that it doesn't pay to be a bully...
Rrrr. Hulk hate puny Banner!
"There's always someone tougher--and smarter--in the schoolyard."
DEEP BENEATH THE (FORMER) BARREN MOUNTAIN.
Can't stop the Juggernaut...
But Hulk is too strong to keep caged...
KKKRR KKKKRAAK
No one is stronger than Hulk!
END

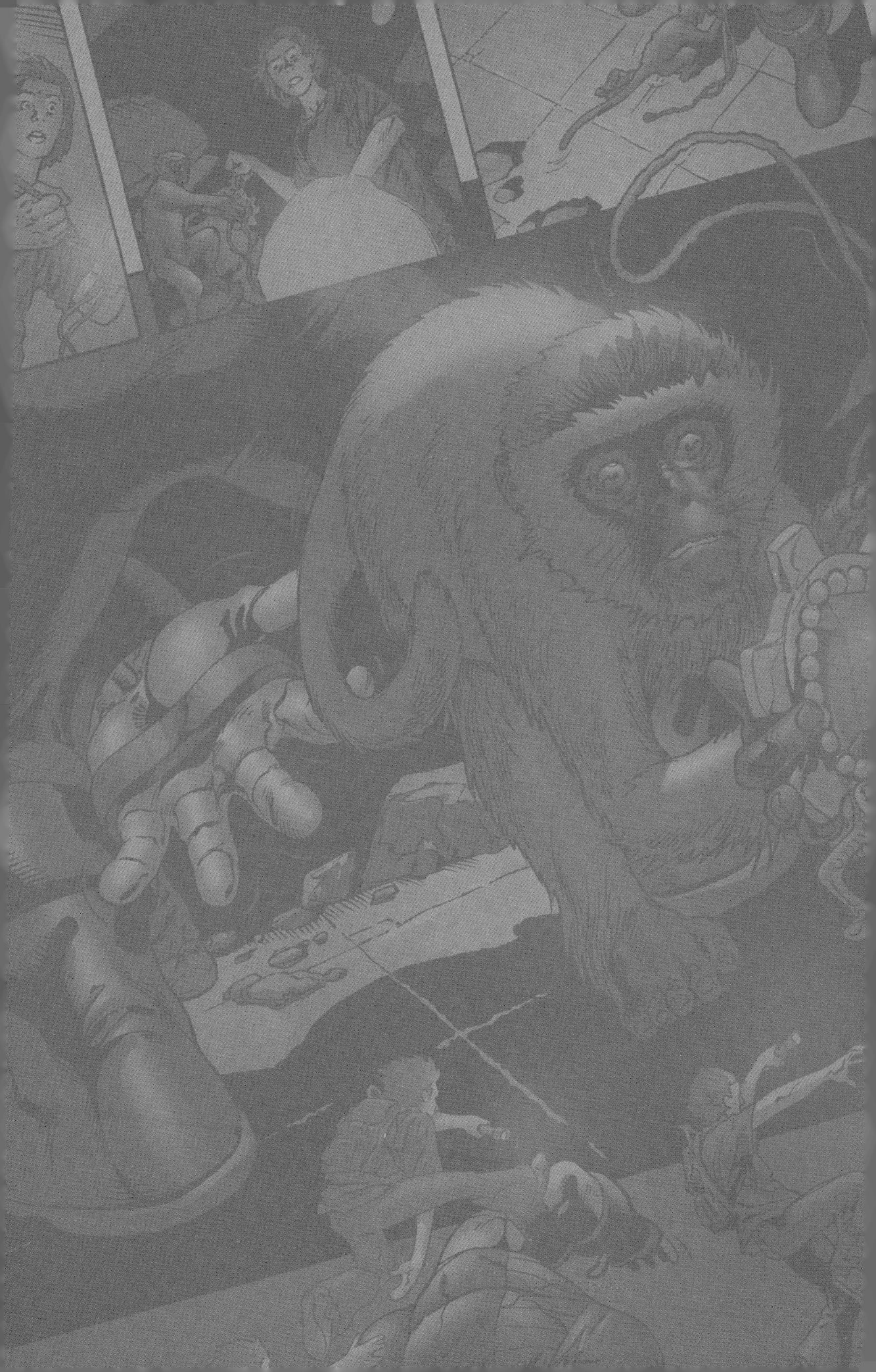

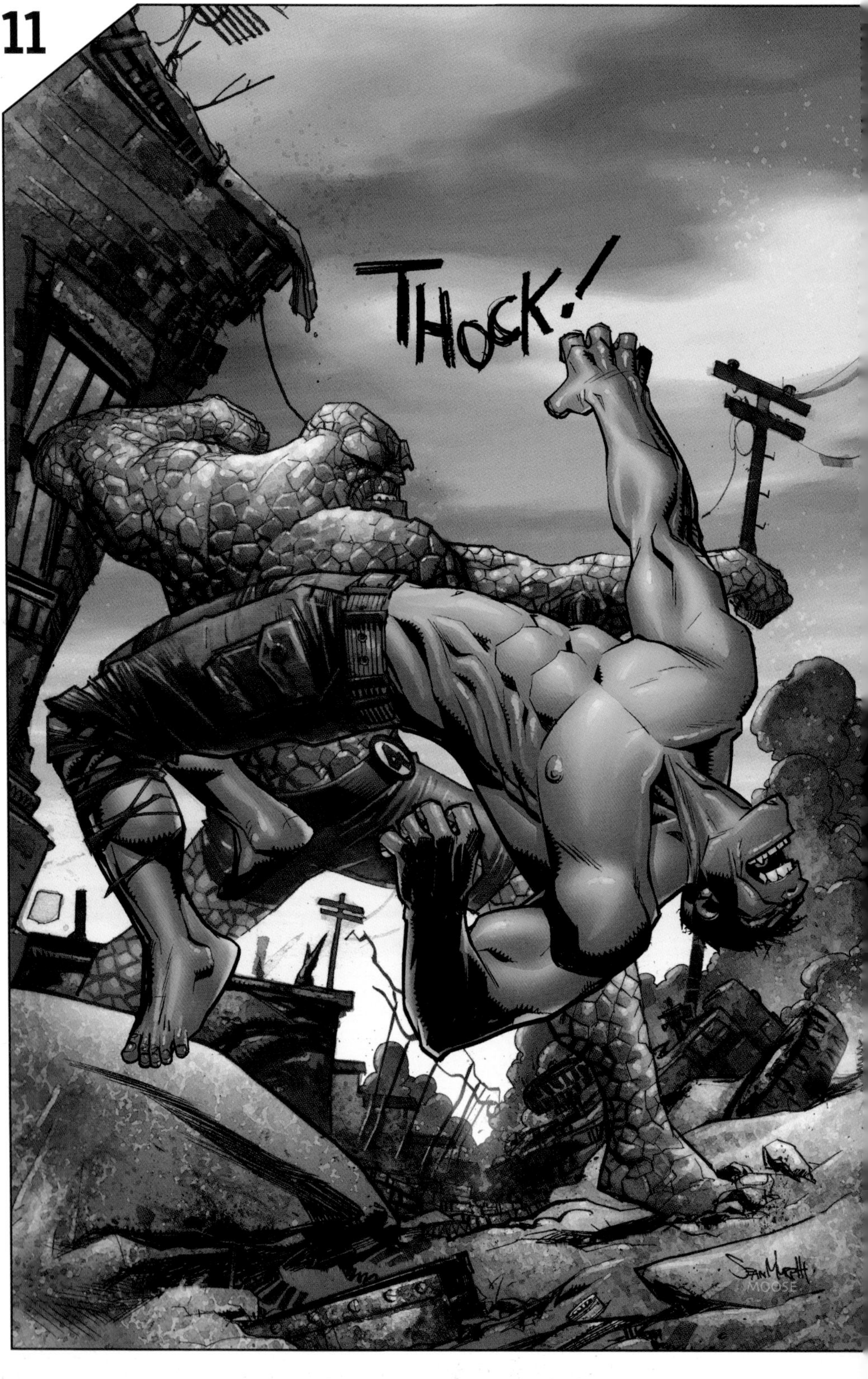
THOCK!
MOOSE

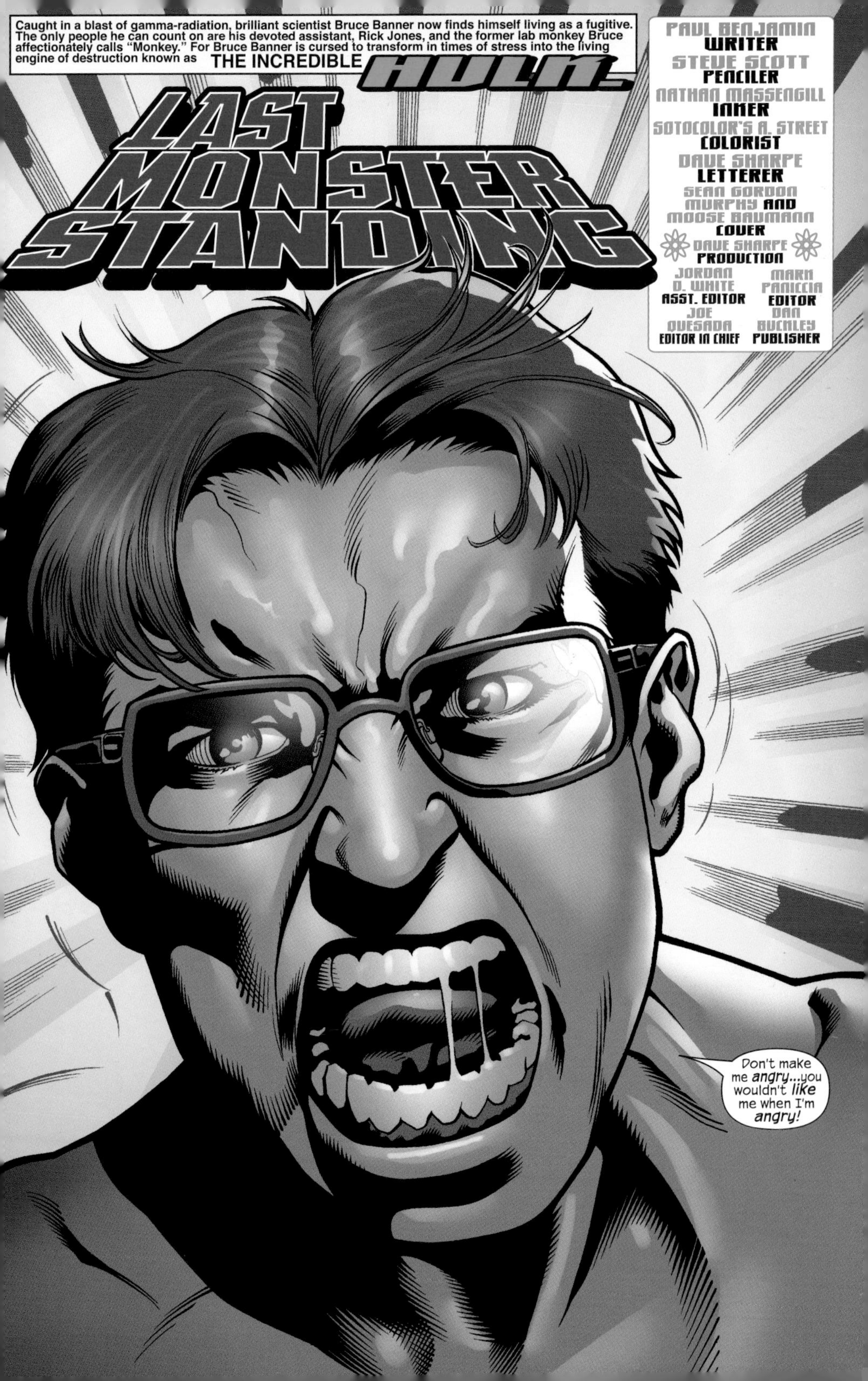

Caught in a blast of gamma-radiation, brilliant scientist Bruce Banner now finds himself living as a fugitive. The only people he can count on are his devoted assistant, Rick Jones, and the former lab monkey Bruce affectionately calls "Monkey." For Bruce Banner is cursed to transform in times of stress into the living engine of destruction known as THE INCREDIBLE HULK.
LAST MONSTER STANDING
PAUL BENJAMIN WRITER
STEVE SCOTT PENCILER
NATHAN MASSENGILL INKER
SOTOCOLOR'S A. STREET COLORIST
DAVE SHARPE LETTERER
SEAN GORDON MURPHY AND MOOSE BAUMANN COVER
DAVE SHARPE PRODUCTION
JORDAN D. WHITE ASST. EDITOR
MARK PANICCIA EDITOR
JOE QUESADA EDITOR IN CHIEF
DAN BUCKLEY PUBLISHER
Don't make me angry...you wouldn't like me when I'm angry!

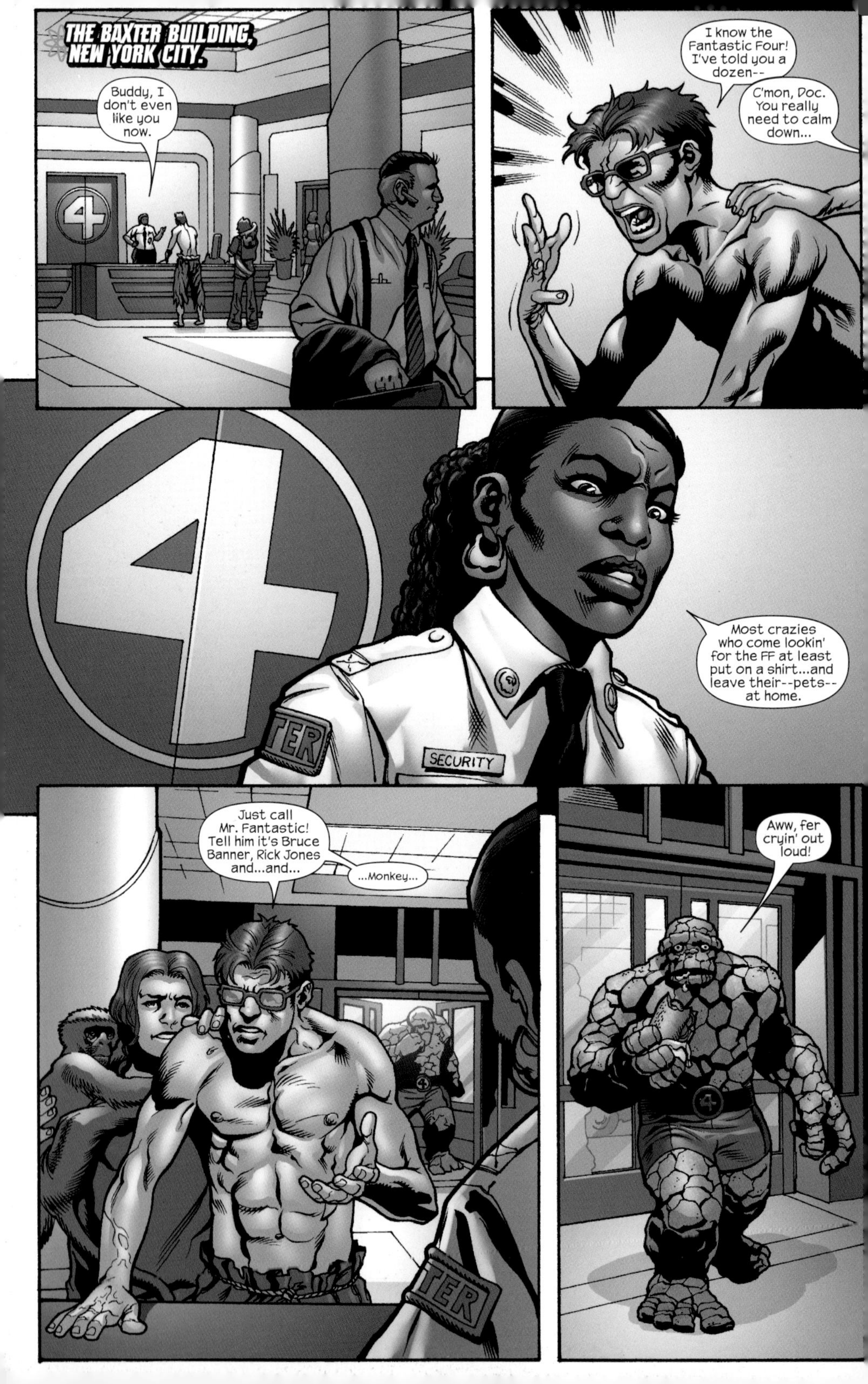
THE BAXTER BUILDING, NEW YORK CITY.
Buddy, I don't even like you now.
I know the Fantastic Four! I've told you a dozen--
C'mon, Doc. You really need to calm down...
Most crazies who come lookin' for the FF at least put on a shirt...and leave their--pets--at home.
SECURITY
Just call Mr. Fantastic! Tell him it's Bruce Banner, Rick Jones and...and...
...Monkey...
Aww, fer cryin' out loud!

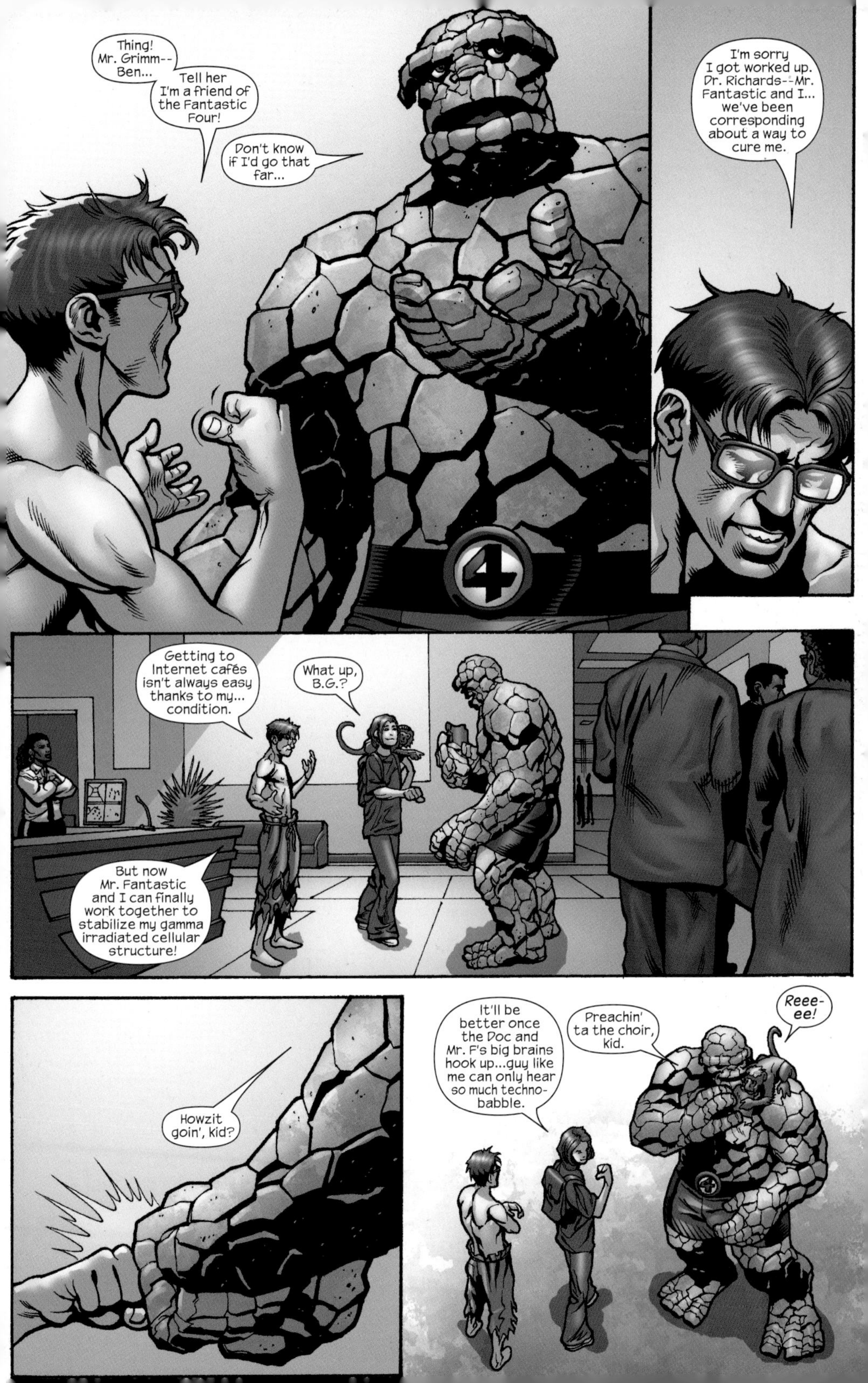
Thing! Mr. Grimm-- Ben...
Tell her I'm a friend of the Fantastic Four!
Don't know if I'd go that far...
I'm sorry I got worked up. Dr. Richards--Mr. Fantastic and I... we've been corresponding about a way to cure me.
Getting to Internet cafés isn't always easy thanks to my... condition.
What up, B.G.?
But now Mr. Fantastic and I can finally work together to stabilize my gamma irradiated cellular structure!
Howzit goin', kid?
It'll be better once the Doc and Mr. F's big brains hook up...guy like me can only hear so much techno-babble.
Preachin' ta the choir, kid.
Reeee-ee!

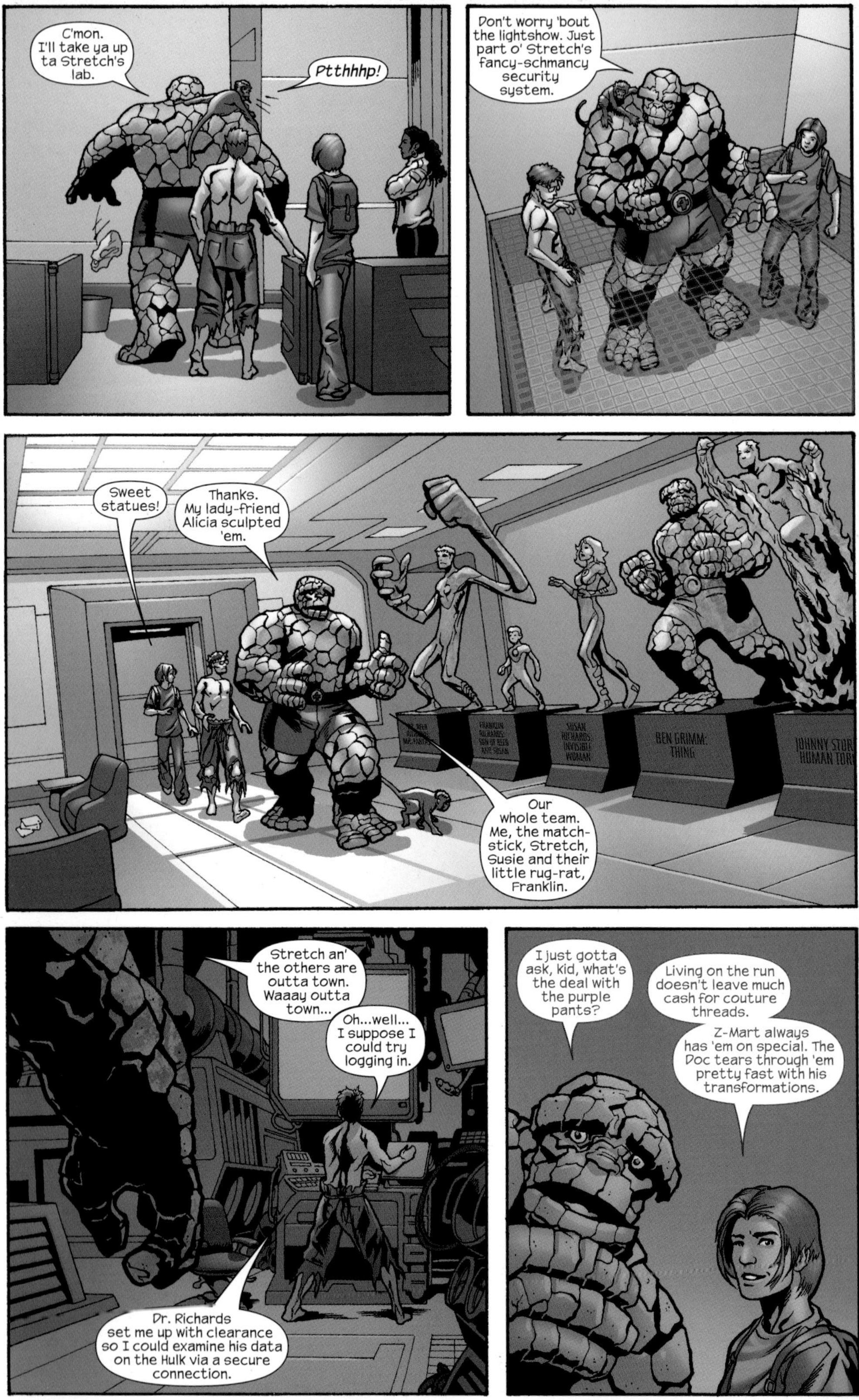

C'mon. I'll take ya up ta Stretch's lab.
Ptthhhp!
Don't worry 'bout the lightshow. Just part o' Stretch's fancy-schmancy security system.
Sweet statues!
Thanks. My lady-friend Alicia sculpted 'em.
BEN GRIMM: THING
Our whole team. Me, the match-stick, Stretch, Susie and their little rug-rat, Franklin.
Stretch an' the others are outta town. Waaay outta town...
Oh...well... I suppose I could try logging in.
Dr. Richards set me up with clearance so I could examine his data on the Hulk via a secure connection.
I just gotta ask, kid, what's the deal with the purple pants?
Living on the run doesn't leave much cash for couture threads.
Z-Mart always has 'em on special. The Doc tears through 'em pretty fast with his transformations.

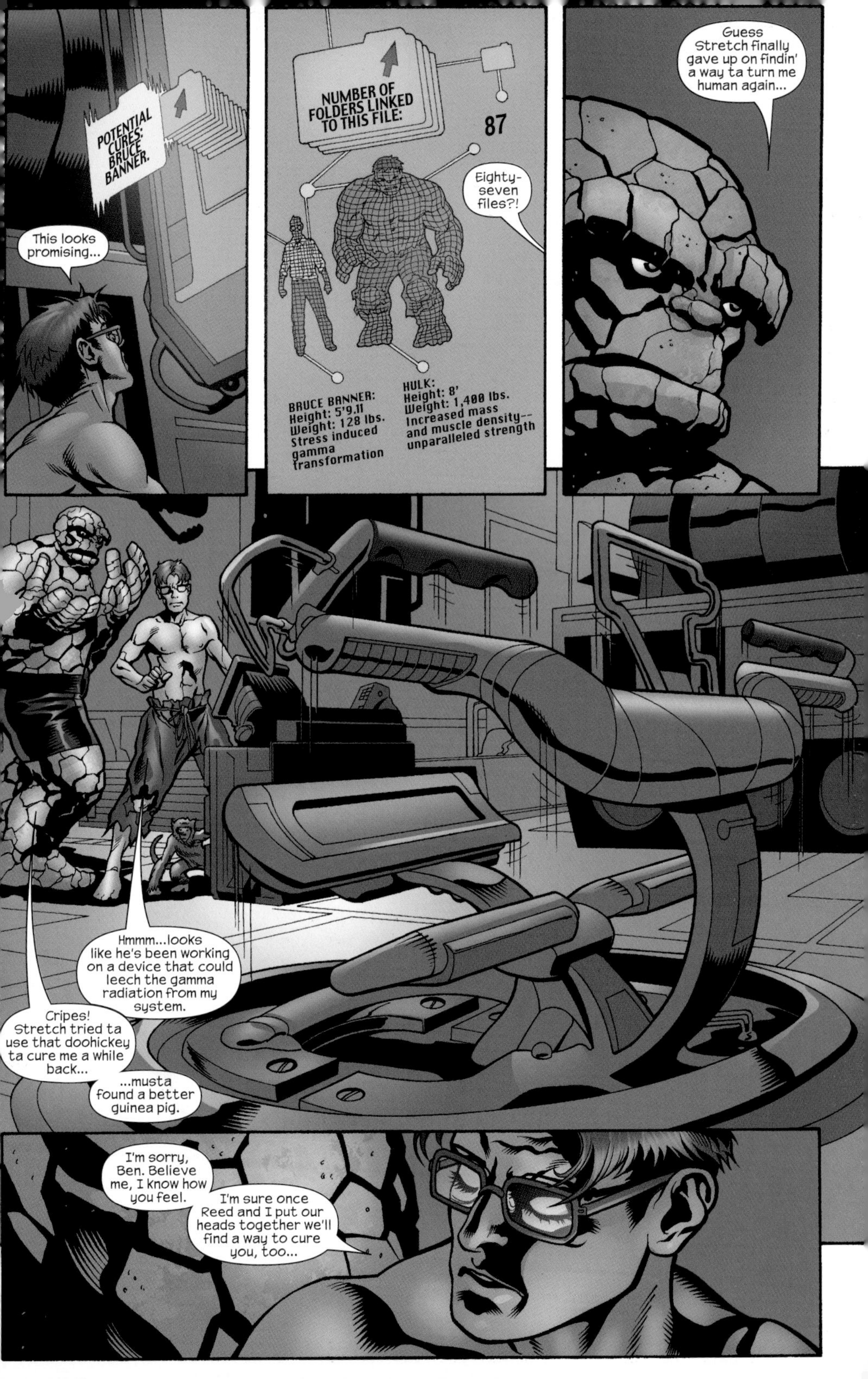
POTENTIAL CURES: BRUCE BANNER.
This looks promising...
NUMBER OF FOLDERS LINKED TO THIS FILE:
87
BRUCE BANNER: Height: 5'9.11 Weight: 128 lbs. Stress induced gamma transformation
HULK: Height: 8' Weight: 1,400 lbs. Increased mass and muscle density-- unparalleled strength
Eighty-seven files?!
Guess Stretch finally gave up on findin' a way ta turn me human again...
Hmmm...looks like he's been working on a device that could leech the gamma radiation from my system.
Cripes! Stretch tried ta use that doohickey ta cure me a while back...
...musta found a better guinea pig.
I'm sorry, Ben. Believe me, I know how you feel.
I'm sure once Reed and I put our heads together we'll find a way to cure you, too...

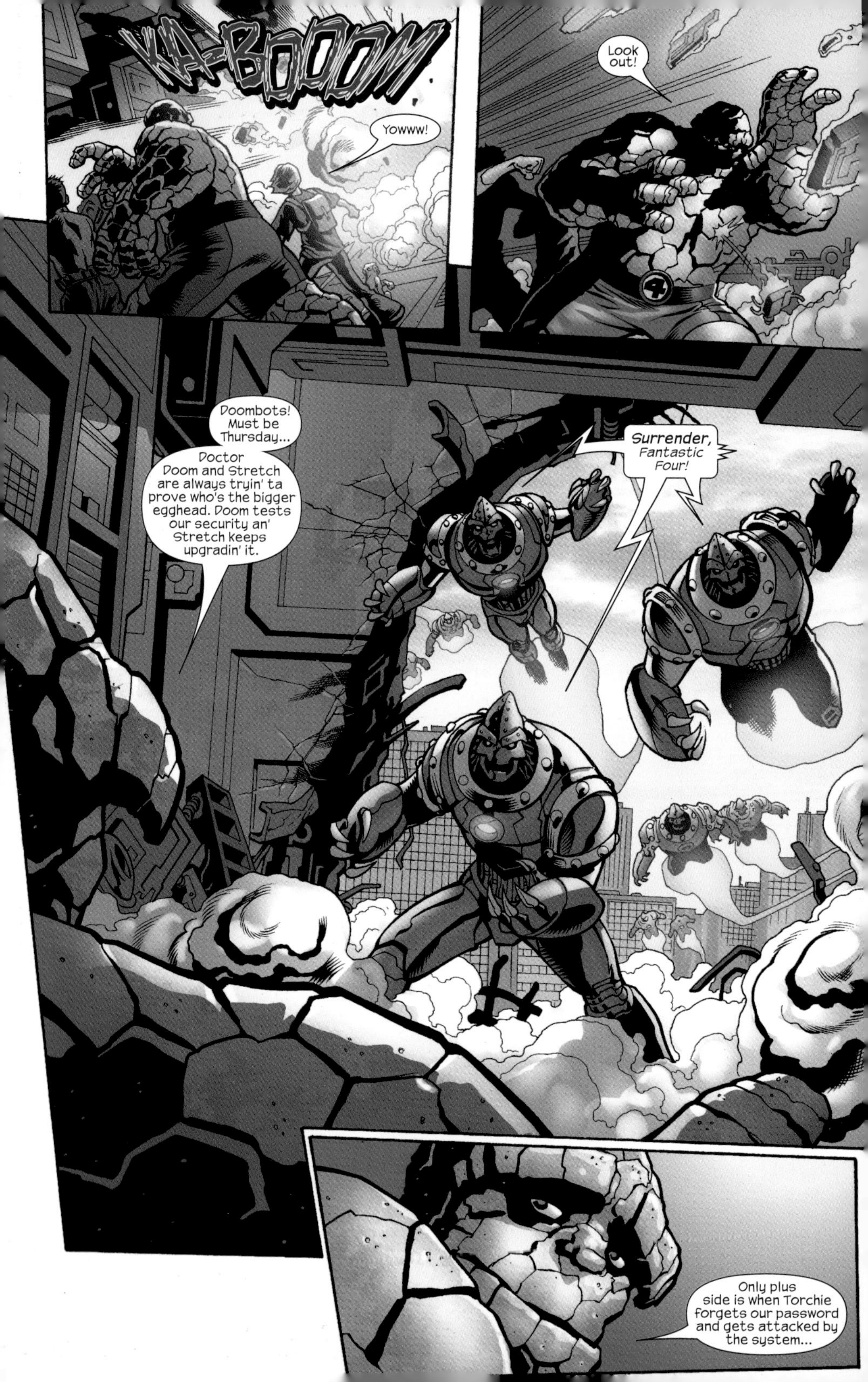
KA-BOOOOM
YOWWW!
Look out!
Doombots! Must be Thursday...
Doctor Doom and Stretch are always tryin' ta prove who's the bigger egghead. Doom tests our security an' Stretch keeps upgradin' it.
Surrender, Fantastic Four!
Only plus side is when Torchie forgets our password and gets attacked by the system...

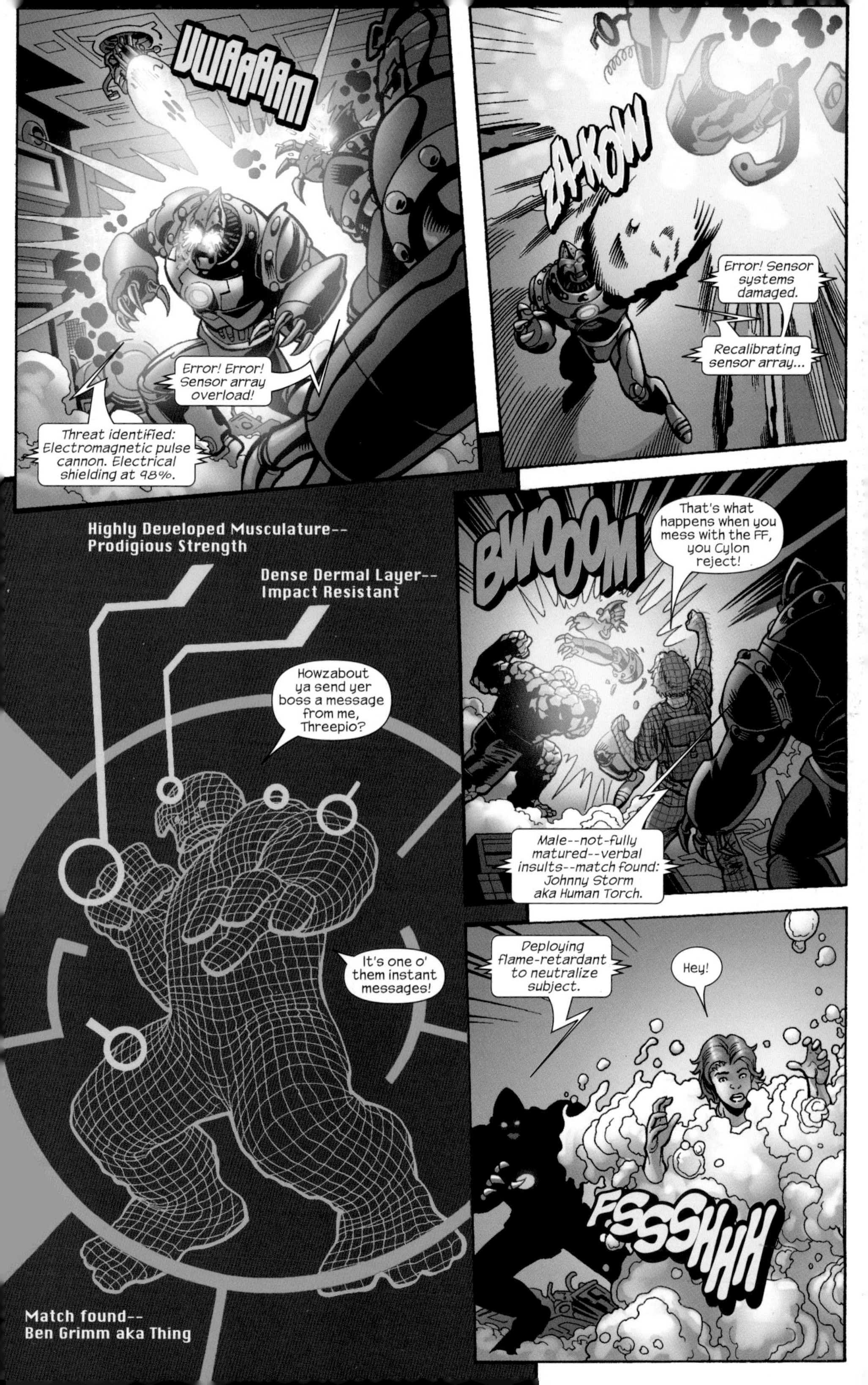
VWAAAAM
Threat identified: Electromagnetic pulse cannon. Electrical shielding at 98%.
Error! Error! Sensor array overload!
ZA-KOW
Error! Sensor systems damaged.
Recalibrating sensor array...
Highly Developed Musculature--Prodigious Strength
Dense Dermal Layer--Impact Resistant
Howzabout ya send yer boss a message from me, Threepio?
It's one o' them instant messages!
Match found--Ben Grimm aka Thing
BWOOOM
That's what happens when you mess with the FF, you Cylon reject!
Male--not-fully matured--verbal insults--match found: Johnny Storm aka Human Torch.
Deploying flame-retardant to neutralize subject.
Hey!
FSSSHHH

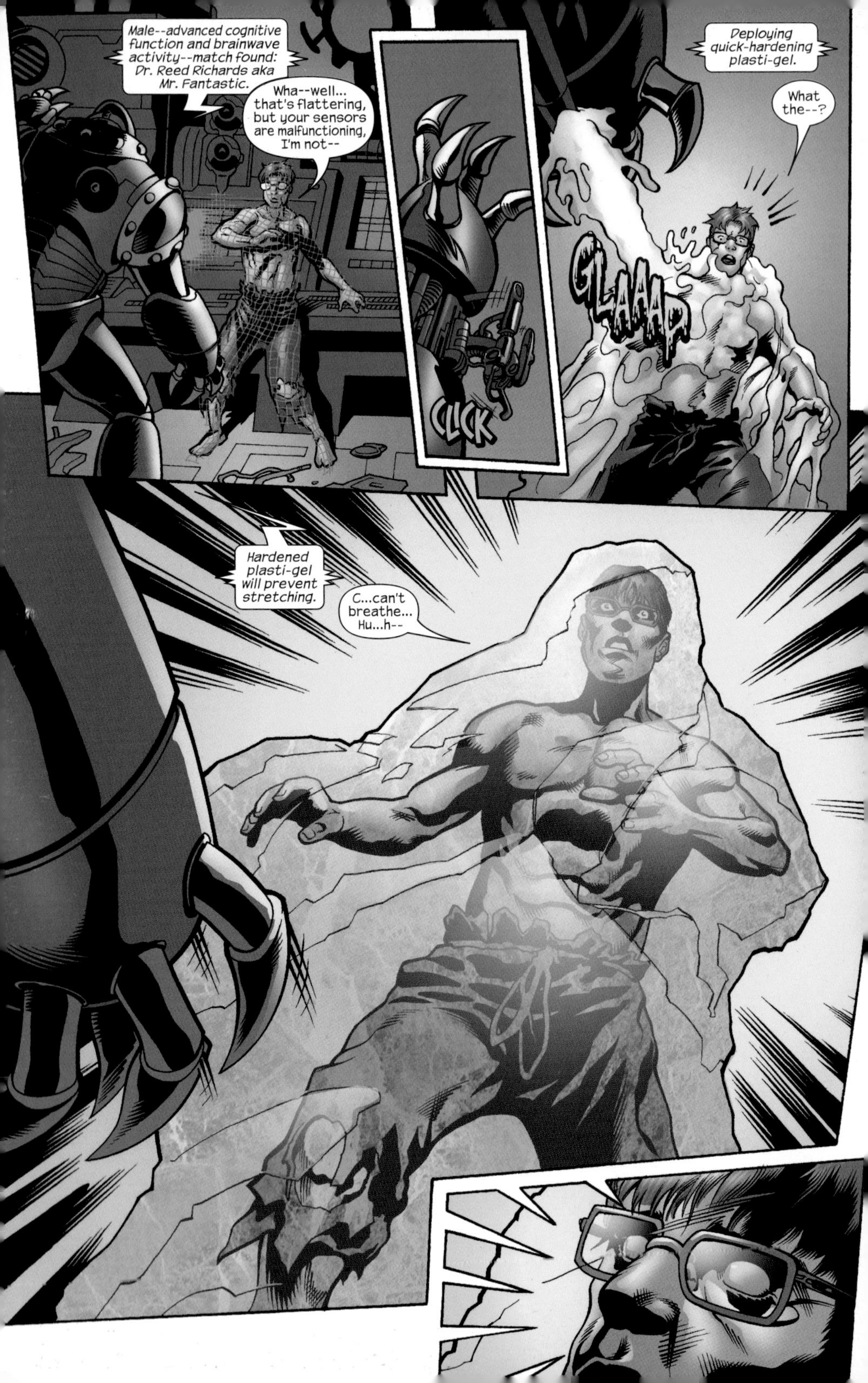
Male--advanced cognitive function and brainwave activity--match found: Dr. Reed Richards aka Mr. Fantastic.
Wha--well... that's flattering, but your sensors are malfunctioning, I'm not--
CLICK
Deploying quick-hardening plasti-gel.
What the--?
GLAAAP
Hardened plasti-gel will prevent stretching.
C...can't breathe... Hu...h--

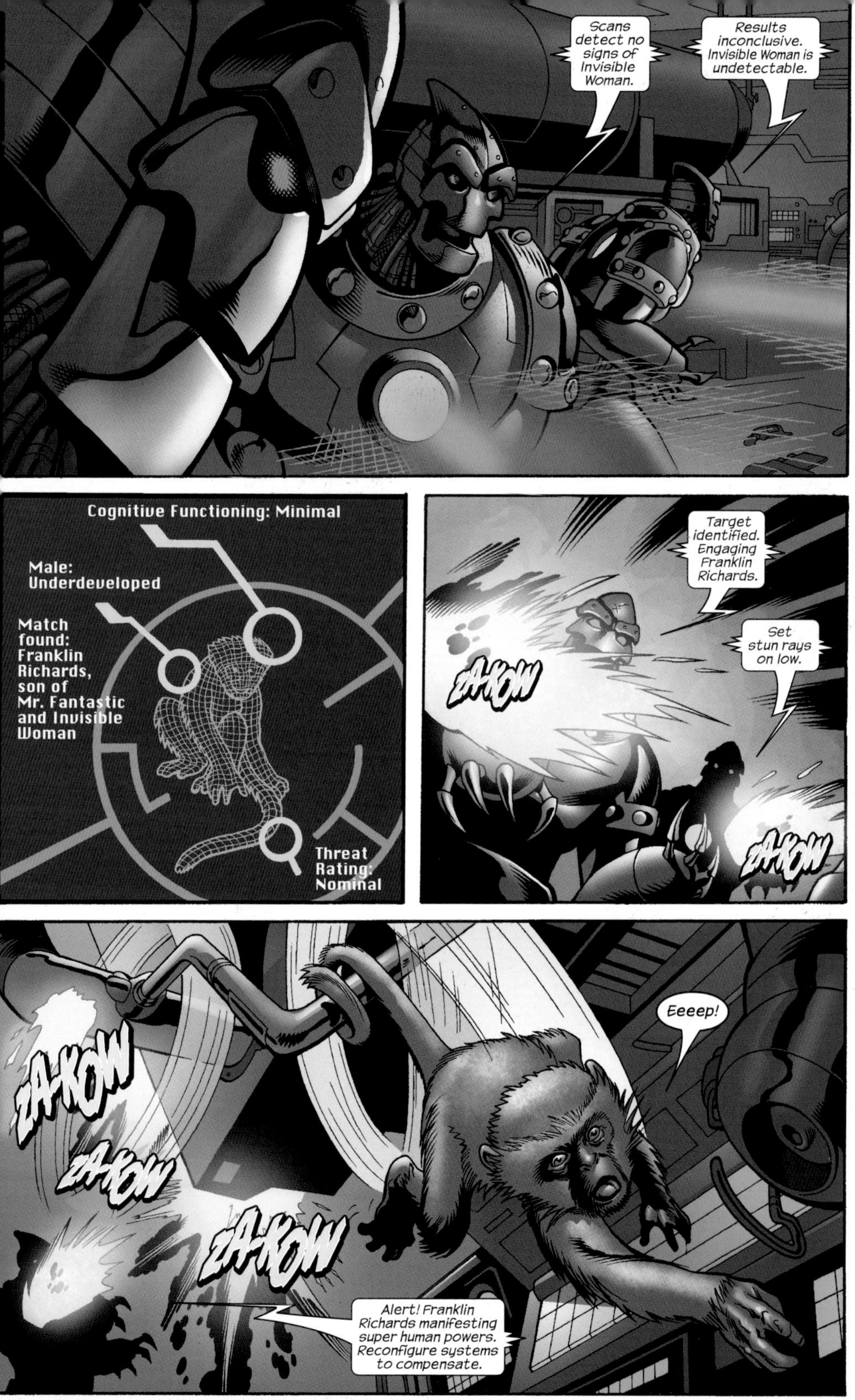
Scans detect no signs of Invisible Woman.
Results inconclusive. Invisible Woman is undetectable.
Cognitive Functioning: Minimal
Male: Underdeveloped
Match found: Franklin Richards, son of Mr. Fantastic and Invisible Woman
Threat Rating: Nominal
Target identified. Engaging Franklin Richards.
Set stun rays on low.
ZA-KOW
ZA-KOW
ZA-KOW
ZA-KOW
ZA-KOW
Eeeep!
Alert! Franklin Richards manifesting super human powers. Reconfigure systems to compensate.

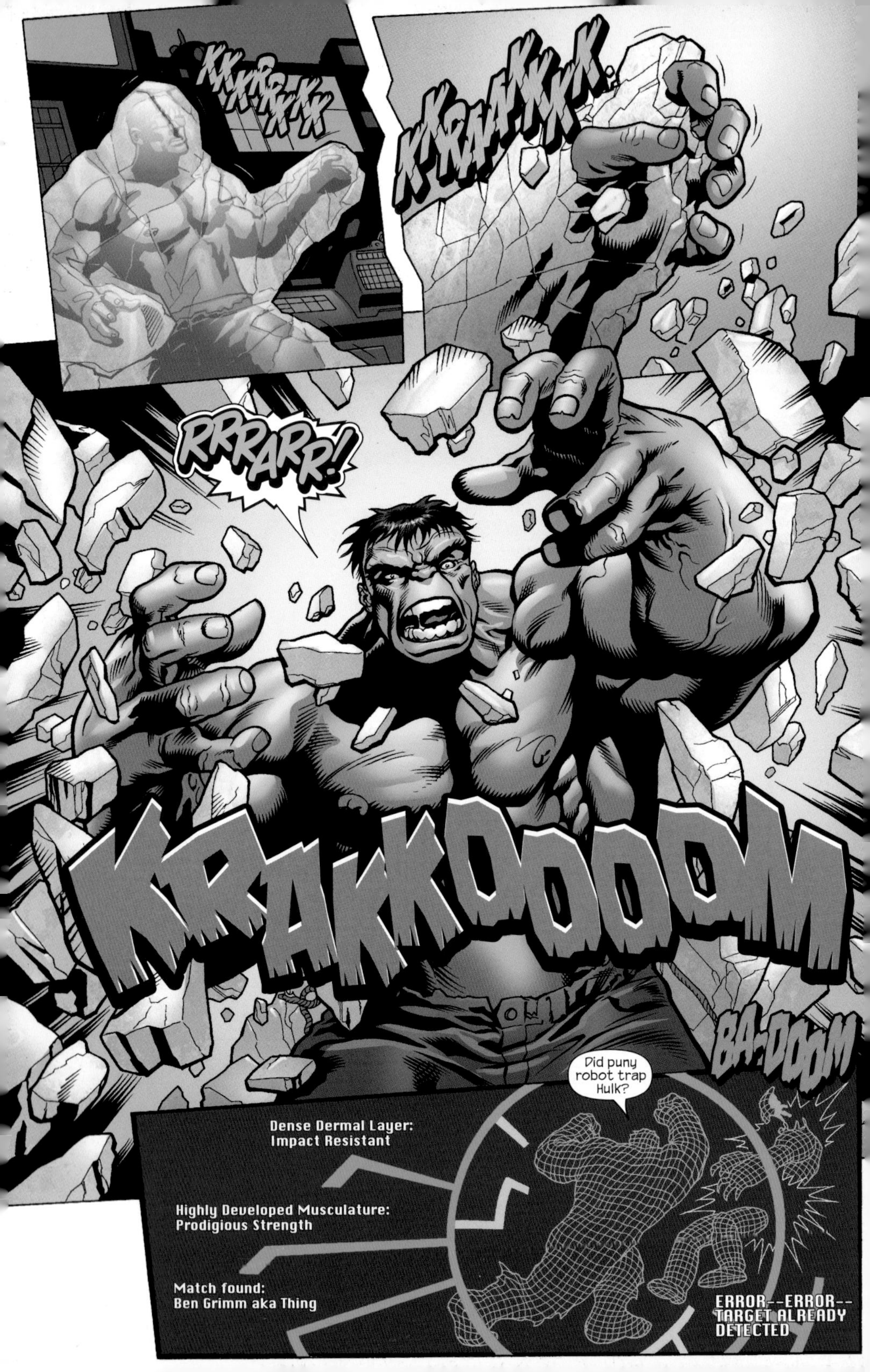
KKKKRRKKKK
KKRAAKKKK
RRRARR!
KRAKKOOOOM
BA-DOOM
Did puny robot trap Hulk?
Dense Dermal Layer:
Impact Resistant
Highly Developed Musculature:
Prodigious Strength
Match found:
Ben Grimm aka Thing
ERROR--ERROR--
TARGET ALREADY
DETECTED

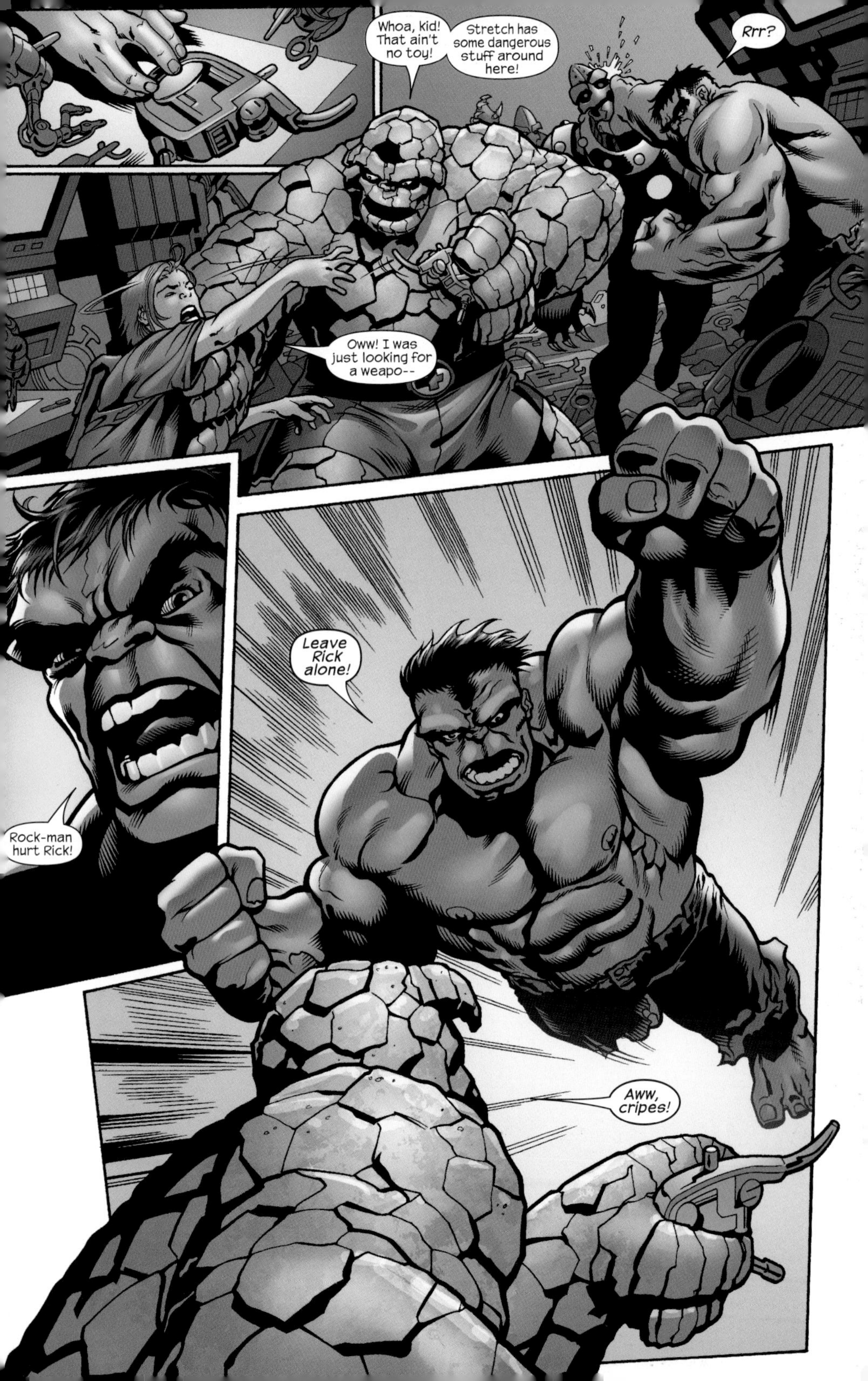
Whoa, kid! That ain't no toy!
Stretch has some dangerous stuff around here!
Rrr?
Oww! I was just looking for a weapo--
Rock-man hurt Rick!
Leave Rick alone!
Aww, cripes!

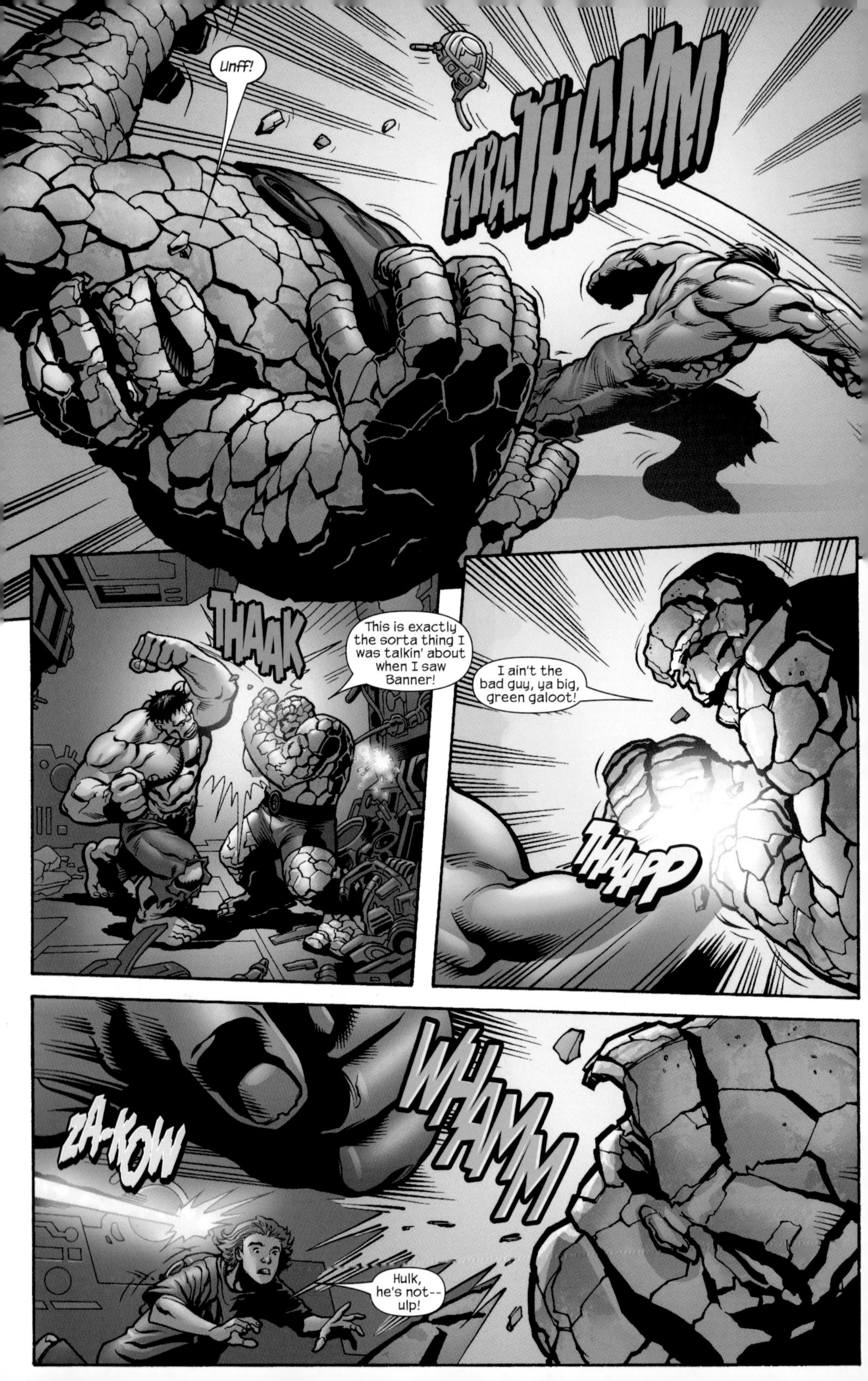
Unff!
KRATHAMM
THAAK
This is exactly the sorta thing I was talkin' about when I saw Banner!
I ain't the bad guy, ya big, green galoot!
THAAPP
ZA-KOW
WHAMM
Hulk, he's not-- ulp!

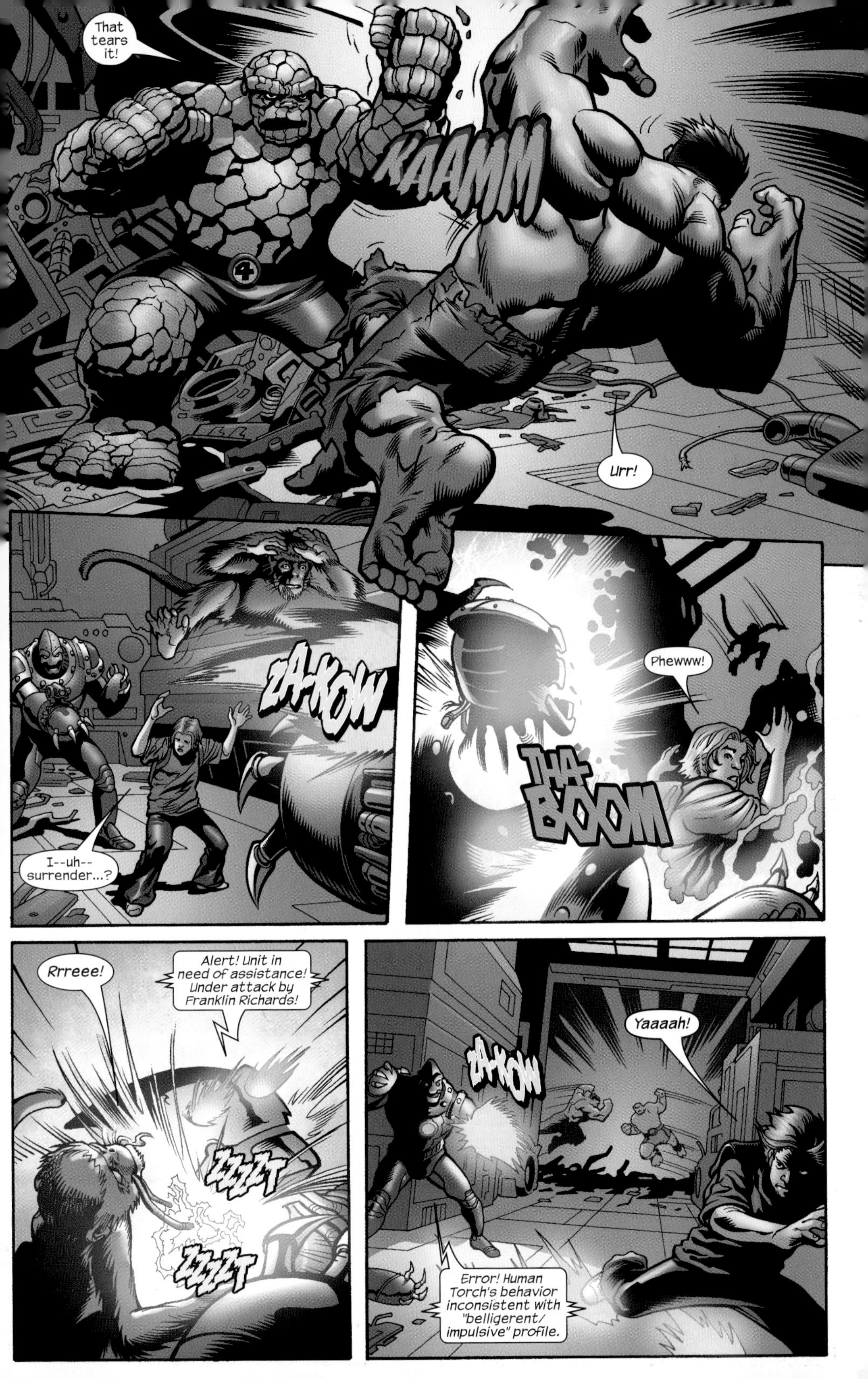
That tears it!
KAAMM
Urr!
ZA-KOW
I--uh-- surrender...?
Phewww!
THA-BOOM
Rrreee!
Alert! Unit in need of assistance! Under attack by Franklin Richards!
ZZZZT
ZZZZT
Yaaaah!
ZA-KOW
Error! Human Torch's behavior inconsistent with "belligerent/ impulsive" profile.

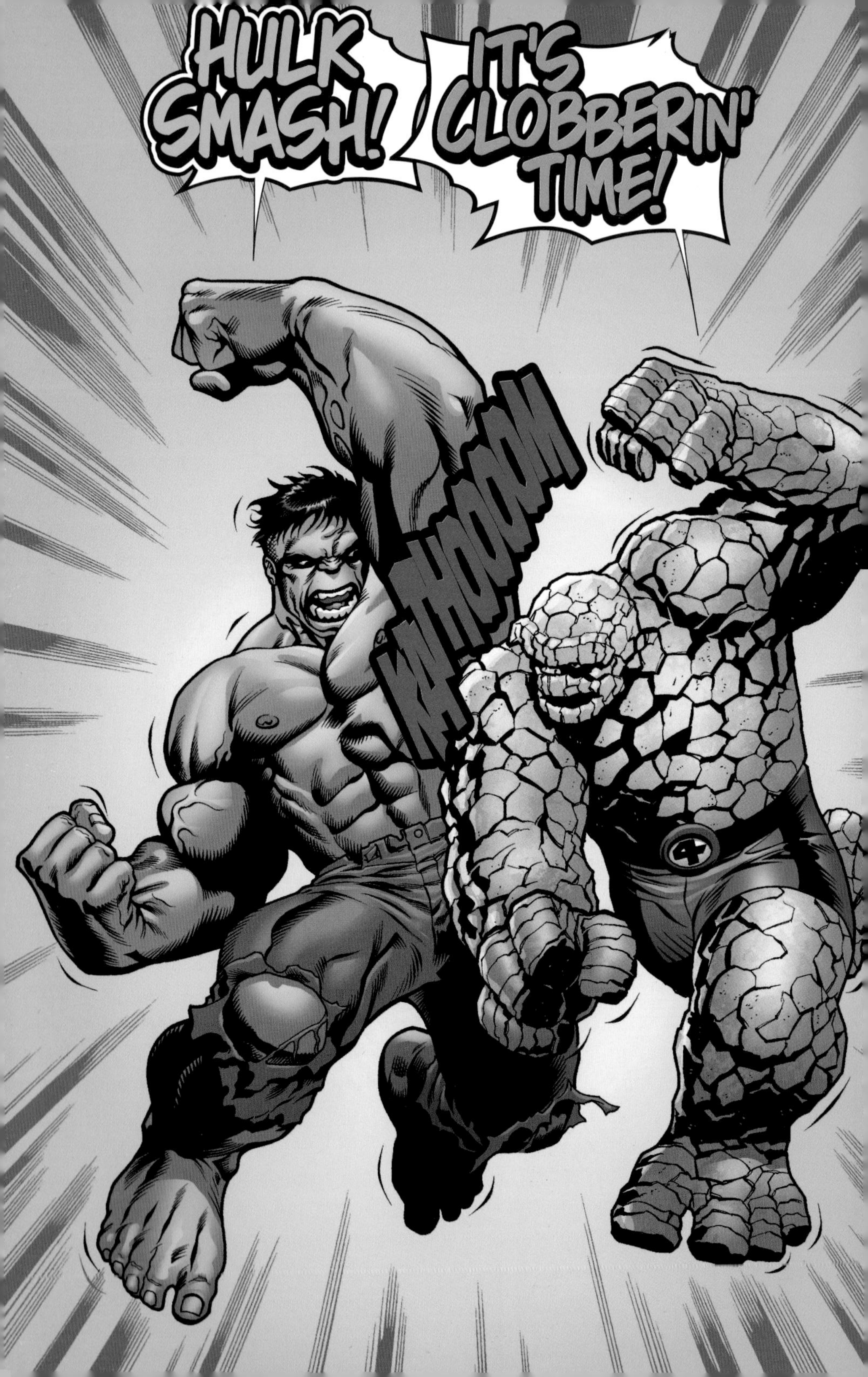
HULK SMASH!
IT'S CLOBBERIN' TIME!
KATHOOOOM

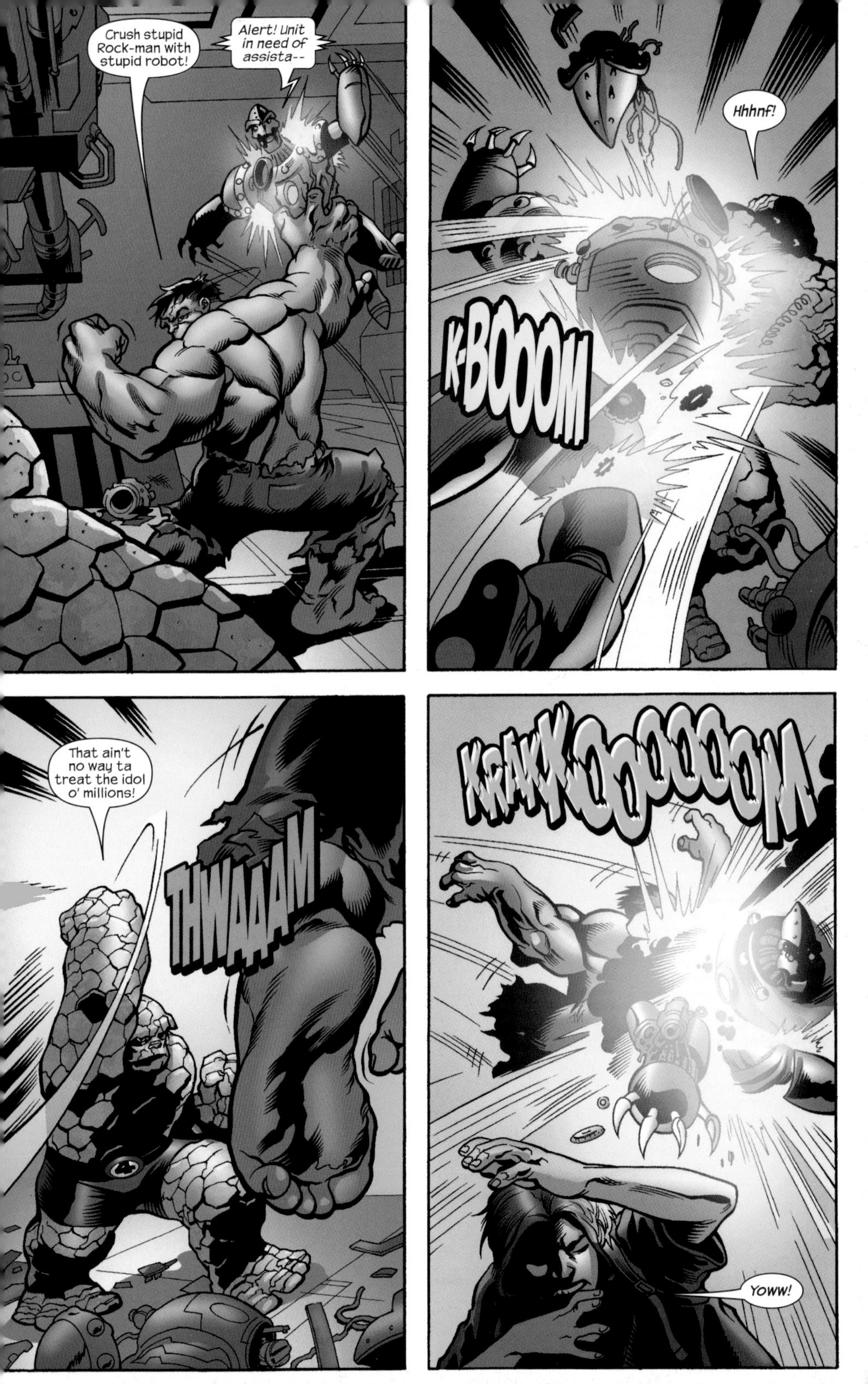
Crush stupid Rock-man with stupid robot!
Alert! Unit in need of assista--
Hhhnf!
K-BOOOM
That ain't no way ta treat the idol o' millions!
THWAAAM
KRAKKOOOOOOM
YOWW!

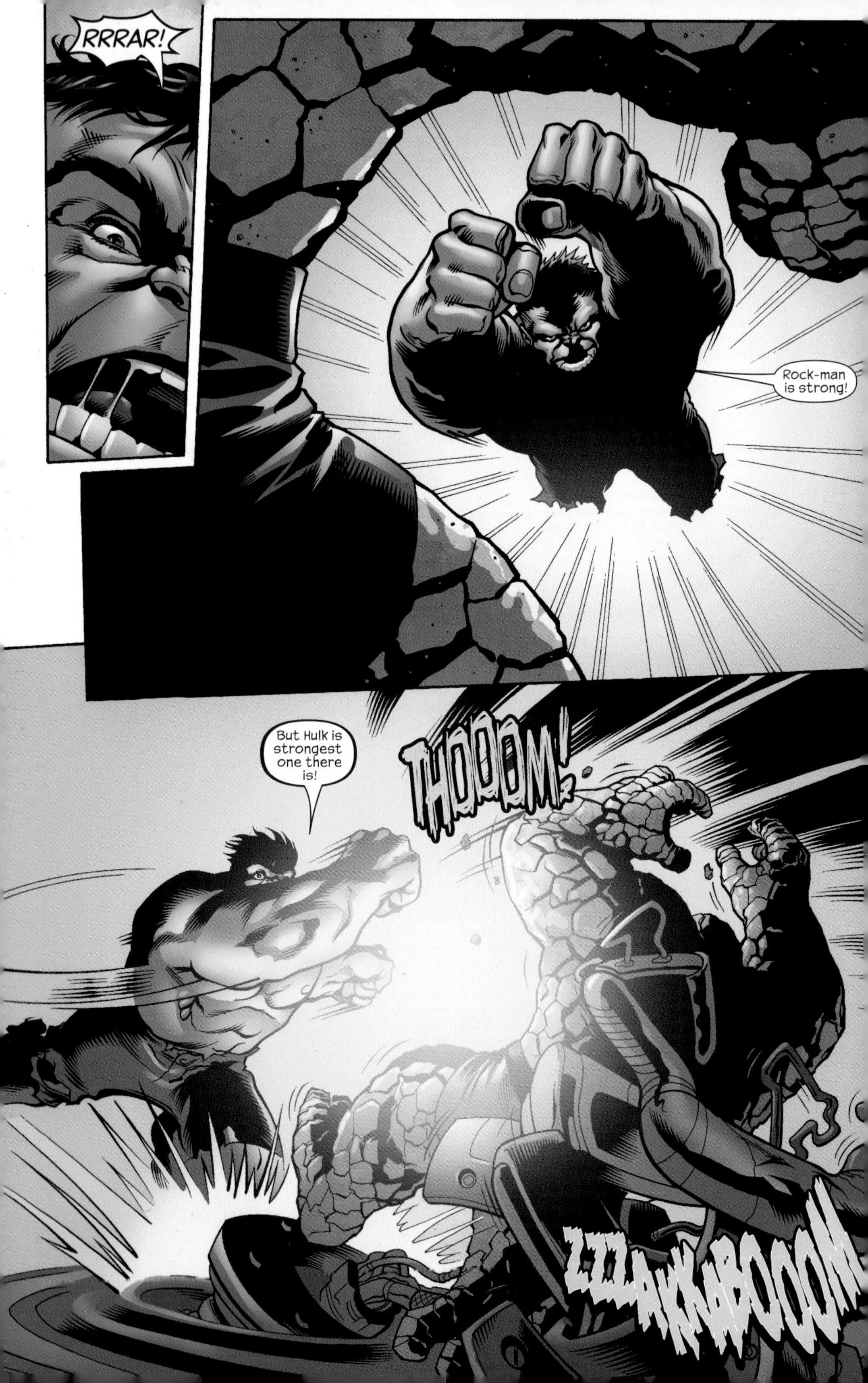
RRRAR!
Rock-man is strong!
But Hulk is strongest one there is!
THOOOM!
ZZZAKKABOOOM

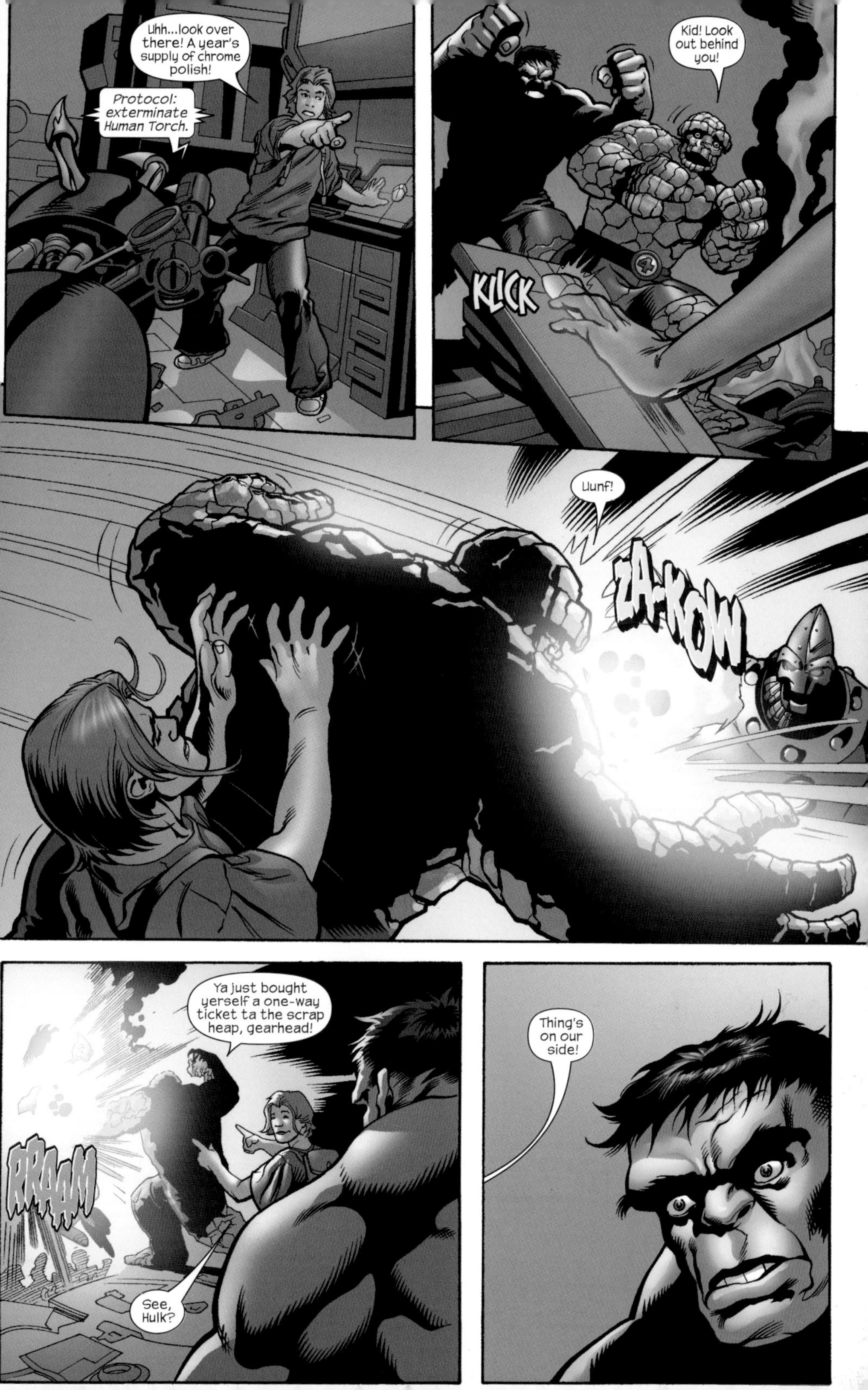
Uhh...look over there! A year's supply of chrome polish!
Protocol: exterminate Human Torch.
Kid! Look out behind you!
KLICK
Uunf!
ZA-KOW
Ya just bought yerself a one-way ticket ta the scrap heap, gearhead!
RRAAM
See, Hulk?
Thing's on our side!

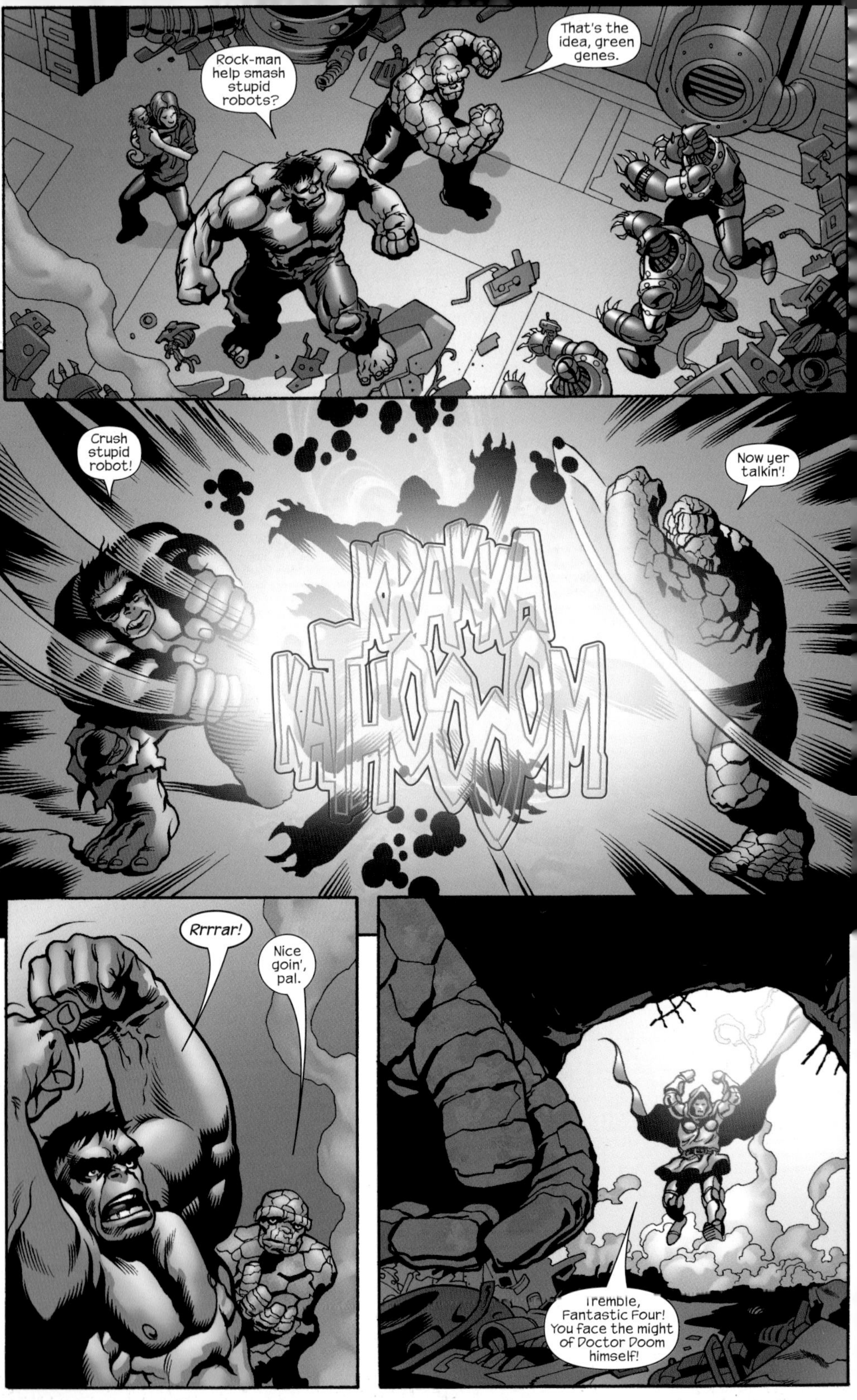
Rock-man help smash stupid robots?
That's the idea, green genes.
Crush stupid robot!
Now yer talkin'!
KRAKKA KATHOOOOOM
Rrrrar!
Nice goin', pal.
Tremble, Fantastic Four! You face the might of Doctor Doom himself!

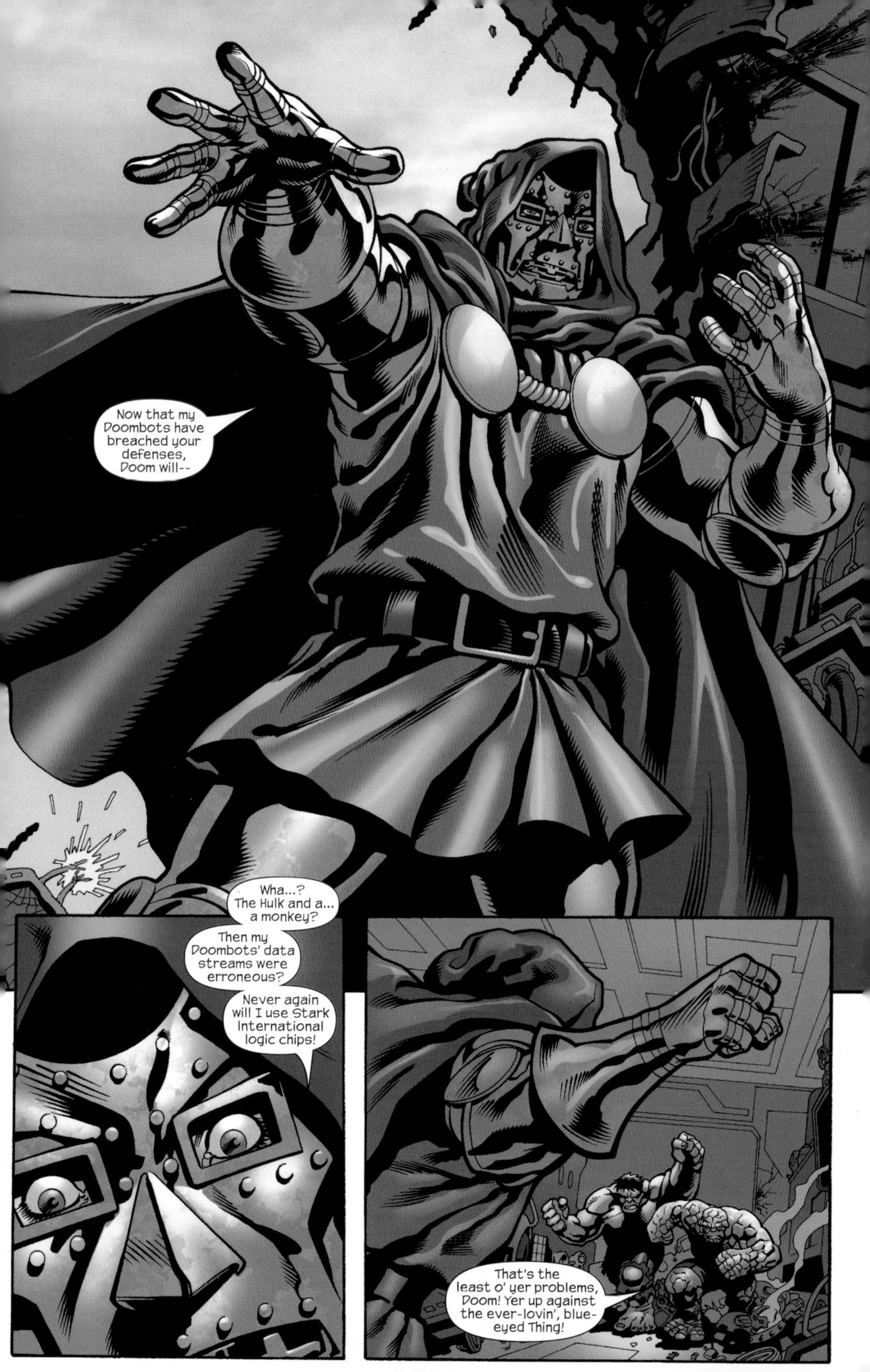

Now that my Doombots have breached your defenses, Doom will--
Wha...? The Hulk and a... a monkey?
Then my Doombots' data streams were erroneous?
Never again will I use Stark International logic chips!
That's the least o' yer problems, Doom! Yer up against the ever-lovin', blue-eyed Thing!

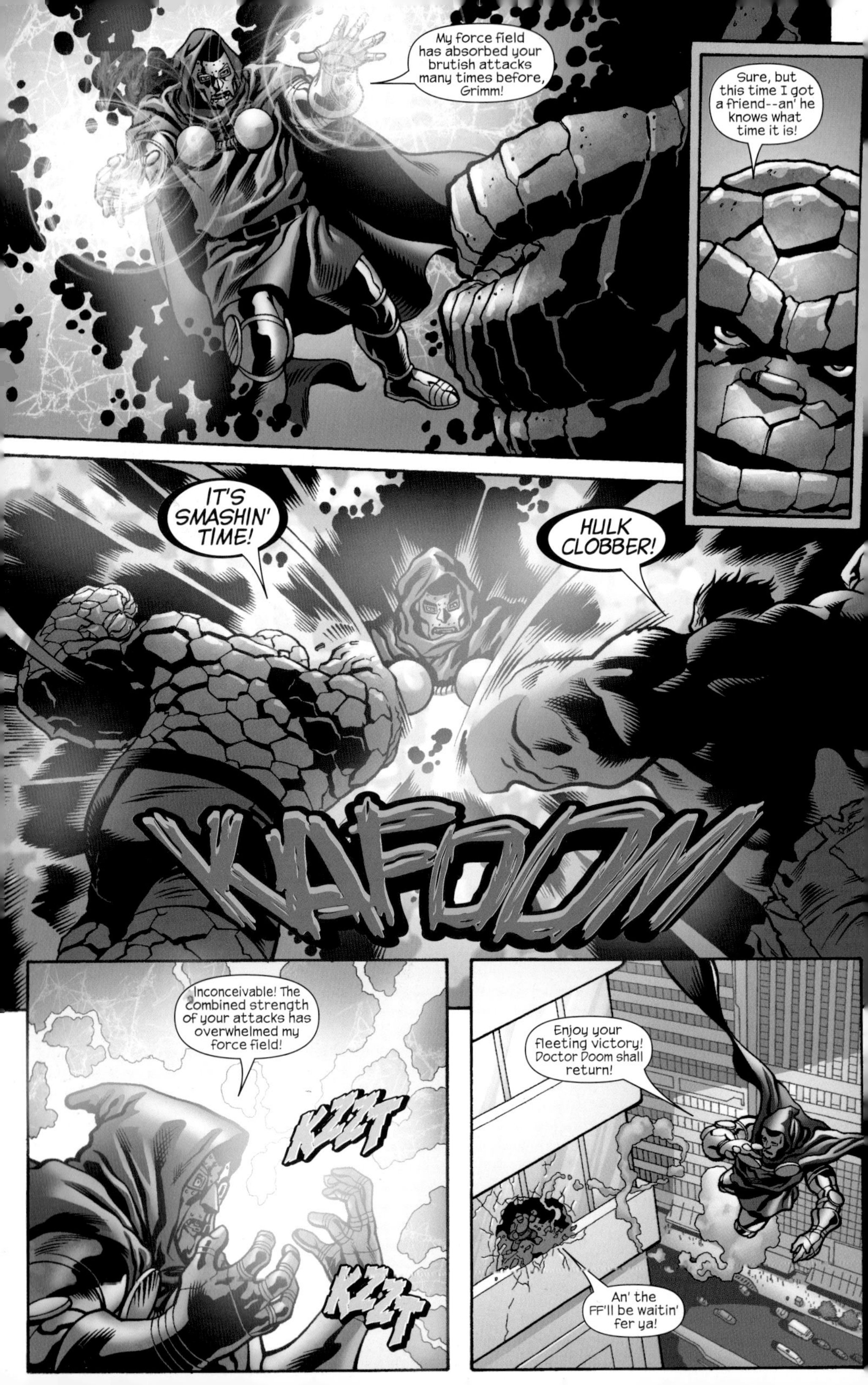
My force field has absorbed your brutish attacks many times before, Grimm!
Sure, but this time I got a friend--an' he knows what time it is!
IT'S SMASHIN' TIME!
HULK CLOBBER!
KAFOOM
Inconceivable! The combined strength of your attacks has overwhelmed my force field!
KZZT
KZZT
Enjoy your fleeting victory! Doctor Doom shall return!
An' the FF'll be waitin' fer ya!

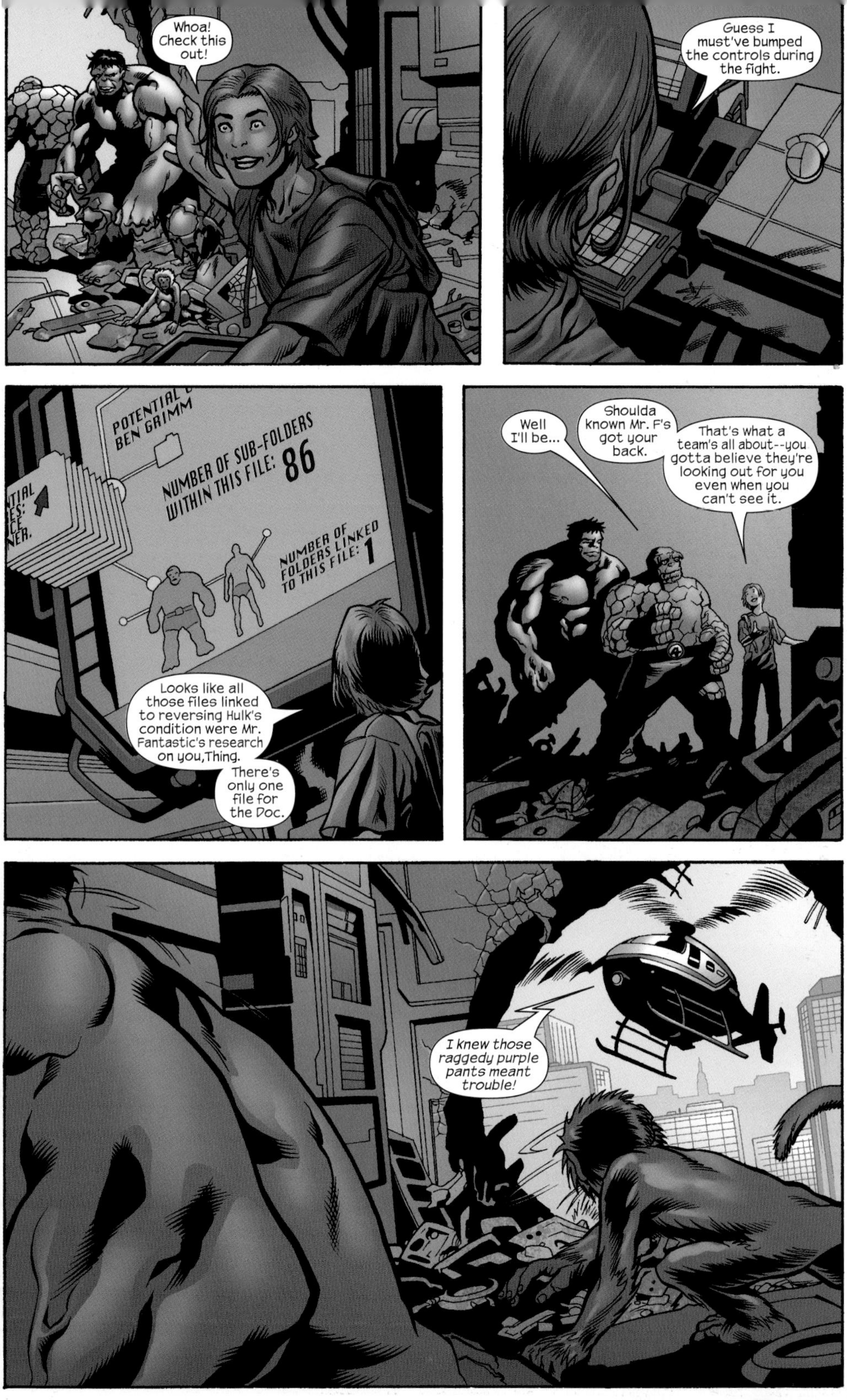
Whoa! Check this out!
Guess I must've bumped the controls during the fight.
POTENTIAL BEN GRIMM
NUMBER OF SUB-FOLDERS WITHIN THIS FILE: 86
NUMBER OF FOLDERS LINKED TO THIS FILE: 1
Looks like all those files linked to reversing Hulk's condition were Mr. Fantastic's research on you, Thing.
There's only one file for the Doc.
Well I'll be...
Shoulda known Mr. F's got your back.
That's what a team's all about--you gotta believe they're looking out for you even when you can't see it.
I knew those raggedy purple pants meant trouble!

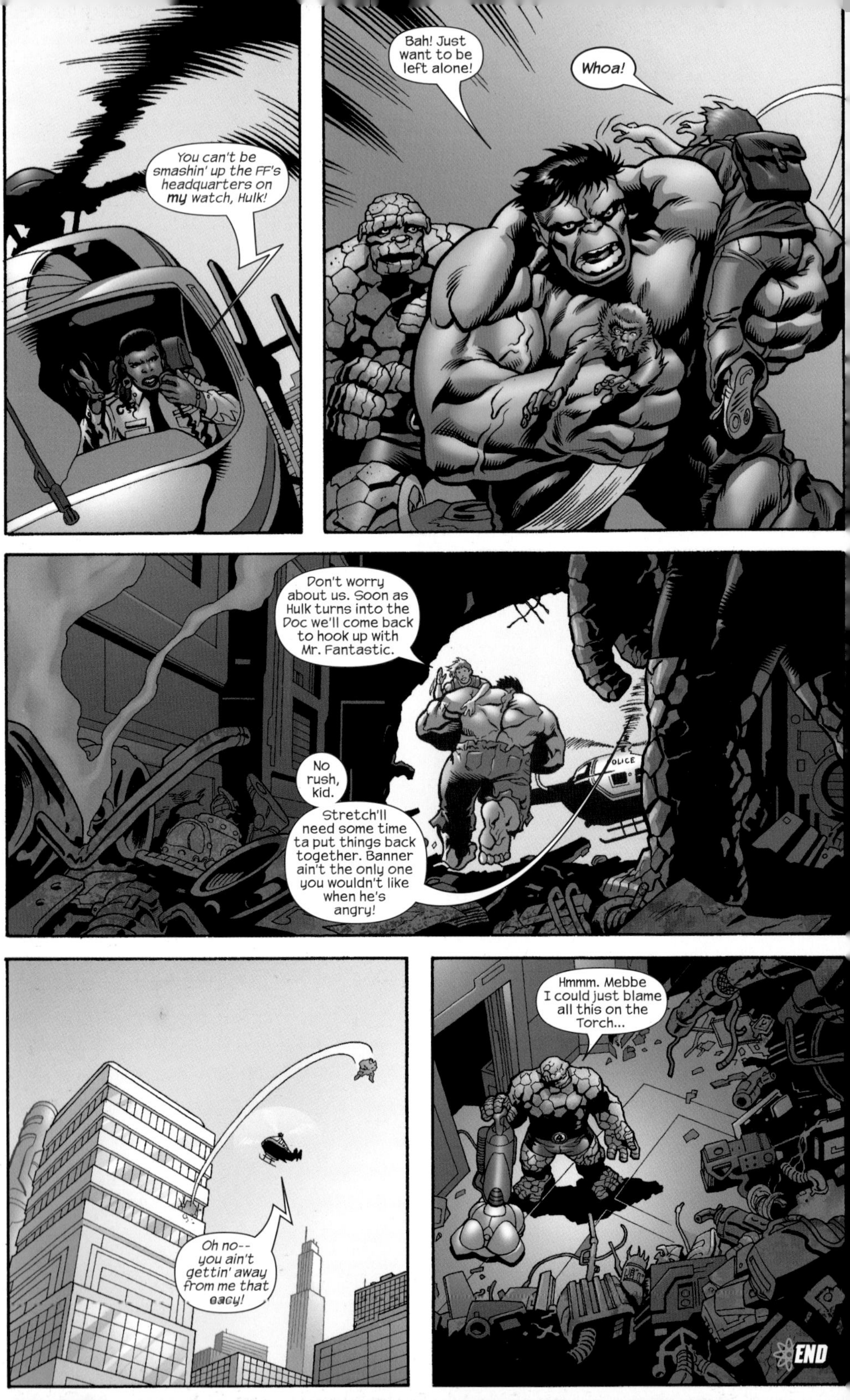
You can't be smashin' up the FF's headquarters on my watch, Hulk!
Bah! Just want to be left alone!
Whoa!
Don't worry about us. Soon as Hulk turns into the Doc we'll come back to hook up with Mr. Fantastic.
No rush, kid.
Stretch'll need some time ta put things back together. Banner ain't the only one you wouldn't like when he's angry!
Oh no-- you ain't gettin' away from me that easy!
Hmmm. Mebbe I could just blame all this on the Torch...
END

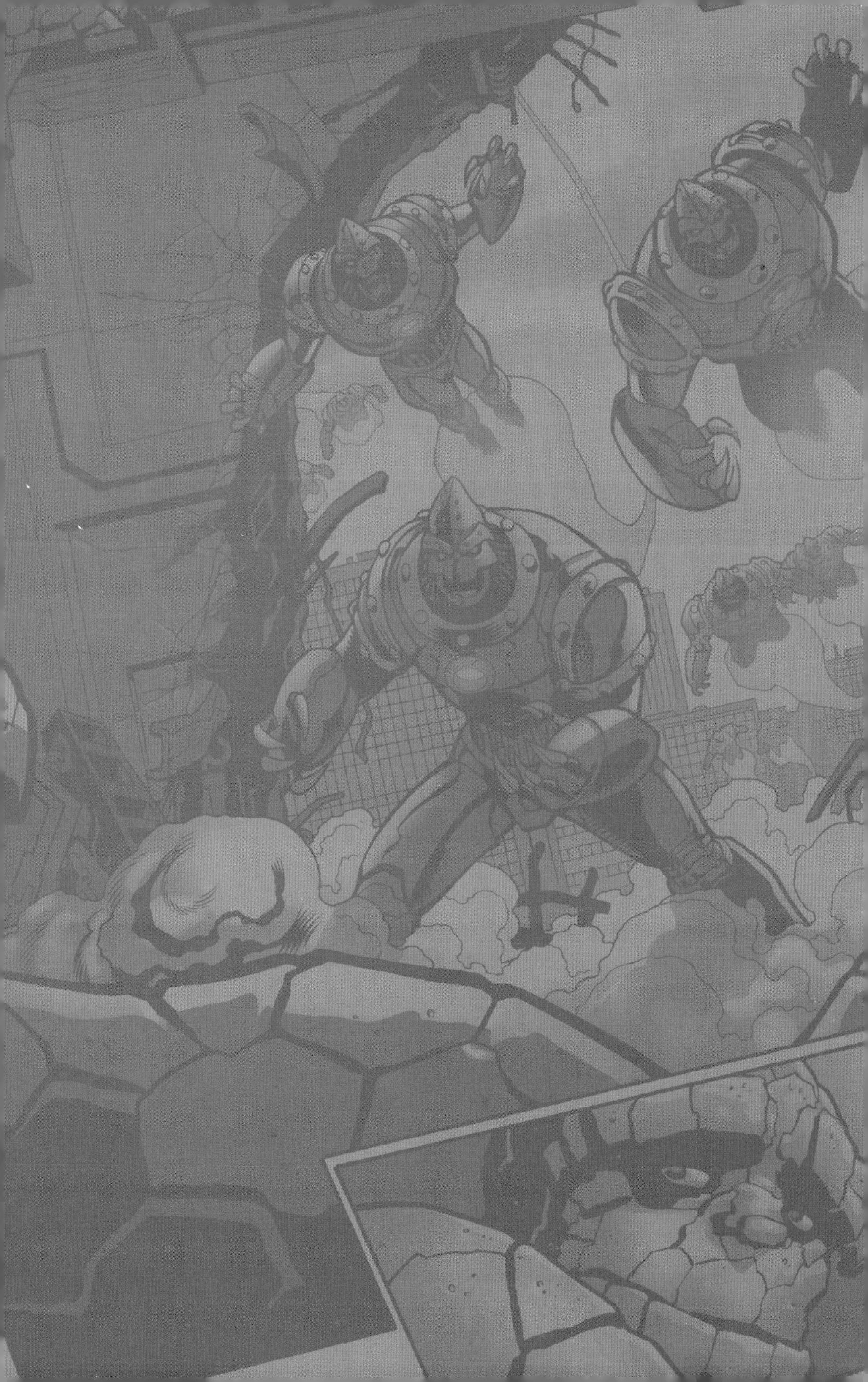

12

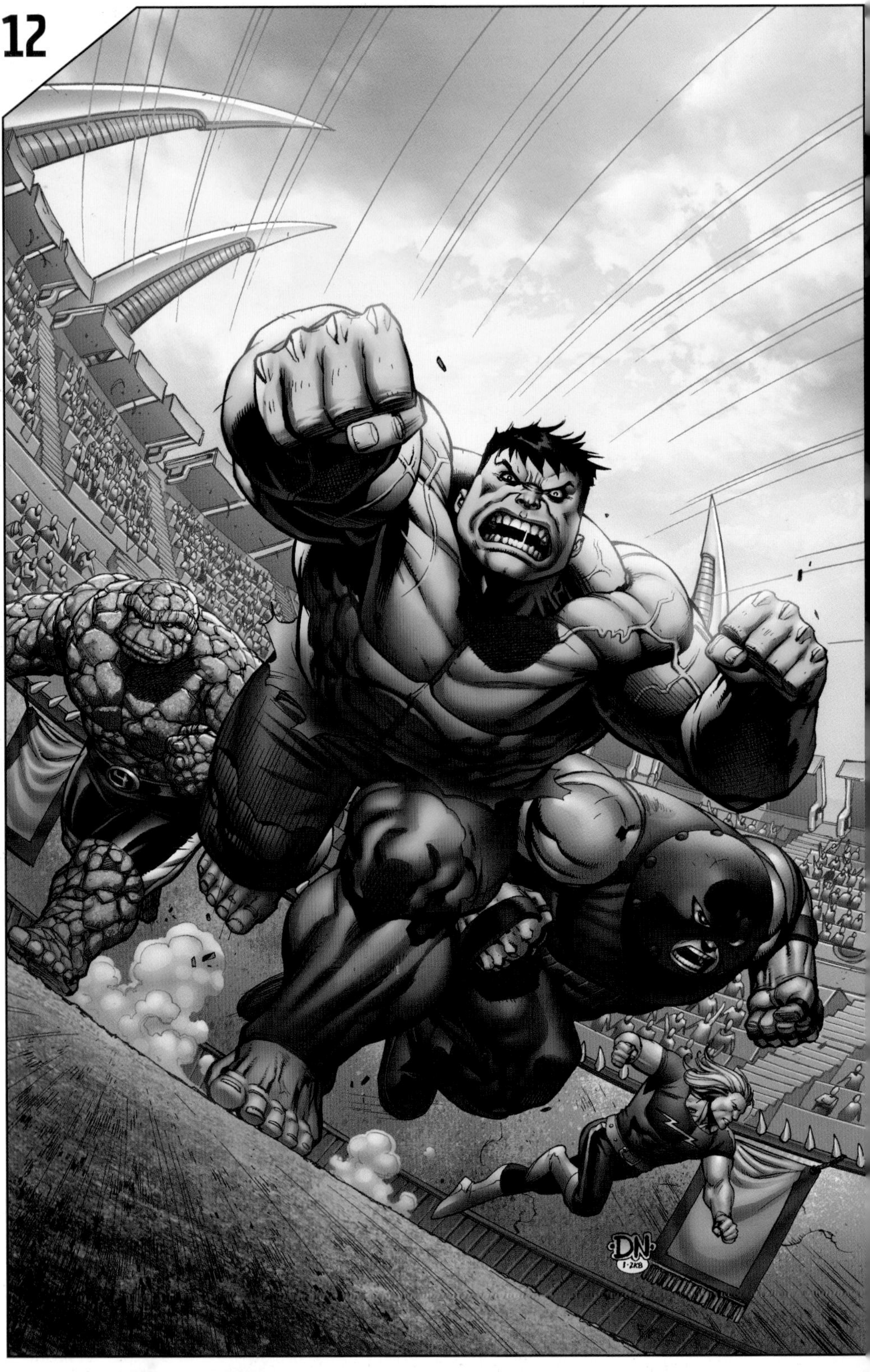
DN

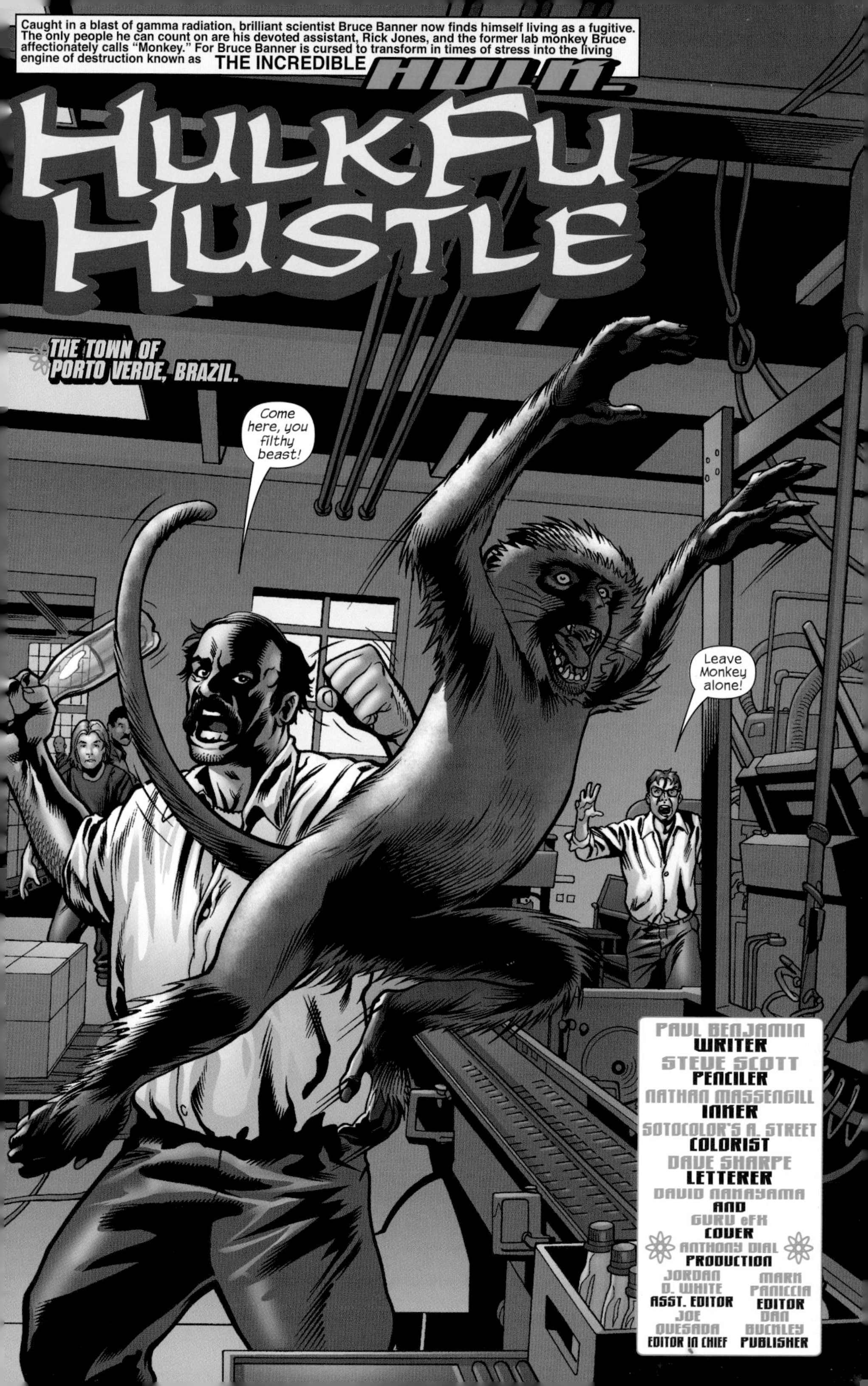
Caught in a blast of gamma radiation, brilliant scientist Bruce Banner now finds himself living as a fugitive. The only people he can count on are his devoted assistant, Rick Jones, and the former lab monkey Bruce affectionately calls "Monkey." For Bruce Banner is cursed to transform in times of stress into the living engine of destruction known as THE INCREDIBLE HULK.
HULK FU HUSTLE
THE TOWN OF PORTO VERDE, BRAZIL.
Come here, you filthy beast!
Leave Monkey alone!
PAUL BENJAMIN WRITER
STEVE SCOTT PENCILER
NATHAN MASSENGILL INKER
SOTOCOLOR'S A. STREET COLORIST
DAVE SHARPE LETTERER
DAVID NAKAYAMA AND GURU eFX COVER
ANTHONY DIAL PRODUCTION
JORDAN D. WHITE ASST. EDITOR
MARK PANICCIA EDITOR
JOE QUESADA EDITOR IN CHIEF
DAN BUCKLEY PUBLISHER

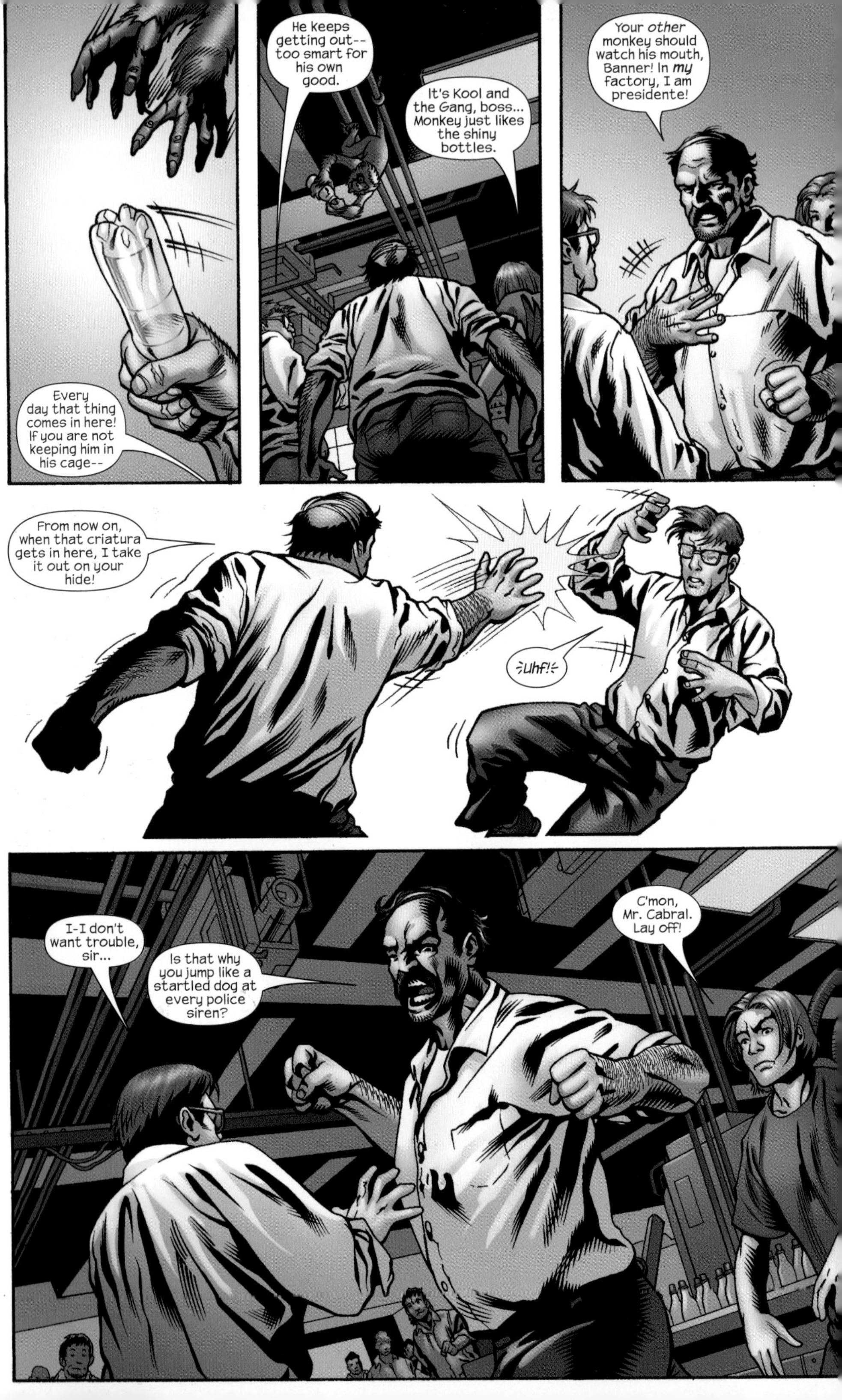
Every day that thing comes in here! If you are not keeping him in his cage--
He keeps getting out-- too smart for his own good.
It's Kool and the Gang, boss... Monkey just likes the shiny bottles.
Your *other* monkey should watch his mouth, Banner! In *my* factory, I am presidente!
From now on, when that criatura gets in here, I take it out on your hide!
UHF!
I-I don't want trouble, sir...
Is that why you jump like a startled dog at every police siren?
C'mon, Mr. Cabral. Lay off!

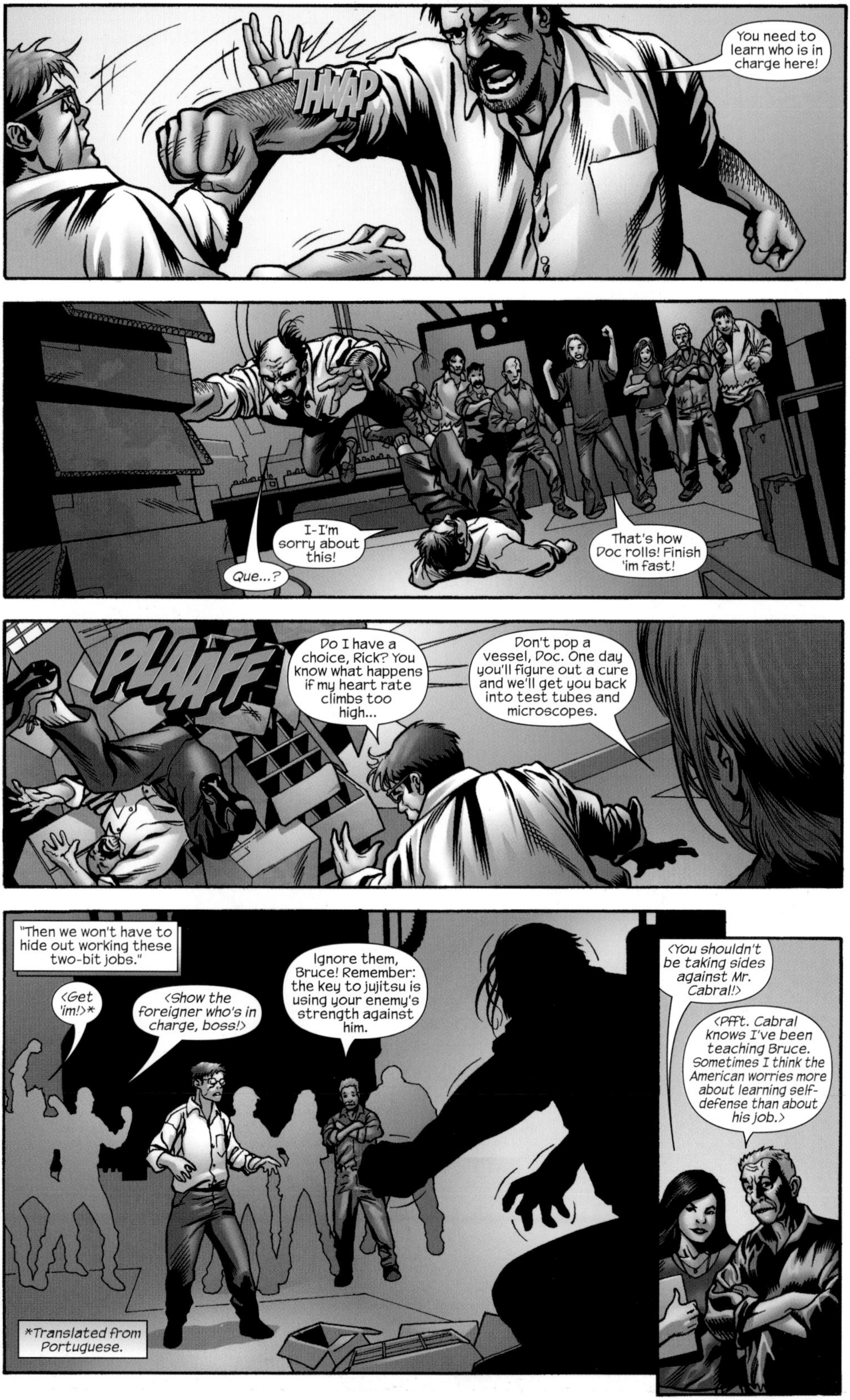
You need to learn who is in charge here!
THWAP
I-I'm sorry about this!
Que...?
That's how Doc rolls! Finish 'im fast!
PLAAFF
Do I have a choice, Rick? You know what happens if my heart rate climbs too high...
Don't pop a vessel, Doc. One day you'll figure out a cure and we'll get you back into test tubes and microscopes.
"Then we won't have to hide out working these two-bit jobs."
<Get 'im!>*
<Show the foreigner who's in charge, boss!>
Ignore them, Bruce! Remember: the key to jujitsu is using your enemy's strength against him.
<You shouldn't be taking sides against Mr. Cabral!>
<Pfft. Cabral knows I've been teaching Bruce. Sometimes I think the American worries more about learning self-defense than about his job.>
*Translated from Portuguese.

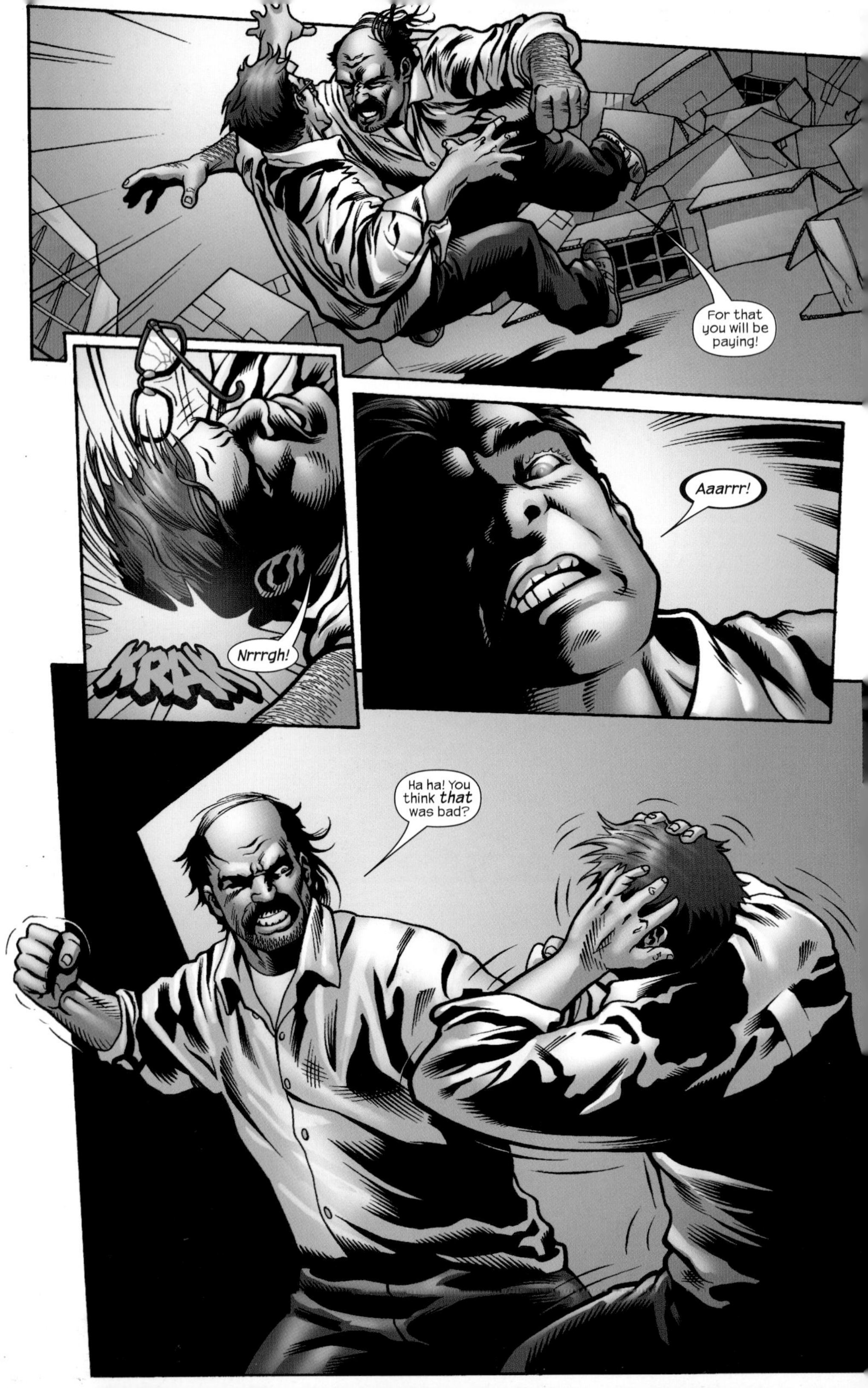
For that you will be paying!
KRAK
Nrrrgh!
Aaarrr!
Ha ha! You think *that* was bad?

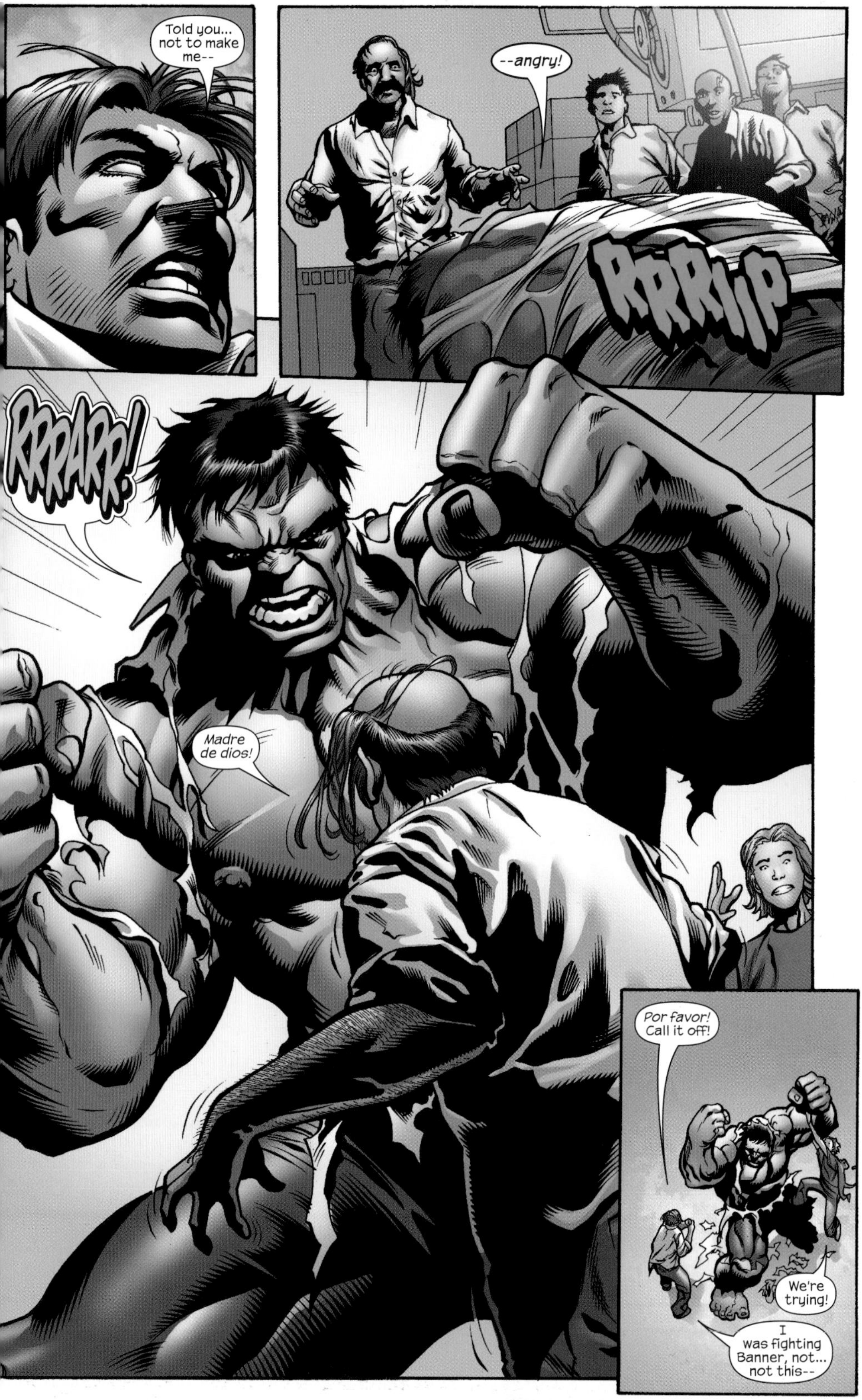
Told you... not to make me--
--angry!
RRRIIIP
RRRARR!
Madre de dios!
Por favor! Call it off!
We're trying!
I was fighting Banner, not... not this--

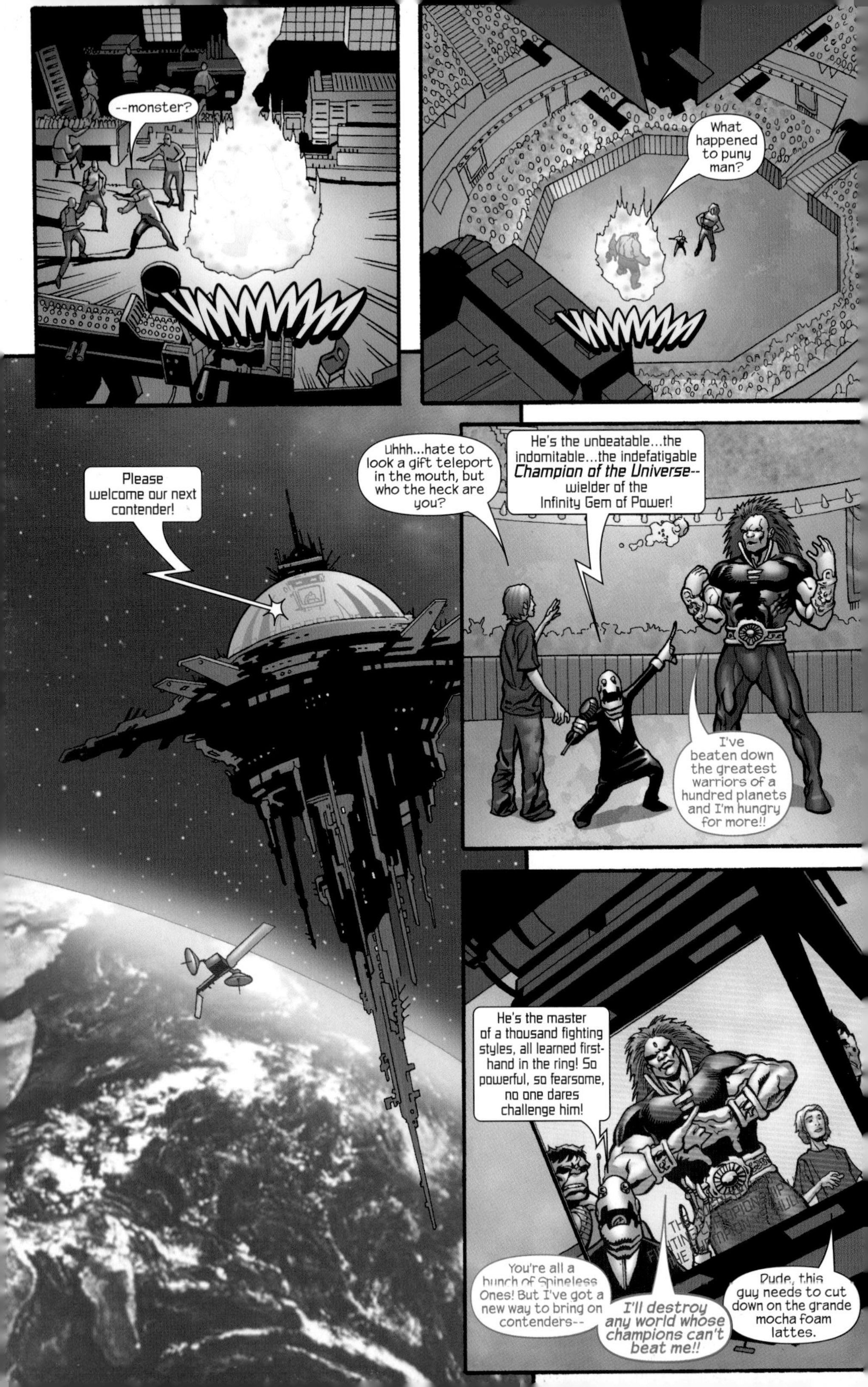
--monster?
VMMMMM
What happened to puny man?
VMMMMM
Please welcome our next contender!
Uhhh...hate to look a gift teleport in the mouth, but who the heck are you?
He's the unbeatable...the indomitable...the indefatigable *Champion of the Universe*-- wielder of the Infinity Gem of Power!
I've beaten down the greatest warriors of a hundred planets and I'm hungry for more!!
He's the master of a thousand fighting styles, all learned first-hand in the ring! So powerful, so fearsome, no one dares challenge him!
You're all a bunch of Spineless Ones! But I've got a new way to bring on contenders--
I'll destroy any world whose champions can't beat me!!
Dude, this guy needs to cut down on the grande mocha foam lattes.

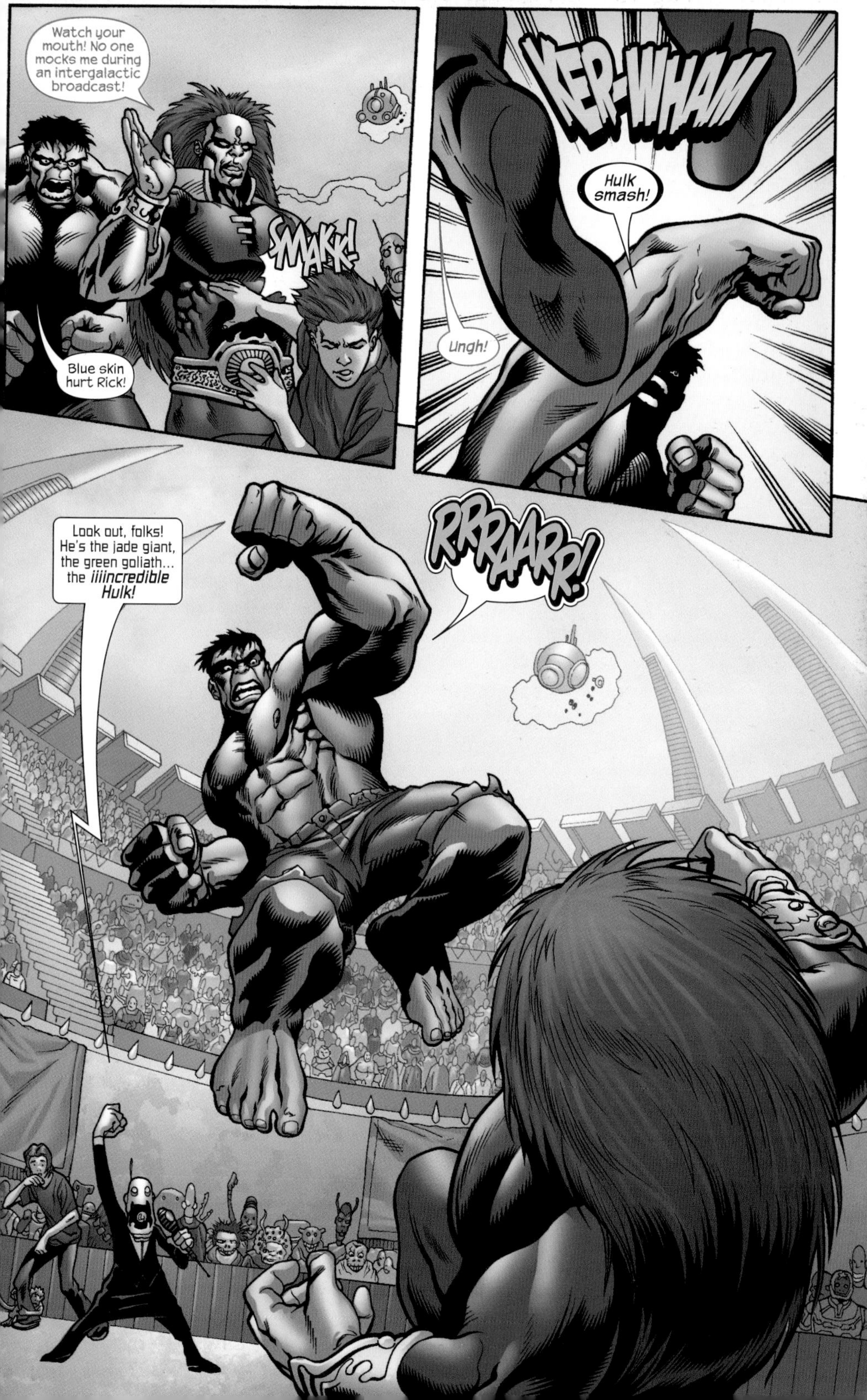
Watch your mouth! No one mocks me during an intergalactic broadcast!
SMAKK!
Blue skin hurt Rick!
KER-WHAM
Hulk smash!
Ungh!
Look out, folks! He's the jade giant, the green goliath... the *iiiincredible Hulk!*
RRRAARR!

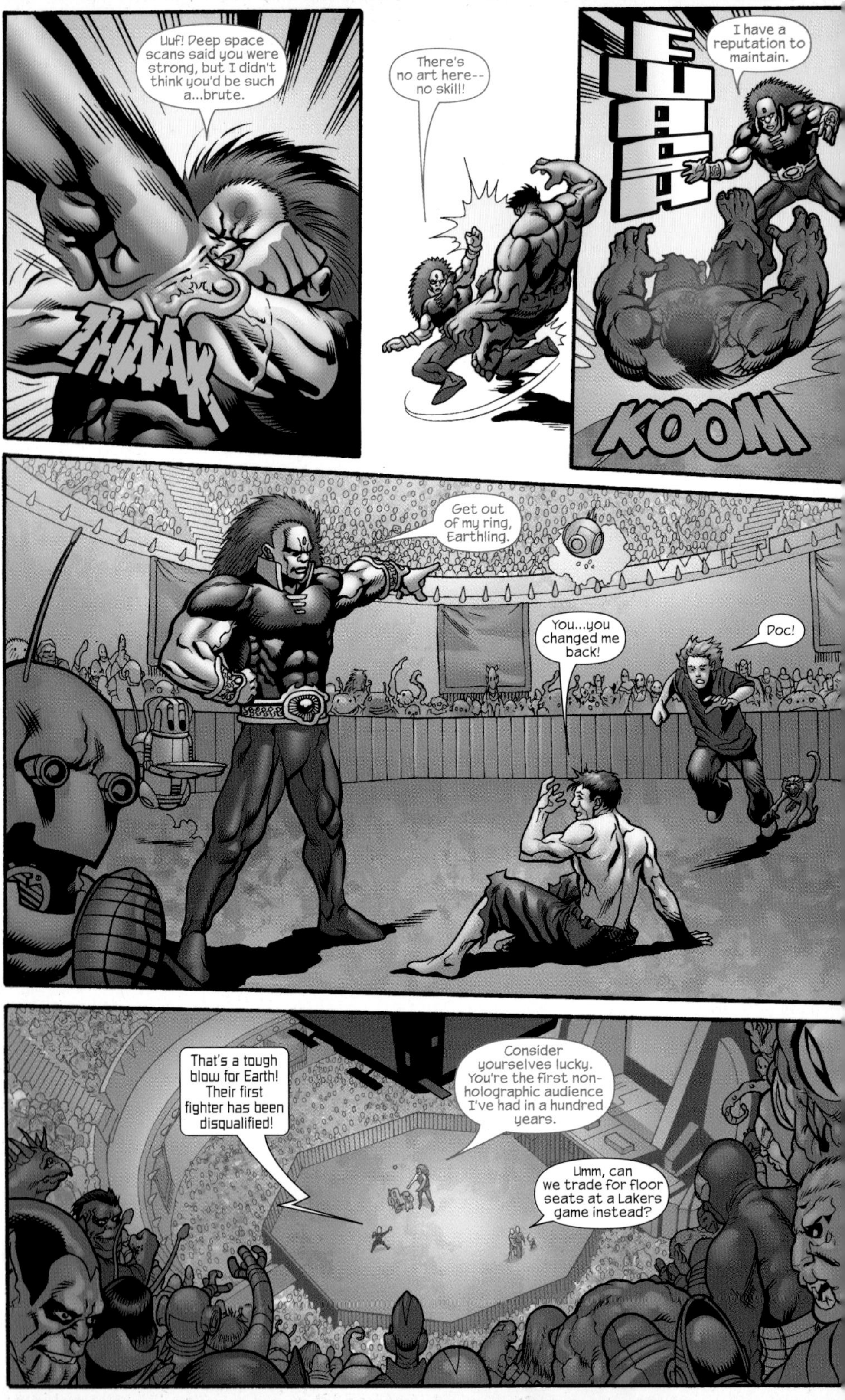
Uuf! Deep space scans said you were strong, but I didn't think you'd be such a...brute.
THWAK
There's no art here--no skill!
FWOOSH
I have a reputation to maintain.
KOOM
Get out of my ring, Earthling.
You...you changed me back!
Doc!
That's a tough blow for Earth! Their first fighter has been disqualified!
Consider yourselves lucky. You're the first non-holographic audience I've had in a hundred years.
Umm, can we trade for floor seats at a Lakers game instead?

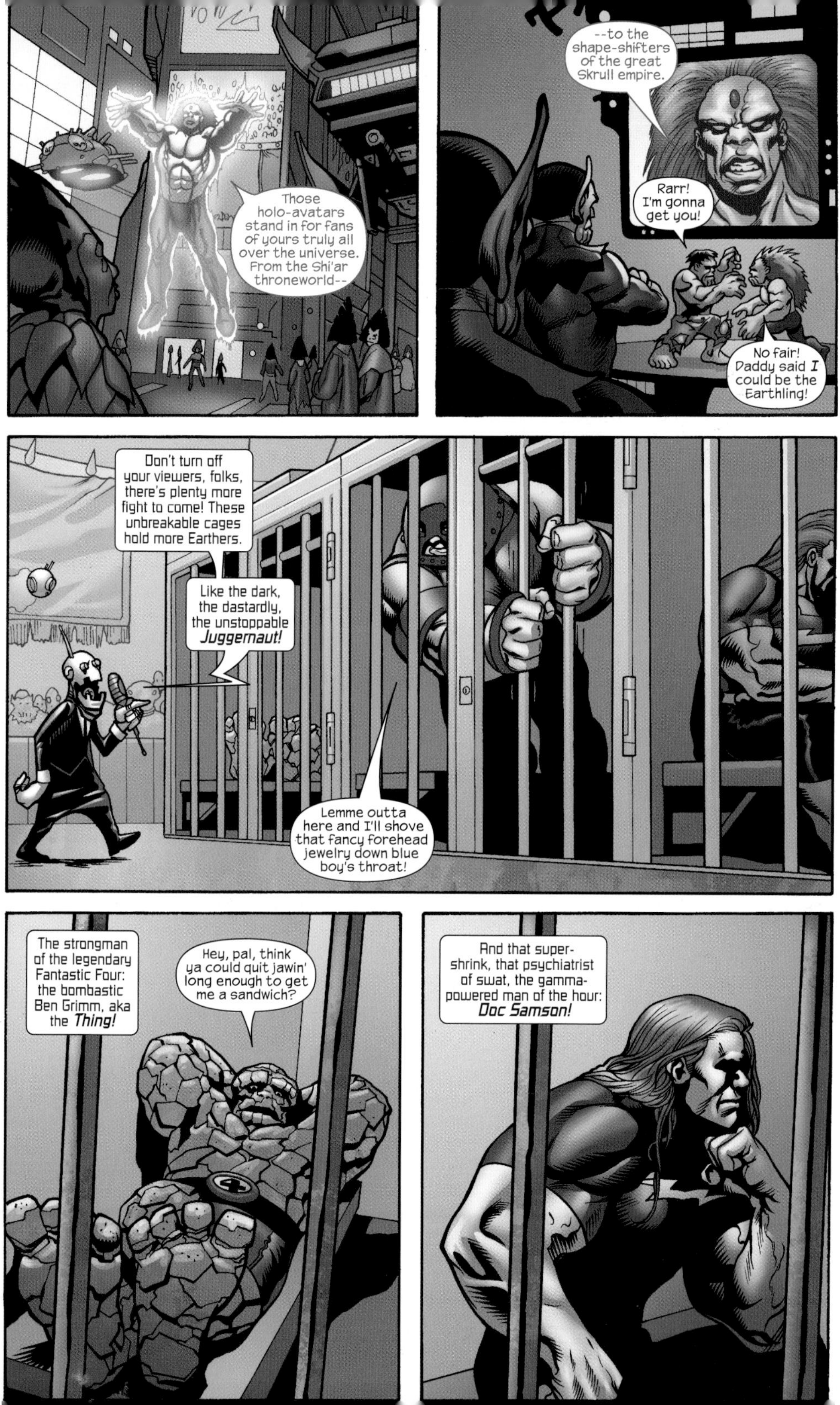

Those holo-avatars stand in for fans of yours truly all over the universe. From the Shi'ar throneworld--
--to the shape-shifters of the great Skrull empire.
Rarr! I'm gonna get you!
No fair! Daddy said I could be the Earthling!
Don't turn off your viewers, folks, there's plenty more fight to come! These unbreakable cages hold more Earthers.
Like the dark, the dastardly, the unstoppable Juggernaut!
Lemme outta here and I'll shove that fancy forehead jewelry down blue boy's throat!
The strongman of the legendary Fantastic Four: the bombastic Ben Grimm, aka the Thing!
Hey, pal, think ya could quit jawin' long enough to get me a sandwich?
And that super-shrink, that psychiatrist of swat, the gamma-powered man of the hour: Doc Samson!

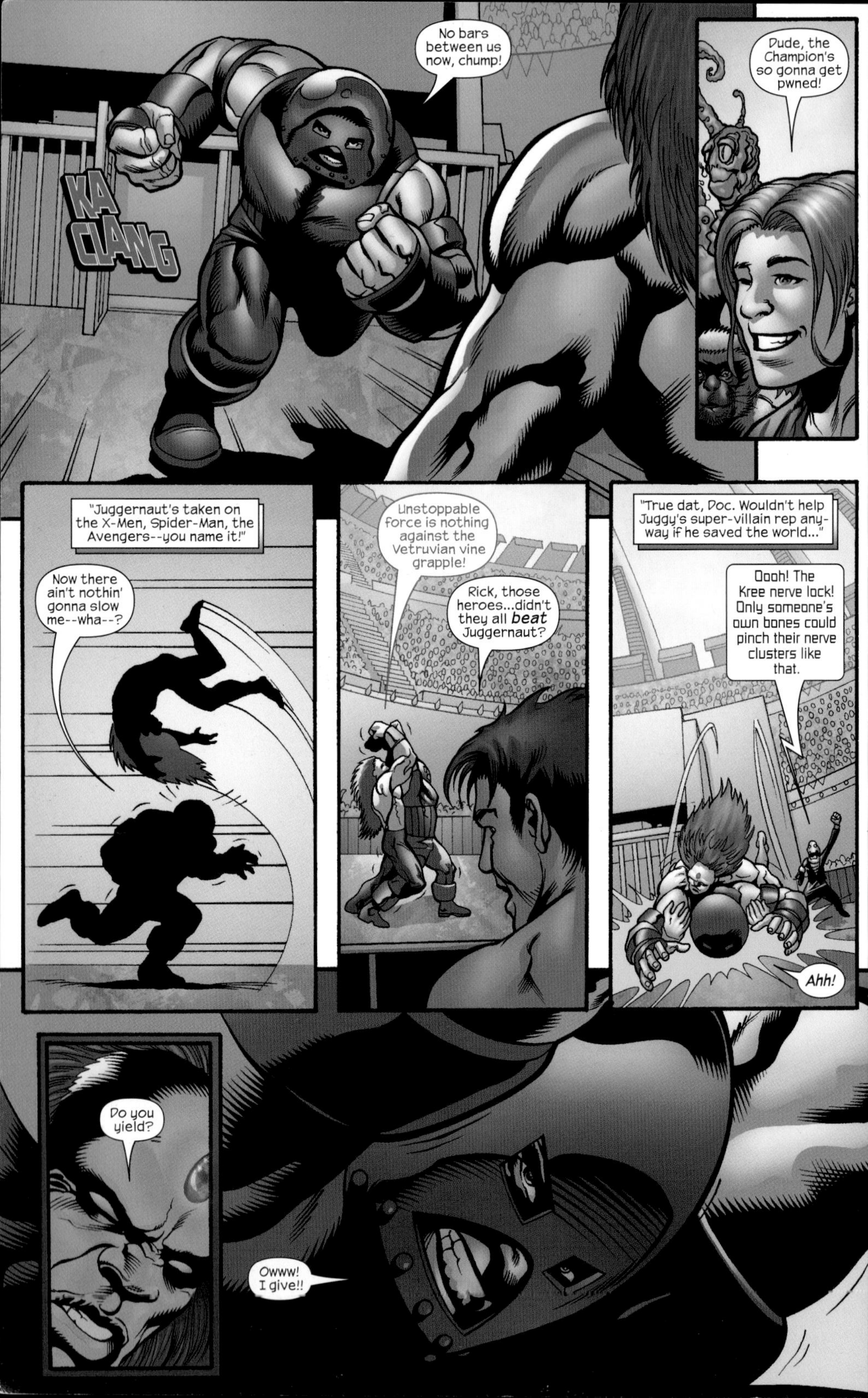

KA CLANG
No bars between us now, chump!
Dude, the Champion's so gonna get pwned!
"Juggernaut's taken on the X-Men, Spider-Man, the Avengers--you name it!"
Now there ain't nothin' gonna slow me--wha--?
Unstoppable force is nothing against the Vetruvian vine grapple!
Rick, those heroes...didn't they all *beat* Juggernaut?
"True dat, Doc. Wouldn't help Juggy's super-villain rep any-way if he saved the world..."
Oooh! The Kree nerve lock! Only someone's own bones could pinch their nerve clusters like that.
Ahh!
Do you yield?
Owww! I give!!

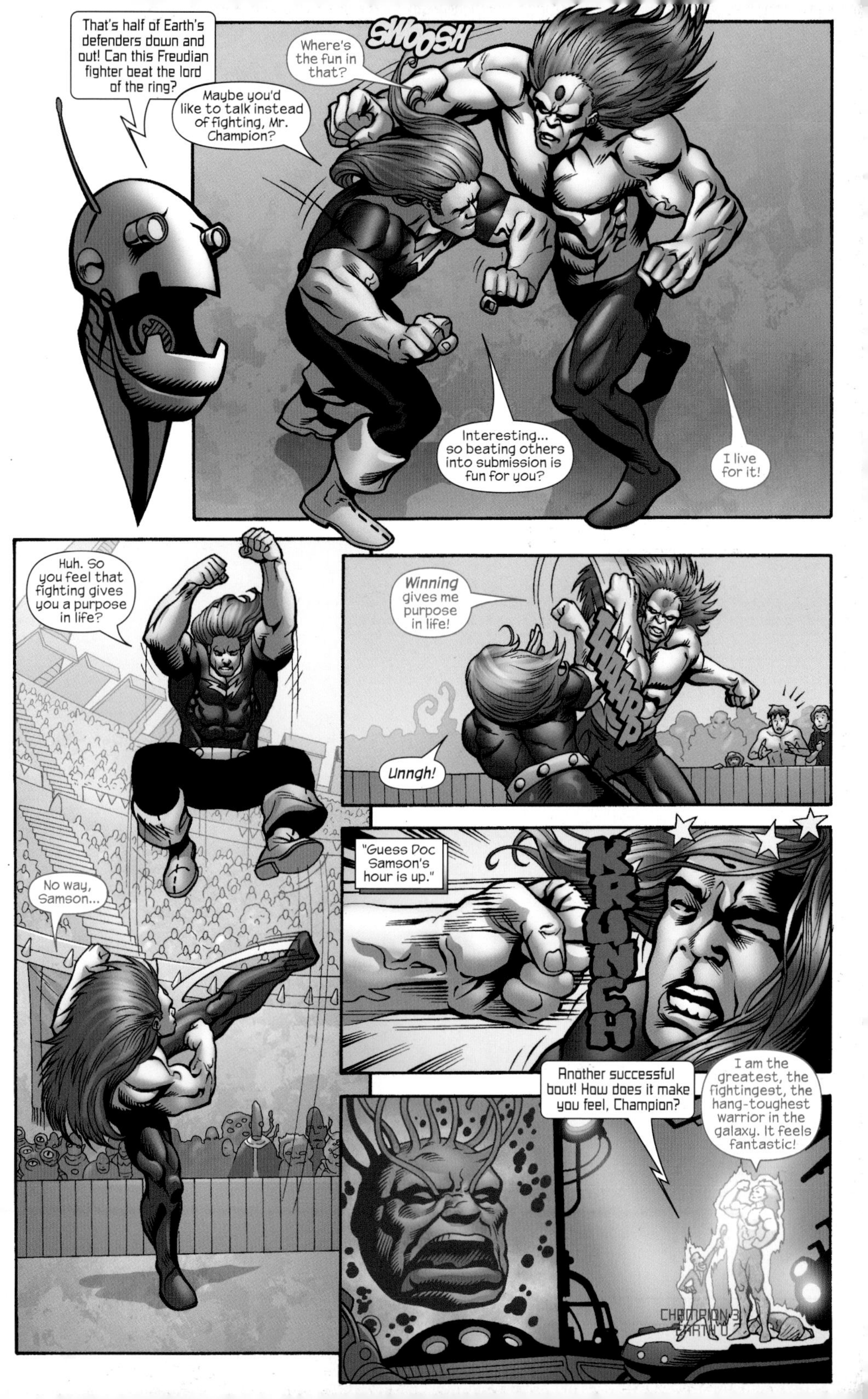
That's half of Earth's defenders down and out! Can this Freudian fighter beat the lord of the ring?
SWOOSH
Where's the fun in that?
Maybe you'd like to talk instead of fighting, Mr. Champion?
Interesting... so beating others into submission is fun for you?
I live for it!
Huh. So you feel that fighting gives you a purpose in life?
Winning gives me purpose in life!
THWAAP
Unngh!
No way, Samson...
"Guess Doc Samson's hour is up."
KRUNCH
Another successful bout! How does it make you feel, Champion?
I am the greatest, the fightingest, the hang-toughest warrior in the galaxy. It feels fantastic!
CHAMPION 3
EARTH 0

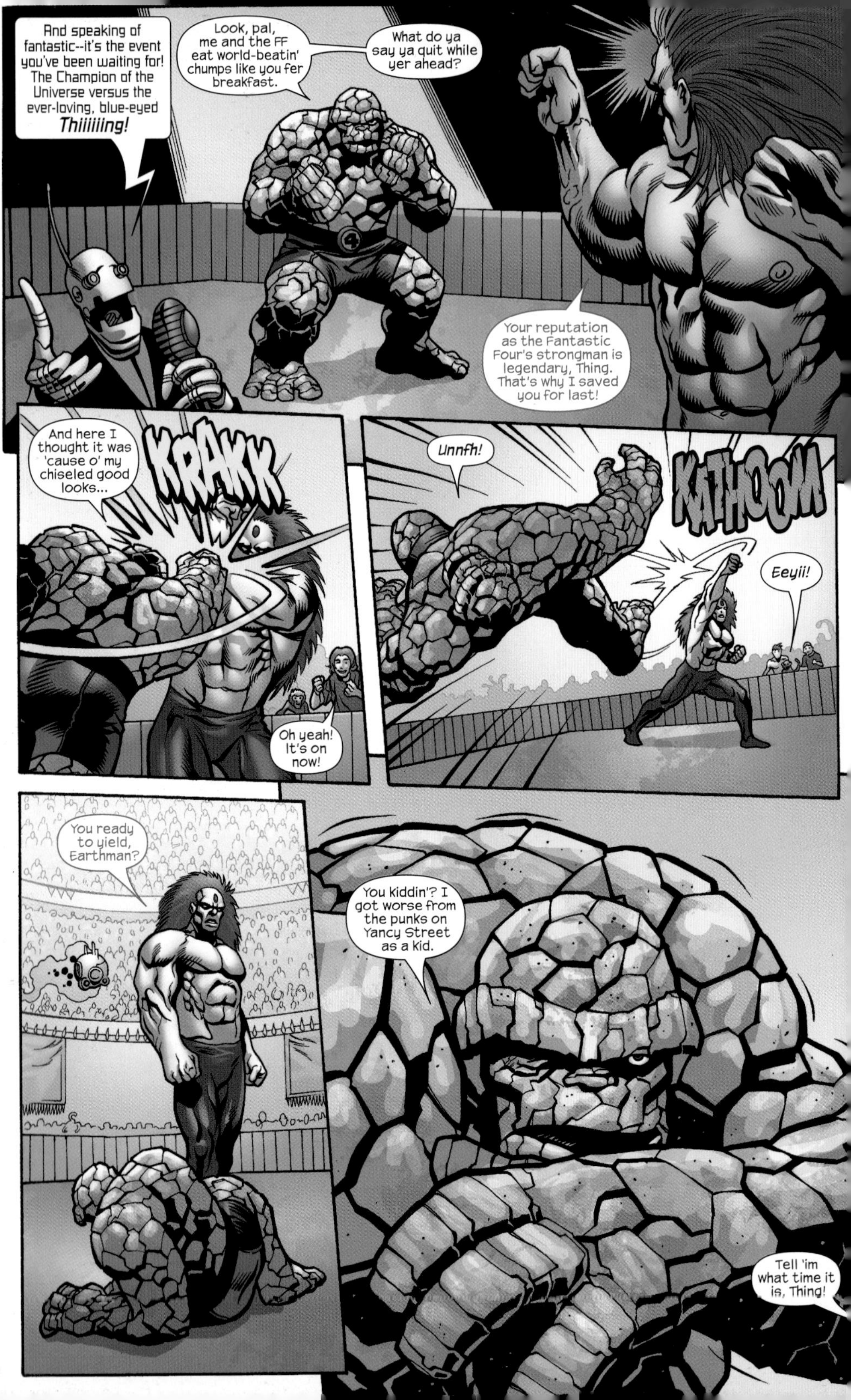
And speaking of fantastic--it's the event you've been waiting for! The Champion of the Universe versus the ever-loving, blue-eyed Thiiiiiing!
Look, pal, me and the FF eat world-beatin' chumps like you fer breakfast.
What do ya say ya quit while yer ahead?
Your reputation as the Fantastic Four's strongman is legendary, Thing. That's why I saved you for last!
And here I thought it was 'cause o' my chiseled good looks...
KRAKK
Oh yeah! It's on now!
Unnfh!
KATHOOM
Eeyii!
You ready to yield, Earthman?
You kiddin'? I got worse from the punks on Yancy Street as a kid.
Tell 'im what time it is, Thing!

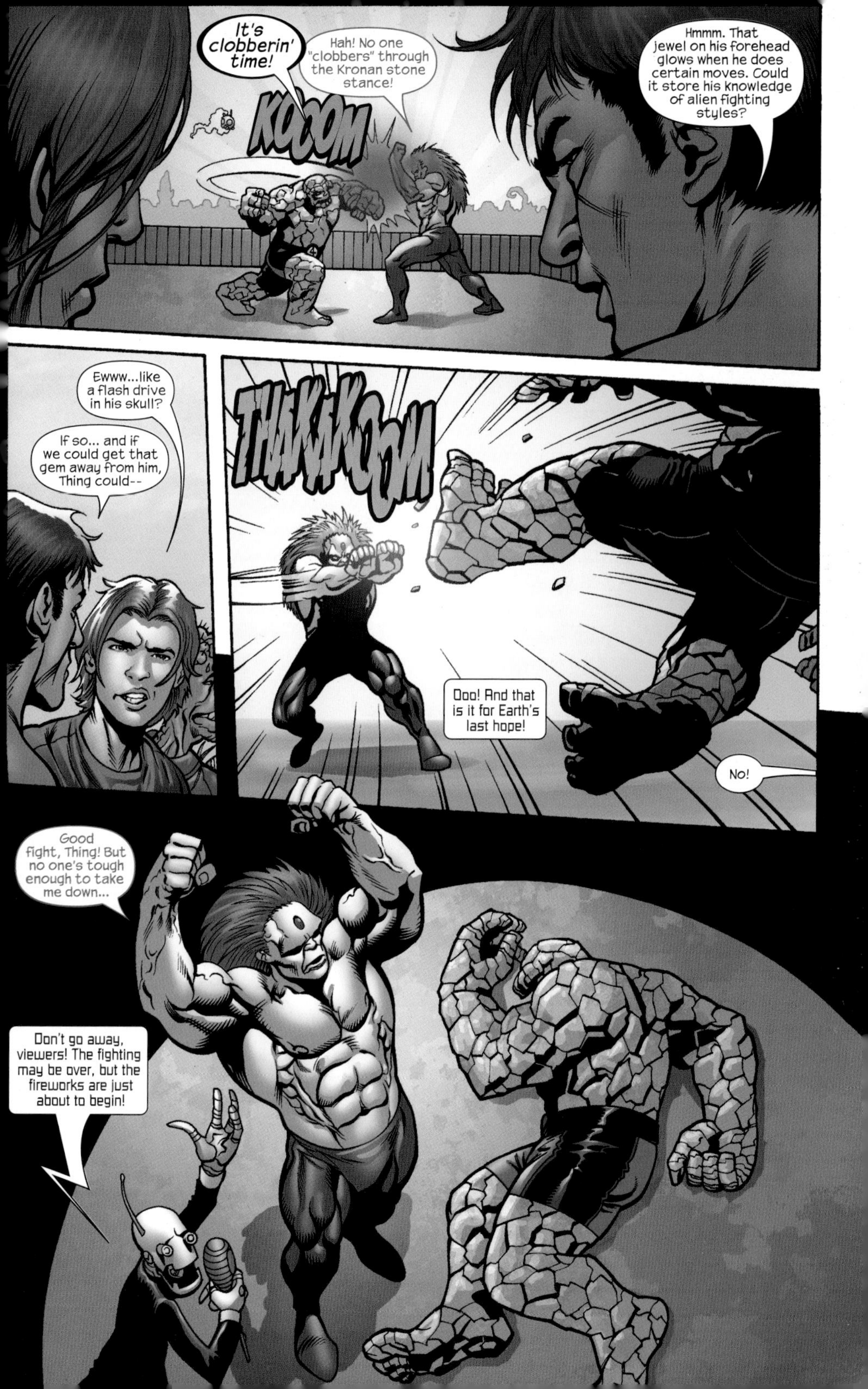
It's clobberin' time!
Hah! No one "clobbers" through the Kronan stone stance!
KOOOM
Hmmm. That jewel on his forehead glows when he does certain moves. Could it store his knowledge of alien fighting styles?
Ewww...like a flash drive in his skull?
If so... and if we could get that gem away from him, Thing could--
THAKAKOOM
Ooo! And that is it for Earth's last hope!
No!
Good fight, Thing! But no one's tough enough to take me down...
Don't go away, viewers! The fighting may be over, but the fireworks are just about to begin!

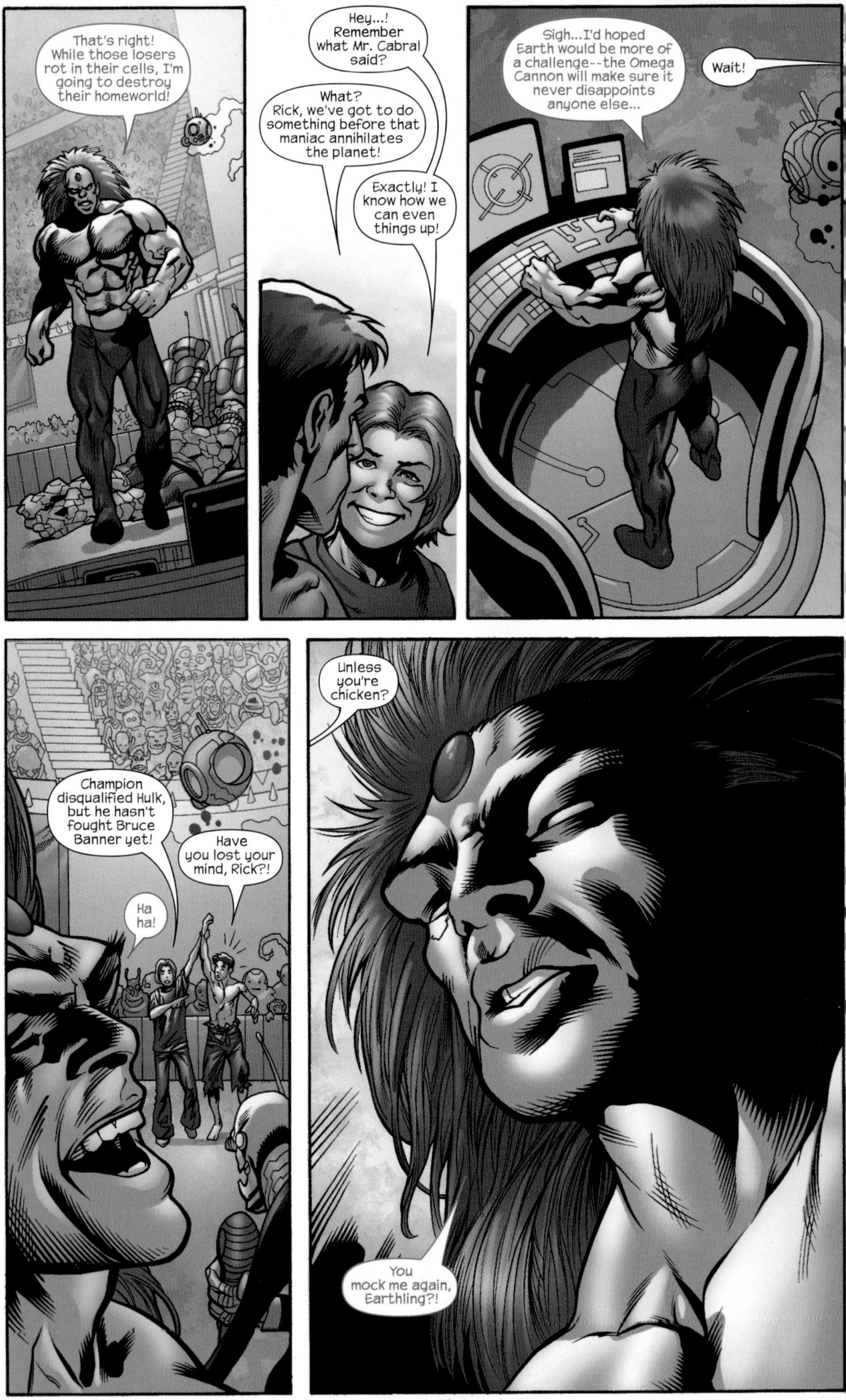
That's right! While those losers rot in their cells, I'm going to destroy their homeworld!
Hey...! Remember what Mr. Cabral said?
What? Rick, we've got to do something before that maniac annihilates the planet!
Exactly! I know how we can even things up!
Sigh...I'd hoped Earth would be more of a challenge--the Omega Cannon will make sure it never disappoints anyone else...
Wait!
Champion disqualified Hulk, but he hasn't fought Bruce Banner yet!
Have you lost your mind, Rick?!
Ha ha!
Unless you're chicken?
You mock me again, Earthling?!

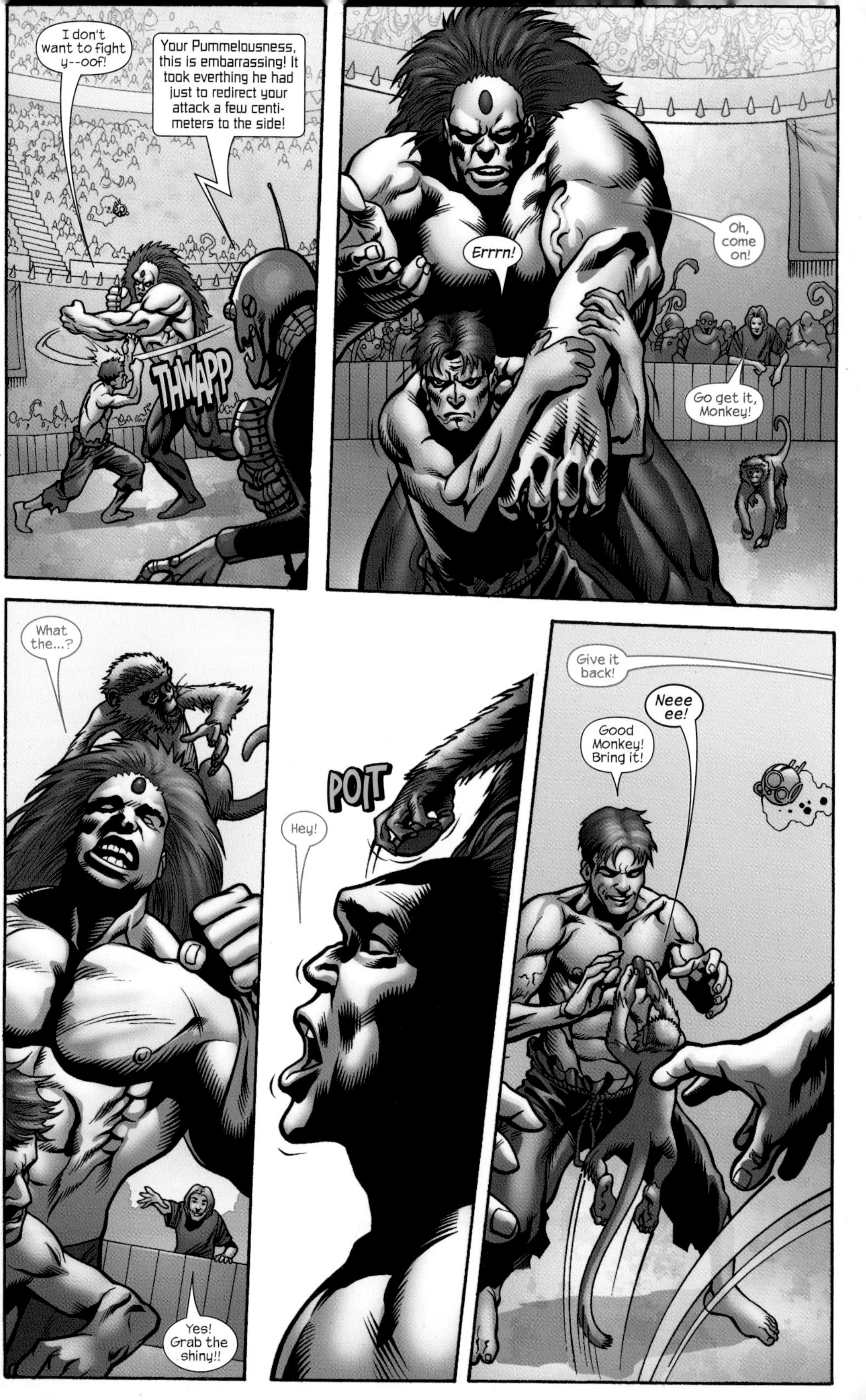
I don't want to fight y--oof!
Your Pummelousness, this is embarrassing! It took everthing he had just to redirect your attack a few centi-meters to the side!
THWAPP
Errrn!
Oh, come on!
Go get it, Monkey!
What the...?
Yes! Grab the shiny!!
POIT
Hey!
Give it back!
Neee ee!
Good Monkey! Bring it!

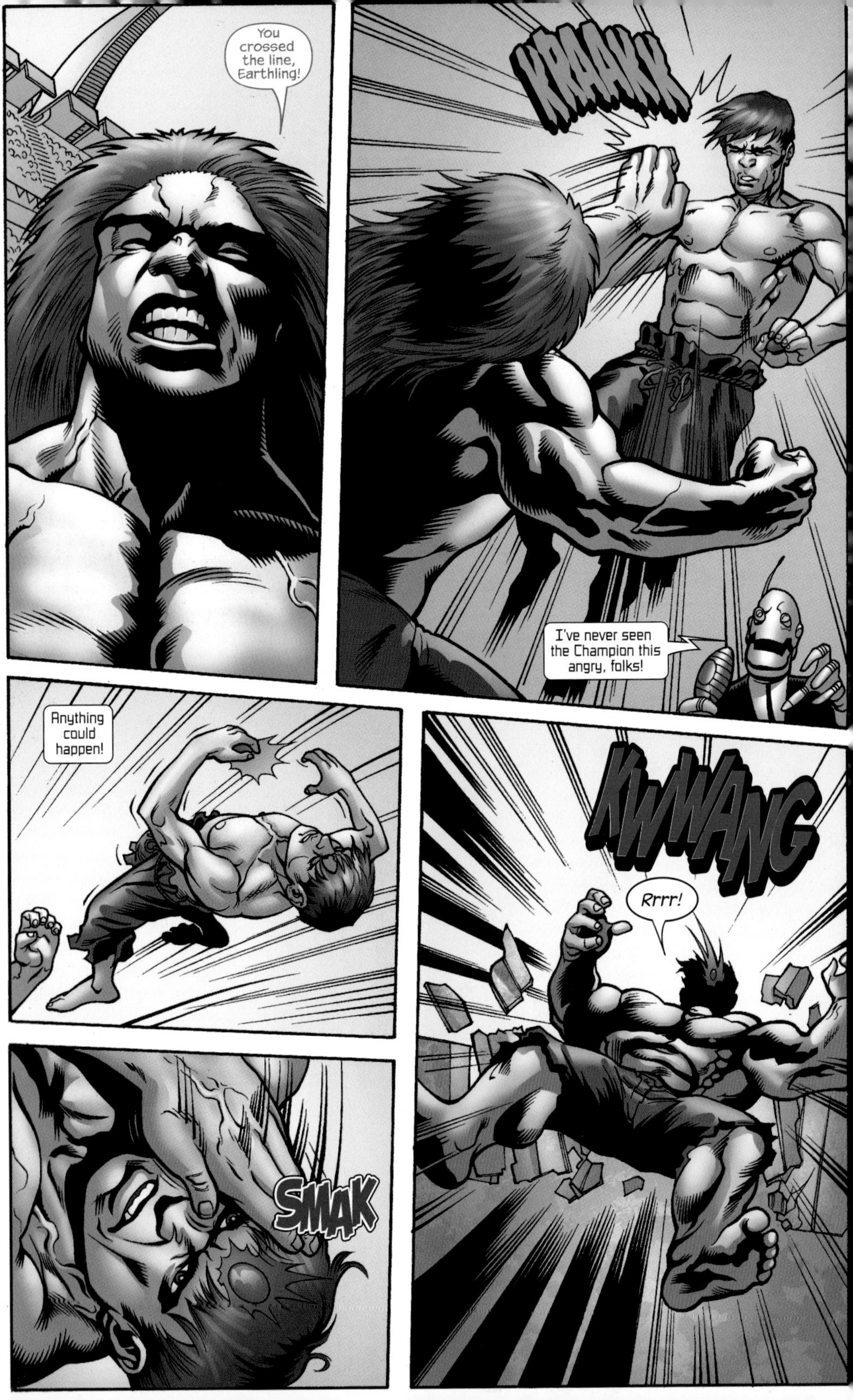
You crossed the line, Earthling!
KRAAKK
I've never seen the Champion this angry, folks!
Anything could happen!
SMAK
KWANG
Rrrr!

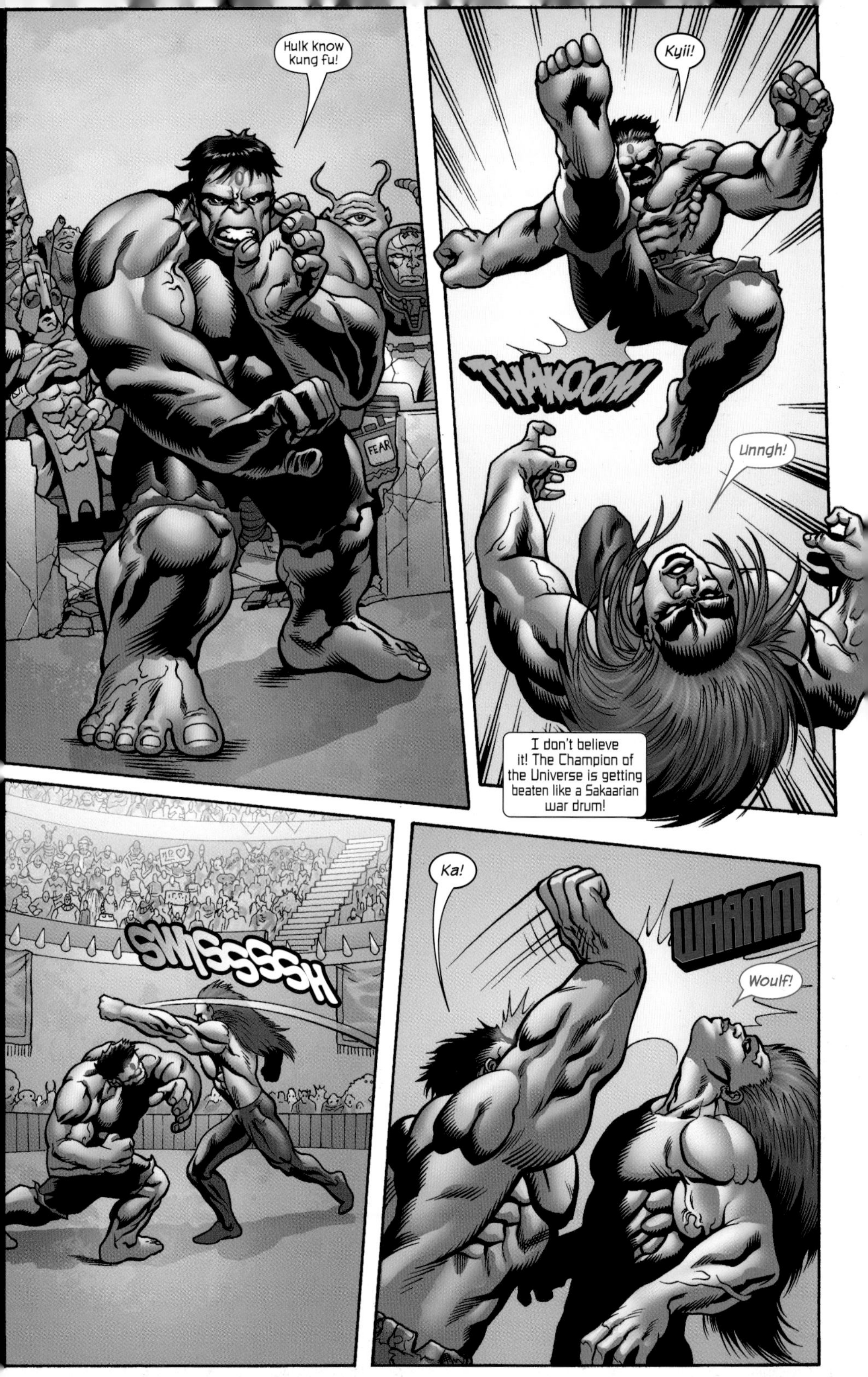
Hulk know kung fu!
Kyii!
THAKOOM
Unngh!
I don't believe it! The Champion of the Universe is getting beaten like a Sakaarian war drum!
SWISSSSSH
Ka!
WHAMM
Woulf!

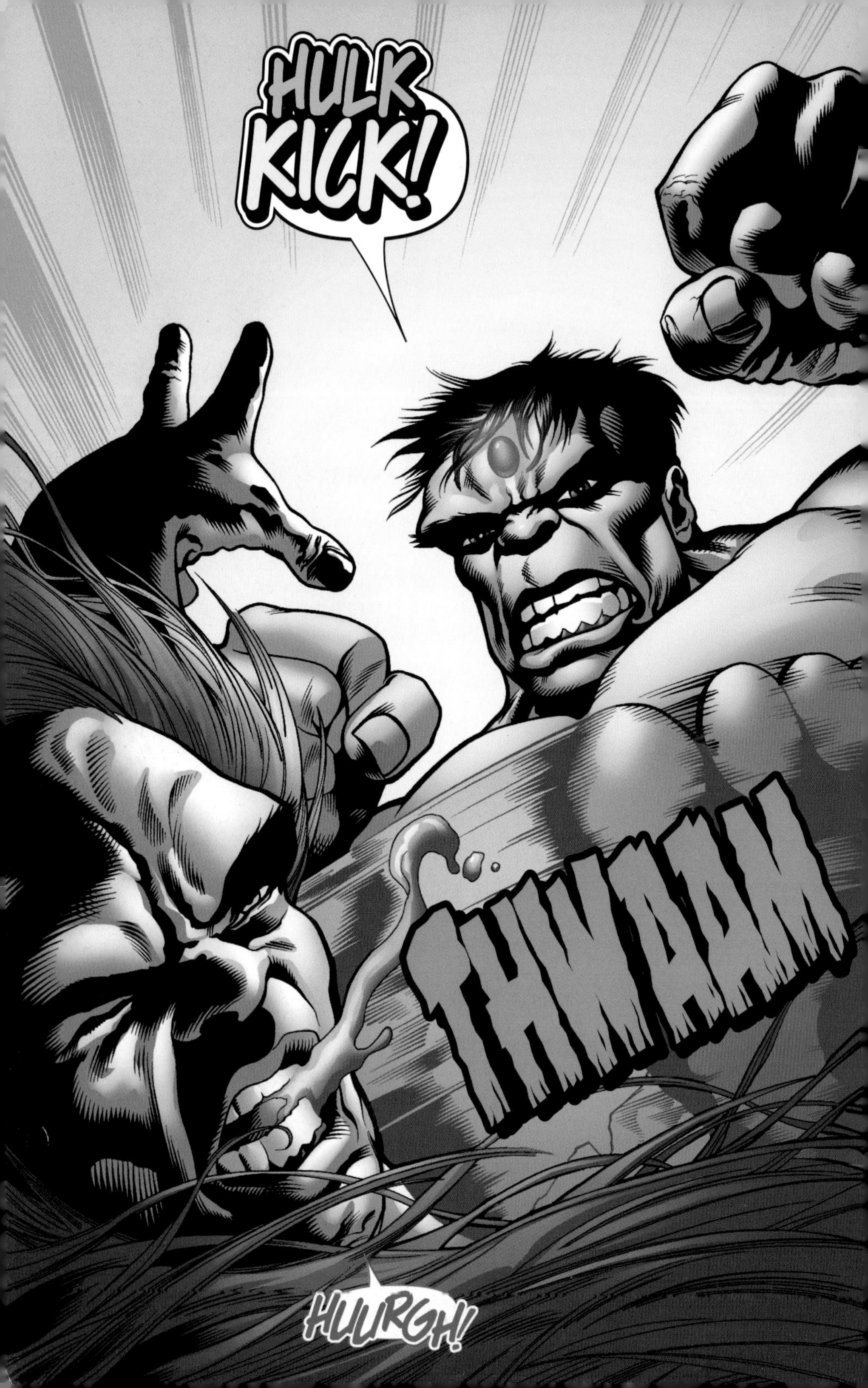
HULK KICK!
THWOOM
HUURGH!

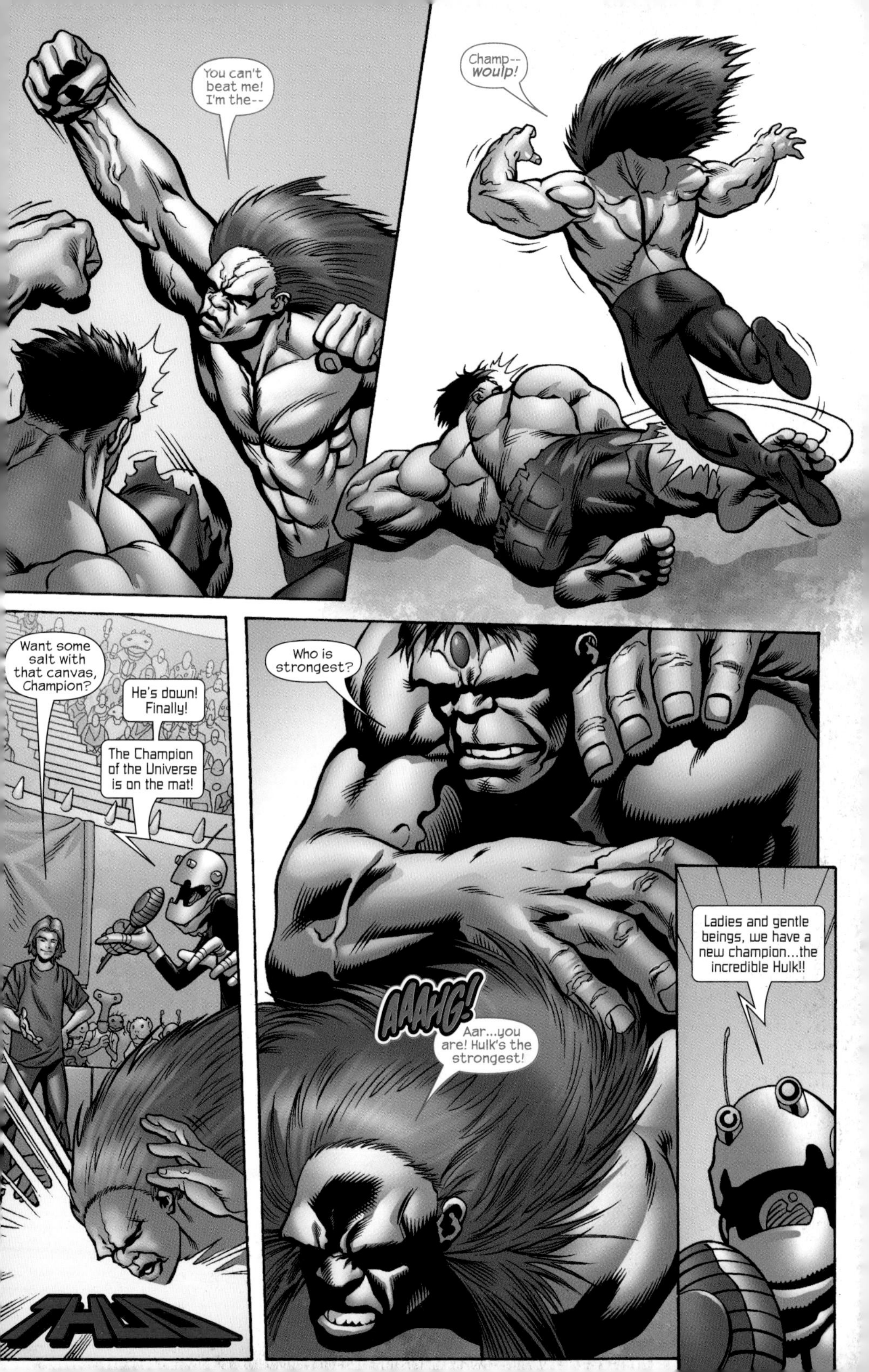
You can't beat me! I'm the--
Champ-- woulp!
Want some salt with that canvas, Champion?
He's down! Finally!
The Champion of the Universe is on the mat!
THUD
Who is strongest?
AAAHG!
Aar...you are! Hulk's the strongest!
Ladies and gentle beings, we have a new champion...the incredible Hulk!!

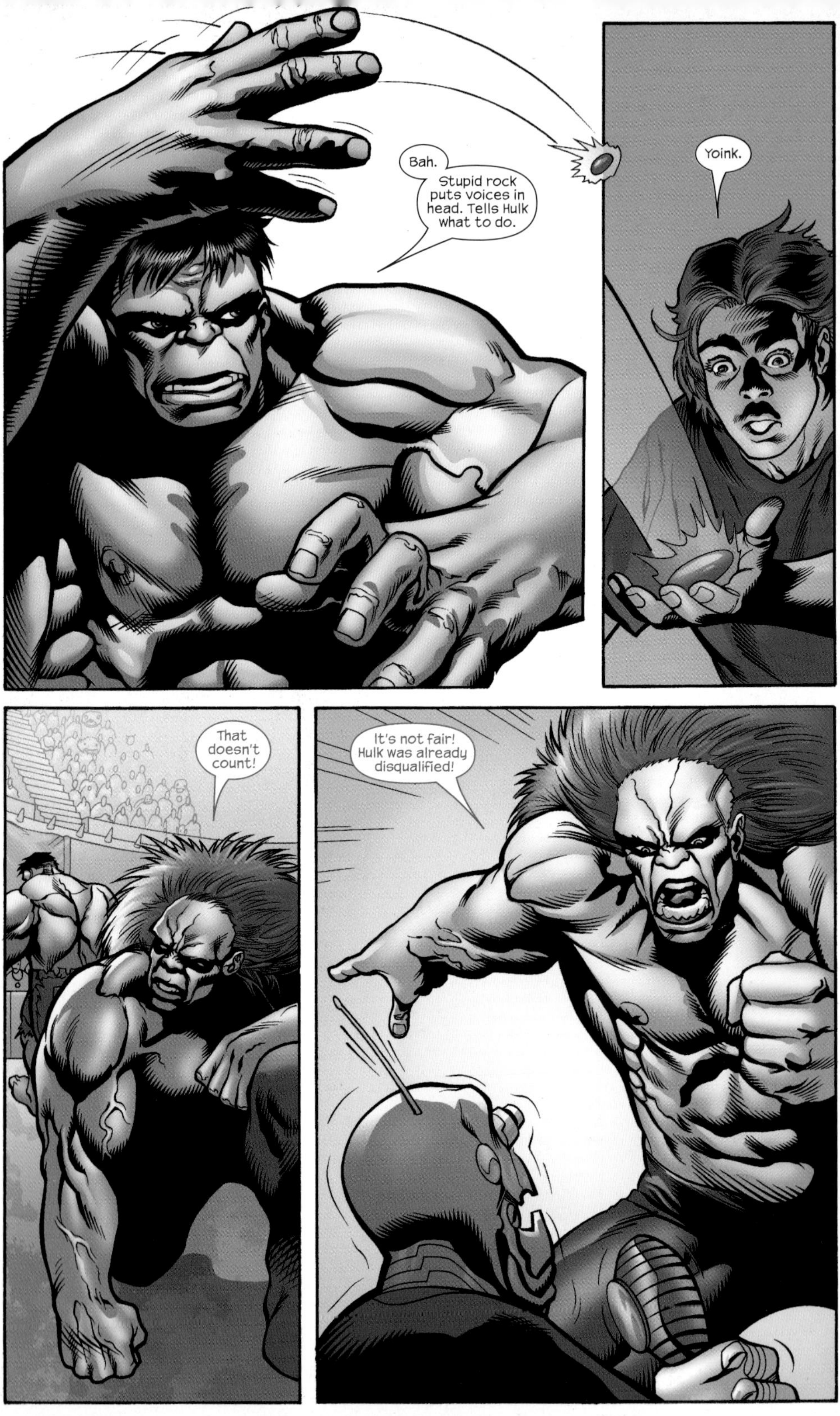
Bah.
Stupid rock puts voices in head. Tells Hulk what to do.
Yoink.
That doesn't count!
It's not fair! Hulk was already disqualified!

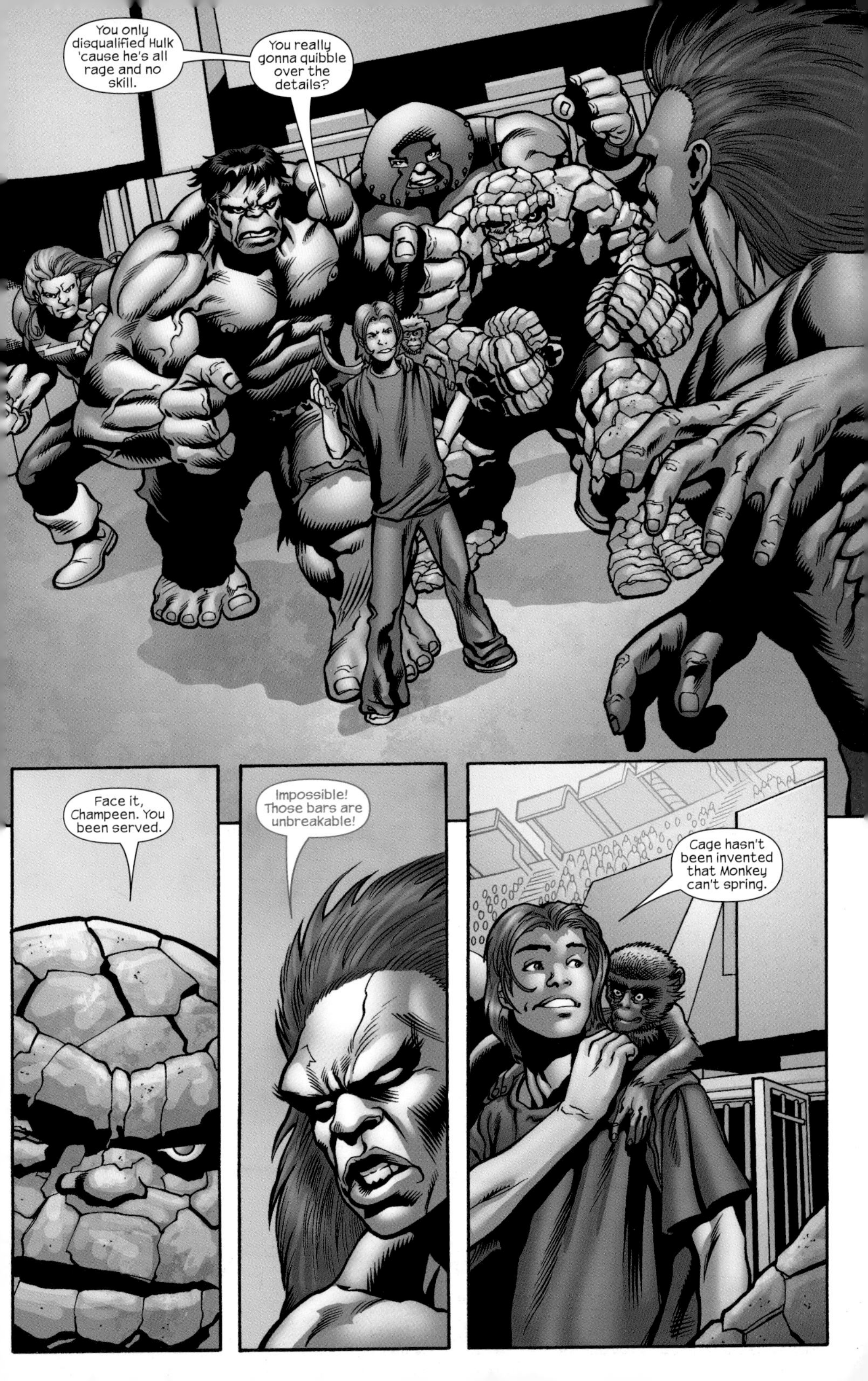
You only disqualified Hulk 'cause he's all rage and no skill.
You really gonna quibble over the details?
Face it, Champeen. You been served.
Impossible! Those bars are unbreakable!
Cage hasn't been invented that Monkey can't spring.

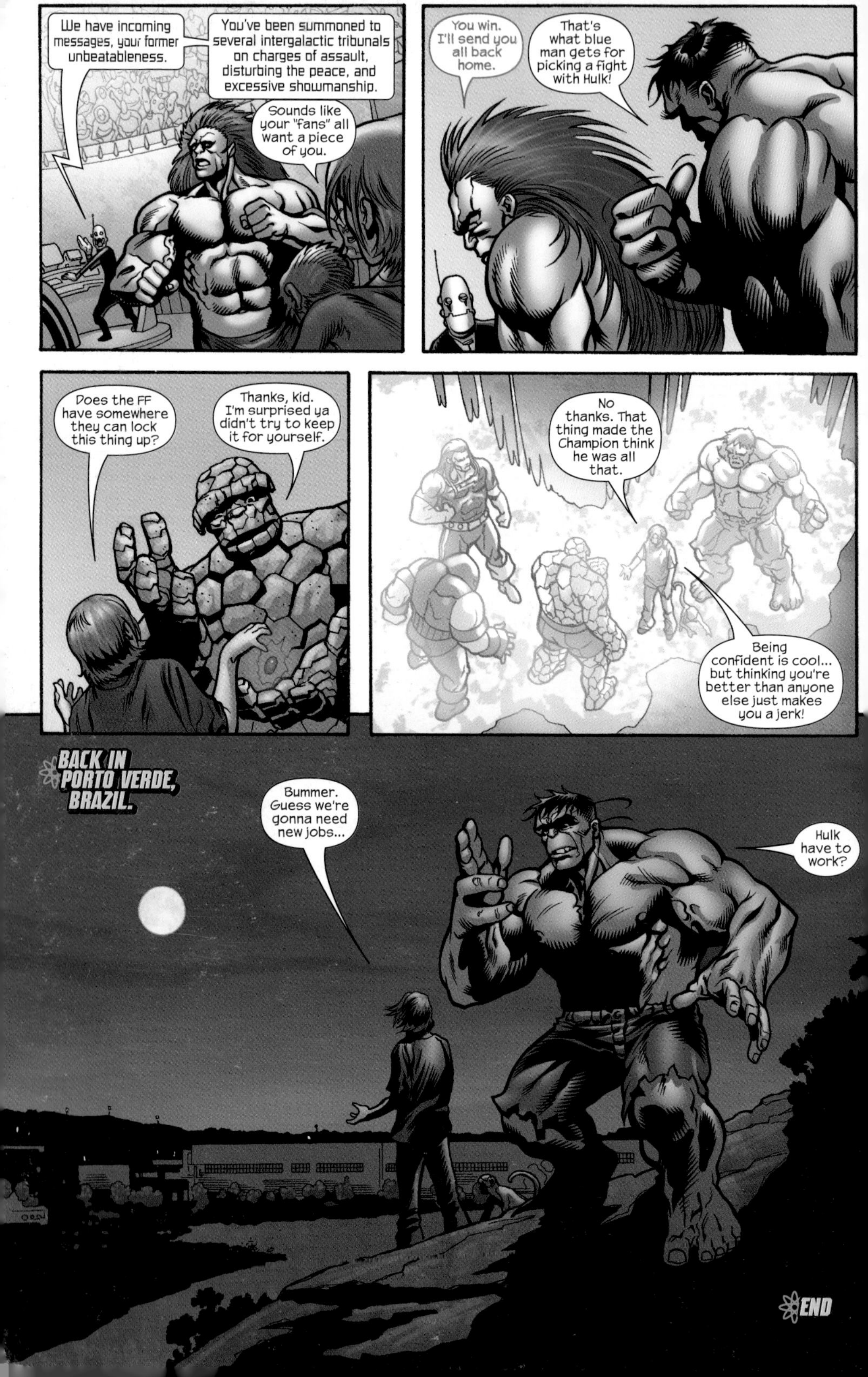
We have incoming messages, your former unbeatableness.
You've been summoned to several intergalactic tribunals on charges of assault, disturbing the peace, and excessive showmanship.
Sounds like your "fans" all want a piece of you.
You win. I'll send you all back home.
That's what blue man gets for picking a fight with Hulk!
Does the FF have somewhere they can lock this thing up?
Thanks, kid. I'm surprised ya didn't try to keep it for yourself.
No thanks. That thing made the Champion think he was all that.
Being confident is cool... but thinking you're better than anyone else just makes you a jerk!
BACK IN PORTO VERDE, BRAZIL.
Bummer. Guess we're gonna need new jobs...
Hulk have to work?
END